ELEVEN ON TOP

ELEVEN ON TOP

Janet Evanovich

ST. MARTIN'S PRESS ≈ NEW YORK

www.stmartins.com

ISBN 0-312-30626-1
EAN 978-0-312-30626-7

First Edition: June 2005

10   9   8   7   6   5   4   3   2   1

This book is a Jan-Jen production, brought to life through the extraordinary powers of SuperEditor Jen Enderlin

*Thanks to Shanna Littlejohn
for suggesting the title for this book.*

ONE

MY NAME IS Stephanie Plum. When I was eighteen I got a job working a hot dog stand on the boardwalk on the Jersey shore. I worked the last shift at Dave's Dogs, and I was supposed to start shutting down a half hour before closing so I could clean up for the day crew. We did chili dogs, cheese dogs, kraut dogs, and bean-topped barking dogs. We grilled them on a big grill with rotating rods. Round and round the rods went all day long, turning the dogs.

Dave Loogie owned the dog stand and came by every night to lock the stand down. He checked the garbage to make sure nothing good was thrown away, and he counted the dogs that were left on the grill.

"You gotta plan ahead," Dave told me every night. "You got more than five dogs left on the grill when we close, I'm gonna fire your ass and hire someone with bigger tits."

So every night, fifteen minutes before closing, before Dave showed up, I ate hot dogs. Not a good way to go when you're working at the shore nights and on the beach in a skimpy bathing suit by day. One night I ate fourteen hot dogs. Okay, maybe it was only nine, but it felt like fourteen. Anyway, it was *too many* hot dogs. Well hell, I needed the job.

For years Dave's Dogs took the number-one slot on my list of all-time crappy jobs held. This morning, I decided my present position had finally won the honor of replacing Dave's Dogs. I'm a bounty hunter. A bond enforcement agent, if you want to make me sound more legitimate. I work for my cousin Vinnie in his bail bonds office in the Chambersburg section of Trenton. At least I used to work for my cousin Vinnie. Thirty seconds ago, I quit. I handed in the phony badge I bought off the Net. I gave back my cuffs. And I dropped my remaining open files on Connie's desk.

Vinnie writes the bonds. Connie shuffles the paperwork. My sidekick, Lula, files when the mood strikes her. And an incredibly sexy, incredibly handsome badass named Ranger and I hunt down the morons who don't show up for trial. Until today. As of thirty seconds ago, all the morons got transferred to Ranger's list.

"Give me a break," Connie said. "You can't quit. I've got a stack of open files."

"Give them to Ranger."

"Ranger doesn't do the low bonds. He only takes the high-risk cases."

"Give them to Lula."

Lula was standing hand on hip, watching me spar with Connie. Lula's a size-sixteen black woman squashed into size-ten leopard print spandex. And the weird thing is, in her own way, Lula looks pretty good in the animal spandex.

"Hell yeah," Lula said. "I could catch them sonsabitches.

I could hunt down their asses good. Only I'm gonna miss you," she said to me. "What are you gonna do if you don't work here? And what brought this on?"

"Look at me!" I said. "What do you see?"

"I see a mess," Lula said. "You should take better care of yourself."

"I went after Sam Sporky this morning."

"Melon-head Sporky?"

"Yeah. Melon-head. I chased him through three yards. A dog tore a hole in my jeans. Some crazy old lady shot at me. And I finally tackled Sporky behind the Tip Top Cafe."

"Looks like it was garbage day," Lula said. "You don't smell too good. And you got something looks like mustard all over your ass. Least I hope that's mustard."

"There were a bunch of garbage bags at the curb and Melon-head rolled me into them. We made sort of a mess. And then when I finally got him in cuffs, he spit on me!"

"I imagine that's the glob of something stuck in your hair?"

"No. He spit on my shoe. Is there something in my hair?"

Lula gave an involuntary shiver.

"Sounds like a normal day," Connie said. "Hard to believe you're quitting because of Melon-head."

Truth is, I don't exactly know why I was quitting. My stomach feels icky when I get up in the morning. And I go to bed at night wondering where my life is heading. I've been working as a bounty hunter for a while now and I'm not the world's best. I barely make enough money to cover my rent each month. I've been stalked by crazed killers, taunted by naked fat men, firebombed, shot at, spat at, cussed at, chased by humping dogs, attacked by a flock of Canadian honkers, rolled in garbage, and my cars get destroyed at an alarming rate.

And maybe the two men in my life add to the icky feeling in my stomach. They're both Mr. Right. And they're both Mr. Wrong. They're both a little scary. I wasn't sure if I wanted a relationship with either of them. And I hadn't a clue how to choose between them. One wanted to marry me, sometimes. His name was Joe Morelli and he was a Trenton cop. Ranger was the other guy, and I wasn't sure what he wanted to do with me beyond get me naked and put a smile on my face.

Plus, there was the note that got slipped under my door two days ago. I'M BACK. What the heck did that mean? And the follow-up note tacked to my windshield. DID YOU THINK I WAS DEAD?

My life is too weird. It's time for a change. Time to get a more sensible job and sort out my future.

Connie and Lula shifted their attention from me to the front door. The bonds office is located on Hamilton Avenue. It's a small two-room storefront setup with a cluttered storage area in the back, behind a bank of file cabinets. I didn't hear the door open. And I didn't hear footsteps. So either Connie and Lula were hallucinating or else Ranger was in the room.

Ranger is the mystery man. He's a half head taller than me, moves like a cat, kicks ass all day long, only wears black, smells warm and sexy, and is 100 percent pure perfectly toned muscle. He gets his dark complexion and liquid brown eyes from Cuban ancestors. He was Special Forces, and that's about all anyone knows about Ranger.

Well hell, when you smell *that* good and look *that* good who cares about anything else, anyway?

I can usually feel Ranger standing behind me. Ranger doesn't ordinarily leave any space between us. Today, Ranger was keeping his distance. He reached around me and dropped a file and a body receipt on Connie's desk.

"I brought Angel Robbie in last night," he said to Connie. "You can mail the check to Rangeman."

Rangeman is Ranger's company. It's located in an office building in center city and specializes in security systems and fugitive apprehension.

"I got big news," Lula said to Ranger. "I've been promoted to bounty hunter on account of Stephanie just quit."

Ranger picked a couple strands of sauerkraut off my shirt and pitched them into Connie's wastebasket. "Is that true?"

"Yes," I said. "I quit. I'm done fighting crime. I've rolled in garbage for the last time."

"Hard to believe," Ranger said.

"I'm thinking of getting a job at the button factory," I told him. "I hear they're hiring."

"I don't have a lot of domestic instincts," Ranger said to me, his attention fixing on the unidentifiable glob of goo in my hair, "but I have a real strong urge to take you home and hose you down."

I went dry mouth. Connie bit into her lower lip, and Lula fanned herself with a file.

"I appreciate the offer," I told him. "Maybe some other time."

"Babe," Ranger said on a smile. He nodded to Lula and Connie and left the office.

No one said anything until he drove off in his shiny black Porsche Turbo.

"I think I wet my pants," Lula said. "Was that one of them double entendres?"

I DROVE BACK to my apartment, took a shower all by myself, and got dressed up in a stretchy white tank top and a tailored black suit with a short skirt. I stepped into four-inch black heels, fluffed up my almost shoulder-length curly brown hair, and added one last layer to my mascara and lipstick.

I'd taken a couple minutes to print out a resume on my computer. It was pathetically short. Graduated with mediocre grades from Douglass College. Worked as a lingerie buyer for a cheap department store for a bunch of years. Got fired. Tracked down scumbags for my cousin Vinnie. Seeking management position in a classy company. Of course, this was Jersey and classy here might not be the national standard.

I grabbed my big black leather shoulder bag and yelled good-bye to my roomie, Rex-the-hamster. Rex lives in a glass aquarium on the kitchen counter. Rex is pretty much nocturnal so we're sort of like ships passing in the night. As an extra treat, once in a while I drop a Cheez Doodle into his cage and he emerges from his soup can home to retrieve the Doodle. That's about as complicated as our relationship gets.

I live on the second floor of a blocky, no-frills, three-story apartment building. My apartment looks out over the parking lot, which is fine by me. Most of the residents in my building are seniors. They're home in front of their televisions before the sun goes down, so the lot side is quiet at night.

I exited my apartment and locked up behind myself. I took the elevator to the small ground-floor lobby, pushed through the double glass doors, and crossed the lot to my car. I was driving a dark green Saturn SL-2. The Saturn had been the special of the day at Generous George's Used Car Emporium. I'd actually wanted a Lexus SC430, but Generous George thought the Saturn was more in line with my budget constraints.

I slid behind the wheel and cranked the engine over. I was heading off to apply for a job at the button factory and I was feeling down about it. I was telling myself it was a new beginning, but truth is, it felt more like a sad ending. I turned onto Hamilton and drove a couple blocks to Tasty Pastry Bakery, thinking a doughnut would be just the thing to brighten my mood.

Five minutes later, I was on the sidewalk in front of the bakery, doughnut bag in hand, and I was face-to-face with Morelli. He was wearing jeans and scuffed boots and a black V-neck sweater over a black T-shirt. Morelli is six feet of lean, hard muscle and hot Italian libido. He's Jersey guy smart, and he's not a man you'd want to annoy . . . unless you're me. I've been annoying Morelli all my life.

"I was driving by and saw you go in," Morelli said. He was standing close, smiling down at me, eyeing the bakery bag. "Boston creams?" he asked, already knowing the answer.

"I needed happy food."

"You should have called me," he said, hooking his finger

into the neckline of my white tank, pulling the neck out to take a look inside. "I have just the thing to make you happy."

I've cohabitated with Morelli from time to time and I knew this to be true. "I have stuff to do this afternoon and doughnuts take less time."

"Cupcake, I haven't seen you in weeks. I could set a new land speed record for getting happy."

"Yeah, but that would be *your* happiness," I said, opening the bag, sharing the doughnuts with Morelli. "What about mine?"

"Your happiness would be top priority."

I took a bite of doughnut. "Tempting, but no. I have a job interview at the button factory. I'm done with bond enforcement."

"When did this happen?"

"About an hour ago," I said. "Okay, I don't actually have an interview *appointment*, but Karen Slobodsky works in the personnel office, and she said I should look her up if I ever wanted a job."

"I could give you a job," Morelli said. "The pay wouldn't be great but the benefits would be pretty decent."

"Gee," I said, "that's the second scariest offer I've had today."

"And the scariest offer would be?"

I didn't think it was smart to tell Morelli about Ranger's offer of a hosing down. Morelli was wearing a gun on his hip, and Ranger wore guns on multiple parts of his body. Seemed like a bad idea to say something that might ratchet up the competition between them.

I leaned into Morelli and kissed him lightly on the

mouth. "It's too scary to share," I told him. He felt nice against me, and he tasted like doughnut. I ran the tip of my tongue along his lower lip. "Yum," I said.

Morelli's fingers curled into the back of my jacket. "*Yum* is a little mild for what I'm feeling. And what I'm feeling shouldn't be happening on the sidewalk in front of the bakery. Maybe we could get together tonight."

"For pizza?"

"Yeah, that too."

I'd been taking a time-out from Morelli and Ranger, hoping to get a better grip on my feelings, but I wasn't making much progress. It was like choosing between birthday cake and a big-boy margarita. How could I possibly decide? And probably I'd be better off without either, but jeez, that wouldn't be any fun.

"Okay," I said. "I'll meet you at Pino's."

"I was thinking my house. The Mets are playing and Bob misses you."

Bob is Morelli's dog. Bob is a big, orange, incredibly huggable shaggy-haired monster with an eating disorder. Bob eats *everything*.

"No fair," I said. "You're using Bob to lure me to your house."

"Yeah," Morelli said. "So?"

I blew out a sigh. "I'll be over around six."

I DROVE A couple blocks down Hamilton and left-turned onto Olden. The button factory is just beyond the city limits of north Trenton. At four in the morning, it's a ten-minute drive from my apartment. At all other hours, the drive time is unpredictable. I stopped for a red light at the corner of Olden and State and just as the light flashed green I heard the pop of gunshot behind me and the *zing, zing, zing* of three rounds tearing into metal and fiberglass. I was pretty sure it was *my* metal and fiberglass, so I floored the Saturn and sailed across the intersection. I crossed North Clinton and kept going, checking my rearview mirror. Hard to tell in traffic, but I didn't think anyone was following me. My heart was racing, and I was telling myself to chill. No reason to believe this was anything more than a random shooting. Probably just some gang guy having fun, practicing his sniping. You've got to practice somewhere, right?

I fished my cell phone out of my purse and called Morelli. "Someone's taking potshots at cars on the corner of Olden and State," I told him. "You might want to send someone over to check things out."

"Are you okay?"

"I'd be better if I had that second doughnut." Okay, so this was my best try at bravado. My hands were white-knuckled gripping the wheel and my foot was shaking on the gas pedal. I sucked in some air and told myself I was just a little excited. Not panicked. Not terrified. Just a little excited. All I had to do was calm down and take a couple more deep breaths and I'd be fine.

Ten minutes later, I pulled the Saturn into the button factory parking lot. The entire factory was housed in a mammoth three-story redbrick building. The bricks were dark with age, the old-fashioned double-hung windows were grimy, and the landscaping was lunar. Dickens would have loved it. I wasn't so sure it was my thing. But then, *my thing* wasn't clearly defined anymore.

I got out and walked to the rear of the car, hoping I'd been wrong about the gunshot. I felt another dump of adrenaline when I saw the damage. I'd taken three hits. Two rounds were embedded in the back panel and one had destroyed a rear light.

No one had followed me into the lot, and I didn't see any cars lingering on the road. Wrong place, wrong time, I told myself. And I would have believed it entirely if it hadn't been for my lousy previous job and the two notes. As it was, I had to back-burner some paranoia so as not to be in a terror-induced cold sweat while trying to talk some guy into hiring me.

I crossed the lot to the large glass double doors leading to the offices, and I sashayed through the doors into the lobby. The lobby was small with a chipped tile floor and seasick green walls. Somewhere, not far off, I could hear machines stamping out buttons. Phones rang in another part of the building. I approached the reception desk and asked for Karen Slobodsky.

"Sorry," the woman said. "You're two hours too late. She just quit. Stormed out of here like hurricane Slobodsky, yelling something about sexual harassment."

"So there's a job opening?" I asked, thinking my day was finally turning lucky.

"Sure looks that way. I'll buzz her boss, Jimmy Alizzi."

Ten minutes later, I was in Alizzi's office, sitting across from him. He was at his desk and his slight frame was dwarfed by his massive furniture. He looked to be in his late thirties to early forties. He had slicked-back black hair and an accent and skin tone that had me thinking Indian.

"I will tell you now that I am not Indian," Alizzi said. "Everyone thinks I am Indian, but that is a false assumption. I come from a very small island country off the coast of India."

"Sri Lanka?"

"No, no, no," he said, wagging his bony finger at me. "Not Sri Lanka. My country is even smaller. We are a very proud people, so you must be careful not to make ethnic slurs."

"Sure. You want to tell me the name of this country?"

"Latorran."

"Never heard of it."

"You see, already you are treading in very dangerous waters."

I squelched a grimace.

"So, you were a bounty hunter," he said, skimming over my resume, eyebrows raised. "That is a quite exciting job. Why would you want to quit such a job?"

"I'm looking for something that has more potential for advancement."

"Oh dear, that would be *my* job you would eventually be seeking."

"Yes, well I'm sure it would take years, and then who knows . . . you might be president of the company by then."

"You are an outrageous flatterer," he said. "I like that. And what would you do if I were to ask you for sexual favors? Would you threaten to sue me?"

"No. I guess I'd ignore you. Unless you got physical.

12

Then I'd have to kick you in a place that hurt a lot and you probably wouldn't be able to father any children."

"That sounds fair," he said. "It happens that I have an immediate position to fill, so you're hired. You can start tomorrow, promptly at eight o'clock. Do not be late."

Wonderful. I have a real job in a nice clean office where no one will shoot at me. I should be happy, yes? This was what I wanted, wasn't it? Then why do I feel so depressed?

I dragged myself down the stairs to the lobby and out to the parking lot. I found my car and the depression deepened. I hated my car. Not that it was a bad car. It just wasn't the *right* car. Not to mention, it would be great to have a car that didn't have three bullet holes in it.

Maybe I needed another doughnut.

A HALF HOUR later, I was back in my apartment. I'd stopped in at Tasty Pastry and left with a day-old birthday cake. The cake said HAPPY BIRTHDAY LARRY. I don't know how Larry celebrated his birthday, but apparently it was without cake. Larry's loss was my gain. If you want to get happy, birthday cake is the way to go. This was a yellow cake with thick, disgusting white frosting made with lard and artificial butter and artificial vanilla and a truckload of sugar. It was decorated with big gunky roses made out of pink and yellow and purple frosting. It was three layers thick with lemon cream between the layers. And it was designed to serve eight people, so it was just the right size.

I dropped my clothes on the floor and dug into the cake. I gave a chunk of cake to Rex, and I worked on the rest. I ate all the pieces with the big pink roses. I was starting to feel nauseous, but I pressed on. I ate all the pieces with the big yellow roses. I had a purple rose and a couple roseless pieces left. I couldn't do it. I couldn't eat any more cake. I staggered into my bedroom. I needed a nap.

I dropped a T-shirt over my head and pulled on a pair of Scooby-Doo boxers with an elastic waist. God, don't you love clothes with elastic? I had one knee on the bed when I saw the note pinned to my pillowcase. BE AFRAID. BE VERY AFRAID. NEXT TIME I'LL AIM HIGHER.

I thought I'd be more afraid if I hadn't just eaten five pieces of birthday cake. As it was, I was mostly afraid of throwing up. I looked under the bed, behind the shower curtain, and in all the closets. No knuckle-dragging monsters anywhere. I slid the bolt home on the front door and shuffled back to the bedroom.

Now, here's the thing. This isn't the first time someone's broken into my apartment. In fact, people regularly break in. Ranger slides in like smoke. Morelli has a key. And various bad guys and psychos have managed to breach the three locks I keep on the door. Some have even left threatening messages. So I wasn't as freaked out as I might have been prior to my career in bounty huntering. My immediate feelings ran more toward numb despair. I wanted all the scary things to go away. I was tired of scary. I'd quit my scary job, and now I wanted the scary people out of my life. I didn't want to be kidnapped ever again. I didn't want to be held at knifepoint or gunpoint. I didn't want to be threatened, stalked, or run off the road by a homicidal maniac.

I crawled under the covers and pulled the quilt over my

head. I was almost asleep when the quilt was yanked back. I let out a shriek and stared up at Ranger.

"What the heck are you doing?" I yelled at him, grabbing at the quilt.

"Visiting, Babe."

"Did you ever think about ringing a doorbell?"

Ranger smiled down at me. "That would take all the fun out of it."

"I didn't know you were interested in fun."

He sat on the side of the bed and the smile widened. "You smell good enough to eat," Ranger said. "You smell like a party."

"It's birthday cake breath. And are we looking at another double entendre?"

"Yeah," Ranger said, "but it's not going anywhere. I have to get back to work. Tank's waiting for me with the motor running. I just wanted to find out if you're serious about quitting."

"I got a job at the button factory. I start tomorrow."

He reached across and removed the note from the pillowcase next to me. "New boyfriend?"

"Someone broke in while I was out. And I guess he shot at me this afternoon."

Ranger stood. "You should discourage people from doing that. Do you need help?"

"Not yet."

"Babe," Ranger said. And he left.

I listened carefully, but I didn't hear the front door open or close. I got up and tiptoed through the apartment. No Ranger. All the locks were locked and the bolt was in place.

I suppose he could have gone out the living room window, but he would have had to climb down the side of the building like Spider-Man.

The phone rang, and I waited to see the number pop up on my caller ID. It was Lula. "Yo," I said.

"Yo, your ass. You got some nerve sticking me with this job."

"You volunteered."

"I must've had sunstroke. A person have to be nuts to want this job."

"Something go wrong?"

"Hell, yes. *Everything's* wrong. I could use some assistance here. I'm trying to snag Willie Martin, and he's not cooperating."

"How uncooperative is he?"

"He hauled his nasty ass out of his apartment and left me handcuffed to his big stupid bed."

"That's pretty uncooperative."

"Yeah, and it gets worse. I sort of don't have any clothes on."

"Omigod! Did he attack you?"

"It's a little more complicated than that. He was in the shower when I busted in. You ever see Willie Martin naked? He is *fine*. He used to play pro ball until he made a mess of his knee and had to turn to boosting cars."

"Un hunh."

"Well, one thing led to another and here I am chained to his hunk-of-junk bed. Hell, it's not like I get it regular, you know. I'm real picky about my men. And besides, anybody would've jumped those bones. He's got muscles on muscles and a butt you want to sink your teeth into."

The mental image had me considering turning vegetarian.

WILLIE MARTIN LIVED in a third-floor loft in a graffiti-riddled warehouse that contained a ground-floor chop shop. It was located on the seven-hundred block of Stark Street, an area of urban decay that rivaled Iraqi bomb sites.

I parked behind Lula's red Firebird and transferred my five-shot Smith & Wesson from my purse to my jacket pocket. I'm not much of a gun person and almost never carry one, but I was sufficiently creeped out by the shooting and the notes that I didn't want to venture onto Stark Street unarmed. I locked the car, bypassed the rickety open-cage service elevator on the ground floor, and trudged up two flights of stairs. The stairwell opened to a small grimy foyer and a door with a size-nine high-heeled boot print on it. I guess Willie hadn't answered on the first knock and Lula got impatient.

I tried the doorknob, and the door swung open. Thank God for small favors because I'd never had any success at kicking in a door. I tentatively stuck my head in and called "Hello."

"Hello, yourself," Lula said. "And don't say no more. I'm not in a good mood. Just unlock these piece-of-crap handcuffs and stand back because I need fries. I need a whole *shitload* of fries. I'm having a fast-food emergency."

Lula was across the room, wrapped in a sheet, one hand cuffed to the iron headboard of the bed, the other hand holding the sheet together.

I pulled the universal handcuff key out of my pocket and looked around the room. "Where are your clothes?"

"He took them. Do you believe that? Said he was going to teach me a lesson not to go after him. I tell you, you can't trust a man. They get what they want and then next thing they got their tighty whities in their pocket and they're out the door. I don't know what he was so upset about, anyway. I was just doing my job. He said, 'Was that good for you?' And I said, 'Oh yeah baby, it was real good.' And then I tried to cuff him. Hell, truth is it wasn't all that good and besides, I'm a professional bounty hunter now. Bring 'em back dead or alive, with or without their pants, right? I had an obligation to cuff him."

"Yeah, well next time put your clothes on *before* you try to cuff a guy."

Lula unlocked the cuffs and tied a knot in the sheet to hold it closed. "That's good advice. I'm gonna remember that. That's the kind of advice I need to be a first-class bounty hunter. At least he forgot to take my purse. I'd be really annoyed if he'd taken my purse." She went to a chest on the far wall, pulled out one of Willie's T-shirts and a pair of gym shorts, and put them on. Then she scooped the rest of the clothes out of the chest, carried them to the window, and threw them out.

"Okay," Lula said, "I'm starting to feel better now. Thanks for coming here to help me. And good news, it looks like no one's stolen your car. I saw it still sitting at the curb." Lula went to the closet and scooped up more clothes. Suits, shoes, and jackets. All went out the window. "I'm on a roll now," she said, looking around the loft. "What else we got that can go out the window? You think we can fit his big-ass TV out the window? Hey, how about some kitchen appliances? Go get me his toaster." She crossed the room, grabbed a table lamp, and brought it to the window. "Hey!" she yelled, head out the window, eyes focused on the street. "Get away from that car. Willie, is that you? What the hell are you doing?"

I ran to the window and looked out. Willie Martin was whaling away at my car with a sledgehammer.

"I'll show you to throw my clothes outta the window," he said, taking a swing at the right rear quarter panel.

"You dumb premature ejaculator," Lula shouted at him. "You dumb-ass moron! That's not my car."

"Oh. Oops," Willie said. "Which one's *your* car?"

Lula hauled a Glock out of her purse, squeezed off two rounds in Willie's direction, and Willie left the scene. One of the rounds pinged off my car roof. And the other round made a small hole in my windshield.

"Must be something wrong with the sight on this gun," Lula said to me. "Sorry about that."

I trudged down the stairs and stood on the sidewalk examining my car. Deep scratch in roof from misplaced bullet. Hole in windshield plus embedded bullet in passenger seat. Bashed-in right rear quarter panel and right passenger-side door from sledgehammer. Previous damage from creepy gun attack by insane stalker. And someone had spray painted EAT ME on the driver's side door.

"Your car's a mess," Lula said. "I don't know what it is with you and cars."

TWO

MORELLI DRIVES AN SUV. He used to own a 4×4 truck, but he traded it in so Bob could ride around with him and be more comfortable. This isn't normal behavior for Morelli men. Morelli men are known for being charming but worthless drunks who rarely care about the comfort of their wife and kids, much less the dog. How Joe escaped the Morelli Man syndrome is a mystery. For a while he seemed destined to follow in his father's footsteps, but somewhere in his late twenties, Joe stopped chasing women and fighting in bars and started working at being a good cop. He inherited his house from his Aunt Rose. He adopted Bob. And he decided, after years of hit-and-run sex, he was in love with me. Go figure that. Joseph Morelli with a house, a dog, a steady job, and an SUV. And on *odd* days of the month he woke up wanting to marry me. It turns out I only want to marry him on *even* days of the month, so to date we've been spared commitment.

When I arrived at Morelli's house his SUV was parked

curbside and Morelli and Bob were sitting on Morelli's tiny front porch. Usually Bob goes gonzo when he sees me, jumping around all smiley face. Today Bob was sitting there drooling, looking sad.

"What's with Bob?" I asked Morelli.

"I don't think he feels good. He was like this when I came home."

Bob stood and hunched. *"Gak,"* Bob said. And he hacked up a sock and a lot of Bob slime. He looked down at the sock. And then he looked up at me. And then he got happy. He jumped around, doing his goofy dance. I gave him a hug and he wandered off, tail wagging, into the house.

"Guess we can go in now," Morelli said. He got to his feet, slid his arm around my shoulders, and hugged me to him for a friendly kiss. He broke from the kiss and his eyes strayed to my car. "I don't suppose you'd want to tell me about the body damage?"

"Sledgehammer."

"Of course."

"You're pretty calm about all this," I said to him.

"I'm a calm kind of guy."

"No, you're not. You go nuts over this stuff. You always yell when people go after me with a sledgehammer."

"Yeah, but in the past you haven't liked that. I'm thinking if I start yelling it might screw up my chances of getting you naked. And I'm desperate. I really need to get you naked. Besides, you quit the bonds office, right? Maybe your life will settle down now. How'd the interview go?"

"I got the job. I start tomorrow."

I was wearing a T-shirt and jeans. Morelli grinned down

at me and slid his hands under my T-shirt. "We should celebrate."

His hands felt nice against my skin, but I was starving and I didn't want to encourage any further celebrating until I got my pizza. He pulled me close and kissed his way up my neck. His lips moved to my ear and my temple and by the time he got to my mouth I was thinking the pizza could wait.

And then we heard it . . . the pizza delivery car coming down the street, stopping at the curb.

Morelli cut his eyes to the kid getting out of the car. "Maybe if we ignore him he'll go away."

The steaming extra-large, extra cheese, green peppers, pepperoni pizza smell oozed from the box the kid was carrying. The smell rushed over the porch and into the house. Bob's toenails clattered on the polished wood hall floor as he took off from the kitchen and galloped for all he was worth at the kid.

Morelli stepped back from me and snagged Bob by the collar just as he was about to catapult himself off the porch.

"*Ulk*," Bob said, stopping abruptly, tongue out, eyes bugged, feet off the ground.

"Minor setback with the celebration plan," Morelli said.

"No rush," I told him. "We have all night."

Morelli's eyes got soft and dark and dreamy. Sort of the way Bob's eyes got when he ate Tastykake Butterscotch Krimpets and then someone rubbed his belly. "All right," Morelli said. "I like the way that sounds."

Two minutes later, we were on the couch in Morelli's living room, watching the pregame show, eating pizza, and drinking beer.

"I heard you were working on the Barroni case," I said to Morelli. "Having any luck with it?"

Morelli took a second piece of pizza. "I have a lot out on it. So far nothing's come in."

Michael Barroni mysteriously disappeared eight days ago. He was sixty-two years old and in good health when he vanished. He owned a nice house in the heart of the Burg on Roebling and a hardware store on the corner of Rudd and Liberty Street. He left behind a wife, two dogs, and three adult sons. One of the Barroni boys graduated with me, and one graduated two years earlier with Morelli.

There aren't a lot of secrets in the Burg and according to Burg gossip Michael Barroni didn't have a girlfriend, didn't play the numbers, and didn't have mob ties. His hardware store was running in the black. He didn't suffer from depression. He didn't do a lot of drinking, and he wasn't hooked on Levitra.

Barroni was last seen closing and locking the back door to the hardware store at the end of the day. He got into his car, drove away . . . and *poof*. No more Michael Barroni.

"Did you ever find Barroni's car?" I asked Morelli.

"No. No car. No body. No sign of struggle. He was alone when Sol Rosen saw him lock up and take off. Sol said he was putting out trash from his diner and he saw Barroni leave. He said Barroni looked normal. Maybe distracted. Sol said Barroni waved but didn't say anything."

"Do you think it's a random crime? Barroni was in the wrong place at the wrong time?"

"No. Barroni lived four blocks from his store. Every day he went straight home from work. Four blocks through the Burg. If something had gone down on Barroni's usual route home someone would have heard or seen something. The day Barroni disappeared he went someplace else. He didn't take his usual route home."

"Maybe he just got tired of it all. Maybe he started driving west and didn't stop until he got to Flagstaff."

Morelli fed his pizza crust to Bob. "I'm going to tell you something that's just between us. We've had two other guys disappear on the exact same day as Barroni. They were both from Stark Street, and a missing person on Stark Street isn't big news, so no one's paid much attention. I ran across them when I checked Barroni's missing-person status.

"Both these guys owned their own businesses. They both locked up at the end of the day and were never seen again. One of the men was real stable. He had a wife and kids. He went to church. He ran a bar on Stark Street, but he was clean. The other guy, Benny Gorman, owned a garage. Probably a chump-change chop shop. He'd done time for armed robbery and grand theft auto. And two months ago he was charged with assault with a deadly weapon. Took a tire iron to a guy and almost killed him. He was supposed to go to trial last week but failed to appear. Ordinarily I'd say he skipped because of the charge but I'm not so sure on this one."

"Did Vinnie bond Gorman out?"

"Yeah. I talked to Connie. She handed Gorman off to Ranger."

"And you think the three guys are connected?"

A commercial came on and Morelli channel surfed

through a bunch of stations. "Don't know. I just have a feeling. It's too strong a coincidence."

I gave Bob the last piece of pizza and snuggled closer to Morelli.

"I have feelings about other things, too," Morelli said, sliding an arm around my shoulders, his fingertips skimming along my neck and down my arm. "Would you like me to tell you about my other feelings?"

My toes curled in my shoes and I got warm in a bunch of private places. And that was the last we saw of the game.

MORELLI IS AN early riser in many ways. I had a memory of him kissing my bare shoulder, whispering an obscene suggestion, and leaving the bed. He returned a short time later with his hair still damp from the shower. He kissed me again and wished me luck with my new job. And then he was gone . . . off on his mission to rid Trenton of bad guys.

It was still dark in Morelli's bedroom. The bed was warm and comfy. Bob was sprawled on Morelli's side of the bed, snuffling into Morelli's pillow. I burrowed under the quilt, and when I reawakened the sunlight was pouring into the room through a break in the curtain. I had a moment of absolute delicious satisfaction immediately followed by panic. According to the bedside clock it was nine o'clock. I was massively late for my first day at the button factory!

I scrambled out of bed, gathered my clothes up off the floor, and tugged them on. I didn't bother with makeup or hair. No time. I took the stairs at a run, grabbed my purse and my car keys, and bolted out of the house.

I skirted traffic as best I could, pulled into the button factory parking lot on two wheels, parked, jumped out of the car, and hit the pavement running. The time was nine-thirty. I was an hour and a half late.

I took the stairs to save time and I was sweating by the time I skidded to a stop in Alizzi's office.

"You are late," Alizzi said.

"Yes, but . . ."

He wagged his finger at me. "This is not a good thing. I told you that you must be on time. And look at you. You are in a T-shirt. If you are going to be late you should at least wear something that is revealing and shows me your breasts. You are fired. Go away."

"No! Give me another chance. Just one more chance. If you give me another chance I'll wear something revealing tomorrow."

"Will you perform a lewd act?"

"What kind of lewd act?"

"Something very, very, very lewd. There would have to be nakedness and body fluids."

"*Ick*. No!"

"Well then, you are still fired."

"That's horrible. I'm going to report you for sexual harassment."

"It will only serve to enhance my reputation."

Unh. Mental head slap.

"Okay. Fine," I said. "I didn't want this job anyway."

I turned on my heel and flounced out of Alizzi's office, down the stairs, through the lobby, and crossed the lot to my bashed-in, bullet-riddled, spray-painted car. I gave the door a vicious kick, wrenched it open, and slid behind the wheel. I punched Metallica into the sound system, cranked it up until the fillings in my teeth were vibrating, and motored across town.

By the time I got to Hamilton I was feeling pretty decent. I had the whole day to myself. True, I wasn't making any money, but there was always tomorrow, right? I stopped at Tasty Pastry, bought a bag of doughnuts, and drove three blocks into the Burg to Mary Lou Stankovic's house. Mary Lou was my best friend all through school. She's married now and has a bunch of kids. We're still friends but our paths don't cross as much as they used to.

I walked an obstacle course from my car to Mary Lou's front door, around bikes, dismembered action figures, soccer balls, remote-control cars, beheaded Barbie dolls, and plastic guns that looked frighteningly real.

"Omigod," Mary Lou said when she opened the door. "It's the angel of mercy. Are those doughnuts?"

"Do you need some?"

"I need a new life, but I'll make do with doughnuts."

I handed the doughnuts off to Mary Lou and followed her into the kitchen. "You have a good life. You like your life."

"Not today. I have three kids home sick with colds. The dog has diarrhea. And I think there was a hole in the condom we used last night."

"Aren't you on the pill?"

"Gives me water retention."

I could hear the kids in the living room, coughing at the television, whining at each other. Mary Lou's kids were cute when they were asleep and for the first fifteen minutes after they'd had a bath. All other times the kids were a screaming advertisement for birth control. It wasn't that they were bad kids. Okay, so they dismembered every doll that came through the door, but they hadn't yet barbecued the dog. That was a good sign, right? It was more that Mary Lou's kids had an excess of energy. Mary Lou said it came from the Stankovic side of the family. I thought it might be coming from the bakery. That's where I got *my* energy.

Mary Lou opened the doughnut bag and the kids came rushing into the kitchen.

"They can hear a bakery bag crinkle a mile away," Mary Lou said.

I'd brought four doughnuts so we gave one to each kid and Mary Lou and I shared a doughnut over coffee.

"What's new?" Mary Lou wanted to know.

"I quit my job at the bonds office."

"Any special reason?"

"No. My reasoning was sort of vague. I got a job at the button factory, but I spent the night with Joe to celebrate and then I overslept this morning and was late for my first day and got fired."

Mary Lou took a sip of coffee and waggled her eyebrows at me. "Was it worth it?"

I took a moment to consider. "Yeah."

Mary Lou gave her head a small shake. "He's been making trouble worthwhile for you since you were five years old. I don't know why you don't marry him."

My reasoning was sort of vague on that one, too.

IT WAS LATE morning when I left Mary Lou. I cut over two blocks to High Street and parked in front of my parents' house. It was a small house on a small lot. It had three bedrooms and bath up and a living room, dining room, kitchen down. It shared a common wall with a mirror image owned by Mabel Markowitz. Mabel was old beyond imagining. Her husband had passed on and her kids were off on their own, so she lived alone in the house, baking coffee cakes and watching television. Her half of the house is painted lime green because the paint had been on clearance when she'd needed it. My parents' house is painted Gulden mustard yellow and dark brown. I'm not sure which house is worse. In the fall my mom puts pumpkins on the front porch and it all seems to work. In the spring the paint scheme is depressing as hell.

Since it was the end of September, the pumpkins were on display and a cardboard witch on a broomstick was stuck to the front door. Halloween was just four weeks away, and the Burg is big on holidays.

Grandma Mazur was at the front door when I set foot on the porch. Grandma moved in with my parents when my Grandpa Mazur got a hot pass to heaven compliments of more than a half century of bacon fat and butter cookies.

"We heard you quit your job," Grandma said. "We've been calling and calling, but you haven't been answering your phone. I need to know the details. I got a beauty parlor appointment this afternoon and I gotta get the story straight."

"Not much of a story," I said, following Grandma into the hallway foyer. "I just thought it was time for a change."

"That's it? Time for a change? I can't tell people that story. It's boring. I need something better. How about we tell them you're pregnant? Or maybe we could say you got a rare blood disease. Or there was a big contract put on your head unless you gave up being a bounty hunter."

"Sorry," I said. "None of those things are true."

"Yeah, but that don't matter. Everybody knows you can't believe everything you hear."

My mother was at the dining room table with a bunch of round pieces of paper spread out in front of her. My sister, Valerie, was getting married in a week, and my mother was still working on the seating arrangements.

"I can't make this work," my mother said. "These round tables don't hold the right number of people. I'm going to have to seat the Krugers at two different tables. And no one gets along with old Mrs. Kruger."

"You should do away with the seating chart," Grandma said. "Just open the doors to the hall and let them fight for their seats."

I love my sister, but I'd deport her to Bosnia if I thought I could get away with it and it'd get me out of her wedding. I'm supposed to be her maid of honor and somehow through my lack of participation and a fabric swatch inaccuracy I've been ordered a gown that makes me look like a giant eggplant.

"We heard you quit your job," my mother said to me. "Thank goodness. I can finally sleep at night knowing you're not running around the worst parts of town chasing after criminals. And I understand you have a wonderful job at the button factory. Marjorie Kuzak called yesterday and told us all about it. Her daughter works in the employment office."

"Actually, I sort of got fired from that job," I said.

"Already? How could you possibly get fired on your first day?"

"It's complicated. I don't suppose you know anybody who's hiring?"

"What kind of job are you looking for?" Grandma asked.

"Professional. Something with career advancement potential."

"I saw a sign up at the cleaners," Grandma said. "I don't know about career advancement, but they do a lot of professional pressing. I see a lot of people taking their business suits there."

"I was hoping for something a little more challenging."

"Dry cleaning's challenging," Grandma said. "It's not easy getting all them spots out. And you gotta have people skills. I heard them talking behind the counter about how hard it was to find someone with people skills."

"And no one would shoot at you," my mother said. "No one ever robs a dry cleaner."

I had to admit, that part appealed to me. It would be nice not to have to worry about getting shot. Maybe working at the dry cleaners would be an okay temporary job until the right thing came along.

I got myself a cup of coffee and poked through the refrigerator, searching for food. I settled on a piece of apple pie and carted the coffee and pie back to the dining room, where my mom was still arranging the paper tables.

"What's going on in the Burg?" I asked her.

"Harry Farstein died yesterday. Heart attack. He's at Stiva's."

"He's gonna have a viewing tonight," Grandma said. "It's gonna be a good one, too. His lodge will be there.

31

And Lydia Farstein is the drama queen of the Burg. She'll be carrying on something awful. If you haven't got anything better to do, you should come to the viewing with me. I could use a ride."

Grandma loved going to viewings. Stiva's Funeral Home was the social center of the Burg. I thought having my thumb amputated would be a preferred activity.

"And everyone's going to be talking about the Barroni thing," Grandma said. "I can't believe he hasn't turned up. It's like he was abducted by Martians."

Okay, now this interested me. Morelli was working on the Barroni disappearance. And Ranger was working on the Gorman disappearance, which might be connected to the Barroni disappearance. I was glad I wasn't working on either of those cases, but on the other hand, I felt a smidgeon left out. So sue me, I'm nosy.

"Sure," I said. "I'll pick you up at seven o'clock."

"Your father got gravy on his gray slacks," my mother said. "If you're going to apply for a job at the cleaner, would you mind taking the slacks with you? It would save me a trip."

A half hour later, I had a job with Kan Klean. The hours were seven to three. They were open seven days a week, and I agreed to work weekends. The pay wasn't great, but I could wear jeans and a T-shirt to work, and they confirmed my mother's suspicion that they'd never been held up and that to date none of their employees had been shot while on the job. I handed over the gravy-stained slacks and agreed to show up at seven the next morning.

I didn't feel quite as nauseated as I had after getting the button factory job. So I was making progress, right?

I drove three blocks down Hamilton and stopped at the bonds office to say hello.

"Look what the wind blew in," Lula said when she saw me. "I heard you got the job at the button factory. How come you're not working?"

"I spent the night with Morelli and overslept. So I was late rolling in to work."

"And?"

"And I got fired."

"That was fast," Lula said. "You're good. It takes most people a couple days to get fired."

"Maybe it all worked out for the best. I got another job already at Kan Klean."

"Do you get a discount?" Lula wanted to know. "I got some dry cleaning to send out. You could pick it up tomorrow here at the office on your way to work."

"Sure," I said. "Why not." I shuffled through the small stack of files on Connie's desk. "Anything fun come in?"

"Yeah, it's all fun," Connie said. "We got a rapist. We got a guy who beat up his girlfriend. We got a couple pushers."

"I'm doing the DV this afternoon," Lula said.

"DV?"

"Domestic violence. My time's real valuable now that I'm a bounty hunter. I gotta use abbreviations. Like I'm doing the DV in the PM."

I heard Vinnie growl from his inner office. "Jesus H. Christmas," he said. "Who would have thought my life would come to this?"

"Hey, Vinnie," I yelled to him. "How's it going?"

Vinnie poked his head out his door. "I gave you a job

when you needed one and now you desert me. Where's the gratitude?"

Vinnie is a couple inches taller than me and has the slim, boneless body of a ferret. His coloring is Mediterranean. His hair looks like it's slicked back with olive oil. He wears pointy-toed shoes and a lot of gold. He's the family pervert. He's married to Harry-the-Hammer's daughter. And in spite of his personality shortcomings (or maybe because of them) he's an okay bail bondsman. Vinnie understands the criminal mind.

"You didn't *give* me the job," I said to Vinnie. "I blackmailed you into it. And I got good numbers when I was working for you. My apprehension rate was close to ninety percent."

"You were lucky," Vinnie said.

This was true.

Lula took her big black leather purse from the bottom file drawer and stuffed it under her arm. "I'm going out. I'm gonna get that DV and I'm gonna kick his ass all the way back to jail."

"No!" Vinnie said. "You're *not* gonna kick his ass *anywhere*. Ass kicking is not entirely legal. You will introduce yourself and you will cuff him. And then you will escort him to the station in a civilized manner."

"Sure," Lula said. "I knew that."

"Maybe you want to go with her," Vinnie said to me. "Since it looks like you don't have anything better to do."

"I start a new job tomorrow. I got a job at Kan Klean."

Vinnie's eyes lit up. "Do you get a discount? I got a shitload of dry cleaning."

"I wouldn't mind if you rode along," Lula said. "This

guy's gonna be slam bam, thank you, ma'am. And then we drop his sorry behind off at the police station and go get some burgers."

"I don't want to get involved," I told her.

"You can stay in the Firebird. It'll only take me a minute to cuff this guy and drag . . . I mean, *escort* him out to the car."

"Okay," I said, "but I *really* don't want to get involved."

A half hour later we were at the public housing project on the other side of town and Lula was motoring the Firebird down Carter Street, looking for 2475A.

"Here's the plan," Lula said. "You just sit tight and I'll go get this guy. I got pepper spray, a stun gun, a head-bashing flashlight, two pairs of cuffs, and the BP in my purse."

"BP?"

"Big Persuader. That's what I call my Glock." She pulled to the curb and jerked her thumb at the apartment building. "This here's the building. I'll be back in a minute."

"Try to keep your clothes on," I said to her.

"Hunh," Lula said. "Funny."

Lula walked to the door and knocked. The door opened. Lula disappeared inside the house and the door closed behind her. I looked at my watch and decided I'd give her ten minutes. After ten minutes I'd do something, but I wasn't sure what it would be. I could call the police. I could call Vinnie. I could run around the outside of the building yelling *fire!* Or I could do the least appealing of all the options—I could go in after her.

I didn't have to make the decision because the front door opened after just two minutes. Lula tumbled out the door, rolled off the stoop, landed on a patch of hard packed dirt that would have been lawn in a more prosperous neighborhood, and the door slammed shut behind her. Lula scrambled to her feet, tugged her spandex lime green miniskirt back down over her ass, and marched up to the door.

"Open this door!" she yelled. "You open this door right now or there's gonna be big trouble." She tried the doorknob. She rang the bell. She kicked the door with her Via Spigas. The door didn't open. Lula turned and looked over at me. "Don't worry," she said. "This here's just a minor setback. They don't understand the severity of the situation."

I slid lower in my seat and became engrossed in the mechanics of my seat belt.

"I'm giving you one more chance to open this door and then I'm going to take action," Lula yelled at the house.

The door didn't open.

"Hunh," Lula said. She backed off from the door and cut over to a front window. Curtains had been drawn across the window, but the flicker of a television screen could faintly be seen through the sheers. Lula stood on tiptoes and tried to open the window, but the window wouldn't budge. "I'm starting to get annoyed now," Lula said. "You know what I think? I think this here's an accident waiting to happen."

Lula pulled her big Maglite out of her purse, set her purse on the ground, and smashed the window with the Maglite. She bent to retrieve her purse and what remained of the window was blown out with a shotgun blast from inside. If Lula hadn't bent down to get her purse, the surgeon of the day at St. Francis would have spent the rest of his afternoon picking pellets out of her.

"What the F!" Lula said. And Lula did a fast sprint to the car. She wrenched the driver's-side door open, crammed herself behind the wheel, and there was a second shotgun blast through the apartment window. "That dumb son of a bitch shot at me!" Lula said.

"Yeah," I said. "I saw. I was impressed you could run like that in those heels."

"I wasn't expecting him to shoot at me. He had no call to do that."

"You broke his window."

"It was an accident."

"It wasn't an accident. I saw you do it with the Maglite."

"That guy's nuts," Lula said, taking off from the curb, leaving a couple inches of rubber on the road. "He should be reported to somebody. He should be arrested."

"*You* were supposed to arrest him."

"I was supposed to *escort* him. Vinnie made that real clear. *Escort him.* And I could escort the hell out of him except I'm hungry. I gotta get something to eat," Lula said. "I work better on a happy stomach. I could take that woman-beating moron in anytime I want, so what's the rush, right? Might as well get a burger first, that's what I think. And anyway, he might be more Ranger's speed. I wouldn't want to step on Ranger's toes. You know how Ranger likes all that shooting stuff."

"I thought you liked the shooting stuff."

"I don't want to hog it."

"Considerate of you."

"Yeah, I'm real considerate," Lula said, turning into a Cluck-in-a-Bucket drive-thru. "I'm seriously thinking of giving this case to Ranger."

"What if Ranger doesn't want it?"

"You think he'd turn down a good case like this?"

"Yeah."

"Hunh," Lula said. "Wouldn't that be a bitch?"

She got a Cluck Burger with cheese, a large side of fries, a chocolate shake, and an Apple Clucky Pie. I wasn't in a Cluck-in-a-Bucket mood so I passed. Lula finished off the last piece of the pie and looked at her watch. "I'd go back and root out that nutso loser, but it's getting late. Don't you think it's late?"

"Almost three o'clock."

"Practically quitting time."

Especially for me, since I quit yesterday.

THREE

I'M NOT THE world's best cook, but I have some special-ties, and almost all of them include peanut butter. You can't go wrong with peanut butter. Today I was having a peanut butter and olive and potato chip sandwich for dinner. Very efficient since it combines legumes and veg-etables plus some worthless white bread carbohydrates all in one tidy package. I was standing in the kitchen, washing the sandwich down with a cold Corona, and Morelli called.

"What are you doing?" he asked.

"Eating."

"Why aren't you eating in my house?"

"I don't live in your house."

"You were living in my house last night."

"I was *visiting* your house last night. That's different from living. Living involves commitment and closet allocation."

"We don't seem to be all that good at commitment, but I'd be happy to give up a couple closets in exchange for wild gorilla sex at least five days out of seven."

"Good grief."

"Okay, four days out of seven, but that's my best offer. How's the new job at the button factory going?"

"Got fired. And it was your fault. I was late for work on my first day."

I could feel Morelli smile at the other end of the line. "Am I good, or what?"

"I got a job at Kan Klean. I start tomorrow."

"We should celebrate."

"No celebrating! That's what lost me the button factory job. Don't you want to ask me if I can get you discount cleaning?"

"I don't clean my clothes. I wear them until they fall apart and then I throw them away."

I finished the sandwich and chugged the beer. "I've got to go," I told Morelli. "I told Grandma I'd pick her up at seven. We're going to Harry Farstein's viewing at Stiva's."

"I can't compete with that," Morelli said.

GRANDMA WAS WAITING at the door when I drove up. She was dressed in powder blue slacks, a matching floral-print blouse, a white cotton cardigan, and white tennis shoes. She had her big black patent-leather purse in the crook of her arm. Her gray hair was freshly set in tight little baloney curls that marched across her pink skull. Her nails were newly manicured and painted fire-engine red. Her lipstick matched her nails.

"I'm ready to go," she said, hurrying over to the car. "We don't get a move on, we're not gonna get a good seat. There's gonna be a crowd tonight and ever since Spiro took off, Stiva hasn't been all that good with organization. Spiro was a nasty little cockroach but he could organize a crowd like no one else."

Spiro was Constantine Stiva's kid. I went to school with Spiro and near the end I guess I inadvertently helped him disappear. He was a miserable excuse for a human being, involved in running guns and God knows what else. He tried to kill Grandma and me, there was a shoot-out and a spectacular fire at the funeral home, and somehow, in the confusion, Spiro vanished into thin air.

When I got the notes saying I'M BACK and DID YOU THINK I WAS DEAD? Spiro was one of the potential psychos who came to mind. Sad to say, he was just one name among many. And he wasn't the most likely candidate. Spiro had been a lot of things . . . dumb wasn't one of them. Plus I couldn't see Spiro being obsessed with revenge. Spiro had wanted money and power.

The funeral home was on Hamilton, a couple blocks down from the bail bonds office. It had been rebuilt after the fire and was now a jumble of new brick construction and old Victorian mansion. The two-story front half of the house was white aluminum siding with black shutters. A large porch wrapped around the front and south side of the house. Some of the viewing rooms and all of the embalming rooms were located in the new brick addition at the rear. The preferred viewing rooms were in the front and Stiva had given them names: the Blue Salon, the Rest in Peace Salon, and the Executive Slumber Salon.

It was a five-minute drive from my parents' house to Stiva's. I dropped Grandma at the door and found street parking half a block away. When I got to the funeral home

Grandma was waiting for me at the entrance to the Executive Slumber Salon.

"I don't know why they call this the Executive Salon," she said. "It's not like Stiva's laying a lot of executives to rest. Think it's just a big phony-baloney name."

The Executive Slumber Salon was the largest of the viewing rooms and was already packed with people. Lydia Farstein was at the far end, one hand dramatically touching the open casket. She was in her seventies and looked surprisingly happy for a woman who had just lost her husband of fifty-odd years.

"Looks like Lydia's been hitting the sauce," Grandma said. "Last time I saw her that happy was . . . never. I'm going back to give her my condolences and take a look at Harry."

Looking at dead people wasn't high on my list of favorite activities, so I separated from Grandma and wandered to the far side of the entrance hall, where complimentary cookies had been set out.

I scarfed down a couple sugar cookies and a couple spice cookies and I felt a prickling sensation at the back of my neck. I turned and looked across the room and saw Morelli's Grandma Bella glaring at me. Grandma Bella is a white-haired old lady who dresses in black and looks like an extra out of a *Godfather* flashback. She has visions, and she puts spells on people. And she scares the crap out of me.

Bitsy Mullen was standing next to me at the cookie table. "Omigod," Bitsy said. "I hope she's glaring at you and not me. Last week she put the eye on Francine

Blainey, and Francine got a bunch of big herpes sores all over her face."

The eye is like Grandma Bella voodoo. She puts her finger to her eye and she mumbles something and whatever calamity happens to you after that you can pin on the eye. I guess it's a little like believing in hell. You hope it's bogus, but you never really know for sure, do you?

"I'm betting Francine got herpes from her worthless boyfriend," I said to Bitsy.

"I'm not taking any chances," Bitsy said. "I'm going to hide in the ladies' room until the viewing is over. Oh no! Omigod. Here she comes. What should I do? I can't breathe. I'm gonna faint."

"Probably she just wants a cookie," I said to Bitsy. Not that I believed it. Grandma Bella had her beady eyes fixed on me. I'd seen the look before and it wasn't good.

"You!" Grandma Bella said, pointing her finger at me. "You broke my Joseph's heart."

"No way," I said. "Swear to God."

"Is there a ring on your finger?"

"N-N-No."

"It's a scandal," she said. "You've brought disgrace to my house. A respectable woman would be married and have children by now. You go to his house and tempt him with your body and then you leave. Shame on you. Shame. Shame. I should put the eye on you. Make your teeth fall out of your head. Turn your hair gray. Cause your female parts to shrink away until there's nothing left of them."

Grandma Mazur elbowed her way through the crush of

people around the cookie table. "What's going on here?" she asked. "What'd I miss about female parts?"

"Your granddaughter is a Jezebel," Grandma Bella said. "Jumping in and out of my Joseph's bed."

"Half the women in the Burg have been in and out of his bed," Grandma Mazur said. "Heck, half the women in the state . . ."

"Not lately," I said. "He's different now."

"I'm going to put the eye on her," Grandma Bella said. "I'm going to make her female parts turn to dust."

"Over my dead body," Grandma Mazur said.

Bella scrunched up her face. "That could be arranged."

"You better watch it, sister," Grandma Mazur said. "You don't want to get me mad. I'm a holy terror when I'm mad."

"Hah, you don't scare me," Bella said. "Stand back. I'm going to give the eye."

Grandma Mazur pulled a .45 long barrel out of her big black patent-leather purse and pointed it at Bella. "You put your finger to your eye and I'll put a hole in your head that's so big you could push a potato through it."

Bella's eyes rolled around in her head. "I'm having a vision. I'm having a vision."

I grabbed the gun from Grandma and shoved it back into her bag. "No shooting! She's just a crazy old lady."

Bella snapped to attention. "Crazy old lady? Crazy old lady? I'll show you crazy old lady. I'll give you a thrashing. Someone get me a stick. I'll put the eye on everyone if someone doesn't give me a stick."

"No one thrashes my granddaughter," Grandma Mazur said. "And besides, look around. Do you see any sticks? It's not like you're in the woods. You know what your problem is? You gotta learn how to chill."

Bella grabbed Grandma Mazur by the nose. She was so fast Grandma never saw it coming. "You're a demon woman!" Bella shouted.

Grandma Mazur clocked Bella on the side of the head with the big patent-leather purse, but Bella had a death grip on Grandma Mazur. Grandma hit her a second time and Bella hunkered in. Bella scrunched up her face and held tight to the nose.

I was in the mix, trying to wrestle Bella away. Grandma accidentally caught me with a roundhouse swing of the purse that knocked me off my feet.

Bitsy Mullen was jumping around, wringing her hands and shrieking. "Help! Stop! Someone do something!"

Mrs. Lubchek was behind Bitsy, at the cookie table, watching the whole thing. "Oh, for the love of God," Mrs. Lubchek said with an eyeroll. And Mrs. Lubchek grabbed the pitcher of iced tea off the cookie table and dumped it on Grandma Bella and Grandma Mazur.

Grandma Bella released Grandma Mazur's nose and looked down at herself. "I'm wet. What is this?"

"Iced tea," Mrs. Lubchek said. "I poured iced tea on you."

"I'll turn you into an artichoke."

"You need to take a pill," Mrs. Lubchek said. "You're nutsy cuckoo."

Stiva hurried across the room with Joe's mother close on his heels.

"We're out of iced tea," Mrs. Lubchek said to Stiva.

"I'm having a vision," Grandma Bella said, her eyes

rolling around in her head. "I see fire. A terrible fire. I see rats escaping, running from the fire. Big, ugly, sick rats. And one of the rats has come back." Bella's eyes snapped open and focused on me. "He's come back to get *you*."

"Omigod," Bitsy said. "Omigod. Omigod!"

"I need to lay down now. I always get tired after I have a vision," Bella said.

"Wait," I said to her. "What kind of a vision is that? A rat? Are you sure about this vision thing?"

"Yeah, and what do you mean the rat's sick?" Grandma Mazur wanted to know. "Does it have rabies?"

"That's all I'm going to say," Bella said. "It's a vision. A vision is a vision. I'm going home."

Bella whirled on her heel and walked to the door with her back ramrod straight and Joe's mom behind her, scurrying to keep up.

Grandma Mazur turned to the cookie tray and picked through the cookies, looking for a chocolate chip. "I tell you a person's gotta get here early or there's only leftovers."

We were both dripping iced tea. And Grandma Mazur's nose was red and swollen.

"We should go home," I said to Grandma Mazur. "I have to get out of this shirt."

"Yeah," Grandma Mazur said. "I guess I could go. I paid my respects to the deceased and this cookie tray's a big disappointment."

"Did you hear anything about Michael Barroni?"

Grandma dabbed at her shirt with a napkin. "Only that he's still missing. The boys are running the store, but Emma Wilson tells me they're not getting along. Emma works there part-time. She said the young one is a trial."

"Anthony."

"That's the one. He was always a troublemaker. Remember there was that business with Mary Jane Roman."

"Date rape."

"Nothing ever came of that," Grandma said. "But I never doubted Mary Jane. There was always something off about Anthony."

We'd walked out of the funeral home and down the street to the car. I looked inside the car and saw a note on the driver's seat.

"How'd that get in there?" Grandma wanted to know. "Don't you lock your car?"

"I stopped locking it. I'm hoping someone will steal it."

Grandma took a good look at the car. "That makes sense."

We both got in and I read the note. YOUR TURN TO BURN, BITCH.

"Such language," Grandma said. "I tell you the world's going to heck in a handbasket."

Grandma was upset about the language. I was upset about the threat. I wasn't exactly sure what it meant, but it didn't feel good. It was crazy and scary. Who *was* this person, anyway?

I pulled away from the curb and headed for my parents' house.

"I can't get that dumb note out of my head," Grandma said when we were half a block from home. "I could swear I even smell smoke."

Now that she mentioned it . . .

I glanced in the rearview mirror and saw flames licking up the backseat. I raced the half block to my parents' house, careened into the driveway, and jerked to a stop.

"Get out," I yelled. "The backseat's on fire."

Grandma turned and looked. "Danged if it isn't."

I ran into the house, told my mother to call the fire department, grabbed the fire extinguisher that was kept in the kitchen under the sink, and ran back to the car. I broke the seal on the extinguisher and sprayed the flaming backseat. My father appeared with the garden hose and between the two of us we got the fire under control.

A half hour later, the backseat of the Saturn was pronounced dead and flame free by the fire department. The fire truck rumbled away down the street, and the crowd of curious neighbors dispersed. The sun had set, but the Saturn could be seen in the ambient light from the house. Water dripped from the undercarriage and pooled on the cement driveway in grease-slicked puddles. The stench of cooked upholstery hung in the air.

Morelli had arrived seconds behind the fire truck. He was now standing in my parents' front yard with his hands in his pockets, wearing his unreadable cop face.

"So," I said to him. "What's up?"

"Where's the note?"

"What note?"

His eyes narrowed ever so slightly.

"How do you know there was a note?" I asked.

"Just another one of those feelings."

I took the note from my pocket and handed it over.

"Do you think this has something to do with the rat?" Grandma asked me. "Remember how Bella had that vision about the fire and the rat? And she said the rat was gonna get you. Well, I bet it was the rat that wrote the note and started the fire."

"Rats can't write," I said.

"What about human rats?" Grandma wanted to know. "What about big mutant human rats?"

Morelli cut his eyes to me. "Do I want to know about this vision?"

"No," I told him. "And you also don't want to know about the fight in the funeral home between Bella and Grandma Mazur when Grandma tried to stop Bella from putting a curse on me for breaking your heart."

Morelli smiled. "I've always been her favorite."

"I didn't break your heart."

"Cupcake, you've been breaking my heart for as long as I've known you."

"How did you know about the fire?" I asked Morelli.

"Dispatch called me. They always call me when your car explodes or goes up in flames."

"I'm surprised Ranger isn't here."

"He got me on my cell. I told him you were okay."

I moved closer to the Saturn and peered inside. Most of the water and fire damage was confined to the backseat.

Morelli had his hand at the nape of my neck. "You're not thinking of driving this, are you?"

"It doesn't look so bad. It probably runs fine."

"The backseat is completely gutted and there's a big hole in the floorboard."

"Yeah, but other than that it's okay, right?"

Morelli looked at me for a couple beats. Probably trying to decide if this was worth a fight.

"It's too dark to get a really good assessment of the damage," he finally said. "Why don't we go home and come back in the morning and take another look. You don't want to drive it tonight anyway. You want to open the windows and let it air out."

He was right about the airing out part. The car reeked. And I knew he was also right about looking at the car when the light was better. Problem was, this was the only car I had. The only thing worse than driving this car would be borrowing the '53 Buick Grandma Mazur inherited from my Great Uncle Sandor. Been there, done that, don't want to do it again.

And the danger involved in driving this car seemed to me to be hardly worth mentioning compared to the threat I was facing from the criminally insane stalker who set the fire.

"I'm more worried about the arsonist than I am about the car," I said to Morelli.

"I haven't got a grip on the arsonist," Morelli said. "I don't know what to do about him. The car I have some control over. Let me give you a ride home."

Five minutes later we were parked in front of Morelli's house.

"Let me guess," I said to Morelli. "Bob still misses me."

Morelli ran a finger along the line of my jaw. "Bob could care less. I'm the one who misses you. And I miss you bad."

"How bad?"

Morelli kissed me. "Painfully bad."

AT SIX-FIFTEEN I dragged myself out of Morelli's bed and into the shower. I'd thrown my clothes in the washer and dryer the night before, and Morelli had them in the bathroom, waiting for me. I did a half-assed job of drying my hair, swiped some mascara on my lashes, and followed my nose to the kitchen, where Morelli had coffee brewing.

Both of the men in my life looked great in the morning. They woke up clear-eyed and alert, ready to save the world. I was a befuddled mess in the morning, stumbling around until I got my caffeine fix.

"We're running late," Morelli said, handing me a travel mug of coffee and a toasted bagel. "I'll drop you off at the cleaner. You can check the car out after work."

"No. I have time. This will only take a minute. I'm sure the car is fine."

"I'm sure the car *isn't* fine," Morelli said, nudging me out of the kitchen and down the hall to the front door. He locked the door behind us and beeped his SUV open with the remote.

Minutes later we were at my parents' house, arguing on the front lawn.

"You're not driving this car," Morelli said.

"Excuse me? Did I hear you give me an order?"

"Cut me some slack here. You and I both know this car isn't drivable."

"I don't know any such thing. Okay, it's got some problems, but they're all cosmetic. I'm sure the engine is fine." I slid behind the wheel and proved my point by rolling the engine over. "See?" I said.

"Get out of this wreck and let me drive you to work."

"No."

"In twenty seconds I'm going to *drag* you out and reignite the fire until there's nothing left of this death trap but a smoking cinder."

"I hate when you do the macho-man thing."

"I hate when you're stubborn."

I hit the door locks and automatic windows, put the car into reverse, and screeched out of the driveway into the road. I changed gears and roared away, gagging on the odor of wet barbecued car. He was right, of course. The car was a death trap, and I was being stubborn. Problem was, I couldn't help myself. Morelli brought out the stubborn in me.

KAN KLEAN WAS a small mom-and-pop dry cleaners that had been operating in the Burg for as long as I can remember. The Macaroni family owned Kan Klean. Mama Macaroni, Mario Macaroni, and Gina Macaroni were the principals, and a bunch of miscellaneous Macaronis helped out when needed.

Mama Macaroni was a contemporary of Grandma Bella and Grandma Mazur. Mama Macaroni's fierce raptor eyes took the world in under drooping folds of parchment-thin skin. Her shrunken body, wrapped in layers of black, curved over her cane and conjured up images of mummified larvae. She had a boulder of a mole set into the roadmap of her face somewhere in the vicinity of Atlanta. Three hairs grew out of the mole. The mole was horrifying and compelling. It was the dermatological equivalent of a seven-car crash with blood and guts spread all over the highway.

I'd never been to Kan Klean that Mama Macaroni wasn't sitting on a stool behind the counter. Mama nodded to customers but seldom spoke. Mama only spoke when there was a problem. Mama Macaroni was the problem solver. Her son Mario supervised the day-to-day operation. Her daughter-in-law, Gina, kept the books and ran day care for the hordes of grandchildren produced by her four daughters and two sons.

"It's not difficult," Gina said to me. "You'll be working the register. You take the clothes from the customer and you do a count. Then you fill out the order form and give a copy to the customer. You put a copy in the bag with the clothes and you put the third copy in the box by the register. Then you put the bag in one of the rolling bins. One bin is laundry and one bin is dry cleaning. That's the way we do it. When a customer comes in to pick up his cleaned clothes you search for the clothes by the number on the top of his receipt. Make sure you always take a count so the customer gets all his clothes."

Mama Macaroni mumbled something in Italian and slid her dentures around in her mouth.

"Mama says you should be careful. She says she's keeping her eye on you," Gina said.

I smiled at Mama Macaroni and gave her a thumbs-up. Mama Macaroni responded with a death glare.

"When you have time between customers you can tag the clothes," Gina said. "Every single garment must get tagged. We have a machine that you use, and you have to make sure that the number on the tag is the same as the number on the customer's receipt."

By noon I'd completely lost the use of my right thumb from using the tagging machine.

"You got to go faster," Mama Macaroni said to me from her stool. "I see you slow down. You think we pay for nothing?"

A man hurried through the front door and approached the counter. He was mid-forties and dressed in a suit and tie. "I picked my dry cleaning up yesterday," he said, "and all the buttons are broken off my shirt."

Mama Macaroni got off her stool and caned her way to the counter. "What?" she said.

"The buttons are broken."

She shook her head. "I no understand."

He showed her the shirt. "The buttons are all broken."

"Yes," Mama Macaroni said.

"You broke them."

"No," Mama said. "Impossible."

"The buttons were fine when I brought the shirt in. I picked the shirt up and the buttons were all broken."

"I no understand."

"What don't you understand?"

"English. My English no good."

The man looked at me. "Do you speak English?"

"What?" I said.

The man whipped the shirt off the counter and left the store.

"Maybe you not so slow," Mama Macaroni said to me. "But don't get any ideas about taking it easy. We don't pay you good money to stand around doing nothing."

I started watching the clock at one o'clock. By three o'clock I was sure I'd been tagging clothes for at least five days without a break. My thumb was throbbing, my feet ached from standing for eight hours, and I had a nervous twitch in my eye from Mama Macaroni's constant scrutiny.

I took my bag from under the counter and I looked over at Mama Macaroni. "See you tomorrow."

"What you mean, *see you tomorrow*? Where you think you going?"

"Home. It's three o'clock. My shift is over."

"Look at little miss clock watcher here. Three o'clock on the dot. *Bing*. The bell rings and you out the door." She threw her parchment hands into the air. "Go! Go home. Who needs you? And don't be late tomorrow. Sunday is big day. We the only cleaner open on Sunday."

"Okay," I said. "And have a nice mole." *Shit!* Did I just say that? "Have a nice *day!*" I yelled. Crap.

I'd parked the Saturn in the small lot adjacent to Kan Klean. I left the building and circled the car. I didn't see any notes. I didn't smell anything burning. No one shot at me. Guess my stalker was taking a day off.

I got into the car, turned my cell phone on, and scrolled to messages.

First message. "Stephanie." That was the whole message. It was from Morelli at seven-ten this morning. It sounded like it had been said through clenched teeth.

Second message. Morelli breathing at seven-thirty.

Third message. "Call me when you turn your phone on." Morelli again.

Fourth message. "It's two-thirty and we just found Barroni's car. Call me."

Barroni's car! I dialed in Joe's cell number.

"It's me," I said. "I just got off work. I had to turn my phone off because Mama Macaroni said it was giving her brain cancer. Not that it would matter."

"Where are you?"

"I'm on the road. I'm going home to take a nap. I'm all done in."

"The car . . ."

"The car is okay," I told Morelli.

"The car is *not* okay."

"Give up on the car. What about Barroni?"

"I lied about Barroni. I figured that was the only way you'd call."

I put my finger to my eye to stop the twitching, disconnected Morelli, and cruised into my lot.

Old Mr. Ginzler was walking to his Buick when I pulled in. "That's some lookin' car you got there, chicky," Mr. Ginzler said. "And it stinks."

"I paid extra for the smell," I told Mr. Ginzler.

"Smart-ass kid," Mr. Ginzler said. But he smiled when he said it. Mr. Ginzler liked me. I was almost sure of it.

Rex was snoozing in his soup can when I let myself into my apartment. There were no messages on my machine. Most people called my cell these days. Even my mother called my cell. I shuffled into the bedroom, kicked my shoes off, and crawled under the covers. The best I could say about today was that it was marginally better than yesterday. At least I hadn't gotten fired. Problem was, it was hard to tell if not getting fired from Kan Klean was a good thing or a bad thing. I closed my eyes and willed myself to sleep, telling myself when I woke up my life would be great. Okay, it was sort of a fib, but it kept me from bursting into tears or smashing all my dishes.

A couple hours later I was still awake and I was thinking less about breaking something and more about eating something. I strolled out to the kitchen and took stock. I could construct another peanut butter sandwich. I could mooch dinner off my mother. I could take myself off to search for fast food. The last two choices meant I'd have to get back into the Saturn. Not an appealing prospect, but still better than another peanut butter sandwich.

I laced up my sneakers, ran a brush through my hair, and applied lip gloss. The natural look. Acceptable in Jersey only if you've had your boobs enhanced to the point where no one looked beyond them. I hadn't had my boobs enhanced, and most people found it easy to look beyond them, but I didn't care a whole lot today.

I took the stairs debating the merits of a chicken quesadilla against the satisfaction of a dozen doughnuts. I was still undecided when I pushed through the lobby door and crossed the lot to my car. Turns out it wasn't a decision I needed to make because my car was wearing a police boot.

I ripped my cell phone out of my bag and punched in Morelli's number.

"There's a police boot on my car," I said to him. "Did you put it on?"

"Not personally."

"I want it off."

"I'm crimes against persons. I'm not traffic."

"Fine. I want to report a crime against a person. Some jerk booted my car."

Morelli blew out a sigh and disconnected.

I dialed Ranger. "I have a problem," I said to Ranger. "And?"

"I was hoping you could solve it."

"Give me a hint."

"My car's been booted."

"And?"

"I need to get the boot off."

"Anything else?"

"I could use some doughnuts. I haven't had dinner."

"Where are you?"

"My apartment."

"Babe," Ranger said, and the connection went dead.

Ten minutes later, Ranger's Porsche rolled to a stop next to the Saturn. Ranger got out and handed me a bag. Ranger was in his usual black. Black T-shirt that looked like it was painted onto his biceps and clung to his washboard stomach. Black cargo pants that had lots of pockets for Ranger's goodies, although clearly not all his goodies were relegated to the pockets. His hair was medium cut and silky straight, falling across his forehead.

"Doughnuts?" I asked.

"Turkey club. Doughnuts will kill you."

"And?"

Ranger almost smiled at me. "If I had to drive this Saturn I'd want to die, too."

FOUR

"CAN YOU GET the boot off?" I asked Ranger.

Ranger toed the big chunk of metal that was wrapped around my tire. "Tank's on his way with the equipment. How'd you manage to get booted in the lot?"

"Morelli. He thinks the car's unsafe."

"And?"

"Okay, so it's got some cosmetic problems."

"Babe, it's got a twelve-inch hole in the floor."

"Yeah, but the hole's in the back and I can't even see it when I'm in the front. And if I leave the back windows open the fumes get sucked out before they get to me."

"Good to know you've thought this through."

"Are you laughing at me?"

"Do I look like I'm laughing?"

"I thought I saw your mouth twitch."

"How'd this happen?"

I took the turkey club out of the bag and unwrapped it. "It was the note guy. I took Grandma to a viewing at

Stiva's, and when we left, there was a note in the car. It said it was my turn to burn . . . and then the backseat caught fire on the way to my parents' house." I took a bite of the sandwich. "I have a feeling about the note guy. I think the note guy is Stiva's kid. Spiro. Joe's Grandma Bella told me she had a vision about rats running away from a fire. And one of the rats was sick and it came back to get me."

"And you think that rat is Spiro?"

"Do you remember Spiro? Beady rat eyes. No chin. Bad overbite. Mousy brown hair."

"Bella's a little crazy, Babe."

I finished the turkey club. "A guy named Michael Barroni disappeared ten days ago. Sixty-two years old. Upstanding citizen. Had a house on Roebling. Owned the hardware store on Rudd and Liberty. Locked the store up at the end of the day and disappeared off the face of the earth. Morelli punched Barroni into missing persons and found there were two other similar cases. Benny Gorman and Louis Lazar. Connie said you're looking for Gorman."

"Yeah, and he feels like a dead end."

"Maybe it's a dead end because he's dead."

"It's crossed my mind."

I crumpled the sandwich bag and tossed it into the back of the Saturn. It bounced off the charred backseat and fell through the hole in the floor, onto the pavement, under the car.

Ranger gave a single, barely visible shake to his head. Hard to tell if he was amused or if he was appalled.

"Did you know Barroni?" Ranger asked me.

"I went to school with his youngest son, Anthony. Here's the thing about Michael Barroni. There's no obvious reason why he disappeared. No gambling debts. No drinking or drug problems. No health problems. No secret sex life. He just locked up the store, got into his car, and drove off into the sunset. He did this on the same day and at the same time Lazar and Gorman drove off into the sunset. It was like they were all going to a meeting."

"I made the Lazar connection," Ranger said. "I didn't know there was a third."

"That's because you're the Stark Street expert and I'm the Burg expert."

"You handed your cuffs and fake badge over to Connie," Ranger said. "Why the interest in Barroni and Lazar and Gorman?"

"In the beginning, Barroni was just Burg gossip and cop talk. Now I'm thinking Spiro's gone psycho and he's back in town and stalking me. And Barroni might be connected to Spiro. I know that sounds like a stretch, but Spiro makes bad things happen. And he drags his friends into the muck with him. All through school, Spiro hung out with Anthony Barroni. Suppose Spiro's back and he's got something bad going on. Suppose Anthony's involved and somehow his dad got in the way."

"That's a lot of supposing. Have you talked to Morelli about this?"

"No. I'm not talking to Morelli about *anything*. He booted my car. I'm doing all my talking to you."

"His loss is my gain?"

"This is your lucky day," I said to Ranger.

Ranger curled his fingers into the front of my jean jacket and pulled me close. "How much luck are we talking about?"

"Not that much luck."

Ranger brushed a light kiss over my lips. "Someday," he said.

And he was probably right. Ranger and I have a strange relationship. He's my mentor and protector and friend. He's also hot and mysterious and oozes testosterone. A while ago, he was my lover for a single spectacular night. We both walked away wanting more, but to date, my practical Burg upbringing plus strong survival instincts have kept Ranger out of my bed. This is in direct contrast to Ranger's instincts. His instincts run more to keeping his eye on the prize while he enjoys the chase and waits for his chance to move in for the kill. He is, after all, a hunter of men . . . and women.

Ranger released my jacket. "I'm going to take a look at Barroni's house and store. Do you want to ride along?"

"Okay, but it's just to keep you company. It's not like I'm involved. I'm done with all that fugitive apprehension stuff."

"Still my lucky day," Ranger said.

My apartment is only a couple miles from the store, but it was after six by the time we got to Rudd and Liberty, and the store was closed. We cruised past the front, turned the corner, and took the service road at the rear. Ranger drove the Porsche down the road and paused at Barroni's back door. There was a black Corvette parked in the small lot.

"Someone's working late," Ranger said. "Do you know the car?"

"No, but I'm guessing it belongs to Anthony. His two older brothers are married and have kids, and I can't see them finding money for a toy like this."

Ranger continued on, turned the corner, and pulled to the curb. There'd been heavy cloud cover all day and now it was drizzling. Streetlights stood out in the gloom and red brake lights traced across Ranger's rain-streaked windshield.

After five minutes, the Corvette rolled past us with Anthony driving. Ranger put the Porsche in gear and followed Anthony at a distance. Anthony wandered through the Burg and stopped at Pino's Pizza. He was inside Pino's for a couple minutes and returned to his car carrying two large pizza boxes. He found his way to Hamilton Avenue, crossed Hamilton, and after two blocks he pulled into a driveway that belonged to a two-story town house. The town house had an attached garage, but Anthony didn't use it. Anthony parked in the driveway and hustled to the small front porch. He fumbled with his keys, got the door open, and rushed inside.

"That's a lot of pizza for a single guy," Ranger said. "And he has something occupying space in his garage. It's raining, and he has his hands full of pizza boxes, and he parked in the driveway."

"Maybe Spiro's in there. Maybe he's got his car parked in Anthony's garage."

"I can see that possibility turns you on," Ranger said.

"It would be nice to find Spiro and put an end to the harassment."

Shades were drawn on all the windows. Ranger idled for a few minutes in front of the town house and moved on. He retraced the route to the hardware store and had me take him from the store to Michael Barroni's house on Roebling.

It was a large house by Burg standards. Maybe two thousand square feet. Upstairs and downstairs. Detached garage. The front of the house was gray fake stone. The other three sides were white vinyl siding. It had a full front porch and a postage-stamp front yard. There was a plaster statue of the Virgin Mary in the front yard. A small basket of plastic flowers had been placed at her feet. Shades were up in the Barroni house and it was easy to look from one end to the other. A lone woman moved in the house. Carla Barroni, Michael Barroni's wife. She settled herself in front of the television in the living room and lost herself to the evening news.

I was spellbound, watching Carla. "It must be awful not to know," I said to Ranger. "To have someone you love disappear. Not to know if he was murdered and buried in a shallow grave, or if you drove him away, or if he was sick and couldn't find his way home. It makes my problems seem trivial."

"Being on the receiving end of threatening letters isn't trivial," Ranger said.

Everything's relative, I thought. The threatening letters weren't nearly as frightening as the prospect of spending another eight hours with Mama-the-Mole Macaroni. And the problems I was thinking about were personal. My life had no clear direction. My goals were small and immediate. Pay the rent. Get a better car. Make a dinner decision. I didn't have a career. I didn't have a husband. I didn't have any special talents. I didn't have a consuming passion. I didn't have a hobby. Even my pet was small . . . a hamster. I liked Rex a lot, but he didn't exactly make a big statement.

Ranger broke into my moment. "Babe, I get the feeling you're standing on a ledge, looking down."

"Just thinking."

Ranger put the Porsche into gear and headed across town. We checked out Louis Lazar's house and bar. Then we went four blocks north on Stark and parked in front of Gorman's garage. The garage was dark. No sign of life inside. A CLOSED sign hung on the office door.

"Gorman's manager kept the garage going for a week on his own and then cut out," Ranger said. "Gorman isn't married. He was living with a woman, but she has no claim to his property. He has a pack of kids, all with different mothers. The kids are too young to run the business. The rest of Gorman's relatives are in South Carolina. I did a South Carolina search, and it came back negative. From what I can tell the business was operating in the black. Gorman had a mean streak, but he wasn't stupid. He would have made arrangements to keep the garage running if he was going FTA. I can't see him just walking away. Usually I pick up a vibe from someone . . . mother, girlfriend, coworker. I'm not getting anything on this."

We cut back two blocks and parked in front of a run-down apartment building.

"This was Gorman's last known address," Ranger said. "His girlfriend didn't wait as long as his manager. The girl-friend had a new guy hanging his clothes in her closet on day five. If she knew Gorman's location, she'd have given him up for a pass to the multiplex."

"No one saw him after he drove away from the garage?"

Ranger watched the building. "No. All I know is he drove north on Stark. Consistent with Lazar."

North on Stark didn't mean much. Stark Street deteriorated as it went north. Eventually Stark got so bad even the gangs abandoned it. At the very edge of the city line Stark was a deserted war zone of fire-gutted brick buildings with boarded-up windows. It was a graveyard for stolen, stripped-down cars and used-up heroin addicts. It was a do-it-yourself garbage dump. North on Stark also led to Route 1 and Route 1 led to the entire rest of the country.

Ranger's pager buzzed, he checked the message, and pulled away from the curb, into the stream of traffic. Ranger is hot, but he has a few personality quirks that drive me nuts. He doesn't eat dessert, he has an overdeveloped sense of secret, and unless he's trying to seduce me or instruct me in the finer points of bounty huntering, conversation can be nonexistent.

"Hey," I finally said, "Man of Mystery . . . what's with the pager?"

"Business."

"And?"

Ranger slid a glance my way.

"It's no wonder you aren't married," I said to him. "You have a lot to learn about social skills."

Ranger smiled at me. Ranger thought I was amusing.

"That was my office," Ranger said. "Elroy Dish went FTA two days ago. I've been waiting for him to show up at Blue Fish, and he just walked in."

Vinnie's bonded out three generations of Dishes. Elroy is the youngest. His specialties are armed robbery and domestic violence, but Elroy is capable of most anything.

When Elroy's drunk or drugged he's fearless and wicked crazy. When he's clean and sober he's just plain mean.

Blue Fish is a bar on lower Stark, dead center in Dish country. No point to breaking down a door and attempting to drag a Dish out of his rat-trap apartment when you can just wait for him to waltz into Blue Fish for a cold one.

Ranger brought the Porsche to the curb two doors from Blue Fish, cut the motor and the lights. Three minutes later, a black SUV rolled down the street and parked in front of us. Tank and Hal, dressed in Rangeman black, got out of the SUV and strapped on utility belts. Tank is Ranger's shadow. He watches Ranger's back, and he's second in the line of command at Rangeman. His name is self-explanatory. Hal is newer to the game. He's not the sharpest tack on the corkboard, but he tries hard. He's just slightly smaller than Tank and reminds me of a big lumbering dinosaur. He's a Halosaurus.

Ranger reached behind him and grabbed a flak vest from the small backseat. "Stay here," he said. "This will only take a couple minutes and then I'll drive you home."

Ranger angled out of the Porsche, nodded to Tank and Hal, and the three of them disappeared inside Blue Fish. I checked my watch, and I stared at the door to the bar. Ranger didn't waste time when he made an apprehension. He identified his quarry, clapped the cuffs on, and turned the guy over to Tank and Hal for the forced march to the SUV.

I was feeling a little left out, but I was telling myself it was much better this way. No more danger. No more mess. No more embarrassing screw-ups. I was focused on the door to the bar, not paying a lot of attention to the street, and suddenly the driver's-side door to the Porsche was wrenched open and a guy slid in next to me. He was in his twenties, wearing a ball cap sideways and about sixty pounds of gold chains around his neck. He had a diamond chip implanted into his front tooth and the two teeth next to the chip were missing. He smiled at me and pressed the barrel of a gleaming silver-plated monster gun into my temple.

"Yo bitch," he said. "How about you get your ass out of my car."

In my mind I saw myself out of the car and running, but the reality of the situation was that all systems were down. I couldn't breathe. I couldn't move. I couldn't speak. I stared openmouthed and glassy-eyed at the guy with the diamond dental chip. Somewhere deep in my brain the word *carjack* was struggling to rise to the surface.

Diamond dental chip turned the key in the Porsche's ignition and revved the engine. "Out of the car," he yelled, pushing the gun barrel against my head. "I'm giving you one second and then I'm gonna blow your brains all over this motherfucker. Now get your *fat ass* out of the car."

The mind works in weird ways, and it's strange how something dumb can push a button. I was willing to overlook the use of the MF word, but getting called a fat ass really pissed me off.

"Fat ass?" I said, feeling my eyes narrow. "Excuse me? Fat ass?"

"I haven't got time for this shit," he said. And he

rammed the car into gear, mashed the gas to the floor, and the Porsche jumped away from the curb.

He was driving with his left hand and holding the gun and shifting with his right. There was light traffic on Stark, and he was weaving around cars and running lights. He came up fast behind a Lincoln Navigator and hit the brake hard. He moved to shift, and I knocked the gun out of his hand. The gun hit the console and fell to the floor on the driver's side.

"Fuck," he said. "Fucking fuck. Fucking bitch."

He leaned forward and reached for the gun, and I punched him in the ear as hard as I could. His head bounced off the wheel, the wheel jerked hard to the left, and we cut across oncoming traffic. The Porsche jumped the curb, plowed through a stack of black plastic garbage bags, and crashed through the plate glass window of a small delicatessen that was closed for the night.

The front airbags inflated with a *bang*, and I was momentarily stunned. I fought my way through the bag, somehow got the door open, and rolled out onto the deli floor. I was on my hands and knees in the dark, and it was wet under my hand. Blood, I thought. Get outside and get help.

A leg came into my field of vision. Black cargo pants, black boots. Hands under my armpits, lifting me to my feet. And then I was face-to-face with Ranger.

"Are you okay?" he asked.

"I must be bleeding. The floor was wet and sticky."

He looked at my hand. "I don't see any blood on you." He put my hand to his mouth and touched his tongue to my palm, giving me a rush that went from my toes to the roots of my hair. "Dill," he said. He looked beyond me, to the crumpled hood of the Porsche. "You crashed into the counter and smashed the pickle barrel."

"I'm sorry about your Porsche."

"I can replace the Porsche. I can't replace you. You need to be more careful."

"I was just sitting in your car!"

"Babe, you're a magnet for disaster."

Tank had the carjacker in cuffs. He shoved him across the floor to the door, the carjacker slid in the pickle juice and went down to one knee, and I heard Tank's boot connect with solid body. "Accident," Tank said. "Didn't see you down there in the dark." And then he yanked the carjacker to his feet and threw him into a wall. "Another accident," Tank said, grabbing the carjacker, jerking him to his feet again.

Ranger cut his eyes to Tank. "Stop playing with him."

Tank grinned at Ranger and dragged the carjacker out to the SUV.

We followed Tank out, and Ranger looked at me under the streetlight. "You're a mess," he said, picking noodles and wilted lettuce out of my hair. "You're covered in garbage again."

"We hit the bags on the curb on the way into the store. And I guess we dragged some of it with us. I probably rolled in it when I fell out of the car."

A smile hung at the corners of Ranger's mouth. "I can always count on you to brighten my day."

A shiny black Ford truck angled to a stop in front of us, and one of Ranger's men got out and handed Ranger the keys. I could see a police car turn onto Stark, two blocks away.

"Tank and Hal and Woody can take care of this," Ranger said. "We can leave."

"You have a guy named Woody?"

Ranger opened the passenger-side door to the truck for me. "Do you want me to explain it?"

"Not necessary."

I WAS IN the Saturn, parked next to Kan Klean. It was Sunday. It was the start of a new day, it was one minute to seven, and Morelli was on my cell.

"I'm in your lot," he said. "I stopped by to take you to work. Where are you? And where's your car?"

"I'm at Kan Klean. I drove."

"What happened to the boot?"

"I don't know. It disappeared."

There was a full sixty seconds of silence while I knew Morelli was doing deep breathing, working at not getting nuts. I looked at my watch, and my stomach clenched.

Mama Macaroni appeared at car side and stuck her face in my open window, her monster mole just inches from my face, her demon eyes narrowed, her thin lips drawn tight against her dentures.

"What you doing out here?" Mama yelled. "You think we pay for talking on the phone? We got work to do. You kids . . . you think you get money for doing nothing."

"Jesus," Morelli said. "What the hell is that?"

"Mama Macaroni."

"She has a voice like fingernails on a chalkboard."

———

I NEEDED A pill really bad. It was noon and I had a fireball behind my right eye and Mama Macaroni screeching into my left ear.

"The pink tag's for dry cleaning and the green tag's for laundry," Mama shrieked at me. "You mixing them up. You make a mess of everything. You ruin our business. We gonna be out on the street."

The tinkle bell attached to the front door jangled, and I looked up to see Lula walk in.

"Hey, girlfriend," Lula said to me. "What's shakin'? What's hangin'? What's the word?"

Lula's hair was gold today and styled in ringlets, like Shirley Temple at age five. Lula was wearing black high-heeled ankle boots, a tight orange spandex skirt that came to about three inches below her ass, and a matching orange top that was stretched tight across her boobs and belly. And Lula's belly was about as big as her boobs.

"What word?" Mama Macaroni asked. "Wadda you mean word? Who is this big orange person?"

"This is my friend Lula," I said.

"You friend? No. No friends. Wadda you think, this is a party?"

"Hey, chill," Lula said to Mama. "I came to pick up my dry cleaning. I'm a legitimate customer."

I had the merry-go-round in motion, looking for Lula's cleaning. The motor whirred, and plastic-sleeved, hangered orders swished by me, carried along on an overhead system of tracks.

"I'll take Vinnie's and Connie's too," Lula said.

Mama was off her stool. "You no take anything until I say so. Let me see the slip. Where's the slip?"

I had Lula's cleaning in hand and Mama stepped in front of me. "What's this on the slip? What's this discount?"

"You said I got a discount," I told her, trying hard not to stare at the mole, not having a lot of luck at it.

"*You* get a discount. This big pumpkin don't get no discount."

"Hey, hold on here," Lula said, lower lip stuck out, hands on hips. "Who you calling a pumpkin?"

"I'm calling *you* a pumpkin," Mama Macaroni said. "Look at you. You a big fat pumpkin. And you don't get no pumpkin discount." Mama turned on me. "You try to pull a fast one. Give everybody a discount. Like we run a charity here. A charity for pumpkins. Maybe you get the kickback. You think you make some money on the side."

"I don't like to disrespect old people," Lula said. "And you're about as old as they get. You're as old as dirt, but that don't mean you can insult my friend. I don't put up with that. I don't take that bus. You see what I'm saying?"

The pain was radiating out from my eye into all parts of my head, and little men in pointy hats and spiky shoes were running around in my stomach. I had to get Lula out of the store. If Mama Macaroni called Lula a pumpkin one more time, Lula was going to squash Mama Macaroni, and Mama Macaroni was going to be Mama Pancake.

I shoved Lula's clothes at her, but Mama got to them first. "Gimme those clothes," Mama said. "She can't have them until she pays full price. Maybe I don't give them to her at all. Maybe I keep them for evidence that you steal from us."

"I need that red sweater," Lula said. "That's my most flattering sweater."

"Too bad for you," Mama said. "You should think of this before you steal from us."

"That does it," Lula said. "I didn't steal from you. And I don't like your attitude. And I'm a bounty hunter now, and I don't got time for this like when I was a file clerk."

Lula got a knee up on the counter and lunged for Mama Macaroni and the dry cleaning.

"Help! Police!" Mama shrieked.

"Police, my patoot," Lula said. And she was over the counter, going for Mama Macaroni.

Mama jumped away and scrambled around a clothes bin, hugging the dry cleaning to her chest. Gina Macaroni and three other women, all shouting in Italian, came running from the back room.

Gina was wielding a broom like a baseball bat. "What's going on?" Gina wanted to know.

"Thieves. Robbers," Mama said. "They trying to steal from us. Hit them with the broom. Hit them good. Knock their heads off."

"This old woman's nuts," Lula said. "I just want my dry cleaning. I paid for it fair and square." Lula pulled her Glock out of her handbag, and all the women shrieked and dropped to the floor. Except for Mama Macaroni. Mama Macaroni flipped Lula the bird.

"You should give her the dry cleaning," I said to Mama Macaroni. "She's real dangerous. She's shot a lot of people." That was sort of a fib. Lula's shot *at* a lot of people. I don't know that she's ever connected.

"She don't scare me," Mama said. And Mama reached

underneath her long black skirt, pulled out a semiautomatic, and started shooting. She was shooting wild, taking out light fixtures and chunks of plaster from the ceiling, but that didn't make it any less terrifying . . . or for that matter, any less dangerous.

Lula and I dove for the front of the store, rolled out the door, and scrambled to the Firebird. Lula jumped behind the wheel, and we roared off.

"Do you frickin' believe that?" Lula yelled. "That crazy old lady shot at us! She could have killed us. You know what she needs?"

I looked expectantly at Lula.

"A dermatologist," Lula said. "Did you see that mole? It should be illegal to have a mole like that. That was a mutant mole. I didn't even bring it up in the conversation either. I was being real polite. Even when she was a meanie, I was still polite."

"You told her she was as old as dirt."

Lula pulled into the Cluck-in-a-Bucket lot. "Yeah, but that was a fact. You can't count a fact. How long do you get for lunch? We might as well have lunch as long as we're out."

"I don't think lunch is an issue. My employer just called me a thief and shot at me. That would lead me to believe I'm unemployed."

"I wouldn't be so sure of that. It's hard to get good help these days. That dry cleaner's lucky to have you. And I didn't hear anybody fire you. The old lady wasn't shooting at you and saying *you're fired*. The old lady was just Anna Banana probably on account of she has that mole."

We went inside, placed our order, and waited for our food to be assembled.

"Well okay, now that I think about it, probably you're fired," Lula said. "It was a nasty job anyway. You had to look at that mole all day. And I'm sorry, that's no normal mole."

"It's the mole from hell."

"Friggin' A," Lula said. "And you shouldn't worry about getting another job. You could get a better job than that. You could even get a job here. Look at the sign by the register. It says they're hiring. And there'd be advantages to working here. I bet you get free chicken and fries." Lula went back to the counter. "We want to see the manager," she said. "My friend's interested in having a job here. I'm not interested myself because I'm a kick-ass bounty hunter, but Stephanie over there just got unemployed."

I had Lula by the arm, and I was trying to drag her away from the counter. "No!" I whispered to Lula. "I don't want to work here. I'd have to wear one of those awful uniforms."

"Yeah, but you wouldn't ruin any of your real clothes that way," Lula said. "Probably you get a lot of grease stains here. And I don't think the uniform's so bad. Besides, your skinny little ass makes everything look good."

"The *hat*!"

"Okay, I see what you're saying about the hat. Suppose the hat had an accident? Suppose the hat fell into the french fry machine first thing? I bet it would take days to get a new hat."

A little guy came up behind me. He was half a head shorter than me, and he looked like a chubby pink pig in pants. His cheeks were round and pink. His hands were pink sausages. His belly jiggled when he moved. His mouth was round and his lips were pink . . . and best not to think about the pig part the mouth most resembled, but it could be found under the curly pig tail.

"I'm the manager," he said. "Milton Mann."

"This here's Stephanie Plum," Lula said. "She's looking for a job."

"Minimum wage," Mann said. "We need someone for the three-to-eleven shift."

"How about food?" Lula wanted to know. "Does she eat free? And what about takeout?"

"There's no eating on the job, but she can eat for free on her dinner break. Takeout gets a twenty percent discount."

"That sounds fair," Lula said. "She'll take the job."

"Come in a half hour early tomorrow," Mann said to me. "I'll give you your uniform and you can fill out the paper-work."

"Look at that," Lula said, claiming her tray of food, steering me back to the table. "See how easy it is to get a job? There's jobs everywhere."

"Yeah, but I don't want this job. I don't want to work here."

"Twenty percent off on takeout," Lula said. "You can't beat that. You can feed your family . . . *and friends.*"

I took a piece of fried chicken from the bucket on the tray. "My car is back at the dry cleaner."

"And I didn't get my sweater. That was my favorite sweater, too. It was just the right shade of red to flatter my skin tone."

I finished my piece of chicken. "Are you going back to get your sweater?"

"Damn skippy I'm going back. Only thing is I'm waiting

until they're closed and it's nice and dark out." Lula looked over my shoulder and her eyes focused on the front door. "Uh oh," Lula said. "Here comes Officer Hottie, and he don't look happy."

Morelli moved behind me and curled his fingers into the back of my jacket collar. "I need to talk to you . . . outside."

"I wouldn't go if I was you," Lula said to me. "He's wearing his mad cop face. At least you should make him leave his gun here."

Morelli shot Lula a look, and she buried her head in the chicken bucket.

When we got outside Morelli dragged me to the far side of the building, away from the big plate glass windows. He still had a grip on my jacket, and he still had the don't-mess-with-me cop face. He held tight to my jacket, and he stared at his shoes, head down.

"Practicing anger management?" I asked.

He shook his head and bit into his lower lip. "No," he said. "I'm trying not to laugh. That crazy old lady shot at you and I don't want to trivialize it, but I totally lost it at Kan Klean. And I wasn't the only one. I was there with three uniforms who responded to the call, and we all had to go around to the back of the building to compose ourselves. Your friend Eddie Gazarra was laughing so hard he wet his uniform. Was there really a shoot-out between the old lady and Lula?"

"Yeah, but Mama Macaroni did all the shooting. She trashed the place. Lula and I were lucky to get out alive. How'd you know where to find me?"

"I did a drive-by on all the doughnut shops and fast-food places in the area. And by the way, Mama Macaroni said to tell you that you're fired." Morelli leaned into me and nuzzled my neck. "We should celebrate."

"You wanted to celebrate when I got the job. Now you want to celebrate because I've lost the job?"

"I like to celebrate."

Sometimes I had a hard time keeping up with Morelli's libido. "I'm not talking to you," I told Morelli.

"Yeah, but we could still celebrate, right?"

"Wrong. And I need to get back inside before Lula eats all the food."

Morelli pulled me to him and kissed me with a lot of tongue. "I *really* need to celebrate," he said. And he was gone, off to file a report on my shoot-out.

Lula was finishing her half gallon of soda when I returned to the table. "How'd that go?" she wanted to know.

"Average." I looked in the chicken bucket. One wing left.

"I'm in a real mean mood after that whole cleaning incident," Lula said. "I figure I might as well make the most of it and go after my DV. When I was a file clerk I didn't usually work on Sunday, unless I was helping you. But now that I'm a bounty hunter I'm on the job twenty-four/seven. You see what I'm saying? And I know how you're missing being a bounty hunter and all, so I'm gonna let you ride with me again."

"I don't miss being a bounty hunter. And I don't want to ride with you."

"Please?" Lula said. "Pretty please with sugar on it? I'm your friend, right? And we do things together, right? Like, look at how we just shared lunch together."

"You ate all the chicken."

"Not *all* the chicken. I left you a wing. 'Course, it's true I don't particularly like wings, but that's not the point. Anyways, I kept you from putting a lot of ugly fat on your skinny ass. You aren't gonna be getting any from Officer Hottie if you get all fat and dimply. And I know you need to be getting some on a regular basis because I remember when you weren't getting *any* and you were a real cranky pants."

"Stop!" I said. "I'll go with you."

FIVE

IT TOOK US a half hour to get to the public housing projects and work our way through the grid of streets that led to Emanuel Lowe, also known as the DV. Lula had the Firebird parked across the street from Lowe's apartment, and we were both watching the apartment door, and we were both wishing we were at Macy's shopping for shoes.

"We need a better plan this time," Lula said. "Last time, I did the direct approach and that didn't work out. We gotta be sneaky this time. And we can't use me on account of everybody here knows me now. So I'm thinking it's going to have to be you to go snatch the DV."

"Not in a million years."

"Yeah, but they don't know you. And there's hardly anybody sneakier than you. I'd even cut you in. I'd give you ten bucks if you collected him for me."

I did raised eyebrows at Lula. "Ten dollars? I used to pay you fifty and up."

"I figure it goes by the pound and a little bitty thing like you isn't worth as much as a full-figured woman like me." Lula took a couple beats. "Well okay, I guess that don't fly. It was worth a try though, right?"

"Maybe you should just sit here and wait for him to come out and then you can run over him with your Firebird."

"That's sarcasm, isn't it? I know sarcasm when I hear it. And it's not attractive on you. You don't usually do sarcasm. You got some Jersey attitude going, don't you?"

I slumped lower in my seat. "I'm depressed."

"You know what would get you out of that depression? An apprehension. You need to kick some butt. You need to get yourself empowered. I bet you'd feel real good if you snagged yourself an Emanuel Lowe."

"*Fine*. Okay. I'll get Lowe for you. The day's already in the toilet. Might as well finish it off right." I unbuckled my seat belt. "Give me your gun and your cuffs."

"You haven't got your own gun?"

"I didn't think I needed to carry a gun because I didn't think I was going to be doing this anymore. When I left the house this morning I thought I was going to be working at the dry cleaners."

Lula handed me her gun and a pair of cuffs. "You always gotta have a gun. It's like wearing undies. You wouldn't go out of the house without undies, would you? Same thing with a gun. Boy, for being a bounty hunter all that time you sure don't know much."

I grabbed the gun from Lula and marched up to Lowe's front door. I knocked twice, Lowe opened the door, and I pointed the gun at him. "On the ground," I said. "*Now*."

Lowe gave a bark of laughter. "You not gonna shoot me.

I'm a unarmed man. You get twenty years for shooting me."

I aimed high, squeezed a round off, and took out a ceiling fixture.

"Crazy bitch," he said. "This here's public housing. You costing the taxpayer money. I got a mind to report you."

"I'm not in a good mood," I said to Lowe.

"I can see that. How you like me to improve your mood? Maybe you need a man to make you feel special."

Emanuel Lowe was five foot nine and rail thin. He had no ass, no teeth, and I was guessing no deodorant, no shower, no mouthwash. He was wearing a wife-beater T-shirt that had yellowed with age, and baggy homeboy-style brown pants precariously perched on his bony hips. And he was offering himself up to me. This was the state of my life. Maybe I should just shoot *myself*.

I leveled the barrel at his head. "On the floor, on your stomach, hands behind your back."

"Tell you what. I'll get on the floor if you show me some pussy. It gotta be good pussy, too. The full show. You aren't bald down there, are you? I don't know what white bitches thinking of, waxing all the bush off. Gives me the willies. It's like bonin' supermarket chicken."

So I shot him. I did it for women worldwide. It was a public service.

"Yow!" he said. "What the fuck you do that for? We just talking, having some fun."

"*I* wasn't having any fun," I said.

I'd shot him in the foot, and now he was hopping around, howling, dripping blood. From what I could see, I'd nicked him somewhere in the vicinity of the little toe.

"If you aren't down on the floor, hands behind your back, in three seconds I'm going to shoot you again," I said.

Lowe dropped to the floor. "I'm dying. I'm gonna bleed to death."

I cuffed him and stood back. "I just tagged your toe. You'll be fine."

Lula poked her head in. "What's going on? Was that gunshot?" She walked over to Lowe and stood hands on hips, staring down at Lowe's foot. "Damn," Lula said. "I hate when I have to take bleeders in my Firebird. I just got new floor mats, too."

"How bad is it?" Lowe wanted to know. "It feels real bad."

"She just ripped a chunk out of the side of your foot," Lula said. "Looks to me like you got all your toes and everything."

I ran to the kitchen and got a kitchen towel and a plastic garbage bag. I wrapped Lowe's foot in the towel and pulled the plastic bag over the foot and the towel and tied it at the ankle. "That's the best I can do," I said to Lula. "You're going to have to deal with it."

We got him to the curb, and Lula looked down at Lowe's foot. "Hold on here," she said. "We ripped a hole in the Baggie when we dragged him out here, and he's bleeding through the towel. He's gonna have to hang his leg out the window."

"I'm not hanging my leg outta the window," Lowe said. "How's that gonna look?"

"It's gonna look like you're on the way to the hospital," Lula said. "How else you think you're gonna get to the hospital and get that foot stitched up? You gonna sit here and wait for an ambulance? You think they're gonna rush to come get *your* sorry behind?"

"You got a point," Lowe said. "Just hurry up. I'm not feeling all that good. It wasn't right of her to shoot me. She had no call to do that."

"The hell she didn't," Lula said. "You gotta learn to co-operate with women. My opinion is she should have shot higher and rearranged your nasty."

Lula rolled the rear side window down, and Lowe got in and hung his legs out the window.

"I feel like a damn fool," Lowe said. "And this here's un-comfortable. My foot's throbbing like a bitch."

Lula walked around to the driver's side. "I saw a picture of what he did to his girlfriend," Lula said. "She had a broken nose and two cracked ribs, and she was in the hos-pital for three days. My thinking is he deserves some pain, so I'm gonna drive real slow, and I might even get lost on the way to the emergency room."

"Don't get too lost. Wouldn't want him to bleed to death since I was the one who shot him."

"I didn't see you shoot him," Lula said. "I especially didn't see you shoot him with my gun that might not be registered on account of I got it from a guy on a street cor-ner at one in the morning. Anyways, I figured Lowe was running away and tore himself up on a broken bottle of hooch. You know how these guys always have broken bottles of hooch laying around." Lula muscled herself be-hind the wheel. "You coming with me or you staying be-hind to tidy up?"

I gave Lula her gun. "I'm staying behind."

"Later," Lula said. And she drove off with Lowe's legs

hanging out her rear side window, the plastic bag rattling in the breeze.

I went into Lowe's apartment and prowled through the kitchen. I found a screwdriver and a mostly empty bottle of Gordon's gin. I used the screwdriver to dig the bullet out of Lowe's floor. I pocketed the round and the casing. Then I dropped the bottle of gin on the bloodiest part of the floor and smashed it with the screwdriver. I went back to the kitchen and washed the screwdriver, washed my hands, and threw the screwdriver into a pile of garbage that had collected in the corner of the kitchen. Discarded pizza boxes, empty soda bottles, fast-food bags, crumpled beer cans, and stuff I preferred not to identify.

"I hate this," I said to the empty apartment. I pulled my cell phone out of my bag and called my dad. A couple years ago my dad retired from his job at the post office, and now he drives a cab part-time.

"Hey," I said when he answered. "It's me. I need a cab."

I locked the doors and secured the windows while I waited for my dad. Not that there was much to steal from Lowe's apartment. Most of the furniture looked like Lowe had shopped at the local Dumpster. Still, it was his and I felt an obligation to be a professional. Probably should have thought about my professional obligation before shooting Lowe in the foot.

I called Ranger. "I just shot a guy in the foot," I told him.

"Did he deserve it?"

"That's sort of a tough moral question. I thought so at the time, but now I'm not so sure."

"Did you destroy the evidence? Were there witnesses? Did you come up with a good lie?"

"Yes. No. Yes."

"Move on," Ranger said. "Anything else?"

"No. That's about it."

"One last word of advice. Stay away from the dough-nuts." And he disconnected.

Great.

Twenty minutes later, my father rolled to a stop at curb-side. "I thought you were working at the button factory," he said.

My father's body showed up at the dinner table every evening. His mind was usually somewhere else. I suppose that was the secret to my parents' marital success. That plus the deal that my father made money and my mother made meatloaf and the division of labor was clear and never challenged. In some ways, life was simple in the Burg.

"The button factory job didn't work out," I told my father. "I helped Lula with an apprehension today and ended up here."

"You're like your Uncle Peppy. Went from one job to the next. Wasn't that he was dumb, either. Was just that he didn't have a direction. He didn't have a passion, you know? It didn't look like he had any special talent. Like take me. I was good at sorting mail. Now, I know that doesn't seem like a big deal, but it was something I was good at. Of course, I got replaced by a machine. But that doesn't take away that I was good at something. Your Uncle Peppy was forty-two before he found out he could do latch hook rugs."

"Uncle Peppy's doing time at Rahway for arson."

"Yeah, but he's doing latch hook there. When he gets out

he can make a good living with rugs. You should see some of his rugs. He made a rug that had a tiger head in it. You ask me, he's better hooking rugs than arson. He never got the hang of arson. Okay, so he set a couple good fires, but he didn't have the touch like Sol Razzi. Sol could set a fire and no one ever knew how it started. Now, *that's* arson."

Jersey's one of the few places where arson is a profession.

"Where are we going?" my father wanted to know.

"What's Mom making for supper?"

"Meatballs with spaghetti. And I saw a chocolate cake in the kitchen."

"I'll go home with you."

THERE WERE TWO cars parked in front of my parents' house. One belonged to my sister. And one belonged to a friend of mine who was helping my mom plan my sister's wedding. My father paused at the driveway entrance and stared at the cars with his eyes narrowed.

"If you smash into them your insurance will go up," I said.

My father gave a sigh, pulled forward, and parked. When my father blew out the candles on his birthday cake I suspect he wished my grandmother would go far away. He'd wish my sister into another state, and my friend Sally Sweet, a.k.a. the Wedding Planner, into another universe. I'm not sure what he wanted to do with me. Maybe ride along on a bust. Don't get me wrong. My dad isn't a mean guy. He wouldn't want my grandmother to suffer, but I think he wouldn't be too upset if she suddenly died in her sleep. Personally, I think Grandma's a hoot. Of course, I don't have to live with her.

All through school my sister, Valerie, looked like the Virgin Mary. Brown hair simply styled, skin like alabaster, beatific smile. And she had a personality to match. Serene. Smooth. Little Miss Perfect. The exact opposite of her sister, Stephanie, who was Miss Disaster. Valerie graduated college in the top 10 percent of her class and married a perfectly nice guy. They followed his job to L.A. They had two girls. Valerie morphed into Meg Ryan. And one day the perfectly nice guy ran off to Tahiti with the baby-sitter. No reflection on Meg. It was just that time in his life. So Valerie moved back home with her girls. Angie is the first-born and a near perfect clone of Valerie the Virgin. Mary Alice is two years behind Angie. And Mary Alice thinks she's a horse.

It's a little over a year now since Valerie returned, and she's since gained sixty pounds, had a baby out of wedlock, and gotten engaged to her boss, Albert Kloughn, who also happens to be the baby's father. The baby's name is Lisa, but most often she's called The Baby. We're not sure who The Baby is yet, but from the amount of gas she produces I think she's got a lot of Kloughn in her.

Valerie and Sally were huddled at the dining room table, studying the seating chart for the wedding reception.

"Hey, girlfriend," Sally said to me. "Long time no see."

Sally drove a school bus during the week, and weekends he played in a band in full drag. He was six foot five inches tall, had roses tattooed on his biceps, hair everywhere, a large hook nose, and he was lanky in a guitar-playing-maniac kind of way. Today Sally was wearing a big wooden cross on a chain and six strands of love beads over a black Metallica T-shirt, black hightop Chucks, and washed-out baggy jeans.

Okay, not your average wedding planner, but he'd sort of adopted us, and he was free. He'd become one of the family with my mom and grandma and they endured his eccentricities with the same eyerolling tolerance that they endured mine. I guess a pothead wedding planner seems respectable when you have a daughter who shoots people.

Angie was doing her homework across from Valerie. The Baby was in a sling attached to Valerie's chest, and Mary Alice was galloping around the table, whinnying. My father went straight to his chair in the living room and remoted the television. I went to the kitchen.

My mother was at the stove, stirring the red sauce. "Emily Restler's daughter got a pin for ten years' service at the bank," my mother said. "Ten years and she was never once in a shootout. I have a daughter who works one day at a dry cleaners and turns it into the gunfight at the O.K. Corral. And on a Sunday, too. The Lord's Day."

"It wasn't me. I didn't even have a gun. It was Mama Macaroni. And she wouldn't give Lula her dry cleaning."

Grandma was at the small kitchen table. "I hate to think you couldn't take down Mama Macaroni. If I'd been there you would have got the dry cleaning. In fact, I got a mind to go over there and get it for you."

"*No*," my mother and I said in unison.

I got a soda from the fridge and eyed the cake on the counter.

"It's for supper," my mother said. "No snitching. It's got to be nice. The wedding planner is eating with us."

Sally is one of my favorite people, but Sally didn't care a lot about what went in his mouth unless it was inhaled from a bong or rolled in wacky tobacky paper.

"Sally wouldn't notice if there were roaches in the icing," I told my mom.

"It has nothing to do with Sally," my mom said. "My water glasses don't have spots. There's no dust on the furniture. And I don't serve guests half-eaten cake at my dinner table."

I didn't serve guests half-eaten cake either. To begin with, I never had guests, unless it was Joe or Ranger. And neither of them was interested in my cake. Okay, maybe Joe would want cake . . . but it wouldn't be the first thing on his mind, and he wouldn't care if it was half-eaten.

I grated parmesan for my mother, and I sliced some cucumbers and tomatoes. In the dining room, Valerie and Sally were yelling at each other, competing with the television and the galloping horse.

"Is there any news about Michael Barroni?" I asked.

"Still missing," Grandma said. "And they haven't found his car, either. I hear he only had it for a day. It was brand-new right out of the showroom."

"I saw Anthony yesterday. He was driving a Corvette that looked new."

Grandma got dishes from the cupboard. "Mabel Such says Anthony's spending money like water. She don't know where he's getting it from. She says he doesn't make all that much at the store. She says he was on a salary just like everybody else. Michael Barroni came up the hard way, and he wasn't a man to give money away. Not even to his sons."

I got silverware and napkins, and Grandma and I set the table around Valerie and Sally and Angie.

"You can stare at that seating chart all you want," Grandma said to Valerie. "It's never gonna get perfect. Nobody wants to sit next to Biddie Schmidt. Everybody wants to sit next to Peggy Linehart. And nobody's going to be happy sitting at table number six, next to the restrooms."

My mother brought the meatballs and sauce to the table and went back for the spaghetti. My father moved from his living room chair to his dining room chair and helped himself to the first meatball. Everyone sat except Mary Alice. Mary Alice was still galloping.

"Horses got to eat," Grandma said. "You better sit down."

"There's no hay," Mary Alice said.

"Sure there is," Grandma said. "See that big bowl of spaghetti? It's people hay, but horses can eat it, too."

Mary Alice plunged her face into the spaghetti and snarfed it up.

"That's disgusting," Grandma said.

"It's the way horses eat," Mary Alice told her. "They stick their whole face in the feed bag. I saw it on television."

The front door opened and Albert Kloughn walked in. "Am I late? I'm sorry I'm late. I didn't mean to be late. I had a client."

Everyone stopped what they were doing and looked at Kloughn. Kloughn didn't get a lot of clients. He's a lawyer and his business has been slow to take off. Partly the problem is that he's a sweetie pie guy . . . and who wants a sweetie pie lawyer? In Jersey you want a lawyer who's a shark, a sonuvabitch, a first-class jerk. And partly the problem is Kloughn's appearance. Kloughn looks like a soft, chubby, not-entirely-with-the-program fourteen-year-old boy.

"What kind of client?" Grandma asked.

Kloughn took his place at the table. "It was a woman from the Laundromat next to my office. She was doing her whites, and she saw my sign and the light on in my office. I went in to do some filing, but I was actually playing poker on my computer. Anyway, she came over for advice." Kloughn helped himself to spaghetti. "Her husband took off on her, and she didn't know what to do. Sounded like she didn't mind him leaving. She said they'd been having problems. It was that he took their car, and she was stuck with the payments. It was a brand-new car, too."

I felt the skin prickle at the nape of my neck. "When did this guy disappear?"

"A couple weeks ago." Kloughn scooped a meatball onto the big serving spoon. The meatball rolled off the spoon, slid down Kloughn's shirt, and ski jumped off his belly into his lap. "I knew that was going to happen," Kloughn said. "This always happens with meatballs. Does it happen with chicken? Does it happen with ham? Okay, sometimes it happens with chicken and ham, but not as much as meatballs. If it was me, I wouldn't make meatballs round. Round things roll, right? Am I right? What if you made meatballs square? Did anybody think of that?"

"That would be meat*loaf*," Grandma said.

"Did this woman report her missing husband to the police?" I asked Kloughn.

"No. It was just one of those personal things. She said she knew he was going to leave her. I guess he was fooling around on the side and things weren't working out for them." Kloughn retrieved the meatball and set it on top of his spaghetti. He dabbed at his shirt with his napkin, but the smear of red sauce only got worse. "I felt sorry for her with the car payment and all, but boy, can you imagine being that dumb? Here she is living with this guy and all of a sudden he just up and leaves her. And it turns out she has nothing but bills. They had two mortgages that she didn't even know about. The bank account was empty. What a dope."

My mother, father, and Grandma and I all sucked in some air and slid our eyes to Valerie. This was exactly what happened to Valerie. This was like calling *Valerie* a dope.

"You think this woman is a dope because her husband managed to swindle her out of everything?" Valerie asked Kloughn.

"Well yeah. I mean, duh. She was probably too lazy to keep track of things and got what she deserved."

The color rose from Valerie's neck clear to the roots of her hair. I swear I could see her scalp glowing like hot coals.

"Oh boy," Grandma said.

Sally inched his chair away from Valerie.

Kloughn was working at the stain on his shirt and not looking at Valerie, and I was guessing he hadn't a clue what he'd just said. Somehow the words got put together into sentences and fell out of his mouth. This happened a lot with Kloughn. Kloughn looked up from his shirt to dead silence. Only a slight sizzle where Valerie's scalp was steaming.

"What?" Kloughn said. He searched the faces in the room. Something was wrong, and he'd missed it. He focused on Valerie, and you could see his mind working backward. And then it hit him. *Kaboom.*

"You were different," he said to Valerie. "I mean, you had a reason for being a dope. Well, not a dope actually. I don't mean to say you were a dope. Okay, you might have been a little dop*ey.* No, wait, I don't mean that either. Not dopey or dope or any of those things. Okay, okay, just a teensy bit dopey, but in a good way, right? Dopey can be good. Like dumb blond dopey. No, I don't mean that either. I don't know where that came from. Did I say that? I didn't say that, did I?"

Kloughn stopped talking because Valerie had gotten to her feet with the fourteen-inch bread knife in her hand.

"You don't want to do anything silly here," I said to Val. "You aren't thinking of stabbing him, are you? Stabbing is messy."

"Fine. Give me your gun, and I'll shoot him."

"It's not good to shoot people," I said. "The police don't like it."

"You shoot people all the time."

"Not *all* the time."

"I'll give you my gun," Grandma said.

My mother glared at my grandmother. "You told me you got rid of that gun."

"I meant I'd give her my gun if I had one," Grandma said.

"Great," Valerie said, flapping her arms, her voice up an octave. "Now I'm dopey. I'm fat, and I'm dopey. I'm a big fat dope."

"I didn't say you were fat," Kloughn said. "You're not fat. You're just . . . chubby, like me."

Valerie went wild-eyed. "*Chubby?* Chubby is awful! I used to be perfect. I used to be serene. And now look at me! I'm a wreck. I'm a big, fat, dopey, chubby wreck. And I look like a white whale in my stupid wedding gown. A big, huge *white whale!*" She narrowed her eyes and leaned across the table at Kloughn. "You think I'm dopey and lazy and chubby, and that I got what I deserved from my philandering husband!"

"No. I swear. I was under stress," Kloughn said. "It was the meatball. I never think. You know I never think."

"I never want to see you again," Valerie said. "The wedding is off." And Valerie gathered up her three kids, her diaper bag, her sling thing, her kids' backpacks, and the collapsible stroller. She went to the kitchen and took the chocolate cake. And she left.

"Dudes," Sally said. "I did the best I could with the dress."

"We're not blaming you," Grandma said. "But she *does* look like a white whale."

Kloughn turned to me. "What happened?"

I looked over at him. "She took the cake."

I CAUGHT A ride home with Sally, and I was parked in front of my television when my doorbell rang at nine o'clock. It was Lula, and she was dressed in black from head to toe, including a black ski mask.

"Are you ready?" Lula wanted to know.

"Ready for what?"

"To get my cleaning. What do you think?"

"I think we should give up on the cleaning and send out for a pizza. Aren't you hot in that ski mask?"

"That Mama Macaroni got my favorite sweater. I need that sweater. And on top of that it's the principle of the thing. It's just not right. I was a hundred percent in the right. I'm surprised at you wanting to let this go. Where's your crusading spirit? I bet Ranger wouldn't let it go. And you got to get your car, anyway. How're you gonna get over there to get your car if you don't go with me?"

My car. Mental head slap. I'd forgotten about the car.

Ten minutes later, we were idling across the street from Kan Klean. "It's nice and dark tonight," Lula said. "We got some cloud cover. Not a star in the sky and it looks like someone already took out the streetlight."

I looked at Lula and grimaced.

"Hey, don't give me that grimace. I expected you'd compliment me on my shooting. I actually hit that freaking lightbulb!"

"How many shots did it take?"

"I emptied a whole clip at it." Lula cut the engine and pulled her ski mask back over her head. "Come on. Time to rock and roll."

Oh boy.

We got out of the Firebird and waited for an SUV to pass before crossing the street. The SUV driver caught a glance at Lula in the ski mask and almost jumped the curb.

"If you can't drive, you shouldn't be on the road," Lula yelled after him.

"It was the mask," I said. "You scared the crap out of him."

"Hunh," Lula said.

We got to the store and Lula tried the front door. Locked. "How many other doors are there?" she asked.

"Just one. It's in back. But it's a fire door. You'll never get through it. There aren't any windows back there either. Just a couple big exhaust fans."

"Then we got to go in through the front," Lula said. "And I don't mind doing it because I'm justified. This here's a righteous cause. It's not every day I can find a sweater like that." She turned to me. "You go ahead and pick the lock."

"I don't know how to pick a lock."

"Hell, you were the big bounty hunter. How could you be the big bounty hunter without knowing how to pick a lock? How'd you ever get in anywhere?" She stood back and looked at the store. "Ordinarily I'd just break a window, but they got one big-ass window here. It's just about the whole front of the place. It might look suspicious if I broke the window."

Lula ran across the street to the Firebird and came back with a tire iron. "Maybe we can pry the door open." She put the tire iron to the doorjamb and another car drove by. The car slowed as it passed us and then took off.

"Maybe we should try the back door," Lula said.

SIX

WE WENT AROUND to the back and Lula tried to wedge the tire iron under the bolt. "Don't fit," she said. "This door's sealed up tight." Lula gave the door a whack with the tire iron and the door swung open. "Will you look at this," Lula said. "Have we got some luck, or what?"

"I don't like it. They always lock up and set the alarm."

"They must have just forgot. It was a traumatic day."

"I think we should leave. This doesn't feel right."

"I'm not leaving without my sweater. I'm close now. I can hear my sweater calling to me. Soon's we get inside I'll switch on my Maglite, and you can work that gizmo that makes the clothes go around, and before you know it we'll be outta here."

We both took two steps forward, the door closed behind us, and Lula hit the button on the Maglite. We cautiously walked past the commercial washers and dryers and the large canvas bins that held the clothes. We stopped and listened for sirens, for someone else breathing, for the beeping of an alarm system ready to activate.

"Feels okay to me," Lula said.

It didn't feel okay to me. All the little hairs on my arm were standing at attention, and my heart was thumping in my chest.

"We got the counter right in front of us," Lula said. "You switch on the whirly clothes thing."

I reached for the switch and every light in the store suddenly went on. It was as bright as day. And there was Mama Macaroni, perched on her chair, a hideous crone dressed in a black shroud, sighting us down the barrel of a gun, her mole hairs glinting under the fluorescent light.

"Holy crap," Lula said. "Holy Jesus. Holy cow."

Mama Macaroni held the gun in one hand and Lula's dry cleaning in the other. "I knew you'd be back," she said. "Your kind has no honor. All you know is stealing and whoring."

"I quit whoring," Lula said. "Okay, maybe I do a little recreational whoring once in a while . . ."

"Trash," Mama Macaroni said. "Cheap trash. Both of you." She turned to me. "I never want to hire you. I tell them anything that come from your family is bad. Hungarians!" And she spat on the floor. "That's what I think of Hungarians."

"I'm not Hungarian," Lula said. "How about giving me my dry cleaning?"

"When hell freezes. And that's where you should be," Mama Macaroni said. "I put a curse on you. I send you to hell."

Lula looked at me. "She can't do that, can she?"

"You never get this sweater," Mama Macaroni said. "*Never*. I take this sweater to the grave with me."

Lula looked at me like she wouldn't mind arranging that to happen.

"It'd be expensive," I said to Lula. "Be cheaper just to buy a new sweater."

"And *you*," Mama Macaroni said to me. "You never gonna see that car again. That *my* car now. You leave it in my lot and that make it mine." She squinted down the barrel at me, leveling it at forehead level. "Give me the key."

"You don't suppose she'd actually shoot you, do you?" Lula asked.

There was no doubt in my mind. Mama Macaroni would shoot me, and I'd be dead, dead, dead. I pulled the car key out of my pocket and gingerly handed it over to Mama.

"I'm gonna leave now," Mama said. "I got a TV show I like to watch. And you gonna stay here." She backed away from us, past the washers and dryers to the rear door. She set the alarm and scuttled through the fire door. The door closed after her, and I could hear her throw the bolt.

I immediately went to the front of the store and stood behind the counter so I could look out the window. "We'll wait until we see her drive away, and then we'll leave," I said to Lula. "We'll trip the alarm when we open the door, but we'll be long gone before the police get here."

I heard the Saturn engine catch, and then there was an explosion that rocked the building. The explosion blew the fire door off its hinges, shattered the big front window, and knocked Lula and me to our knees.

"Fudge!" Lula said.

My instinct was to leave the building. I didn't know what caused the explosion, but I wanted to get out before it happened again. And I didn't know if the building was structurally sound. I grabbed Lula and got her to her feet and pulled her to the front door. We were walking carefully, crunching over glass shards. Lucky we'd been behind the counter when the explosion occurred. The door had been blown open, and Lula and I picked our way through the debris, onto the sidewalk.

Kan Klean was in a mixed neighborhood of small businesses and small homes, and people were coming out of their houses, looking around for the source of the explosion.

"What the heck was that?" Lula said. "And why's there a tire in the middle of the sidewalk?"

I looked at Lula and Lula looked at me, and we knew why there was a tire in the middle of the sidewalk.

"Car bomb," Lula said.

We ran around to the parking lot on the side of the building and stopped short. The Saturn was a blackened skeleton of smoking, twisted metal. Difficult to see details in the dark. Chunks of shredded fiberglass body, upholstered cushion, and odds and ends of car parts were scattered over the lot.

Lula had her flashlight out, playing it across the disaster. She momentarily held the light on a segment of steering wheel. Part of a hand still gripped the wheel. A ragged shred of black cloth was attached to the hand.

"Uh oh," Lula said. "It don't look good for my dry cleaning."

I felt a wave of nausea slide through my stomach. "We should secure this area until the police get here."

Fifteen minutes later, the entire block was cordoned. Yellow police tape stretched everywhere and fire trucks and emergency vehicles were angled between police cars, lights flashing. Banks of portable lights were going up to better see the scene. Macaronis from all parts of the Burg were gathered in a knot to one side of the lot.

Morelli arrived shortly after the first blue-and-white, and he immediately whisked me away, lest I be torn limb from limb by Macaronis. He got the story, and then he stuffed me into his SUV with police escort. Forty-five minutes later, he returned and slid behind the wheel.

"Tell me again how this happened," Morelli said.

"Lula and I were driving by and I saw the light on, so I thought I'd go in and try to get Lula's dry cleaning. Mama Macaroni was alone in the store, she pulled a gun on me, demanded the keys to the Saturn, and left through the back door. Moments later, I heard the explosion."

"Good," Morelli said. "Now tell me what really happened."

"Lula and I broke in through the back door so we could steal her dry cleaning. Mama Macaroni was waiting for us, and the rest of the story is the same."

"Definitely go with the first version," Morelli said.

"Did they find the rest of Mama Macaroni?"

"Most of her. They're still looking through the bushes. Mama Macaroni covered a lot of ground." Morelli turned the key in the ignition. "Do you want to go home with me?"

"Yeah. I'm a little creeped out."

"I was hoping you'd want to go home with me because I'm smart and sexy and fun."

"That, too. And I like your dog."

"That car bomb was meant for you," Morelli said.

"I thought my life would get better if I stopped chasing after bad guys."

"You've made some enemies."

"It's Spiro," I told him.

Morelli stopped for a light and looked at me. "Spiro Stiva? Constantine's kid? Do you know this for sure?"

"No. It's just a gut feeling. The notes sound like him. And he was friends with Anthony Barroni. And now Barroni's dad is missing, and people say Anthony is spending money he shouldn't have."

"So you think something's going on with Anthony Barroni and Spiro Stiva?"

"Maybe. And maybe Spiro's whacko and decided I ruined his life and now he's going to end mine."

Morelli thought about it for a moment and shrugged. "It's not much, but it's as good as anything I've got. How do the other two disappearances fit in?"

"I don't know, but I think there might be one more." And I told him about Kloughn's client. "And there's something else. Kloughn's client's husband disappeared in their brand-new car. Michael Barroni also disappeared in a brand-new car."

Morelli slid a sideways look at me.

"Okay, so I know lots of people have new cars. Still, it's something they had in common."

"Barroni, Gorman, and Lazar were the same age within two years, and they all owned small businesses. Does Kloughn's client fit that profile?"

"I don't know."

Morelli turned a corner, drove two blocks, and parked in front of his house. "You'd think someone would have seen

Spiro if he was back. The Burg's not good at keeping a secret."

"Maybe he's hiding."

My mother called on my cell phone. "People are saying
you blew up Mama Macaroni."

"She was in my car, and she accidentally blew herself up.
I did not blow her up."

"How can someone accidentally blow themself up? Are
you okay?"

"I'm fine. I'm going home with Joe."

IT WAS EARLY morning, and I was sitting on the side of
the bed, watching Morelli get dressed. He was wearing
black jeans, cool black shoes with a thick Vibram sole, and
a long-sleeved blue button-down shirt. He looked like a
movie star playing an Italian cop.

"Very sexy," I said to Morelli.

He strapped his watch on and looked over at me. "Say it
again and the clothes come off."

"You'll be late."

Morelli's eyes darkened, and I knew he was weighing
pleasure against responsibility. There was a time in
Morelli's life when pleasure would have won, no contest.
I'd been attracted to that Morelli, but I hadn't especially
liked him. The moment passed and Morelli's eyes regained
focus. The guy part was under control. Not to give him
more credit than he deserved, I suspected this was made
possible by the two orgasms he'd had last night and the
one he'd had about a half hour ago.

"I can't be late today. I have an early meeting, and I'm

way behind on my paperwork." He kissed the top of my head. "Will you be here when I come home tonight?"

"No. I'm working the three-to-eleven shift at Cluck-in-a-Bucket."

"You're kidding."

"It was one of those impulse things."

Morelli grinned down at me. "You must need money real bad."

"Bad enough."

I followed him down the stairs and closed the door after him. "Just you and me," I said to Bob.

Bob had already eaten his breakfast and gone for a walk so Bob was feeling mellow. He wandered away, into the living room where bars of sunshine were slanting through the window onto the carpet. Bob turned three times and flopped down onto the sunspot.

I shuffled out to the kitchen, got a mug of coffee, and took it upstairs to Morelli's office. The room was small and cluttered with boxes of income tax files, a red plastic milk carton filled with old tennis balls collected during dog walks in the park, a baseball bat, a stack of phone books, gloves and wraps for a speed bag, a giant blue denim dog bed, a well-oiled baseball glove, a power screwdriver, roles of duct tape, a dead plant in a clay pot, and a plastic watering can that had obviously never been used. He had a computer and a desktop printer on a big wood desk that had been bought used. And he had a phone.

I sat at the desk, and I took a pen and a yellow legal pad from the top drawer. I had the morning free, and I was going to use it to do some sleuthing. Someone wanted me dead, and I didn't feel comfortable sitting around doing nothing, waiting for it to happen.

First on my list was a call to Kloughn.

"She wouldn't let me in the house," he said. "I had to sleep here in the office. It wasn't so bad since I have a couch, and the Laundromat is next door. I got up early and did some laundry. What should I do? Should I call? Should I go over there? I had this terrible nightmare last night. Valerie was floating over top of me in the wedding gown except she was a whale. I bet it was because she kept saying how she was a whale in the wedding gown. Anyway, there she was in my dream . . . a big huge whale all dressed up in the white wedding gown. And then all of a sudden she dropped out of the sky, and I was squashed under her, and I couldn't breathe. Good thing I woke up, hunh?"

"Good thing. I need to know your client's name," I told him. "The one with the missing husband."

"Terry Runion. Her husband's name is Jimmy Runion."

"Do you know what kind of car he just bought?"

"Ford Taurus. He got it at that big dealership on Route One. Shiller Ford."

"His age?"

"I don't know his exact age, but his wife looks like she's late fifties."

"What about his job? Did he quit his job when he disappeared?"

"He didn't have a job. He used to work for some computer company, but he took early retirement. About Valerie . . ."

"I'll talk to Valerie for you," I said. And I hung up.

Valerie answered on the second ring. "Yuh," she said.

"I just talked to Albert. He said he slept in his office."

"He said I was fat."

"He said you were chubby."

"Do you think I'm chubby?" Val asked.

"No," I told her. "I think you're fat."

"Oh God," Valerie wailed. *"Oh God!* How did this happen? How did I get *fat*?"

"You ate everything. And you ate it with gravy."

"I did it for the baby."

"Well, something went wrong because only seven pounds went to the baby, and you got the rest."

"I don't know how to get rid of it. I've never been fat before."

"You should talk to Lula. She's good at losing weight."

"If she's so good at losing weight, why is she so big?"

"She's also good at *gaining* weight. She gains it. She loses it. She gains it. She loses it."

"The wedding is on Saturday. If I really worked at it, do you think I could lose sixty pounds between now and Saturday?"

"I guess you could have it sucked out, but I hear that's real painful and you get a lot of bruising."

"I hate my life," Val said.

"Really?"

"No. I just hate being fat."

"That doesn't mean you should hate Albert. He didn't make you fat."

"I know. I've been awful to him, and he's such an adorable oogie woogams."

"I think it's great that you're in love, Val. And I'm happy

for you . . . I really am. But the baby talk cuddle umpkins oogie woogams thing is making me a little barfy warfy. What about the Virgin Mary, Val? Remember when everyone said you were just like the Virgin Mary? You were cool and serene like the Virgin Mary, like a big pink plaster statue of the Virgin. Would the Virgin refer to God as her cuddle umpkins? I don't think so."

The next call was to my cousin Linda at the DMV. "I need some information," I said to Linda. "Benny Gorman, Michael Barroni, Louis Lazar. I want to know if they got a new car in the last three months and what kind?"

"I heard you quit working for Vinnie. So what's up with the names?"

"Part-time job. Routine credit check for CBNJ." I had no idea what CBNJ stood for, but it sounded good, right?

I could hear Linda type the names into her computer. "Here's Barroni," she said. "He bought a Honda Accord two weeks ago. Nothing on Gorman. And nothing's coming up on Lazar."

"Thanks. I appreciate it."

"Boy, the wedding's almost here. I guess everyone's real excited."

"Yeah. Valerie's a wreck."

"That's the way it is with weddings," Linda said.

I disconnected and took a moment to enjoy my coffee. I liked sitting in Morelli's office. It wasn't especially pretty, but it felt nice because it was filled with all the bits and pieces of Morelli's life. I didn't have an office in my apartment. And maybe that was a good thing because I was afraid if I had an office it might be empty. I didn't have a hobby. I didn't play sports. I had a family, but I never got around to framing pictures. I wasn't learning a foreign language, or learning to play the cello, or learning to be a gourmet cook.

Well hell, I thought. I could just pick one of those things. There's no reason why I can't be interesting and have an office filled with stuff. I can collect tennis balls in the park. And I can get a plant and let it die. And I can play the damn cello. In fact, I could probably be a terrific cello player.

I took my coffee mug downstairs and put it in the dishwasher. I grabbed my bag and my jacket. I yelled good-bye to Bob as I was going out the door. And I set off on foot for my parents' house. I was going to borrow Uncle Sandor's Buick. Again. I had no other option. I needed a car. Good thing it was a long walk to my parents' house and I was getting all this exercise because I was going to need a doughnut after taking possession of the Buick.

Grandma was at the door when I strolled down the street. "It's Stephanie!" Grandma yelled to my mother.

Grandma loved when I blew up cars. Blowing up Mama Macaroni would be icing on the cake for Grandma. My mother didn't share Grandma's enthusiasm for death and disaster. My mother longed for normalcy. Dollars to doughnuts, my mother was in the kitchen ironing. Some people popped pills when things turned sour. Some hit the bottle. My mother's drug of choice was ironing. My mother ironed away life's frustrations.

Grandma opened the door for me, and I stepped into the house and dropped my bag on the hall table.

"Is she ironing?" I asked Grandma Mazur.

"Yep," Grandma said. "She's been ironing since first thing this morning. Probably would have started last night but she couldn't get off the phone. I swear, half the Burg called about you last night. Finally we disconnected the phone."

I went to the kitchen and poured myself a cup of coffee. I sat down at the little kitchen table and looked over at my mother's ironing basket. It was empty. "How many times have you ironed that shirt you've got on the board?" I asked my mother.

"Seven times," my mother said.

"Usually you calm down by the time the basket's empty."

"Somebody blew up Mama Macaroni," my mother said. "That doesn't bother me. She had it coming. What bothers me is that it was supposed to be you. It was your car."

"I'm being careful. And it's not certain that it was a bomb. It could have been an accident. You know how it is with my cars. They catch on fire, and they explode."

My mother made a strangled sound in her throat, and her eyes sort of glazed over. "That's true," she said. "Hideously true."

"Marilyn Rugach said Stiva's got most of Mama Macaroni at the funeral parlor," Grandma said. "Marilyn works there part-time doing bookkeeping. I talked to Marilyn this morning, and she said they brought the deceased to the home in a zippered bag. She said there was still some parts missing, but she wouldn't say if they found the mole. Do you think there's any chance that they'll have an open casket at the viewing? Stiva's pretty good at patching people up, and I sure would like to see what he'd do with that mole."

My mother made the sign of the cross, a hysterical giggle gurgled out of her, and she clapped a hand over her mouth.

"You should give up on the ironing and have a snort," Grandma said to my mother.

"I don't need a snort," my mother said. "I need some sanity in my life."

"You got a lot of sanity," Grandma said. "You got a real stable lifestyle. You got this house and you got a husband . . . sort of. And you got daughters and granddaughters. And you got the Church."

"I have a daughter who blows things up. Cars, trucks, funeral parlors, people."

"That only happens once in a while," I said. "I do lots of other things besides that."

My mother and grandmother looked at me. I had their full attention. They wanted to know what other things I did besides blowing up cars and trucks and funeral parlors and people.

I searched my mind and came up with nothing. I did a mental replay of yesterday. What did I do? I blew up a car and an old lady. Not personally but I was somewhere in the mix. What else? I made love to Morelli. A lot. My mother wouldn't want to hear about that. I got fired. I shot a guy in the foot. She wouldn't want to hear that either.

"I can play the cello," I said. I don't know where it came from. It just flew out of my mouth.

My mother and grandmother stood frozen in open-mouthed shock.

"Don't that beat all," Grandma finally said. "Who would have thought you could play the cello?"

"I had no idea," my mother said. "You never mentioned it before. Why didn't you tell us?"

"I was . . . shy. It's one of those personal hobbies. Personal cello playing."

"I bet you're real good," Grandma said.

My mother and grandmother looked at me expectantly. They wanted me to be good.

"Yep," I said. "I'm pretty good."

Stephanie, Stephanie, Stephanie, I said to myself. What are you doing? You are such a goofus. You don't even know what a cello looks like. Sure I do, I answered. It's a big violin, right?

"How long have you been taking lessons?" Grandma wanted to know.

"A while." I looked at my watch. "Gee, I'd like to stay, but I have things to do. I was hoping I could borrow Uncle Sandor's Buick."

Grandma took a set of keys out of a kitchen drawer. "Big Blue will be happy to see you," she said. "He doesn't get driven around too much."

Big Blue corners like a refrigerator on wheels. It has power brakes but no power steering. It guzzles gas. It's impossible to park. And it's powder blue. It has a shiny white top, powder blue body, silver-rimmed portholes, fat whitewall tires, and big gleaming chrome bumpers.

"I guess you need a big car like Blue so you can carry that cello around with you," Grandma said.

"It's a perfect fit for the backseat," I told her.

I took the keys and waved myself out of the house. I walked to the garage, opened the door, and there it was . . . Big Blue. I could feel the vibes coming off the car. The air hummed around me. Men loved Big Blue. It was a muscle car. It rode on a sweaty mix of high-octane gas and testosterone. Step on the gas and hear me roar, the car whispered. Not the growl of a Porsche. Not the *vroooom* of a Ferrari. This car was a bull walrus. This car had cajones that hung to its hubcaps.

Personally, I prefer cajones that sit a little higher, but hey, that's just me. I climbed aboard, rammed the key in, and cranked Blue over. The car came to life and vibrated under me. I took a deep breath, told myself I'd own a Lexus someday, and slowly backed out of the garage.

Grandma trotted over to the car with a brown grocery bag. "Your mother wants you to drop this off at Valerie's house. Valerie forgot to take it last night."

Valerie was renting a small house at the edge of the Burg, about a half mile away. Until yesterday, she was sharing the house with Albert Kloughn. And since she was back to calling him her oogie woogams, I suppose he was about to return.

I wound through a maze of streets, brought Big Blue to the curb in front of Val's house, and stared at the car parked in front of me. It was Lula's red Firebird. Two possibilities. One was that Valerie had skipped out on a bond. The other was that she'd taken my smart-mouth advice and called Lula for diet tips. I rolled out of the Buick and got on with the brown-bag delivery.

Val opened the door before I reached the porch. "Grandma called and said you were on your way."

"Looks like Lula's here. Are you FTA?"

"No. I'm F-A-T. So I called Lula like you suggested. And she came right over."

"I take other people's dieting seriously," Lula said to Valerie. "I'm gonna have you skinny in no time. This might even turn out to be a second career for me. Of course, now that I'm a bounty hunter I've got a lot of demands on my time. I've got a real nasty case that I'm working on. I should be out tracking this guy down right now, only I figured I could take a break from it and help you out."

"What kind of case is it?" Val asked.

"He's wanted for AR and PT," Lula said. "That's bounty hunter shorthand for armed robbery and public tinkling. He held up a liquor store and then took a leak in the domestic table wines section. I bet Stephanie here is gonna be so happy I'm helping you that she's gonna ride along and help out with the apprehension."

"Not likely," I said. "I have to be at work at three."

"Yeah, but at the rate you're going, you'll be fired by five," Lula said. "I just hope you last through dinnertime because I was planning on coming in for a bucket of extra crispy."

"Is that on *my* diet?" Val asked.

"Hell no," Lula said. "Ain't nothing on your diet. You want to lose weight, you gotta starve. You gotta eat a bunch of plain-ass carrots and shit."

"What about that no-carb diet? I hear you can eat bacon and steak and lobster."

"You didn't tell me what kind of diet you wanted to do. I just figured you wanted the starvation diet on account of it's the easiest and the most economical. You don't have to weigh anything. And you don't have to cook anything. You just don't eat anything." Lula motored off to the kitchen.

"Let's check out your cupboards and see if you got *good* food or *bad* food." Lula poked around. "Uh oh, this don't look like skinny food. You got chips in here. Boy, I sure would like some of these chips. I'm not gonna eat them, though, 'cause I got willpower."

"Me, too," Valerie said. "I'm not going to eat them either."

"I bet you eat them when we leave," Lula said.

Valerie bit into her lower lip. Of course she'd eat them. She was human, wasn't she? And this was Jersey. And the *Burg,* for crissake. We ate chips in the Burg. We ate *everything*.

"Maybe I should take those chips," Lula said. "It would be okay if *I* ate the chips later being that *I'm* currently not in my weight-losing mode. I'm currently in my weight-*gaining* mode."

Valerie pulled all the bags of chips out of the cupboard and dumped them into a big black plastic garbage bag. She threw boxes of cookies and bags of candy into the bag. She added the junk-sugar-loaded cereals, the toaster waffles, the salted nuts. She handed the bag over to Lula. "And I'm only going to eat one pork chop tonight. And I'm not going to smother it in gravy."

"Good for you," Lula said. "You're gonna be skinny in no time with an attitude like that."

Valerie turned to me. "Grandma was all excited when she called. She said they just found out you've been playing the cello all these years."

Lula's eyes bugged out. "Are you shitting me? I didn't know you played a musical instrument. And the cello!

That's real fancy-pants. That's fuckin' classy. How come you never said anything?"

Small tendrils of panic curled through my stomach. This was getting out of control. "It's no big thing," I said. "I'm not very good. And I hardly ever play. In fact, I can't remember the last time I celloed."

"I don't ever remember seeing a cello in your apartment," Valerie said.

"I keep it in the closet," I told her. *I was such a good fibber!* It had been my one real usable talent as a bounty hunter. I made a show of checking my watch. "Boy, look at the time. I have to go."

"Me, too," Lula said. "I gotta go get that stupid AR." She wrapped her arms around the bag of junk food and lugged it out to her car. "It would be like old times if you rode with me on this one," Lula said to me. "It wouldn't take us long to round up Mr. Pisser, and then we could eat all this shit."

"I have to go home and take a shower and get dressed for work. And I have to feed Rex. And I don't want to do bond enforcement anymore."

"Okay," Lula said. "I guess I could understand all that."

Lula roared off in her Firebird. And I slowly accelerated in the Buick. The Buick was like a freight train. Takes a while to get a full head of steam, but once it gets going it'll plow through anything.

I stopped at Giovichinni's Meat Market on the way home. I idled in front of the store and looked through the large front window. Bonnie Sue Giovichinni was working the register. I dialed Bonnie Sue and asked her if there were any Macaronis in the store.

"Nope," Bonnie Sue said. "The coast is clear."

I scurried around, gathering the bare essentials. A loaf of bread, some sliced provolone, a half pound of sliced ham, a small tub of chocolate ice cream, a quart of skim milk, and a handful of fresh green beans for Rex. I added a couple Tastykakes to my basket and lined up behind Mrs. Krepler at the checkout.

"I just talked to Ruby Beck," Mrs. Krepler said. "Ruby tells me you've left the bonds office so you can play cello with a symphony orchestra. How exciting!"

I was speechless.

"And have you heard if they found the mole yet?" Mrs. Krepler asked.

I paid for my groceries and hurried out of the store. The cello-playing thing was going through the Burg like wildfire. You'd think with something as good as Mama Macaroni getting blown to bits there wouldn't be time to care about my cello playing. I swear, I can't catch a break here.

I drove home and docked the boat in a spot close to the back door. I figured the closer to the door, the less chance of a bomb getting planted. I wasn't sure the theory held water, but it made me feel better. I took the stairs and opened the door to my apartment cautiously. I stuck my head in and listened. Just the sound of Rex running on his wheel in his cage in the kitchen. I locked and bolted the door behind me and retrieved my gun from the cookie jar. The gun wasn't loaded because I'd forgotten to buy bullets, but I crept through the apartment, looking in closets and under the bed with the gun drawn anyway. I couldn't shoot anyone, but at least I looked like I could kick ass.

I took a shower and got dressed in jeans and a T-shirt. I didn't spend a lot of time on my hair since I'd be wearing the dorky Cluck hat. I lined my eyes and slathered on mascara to make up for the hair. I gave Rex a couple beans, and I made myself a ham and cheese sandwich. I glanced at my gun while I ate my sandwich. The gun was loaded. I went to the cookie jar and looked inside. There was a Rangeman business card in the bottom of the jar. A single word was handwritten on the card. BABE!

I had a momentary hot flash and briefly considered checking out my underwear drawer for more business cards. "He's trying to protect me," I said to Rex. "He does that a lot."

I got the tub of ice cream from the freezer and took it to the dining room table, along with a pad. I sat at the table and ate the ice cream and made notes for myself. I had four guys who were all about the same age. They all had a small business at one time or another. Two bought new cars. They all disappeared on the same day at about the same time. None of their cars were ever retrieved. That was all I knew.

My hunch about Anthony and Spiro didn't really amount to much. Probably I was trying to make a connection where none existed. One thing was certain. Someone was stalking me, trying to scare me. And now it looked like that person was trying to kill me. Not a happy thought.

I'd eaten about a third of the tub of ice cream. I put

the lid on the tub and walked it back to the freezer. I put all the food away and wiped down the countertop. I wasn't much of a housekeeper, but I didn't want to be killed and have my mother discover my kitchen was a mess.

SEVEN

I LEFT MY apartment at two-thirty and gingerly circled the Buick, looking for signs of tampering. I looked in the window. I crouched down and looked under the car. Finally I put the key in the lock, squinched my eyes closed, and opened the door. No explosion. I slid behind the wheel, took a deep breath, and turned the engine over. No explosion. I thought this was good news and bad news. If it had exploded I'd be dead, and that would be bad. On the other hand, I wouldn't have to wear the awful Cluck hat, and that would be very good.

Twenty minutes later, I was standing in front of Milton Mann, receiving instructions.

"We're going to start you off at the register," he said. "It's all computerized so it's super simple. You just punch in the order and the computer sends the order to the crew in the back and tells you how much to charge the customer. You have to be real friendly and polite. And when you give the customer their change you say, 'Thank you for visiting

Cluck-in-a-Bucket. Have a clucky day.' And always remember to wear your hat. It's our special trademark."

The hat was egg-yolk yellow and rooster-comb red. It had a bill like a ball cap, except the bill was shaped like a beak, and the rest of the hat was a huge chicken head, topped off with the big floppy red comb. Red chicken legs with red chicken toes hung from either side of the bottom of the hat. The rest of the uniform consisted of an egg-yolk yellow short-sleeve shirt and elastic-waist pants that had the Cluck-in-a-Bucket chicken logo imprinted everywhere in red. The shirt and pants looked like pajamas designed for the criminally insane.

"You'll do a two-hour shift at the register and then we'll rotate you to the chicken fryer," Mann said.

If it was in the cards that the bomber was going to succeed in killing me, I prayed that it happened before I got to the chicken fryer.

It turns out the three-to-five shift at the register is light. Some after-school traffic and some construction workers.

A woman and her kid stepped up to the counter.

"Tell the chicken what you want," the woman said.

"It's not a chicken," the kid said. "It's a girl in a stupid chicken hat."

"Yes, but she can cluck like a chicken," the woman said. "Go ahead," she said to me. "Cluck like a chicken for Emily."

I looked at the woman.

"Last time we were here the chicken clucked," the woman said.

I looked down at Emily. "Cluck."

"She's no good," Emily said. "The other chicken was *way* better. The other chicken flapped her arms."

I took a deep breath, stuffed my fists under my armpits, and did some chicken-wing flapping. "Cluck, cluck, cluck, cluck, clu-u-u-u-ck," I said.

"I want french fries and a chocolate shake," Emily said.

The next guy in line weighed three hundred pounds and was wearing a torn T-shirt and a hard hat. "You gonna cluck for me?" he asked. "How about I want you to do something besides cluck?"

"How about I shove my foot so far up your ass your nuts get stuck in your throat?"

"Not my idea of a good time," he said. "Get me a bucket of extra crispy and a Diet Coke."

At five o'clock I was marched back to the fryer.

"It's a no-brainer," Mann said. "It's all automated. When the green light goes on the oil is right for frying, so you dump the chicken in."

Mann pulled a huge plastic tub of chicken parts out of the big commercial refrigerator. He took the lid off the tub, and I almost passed out at the site of slick pink muscle and naked flesh and cracked bone.

"As you can see, we have three stainless-steel tanks," Mann said. "One is the fryer and one is the drainer and one is the breader. It's the breader that sets us apart from all the other chicken places. We coat our chicken with the specially seasoned secret breading glop right here in the store." Mann dumped a load of chicken into a wire basket and lowered it into the breader. He swished the basket around, raised it, and gently set it into the hot oil. "When you put the chicken into the oil you push the Start button and the machine times the chicken. When the bell rings you take the chicken out and set the basket in the drainer. Easy, right?"

I could feel sweat prickle at my scalp under my hat. It was about two hundred degrees in front of the fryer, and the air was oil saturated. I could smell the hot oil. I could taste the hot oil. I could feel it soaking into my pores.

"How do I know how much chicken to fry?" I asked him.

"You just keep frying. This is our busy time of day. You go from one basket to the next and keep the hot chicken rolling out."

A half hour later, Eugene was yelling at me from the bagging table. "We need extra-spicy. All you're doing is extra-crispy. And there's all wings here. You gotta give us some backs and some thighs. People are bitchin' about the friggin' wings. If they wanted all wings, they'd order all wings."

At precisely seven o'clock, Mann appeared at my side. "You get a half-hour dinner break now, and then we're going to rotate you to the drive-thru window until closing time at eleven."

My muscles ached from lifting the chicken baskets. My uniform was blotched with grease stains. My hair felt like it had been soaked in oil. My arms were covered with splatter burns. I had thirty minutes to eat, but I didn't think I could gag down fried chicken. I shuffled off to the ladies' room and sat on the toilet with my head down. I think I fell asleep like that because next thing I knew, Mann was knocking on the ladies' room door, calling my name.

I followed Mann to the drive-thru window. The plan was that I remove my Cluck hat, put the headset on, and put the Cluck hat back over the headset. Problem was, after tending the fryer, my hair was slick with grease and the headset kept sliding off.

"Ordinarily I don't put people in the drive-thru after the fryer just for this problem," Mann said, "but Darlene went home sick and you're all I got." He disappeared into the storeroom and came back with a roll of black electrical tape. "Necessity is the mother of invention," he said, holding the headset to my head, wrapping my head with a couple loops of tape. "Now you can put your hat on and get clucky, and that headset isn't going anywhere."

"Welcome to Cluck-in-a-Bucket," I said to the first car.

"I wanna crchhtra skraapyy, two orders of fries, and a large crchhhk."

Mann was standing behind me. "That's extra crispy chicken, two fries, and a large Coke." He gave me a pat on the shoulder. "You'll get the hang of it after a couple cars. Anyway, all you have to do is ring them up, take their money, and give them their order. Fred is in back filling the order." And he left.

"Seven-fifty," I said. "Please drive up."

"What?"

"Seven-fifty. Please drive up."

"Speak English. I can't understand a friggin' thing you're saying."

"Seven-fifty!"

The car pulled to the window. I took money from the driver, and I handed him the bag. He looked into the bag and shook his head. "There's only one fries in here."

"Fred," I yelled into my mouthpiece, "you shorted them a fries."

Fred ran over with the fries. "Sorry, sir," he said to the guy in the car. "Have a clucky day."

Fred was a couple inches taller than me and a couple pounds lighter. He had pasty white skin that was splotched with grease burns, pale blue eyes, and red dreads that stuck out from his hat, making him look a little like the straw man in *The Wizard of Oz*. I put him at eighteen or nineteen.

"Cluck you," the guy said to Fred, and drove off.

"Thank you, sir," Fred yelled after him. "Have a nice day. Go cluck yourself." Fred turned to me. "You gotta go faster. We have about forty cars in line. They're getting nasty."

After a half hour I was hoarse from yelling into the microphone. "Seven-twenty," I croaked. "Please drive up."

"What?"

I took a sip of the gallon-size Coke I had next to my register. "Seven-twenty."

"What?"

"Seven fucking twenty."

An SUV pulled up to the window, I reached for the money, and I found myself staring into Spiro Stiva's glittering rat eyes. The lighting was bad, but I could see that his face had obviously been badly burned in the funeral home fire. I stood rooted to the spot, unable to move, unable to speak.

His mouth had become a small slash in the scarred face. The mouth smiled at me, but the smile was tight and joyless. He handed me a ten. His hand shook, and the skin on his hand was mottled and glazed from burn scars.

Fred gave me a bag, and I automatically passed it through to Spiro.

"Keep the change," Spiro said. And he tossed a medium-size box wrapped in Scooby-Doo paper and tied with a red ribbon through the drive-thru window. And he drove away.

The box bounced off the small service counter and landed on the floor between Fred and me. Fred picked the box up and examined it. "There's a gift tag attached. It says 'Time is ticking away.' What's that supposed to mean? Hey, and you know what else? I think this thing is ticking. Do you know that guy?"

"Yeah, I know him." I took the box and turned to throw it out the drive-thru window. No good. Another car had already pulled up.

"What's the deal?" Fred asked.

"I need to take this outside."

"No way. There are a bazillion cars lined up. Mann will have a cow." Fred reached for the box. "Give it to me. I'll put it in the back room for you."

"No! This might be a bomb. I want you to *very quietly* call the police while I take this outside."

"Are you shitting me?"

"Just call the police, okay?"

"Holy crap! You're serious. That guy gave you a bomb?"

"Maybe . . ."

"Put it under water," Fred said. "I saw a show on television and they put the bomb under water."

Fred ripped the box out of my hand and dumped it into the chicken fryer. The boiling oil bubbled up and spilled over the sides of the fryer. The oil slick carried to the grill, there was a sound like *phuunf,* and suddenly the grill was covered in blue flame.

Fred's eyes went wide. "Fire!" he shrieked. He grabbed a super-size cup and scooped water from the rinse sink.

"No!" I yelled. "Get the chemical extinguisher."

Too late. Fred threw the water at the grill fire, a whoosh of steam rose in the air, and fire raced up the wall to the ceiling.

I pushed Fred to the front of the store and went back to make sure no one was left in the kitchen area. Flames were running down the walls and along the counters and the overhead sprinkler system was shooting foam. When I was sure the prep area was empty I left through a side door.

Sirens were screaming in the distance and the flash of emergency-vehicle strobes could be seen blocks away. Black smoke billowed high in the sky and flames licked out windows and doors and climbed up the stucco exterior.

Customers and employees stood in the parking lot, gawking at the spectacle.

"It wasn't my fault," I said to no one in particular.

Carl Costanza was the first cop on the scene. He locked eyes with me and smiled wide. He said something to Dispatch on his two-way, and I knew Morelli would be getting a call. Fire trucks and EMT trucks roared into the parking lot. More cop cars. The crowd of spectators was growing. They spilled onto the street and clogged the sidewalk. The evening news van pulled up. I moved away from the building to stand by the Buick at the outermost perimeter of the lot. I would have driven home, but the keys were in my bag, and my bag was barbecued.

The flashing strobes and the glare of headlights made it difficult to see into the jumble of parked cars and emergency trucks. Fire hoses snaked across the lot and silhouettes of men moved against the glare. Two men walked toward me, away from the pack. The silhouettes were familiar. Morelli and Ranger. They had a strange alliance. They were two very different men with similar goals. They were teammates of a sort. And they were competitors. They were both smiling when they reached me. I'd like to think it was because they were happy to see me alive. But probably it was because I was my usual wreck. I was grease stained and smoke smudged. I still had the headset taped to my head. I was still wearing the awful chicken hat and Cluck pajamas. And globs of pink foam hung from the hat and clung to my shirt.

They both stood hands on hips when they reached me. They were smiling, but there was a grim set to their mouths.

Morelli reached over and swiped at the pink gunk on my hat.

"Fire extinguisher foam," I said. "It wasn't my fault."

"Costanza told me the fire was started with a bomb."

"I guess that might be true . . . indirectly. I was working the drive-thru window, and Spiro pulled up. He tossed a gift-wrapped box at me and drove away. The box was ticking, and Fred got all excited and dumped the box in the vat of boiling oil. The oil bubbled over onto the grill and next thing the place was toast."

"Are you sure it was Spiro?"

"Positive. His face and hands are scarred, but I'm sure it was him. The card on the box said 'Time is ticking away.'"

Morelli took a quarter from his pocket and flipped it into the air. "Call it," he said to Ranger.

"Heads."

Morelli caught the quarter and slapped it over. "Heads. You win. I guess I have to clean her up."

"Good luck," Ranger said. And he left.

I was too exhausted to get totally irate, but I managed to muster some half-assed outrage. I glared at Morelli. "I don't believe you tossed for me."

"Cupcake, you should be happy I lost. He would have put you through the car wash at the corner of Hamilton and Market." He took my hand and tugged me forward. "Let's go home."

"Will Big Blue be safe here?"

"Big Blue is safe *everywhere*. That car is indestructible."

MORELLI WAS IN the shower with me. "Okay," he said. "There's some bad news, and then there's some bad news. The bad news is that it would seem some clumps of hair got yanked out of your head when we ripped the electrician's tape off. The other bad news is that you still smell like fried chicken, and it's making me hungry. Why don't we towel you off and send out for food?"

I put my hand to my hair. "How bad is it?"

"Hard to tell with all that oil in it. It's sort of clumping together."

"I shampooed three times!"

"I don't think shampoo is going to cut it. Maybe you need something stronger . . . like paint stripper."

I grabbed a towel, stepped out of the shower, and

looked at myself in the mirror over the sink. He was right. Shampoo wasn't working, and I had bald spots at the side of my head where the tape had been bound to me.

"I'm not going to cry," I said to him.

"Thank God. I hate when you cry. It makes me feel really shitty."

A tear slid down my cheek.

"Oh crap," Morelli said.

I wiped my nose with the back of my hand. "It's been a long day."

"We'll figure this out tomorrow," Morelli said. He took the cap off a tube of aloe ointment and carefully dabbed the ointment on my chicken-fryer burns. "I bet if you go to that guy at the mall, Mr. Whatshisname . . ."

"Mr. Alexander."

"Yeah, he's the one. I bet he'll be able to fix your hair." Morelli recapped the tube and reached for his cell phone. "I'm calling Pino. What do you want to eat?"

"Anything but chicken."

I WOKE UP thinking Morelli was licking me, but it turned out to be Bob. My face was wet with Bob slurpees, and he was gnawing on my hair. I made a sound that was halfway between laughing and crying, and Morelli opened an eye and batted Bob away.

"It's not his fault," Morelli said. "You still smell like fried chicken."

"Great."

"Could be worse," Morelli said. "You could still smell like cooked car."

I rolled out of bed and shuffled into the bathroom. I soaped myself in the shower until there was no more hot water. I got out and sniffed at my arm. Fried chicken. I returned to the bedroom and checked out the bed. Empty. Large grease stain on my pillowcase. I borrowed some sweats from Morelli's closet and followed the coffee smell to the kitchen.

Bob was sprawled on the floor next to his empty food bowl. Morelli was at the table, reading the paper.

I poured out a mug of coffee and sat across from Morelli. "I'm not going to cry."

"Yeah, I've heard that before," Morelli said. He put the paper aside and slid a bakery bag over to me. "Bob and I went to the bakery while you were in the shower. We thought you might need happy food."

I looked inside the bag. Two Boston cream doughnuts. "That's so nice of you," I said. And I burst into tears.

Morelli looked pained.

"My emotions are a little close to the surface," I told him. I blew my nose in a paper napkin and took a dough-nut. "Any word on the fire?"

"Yeah. First, some good news. Cluck-in-a-Bucket is closed indefinitely, so you don't have to go back to work there. Second, some mixed news. Big Blue is parked at the curb in front of my house. I'm assuming this is Ranger's handiwork. Unfortunately, unless you have an extra key you're not going to be driving it until you get a locksmith out here. And now for the interesting stuff. They were able to retrieve the gift box from the chicken fryer."

I pulled the second doughnut out of the bag. "And?"

"It was a clock. No evidence that it was a bomb."

"Is that for sure?"

"That's what the lab guys said. I also got a report back on the car bomb. It was detonated from an outside source."

"What does that mean?"

"It means it didn't go off when Mama Macaroni stepped on the gas or turned the key in the ignition. Someone pushed the button on Mama Macaroni when they saw her get into the car. We'll assume it was Spiro since he gave you the box. Hard to believe he'd mistake Mama Macaroni for you, so I have to think he blew her away for giggles."

"Yikes."

Bob lumbered over and sniffed at the empty doughnut bag. Morelli crumpled the bag and threw it across the room, and Bob bounded after it and tore it to shreds.

"I'm guessing Spiro was waiting for you and when Mama Macaroni showed up he couldn't resist blowing her to smithereens. Hell, I'm not sure *I* could resist." Morelli took a sip of my coffee. "Anyway, it looks like he isn't trying to kill you . . . yet."

I drank a second cup of coffee. I called Mr. Alexander and made an appointment for eleven o'clock. I stood to leave and realized I had nothing. No key to the Buick. No key to my apartment. No credit cards. No money. No shoes. No underwear. We'd thrown all my clothes, including my shoes, into the trash last night.

"Help," I said to Morelli.

Morelli smiled at me. "Barefoot and desperate. Just the way I like you."

"Unless you also like me with a greasy head you'd better find a way to get me dressed and out to the mall."

"No problemo. I have a key to your apartment. And I have the day off. I'm ready to roll anytime you are."

"HOW DID THIS happen?" Mr. Alexander asked, studying my hair. "No. On second thought, don't tell me. I'm sure it's something awful. It's *always awful*!" He leaned over me and sniffed. "Have you been eating fried chicken?"

Morelli was slouched in a chair, hiding behind a copy of *GQ*. He was armed, he was hungry, and he was hoping for a nooner. From time to time, women walked in and checked Morelli out, starting with the hip work boots, going to the long legs in professionally faded jeans, pausing at the nicely packaged goods. He didn't have a ring on his left hand. He didn't have a diamond stud in his ear. He didn't look civilized enough to be gay. He also didn't return the interest. If he looked beyond the magazine it was to assess the progress Mr. Alexander was making. If he locked eyes with an ogling woman his message wasn't friendly and the woman hurried on her way. I suspected the unfriendly disinterest was more a reflection of Morelli's impatience than of his single-minded love for me.

"I'm done!" Mr. Alexander said, whipping the cape off me. "This is the best I can do to cover up the bald spots. And we've gotten all the oil out." He looked over at Morelli. "Do you want me to tame the barbarian?"

"Hey, Joe," I yelled to him. "Do you need a haircut?"

Morelli *always* needed a haircut. Ten minutes after he got a haircut he still needed a haircut.

"I just got a haircut," Morelli said, getting to his feet.

"It would look wonderful if we took a smidgeon more off the sides," Mr. Alexander said to Morelli. "And we could put the tiniest bit of gel in the top."

Morelli stood hands on hips, his jacket flared, his gun obvious on his hip.

"But then maybe not," Mr. Alexander said. "Maybe it's perfect just as it is."

Morelli's cell phone rang. He answered the phone and passed it over to me. "Your mother."

"I've been calling and calling you," my mother said. "Why don't you answer your cell phone?"

"My phone was in my bag and my bag was in Cluck-in-a-Bucket when it burned down."

"Omigod, it's true! People have been calling night and day, and I thought they were joking. Since when do you work at Cluck-in-a-Bucket?"

"Actually, I don't work there anymore."

"Where are you? You're with Joseph. Are you in jail?"

"No. I'm at the mall."

"Four days to your sister's wedding and you're burning down the Burg. You have to stop exploding things and burning things. I need help. Someone has to check on the cake. Someone has to pick up the decorations for the cars. And the flowers for the church."

"Albert is in charge of the flowers."

"Have you seen Albert lately? Albert is drinking. Albert is locked away in his office having conversations with Walter Cronkite."

"I'll talk to him."

"No! No talking. It's better he's drunk. If he gets sober he might back out. And leave him in the office. The less

135

time spent with Valerie the more likely he is to marry her."

I could see Morelli losing patience. He wasn't much of a mall person. He was more a bedroom and bar and playing-football-in-the-park person.

My grandmother was yelling in the background. "I gotta go to a viewing tonight. Stiva's laying out Mama Mac. I need a ride."

"Are you insane?" my mother said to my grandmother. "The place will be filled with Macaronis. They'll tear you to pieces."

MORELLI PARKED THE SUV in front of my parents' house and looked over at me. "Don't get any ideas about your powers of persuasion. I'm only doing this for the meatloaf."

"And later you're going to play detective with me."

"Maybe."

"You promised."

"The promise doesn't count. We were in bed. I would have promised *anything*."

"Spiro's going to make an appearance, one way or another. I know it. He's going to have to see his handiwork. He's going to want to be part of the process."

"He won't see any of his handiwork tonight. The lid will be nailed down. I know Stiva's good, but trust me, all the king's horses and all the king's men couldn't put Mama Macaroni together again."

Morelli and I got out of the SUV and watched a car creep down the street toward us. It was a blue Honda

Civic. It was Kloughn's car. Kloughn hit the curb and eased one tire over before coming to a complete stop. He looked through the windshield at us and waved with just the tips of his fingers.

"Snockered," I said to Morelli.

"I should arrest him," Morelli said.

"You can't arrest him. He's Valerie's cuddle umpkins."

Morelli closed the distance, opened the door for Kloughn, and Kloughn fell out of the car. Morelli dragged Kloughn to his feet and propped him against the Civic.

"You shouldn't be driving," Morelli said to Kloughn.

"I know," Kloughn said. "I tried walking, but I was too drunk. It's okay. I was driving very slooooowly and 'sponsibly."

Kloughn started to sink to the ground, and Morelli grabbed him by the back of his coat. "What do you want me to do with him?" Morelli asked.

Here's the thing. I like Albert Kloughn. I wouldn't marry him. And I wouldn't hire him to defend me if I was accused of murder. I might not even trust him to baby-sit Rex. Kloughn sort of falls into the Bob Dog category. Kloughn inspires maternal pet instincts in me.

"Bring him inside," I told Morelli. "We'll put him to bed and let him sleep it off."

Morelli carted Kloughn into the house and up the stairs with Grandma trotting behind.

"Put him in the third bedroom," Grandma said to Morelli. "And then let's get to the table. Dinner's almost ready, and I don't want to get a late start on the meatloaf. I gotta get to the viewing."

"Over my dead body," my mother yelled from the bottom of the stairs.

My father was already at the table. He had his fork in his hand, and he was watching the kitchen door, as if the food would come marching out to him without my mother's help.

A car pulled up outside. Car doors opened and slammed shut, and then there was chaos. Valerie, Angie, The Baby, and the horse were in the house, and the house suddenly got very small.

Grandma bustled down the stairs and took the diaper bag off Valerie's shoulder. "Everybody sit," Grandma said. "The meatloaf's done. We got meatloaf and gravy and mashed potatoes. And we got pineapple upside-down cake for dessert. And we put lots of whipped cream on the cake." Grandma eyed Mary Alice. "And only horses who sit at the table and eat their vegetables and meatloaf are gonna get any of the whipped cream and cake."

"Where's my oogie woogie bear?" Valerie wanted to know. "I saw his car on the curb."

"He's upstairs drunk as a skunk," Grandma said. "I just hope his liver don't explode before we get you married off. You should make sure he's got life insurance."

My mother brought the meatloaf and green beans to the table. Grandma brought the red cabbage and a bowl of mashed potatoes. I pushed my chair back and went to the kitchen to fetch the gravy and get milk for the girls.

Dinner at my parents' house is survival of the fastest. We all sit down at the table. We all put napkins on our laps. And that's where the civility ends and the action heats up. Food is passed, shoveled onto plates, and consumed at warp speed. To date, no one has been stabbed with a fork for taking the last dinner roll, but that's only because we all understand the rules. Get there first and fast. So we were all a little stunned when Valerie put five green beans on her big empty plate and angrily stabbed them with her fork. *Thunk, thunk, thunk.*

"What's with you?" Grandma said to Valerie.

"I'm on a diet. All I get to eat are these beans. Five boring hideous beans." The grip on her fork was white-knuckled, her lips were pressed tightly together, and her eyes glittered feverishly as she took in Joe's plate directly across from her. Joe had a mountain of creamy mashed potatoes and four thick slabs of meatloaf, all drenched in gravy.

"Maybe this isn't a good time to be on a diet, what with all the stress over the wedding and all," Grandma said.

"It's *because* of the wedding that I have to diet," Valerie said, teeth clenched.

Mary Alice forked up a piece of meatloaf. "Mommy's a blimp."

Valerie made a growling sound that had me worrying her head was going to start doing full rotations on her neck.

"Maybe I should check on Albert," Morelli said to me.

I narrowed my eyes and looked at him sideways. "You're going to sneak out, aren't you?"

"No way. Honest to God." He blew out a sigh. "Okay, yeah, I was going to sneak out."

"I had a good idea today," Grandma said, ignoring the possibility that Valerie might be possessed. "I thought it would be special if we could have Stephanie play the cello at Valerie's wedding. She could play it at the church while the people are coming in. Myra Sklar had a guitar player at her wedding, and it worked out real good."

My mother's face brightened. "That's a wonderful idea!"

Morelli turned to me. "You play the cello?"

"You bet she does," Grandma said. "She's good, too."

"No, really, I'm not that good. And I don't think it would work if I played at the church. I'm in the wedding party. I have to be with Valerie."

Valerie was momentarily distracted from her green-bean stabbing. "It would just be while the people are walking in," Valerie said. "And then you can put the cello aside and take your place in line."

Morelli was smiling. He knew I didn't play the cello. "I think you should do it," Morelli said. "You wouldn't want all those years of cello lessons to go to waste, would you?"

I shot him a warning look. "You are *so toast*."

EIGHT

"THIS IS GOING to be a humdinger of a wedding," Grandma said, returning her attention to her meatloaf and potatoes. "And it's going to be smooth sailing because we got a wedding planner."

Morelli and I exchanged glances. The Kloughn wedding was going to be a disaster of epic proportions.

We heard some scuffling and mumbling from the second floor. There was a moment of silence. And then Kloughn rolled down the stairs and landed at the bottom with a good solid thud. We all pushed back from the table and went to assess the damage.

Kloughn was spread-eagled on his back. His face was white and his eyes were wide. "I had the nightmare again," he said to me. "The one I told you about. It was awful. I couldn't breathe. I was suffocating. Every time I go to sleep I get the nightmare."

"What nightmare is he talking about?" Valerie wanted to know.

I didn't want to tell Valerie about the whale. It wasn't the sort of recurring dream a bride could get all gushy about. Especially since Val had almost gone into cardiac arrest when Mary Alice had called her a blimp. "It's a nightmare about an elevator," I said. "He's in this elevator, and all the air gets sucked out, and he can't breathe."

"All that white," Kloughn said, sweat popping out on his forehead. "It was all I could see. I could only see white. And then I couldn't breathe."

"It was a white elevator," I said to Valerie. "You know how dreams can get weird, right?"

Morelli had Kloughn on his feet, holding him up by the back of his jacket again. "Now what?" Morelli said. "Where do you want him this time?"

"We should lock him up someplace safe where he can't get away," Grandma said. "Someplace like jail. Maybe you should bust him."

"What's in his jacket pocket?" Valerie asked, patting the pocket. "It's a candy bar!" She ran her fingers over it. "It feels like a Snickers."

Some people can read Braille . . . my sister can feel up a candy bar in a pocket and identify it.

"I need that candy bar," Valerie said.

"It wouldn't be good for your diet," I told her.

"Yeah," Grandma said. "Go eat another green bean."

"I *need* that candy bar," Valerie said, eyes narrowed. "I *really need* it."

Kloughn pulled the candy bar out of his pocket, the candy bar slipped through his fingers, flew through the air, and bounced off Valerie's forehead.

Valerie blinked twice and burst into tears. "You hit me," she wailed.

"You're a nutso bride," Grandma said, retrieving the candy bar, tucking it into the zippered pocket of her warm-up suit jacket. "You're imagining things. Just look at Snoogie Boogie here. Does he look like he could hit someone? He don't know the time of day."

"I don't feel so good," Kloughn said. "I want to lie down."

"Put him on the couch," my mother said to Morelli. "He'll be safer there. He's lucky he didn't break his neck when he fell down the stairs."

We went back to the table and everybody dug in again.

"Maybe I don't want to get married," Valerie said.

"Of course you want to get married," Grandma told her. "How could you pass up Snogle Wogle out there? It'll be his job to take the garbage out on garbage day. And he'll get the oil changed in the car. You want to do those things all by yourself? And after we get you married off we gotta work on Stephanie." Grandma fixed an eye on Morelli. "How come you don't marry her?"

"Not my fault," Morelli said. "She won't marry *me*."

"Of course it's your fault," Grandma said. "You must be doing something wrong, if you know what I mean. Maybe you need to buy a book that tells you how to do it. I hear there are books out there with pictures and everything. I saw one in the store the other day. It was called *A Sex Guide for Dummies*."

Morelli paused with a chunk of meatloaf halfway to his mouth. No one had ever questioned his expertise in the sack before. His sexual history was legend in the Burg.

My sister gave a bark of laughter and quickly clapped a hand over her mouth. My mother went pale. And my father kept his head down, not wanting to lose the fork-to-mouth rhythm he had going.

Morelli sat frozen in his seat for a long moment and then obviously decided no answer was the way to go. He gave me a small tight smile and got on with his meal. Things quieted down after that until Grandma started checking her watch halfway through dessert.

"No," my mother said to her. "Don't even think it."

"Think what?" Grandma asked.

"You know what. You're not going to the viewing. It would be in terrible taste. The Macaronis have suffered enough without us adding to their grief."

"The Macaronis are probably dancing in their socks," Grandma said. "Susan Mifflin saw them eating at Artie's Seafood House the day after the accident. She said they were going at the all-you-can-eat crab legs like it was a party."

When the only thing left of the pineapple upside-down cake was a smudge of whipped cream on the cake plate, I helped my mother clear the table. I promised I'd get the decorations for the cars. And I made a mental note that in the future I would avoid weddings, mine or anyone else's. And while I was making my never-again list, I might add never have another dinner at my parents' house . . . although it was pretty funny when Grandma suggested Morelli get a *Dummies'* guide to good sex.

Ten minutes later, Morelli and I were parked on Hamilton, across from the funeral home.

"Tell me again why we're doing this," Morelli said.

"The bad guy always returns to the scene of the crime. Everybody knows that."

"This isn't the scene of the crime."

"Work with me here, okay? It's close enough. Spiro seems like the kind of guy who would hate to be left out. I think he'd want to watch the spectacle."

We sat for a couple minutes in silence and Morelli turned to me. "You're smiling," Morelli said. "It's making me uneasy. Anyone in their right mind wouldn't be smiling after that dinner."

"I thought there were some good moments."

Morelli was dividing his attention between the people arriving for the viewing and me. "Like when your grandmother suggested I get a book?"

"That was the *best* moment."

It was deep twilight. Light pooled on the sidewalk and road from overhead halogens, and Stiva's front porch was glowing. Stiva didn't want the old folks falling down the stairs after visiting with the deceased.

Morelli reached out to me in the darkened car. His fingertips traced along my hairline. "Do you want to throw out a comment here? Was your grandmother right? Is that why we're not married?"

"You're fishing for compliments."

That got Morelli smiling. "Busted."

Someone rapped on the driver's-side window, and we both flinched. Morelli rolled the window down a crack, and Grandma squinted in at us.

"I thought I recognized the car," Grandma said.

"What are you doing here?" I asked Grandma. "I thought it was settled that you'd stay away."

"I know your mother means well, but sometimes she can be a real pain in the patoot. This viewing will be the talk of the town. How can I go to the beauty parlor tomorrow if I don't know anything about the viewing? What will I say to people? I got a reputation to uphold. People expect me to know the dirt. So I sneaked out when your mother went to the bathroom. I was lucky to be able to hitch a ride with Mabel from next door."

"We can't let Grandma go to that viewing," I said to Morelli. "She'll be nothing but a grease spot on Stiva's carpet after the Macaronis get done with her."

"You really shouldn't go to the viewing," he said to Grandma. "Why don't you get in the car, and we'll go to a bar and get wasted?"

"Not a bad offer," Grandma said. "But no can do. I can't take a chance on them having the lid up."

"There's no chance they'll have the lid up," Morelli said. "I saw them collecting the pieces, and they're not going to fit together."

Grandma slid her dentures around in her mouth while she weighed her choices. "Don't seem right not to pay my respects," she finally said.

"Here's the deal," Morelli said. "I'll go in and scope things out. If the lid is up I'll come get you. If the lid is down I'll drive you home."

"I guess that sounds reasonable," Grandma said. "I don't want to get torn limb from limb by the Macaronis for no good cause. I'll wait here."

"And ask Constantine if he's seen Spiro," I told Morelli.

Morelli got out, and Grandma took his place behind

the wheel. We watched Morelli walk into the funeral home.

"He's a keeper," Grandma said. "He's turned into a real nice young man. And he's nice looking, too. Not as hot as that Ranger but pretty darn close."

Cars rolled past us on Hamilton. People parked in the lot next to Stiva's and made their way to the big front porch. A group of men stood just outside the door. They were smoking and talking and occasionally there'd be a bark of laughter.

"I guess you're unemployed again," Grandma said. "You have any ideas where you'll go next?"

"I hear they're hiring at the sanitary products plant."

"That might work out. That plant is way down Route One and they might not have heard about you yet."

The light changed at the end of the block and cars began moving again. An SUV slid by us going in the opposite direction . . . and Spiro was behind the wheel.

I started climbing over the console. "Get out of the car," I yelled. "I need to follow that SUV."

"No way. I'm not missing out on this. I can catch him," Grandma said. "Buckle your seat belt."

I opened my mouth to say no, but Grandma already had the car in gear. She shot back and rammed the car behind us, knocking him back a couple feet.

"That's better," Grandma said. "Now I got room to get out." She wheeled Morelli's SUV into traffic, stopped short, laid on the horn, and cut into the stream of oncoming cars.

Grandma learned to drive a couple years ago. She

immediately racked up points for speeding and lost her license. She wasn't all that good a driver back then, and she wasn't any better now. I tightened my seat belt and started making deals with God. I'll be a better person, I told God. I swear I will. I'll even go to church. Okay, maybe that's not going to happen. I'll go to church on holidays. Just don't let Grandma kill us both.

"I'm coming up on him," Grandma said. "He's just two cars ahead of us."

"Keep the two cars between us," I told her. "I don't want him to see us."

The light changed at the corner. Spiro went through on the yellow, and we were stopped behind the two cars. Grandma yanked the wheel to the right, jumped the curb, and drove on the sidewalk to the intersection. She leaned on the horn, smashed her foot to the floor, and rocketed across two lanes of traffic. I had my feet braced against the dash and my eyes closed.

"I have a better idea," I said. "Why don't we go back to the funeral home? You wouldn't want to miss hearing that the lid was up. And maybe it would be a good idea to pull over and let me drive, since you don't have a license."

"I got him in my sights," Grandma said, hunched over the wheel, eyes narrowed.

Spiro turned right and Grandma raced to the corner and took it on two wheels. One block ahead of us we saw Spiro right-turn again. Grandma stuck with him, and two turns later we found ourselves back on Hamilton, heading for the funeral home. Spiro was going to make another pass.

"This is convenient," Grandma said. "We can see if Joseph is waiting for us."

"Not good," I said. "He won't be happy to see you behind the wheel. He's a cop, remember? He arrests people who drive without a license."

"He can't arrest me. I'm an old lady. I got rights. And besides, he's practically family."

Was that true? Was Morelli practically family? Had I become accidentally married?

My attention returned to Spiro, and I realized Grandma had closed the gap, and we were one car behind him. We sailed past the funeral home, past Morelli standing at the side of the road, hands on hips. He gave his head a small shake as we whizzed by. Probably best not to second-guess his thoughts . . . they didn't look happy.

"I know I should have stopped to find out about the viewing," Grandma said, "but I hate to lose this guy. I don't know why I'm following him, but I can't seem to quit."

Spiro drove three blocks and did another loop, taking himself back down Hamilton. We lost the single-car buffer, and Grandma got on Spiro's bumper just as he came up to the funeral home. Spiro flashed his right-turn signal and after that it was all horror and panic and life in slow motion, because Spiro jumped the curb and plowed into a group of men on the sidewalk. He hit two men I'd never seen before and Morelli. One of the men was knocked aside. One was pitched off the hood. And Morelli spiraled off the right front fender of Spiro's SUV and was thrown to the ground.

Probably I should have gone after Spiro, but I acted without thought. I was out of the car and running to Morelli before Grandma had come to a complete stop. He was on his back, his eyes open, his face white.

"Are you okay?" I asked, dropping to my knees.

"Do I look okay?"

"No. You look like you've just been run over by an SUV."

"Last time this happened I got to look up your skirt," he said. And then he passed out.

IT WAS CLOSE to midnight when I was told Morelli was out of surgery. His leg had been broken in two places but aside from that he was fine. I'd taken Grandma home, and I was alone in the hospital. A bunch of cops had stopped by earlier. Eddie Gazarra and Carl Costanza had offered to stay with me, but I'd assured them it wasn't necessary. I'd already been informed Morelli's injuries weren't life threatening. The two other guys that were mowed down by Spiro were going to be okay, too. One had been sent home with scrapes and bruises. The other was being kept overnight with a concussion and broken collarbone.

I was allowed to see Morelli for a moment when he was brought up to his room. He was hooked to an IV drip, his leg was elevated on the bed, and he was still groggy. He was half a day beyond a five o'clock shadow. He had a bruise on his cheek. His eyes were partly closed, and his dark lashes shaded his eyes.

I brushed a light kiss across his lips. "You're okay," I told him.

"Good to know," he said. And then the drugs dragged him back into sleep.

I walked the short distance to the parking garage and found a blue-and-white parked next to Morelli's SUV. Gazarra was at the wheel.

"I had late shift and this is as good a place as any to hang," he said. "Lock the car in Morelli's garage tonight. I wouldn't want to see you in the room next to Mama Mac tomorrow."

I left the garage and followed Gazarra's instructions. It was a dark moonless night with a chill in the air that ordinarily would have me thinking about pumpkins and winter clothes and football games. As it was, I had a hard time pushing the anger and fear generated by Spiro into the background. Hard to think about anything other than the pain he'd caused Morelli.

Morelli's garage was detached from his house and at the rear of his property. Bob was waiting for me when I let myself into the house through the back door. He was sleepy-eyed and lethargic, resting his big shaggy orange head against my leg. I scratched him behind his ear and gave him a dog biscuit from the cookie jar on the counter.

"Do you have to tinkle?" I asked Bob.

Bob didn't look especially interested in tinkling.

"Maybe you should try," I told him. "I'm going to sleep late tomorrow."

I opened the back door, Bob picked his head up, his nose twitched, his eyes got wide, and Bob bolted through the door and took off into the night. Shit! I could hear Bob galloping two yards over, and then there was nothing but the sound of distant cars and the whir of Morelli's refrigerator in defrost cycle behind me.

Great job, Stephanie. Things aren't bad enough, now you've lost Morelli's dog. I got a flashlight, pocketed the house key, and locked up behind me. I crossed through two yards and stopped and listened. Nothing. I kept walking through yards, occasionally sweeping the area with the light. At the very end of the block I found Bob munching his way through a big black plastic garbage bag. He'd torn a hole in the bag and had pulled out chicken remains, wads of paper towels, empty soup cans, lunch-meat wrappers, and God knows what else.

I grabbed Bob by the collar and dragged him away from the mess. Probably I should clean up the garbage, but I was in no mood. With any luck, a herd of crows would descend on the carnage and cart everything off to Crowland.

I dragged Bob all the way home. When I got to the house there was a piece of notebook paper tacked to the back door. A smiley face was drawn on the paper. ISN'T THIS FUN? was printed under the smiley face.

I got Bob inside and threw the bolt. And then as a double precaution I locked us into Morelli's bedroom.

IT WAS A little after nine, and I had the phone cradled between my ear and shoulder as I scoured Morelli's kitchen floor, cleaning up the chicken bones Bob had hacked up.

"I can come home," Morelli said. "I need some shorts and a ride."

"I'll be there as soon as I finish cleaning the kitchen." I disconnected and looked over at Bob. "Are you done?"

Bob didn't say anything, but he didn't look happy. His eyes cut to the back door.

I hooked a leash to Bob and took him into the yard. Bob hunched over and pooped out a red lace thong. I was going to have to check upstairs to be sure, but I strongly suspected it was mine.

MORELLI WAS ON the couch with his foot propped up on a pillow on the coffee table. He had the television remote, a bowl of popcorn, his cell phone, a six-pack of soda, crutches, a week's supply of pills for pain, an Xbox remote, his iPod with headset, a box of dog biscuits, and a gun, all within reach. Bob was sprawled on the floor in front of the television.

"Is there anything else before I go?" I asked him.

"Do you have to go?"

"Yes! I promised my mother I'd get the decorations for the cars. I need to check in on Valerie. We have no food in the house. I used up all the paper towels cleaning up Bob barf. And I need to stop at the personal products plant and get a job application."

"I think you should stay home and play with me. I'll let you write dirty suggestions on my cast."

"Appealing, but no. Your mother and your grandmother are going to show up. They're going to need to see for themselves that you're okay. They're going to bring a casserole and a cake, because that's what they always do. And if I'm here they're going to grill us about getting married, because that's what they always do. And then Bella is going to have a vision that involves my uterus, because that's also a constant. Better to take the coward's way out and run errands." Plus, I wanted to drop in at the funeral home and talk to Constantine Stiva about his son.

"What if I fall and I can't get up?"

"Nice try, but I've got it covered. I've got a baby-sitter for you. Someone who will attend to your every need while I'm gone."

There was a sharp rap on the front door, and Lula barged in. "Here I am, ready to baby-sit your ass," she said to Morelli. "Don't you worry about a thing. Lula's here to take care of you."

Morelli looked over at me. "You're kidding."

"I wanted to make sure you were safe."

And that was true. I was worried about Spiro returning and setting the house on fire. Spiro was nuts.

Lula set her bag in the hall and walked to the curb with me. Big Blue was soaking up sun on the street, ready to spring into action. I had an extra car key from Grandma. I'd gotten an extra apartment key from my building super, Dillon Ruddick. I had Morelli's credit card for the food. I was ready to roll. It was early afternoon, and if I didn't hit too much traffic on Route One I'd be home to feed Morelli dinner.

"We'll be fine," Lula said. "I brought some videos to watch. And I got the whole bag of tricks with me if anything nasty goes down. I even got a taser. It's brand-new. Never been used. I bet I could give a guy the runs with that taser."

"I should be back in a couple hours," I told her. I slid behind the wheel and turned the key in the ignition. Something under the car went *phunnnf*, and flames shot out on all sides and the car instantly died. I got out, and Lula and I got on our hands and knees and checked the undercarriage.

"Guess that was a bomb," Lula said.

Little black dots floated in front of my eyes, and there was a lot of clanging in my head. When the clanging stopped, I stood and brushed road gravel off my knees, using the activity to get myself under control. I was freaking out deep inside, and that wasn't a good thing. I needed to be brave. I needed to think clearly. I needed to be Ranger. Get a grip, I said to myself. Don't give in to the panic. Don't let this bastard run your life and make you afraid.

"You're starting to scare me," Lula said. "You look like you're having a whole conversation with someone and it isn't me."

"Giving myself a pep talk," I said. "Tell Morelli about the bomb. I'm taking his SUV."

"You're whiter than usual," Lula said.

"Yeah, but I didn't totally faint or throw up, so I'm doing good, right?"

I backed Morelli's car out of the garage and hit the first stop on my list. A party store on Route 33 in Hamilton Township. Valerie had, at last count, three bridesmaids, one maid of honor (me), and two flower girls (Angie and Mary Alice). We were riding in six cars. The party store had dolls in fancy gowns for the hood, bows for all the door handles, and streaming ribbons that got attached to the back of each car. Everything corresponded to the color of the gown inside the car. Mine was eggplant. Could it get any worse? I was going to look like the attendant to the dead.

"I'm here to pick up the car decorations for the Plum wedding," I said to the girl at the counter.

"We have them right here, ready to go," she said, "but there's a problem with one of them. I don't know what happened. The woman who makes these is always so careful. One of the dolls looks like . . . an eggplant."

"It's a vegetarian wedding," I told her. "New Age."

I lugged the six boxes out to the car and drove them to my parents' house. I left the SUV idling at the curb, ran in with the boxes, dumped them on the kitchen table, and turned to leave.

"Where are you going so fast?" Grandma wanted to know. "Don't you want a sandwich? We have olive loaf."

"No time. Lots of errands today. And I need to get back to Morelli." Also I didn't want to leave the car unattended long enough for Spiro to set another bomb.

My mother was at the stove, stirring a pot of vanilla pudding. "I hope Joseph is feeling better. That was a terrible thing last night."

"He's on the couch, watching television. His leg is achy, but he's going to be okay." I looked over at Grandma Mazur. "He said to tell you the lid was down, and rumor has it Mama Mac went to the hereafter without the mole. Morelli said the medical examiner thinks the mole is still in the parking lot somewhere, but there might not be a lot left of it due to all the foot traffic around the scene."

"I get a chill just thinking about it," Grandma said. "Someone could be walking around with Mama Mac's mole on the bottom of their shoe."

From the corner of my eye I saw my mother take a bottle out of a cupboard, pour two fingers of whisky into a juice glass, and knock it back. Guess the ironing wasn't doing it for her anymore.

"Gotta go," I said. "If you need me I'll be staying with Morelli. He needs help getting around."

"The organist at the church would like to know if you want her to accompany you when you play the cello," Grandma said. "I saw her at the market this morning."

I smacked my forehead with the heel of my hand. "With all the excitement I forgot to tell you. I don't have a cello anymore. I gave it away. It was taking up too much space in my closet. You know how it is when you live in an apartment. Never enough closet space."

"But you loved your cello," Grandma said.

I tried to plaster an appropriate expression of remorse on my face. "That's the way it goes. A girl has to have priorities."

"Who got the cello?"

"Who?" My mind was racing. Who got the cello? "My cello teacher," I said. "I gave it to my cello teacher."

"Do we know her?"

"Nope. She lived in New Hope. But she's moved. She moved to South Carolina. That's another reason I stopped playing. My cello teacher moved, and I didn't feel like finding a new cello teacher. So I gave the cello back to her. It was originally hers, anyway." Sometimes I was really impressed with my ability to come up with this shit. Once I got going, it just rolled out of me. I could compose a whole parallel universe for myself in a matter of seconds.

I glanced down at my watch. "Look at the time! I'm late."

I snatched a couple cookies off the plate on the kitchen table and ran through the house to the car. I jumped in the SUV and roared away. Next stop was Valerie. I didn't have any real reason to visit Valerie. It was just that I was her sister and her maid of honor and Val wasn't entirely together these days. I thought it wouldn't hurt to check on her once in a while until she made it through the wedding.

The first thing I noticed when I got to her house was the absence of Kloughn's car. Not surprising since this was a workday. Sort of surprising that he was able to get himself up and out on the road with a raging hangover.

"What?" Val yelled when she opened the door to me.

"I just stopped by to say hello."

"Oh. Sorry I yelled at you. I'm having a problem with volume control. It turns out when you're starving to death you do a lot of yelling."

"Where's Albert? I thought he'd still be in bed with a hangover."

"He decided he was better off at the office. He couldn't stand the galloping and whinnying. You might want to see how he's doing. He left in his pajamas."

"You know, Val, not everyone's cut out to have a big wedding. Maybe you should reconsider the eloping option."

"I wish I'd never started this wedding thing," Val wailed. "What was I thinking?"

"It's not too late to bail."

"It is. And I'm too chicken. Everybody's made all these plans!"

"Yeah, but it's your wedding. It shouldn't be some horrible stressful thing. It should be something you enjoy." Not to mention, if Valerie eloped I wouldn't have to wear the hideous eggplant getup.

I left Valerie and drove to Kloughn's office. There was a CLOSED sign on his door and when I looked in the window I could see Kloughn was stretched out on the floor in his pajamas with a wet towel over his face. I didn't want to make him get up, so I tiptoed away and headed down Route 1 to the personal products plant. I parked in a visitor slot, ran in, and got a job application from the personnel office. I had no illusions of getting an office job here. I had no references and few skills. I'd be lucky if I could get a job on the line. I'd bring the application back tomorrow and wait for a phone call for an interview.

I slid to a stop in front of Giovichinni's Market and didn't bother to call to check on Macaronis. I figured I had bigger problems than Macaronis. I was being stalked by a homicidal maniac. Spiro was officially over the edge.

I ran through the store gathering together some basic foods. Bread, cheese, Tastykakes, peanut butter, cereal, milk, Tastykakes, eggs, frozen pizza, Tastykakes, orange juice, apples, lunch meat, and Tastykakes. I checked out and muscled my way through the door with bags in my arms.

Ranger was leaning against the SUV, waiting for me. He pushed off, took the bags, and put them in the car. "Looks like you're playing house," he said.

"More like nurse. Morelli needs some help."

"Is that your job application on the front seat?"

"Yep."

"Personal products plant?"

"It's halfway to New Brunswick. I'm hoping they won't have heard about me. That's Grandma's line, but it's true."

"Babe," Ranger said. He was smiling, but there was a quality to his voice that told me it wasn't actually funny. We both knew that my life wasn't going in the carefree direction I'd hoped for.

NINE

"I HAVE AN office position open," Ranger said. "Are you interested in working for Rangeman?"

"Oh great. A pity position."

"If I gave you a pity position it wouldn't be in the office."

This got a burst of laughter out of me because I knew he
was taking a zing at my sex life with Morelli. For the most
part, Ranger had a consistent personality. He wasn't a guy
who wasted a lot of unnecessary energy and effort. He
moved and he spoke with an efficient ease that was more
animal than human. And he didn't telegraph his emotions.
Unless Ranger had his tongue in my mouth it was usually
impossible to tell what he was thinking. But every now and
then, Ranger would step out of the box, and like a little
treat that was doled out on special occasions, Ranger
would make an entirely outrageous sexual statement. At
least it would be outrageous coming from an ordinary
guy . . . from Ranger it seemed on the mark.

"I didn't think you hired women," I said to him. "The

only woman you have working for you is your house-keeper."

"I hire people who have the skills I need. Right now I could use someone in the building who can do phone work and paperwork. You'd be an easy hire. You already know the drill. Nine to five, five days a week. You can discuss salary with my business manager. You should consider it. The garage is secure. You wouldn't have to worry about getting blown up when you leave at the end of the day."

Ranger owns a small seven-story office building in downtown Trenton. The building is unspectacular on the outside. Well maintained but not architecturally interesting. The interior of the building is high tech and slick, equipped with a state-of-the-art control center, offices, a gym, studio apartments for some of Ranger's crew, plus an apartment for Ranger on the top floor. I'd stayed in Ranger's apartment for a short time on a nonconjugal basis not long ago. It had been equal parts pleasure and terror. Terror because it was Ranger's apartment and Ranger could sometimes be a scary guy. Pleasure because he lives well.

The job offer was tempting. My car would be safe. I'd be safe. I'd be able to pay my rent. And the chances of rolling in garbage were slim.

"Okay," I said. "I'll take the job."

"Use the intercom at the gate when you come in tomorrow. Dress in black. You'll be working on the fifth floor."

"Any leads on Benny Gorman?"

"No. That's one of the things I want you to do. I want you to see what you can turn up."

Ranger's pager buzzed, and he checked the readout. "Elroy Dish is back at Blue Fish. Do you want to ride along?"

"No thanks. Been there, done that."

"Be careful."

And he was gone.

I looked at my watch. Almost five. Perfect. Stiva would be between afternoon and evening viewings. I drove the short distance up Hamilton and parked on the street. I found Stiva in his office just off the large entrance foyer. I rapped on the doorjamb, and he looked up from his computer.

"Stephanie," he said. "Always nice to see you."

I appreciated the greeting, but I knew it was a big fat lie. Stiva was the consummate undertaker. He was an island of professional calm in an ocean of chaos. And he never alienated a future customer. The ugly truth is, Stiva would rather shove a sharp stick in his eye than see Grandma or me alive on his doorstep. Dead would be something else.

"I hope this visit isn't due to bad news," Stiva said.

"I wanted to talk to you about Spiro. Have you seen him since the fire?"

"No."

"Spoken to him?"

"No. Why do you ask?"

"He was driving the car that ran over Morelli."

Stiva went as still as stone, and his pale vanilla custard cheeks flushed pink. "Are you serious?"

"Unfortunately, yes. I'm sorry. I saw him clearly."

"How does he look?" Stiva asked.

I felt my heart constrict at his response. He was a concerned parent, anxious to hear word of his missing son. What on earth could I say to Stiva?

"I only saw him briefly," I said. "He seemed healthy. Maybe some scars on his face from the fire."

"He must have been driving by and lost control of his car," Stiva said. "At least I know he's alive. Thank you for coming in to tell me."

"I thought you'd want to know."

No point to saying more. Stiva didn't have information to share, and I didn't want to tell him the whole story. I left the funeral home and returned to the SUV. I drove two blocks to Pino's and got two meatball subs, a tub of coleslaw, and a tub of potato salad. Morelli was going to be in a bad mood after spending the afternoon with Lula. I figured I'd try to mellow him out with the sub before I dropped the news about my new job. Morelli wasn't going to be happy to hear I was working for Ranger.

I went out of my way on the trip home to drive by Anthony Barroni's house. I had no real basis for believing he was involved with Spiro and the missing men. Just a gut feeling. Maybe it was desperation. I wanted to think I had a grip on the problem. The grip loosened when I got to Barroni's house. No lights shining. Curtains drawn. Garage door closed. No car in driveway.

I turned at the corner and wound my way through the Burg to Chambers Street. I crossed Chambers and two blocks later I pulled the SUV into Morelli's garage. Big Blue and Lula's Firebird were still at the curb. I made sure the garage door was locked, and I carted the bags in through the back door.

"Is that Stephanie Plum coming through the back

door?" Lula yelled. "'Cause if it's some maniac pervert I'm gonna kick his ass."

"It's me," I yelled back. "Sorry you don't get to do any ass kicking."

I put the bags on the counter and went into the living room to see Lula and Morelli. Morelli was still on the couch. Bob was still on the floor. And Lula was packing up.

"This wasn't so bad," Lula said. "We played poker and I won three dollars and fifty-seven cents. I would have won more, but your boyfriend fell asleep."

"It's the drugs," Morelli said. "You're a sucky poker player. I would have won if I wasn't all drugged up. You took advantage."

"I won fair and square," Lula said. "Anytime you want to get even you let me know. I can always use extra cash."

"Any other fun things happen that I should know about?"

"Yeah," Lula said. "His mother and grandmother came over. And they're nuts. The old lady said she was putting the eye on me. I told her she better not pull any of that voodoo shit with me or I'll beat her like a piñata."

"I bet that went over big."

"They left after that. They brought a casserole, and I put it in the refrigerator. I didn't think it looked all that good."

"No cake?"

"Oh yeah, the cake. I ate the cake."

"All of it?"

"Bob had some. I would have given some to Morelli, but he was sleeping." She had her bag over her shoulder and her car keys in her hand. "I walked Bob about an hour ago, and he pooped twelve times, so he should be good for the night. I didn't feed him, but he ate one of Morelli's sneakers around three o'clock. You might want to go light on the dog crunchies until he horks the sneaker up."

Morelli waited until he heard Lula's car drive off before speaking. "Another fifteen minutes and I would have shot her. I would have gone to jail for the rest of my life, and it would have been worth it."

I brought out the subs and the cole slaw and the potato salad. "Don't you want to know how my day went?"

He unwrapped his sub. "How did your day go?"

"I didn't get blown up."

"Speaking of getting blown up, the lab took a look at your Buick. The bomb was very similar to the bomb that killed Mama Mac. The difference being that this bomb was detonated when you turned the key in the ignition, and it was much smaller. It wasn't intended to kill."

"Spiro is still playing with me."

"You're sure it's Spiro?"

"Yes. I stopped in to see Stiva. He had no idea Spiro was back. Said he hasn't heard from him since the fire."

"You believed him?"

"Yeah."

"I talked to Ryan Laski today. He's been working the Barroni case with me. I told him about Spiro, and I asked him to keep an eye on Anthony Barroni. And I asked my mother about Spiro. So far as I can tell, you're the only one who's seen him. There's no gossip on Spiro circulating in the Burg."

AT TEN O'CLOCK Morelli and I were still on the couch. We'd watched the news while we ate our subs. And then we watched some sitcom reruns. And then we watched a ball game. And now Morelli was getting *that look*.

"You have a cast on your leg, and you're full of painkillers," I said to him. "One would think it would slow you down."

"What can I say . . . I'm Italian. And that part of me isn't broken."

"There are some logistical things involved here. Can you get up to the bedroom?"

"I might need motivation to get through the pain . . . like, seeing you naked and gyrating at the top of the stairs."

"And what about a shower?"

"Can't take a shower," Morelli said. "I'm going to have to lie on the bed and let you wash me . . . everywhere."

"I can see you've given this some thought."

"Yeah. That's why it's not just my cast that's hard."

Okay, so this might not be so bad. I thought I could probably get into the naked gyrating and the washing. And it seemed to me I'd pick up some perks from the injury. Morelli wasn't going to be especially mobile with that heavy cast. Once I got him on his back he was going to stay there, and I'd have the top all to myself.

I'D SET THE alarm for 7:00 A.M. I didn't have to be at work until 9:00, but I had to shower and do the hair and makeup thing, walk and feed Bob, get Morelli set for the day, and make a fast trip back to my apartment in search of black clothes. And I needed to get Rex. He didn't require a lot of care, but I didn't like to leave him alone for more than a couple days.

Morelli threw an arm over me when the alarm went off. "Did you set it for sex?" he asked.

"No, I set it for *get up*."

"We don't have to get up early this morning."

I slipped out from under the arm and rolled out of bed. "*You* don't have to get up early. I have lots of things to do."

"Again? You're not going to bring Lula back, are you?"

"No. Based on your performance last night, I'd say you're not in the least impaired."

I didn't want to give details on the day's activities, so I hurried off to the bathroom. I showered, did the blow-dry thing, slathered on some makeup, and bumped into Morelli when I opened the bathroom door.

"Sorry," I said. "Are you waiting to use the bathroom?"

"No, I'm waiting to talk to you."

"Jeez, I'm in kind of a hurry. Maybe we can talk after I walk Bob."

Morelli pinned me to the wall. "Let's talk now. Where are you going today?"

"I need to go back to my apartment for clothes."

"And?"

"And I have a job."

"I hate to ask. Your jobs have been getting progressively worse. I can't imagine who would hire you after the Cluck-in-a-Bucket fiasco. Is it the personal products plant?"

"It's Ranger."

"That makes sense," Morelli said. "I should have guessed. I can hardly wait to hear your job description."

"It's a good job. I'm doing phone work from the office. Nothing in the field. And I get to park in the Rangeman garage, so my car will be secure. Is this where you start yelling?"

Morelli released me. "Hard to believe, but I'm actually relieved. I was afraid you were going to be out there trying to find Spiro today."

Go figure this. "You love me," I said to Morelli.

"Yeah. I love you." He looked at me expectantly. "And?"

"I . . . l-l-like you, too." *Shit.*

"Jesus," Morelli said.

I did a grimace. "I feel it. I just can't say it."

Bob padded out of the bedroom. *"Gak,"* Bob said, and he barfed out a slimy mess on the hall carpet.

"Guess that's what's left of my sneaker," Morelli said.

I PARKED MORELLI'S SUV in my lot and ran upstairs to change my clothes. I unlocked my apartment door, rushed inside, and almost stepped on a small, gift-wrapped box. Same wrapping paper Spiro had used for the clock. Same little ribbon bow.

I stared down at the box for a full minute without breathing. I didn't have a gun. I didn't have pepper spray. I didn't have a stun gun. My toys had all gone up in smoke at Cluck-in-a-Bucket.

"Anyone here?" I called out.

No one answered. I knew I should call Ranger and have him go through the apartment, but that felt wimpy. So I backed out, closed the door to my apartment, and called Lula.

Ten minutes later, Lula was standing alongside me in front of the door.

"Okay, open it," Lula said, gun in hand, taser on her hip, pepper spray stuck into her pocket, bludgeoning flashlight shoved under the waistband of her rhinestone-studded spandex jeans, flak vest stretched to the max over her basketball boobs.

I opened the door and we both peeked inside.

"One of us should go through and check for bad guys," Lula said.

"You've got the gun."

"Yeah, but it's your apartment. I could check, but I don't want to be intrusive. It's not that I'm chicken or anything, I just don't want to deprive you of checking."

I rolled my eyes at her.

"Don't you roll eyes at me," Lula said. "I'm being considerate. I'm giving you the opportunity to get shot before me."

"Gee, thanks. Can I at least have the gun?"

"Damn skippy. It's loaded and everything."

I was 99 percent sure the apartment was empty. Still, why take a chance with the 1 percent, right? I crept through the apartment with Lula three steps behind me. We looked in closets, under the bed, behind the shower curtain. No spooky Spiro. We returned to the front door and stared down at the box.

"I guess you should open it," Lula said.

"Suppose it's a bomb?"

"Then I guess you should open it far away from me."

I cut a look to her.

"Well, if it's a bomb it's a little bitty one," Lula said. "Anyway, maybe it's not a bomb. Maybe it's a diamond bracelet."

"You think Spiro's sending me a diamond bracelet?"

"It would be a long shot," Lula said.

I blew out a sigh and gingerly picked the box up. It wasn't heavy. It wasn't ticking. I shook it. It didn't rattle. I carefully unwrapped the box. I lifted the lid and looked inside.

Lula looked over my shoulder. "What the hell is that?" Lula asked. "It's got hairs growing out of it. *Holy fuck!* Is that what I think it is?"

It was Mama Mac's mole. I dropped the box and ran into the bathroom and threw up. When I came out of the bathroom, Lula was on the couch, flipping through television channels.

"I scooped the mole up and put it back in the box," Lula said. "And then I put it in a plastic baggie. It doesn't smell all that great. It's on the counter in the kitchen."

"I have to change clothes. I took a job working for Ranger, and I need to wear black."

"Does this job involve fancy underwear? Oral sex? Lap dancing?"

"No. It involves phone investigation."

Lula remoted the television off and stood to leave. "I bet it'll work its way around to one of those other things. You'd tell me, right?"

"You'll be the first to know."

I bolted the door after Lula and got dressed in black jeans, black Puma sneakers, and a stretchy black V-neck T-shirt. I took Mama's mole, shrugged into my denim jacket, and looked out the window at Morelli's SUV. No one lurking around, planting bombs. Hooray. I grabbed Rex's cage and vacated the apartment, locking up after me.

Lot of good that did. Everybody and their brother broke into my apartment.

I drove the mole to Morelli's house, handed it over, and took Rex into the kitchen.

"This is disgusting," Morelli said, opening the box, checking the mole out. "This is sick."

"Yeah. You'd better call Grandma and let her come over to have a look before you turn it in. Grandma will never forgive you if you don't let her see the mole."

Morelli looked at the packet of painkillers on his coffee table. "I need more drugs," he said. "If I have to have your grandmother over here examining the mole I definitely need more drugs."

I gave him a fast kiss and ran back to the SUV. If I got all the lights right I might make work on time.

I PARKED IN the underground garage and took the elevator to the fifth floor. I already knew most of the guys who worked for Ranger. No one looked surprised to see me when I came onto the floor of the control room. Everyone was dressed in black jeans or cargo pants and black T-shirts. Ranger and I were the only ones without, Rangeman embroidered on the front of the shirt. Ranger had been slouched in a chair, watching a monitor, when I stepped out of the elevator. He came to my side and walked me station to station.

"As you can see there are two banks of monitors," Ranger said. "Hal's watching the cameras in the building and listening to police scanners. He also watches the GPS screen that tracks Rangeman vehicles. Woody and Vince are monitoring private security systems. Rangeman provides personal, commercial and residential security to select clients. It's not a large operation in the world of security specialists, but the profit margin is good. I have similar operations in Boston, Miami, and Atlanta. I'm in the middle of a sellout to my Atlanta partner, and I'll probably sell Boston. I like being out on the street. I'm not crazy about running a national empire. Too difficult to control quality.

"I'm going to give you the cubby on the far side of the room. It's the area we set aside for investigation. Silvio has been doing this job, but he's transferring to the Miami office on Monday. He has family there. He'll sit with you today and make sure you know how to get into the search programs. Initially, I want you to concentrate on Benny Gorman. We've already run him through the system. Silvio will give you the file. I want you to read the file and then start over.

"The gym is open to you. Unfortunately, the locker room is men only. I'm sure they'd be happy to share, but I don't think it's a good idea. If you need to change clothes or shower you can use my apartment. Tank will issue you a key fob similar to mine. It'll get you into the building and into my apartment. My housekeeper, Ella, keeps food in the kitchen at the end of the hall. It's for staff use. There are always sandwiches, raw vegetables, and fruit. You're going to have to bring your own Cheez Doodles and Tastykakes. My business manager will stop by later this morning to discuss salary and benefits. I'll have Ella order some Rangeman shirts for you. If you decide to go back to Vinnie you can keep the shirts." Ranger almost smiled. "I like the idea of you wearing my name on your breast." He had his hand at the back of my waist, and he guided me into the cubby. "Make yourself comfortable. I'll send Silvio in to you. I'll be out of the office all day, but you can reach me on my cell if there's a problem. Are there any new disasters you want to share with me before I take off?"

"Spiro sent me Mama Mac's mole."

"Her mole?"

"Yeah, she had this horrible mutant mole on her face that the crime lab was never able to find. Spiro left it for me in my apartment. He had it all gift wrapped in a little box."

"Walk me through this."

"I went back to my apartment this morning to find something black to wear to work. I opened my locked door and the little gift-wrapped package was on the floor in the foyer. I was worried Spiro might still be in the apartment, so I called Lula and we went through together."

"Why didn't you call me?"

"It felt wimpy."

"Do you honestly think Lula would protect you against Spiro?"

"She had a gun."

There was an awkward pause while Ranger came to terms with the possibility that I didn't have my own gun.

"My gun melted down in the Cluck-in-a-Bucket fire," I told him. Not nearly so much of a loss as my lip gloss.

"Tank will also outfit you with a gun," Ranger said. "I expect you to carry it. And I expect it to be loaded. We have a practice range in the basement. Once a week I expect you to visit the practice range."

I snapped him a salute. "Aye, aye, sir!"

"Don't let the rest of the men see you being a smart-ass," Ranger said. "They're not allowed."

"I'm allowed?"

"I have no illusions over my ability to control you. Just try to keep the power play private, so you don't undermine my authority with my men."

"You're assuming we'll have private time?"

"It would be nice." The almost smile turned into a for-sure smile. "Are you flirting with me?"

"I don't think so. Did it feel like flirting?" Of course I was flirting with him. I was a horrible person. Morelli was home with a broken leg and a mutant mole, and I was flirting with Ranger. God, I was such a slut.

"Finish walking me through your latest disaster."

"Okay, so Lula and I went through the apartment and there was no Spiro. So we went back to the box, and I opened it."

"You weren't worried that it was a bomb?"

"It would have been a little bomb."

Ranger looked like he was trying hard not to grimace. "What happened after you opened it?"

"I threw up."

"Babe," Ranger said.

"Anyway, I gave the mole to Morelli. I figured he'd know what to do with it."

"Good thinking. Anything else you want to share?"

"Maybe later."

"You're flirting again," Ranger said.

And he left.

I saw him stop to talk to Tank on his way out. Tank

nodded and looked my way. I gave Tank a little finger wave and both men smiled.

The cubby walls were corkboard. Good for deadening sound, and also good for posting notes. I could see holes where Silvio had tacked messages and whatever, but the messages had all been removed, and only the pushpins remained. I had a workstation desk, a comfy-looking leather desk chair, a computer that could probably e-mail Mars, a phone that had too many buttons, a headset to go with the phone, file cabinets, in/out baskets that were empty, a second chair for guests, and a printer.

I sat in my chair and swiveled around. If I leaned back I could see out of the cubby, into the control room. The computer was different from the one I had at home. I hadn't a clue how to work the darn thing. Ditto the multiline phone. Maybe I shouldn't throw the personal products plant application away. Maybe overseeing the boxing machine was more my speed. I looked in the desk drawers. Pens, sticky-note pads, tape, stapler, lined pads, Advil. The Advil might not be a good sign. I was dying to go to the kitchen for coffee, but I didn't want to leave my cubby. It felt safe in the cubby. I didn't have to make eye contact with any of the guys. Some of Ranger's men looked like they should be wearing orange jumpsuits and ankle monitors.

Five minutes after Ranger left, Tank came into my cubicle with a small box. He set the box on my desk and removed the contents. Key fob for the garage and Ranger's apartment, Sig Sauer 9 with extra mag, stun gun, cell phone, laminated photo ID on a neck chain identifying me as a Rangeman employee. I hadn't posed for the photo and decided not to ask how it was obtained.

"I don't know how to work this kind of gun," I told Tank. "I use a revolver."

"Ranger has practice time reserved for you tomorrow at ten A.M. You're required to carry the gun, the phone, and the ID with you at all times. You don't have to wear the ID. It's for fieldwork. It's a good idea to keep it on you in case you're questioned about the gun."

Silvio arrived with a cup of coffee, and Tank disappeared. "I brought you cream, no sugar," he said, setting the coffee on the desk in front of me. "If you want sugar there are some packets in the left-hand drawer." He pulled the extra chair next to mine. "Okay," he said. "Let's see what you know about computers."

Oh boy.

BY NOON I had the phone figured out, and I could navigate the Net. I was already familiar with most of the search programs used by Rangeman. I'd used them from time to time on Connie's computer. Beyond the standard search programs that Connie used, Rangeman had a few extra that were frighteningly invasive. Just for the heck of it, I typed my name in on one of the super searchers and blanched at what appeared on my screen. I had no secrets. The file stopped just short of a Webcam view of my last gyn exam.

I followed Silvio to the kitchen and took a food survey. Fresh fruit and vegetables, cut and washed. Turkey, roast beef, tuna sandwiches on seven-grain bread. Low-fat yogurt. Energy bars. Juice. Skim milk. Bottles of water.

"No Tastykakes," I said to Silvio.

"Ella used to set out trays of cookies and brownie bars, but we started to get fat so Ranger banned them."

"He's a hard man."

"Tell me about it," Silvio said. "He scares the crap out of me."

I took a turkey sandwich and a bottle of water and returned to my cubicle. Hal, Woody, and Vince were watching their screens. Silvio went off to clean out his locker. So I was now officially Miz Computer Wiz. Three requests for security searches were sitting in my in-box. Mental note. Never leave cubby. Work appears when cubby is left unattended. I looked at the name requesting the search requests. Frederick Rodriguez. Didn't know him. Didn't see him out and about in the control room. There was another floor of offices. I guessed Frederick Rodriguez was in one of those offices.

I called my mom on my new cell phone and gave her the number. I could hear my grandmother yelling in the background.

"Is that Stephanie?" Grandma Mazur hollered. "Tell her the Macaroni funeral is tomorrow morning, and I need a ride."

"You're not going to the funeral," my mother said to Grandma Mazur.

"It's gonna be the big event of the year," Grandma said. "I have to go."

"Joseph let you see the mole before he gave it over to the police," my mother said. "You're going to have to be satisfied with that." My mother's attention swung back to me. "If you take her to that funeral there's no more pineapple upside-down cake for the rest of your life."

I disconnected from my mother, ate my sandwich, and ran the first name. It was close to three by the time I was done running the second name. I set the third request aside and paged through the Gorman file. Then I did as Ranger suggested and ran Gorman through all the searches again. I called Morelli to make sure he was okay and to tell him I might be late. There was a stretch of silence while he wrestled with trust, and then he put in a request for a six-pack of Bud and two chili dogs.

"And by the way," Morelli said. "The lab guy called and told me the mole was made out of mortician's putty."

"Don't tell Grandma," I said. "It'll ruin everything for her."

TEN

I PRINTED THE Gorman search, and then I searched Louis Lazar. Both men yielded volumes of information. Date of birth, medical history, history of employment, military history, credit history, history of residence, class standings through high school. Neither man attended college. Personal history included photos, wives, kids, assorted relatives.

I printed Lazar and moved to Michael Barroni. Most of this information I already knew. Some was new and felt embarrassingly intrusive. His wife had miscarried two children. He'd gotten psychiatric counseling a year ago for anxiety. He'd had a hernia operation when he was thirty-six. He'd been asked to repeat the third grade.

I'd just started a credit check on Barroni when my cell rang.

"I'm hungry," Morelli said. "It's seven o'clock. When are you coming home?"

"Sorry. I lost track of the time."

"Bob is standing by the door."

"*Okay!* I'll be right there."

I put the Barroni search on hold and dropped the Lazar file and the Gorman file into my top desk drawer. I grabbed my bag and my jacket and dashed out of my cubby. There was an entirely new crew in the control room. Ranger ran the control room in eight-hour shifts around the clock. A guy named Ram was at one of the monitor banks. Two other men were at large.

I crossed the room at a run, barreled through the door to take the stairs, and crashed into Ranger. We lost balance and rolled tangled together to the fourth-floor landing. We lay there for a moment, stunned and breathless. Ranger was flat on his back, and I was on top of him.

"Oh my God," I said. "I'm so sorry! Are you okay?"

"Yeah, but next time it's my turn to have the top."

The door opened above us and Ram stuck his head out. "I heard a crash . . . oh, excuse me," he said. And he pulled his head back and closed the door.

"I wish this was as bad as it looks," Ranger said. He got to his feet, scooping me up with him. He held me at arm's length and looked me over. "You're a wreck. Did I do all this damage?"

I had some scratches on my arm, the knee had gotten torn on my jeans, and there was a rip in my T-shirt. Ranger was perfect. Ranger was like Big Blue. Nothing ever touched Ranger.

"Don't worry about it," I said. "I'm fine. I'm late. Gotta go." And I took off, down the rest of the stairs and out the door to the garage.

I crossed town and stopped at Mike the Greek's deli for the hot dogs and beer. Five minutes later, I had the SUV locked up in Morelli's garage. I took his back porch steps two at a time, opened the back door, and Bob rushed past me and tinkled in the middle of Morelli's backyard.

The instant the last drop hit grass, Bob bolted off into the night. I rustled the hot dog bag, pulled out a hot dog, and waved it in Bob's direction. I heard Bob stop galloping two houses down, there was a moment of silence, and then Bob came thundering back. Bob can smell a hot dog a mile away.

I lured him into the house with the hot dog and locked up. Morelli was still on the couch with his foot on the coffee table. The room was trashed around him. Empty soda cans, newspapers, a crumpled fast-food bag, a half-empty potato chip bag, an empty doughnut box, a sock (probably Bob ate the mate), assorted sports and girlie magazines.

"This room is a Dumpster," I said to him. "Where'd all this stuff come from?"

"Some of the guys visited me."

I doled out the hot dogs. Two to Morelli, two to Bob, two to me. Morelli and I got a Bud. Bob got a bowl of water. I kicked through the clutter, brushed potato chip crumbs off a chair, and sat down. "You need to clean up."

"I can't clean up. I'm supposed to stay off my leg."

"You weren't worrying about your leg last night."

"That was different. That was an emergency. And anyway, I wasn't on my leg. I was on my back. And what's with the scratches on your arm and the torn clothes? What the hell were you doing? I thought you were supposed to be working in the office."

"I fell down the stairs."

"At Rangeman?"

"Yep. Do you want another beer? Ice cream?"

"I want to know how you managed to fall down the stairs."

"I was rushing to leave, and I sort of crashed into Ranger, and we fell down the stairs."

Morelli stared at me with his unreadable cop face. I was ready for him to morph into the jealous Italian boyfriend with a lot of arm flapping and yelling, but he gave his head a small shake and took another pull on his Bud. "Poor dumb bastard," he said. "I hope he's got insurance on that building."

I was pretty sure I'd just been insulted, but I thought it was best to let it slide.

Morelli leaned back into the couch and smiled at me. "And before I forget, your cello is in the front hall."

"My cello?"

"Yeah, every great cello player needs a cello, right?"

I ran to the hall and gaped at the big bulbous black case leaning against the wall. I dragged the case into the living room and opened it. There was a large violin sort of thing in it. I supposed it was a cello.

"How did this get here?" I asked Morelli.

"Your mother rented it for you. She said you gave yours away, and she knew how much you were looking forward to playing at Valerie's wedding, so she rented a cello for you. I swear to God, those were her exact words."

I guess the panic showed on my face because Morelli stopped smiling.

"Maybe you should fill me in on your musical accomplishments," Morelli said.

I plunked down on the couch beside him. "I don't have any musical accomplishments. I don't have any accomplishments of any kind. I'm stupid and boring. I don't have any hobbies. I don't play sports. I don't write poetry. I don't travel to interesting places. I don't even have a good job."

"That doesn't make you stupid and boring," Morelli said.

"Well, I *feel* stupid and boring. And I wanted to feel interesting. And somehow, someone told my mother and grandmother that I played the cello. I guess it was me . . . only it was like some foreign entity took possession of my body. I heard the words coming out of my mouth, but I'm sure they originated in some other brain. And it was so simple at first. One small mention. And then it took on a life of its own. And next thing, *everyone* knew."

"And you can't play the cello."

"I'm not even sure this *is* a cello."

Morelli went back to smiling. "And you think you're boring? No way, Cupcake."

"What about the stupid part?"

Morelli threw his arm around me. "Sometimes that's a tough call."

"My mother expects me to play at Valerie's wedding."

"You can fake it," Morelli said. "How hard can it be? You just make a couple passes with the bow and then you faint or pretend you broke your finger or something."

"That might work," I said. "I'm good at faking it."

This led to a couple moments of uncomfortable silence from both of us.

"You didn't mean . . . ?" Morelli asked.

"No. Of course not."

"Never?"

"Maybe once."

His eyes narrowed. "Once?"

"It's all that comes to mind. It was the time we were late for your Uncle Spud's birthday party."

"I remember that. That was great. You're telling me you faked it?"

"We were late! I couldn't concentrate. It seemed like the best way to go."

Morelli took his arm away and started flipping through channels with the remote.

"You're mad," I said.

"I'm working on it. Don't push me."

I got up and closed the cello case and kicked it to the side of the room. "Men!"

"At least we don't fake it."

"Listen, it was *your* uncle. And we were *late*, remember? So I made the sacrifice and got us there in time for dessert. You should be thanking me."

Morelli's mouth was open slightly and his face was registering a mixture of astonished disbelief and wounded, pissed-off male pride.

Okay, it wasn't that much of a sacrifice at the time, and I knew he shouldn't be thanking me, but give me a break here . . . this wasn't famine in Ethiopia. And it wasn't as if I hadn't *tried* to have an orgasm. And it wasn't as if we didn't fib to each other from time to time.

"I should be thanking you," Morelli repeated, sounding like he was making a gigantic but futile effort to understand the female mind.

"All right, I'll concede the *thanking* thing. How about if you're just happy I got you to the party in time for dessert?"

Morelli cut me a sideways look. He wasn't having any of it. He returned his attention to the television and settled on a ball game.

This is the reason I live with a hamster, I thought.

MORELLI WAS STILL on the couch watching television when I went downstairs to take Bob for his morning walk. I was wearing sweats that I'd found in Morelli's dresser, and I'd borrowed his Mets hat. I clipped the leash on Bob, and Morelli glanced over at me. "What's with the clothes? Trying to fake being me?"

"Get a grip," I said to Morelli.

Bob was dancing around, looking desperate, so I hurried him out the front door. He took a big tinkle on Morelli's sidewalk and then he got all smiley and ready to walk. I like walking Bob at night when it's dark and no one can see where he poops. At night Bob and I are the phantom poopers, leaving it where it falls. By day, I have to carry plastic pooper bags. I don't actually mind scooping the poop. It's carrying it around for the rest of the walk that I hate. It's hard to look hot when you're carrying a bag of dog poop.

I walked Bob for almost an hour. We returned to the house. I fed Bob. I made coffee. I brought Morelli coffee, juice, his paper, and a bowl of raisin bran. I ran upstairs, took a shower, did some makeup and hair magic, got dressed in my black clothes, and came downstairs ready for work.

"Is there anything you need before I leave?" I asked Morelli.

Morelli gave me a full body scan. "Dressing sexy for Ranger?"

I was wearing black jeans, black Chucks, and a stretchy V-neck black T-shirt that didn't show any cleavage. "Is that sarcasm?" I asked.

"No. It's an observation."

"This is *not* sexy."

"That shirt is too skimpy."

"I've worn this shirt a million times. You've never objected to it before."

"That's because it was worn for me. You need to change that shirt."

"Okay," I said, arms in air, nostrils flaring. "You want me to change my shirt. I'll change my shirt." And I stomped up the stairs and stripped off all my clothes. I'd brought every piece of black I owned to Morelli's house, so I pawed through my wardrobe and came up with skintight black spandex workout pants that rode low and were worn commando. I changed my shoes to black Pumas. And I wriggled into a black spandex wrap shirt that didn't quite meet the top of the workout pants and showed *a lot* of cleavage . . . at least as much as I could manage without implants. I stomped back down the stairs and paraded into the living room to show Morelli.

"Is this better?" I asked.

Morelli narrowed his eyes and reached for me, but he

couldn't move far without his crutches. I beat him to the crutches and ran to the kitchen with them. I hustled out of the house, backed Morelli's SUV out of the garage, and motored off to work.

I used my new key fob to get into the underground garage and parked in the area reserved for noncompany cars. I took the elevator to the fifth floor, stepped into the control room, and six sets of eyes looked up from the screens and locked onto me. Halfway to work, I'd pulled Morelli's sweatshirt out of my shoulder bag and put it on over my little stretchy top. It was a nice, big shapeless thing that came well below my ass and gave me a safe unisex look. I smiled at the six men on deck. They all smiled back and returned to their work.

I was a half hour early and for the first time in a long time I was excited to get to work. I wanted to finish the Barroni search, and then I wanted to move on to Jimmy Runion. I still had one file left to search for Frederick Rodriguez. I decided to do it first and get it off my desk. I was still working on the Rodriguez file when Ranger appeared in my cubby entrance.

"We have a date," Ranger said. "You're scheduled for ten o'clock practice downstairs."

Here's the thing about guns. I hate them. I don't even like them when they're not loaded. "I'm in the middle of something," I said. "Maybe we could reschedule for some other time." Like never.

"We're doing this now," Ranger said. "This is important. And I don't want to find your gun in your desk drawer when you leave. If you work for me, you carry a gun."

"I don't have permission to carry concealed."

Ranger shoved my chair with his foot and rolled me back from the computer. "Then you carry exposed."

"I can't do that. I'll feel like Annie Oakley."

Ranger pulled me out of the chair. "You'll figure it out. Get your gun. We have the range for an hour."

I took the gun out of the desk drawer, shoved it into my sweatshirt pocket, and followed Ranger to the elevator. We exited into the garage and walked to the rear. Ranger unlocked the door to the range and switched the light on. The room was windowless and appeared to stretch the length of the building. There were two lanes for shooters. Remote-controlled targets at the far end. Shelves and a thick bulletproof glass partition that separated the shooters at the head of each lane.

"With a little effort you could turn this into a bowling alley," I said to Ranger.

"This is more fun," Ranger said. "And I'm having a hard time seeing you in bowling shoes."

"It's not fun. I don't like guns."

"You don't have to like them, but if you work for me you have to feel comfortable with them and know how to use them and be safe."

Ranger took two headsets and a box of ammo and put them on my shelf. "We'll start with basics. You have a nine-millimeter Sig Sauer. It's a semiautomatic." Ranger removed the magazine, showed it to me, and shoved it back into the gun. "Now you do it," he said.

I removed the magazine and reloaded. I did it ten times. Ranger did a step-by-step demonstration on firing. He gave the gun back to me, and I went through the process ten times. I was nervous, and it felt stuffy in the narrow room, and I was starting to sweat. I put the gun on the shelf, and I took off Morelli's sweatshirt.

"Babe," Ranger said. And he pulled his key fob out of his pocket and hit a button.

"What did you just do?" I asked him.

"I scrambled the security camera in this room. Hal will fall out of his seat upstairs if he sees you in this outfit."

"You don't want to know the long story, but the short story is I wore it to annoy Morelli."

"I'm in favor of anything that annoys Morelli," Ranger said. He moved in close and looked down at me. "This wouldn't be my first choice as a work uniform, but I like it." He ran a finger across the slash of stomach not covered by clothing, and I felt heat rush into private places. He splayed his hand at my hip and turned his interest to my workout pants. "I especially like these pants. What do you wear under them?"

And here's where I made my mistake. I was hot and flustered and a flip answer seemed in order. Problem was the answer that popped out of my mouth was a tad flirty.

"There are some things a man should find out for himself," I said.

Ranger reached for the waistband on the spandex pants, and I shrieked and jumped back.

"Babe," Ranger said, smiling. I was amusing him, again.

I glanced at my watch. "Actually, I need to leave the building for a while."

"Looking for another job?"

"No. This is personal."

Ranger pushed the button to unscramble the surveillance camera. "Wear the sweatshirt when you're on deck in the control room."

"Deal."

A HALF HOUR later, I was idling across the street from Stiva's. The hearse and the flower cars were in place at the side entrance. Three black Town Cars lined up behind the flower cars. I sat and watched the casket come out. Macaronis followed. The flower cars were already loaded. The cars slowly moved out and drove the short distance to the church. I saw no sign of Spiro. I followed at a distance and parked half a block from the church. I had a clear view of the parking lot and the front of the church. I settled back to wait. This would take a while. The Macaronis would want Mass. The parking lot was full and the surrounding streets were bumper-to-bumper cars. The entire Burg had turned out.

An hour later, I was worrying about my cubicle sitting empty. I was getting paid to do computer searches, not hang out at funerals. And then just as I was thinking about leaving and returning to work, the doors to the church opened and people began to file out. I caught a glimpse of the casket being rolled out a side door to the waiting hearse. Engines caught up and down the street. Stiva's assistants were out, lining up cars, attaching flags to antennae. I was intently watching the crowd at the church and jumped when Ranger rapped on my side window.

"Have you seen Spiro?"

"No."

"I'm right behind you. Lock up and we'll take my car."

Ranger was driving a black Porsche Cayenne. I slid onto the passenger seat and buckled up. "How did you find me?"

"Woody picked you up on the screen, realized you were following the funeral, and told me."

"It'll be ugly if Morelli finds out you're tracking his SUV."

"I'll remove the transponder when you stop using the car."

"I don't suppose there's any way I can get you to stop tracking *me*?"

"You don't want me to stop tracking you, Babe. I'm keeping you safe."

He was right. And I was sufficiently freaked out by Spiro to tolerate the intrusion.

"This isn't personal leave time," Ranger said. "This is work. You should have run it by me. We had to scramble to coordinate this."

"Sorry. It was a last-minute decision . . . as you can see from my clothes. My mother will need a pill after she starts getting the reports back on my cemetery appearance."

"We're wearing black," Ranger said. "We're in the ball-park. Just keep your sweatshirt zipped, so the men don't accidentally fall into the grave."

Cars were moving around in front of the church, jockey-ing for position. The hearse pulled into the street and the procession followed, single file, lights on. Ranger waited for the last car to go by before he fell into line. There'd been no sign of Spiro, but then I hadn't expected him to show up at church, shaking hands and chatting. I'd expected him to do another drive-by or maybe hang in a shadow somewhere. Or maybe he'd be hidden at some distance, waiting for the graveside ceremony, using binoculars to see the results of his insanity.

"Tank's already at the cemetery," Ranger said. "He's watching the perimeter. He's got Slick and Eddie working with him."

It was a slow drive to Mama Mac's final resting place. Ranger wasn't famous for making small talk, so it was also a quiet drive. We parked and got out of the Cayenne. The sky was overcast, and the air was unusually cool for the time of year. I was happy to have the sweatshirt. We'd been the last to arrive, and that meant we had the longest walk. By the time we made it to the grave site, the principals were seated and the large crowd had closed around them. This was perfect for our purpose. We were able to stand at a distance and keep watch.

Ranger and I were shoulder to shoulder. Two professionals, doing a job. Problem was, one of the professionals didn't do well at funerals. I was a funeral basket case. Possibly the only thing I hated more than a gun was a funeral. They made me sad. *Really sad.* And the sadness had nothing to do with the deceased. I got weepy over perfect strangers.

The priest stood and repeated the Lord's Prayer and I felt my eyes well with tears. I concentrated on counting blades of grass at my feet, but the words intruded. I blinked the tears back and swung my thoughts to Bob. I tried to envision Bob hunching. He was going to hork up a sock. The tears ran down my cheeks. It was no good. Bob thoughts couldn't compete with the smell of fresh-turned earth and funeral flowers. "Shit," I whispered. And I sniffed back some snot.

Ranger turned to me. His brown eyes were curious and the corners of his mouth were tipped up ever so slightly. "Are you okay?" he asked.

I found a tissue in one of the sweatshirt pockets, and I blew my nose. "I'm fine. I just have this reaction to funerals!"

Several people on the outermost ring of mourners glanced our way.

Ranger put his arm around me. "You didn't like Mama Mac. You hardly knew her."

"It doesn't m-m-matter," I sobbed.

Ranger drew me closer. "Babe, we're starting to attract a lot of attention. Could you drop the sobbing down a level?"

"Ashes to ashes . . ." the priest said.

And I totally lost it. I slumped against Ranger and cried. He was wearing a windbreaker, and he wrapped me in the open windbreaker, hugging me in to him, his face pressed to the side of my head, shielding me as best he could from people turning to see the sobbing idiot. I was burrowed into him, trying to muffle the sobs, and I could feel him shaking with silent laughter.

"You're despicable," I hissed, giving him a punch in the chest. "Stop laughing. This is s-s-s-sad."

Several people turned and shushed me.

"It's okay," Ranger said, still silently laughing, arms wrapped tight around me. "Don't pay any attention to them. Just let it all out."

I hiccupped back a couple small sobs, and I wiped my

nose with my sleeve. "This is nothing. You should see me at a parade when the drums and the flag go by."

Ranger cradled my face in his hands, using his thumbs to wipe the tears from my eyes. "The ceremony is over. Can you make it back to the car?"

I nodded. "I'm okay now. Am I red and blotchy from crying?"

"Yes," Ranger said, brushing a kiss across my forehead. "I love you anyway."

"There's all kinds of love," I said.

Ranger took me by the hand and led me back to the SUV. "This is the kind that doesn't call for a ring. But a condom might come in handy."

"That's not love," I told him. "That's lust."

He was scanning the crowd as we walked and talked, watching for Spiro, watching for anything unusual. "In this case, there's some of both."

"Just not the marrying type?"

We'd reached the car, and Ranger remoted it open. "Look at me, Babe. I'm carrying two guns and a knife. At this point in my life, I'm not exactly family material."

"Do you think that will change?"

Ranger opened the door for me. "Not anytime soon."

No surprise there. Still, it was a teeny, tiny bit of a downer. How scary is that?

"And there are things you don't know about me," Ranger said.

"What kind of things?"

"Things you don't *want* to know." Ranger rolled the engine over and called Tank. "We're heading back," he said. "Anything on your end?"

The answer was obviously negative because Ranger disconnected and pulled into the stream of traffic. "Tank didn't see any bad guys, but it wasn't a total wash," Ranger said, handing his cell phone over to me. "I managed to take a picture for you while you were tucked into my jacket."

Ranger had a picture phone, exactly like the one I'd been issued. I went to the album option and brought up four photos of Anthony Barroni. The images were small. I chose one and waited while it filled the screen. Anthony appeared to be talking on his phone. Hold on, he wasn't talking . . . he was taking a picture. "Anthony's taking photos with his phone," I said. "Omigod, that's so creepy."

"Yeah," Ranger said. "Either Anthony's really into dead people or else he's sending photos to someone not fortunate enough to have a front-row seat."

"Spiro." Maybe.

Most of the cars left the cemetery and turned toward the Burg. The wake at Gina Macaroni's house would be packed. Anthony Barroni peeled away from the herd at Chambers Street. Ranger stuck to him, and we followed him to the store. He parked his Vette in the rear and sauntered inside.

"You should go talk to him," Ranger said. "Ask him if he had a good time."

"You're serious."

"Time to stir things up," Ranger said. "Let's raise the stakes for Anthony. Let him know he's blown his cover. See if anything happens."

I chewed on my lower lip. I didn't want to face Anthony. I didn't want to do this stuff anymore. "I'm an office worker," I said. "I think *you* should talk to him."

Ranger parked the SUV in front of the store. "We'll both talk to Anthony. Last time I left you alone in my car someone stole you."

It was early afternoon on a weekday, and there wasn't a lot of activity in the store. There was an old guy behind the counter, waiting on a woman who was buying a sponge mop. No other customers. Two of the Barroni brothers were working together, labeling a carton of nails in aisle four. Anthony was on his cell phone to the rear of the store. He was shuffling around, nodding his head and laughing.

I always enjoy watching Ranger stalk prey. He moves with single-minded purpose, his body relaxed, his gait even, his eyes unswerving and fixed on his quarry. The eye of the tiger.

I was one step behind Ranger, and I was thinking this wasn't a good idea. We could be wrong and look like idiots. Ranger never worried about that, but I worried about it constantly. Or we could be right, and we could set Anthony and Spiro off on a killing spree.

Anthony saw us approaching. He closed his phone and slipped it into his pants pocket. He looked to Ranger and then to me.

"Stephanie," he said, grinning. "Man, you were really bawling at the cemetery. Guess you got real broken up having Mama Melanoma blown to bits in your car."

"It was a touching ceremony," I said.

"Yeah," Anthony said, snorting and laughing. "The Lord's Prayer always gets to me, too."

Ranger extended his hand. "Carlos Manoso," he said. "I don't believe we've met."

Anthony shook Ranger's hand. "Anthony Barroni. What can I do for you? Need a plunger?"

Ranger gave him a small cordial smile. "We thought we'd stop by to say hello and see if Spiro liked the pictures."

"Waddaya mean?"

"It's too bad he couldn't have been there in person," Ranger said. "So much is lost in a photograph."

"I don't know what you're talking about."

"Sure you do," Ranger said. "You made a bad choice. And you're going to die because of it. You might want to talk to someone while there's still time."

"Someone?"

"The police," Ranger said. "They might be able to cut you a deal."

"I don't need a deal," Anthony said.

"He'll turn on you," Ranger said. "You made a bad choice for a partner."

"You should talk. Look who you've got for a partner. Little Miss Cry-Her-Eyes-Out." Anthony rubbed his eyes like he was crying. "Boohoohoo."

"This is embarrassing," I said. "I *hate* when I cry at funerals."

"Boohoo-ooo."

"Stop. That's enough," I said. "It's not funny."

"Boohoo boohoo boohoo."

So I punched him. It was one of those bypass-the-brain impulse actions. And it was a real sucker punch. Anthony never saw it coming. He had his hands to his eyes doing the boohoo thing, and I guess I threw all my fear and frustration into the punch. I heard his face crunch under my fist, and blood spurted out of his nose. I was so horrified I froze on the spot.

Ranger gave a bark of laughter and dragged me away so I didn't get splattered.

Anthony's eyes were wide, his mouth open, his hands clapped over his nose.

Ranger shoved a business card into Anthony's shirt pocket. "Call me if you want to talk."

We left the store and buckled ourselves into the Cayenne. Ranger turned the engine over and slid a glance my way. "I usually spar with Tank. Maybe next time I should get in the ring with you."

"It was a lucky punch."

Ranger had the full-on smile and there were little laugh lines at the corners of his eyes. "You're a fun date."

"Do you really think Spiro and Anthony are partners?"

"I think it's unlikely."

ELEVEN

I LEFT RANGER in the control room and hurried into my cubicle, anxious to finish running the check on Barroni. I came to a skidding stop when I saw my in-box. Seven new requests for computer background searches. All from Frederick Rodriguez.

I stuck my head out of my cubicle and yelled at Ranger. "Hey, who's this Frederick Rodriguez guy? He keeps filling up my in-box."

"He's in sales," Ranger said. "Let them sit. Work on Gorman."

I finished Barroni, printed his entire file, and dropped it into the drawer with Gorman and Lazar. I entered Jimmy Runion into the first search program and watched as information rushed onto my screen. I'd been scanning the searches as they appeared, taking notes, trying to find the one thing that bound them together in life and probably in death. So far, nothing had jumped out at me. There were a few things that were common to the men, but nothing significant. They were all approximately the same age. They had all owned small businesses. They were all married. When I finished Runion I'd take all the files and read through them more carefully.

I was halfway through Runion when my mom called on my cell.

"Where are you?" she wanted to know.

"I'm at work."

"It's five-thirty. We're supposed to be at the church for rehearsal. You were going to stop here first, and then we were all going over to the church. We've been waiting and waiting."

Crap! "I forgot."

"How could you forget? Your sister's getting married tomorrow. How could you forget?"

"I'm on my way. Give me twenty minutes."

"I'll take your grandmother with me. You can meet us at the church. You just bring Joseph and the cello."

"Joseph and the cello," I dumbly repeated.

"Everyone's waiting to hear you play."

"I might be late. There might not be time."

"We don't have to be at Marsillio's for the rehearsal dinner until seven-thirty. I'm sure there'll be time for you to practice your cello piece."

Crap. *Crap.* And *double crap!*

I grabbed my bag and took off, across the control room, down the stairs, into the garage. Ranger had just pulled in. He was getting out of his car as I ran to Morelli's SUV.

"I'm late!" I yelled to him. "I'm frigging late!"

"Of course you are," Ranger said, smiling.

IT TOOK ME twelve minutes to get across town to the Burg and then into Morelli's neighborhood. I'd had to drive on the sidewalk once when there was traffic at a light. And I'd saved two blocks by using Mr. Fedorka's driveway and cutting through his backyard to the alley that led to Morelli's house.

I locked the SUV in the garage, ran into the house, into the living room.

"The wedding rehearsal is tonight," I yelled at Morelli. "The wedding rehearsal!"

Morelli was working his way through a bag of chips. "And?"

"And we have to be there. We're in the wedding party. It's my sister. I'm the maid of honor. You're the best man."

Morelli set the chips aside. "Tell me those aren't blood splatters on your shoes."

"I sort of punched Anthony Barroni in the nose."

"Anthony Barroni was at Rangeman?"

"It's a long story. I haven't time to go into it all. And you don't want to hear it anyway. It's . . . embarrassing." I had Bob clipped to his leash. "I'm taking Bob out, and then I'm going to help you get dressed." I dragged Bob out the back door and walked him around Morelli's yard. "Do you have to go, Bob?" I said. "Gotta tinkle? Gotta poop?"

Bob didn't want to tinkle or poop in Morelli's yard. Bob needed variety. Bob wanted to tinkle on Mrs. Rosario's hydrangea bush, two doors down.

"This is it!" I yelled at Bob. "You don't go here and

you're holding it in until I get back from the stupid rehearsal dinner."

Bob wandered around a little and tinkled. I could tell he didn't have his heart in it, but it was good enough, so I dragged Bob inside, fed him some dog crunchies for dinner, and gave him some fresh water. I ran upstairs and got clothes for Morelli. Slacks, belt, button-down shirt. I ran back downstairs and shoved him into the shirt, and then realized he couldn't get the slacks over the cast. He was wearing gray sweatpants with one leg cut at thigh level.

"Okay," I said, "the sweats are good enough." I took a closer look. Pizza sauce on the long leg. Not good enough.

I ran upstairs and rummaged through Morelli's closet. Nothing I could use. I rifled his drawers. Nothing there. I went through the dirty clothes basket, found a pair of khaki shorts, and ran downstairs with the shorts.

"Ta-*dah!*" I announced. "Shorts. And they're almost clean." I had Morelli out of his sweatpants in one fast swoop. I tugged the shorts up and zipped them.

"Jeez," Morelli said. "I can zip my own shorts."

"You weren't fast enough!" I looked at my watch. It was almost six o'clock! *Yikes.* "Put your foot on the coffee table, and I'll get shoes on you."

Morelli put his foot on the coffee table, and I stared up his shorts at Mr. Happy.

"Omigod," I said. "You're wearing boxers. I can see up your shorts."

"Do you like what you see?"

"Yes, but I don't want the world seeing it!"

"Don't worry about it," Morelli said. "I'll be careful."

I pulled a sock on Morelli's casted foot, and I laced a sneaker on the other. I raced upstairs, and I changed into a skirt and short-sleeved sweater. I threw my jean jacket over the sweater, grabbed my bag, got Morelli up on his crutches, and maneuvered him to the kitchen door.

"I hate to bring this up," Morelli said. "But aren't you supposed to take the cello?"

The cello. I squinched my eyes closed, and I rapped my head on the wall. *Thunk, thunk, thunk.* I took a second to breathe. I can do this, I told myself. Probably I can play a little something. How hard can it be? You just do the bowing thing back and forth and sounds come out. I might even turn out to be good at it. Heck, maybe I should take some lessons. Maybe I'm a natural talent and I don't even *need* lessons. The more I thought about it, the more logical it sounded. Maybe I was always meant to play the cello, and I'd just gotten sidetracked, and this was God's way of turning me in the direction of my true calling.

"Wait here," I said to Morelli. "I'll put the cello in the car, and I'll come back to get you."

I ran into the living room and hefted the cello. I carted it into the kitchen, past Morelli, out the door, and crossed the yard with it. I opened the garage door, rammed the cello into the back of the SUV, dropped my purse onto the driver's seat, and returned to the kitchen for Morelli. I realized he was just wearing a cotton shirt. No sweater on him. No jacket. And it was cold out. I ran upstairs and got a jacket. I helped him into the jacket, stuffed the crutches back under his arms, and helped him navigate through the back door and down the stairs.

We started to cross the yard, and the garage exploded with enough force to rattle the windows in Morelli's house.

The garage was wood with an asbestos-shingle roof. It hadn't been in the best of shape, and Morelli seldom used it. I'd been using it to keep the SUV bomb-free, but I now saw the flaw in the plan. It was an old garage without an automatic door opener. So to make things easier, I'd left the garage open when not in use. Easy to pull in and park. Also easy to sneak in and plant a bomb.

Morelli and I stood there, dumbstruck. His garage had gone up like fireworks and had come down like confetti. Splintered boards, shingles, and assorted car parts fell out of the sky into Morelli's yard. It was Mama Mac all over again. Almost nothing was left of the garage. Morelli's SUV was a fireball. His yard was littered with smoldering junk.

"Omigod!" I said. "The cello was in your SUV." I pumped my fist into the air and did a little dance. "*Yes!* Way to go! *Woohoo!* There is a God and He loves me. It's good-bye cello."

Morelli gave his head a shake. "You're a very strange woman."

"You're just trying to flatter me."

"Honey, my garage just blew up, and I don't think it was insured. We're supposed to be upset."

"Sorry. I'll try to look serious now."

Morelli glanced over at me. "You're still smiling."

"I can't help it. I'm trying to be scared and depressed, but it's just not working. I'm just so frigging relieved to be rid of that cello."

There were sirens screaming from all directions, and the

first of the cop cars parked in the alley behind Morelli's house. I borrowed Morelli's cell phone and called my mother.

"Bad news," I said. "We're going to be late. We're having car trouble."

"How late? What's wrong with the car?"

"Real late. There's a lot wrong with the car."

"I'll send your father for you."

"Not necessary," I said. "Have the rehearsal without me, and I'll meet you at Marsillio's."

"You're the maid of honor. You have to be at the rehearsal. How will you know what to do?"

"I'll figure it out. This isn't my first wedding. I know the drill."

"But the cello . . ."

"You don't have to worry about that either." I didn't have the heart to tell her about the cello.

Two fire trucks pulled up to the garage. Emergency-vehicle strobes flashed up and down the alley, and headlights glared into Morelli's yard. The garage had been blown to smithereens, and the remaining parts had rained down over a three-house area. Some parts had smoked but none had flamed. The SUV had burned brightly but not long. So the fire had almost entirely extinguished itself before the first hose was unwound.

Ryan Laski crossed the yard and found Morelli. "I'm seeing a disturbing pattern here," Laski said. "Was anyone hurt . . . or vaporized?"

"Just property damage," Morelli said.

"I've sent some uniforms off to talk to neighbors. Hard

to believe no one ever sees this guy. This isn't the sort of place where people mind their own business."

A mobile satellite truck for one of the local television stations cruised into the alley.

Laski cut his eyes to it. "This is going to be a big disappointment. I'm sure they're hoping for disintegrated bodies."

THERE'S SOMETHING HYPNOTIC about a disaster scene, and time moves in its own frame of reference, lost in a blur of sound and color. When the first fire truck rumbled away I looked at my watch and realized I had ten minutes to get to Marsillio's.

"The rehearsal dinner!" I said to Morelli. "I forgot about the rehearsal dinner."

Morelli was blankly staring at the charred remains of his garage and the blackened carcass of his SUV. "Just when you think things can't get any worse . . ."

"The rehearsal dinner won't be that bad." This was a blatant lie, but it didn't count since we both knew it was a blatant lie. "We need a car," I said. "Where's Laski? We can use his car."

"That's a department car. You can't borrow a department car to go to a rehearsal dinner."

I looked at my watch. Nine minutes! *Shit.* I didn't want to call anyone in the wedding party. I'd rather they read about this in the paper tomorrow. I didn't think Joe would be excited about getting a lift from Ranger. There was Lula, but it would take her too long to get here. I searched the crowd of people still milling around in Morelli's yard. "Help me out here, will you?" I said to Morelli. "I'm running down roads of blind panic."

"Maybe I can get someone to drop us off," Morelli said.

And then it came to me. Big Blue. "Wait a minute! I just had a brain flash. The Buick is still sitting in front of the house."

"You mean the Buick that's been sitting there unprotected? The Buick that's very likely booby-trapped?"

"Yeah, that one."

Now Morelli was seriously looking around. "I'm *sure* I can find someone . . ."

I could hear time ticking away. I looked down at my watch. Seven minutes. "I have seven minutes," I said to him.

"This is an extreme circumstance," Morelli said. "It's not every day someone blows up my garage. I'm sure your family will understand."

"They won't understand. This is an everyday occurrence for me."

"Good point," Morelli said. "But I'm not getting in the Buick. And you're not getting in it either."

"I'll be careful," I said. And I ran through the house, locking up behind myself. I got to the Buick, and I hesitated. I wasn't crazy about my life, but I wasn't ready to die. I especially didn't like the idea that my parts could be distributed over half the county. Okay, so what was stronger . . . my fear of death or my fear of not showing up at the rehearsal dinner? This one was a no-brainer. I unlocked the Buick, jumped behind the wheel, and shoved the key into the ignition. No explosion. I drove around the block, turned into the alley, and parked as close as I could to Morelli. I left the motor running and ran to retrieve him.

"You're a nut," he said.

"I looked it all over. I swear."

"You didn't. I know you didn't. You didn't have time. You just took a deep breath, closed your eyes, and got in."

"Five minutes!" I shrieked. "I've got five friggin' minutes. Are you going with me or what?"

"You're unglued."

"And?"

Morelli blew out a sigh and hobbled over to the Buick. I put the crutches in the trunk and loaded Morelli into the car with his back to the door, his casted leg stretched flat on the backseat.

"I guess you're not that unglued," Morelli said. "You just spared a few seconds to look up my pants leg again."

He was right. I'd taken a few seconds to look up his pants leg. I couldn't help myself. I liked the view.

I got behind the wheel and put my foot to the floor. When I reached the corner the Buick was rolling full-steam-ahead and I didn't want any unnecessary slow-downs, so I simply jumped the curb and cut across Mr. Jankowski's lawn. This was the hypotenuse is shorter than the sum of two sides school of driving, and the only thing I remember from high school trigonometry.

Morelli fell off the backseat when I jumped the curb, and a lot of creative cursing followed.

"Sorry," I yelled to Morelli. "We're late."

"You keep driving like this and we're going to be *dead*."

I got there with no minutes to spare. And there were no

parking places. It was Friday night, and Marsillio's was packed.

"I'm dropping you off," I said.

"No."

"Yes! I'm going to have to park a mile away, and you can't walk with that cast." I double-parked, jumped out, and hauled Morelli out of the backseat. I gave him his crutches, and I left him standing on the curb while I ran inside and got Bobby V. and Alan. "Get him up the stairs and into the back room," I told them. "I'll be there in a minute."

I roared away, circling blocks, looking in vain for a place to park. I looked for five minutes and decided parking wasn't going to happen. So I parked in front of a fire hydrant. It was very close to Marsillio's, and if there was a fire I'd run out and move the car. Problem solved.

I rolled into the back room just as the antipasto was set on the table. I took my seat beside Morelli and shook out my napkin. I smiled at my mother. I smiled at Valerie. No one smiled back. I looked down the line at Kloughn. Kloughn smiled at me and waved. Kloughn was wasted. Drunk as a skunk. Grandma didn't look far behind.

Morelli leaned over and whispered in my ear. "Your ass is grass. Your mother's going to cut you off from pineapple upside-down cake."

"THIS IS THE big day," Morelli said.

I was slumped in a kitchen chair, staring at my mug of coffee. It was almost eight o'clock, and I wasn't looking forward to what lay in front of me. I was going to have to call my mom and tell her about the cello. Then I was going to have to give her the fire details. Then I was going to dress up like an eggplant and walk down the aisle in front of Valerie.

"Your big day, too," I said. "You're Albert's best man."

"Yeah, but I don't have to be a vegetable."

"You have to make sure he gets to the church."

"That could be a problem," Morelli said. "He wasn't looking good last night. I hate to be the bearer of bad news, but I don't think he's hot on marriage."

"He's confused. And he keeps having this nightmare about Valerie smothering him with her wedding gown."

Morelli was looking beyond me, out the back window to the place where he used to have a garage.

"Sorry about your garage," I said. "And your SUV."

"Tell you the truth, it wasn't much of a loss. The garage was falling apart. And the SUV was boring. Bob and I need something more fun. Maybe I'll buy a Hummer."

I couldn't see Morelli in a Hummer. I thought Morelli was more suited to his Duc. But of course, Bob couldn't ride on the Duc. "Your Ducati wasn't in the garage," I said. "Where's the Ducati?"

"Getting new pipes and custom paint. No rush now. By the time I get the cast off it'll be too cold to ride."

The phone rang and I froze. "Don't answer it."

Morelli looked at the caller ID and handed the phone over to me. "Guess who."

"Stephanie," my mother said. "I have terrible news. It's about your sister. She's gone."

"Gone? Gone where?"

"Disney World."

I covered the phone with my hand. "My mother's been drinking," I whispered to Morelli.

"I heard that," my mother said. "I haven't been drinking. For goodness sakes, it's eight o'clock in the morning."

"You have too been drinking," Grandma yelled from the background. "I saw you take a nip from the bottle in the cupboard."

"It was either that or kill myself," my mother said. "Your sister just called from the airport. She said they were all on a plane . . . Valerie, the three girls, and cuddle umpkins. And they were going to Disney World, and she had to disconnect because they were about to take off. I could hear the announcements over the phone. I sent your father over to her apartment, and it's all locked up."

"So there's no wedding?"

"No. She said she didn't lose enough weight. She said she was sixty pounds short. And then she said something about cuddle umpkins having an asthma attack from her wedding gown. I couldn't figure out what that was about."

"What about the reception? Is there a reception?"

"No."

"Never?"

"Never. She said if they liked Disney World they were going to live there and never return to Jersey."

"We should get the cake," I said. "Be a shame to waste the cake."

"At a time like this, you're thinking of cake? And what's wrong with your new cell phone?" my mother asked. "I tried to call you, and it's not working."

"It got blown up in Joe's garage."

"Be sure to give me your new number when you replace

your phone," my mother said. "I'm sorry you didn't get to play the cello for everyone."

"Yeah, that would have been fun."

I disconnected and looked across the table at Morelli. "Valerie's going to Disney World."

"Good for her," Morelli said. "Guess that leaves the rest of the day open. It'll give you a chance to look up my pants leg again."

Here's a basic difference between Morelli and me. My first thought was always of cake. His first thought was always of sex. Don't get me wrong. I like sex . . . a lot. But it's never going to replace cake.

Morelli topped off our coffee. "What did your mother say when you told her about your cell phone?"

"She said I should tell her my new number when I got a new phone."

"That was it?"

"Pretty much. Guess your garage wasn't big news."

"Hard to top the Mama Macaroni explosion," Morelli said.

Last night, Morelli's garage had been cordoned off with crime-scene tape, and men were now carefully moving around inside the tape, gathering evidence, photographing the scene. A couple cop cars and crime-scene vans were parked in the alley. A few neighbors were standing, hands in pockets, watching at the edge of Morelli's yard.

I saw Laski cross the yard and come to the back door. Laski let himself in and put a white bakery bag on the table. "Doughnuts," he said. "You got coffee?"

Two uniforms followed Laski into the kitchen.

"Was that a bakery bag I saw come in here?" one of them asked.

I started a new pot of coffee going and excused myself. The house was going to be filled with cops today. Morelli wasn't going to need Nurse Stephanie. I took a shower, pulled my hair back into a half-assed ponytail, and dressed in black jeans, a black T-shirt, and the Pumas. I grabbed the black sweatshirt and the keys to the Buick and returned to the kitchen to give the good news to Morelli.

"I'm going to work," I told him. "I wasn't able to get through everything yesterday."

Our eyes held and I guess Morelli decided I was actually going in to work and not going in to boff Ranger. "Are you taking the Buick?"

"Yes."

"Let Ryan go over the car before you touch it."

That worked just fine for me. I wasn't in the mood to get exploded.

I HAD THREE complete files in front of me. Barroni, Gorman, and Lazar. I had Runion running on the first of the search programs. I had my pad half filled with notes, but so far, nothing had added up to anything resembling *a clue*.

I knew by the sudden silence that Ranger was in the control room. When the men were alone there was constant low-level chatter. When Ranger appeared there was silence. I rolled back so I could see into the room. Ranger was standing, quietly talking to Tank. He glanced my way and our eyes met. He finished his conversation with Tank, and he crossed the room to speak to me.

His hair was still damp from his shower, and when he entered my cubicle he brought the scent of warm Ranger and Bulgari shower gel with him. He leaned against my desk and looked down at me. "Aren't you supposed to be in a wedding?"

"Valerie took off for Disney World."

"Alone?"

"With Albert and the three kids. It's almost ten o'clock. Aren't you getting a late start? Have a late night?"

"I worked out this morning. I understand you had an interesting evening. You stopped sending signals abruptly at six-oh-four. We heard the fire and police request go out on the scanner at six-ten. Tank reported to me at six-twelve that there were no injuries. Next time call me, so I don't have to send a man out."

"Sorry. My phone went with the garage."

Ranger flipped my top drawer open. I'd left my gun and stun gun and pepper spray in the drawer overnight.

"I forgot to take them," I said.

"Forget them again, and you don't have a job."

"That's harsh."

"Yeah, but you can keep the key to my apartment."

TWELVE

RANGER TOOK MY pad and read through my notes. He looked over at the thick printouts on my desk. "Files on Barroni, Gorman, and Lazar?"

"Yes. I'm running Runion now. I think he fits the profile. If you haven't got anything better to do, you might go over the files for me. Maybe you'll see something I missed."

Ranger slouched in the chair next to me and started with Barroni.

I finished Runion a little after noon. I printed him out and pushed back from my station. Ranger looked over at me. He was on the third file.

"How long are you staying?" Ranger asked.

"As long as it takes. I'm going to the kitchen for a sandwich."

"Bring something back for me. I want to keep reading."

"Something?"

"Anything."

"You don't mean that. You have all these rules about eating. No fat. No sugar. No white bread."

"Babe, I don't keep things in my kitchen that I don't eat."

"You want tuna?"

"No. I don't want tuna."

"You see!"

Ranger put the file aside and stood. He crooked an arm around my neck, kissed the top of my head, and dragged me off to the kitchen. We got chicken salad on wheat, bottles of water, and a couple apples and oranges.

"No chips," I said. "Where are the chips?"

"I have chips upstairs in my apartment," Ranger said.

"Are you trying to lure me to your apartment with chips?"

Ranger smiled.

"Okay, tell me the truth. Do you really have chips?"

"There are some things a woman should find out for herself," Ranger said.

I thought that was as far as I wanted to go under the present circumstances. Going upstairs with Ranger, chips or no chips, was a complication I didn't think I could manage right now. So I returned his smile and carted my food back to the cubicle.

I was almost done rereading Runion when it hit me. The one possible thing that would tie the four men to each other. I looked over at Ranger and saw that he was watching me. Ranger had seen it, too. He was a step ahead of me.

"I haven't read Runion yet," Ranger said. "Tell me he was in the army."

"He was in the army."

"Thirty-six years ago he was stationed at Fort Dix."

"Bingo."

"A lot of people pass through Fort Dix," Ranger said. "But it feels good."

I agreed. It felt good. "I'm tired of sitting," I told him. "I think we need a field trip."

"Babe, you're not going to make me go to the mall, are you?"

"I was thinking more along the lines of doing some B and E on Anthony's house."

"I thought you were out of the B and E business."

"Here's the thing, someone keeps blowing up my cars, and it's getting old."

Ranger's cell rang. He answered it and passed it over to me. "It's Morelli," he said.

"I see you're working very closely with the boss," Morelli said.

"Don't start."

"I heard from the crime lab. The bomb was inside the garage, next to a wall, halfway to the rear. It was manually detonated."

"Like the Mama Macaroni bomb."

"Exactly. They found another interesting piece of equipment. Did you know you were being tracked?"

"Yes."

"And last but not least, your mother called and said she was having meatballs and wedding cake for dinner."

"I'll pick you up at six."

"It's amazing what you'll do for a piece of cake," Morelli said.

I gave the phone back to Ranger. "He could have killed me, but he didn't."

"Morelli?"

"The bomber. The bomb was detonated manually, like the bomb that killed Mama Macaroni."

"So this guy is still taking risks to play with you."

"I guess I can sort of understand his motivation. If he thinks I ruined his life, his face, maybe he wants to torment me."

"The notes felt real. The sniping felt real. The first car bomb made sense to me. They were all consistent with increasing harassment and intimidation. After the Mama Macaroni bombing he loses me."

"What's your theory?"

"I don't have a theory. I just think it feels off."

"Do you think there's a copy cat?"

"Possible, but you'd think the crime lab would have noticed differences in the bomb construction." Ranger slid the files into my file cabinet. "Let's roll. If we're going to break into Anthony's house we want to do it before the store closes and he comes home."

I grabbed my jean jacket and got halfway out of my cubby when I was yanked back by my ponytail.

"What did you forget?" Ranger asked.

"My orange?"

"Your gun."

I blew out a sigh, took the gun out of my desk drawer, and then didn't know what to do with it. If I carry a gun, I almost always carry it in my purse, but guess what, no purse. My purse was a cinder in what was left of Morelli's SUV.

Ranger took the gun, pulled me flat against him, and slid the gun under the waistband of my jeans, so that it was nestled at the small of my back.

"This is uncomfortable," I said. "It's going to give me a bruise."

Ranger reached around and removed the gun. And before I realized what he was doing, he had the gun tucked into the front of my jeans at my hipbone. "Is this better?"

"No, but I can't imagine where you'll put it next, so let's just leave it where it is and forget about it."

We rode the elevator to the garage, and Ranger confiscated one of the black Explorers normally set aside for his crew. "Less memorable than a Porsche," he said. "In case we set off an alarm."

We got into the Explorer, and I couldn't sit with the gun rammed into my pants. "I can't do this," I said to Ranger. "This dumb gun is too big. It's poking me."

Ranger closed his eyes and rested his forehead against the wheel. "I can't believe I hired you."

"Hey, it's not my fault. You picked out a bad gun."

"Okay," he said, swiveling to face me. "Where's it poking you?"

"It's poking me in my . . . you know."

"No. I don't know."

"My pubic area."

"Your pubic area?"

I could tell he was struggling with some sort of emotion. Either he was trying hard not to laugh or else he was trying hard not to choke me.

"Give me the gun," Ranger said.

I extracted the gun from my pants and handed it over.

Ranger held the gun in the palm of his hand and smiled. "It's warm," he said. He put the gun in the glove compartment and plugged the key into the ignition.

"Am I fired?"

"No. Any woman who can heat up a gun like that is worth keeping around."

In twenty minutes we were parked across the street and two houses down from Anthony. Ranger cut the engine and dialed Anthony's home number. No answer.

"Try the door," he said to me. "If someone opens it tell them you're selling Girl Scout cookies and keep them talking until I call you. I'm going in through the back. I'm parking one street over."

I swung out of the Explorer and watched Ranger drive away. I waited a couple minutes and then I crossed the street, marched up to Anthony's front door, and rang the bell. Nothing. I rang again and listened. I didn't hear any activity inside. No television. No footsteps. No dog barking. I was about to ring a third time when the door opened, and Ranger motioned me in. I followed him to the second floor, and we methodically worked our way through all three levels.

"I don't see any evidence of a second person living here," Ranger said when we reached the basement.

"This is a real bummer," I said. "No books on how to build a bomb. No sniper rifles. No dirty underwear with 'Spiro' embroidered on it."

We were in the kitchen and only the garage remained. We knew there was something in the garage because Anthony never parked his fancy new Vette in the garage. Ranger drew his gun and opened the door that led to the garage, and we both looked in at wall-to-wall boxes. Never-been-opened cartons containing toaster ovens, ceiling fans, nails, duct tape, grout guns, electric screwdrivers.

"I think the little jerk is stealing from his brothers," I said to Ranger.

"I think you're right. There'd be larger quantities of single items if he was hijacking trucks or legally storing inventory. This looks like he randomly fills his trunk every night when he leaves."

We backed out and closed the garage door.

Ranger looked at his watch. "We have a little time. Let's see what he's got on his computer."

Anthony had a small office on the first floor. Cherry built-ins lined the walls, but Anthony hadn't yet filled them with books or objets d'art. The cherry desk was large and masculine. The cushy desk chair was black leather. The desktop held a phone, a computer and keyboard, and small printer.

Ranger sat in the chair and turned the computer on. A strip of icons appeared on the screen. Ranger hit one of the icons and Anthony's e-mail program opened. Ranger scrolled through new mail and sent mail and deleted mail. Not much there. Anthony didn't do a lot of e-mailing. Ranger opened Anthony's address book. No Spiro listed. Ranger closed the program and tried another icon.

"Let's see what he surfs," Ranger said. He went to the bookmarked sites. They were all porn.

Ranger closed the program and returned his attention to the icon strip. He hit iPhoto and worked his way through the photo library. There were a couple pictures of

Anthony's Vette. A couple pictures of the front of his town house. And three photos from the Macaroni funeral. The quality wasn't great since they were downloaded from his phone, but the subject matter was clear. He'd been taking pictures of Carol Zambelli's hooters. Zambelli had just purchased the set, and couldn't get her coat closed at graveside.

Ranger shut the computer down. "Time to get out of here."

We left through the back door and followed a bike path through common ground to the street. Ranger remoted the SUV open, we buckled ourselves in, and Ranger hung a U-turn and headed back to the office.

"This trip doesn't take Anthony Barroni out of the picture," Ranger said, "but it definitely back-burners him."

We pulled into the Rangeman garage at five-thirty. Ranger parked and walked me to the Buick. "You have a half hour to get to Morelli. Where are you taking him?"

"We're having dinner with my parents. They have wedding cake for two hundred."

"ISN'T THIS NICE," my mother said, glass in hand, amber liquid swirling to the rim, stopping just short of sloshing onto the white tablecloth. "It's so quiet. I hardly have a headache."

Two leaves had been taken out of the dining room table, and the small dining room seemed strangely spacious. The table had been set for five. My mother and father sat at either end, and Morelli and I sat side by side and across from Grandma, who was lost behind the massive three-tier wedding cake that had been placed in the middle of the table.

"I was looking forward to a party," Grandma said. "If it was me, I would have had the reception anyway. I bet nobody would even have noticed Valerie wasn't there. You could have just told everybody she was in the ladies' room."

Morelli and my father had their plates heaped with meatballs, but I went straight for the cake. My mother was going with a liquid diet, and I wasn't sure what Grandma was eating since I couldn't see her.

"Valerie called when they got off the plane in Orlando, and she said Albert was breathing better, and the panic attacks were not nearly as severe," my mother said.

My father smiled to himself and mumbled something that sounded like "friggin' genius."

"How'd Sally take the news?" I asked my mother. "He must have been upset."

"He was upset at first, but then he asked if he could have the wedding gown. He thought he could have it altered so he could wear it onstage. He thought it would give him a new look."

"You gotta credit him," Grandma said. "Sally's always thinking. He's a smart one."

I had the cake knife in hand. "Anyone want cake?"

"Yeah," Morelli said, shoving his plate forward. "Hit me."

"I heard your garage got blown up," Grandma said to Morelli. "Emma Rhinehart said it went up like a bottle rocket. She heard that from her son, Chester. Chester delivers pizza for that new place on Keene Street, and he was making a delivery a couple houses down from you. He said he was taking a shortcut through the alley, and all of a sudden the garage went up like a bottle rocket. Right in front of him. He said it was real scary because he almost hit this guy who was standing in the alley just past your house. He said the guy looked like his face had melted or something. Like some horror movie."

Morelli and I exchanged glances, and we were both thinking *Spiro*.

An hour later, I helped Morelli hobble down the porch stairs and cross the lawn. I'd parked the Buick in the driveway, and I'd bribed one of the neighborhood kids into baby-sitting the car. I loaded Morelli into the car, gave the kid five dollars, and ran back to the house for my share of the leftovers.

My mother had bagged some meatballs for me, and now she was standing in front of the cake. She had a cardboard box on the chair and a knife in her hand. "How much do you want?" she asked.

Grandma was standing beside my mother. "Maybe you should let me cut the cake," Grandma said. "You're tipsy."

"I'm not tipsy," my mother said, very carefully forming her words.

It was true. My mother wasn't tipsy. My mother was shit-faced.

"I tell you, we're lucky if we don't find ourselves talking to Dr. Phil one of these days," Grandma said.

"I like Dr. Phil," my mother said. "He's cute. I wouldn't mind spending some time with him, if you know what I mean."

"I know what you mean," Grandma said. "And it gives me the creeps."

"So how much of the cake do you want?" my mother asked me again. "You want the whole thing?"

"You don't want the whole thing," Grandma said to me. "You'll give yourself the diabetes. You and your mother got no control."

"Excuse me?" my mother said. "No control? Did you say I had no control? I am the queen of control. Look at this family. I have a daughter in Disney World with oogly woogly smoochikins. I have a granddaughter who thinks she's a horse. I have a mother who thinks she's a teenager." My mother turned to me. "And you! I don't know where to begin."

"I'm not so bad," I said. "I'm taking charge of my life. I'm making changes."

"You're a walking disaster," my mother said. "And you just ate seven pieces of cake."

"I didn't!"

"You did. You're a cakeaholic."

"I don't mind thinking I'm a teenager," Grandma said. "Better than thinking I'm an old lady. Maybe I should get a boob job, and then I could wear them sex-kitten clothes."

"Good God," my mother said. And she drained her glass.

"I'm not a cakeaholic," I said. "I only eat cake on special occasions." Like Monday, Tuesday, Wednesday, Thursday . . .

"You're one of them comfort eaters," Grandma said. "I saw a show about it on television. When your mother gets stressed, she irons and tipples. When you get stressed, you eat cake. You're a cake abuser. You need to join one of them help groups, like Cake Eaters Anonymous."

My mother sliced into the cake and carved off a chunk

for herself. "Cake Eaters Anonymous," she said. "That's a good one." She took a big bite of the cake and got a smudge of icing on her nose.

"You got icing on your nose," Grandma said.

"Do not," my mother said.

"Do, too," Grandma Mazur said. "You're three sheets to the wind."

"Take that back," my mother said, swiping her finger through the frosting on the top tier and flicking a glob at Grandma Mazur. The glob hit Grandma in the forehead and slid halfway down her nose. "Now you've got icing on your nose, too," my mother said.

Grandma sucked in some air.

My mother flicked another glob at Grandma.

"That's it," Grandma said, narrowing her eyes. "Eat dirt and die!" And Grandma scooped up a wad of cake and icing and smushed it into my mother's face.

"I can't see!" my mother shrieked. "I'm blind." She was wobbling around, flailing her arms. She lost her balance and fell against the table and into the cake.

"I tell you it's pathetic," Grandma said. "I don't know how I raised a daughter that don't even know how to have a food fight. And look at this, she fell into a three-tiered wedding cake. This is gonna put a real crimp in the leftovers." She reached out to help my mother, and my mother latched on to Grandma and wrestled her onto the table.

"You're going down, old woman," my mother said to Grandma.

Grandma yelped and struggled to scramble away, but she couldn't get a grip. She was as slick as a greased pig, in lard icing up to her elbows.

"Maybe you should stop before someone falls and gets hurt," I told them.

"Maybe you should mind your own beeswax," Grandma said, mashing cake into my mother's hair.

"Hey, wait a minute," my mother said. "Stephanie didn't get her cake."

They both paused and looked over at me.

"How much cake did you want?" my mother asked. "This much?" And she threw a wad of cake at me.

I jumped to dodge the cake, but I wasn't quick enough, and it caught me in the middle of the chest. Grandma nailed me in the side of my head, and before I could move she got me a second time.

My father came in from the living room. "What the devil?" he said.

Splat, splat, splat. They got my father.

"Jesus Marie," he said. "What are you, friggin' nuts? That's good wedding cake. You know how much I paid for that cake?"

My mother threw one last piece of cake. It missed my father and hit the wall.

I had cake and icing in my hair, on my hands and arms, on my shirt, my face, my jeans. I looked over at the cake plate. It was empty. The aroma of sugar and butter and vanilla was enticing. I swiped at the cake sliding down the wall and stuck my finger in my mouth. If I'd been alone I probably would have licked the wall. My mother was right. I was a cakeaholic.

"Boy," my grandmother said to my mother. "You're fun when you've got a snootful."

My mother looked around the room. "Do you think that's how this happened?"

"Do you think you'd do this if you were sober?" Grandma asked. "I don't think so. You got a real stick up your ass when you're sober."

"That's it," my mother said. "I'm done tippling."

I caught myself licking cake off my arm. "And maybe I should cut back on the cake," I said. "I *do* feel a little addicted."

"We'll have a pact," my mother said. "No more tippling for me and no more cake for you."

We looked at Grandma.

"I'm not giving up nothing," Grandma said.

I took my bag of meatballs and went out to the car. I slid behind the wheel, turned the key in the ignition, and Morelli leaned over the seat at me.

"What the hell happened to you?" he asked.

"Food fight."

"Wedding cake?"

"Yep."

Morelli licked icing off my neck, and I accidentally jumped the driveway and backed out over my parents' front lawn.

"OKAY, LET ME get this correct," Morelli said. "You're giving up sweets."

We were sitting at Morelli's kitchen table, having a late breakfast.

"If it's got sugar on it, I'm not eating it," I told Morelli.

"What about that cereal you've got in front of you?"

"Frosted Flakes. My favorite."

"Coated with sugar."

Shit. "Maybe I got carried away last night. Maybe I was overreacting to Valerie gaining all that weight, and then Kloughn dreaming about her smothering him. And my mother said I ate seven pieces of wedding cake, but I don't actually remember eating anything. I think she must have been exaggerating."

Morelli's phone rang. He answered and passed it to me. "Your grandmother."

"Boy, that was some mess we made last night," Grandma said. "We're gonna have to put up new paper in the dining room. It was worth it, though. Your mother got up this morning and cleaned the bottles out of the cupboard. 'Course, I still got one in my closet, but that's okay on account of I can handle my liquor. I'm not one of them anxiety-ridden drunks. I just drink because I like it. Anyway, your mother's not drinking so long as you're off the sugar. You're off the sugar, right?"

"Right. Absolutely. No sugar for me."

I gave the phone back to Morelli, and I went to look in the cupboard. "Do we have cereal that's not coated with sugar?"

"We have bagels and English muffins."

I popped a bagel into the toaster and drank coffee while I waited. "Ranger thinks some of the bombings feel off."

"I agree," Morelli said. "Laski's double-checking the crime-lab reports to make sure we don't have an opportunist at work. And I left a message for him to talk to Chester Rhinehart. So far Chester's the only other person besides you to see Spiro."

"So, what's up for today? How's your leg?"

"The leg is a lot better. No pain. My foot isn't swollen."

There was a lot of loud knocking on the front door. I grabbed my bagel and went to investigate.

It was Lula, dressed in a poison green tank and spandex jeans with rhinestones running down the side seam. "I heard about the wedding," Lula said. "I bet your mama had a cow. Imagine having to call all those people and tell them they're on their own for burgers tonight. But there's some good news in all this, right? You didn't have to go parading around like a freakin' eggplant."

"It all worked out for the best," I said.

"Damn skippy. Glad you feel that way. Wouldn't want you to be in a bad mood since I need a little help."

"Oh boy."

"It's just a little help. Moral support. But you can jump in on the physical stuff if you want. Not that I expect anyone's gonna shoot at us or anything."

"No. Whatever it is . . . I'm not doing it."

"You don't mean that. I can see you don't mean that. Where's Officer Hottie? He in the kitchen?" Lula swept past me and went in search of Morelli. "Hey," she said to him. "How's it shakin'? You don't mind if I borrow Stephanie today, do you?"

"He does," I said. "We were going to do something . . ."

"Actually, it's Guy Day," Morelli said to me. "I promised the guys we could hang out today."

"You hung out with the guys yesterday. And the day before."

"Those were cop guys. These are just guy guys. My brother Tony and my cousin Mooch. They're coming over to watch the game."

"Lucky for you I came along," Lula said to me. "You would have had to hide upstairs in your room so you didn't ruin Guy Day."

"You can stay and watch the game with us," Morelli said to me. "It's not like it's a stag party. It's just Tony and Mooch."

"Yeah," Lula said. "They probably be happy to have someone do the pizza run and open their beer bottles for them."

"Think I'll pass on Guy Day," I said to Morelli. "But thanks for inviting me." I grabbed my jacket and followed Lula out to the Firebird. "Who are we looking for?"

"I'm gonna take another shot at Willie Martin. I'm gonna keep my clothes on this time. I'm gonna nail his ass."

"He didn't leave town?"

"He's such an arrogant so-and-so. He thinks he's safe. He thinks no one can touch him. He's still in his cheap-ass apartment over the garage. My friend Lauralene made a business call on him last night. Do you believe it?"

In a former life, Lula was a 'ho, and she still has a lot of friends in the industry. "Is Lauralene still there?"

"No. Willie's too cheap to pay for a night. Willie's strictly pay by the job."

We crossed town, turned onto Stark, and Lula parked in

front of the garage. We both looked up at Willie's apartment windows on the third floor.

"You got a gun?" Lula asked.

"No."

"Stun gun?"

"No."

"Cuffs?"

"Negative."

"I swear, I don't know why I brought you."

"To make sure you keep your clothes on," I said.

"Yeah, that would be it."

We got out of the Firebird and took the stairs. The air was foul, reeking of urine and stale fast-food burgers and fries. We got to the third-floor landing, and Lula started arranging her equipment. Gun shoved into the waistband of her jeans. Cuffs half out of her pocket. Stun gun rammed into her jeans at the small of her back. Pepper spray in hand.

"Where's the taser?" I asked.

"It's in my purse." She rooted around in her big shoulder bag and found the taser. "I haven't had a chance to test-drive this baby yet, but I think I could figure it out. How hard can it be, right?" She powered up and held on to the taser. She motioned me to the door. "Go ahead and knock."

"Me?"

"He won't open the door if it's me. I'm gonna hide to the side, here. He see a skinny white girl like you standing at his door, he's gonna get all excited and open up."

"He'd better not get *too* excited."

"Hell, the more excited the better. Slow him down running. Make him do some pole vaulting."

I rapped on the door, and I stood where Martin could see me. The door opened, and he looked me over.

"I don't know what you're selling, but I might be willing to buy it," Willie said.

"Boy, that's real original," I said, walking into his apartment. "I bet you had a hard time coming up with that one."

"Wadda ya mean?"

I turned to face him. Was he really that dumb? I looked into his eyes and decided the answer was yes. And the frightening part is that he outsmarted Lula last time she tried to snag him. Best not to dwell on that realization. The door was still open, and I could see Lula creeping forward behind Willie Martin. She had pepper spray in one hand and the taser in the other.

"I was actually looking for Andy Bartok," I said to Martin. "This is his apartment, right?"

"This is my apartment. There's no Andy here. Do you know who I am? You follow football?"

"No," I said, putting the couch between me and Martin. "I don't like violent sports."

"I like violent sports," Lula said. "I like the sport called kick Willie Martin in his big ugly blubber butt."

Martin turned to Lula. "You! Guess you didn't get enough of Will Martin, hunh? Guess you came back for more. And look at this here present you brought me . . . a candy-ass white woman."

"The only thing I brought you is a ticket to the lockup," Lula said. "I'm hauling your nasty blubber butt off to jail."

"I haven't got no blubber butt," Martin said. He turned

again so he could moon Lula, and he dropped his drawers to prove his point.

I was standing in front of him so I got the pole-vaulting demonstration. Lula got the rear view, and whether it was intentional or just a jerk-action reflex was hard to say, but Lula shot Martin in the ass with the taser.

Martin went down with his pants at half-mast and flopped around on the floor, twitching on the taser line like a fresh-caught fish.

"Get your finger off the button," I yelled to Lula. "You're going to kill him!"

"Oops," Lula said. "Guess I should have read the instruction book."

Martin was facedown, doing shallow breathing. He was about six foot five and close to three hundred pounds. I had no idea how we were going to get him to the Firebird.

"I'll cuff him, and you pull his pants up," Lula said.

"Good try, but this is your party. I'm not doing pants wrangling."

"The bounty hunter assistant is supposed to take orders," Lula said.

I cut my eyes to her.

"Of course, that don't count for you," she said. "On account of you're not an official assistant. You're the . . ."

"The friend of the bounty hunter," I said.

"Yeah, that's it. The friend of the bounty hunter. How about you cuff him, and I'll get his pants up."

I took the cuffs from Lula. "Works for me."

I cuffed Martin's hands behind his back and stepped

away, and Lula straddled him and yanked the taser leads off. By the time she got his pants up, she was sweating.

"Usually I'm taking pants *off* a man," Lula said. "It's a lot more work getting them up than down."

Especially when you're wrestling them up the equivalent of a 280-pound sandbag.

Willie had one eye open, and he was making some low-level gurgling sounds.

"He's gonna be pissed off when he comes around," Lula said. "I'm thinking we want to get him into the car before that happens."

"I'd feel a lot better about this if you had ankle shackles," I said.

"I forgot ankle shackles."

I grabbed a foot and Lula grabbed a foot, and we threw our weight into dragging Martin to the door. We got him through the door and onto the cement landing and realized we were going to have to use the rickety freight elevator.

"It's probably okay," Lula said, pushing the button.

I closed and locked Martin's door. I repeated Lula's words. It's probably okay. It's probably okay.

The elevator made a lot of grinding, clanking noises, and we could see it shudder as it rose from the bottom floor.

"It's just three floors," Lula said, more to herself than to me. "Three floors isn't a whole lot, right? Probably you could jump from three floors if you had to. Remember when you fell off that fire escape? That was three floors, right?"

"Two floors by the time I actually started free falling." And it knocked me out and hurt like hell.

The open-air car came to a lurching stop three inches below floor level. Lula struggled with the grate and finally got it half open.

"You got the least weight," Lula said. "You go in first and see if it holds you."

I gingerly got into the cage. It swayed slightly but held. "Feels okay," I said.

Lula crept in. "See, this is gonna be fine," Lula said, standing very still. "This is one sturdy-ass elevator. You give this elevator a coat of paint and it'll be like new."

The elevator groaned and dropped two inches.

"Just settling in," Lula said. "I'm sure it's fine. I could see this is a real safe elevator. Still, maybe we should get off and reconsider our options."

Lula took a step forward and the elevator went into a downslide, banging against the side of the building, groaning and screeching. It reached the second floor and the bottom dropped out from under us. Lula and I hit the ground level and lay there stunned, knocked breathless, with rust sifting down on us like fairy dust.

"Fuck," Lula said. "Take a look at me and tell me if anything's broken."

I got to my hands and knees and crawled out of the elevator. It was Sunday and the garage was closed, thank God. At least we didn't have an audience. And probably the guys who worked in the garage wouldn't be real helpful when it came to capturing Martin. Lula crawled out after me, and we slowly got to our feet.

"I feel like a truck rolled over me," Lula said. "That was a dumb idea to take the elevator. You're supposed to stop me from acting on those dumb ideas."

I tried to dust some of the rust and elevator grit off my jeans, but it was sticking like it was glued on. "I don't know how to break this to you," I said. "But your FTA is still on the third floor."

THIRTEEN

"WE'RE JUST GONNA have to carry Willie down the stairs," Lula said. "I got him cuffed. I'm not giving up now."

"We can't carry him. He's too heavy."

"Then we'll drag him. Okay, so he might get a little bruised, but we'll say we were walking him down and he slipped. That happens, right? People fall down the stairs all the time. Look at us, we just fell down an elevator, and are we complaining?"

We were standing next to a stack of tires that were loaded onto a hand truck. "Maybe we could use this hand truck," I said. "We could strap Martin on like a refrigerator. It'll be hard to get him down the two flights of stairs, but at least we won't crack his head open."

"That's a good idea," Lula said. "I was just going to think of that idea."

We off-loaded the tires and carted the truck up the stairs. Martin was still out. He was drooling and his expression was dazed, but his breathing had normalized, and he now had both eyes open. We laid the hand truck flat and rolled Martin onto it. I'd brought about thirty feet of strapping up with the hand truck, and we wrapped Martin onto the truck until he looked like a mummy. Then we pushed and pulled until we had Martin and the truck upright.

"Now we're going to ease him down, one step at a time," I said to Lula. "We're both going to get a grip on the truck, and between the two of us we should be able to do this."

By the time we got Martin to the second-floor landing we were soaked through. The air in the stairwell was hot and stagnant, and lowering Martin down the stairs one at a time was hard work. My hands were raw from gripping the strapping and my back ached. We stopped to catch our breath, and I saw Martin's fingers twitch. Not a good sign. I didn't want him struggling to get free on the next set of stairs.

"We have to get moving," I said to Lula. "He's coming around."

"I'm coming around, too," Lula said. "I'm having a heart attack. I think I gave myself a hernia. And look . . . I broke a nail. It was my best nail, too. It was the one with the stars and stripes decal."

We shifted the hand truck into position to take the first step, and Martin turned his head and looked me in the eye.

"What the . . ." he said. And then he went nuts, yelling and struggling against the strapping. He was crazy-eyed and a vein was popped out in his forehead. I was having a hard time hanging on to the hand truck, and I was watching the strapping around his chest go loose and show signs of unraveling.

"The stun gun," I yelled to Lula. "Give him a jolt with the stun gun. I can't hang on with him struggling like this."

Lula reached around back for the stun gun and came up empty. "Must have fallen out when the elevator crashed," she said.

"Do something! The strap is unraveling. Shoot him. Zap him. Kick him in the nuts. *Do something! Anything!*"

"I got my spray!" Lula said. "Stand back, and I'll spray the snot out of him."

"No!" I shrieked. "Don't spray in the stairwell!"

"It's okay, I got plenty," Lula said.

She hit the button, and I got a faceful of pepper spray. Martin gave an enraged bellow and wrenched the hand truck away from Lula and me. I was blinded and gagging, and I could hear the hand truck banging down the stairs like a toboggan. There was some scuffling at ground level, the door opened, and then it was quiet at the bottom of the stairs. At the top of the stairs, Lula and I were gasping for breath, feeling our way down, trying to get away from the droplets that were still hanging in the torpid air on the second-floor landing.

We stumbled over the hand truck when we got to the bottom. We pushed through the door and stood bent at the waist, waiting for the mucus production to slow, eyes closed and tearing, nose running.

"Guess pepper spray wasn't a good idea," Lula finally said.

I blew my nose in my T-shirt and tried to blink my eyes clear. I didn't want to touch them with my hand in case I still had some spray left on my skin. Martin was nowhere to be seen. The wrapping was in a heap on the sidewalk.

"You don't look too good," Lula said. "You're all red and blotchy. I'm probably red and blotchy, too, but I got superior skin tone. You got that pasty white stuff that only looks good after you get a facial and put on makeup."

We were squinting, not able to fully open our eyes, my throat burned like fire, and I was a mucus factory.

"I need to wash my hands and my face," I said. "I have to get this stuff off me."

We got into Lula's Firebird, and Lula crept down Stark to Olden. She turned on Olden and somehow the Firebird found its way to a McDonald's. We parked and dragged ourselves into the ladies' room.

I stuck my entire head under the faucet. I washed my face and hair and hands as best I could, and I dried my hair under the hot-air hand dryer.

"You're a little scary," Lula said. "You got a white-woman-Afro thing going."

I didn't care. I shuffled out of the ladies' room and got a cheeseburger, fries, and a bottle of water.

Lula sat across from me. She had a mountain of food and a gallon of soda. "What's with you?" she wanted to know. "Where's your soda? Where's your pie? You gotta have a pie when you come here."

"No soda and no pie. I'm off sweets."

"What about cake? What about doughnuts?"

"No cake. No doughnuts."

"You can't do that. You need cake and doughnuts. That's your comfort food. That's your stress buster. You don't eat cake and doughnuts, and you'll get all clogged up."

"I made a deal with my mother. She's off the booze as long as I'm off the sugar."

"That's a bad deal. You're not good at that deprivation stuff. You're like a big jelly doughnut. You give it a squeeze and the jelly squishes out. You don't let it squish out where it wants and it's gotta find a new place to squish out. Remember when your love life was in the toilet and you weren't getting any? You were eating bags of candy bars. You're a compensator. Some people can hold their jelly in, but not you. Your jelly gotta squish out somewhere."

"You've got to stop talking about doughnuts. You're making me hungry."

"See, that's what I'm telling you. You're one of them hungry people. You deprive yourself of cake and you're gonna want to eat something else."

I shoved some fries into my mouth and crooked an eyebrow at Lula.

"You know what I'm saying," Lula said. "You better be careful, or you'll send Officer Hottie to the emergency room. And you're working for Ranger now. How're you gonna keep from taking a bite outta that? He's just one big hot sexy doughnut far as I'm concerned."

"What are you going to do about Willie Martin?"

"I don't know. I'm gonna have to think about it. Taking him down in his apartment doesn't seem to be working."

"Does he have a job?"

"Yeah, he works nights, stealing cars and hijacking trucks."

I drained my bottle of water and bundled my trash. "I need to go back to Morelli's house and get out of these clothes. Call me when you get a new plan for Martin."

"You mean you'd go out with me again?"

"Yeah." Go figure that. Truth is, it was getting pretty obvious that being a bounty hunter wasn't the problem. In fact, maybe being a bounty hunter was the solution. At least I'd acquired a few survival skills. When trouble followed me home I was able to cope. I was never going to be Ranger, but I wasn't Ms. Wimp either.

THERE WERE A bunch of cars parked in front of Morelli's house when Lula dropped me off.

"You sure you want to go in there?" Lula asked. "Looks like it's still Guy Day."

"I don't care what day it is. I'm beat. I want to take a shower, get into clean clothes, and turn into a couch potato."

I straggled into the house and found five guys slouched in front of the television. I knew them all. Mooch, Tony, Joe, Stanley Skulnik, and Ray Daily. There were pizza boxes, boxes of doughnuts, discarded candy bar wrappers, beer bottles, and chip bags on the coffee table. Bob was sound asleep on the floor by Morelli. He had orange Cheez Doodle dust on his nose, and a red jelly bean stuck in the fur on his ear. Everyone but Bob was eyes glued to the television. They all turned and stared at me when I walked into the room.

"How's it going?" Mooch said.

"Looking good," Stanley said.

"Yo," from Tony.

"Long time no see," Ray said.

And they turned back to the game.

I had hair from hell, I'd blown my nose in my shirt, I was covered with rust and crud, my jeans were torn, and I was holding a roll of toilet paper from McDonald's, and no one noticed. Not that I was surprised by this. After all, these guys were from the Burg, and a game was on television.

Morelli continued to stare after the others had turned away.

"Fell down an elevator shaft and got sprayed with pepper spray," I said to him. "Picked up the toilet paper at McDonald's."

"And you're okay?"

I nodded.

"Could you get me a cold one?"

I GOT INTO the shower and stood there until there was no more hot water. I got dressed in Morelli's sweats, blasted my hair with the dryer, and crawled into bed. It was close to seven when I woke up. The house was quiet. I shuffled into the bathroom, glanced in the mirror, and realized there was a note pinned to my sweatshirt.

WENT OUT TO EAT WITH MOOCH AND TONY. DIDN'T WANT TO WAKE YOU. CALL MY CELL IF YOU WANT ME TO BRING SOMETHING HOME. THERE'S LEFTOVER PIZZA IN THE FRIDGE.

Apparently Guy Day continued into Guy Night. I shuffled downstairs and ate the leftover pizza. I washed it down with a Bud. I checked out the doughnut box. Three doughnuts left in the box. I blew out a sigh. I wanted a doughnut. I paced in the kitchen. I finished off a bag of chips. I drank another Bud. I couldn't stop thinking about the doughnuts. It's only been one friggin' day, I thought. Surely I can make it through one lousy day without a doughnut. I went to the living room and remoted the television. I flipped through the channels. I couldn't concentrate. I was haunted by the doughnuts. I stormed into the kitchen space, got the doughnuts, and threw them in the garbage. I paced around, and I got the doughnuts out of the garbage. I rammed them down the garbage disposal and ran the disposal. I stared into the sink at the empty drain. No doughnuts. I couldn't believe I had to disposal the doughnuts. I was pathetic.

I went back to the living room and tried television again. Nothing held my attention. I was restless. Big Blue was at the curb, but I had nowhere to go. It was Sunday night. The mall was closed. I wasn't up to a visit with my parents. Probably I shouldn't be driving Big Blue anyway. It was sitting out there unprotected.

A couple minutes after nine, Morelli swung in on his crutches. "You're looking better," he said. "You were out like a light when I left. I guess falling down an elevator shaft is exhausting. Did you get your man?"

"No. He ran away."

Morelli grinned. "You're not supposed to let them do that."

"Did I miss anything important?"

"Yeah. I just got a call from Laski. Four bodies were found in a shallow grave in a patch of woods off upper Stark this afternoon. Some kids stumbled across it. They said they were looking for their dog, but they were probably looking for a place to smoke weed." Morelli eased himself onto the couch. "Laski said the bodies were pretty decomposed, but there were rings and belt buckles. None of the bodies has been officially identified yet, but Laski's certain one of them is Barroni. He was wearing an initialed belt buckle when he disappeared, and the wedding ring matches the description his wife, Carla, gave when she filed missing persons."

I sat next to Morelli. "That's so sad. I always hoped they'd suddenly reappear. Did Laski know how they were killed?"

"Shot. Multiple times. All in the chest, as if they'd been standing together and someone sprayed them with bullets like in an old Al Capone movie."

"What about the cars?"

"Laski said there was a dirt road going in. Most likely used by kids looking for privacy for one reason or another. So cars could have driven in there. But no cars were found with the bodies."

"I have profiles on the four missing men. I've been trying to tie them together. And I had a feeling Anthony Barroni and Spiro Stiva were involved somehow. Now I'm not so sure. Maybe Spiro came back for the sole purpose of terrorizing me and eventually killing me. Maybe he's a lone gun out there and not hanging with anyone. That would partially explain why no one's seen him."

"There's a description out on him now. There's a corroborating witness that Spiro, or at least someone with a badly scarred face, was seen in the area when my garage went up. I don't know what to say about the men who were just found. It's pretty clear that someone called a meeting and executed them."

"They had to have known the gunman," I said. "I can't

see any of these men getting in his car and driving off to a meeting on upper Stark at the request of a stranger."

"I agree, but we don't know the relationship. It could have been something impersonal, like blackmail. And the blackmailer decided to terminate."

"Do you think that's it?"

"No," Morelli said. "I think they all knew each other, and there was a fifth member of the group who had his own agenda."

"They were all in the same unit at Fort Dix."

Morelli turned and looked at me. "You found that out?"

"Yeah."

"So, not only are you hot but you're smart, too?"

"You think I'm hot?"

Morelli had his hand up my shirt, tinkering with my bra. "Cupcake, I'm not sharing my house with you because you can cook."

I cut my eyes to him. "Are you telling me I'm here just for the sex?"

Morelli was concentrating on getting me undressed and not paying attention to the tone of my voice. "Yeah, the sex has been great."

"What about the companionship, the friendship, the relationship part of this?"

Morelli paused in his effort to release the clasp on my bra. "Uh oh, did I just say something stupid?"

"Yes. You said I was just here for the sex."

"I didn't mean that."

"Yes, you did! It's all you think about with me."

"Cut me some slack," Morelli said. "I have a broken leg. I sit here all day, eating jelly beans and thinking about you naked. It's what guys do when they have a broken leg."

"You did that *before* you broke your leg."

"Oh man," Morelli said. "This isn't going to turn into one of those issue discussions, is it? I hate those discussions."

"Suppose for some reason we couldn't have sex. Would you still love me?"

"Yeah, but not as much."

"What kind of an answer is that? That's not the right answer."

Okay, so I knew his answer wasn't serious, and I didn't really think my relationship with Morelli was entirely sexual, but I couldn't seem to stop myself from getting crazy. I was on my feet, flapping my arms and yelling. This was usually Morelli's role, and here I was, working myself into a frenzy, going down a one-way street to nowhere. And I suspected it was Lula's jelly doughnut. The doughnut was bursting with jelly, and the jelly was squishing out in all the wrong places. And if that wasn't frightening enough, I was turning myself on. All the while I was yelling about Morelli wanting nothing but sex, the truth is, I could think of nothing else.

"Can we finish this upstairs?" Morelli asked. "My leg wants to go to bed."

"Sure," I said. "There are parts of me that want to go to bed, too."

I WAS SHOWERED and dressed and ready to go to work. I'd had two mugs of coffee and an English muffin. It was 8:00 A.M., and Morelli was still in bed.

"Hey," I said. "What's up with you? You're always the early riser."

"Mmmmph," Morelli said, pillow over his face. "Tired."

"How could you be tired? It's eight o'clock. It's time to get up! I'm leaving. Don't you want to kiss me good-bye?"

Nothing. No answer. I whipped the sheet off him and left him lying there in all his glorious nakedness. Morelli still didn't move.

I sat on the bed next to him. "Joe?"

"I thought you were going to work."

"You're looking very sexy . . . except for Mr. Happy, who seems to be sleepy."

"He's not sleepy, Steph. He's in a coma. You woke him up every two hours and now he's dead."

"He's dead?"

"Okay, not dead, but he's not going to be up and dancing anytime soon. You might as well go to work. Did you walk Bob?"

"I walked Bob. I fed Bob. I cleaned the living room and the kitchen."

"Love you," Morelli said from under the pillow.

"I l-l-l-like you, too." *Shit.*

I went downstairs and stood at the front door, looking out at Big Blue. Probably perfectly safe, but I didn't feel comfortable taking the chance. Bob came to stand next to me. "I have no way to get to work," I said to Bob. "I could call Ranger, but lately it feels like I'm on a date when I'm in a car with Ranger, and it would be tacky to have a date pick me up here. Lula probably isn't up yet." I went to the kitchen and dialed my parents' number.

"I need a ride to work," I told my mom. "Can you or Dad take me?"

"Your father can pick you up," my mom said. "He's driving the cab today, anyway. Are you still off dessert?"

"Yes. How about you?"

"It's amazing. I don't even have the slightest need to tipple now that the wedding is behind us and Valerie's in Disney World."

Great. My mother doesn't need to tipple, and I'm so strung out with doughnut cravings I put Mr. Happy into a coma.

My dad showed up ten minutes later. "What's wrong with the Buick?" he said.

"Broken."

"I figured you were worried it was booby-trapped."

"Yep. That, too."

RANGER WAS WAITING for me when I arrived. He was in my cubby, slouched in the extra chair, reading through the files on Gorman, Lazar, Barroni, and Runion. There was a new cell phone on my desk, plus a new key fob, and my Sig. The Sig was in a holster that clipped to a belt.

"They found them," I said.

"I heard. How'd you get in to work?"

"My dad."

"I have a bike set aside for you downstairs. If you park it exposed, be sure to look it over before getting on. It's hard to hide a bomb on a bike, but you still need to be careful. The key is on your keychain.

"As far as Rangeman is concerned, Gorman is found, and the file is closed," Ranger said. "If you still think there's a connection between the murdered men and your stalker and you want to use this office to continue searching, you have permission to do that."

I looked at my in-box and stifled a groan. It was packed with search requests.

Ranger followed my eyes. "You're going to have to divide your time and get through some of those files. They're not just from Rodriguez. You do the searches for everyone here, including me."

He stood and brushed against me, and I had a wave of desire rush into my chest and shoot south.

"What?" Ranger said.

"I didn't say anything."

"You moaned."

"I was thinking of Butterscotch Krimpets."

Our eyes locked for a long moment. "I'll be in my office the rest of the morning," Ranger said. "Let me know if you need anything."

Oh boy.

I sorted through the requests that had come in over the weekend. Three were from Ranger. I'd do them first. He was the boss. And he was hot. One was from someone named Alvirez. The rest were Rodriguez.

Ranger's files were all standard searches. Nothing unusual. I had them done by noon. My plan was to get a quick lunch, run the Alvirez and two for Rodriguez, and then see what I could turn up at Fort Dix. I prowled through the kitchen, not finding anything inspiring to eat.

I settled on the turkey again and took it back to my cubicle with a bottle of water. I finished lunch, finished Alvirez and Rodriguez, and started surfing Fort Dix.

I called my mother, Morelli, Lula, and Valerie and told them I had a new cell phone. Valerie was in the Magic Kingdom and said she'd be home at the end of the week. They liked Florida, but the girls missed their friends, and Albert had broken out in hives when he was approached by a six-foot-tall, four-foot-wide Pooh Bear. Lula wasn't answering. I left a message. Morelli wasn't answering. I left a message. My mother invited me for dinner, and I declined.

It was midafternoon when Ranger returned to my cubby. I was pacing, unable to focus on anything beyond my need for a cupcake.

"Babe," Ranger said. "You're looking a little strung out. Is there anything I should know?"

"I'm in sugar withdrawal. I've given up dessert, and it's all I can think about." That had been true five minutes ago. Now that Ranger was standing in front of me I was thinking a cupcake wasn't what I actually wanted.

"Maybe I can help get your mind off doughnuts," Ranger said.

My mouth dropped open, and I think some drool might have dribbled out.

"Did Silvio show you how to search the newspapers?" Ranger asked.

"No."

"Sit down and I'll show you how to get into the programs. It's tedious work, but it accesses a lot of information. You want to go to the local paper and look for something bad that happened when the four men were at Dix. An unsolved murder, a high-stakes robbery, unsolved serial crimes like multiple burglaries."

"Morelli thinks there were five men involved. Originally, I thought Anthony Barroni was the fifth guy, but now I'm not sure. Is there a way to get a list of men who were in that unit at Dix?"

"I don't have access to those records. I could get someone to hack in but I'd rather not. It would be safer to have Morelli do it."

I was hearing the words, but they weren't sticking. My brain was clogged with naked and sweaty Ranger thoughts.

"Babe," Ranger said, smiling. "You just looked me up and down like I was lunch."

"I need a doughnut," I told him. "I *really* need a doughnut."

"That would have been my second guess."

"I'll feel better tomorrow. The sugar will be out of my system. The cravings will be gone." I sat down and faced the keyboard. "How do I do this?"

Ranger pulled a chair next to me. His leg pressed against mine and when he leaned forward to get to my keyboard we were shoulder to shoulder, his arm brushing the side of my breast when he typed. He was warm and he smelled delicious. I felt my eyes glaze over, and I worried I might start panting.

"You should take notes," Ranger said. "You're going to need to remember some passwords."

Get a grip, I said to myself. It wouldn't be good to jump on him here. You'd be on television. And you haven't got a door on your cubby. And then there was Morelli. I was liv-

ing with Morelli. It wouldn't be right to live with Morelli
and boink Ranger. And what was wrong with me, anyway,
that I needed two men? Especially when the second man
was Ranger. Ever since we'd had the discussion about marriage my imagination had been running wild dredging up
possibilities for his deep dark secret. I knew it had nothing
to do with killing people because that was no secret. I
knew he wasn't gay. I'd seen that one firsthand. The
memory brought a new rush of heat, and I resisted squirm-
ing in my seat. Was he scarred by a terrible childhood? Had
his heart been so badly broken he was unable to recover?

"Earth to Babe," Ranger said.

I looked at him and unconsciously licked my lips.

"I'm going to have to disconnect your cubby's security
camera," Ranger said. "I just heard everyone in the control
room gasp when you licked your lips. I could have a
hatchet murder taking place in full monitor view on one of
my accounts, and I don't think anyone would notice as long
as you're sitting in here." Ranger signed off the search he'd
just pulled up. He took my pad and wrote out instructions
for retrieving information from newspapers. He returned
the pad to my desk and stood. "Let's go on a field trip," he
said. "I want to see the area where the bodies were
recovered."

I thought that sounded sufficiently grim to be a good
doughnut diversion. I stood and clipped my new cell
phone onto the waistband of my jeans. I pocketed the key
fob. And I stared at the gun. The gun was in a holster that
attached to a belt, and I wasn't wearing a belt.

"No belt," I said to Ranger.

"Ella has some clothes for you upstairs in my apartment.

Try them on. I'm sure she's included a belt. I'll meet you in the garage. I need to talk to Tank."

I took the elevator to the top floor and stepped out into the small marble-floored foyer. I'd lived here for a brief time not long ago, so I was familiar with the apartment. I opened the locked door with the key he'd given me and stepped inside. His apartment always felt cool and serene. His furniture was comfortable, with clean lines and earth tones, and felt masculine without being overbearing. There were fresh flowers on the sideboard by the door. I doubted Ranger ever noticed the flowers, but Ella liked them. They were part of Ella's campaign to civilize Ranger and make his life nicer.

I dropped my keys in the silver dish beside the flowers. I walked through the apartment and found my clothes stacked on a black leather upholstered bench in Ranger's dressing room. Two black shirts, two black cargo pants, a black belt, a black windbreaker, a black sweatshirt, a black ball cap. I was going to look like a mini-Ranger. I stepped into the cargo pants. Perfect fit. Ella had remembered my size from the last time I'd stayed here. I belted the cargo pants, and I tugged the shirt over my head. It was a short-sleeved shirt, female cut with some spandex. It had a V-neck that was relatively high. Rangeman was em-broidered on the left breast with black thread. The shirt was a good fit with the exception of being too short to tuck into the cargo pants. The shirt barely touched the top of the cargo pants waistband.

I called Ranger on his cell. "This shirt is short. I'm not sure you're going to like it on the control room floor."

"Put a jacket over it and come down to the garage."

I shrugged into the windbreaker. Black on black again, with Rangeman embroidered on the left breast of the jacket. I took my phone off my jeans and clipped it onto the cargo pants. I grabbed the black-on-black ball cap, and I left Ranger's apartment and rode the elevator to the garage.

Ranger was waiting by his truck. He was wearing a windbreaker exactly like mine, and the almost smile expression was fixed on his face.

"I feel like a miniature Ranger," I said to him.

Ranger unzipped the windbreaker and looked me over. "Nice, but you're no miniature Ranger." He took my Sig out of his jacket pocket and snapped it onto my belt just in front of my hip, his knuckles grazing bare skin. "There are some advantages to this short shirt," he said, sliding his hands under, fingertips stopping short of my bra.

"Okay, here's the deal," I said to him. "You know how when you squeeze a jelly doughnut and the jelly squirts out in the weakest spot of the doughnut? Well, if I'm a jelly doughnut then my weak spot is dessert. Every time I get stressed I head for the bakery. I'm trying to stop the dessert thing now, and so the jelly is squirting out someplace else."

"And?"

"And this place that it's squirting out . . . maybe squirting out isn't a good way to put this. Forget squirting out."

"You're trying to tell me something," Ranger said.

"Yes! And it would be a lot easier if you didn't have your hands under my shirt. It's hard for me to think when you've got your hands on me like this."

"Babe, has it occurred to you that you might be giving information to the enemy?"

"The thing is, I have all these excess hormones. They used to be jelly-doughnut hormones, but somehow they got switched over to sex-drive hormones. Not that sex-drive hormones are bad, it's just that my life is so complicated right now. So I'm trying to control all these stupid hormones, to keep them locked up in the doughnut. And you're going to have to help."

"Why?"

"Because you're a good guy."

"I'm not that good," Ranger said.

"So I'm in trouble?"

"Big time."

"You told Ella to get me this short shirt, didn't you?"

Ranger's fingers were slowly creeping up my breast. "No. I told her to get you something that didn't look like it was made for Tank. She probably didn't realize it was cut off at the waist."

"The hand," I said. "You have to remove the hand. You're poaching."

Ranger smiled and kissed me. Light. No tongue. The appetizer on Ranger's dinner menu. "Don't count on my help with the overactive sex drive," he said. "You're on your own with this one."

I looked up at the security camera focused on us. "Do you think Hal will sell this tape to the evening news?"

"Not if he wants to live." Ranger took a step back and opened the passenger-side door to the truck for me.

FOURTEEN

RANGER TOOK THE wheel, drove out of the garage, and headed for the patch of scrub woods east of center city where the four men had been found. Neither of us spoke. Understandable since there wasn't a lot to say after I explained my jelly doughnut dilemma, and Ranger'd declared open season on Stephanie. Still, it was good to have cleared the air, and now if I accidentally ripped his clothes off he'd understand it was one of those odd chemical things.

The crime-scene tape blocked the dirt road leading back to the crime site and covered a couple acres along the road and into the woods. Ranger parked the truck, and we got out and scooted under the yellow tape. I could see a van through the trees, and snatches of conversation carried to me. Men's voices. Two or three.

We walked the dirt road through the scrubby field and into the woods. The graves weren't far in. There was an area about the size of a two-car garage where the vegetation had been trampled over the years, leaving hard-packed dirt and some hardscrabble grass. This was the end of the road, the turnaround point. This was the place where drug deals were made, sex was sold, and kids got drunk, stoned, pregnant.

The van belonged to the state lab. The side door was open. One guy stood by the open door, writing on a pad. Two guys in shirtsleeves were working at the grave site. They were wearing disposable gloves and carrying evidence bags. They looked our way and nodded, recognizing Ranger.

"Your FTA's long gone," the guy at the van said.

"Just curious," Ranger told him. "Wanted to see what the scene looked like."

"Looks like you got a new partner. What happened to Tank?"

"It's Tank's day off," Ranger said.

"Hey, wait a minute," the guy said, smiling at me. "Aren't you Stephanie Plum?"

"Yes," I said. "And whatever you've heard . . . it isn't true."

"You two are kind of cute together," the guy said to Ranger. "I like the matching clothes. Does Celia know about this?"

"This is business," Ranger said. "Stephanie's working for Rangeman. Are you finding anything interesting?"

"Hard to say. There was a lot of trash here. Everything from left-behind panties to crack cookers. A lot of used condoms and needles. You want to watch where you walk. Be best if you stay on the road. The road's clean."

"How deep was the grave?"

"A couple feet. I'm surprised they weren't found sooner. It's on the far perimeter of the cleared area so maybe it wasn't noticed. Or maybe no one cared. From the way the ground's settled I'd say they were here for a while. Couple weeks at least. Looks to me like they were shot here. Won't know for sure until the lab tests come back."

"Did he leave the shells?"

"Took the shells."

Ranger nodded. "Later."

"Later. Give Celia a hug for me."

We got back to the truck and Ranger shielded his eyes from the low-angled sun and studied the road we'd just walked.

"There was just barely enough room back there for five cars," Ranger said. "We know two of them were SUVs. Probably they could at least partially be seen from the main road. And that probably ensured their privacy. We know when three of the men left work and got into their cars. If they came directly here they'd arrive around six-thirty, which meant there was still daylight."

"You'd think someone would have heard gunshots. This guy didn't just pop off a couple rounds."

"It's an isolated area. And if you were a passing motorist it might be hard to tell where the shots originated. Most likely you'd just get the hell out of here."

We climbed into the truck and buckled ourselves in.

"Who's Celia?" I asked Ranger.

"My sister. Marty Sanchez, the guy by the van, went to school with Celia. They dated for a while."

"Is she your only sister?"

"I have four sisters."

"Any brothers?"

"One."

"And you have a daughter," I said.

Ranger swung the truck onto the paved road. "Not many people know about my daughter."

"Understood. Do I get to ask more questions?"

"One."

"How old are you?"

"I'm two months older than you," Ranger said.

"You know my birthday?"

"I know lots of things about you. And that was two questions."

IT WAS FIVE o'clock when we pulled into the garage.

"How's Morelli doing?" Ranger asked.

"Good. He's going back to work tomorrow. The cast won't come off for a while, so he's limited. He's on crutches, and he can't drive, and he can't walk Bob. I'm going to stay until he's more self-sufficient. Then I'll go back to my apartment."

Ranger walked me to the bike. "I don't want you going back to your apartment until we get this guy."

"You don't have to worry about me," I said. "I've got a gun."

"Would you feel comfortable using it?"

"No, but I could hit someone over the head with it."

The bike was a black Ducati Monster. I'd driven Morelli's Duc, so I was on familiar ground. I took the black full-face helmet off the grip and handed it to Ranger. I took the key out of my pocket, and I swung my leg over the bike.

Ranger was watching me, smiling. "I like the way you straddle that," he said. "Someday . . ."

I revved the engine and cut off the rest of the sentence. I didn't have to read his lips to know where he was going. I put the helmet on, Ranger remoted the gate open for me, and I wheeled out of the garage.

It felt great to be on the bike. The air was cool, and traffic was light. It was just a few minutes short of rush hour. I took it slow, getting the feel of the machine. I cut to the alley and brought the bike in through Morelli's backyard. Morelli had an empty tool shed next to his house. The shed was locked with a combination lock, and I knew the combination. I spun the dial, opened the shed, and locked the bike away.

Morelli was waiting for me in the kitchen. "Let me guess," Morelli said. "He gave you a bike. A Duc."

"Yeah. It was terrific riding over here." I went to the fridge and studied the inside. Not a lot there. "I'll take Bob out, and you can dial supper," I said.

"What do you want?"

"Anything without sugar."

"You're still on the no-sugar thing?"

"Yeah. I hope you took a nap this afternoon."

Morelli poked me with his crutch. "Where are your clothes? You weren't wearing this when you left this morning."

"I left them at work. I didn't have a way to carry them on the bike. I could use a backpack." I still had the windbreaker zipped over the shirt. I thought it was best to delay the short-shirt confrontation until after we'd eaten. I clipped Bob to his leash and took off. I got back just as the Pino's delivery kid was leaving.

"I ordered roast beef subs," Morelli said. "Hope that's okay."

I took a sub and unwrapped it and gave it to Bob. I handed a sub to Morelli, and I unwrapped the third for myself. We were in the living room, on the couch, as always. We ate, and we watched the news.

"The news is always the same," I said. "Death, destruction, blah, blah, blah. There should be a news station that only does happy news."

I collected the wrappers when we were done eating and carted them off to the kitchen. Morelli followed after me on his crutches.

"Take your jacket off," Morelli said. "I want to see the rest of the uniform."

"Later."

"Now."

"I was thinking I might go back to work just for a couple hours. I started a search and didn't get to finish it."

Morelli had me backed into a corner. "I don't think so. I have plans for tonight. Let's see the shirt."

"I don't want to hear any yelling."

"It's that bad?"

It wasn't just the shirt. It was also the gun. Morelli was going to be unhappy that I was carrying. He knew I was a moron when it came to guns.

I took the jacket off and twirled for him. "What do you think?"

264

"I'm going to kill him. Don't worry. I'll make it look like an accident."

"He didn't pick out the shirt. His housekeeper picked out the shirt. She's short. It probably came to her knees."

"Who picked out the gun?"

"Ranger picked out the gun."

"Is it loaded?"

"I don't know. I didn't look."

"You aren't really going to keep working for him, are you? He's a nut. Plus half his workforce has graduated from Jersey Penal," Morelli said. "And what about not wanting a dangerous job?"

"The job isn't dangerous. It's boring. I sit at a computer all day."

I HAD MORELLI up and dressed. I got him down the stairs and into the kitchen. I sat him at the table, put the coffee on, and left for a short walk with Bob. When I came back, Morelli was asleep with his head on the table. I put a mug of coffee in front of him, and he opened an eye.

"You have to open *both* eyes," I said. "You're going to work today. Laski's picking you up in five minutes."

"That gives me five minutes to sleep," Morelli said.

"No! Drink some coffee. Get some legal stimulants into your system." I danced in front of him. "Look at me. I'm wearing a gun! And look at the short shirt. Are you going to let me go to work like this?"

"Cupcake, I haven't got the energy to stop you. Anyway, maybe if you look slutty enough, Ranger will take up some of the slack in the bedroom before you make a permanent cripple out of me. Maybe you should wear that shirt with the neckline that lets your boobs hang out." Morelli squinted at me. "Why aren't you tired?"

"I don't know. I feel all energized. I always thought I couldn't keep up with you, but maybe you've just been slowing me down all these years."

"Stephanie, I'm begging you. Eat some doughnuts. I can't keep going like this."

I poured his coffee into a travel mug and got him to his feet. I shoved the crutches under his arms and pushed him to the front door. Laski was already at the curb. I helped Morelli hobble down the stairs and maneuver himself into the car. I threw his crutches onto the backseat and handed Morelli his mug of coffee.

"Have a nice day," I said. I gave him a kiss, closed the car door, and watched as Laski motored them away, down the street.

There was a chill to the air, so I went back to the house, ran upstairs, and borrowed Morelli's leather biker jacket. I tied the Rangeman windbreaker around my waist, I gave Bob a hug, and I let myself out through the back door. I unlocked the shed and rolled the bike out, and a half hour later, I was at my desk.

I went straight into the newspaper search. I limited the search to the last three months the men were at Dix. It seemed to me that was the most likely time frame for them to do something catastrophic. I began with a name search and came up empty. None of the men were mentioned in any of the local papers. My next search was front page. I was only reading headlines, but it was still a slow process.

I stopped the Fort Dix search at nine-thirty and switched to Rangeman business, working my way through the security check requests. By noon I was questioning my ability to do the job long-term. The words were swimming on the screen, and I felt creaky from sitting. I went to the kitchen and poked at the sandwiches. Turkey, tuna, grilled vegetables, roast beef, chicken salad. I dialed Ranger on my cell phone.

"Yo," Ranger said. "Is there a problem?"

"I don't like any of these sandwiches."

There was a moment of dead phone time before Ranger answered. "Go upstairs to my apartment. I think there's some peanut butter left from last time you stayed there."

"Where are you?"

"I'm with an account. I'm inspecting a new system."

"Are you coming home for lunch?"

"No," Ranger said. "I won't be back until three. Are you still off sugar?"

"Yes."

"Maybe I can get back sooner."

"No rush," I said. "I'm happy with peanut butter."

"I'm counting on that being a lie," Ranger said.

I let myself into Ranger's apartment and went straight to the kitchen. He still had the peanut butter in his fridge, and there was a loaf of bread on the granite countertop. I made myself a sandwich and washed it down with a beer. I was tempted to take a nap in Ranger's bed, but that felt too much like Goldilocks.

I was on my way out when I got a call from Lula. "I got him trapped," she yelled into the phone. "I got Willie Martin trapped in the deli at the corner of Twenty-fifth Street and Lowman Avenue. Only I'm gonna need help to bag him. If you're at Rangeman it's just around the corner."

"Are you sure you need my help?"

"Hurry!"

I took the elevator to the first floor and went out the front door. No point taking the bike. The deli was only a block away. I jogged to Lowman, and saw Lula standing in front of Fennick's Deli.

"He's in there eating," she said to me. "I just happened on him. I was going in for sandwiches for Connie and me and there he was. He's in the back where they have some tables."

"Did he see you?"

"I don't think so. I got out right away."

"So what do you need me for?"

"I thought you could be a diversion. You could go in there and get his attention, and then I'll sneak up and zap him with the stun gun."

"Didn't we already try that?"

"Yeah, but we'd be better this time on account of we got some practice at it."

"Okay, but you'd better not screw up. If you screw up he's going to beat the crap out of me."

"Don't worry," Lula said. "The third time's a charm. This is going to work. You'll see. You go on up to him, and I'll sneak around from the side and get him from the back."

"Have you tested the stun gun? Does it work?"

We were standing next to a bus stop with a bench. Three elderly men were sitting on the bench. One was reading a paper, and the other two were zoned out, staring blankly into space. Lula reached out and pressed the stun gun to one of the men. He gave a twitch and slumped onto the man next to him.

"Yep," Lula said. "It works."

I was speechless. My mouth was open and my eyes were wide.

"What?" Lula said.

"You just zapped that poor old man."

"It's okay. I know him. That's Gimp Whiteside. He don't do nothing all day. Might as well help us hardworking bounty hunters. Anyway, he didn't feel any pain. He's just taking a snooze now." Lula looked me over and grinned. "Look at you! You look like Rangeman Barbie. You got a gun and everything."

"Yeah, and I have to get back to work, so let's do this. I'm going to talk to Willie and see if I can get him to surrender. Give me your cuffs, and don't use the stun gun until I tell you to use it."

Lula handed her cuffs over to me. "You're taking some of the fun out of it, but I guess I could do it that way."

I walked straight back to Willie Martin. He was sitting alone at a small bistro table. He'd finished his sandwich, and he was picking at a few remaining fries. There was a second chair at his table. I slid the chair over next to him and sat down. "Remember me?" I asked him.

Willie looked at me and laughed. It was a big open-mouthed, mashed-up-french-fries-and-ketchup laugh that sounded like *haw, haw, haw*. "Yeah, I remember you," he said. "You're the dumb white bitch who came with fat-ass Lula."

He dipped a french fry into a glob of ketchup with his right hand, and I clamped a cuff onto his left.

He looked down at the cuff and grinned. "I already got a pair of these. You giving me another?"

"I'm asking you nicely to return to the courthouse with me, so we can get you rescheduled."

"I don't think so."

"It's just a formality. We'll rebond you."

"Nope."

"I have a gun."

"You gonna use it?"

"I might."

"I don't think so," Willie said. "I'm unarmed. You shoot me, and you'll do more time than I will. That's assault with a deadly weapon."

"Okay, how about this. If you don't let me cuff your other hand, and you don't quietly walk out with me and get in Lula's car, we're going to send enough electricity through you to make you mess your pants. And that's going to be an embarrassing experience. It'll probably make the papers—pro ball all-star Willie Martin messed his pants in Fennick's Deli yesterday . . ."

"I didn't mess my pants last time."

"Do you want to risk it? We'd be happy to give you a few volts."

"You swear you'll rebond me?"

"I'll call Vinnie as soon as we get you into the car."

"Okay," Willie said. "I'm gonna stand and put my hands behind my back. And we'll do this real quiet so nobody notices."

Lula was a short distance away with the stun gun in hand, her eyes glued to Willie. I stood, and Willie stood, and next thing I knew I was flying through the air. He'd moved so fast and scooped me up so effortlessly, I never saw it coming. He threw me about fifteen feet, and I crash-landed on a table of four. The table gave way and I was on the floor with the burgers and shakes and soup of the day. I was flat on my back, the wind knocked out of me, dazed for a moment, the world swirling around me. I rolled to my hands and knees and crawled over smashed food and dishes to get to my feet.

Willie Martin was facedown on the floor just beyond the table debris. Lula was sitting on him, struggling with the second cuff. "Boy, you really know how to make a diversion," Lula said. "I zapped him good. He's out like a light. Only I can't get his second hand to cooperate."

I limped over and held Martin's hand behind his back while she cuffed him. "Do you have shackles in the car?"

"Yeah. Maybe you should go get them while I baby-sit here."

I took the key to the Firebird, got the shackles, and brought them back to Lula. We got the shackles on Martin, and a squad car pulled up outside the deli. It was my pal Carl Costanza and his partner, Big Dog.

Costanza grinned when he saw me. "We got a call that two crazy fans were on Willie like white on rice."

"That would be Lula and me," I said. "Except we're not fans. He's FTA."

"Looks like you're wearing lunch."

"Willie threw me into the table. And then he decided to take a nap."

"We'd appreciate it if you could help us drag his sorry ass out of here," Lula said. "He weighs a ton."

Big Dog got Willie under the armpits, Carl took the feet,

and we hauled Willie out of the deli and dumped him into the back of Lula's Firebird.

"We need to do a property damage report," Costanza said to me. "You're wearing Rangeman clothes. Are you hunting desperadoes for Vinnie or for Ranger?"

"Vinnie."

"Works for me," Costanza said. And they disappeared inside the deli.

Lula and I looked over at the bench by the bus stop. Two of the three men were gone from the bench. The guy Lula stun-gunned was still there.

"Looks like Gimp missed his bus," Lula said. "Guess he didn't come around fast enough. Hey, Gimp," she yelled. "You want a ride? Get your bony behind over here."

"You're a big softy," I said.

"Yeah, don't tell nobody."

I walked back to Rangeman and entered through the front door. "Don't say anything," I told the guy at the desk. "I've just walked two blocks through town, and I've heard it all. And just in case you're wondering, those are noodles stuck in my hair, not worms."

I rode the elevator to the control room and had the full attention of everyone there as I crossed to my desk.

"I got tired of turkey so I went out for lunch," I told them.

I retrieved the key fob I'd left on my desk, got back into the elevator, and rode to Ranger's floor. I knocked on his door and didn't get an answer, so I let myself in. I took my shoes off in the hall and left them on the marble floor. I didn't want to trash Ranger's apartment, and the shoes were coated with chocolate milkshake and some smushed cheeseburger. I padded into Ranger's bathroom, locked the door, and dropped the rest of my clothes. I washed with his delicious shower gel and stood under the hot water until I was relaxed and no longer cared that just minutes before I'd had chicken noodle soup in my hair.

I wrapped myself in Ranger's luxuriously thick terry-cloth robe, unlocked the door, and stepped into his bedroom. Ranger was stretched out on the bed, ankles crossed, arms behind his head. His was fully clothed, and he was obviously waiting for me.

"I had a small mishap," I said.

"That's what they tell me. What happened?"

"I was helping Lula snag Willie Martin at Fennick's and next thing I knew I was airborne. He threw me about fifteen feet, into a table full of food and people."

"Are you okay?"

"Yeah, but my sneakers are history. They're covered with chocolate milkshake."

Ranger crooked a finger at me. "Come here."

"No way."

"What about the jelly-doughnut hormones and the sex-drive hormones?"

"Getting thrown across a room seems to have a calming effect on them."

"I could fix that," Ranger said.

I smiled at him. "There's no doubt in my mind, but I'd rather you didn't. I have a lot of things going on in my head right now, and you could make it a lot more confusing."

"That's promising," Ranger said. He got off the bed and

crossed the room. He grabbed me by the big shawl collar on the robe and pulled me to him. "I like when you wear my robe."

"Because I'm cute in it?"

"No, because it's all you're wearing."

"You don't know that for sure," I said. "I could have clothes under this."

"Is this another one of those things I should find out for myself?"

I was skating on thin ice here. I had the jelly-doughnut hormone problem going on, and I didn't want it to get out of control. I'd spent a night with Ranger a while ago, and I knew what happened when he was encouraged. Ranger knew how to make a woman want him. Ranger was magic.

"Let's take a look at my life," I said to Ranger. "I keep rolling in garbage."

"Mind-boggling," Ranger said.

"And let's take a look at your life. You have a deep dark secret."

"Let it go," Ranger said.

"Are you sick?"

"No, I'm not sick. Not physically, anyway. I'm not so sure sometimes about the mental, emotional, and sexual."

I locked myself in Ranger's dressing room and got dressed in the second Rangeman outfit. Short black T-shirt, black cargo pants, black socks. Ella hadn't provided underwear or shoes, so I sent my soda-and-ketchup-soaked underwear and my chocolate-shake-covered shoes off to the laundry with the first Rangeman outfit. I was feeling a little strange without underwear, but a girl's gotta do what a girl's gotta do, right?

I returned to my desk, and I ignored the search requests piling up in my in-box. I picked up where I left off with the Dix search, reading the front pages. By five o'clock I had a list of crimes that I thought had potential. Nothing sensational. Just good solid crimes like a rash of unsolved burglaries, an unsolved murder, an unsolved hijacking. None of the crimes really grabbed me, and I still had lots of front pages to read, so I decided to keep searching.

I called Morelli and told him I was working late.

"How late?" he said.

"I don't know. Does it matter?"

"Only if you come home with your underwear on backwards."

I could go him one better than that. How about no underwear at all?

"Dial yourself some food," I said. "And tie Bob out back. I need to finish this project. How was your day? Is your leg okay?"

"The leg is okay. The day was long. I don't like being stuck in the building."

"Anything on Barroni and the three other guys?"

"They've all been positively identified. You were right about all of them. They were killed on-site. That's it so far."

"No one's seen Spiro?"

"No, but the pizza kid gave a good description, and it matches yours."

I STRUGGLED UP from a deep sleep and opened my eyes to Ranger.

"Babe," he said softly. "You need to wake up. You need to go home."

I had my arms crossed on my desk and my head on my arms. The screen saver was up on my computer. "What time is it?"

"It's a little after eleven. I just came back from a break-in on one of the Rangeman accounts and saw you were still here."

"I was looking for a crime."

"Did you call Morelli?"

"Earlier. He knows I'm working late."

Ranger looked down at my feet. "Have you heard anything about your shoes? Ella was going to wash them."

"Haven't heard anything."

Ranger punched Ella's extension on my phone. "Sorry to call so late," he said. "What's happening with Stephanie's shoes?"

Ranger smiled at Ella's answer. He disconnected and slung an arm around my shoulder. "Bad news on the shoes. They melted in the dryer. Looks like you're going home in your socks." He pulled me to my feet. "I'll drive you. You can't ride the bike like this."

FIFTEEN

WE TOOK THE elevator to the garage, and Ranger went to the Porsche. Of all his cars, this was my favorite. I loved the sound of the engine, and I loved the way the seat cradled me. At night, the dash looked like controls on a jet, and the car felt intimate.

I was groggy from sleep and exhausted from the events of the day. And I suspected the last two nights were catching up with me. I closed my eyes and melted into the cushy leather seat. I felt Ranger reach across and buckle my seat belt. I heard the Porsche growl to life and move up the ramp to exit the garage. I dozed on the way home and came awake when the car stopped. I looked out at the darkened neighborhood. Not a lot of lights shining in windows at this time of the night. These were hardworking people who rose early and went to bed early. We were stopped half a block from Morelli's house.

"Why are we stopped here?" I asked Ranger.

"I have a working relationship with Morelli. I think he's a good cop, and he thinks I'm a loose cannon. Since we both carry guns, I try not to do things that would upset the balance in an insulting way. I wanted to give you a chance to wake up, so we didn't sit at the curb in front of his house like a couple teenagers adjusting their clothes." Ranger looked over at me. "You got the rest of your clothes from Ella, didn't you?"

Damn. "I forgot! I was working, and then I fell asleep. She's got my underwear."

Ranger laughed out loud, and when he looked back at me he was smiling the full-on Ranger smile. "I'm worrying about parking too long in front of Morelli's house, and I'm bringing his girlfriend home without her underwear. I'll have to put double security on the building tonight." He put the Porsche in gear, drove half a block, and parked. Lights were on in the downstairs rooms. "Are you going to be okay?" he asked.

"Morelli's a reasonable person. He'll understand." Plus he had a cast on his leg. He couldn't move fast. I'd head straight for the stairs, and I'd be changed before he could get to me.

Ranger locked eyes with me. "Just so you know, for future reference, *I* wouldn't understand. If you were living with me, and you came home without underwear, I'd go looking for the guy who had it. And it wouldn't be pretty when I found him."

"Something to remember," I said. And the truth is, Morelli wasn't so different from Ranger. And Morelli wasn't usually a reasonable person. Morelli was being uncharacteristically mellow. I wasn't sure why I was seeing the mellow, and I wasn't sure how long it would last. The main difference between Morelli and Ranger was that when Morelli got mad he got loud. And when Ranger got mad he got quiet. They were both equally scary.

I jumped out of the Porsche and ran to the house. I let myself in, called to Morelli, and ran up the stairs and into the bedroom to get clothes. I smacked into Morelli en route to the bathroom. He dropped a crutch and put an arm out to steady me.

"What are you doing up here?" I asked.

"Going to bed? I live here, remember?"

"I thought you were downstairs."

"You were wrong." He looked over at me. "Where's your bra?"

"What?"

"I know your body better than I know my own. And I know when you're not wearing a bra."

I slumped against the doorjamb. "It's in Ranger's dryer. You're not going to make a big deal about this, are you?"

"I don't know. I'm waiting to hear the whole story."

"I helped Lula capture Willie Martin this morning, and I sort of got thrown into a table filled with food and people."

"Costanza told me."

"Yeah, he responded to the call from Fennick's. Anyway, my clothes and my shoes were a mess, and I had chicken soup in my hair, so I used Ranger's shower to get cleaned up. And I put clean clothes on, except Ella hadn't gotten me any underwear or shoes." We both looked down at my feet. Black socks. No shoes. "So here I am, and I don't have any underwear."

"Was Ranger in the shower with you?"

"Nope. Just me."

"And you were actually working tonight?"

"Yep."

"If I had anyone else for a girlfriend I'd be out the door with a gun in my hand, looking for Ranger—but your life is so insane I'm willing to believe anything. Living with you is like being in one of the reality shows on television where people keep getting covered with bees and dropped off forty-story buildings into a vat of Vaseline."

"I admit it's been a little . . . hectic."

"Hectic is getting three kids to soccer practice on time. Your life is . . . there are no words for your life."

"That's what my mother says. Is this leading to something?"

"I don't know. I'm really tired right now. Let's talk about it tomorrow."

I picked Morelli's crutch up for him, and he moved toward the little guest room.

"Where are you going?" I asked him.

"I'm sleeping in the guest room, and I'm locking the door. I need a night of uninterrupted sleep. I'm running on empty. I was a mess at work. I couldn't keep my eyes open. And my guys feel like they've been run over by a truck. They need a day off."

"What about *my* guys?"

"Cupcake, you don't have guys."

"I have *something.*"

"You do. And I love it. But you're on your own tonight. You're going to have to fly solo."

I ROLLED OUT of bed and crossed the hall to the little guest room. The door was open, and the room was empty. No Morelli in the bathroom or study, but Bob was sleeping in the bathtub. I crept down the stairs and walked through the house to the kitchen. There was hot coffee, and a note had been left by the coffeemaker.

SORRY ABOUT LAST NIGHT. THE GUYS MISSED YOU THIS MORNING. DON'T WORK LATE.

That sounded hopeful. I poured a mug of coffee, added milk, and took it upstairs. An hour later, I was dressed in black jeans and black T-shirt, and I was ready for work. I'd called my dad and mooched a ride. He was at the curb when I came down the stairs.

"You're doing pretty good on the new job," he said. "Almost a week. And nothing's caught fire or blown up."

It'd be a real challenge for Spiro to penetrate Rangeman. And that's probably the reason Morelli's garage got destroyed. Spiro went for what was available. Truth is I was beginning to be bothered by the lack of activity. The garage went five days ago and there hadn't been any threatening notes, snipings, or bombings since the Buick.

"They're holding a memorial service for Michael Barroni today," my father said. "Your mother said to tell you she's taking your grandmother. It's being held at Stiva's. Ordinarily they'd hold it at the church, but Stiva and Barroni were old friends, and I guess Stiva gave the Barronis a discount if they held the service in his chapel."

"I didn't realize Stiva and Barroni were that close."

"Yeah, me neither. I didn't see them spending a lot of time together. But then that happens when you got a big family and a business to run. You lose touch with your buddies."

I had a chill run up my spine to the roots of my hair, and my scalp was tingling like I was electric. "How'd Stiva and Barroni get to be friends?" I asked, holding my breath, my heart skipping beats.

"They were in the army together. They were both at Dix."

I might have the fifth man. I was so excited I was hyperventilating. Now here's the thing, *why was I so excited?* Ranger had his FTA, so the excitement didn't come from case closure. I barely knew Barroni and I didn't know the other three men at all, so there was nothing personal. My original long jump tying Anthony Barroni to Spiro and the missing men proved to be groundless. So why did I care? The four missing men seemed to be completely unrelated to anything I'd care about. And even if Spiro *did* turn out to have a tie to the four men, even if there *was* a crime involved, it really didn't matter to me, did it? Finding Spiro and stopping the harassment was really the only thing that mattered, right? Right. But stopping the harassment could be a problem. There were really only two ways the harassment would stop. Ranger could kill Spiro. Or Spiro could get convicted of a crime, like murdering Mama Macaroni, and get locked away. The latter was definitely the preferred. Okay, maybe I was excited about the fifth man because it might be Constantine Stiva. And if Con was involved, then Spiro might be involved. And if there wasn't evidence that convicted Spiro of the bombings, there might be evidence to convict him of the shallow grave homicides. So, was this why I couldn't wait to plug Con's name into the search program? I didn't think so. I suspected the hard reality was that it all just came down to tasteless curiosity. I was a product of the Burg. I had to know all the dirt.

My dad pulled up to the front of the building and I jumped out. "Thanks," I yelled, hitting the ground running.

I was supposed to sign in and sign out when I entered and left the building. And I was supposed to show my picture ID when I came through the first-floor lobby. I never remembered to sign in or out, and my picture ID was lost in the garage fire. Good thing everyone knew me. Being the only woman in an organization had its upside.

I waved to the guy at the desk and danced in place, waiting for the elevator. I barreled out of the elevator on the fifth floor and crossed to my cubby. I got my computer up and running and punched "Constantine Stiva" into the newspaper search program. A single article appeared. It was small and on page thirteen. I would have missed it on my front-page search.

Private first class Constantine Stiva had been injured in his attempt to thwart a robbery. A government armored truck carrying payroll had been hijacked when it had stopped for a routine gate check at Fort Dix. Stiva had been on guard duty, along with two other men. Stiva was the only guard to survive. He'd been shot in the leg. There'd been no mention of the amount of money involved. And there weren't a lot of details on the hijacking, other than a few brief sentences that the truck had been recovered. I searched papers for two weeks following the incident but came up empty. There'd only been the one article.

I called Ranger on his cell and got a message. I left my cubby and went to the console that monitored Rangeman cars. "Where's Ranger?" I asked Hal. "He's not answering his cell, and I don't see him on the board."

"He's on a plane," Hal said. "He had to bring an FTA up from Miami. He'll be back tonight. Manny was supposed to bring the guy up on a red-eye yesterday, but he had problems with security, so Ranger had to go down this morning." Hal tapped Ranger's number into his computer and a screen changed and brought Ranger's car up. Philadelphia airport. "He should be on the ground in three hours," Hal said. "His cell will come back on then."

I went back to my cubby and I called Morelli.

"I might know the fifth guy," I told him. "It might be Constantine Stiva. He was at Dix when Barroni was there. They were army buddies."

"I can't imagine Con in the army," Morelli said. "I can't imagine him ever being anything other than a funeral director."

"It gets even stranger. He was on guard duty, and he was shot during an armored car hijacking."

"How do you know all this?"

"I've been searching newspapers. I'm going to e-mail you the article on Con. I know it's stupid, but I just have this feeling everything fits somehow. Like maybe the four missing men were involved in the armored car hijacking and Con recognized them."

"Then it would seem to me Con should be the one in the shallow grave."

"Yes, but suppose Con told Spiro and Spiro came back and was extorting money from the four men? And then when he didn't think he could get any more he shot them."

"It's a lot of supposing," Morelli said.

"And here's something else that's interesting. There's been no activity since your garage got blown up. Five days without a note, a sniping, or a bombing. Don't you think that's odd?"

"I think it's all odd."

I sent the news article to Morelli, and then I went to the kitchen, got coffee with milk, no sugar, and went back to my desk and called my mother. "Are you tippling yet?" I asked her.

"No," she said.

Damn. "Dad said you and Grandma were going to the memorial service."

"Yes. It's at one o'clock. I feel so sorry for Carla and the three boys. What a terrible thing. I might have to tipple after the service. Do you think that would be bad?"

"Everybody tipples after a memorial service," I told her. I knew it was the wrong thing to say. God help me, I was a rotten daughter, but I really needed dessert!

I disconnected and started working my way through the search requests. I called Morelli at noon.

"How's it going?"

"I talked to Con."

"Just for the heck of it."

"Yeah. Just for the heck of it. He said the army tried to keep the armored truck robbery as quiet as possible. The two guards that Con was working with were shot and killed. Con said he was alive because he fainted when he got shot in the leg, and he supposed the hijackers thought he was dead. He couldn't identify any of the hijackers. They were all dressed in fatigues, wearing masks. For security purposes the army never released the entire death toll, but Con said it was rumored that there were three men in the truck who were killed."

"Did he say how much money was involved?"

"He didn't know."

"Did you ask him if he thought Barroni might have been involved in that hijacking?"

"Yeah. He looked at me like I was on drugs."

"Did Spiro know about the hijacking?"

"Spiro knew his dad was shot. Con said there was a time when Spiro was a kid, and he was sort of obsessed with it. Kept the newspaper article in a scrapbook."

"What does he have to say about the Spiro sightings?"

"Not much. He seemed confused more than anything else. He said he thought Spiro had perished in the fire. If he's telling the truth he's in a strange spot, not sure if he should be happy Spiro's alive or sad that Spiro blew up Mama Macaroni."

"Do you think he's telling the truth?"

"Don't know. He sounds convincing enough. The big problem for me isn't that Spiro came back to harass you. That I could easily believe, and you've actually seen him. My problem is I don't feel comfortable involving him in the Barroni murder."

"You don't think Spiro's a multitasker."

"Spiro's a rodent. You put a rodent in a maze, and he focuses on one thing, he goes for the piece of cheese."

"Then who killed Michael Barroni?"

"Don't know. If I was going on gut instinct, I'd have to say it feels like Spiro's got his finger in that pie, but there's absolutely no evidence. We don't know *why* Barroni was killed, and we have no reason to believe he was involved in the hijacking."

"Jeez, you're such a party pooper."

"Yeah, insisting on evidence is always a downer."

I hung up and went back to my searches, but I couldn't keep my mind on them. I was getting double vision from looking at the computer, and I was tired of sitting in the cubby. And even worse, I was feeling friendly. I was thinking Morelli's voice had sounded nice on the phone. I was wondering what he was wearing. And I was remembering what he looked like when he wasn't wearing anything. And I was thinking I might have to leave work early, so I could be naked by the time Morelli walked through the door at four o'clock.

I pushed away from my desk, stuffed myself into the windbreaker, and grabbed the key fob.

"I need to get some air," I told Hal. "I won't be gone long."

I rode the elevator to the garage and got on the bike. When I pushed away from my desk I didn't have a direction in mind. By the time I'd reached the garage I knew where I was going. I was going to the memorial service.

I got to Stiva's exactly at one o'clock. Latecomers were hunting parking places and hustling up to the big front porch. I zipped into the lot with the Duc and parked on a patch of grass separating the lot from the drive-thru lane for the hearse and the flower car. My mother's gray Buick was in the lot. From the location of her parking place I was guessing she'd gotten there early. Grandma always liked a seat up front.

Stiva had a chapel on the first floor to the rear of the building. When there was a large crowd he opened the doors and seated the overflow on folding chairs in the wide hallway. Today was standing room only. Since I was one of the last to arrive, I was far down the hall, catching the service over the speaker system.

I wandered away after fifteen minutes and peeked in some of the other rooms. Mr. Earls was in Slumber Salon number three. I thought he was sort of a sad sack in there all by himself while everyone else was at the service. It felt like poor Mr. Earls didn't get an invitation to the party. I snooped in the kitchen and spent a moment considering the cookie tray. I told myself they weren't that good. They were store-bought cookies, and there weren't any of my favorites on the tray. There were better things to nibble on, I told myself. Fresh doughnuts, homemade chocolate chip cookies . . . Ranger. I left the kitchen and tiptoed into Con's office. He'd left the door open. It was an announcement that he had nothing to hide. If you can't trust your undertaker, who *can* you trust, eh?

I don't ordinarily do recreational mortuary tours, and I'd absolutely believed Con when he said he hadn't seen Spiro, so I wasn't sure why I felt compelled to search the building. I guess it just wasn't adding up for me. I kept coming back to the mole. It had been made from mortician's putty. Stiva doesn't run the only funeral home in the greater Trenton area. And for that matter, you can probably order mortician's putty on the Net. Still, this was the easiest and most logical place for Spiro to get a chunk of the stuff. I had a feeling that if I opened enough doors here, I'd find Spiro or at least some evidence that Spiro had passed through.

I went upstairs and checked out the storage room and the two additional viewing rooms Con reserved for peak periods, like the week after Christmas. I returned to the ground level, exited the side door, and looked in the garage. Two slumber coaches, waiting for the call. Two flower cars that were somber, even when filled with flowers. Two Lincoln Town Cars. And Con's black Navigator, the vehicle of choice when someone inconveniently dies during a blizzard.

I returned to the main building through the back door. The chapel was straight ahead, at the end of a short corridor. The embalming rooms were in the new wing, to my left. These rooms were added after the fire. The new structure was cinder block and the equipment supposedly was state of the art, whatever that meant.

I took a deep breath and turned left. I'd gone this far, I should finish the search. I tested the door that led to the new wing. Locked. Gee, too bad. Guess God doesn't want me to see the embalming rooms.

The basement also remained unexplored. And that's the way it was going to stay. The furnaces and meat lockers are in the basement. This is where the fire started. I've been told the basement's all rebuilt and shiny and bright, but I'd rather not see for myself. I'm afraid the ghosts are still there . . . and the memories.

Con lived in a house that sat next to the mortuary. It was

a good-size Victorian, not as big as the original mortuary house, but twice the size of my parents' house. Spiro had grown up in that house. I'd never been inside. Spiro hadn't been one of my friends. Spiro had been a kid who lived in shadows, scheming and spying on the rest of the world, occasionally sucking another kid into the darkness.

I went out through the back door and followed the walkway past the garages to Con's house. It was a pretty house, well maintained, the property professionally landscaped. It was painted white with black shutters, like the mortuary. I circled the house and stepped up onto the small back porch that sheltered the kitchen door. I looked in the windows. The kitchen was dark. I could see through to the dining room. It was also dark. Nothing out of place. No dirty dishes on the counter. No cereal boxes. No sweatshirt draped over a chair. I stood very still and listened. Nothing. Just the beating of my heart, which seemed frighteningly loud.

I tried the door. Locked. I worked my way around the side of the house. No open windows. I returned to the back of the house and looked up at the second floor. An open window. People felt safe leaving windows open on the second floor. And most of the time they were safe. But not this time. This window was over the little back porch, and I was good at climbing up back porches. When I was in high school my parents' back porch had been my main escape route when I was grounded. And I was grounded a lot.

Stephanie, Stephanie, Stephanie, I said to myself. This is insane. You're obsessed with this Spiro thing. There's no good reason to believe you'll find anything helpful in Con's house. What if you get caught? How embarrassing will that be? Then the stupid Stephanie spoke up. Yes, but I won't get caught, the stupid Stephanie said. Everyone's at the memorial service and it'll go on for another half hour at least. And no one can see this side of the house. It's blocked by the garage. The smart Stephanie didn't have an answer to that, so the stupid Stephanie shimmied up the porch railing and climbed through the second-story window and dropped into the bathroom.

The bathroom was white tile, white walls, white towels, white fixtures, white shower curtain, white toilet paper. It was blindingly antiseptic. The towels were perfectly folded and lined up on the towel bar. There was no scum in the soap dish. I took a quick peek in the medicine cabinet. Just the usual over-the-counter stuff you'd expect to find.

I walked through the three upstairs bedrooms, looking in closets and drawers and under beds. I went downstairs and walked through the living room, dining room, and den. The house was eerily unlived-in. No wrinkles on the pillowcases, and all the clothes hanging in the closet and folded in the chest were perfectly pressed. Just like Con, I thought. Lifeless and perfectly pressed.

I went to the kitchen. No food in the fridge. A bottle of water and a bottle of cranberry juice. The poor man was probably anemic from starvation. No wonder he was always so pale. His complexion frequently mirrored the deceased. Not flawed by death or disease but not quite human either. I thought it was by association, but Grandma said she thought Con dabbled in the makeup tray in the prep room.

Constantine Stiva was surrounded by grieving people

every night, left alone with the dead by day, and went home to this sterile house after the evening viewings. And if we're to believe him, he has a son who came back to the Burg but never stopped by to say hello. Morelli thought Spiro was a single-minded rodent. I thought Spiro was a fungus. I thought Spiro fed off a host, and his host had always been Con.

I opened the door to the cellar, switched the light on, and cautiously crept down the stairs. *Eureka.* This was the room I'd been looking for. It was a windowless basement room that had been made into a do-it-yourself apartment. There was a couch covered by a rumpled sleeping bag and pillow. A television. A comfy chair that had seen better days. A scarred coffee table. A bookshelf that had been stocked with cans of soup and boxes of crackers. At the far end someone had installed a sink and a makeshift counter. There was a hotplate on the counter. And there was a small under-the-counter refrigerator. This was the perfect hiding hole for Spiro. There was a door next to the refrigerator. Bathroom, I thought.

I opened the door and looked around the room. I'd expected to find a small bathroom. What I had in front of me was a mortician's workroom. Two long tables covered with tubes of paint, artists' brushes, a couple large plastic containers of mortician's modeling clay, wigs and hairpieces, trays of cosmetics, jars of replacement teeth. And on a chair in the corner was a jacket and hat. Spiro's.

I had my cell phone clipped to my belt alongside my gun. I unclipped the phone and went to dial. No service in the basement. I was on my way through the door when a flash of color caught my eye. It was a rubbery blob that looked a lot like uncooked bacon. I moved closer and realized it was several pieces of the material morticians used for facial reconstruction. I didn't know a lot about the mechanics of preparing the dead for their last appearance, but I'd seen shows on movie makeup, and this looked similar. I knew it was possible to transform people into animals and aliens with this stuff. It was possible to make young actors look old, and it was possible to give the appearance of health and well-being to the newly departed. Stiva was a genius when it came to reconstructing the dead. He added fullness to the cheeks, smoothed over wrinkles, tucked away excess skin. He filled in bullet holes, added teeth, covered bruises, straightened noses when necessary.

Stiva was Burg comfort food. Burg residents knew their secrets and flaws were safe in Stiva's hands. At the end of the day, Stiva would make the fat look thin and the jaundiced look healthy. He wiped away time and alcoholism and self-indulgence. He chose the most flattering lipstick shade for the ladies. He hand-selected men's ties. Even fifty-two-year-old Mickey Branchek, who had a heart attack while laboring over Mrs. Branchek and died with an enormous erection that gave new meaning to the term stiffy, looked rested and respectable for his last hoohah. Best not to consider the process used to achieve that result.

Spiro had watched his father at work and would know the same techniques. So it wasn't shocking that the mole had been made from mortician's putty. The pieces of plastic that were lying on the table were more disturbing. They reminded me of Spiro's scars, and I realized Spiro would have the ability to change his appearance. A perfectly healthy Spiro could make himself horribly disfigured. He wouldn't fool anyone up close, but I'd only seen him at a distance, in a car. And Chester Rhinehart had seen him at night. If I was, in fact, looking at a disguise, it was pretty darn creepy.

I heard movement behind me, and I turned to find Con standing in the doorway.

"What are you doing? How'd you get in here?" he asked. "The doors to the house were closed and locked."

"The back door was open." When in a jam always go with a fib. "Is the service done?"

"No. I came back here because you tripped my alarm."

"I didn't hear it."

"It rings in my office. It monitors the cellar door, among others."

"You're hiding Spiro," I said. "I recognize the coat and hat on the chair. I'm sorry. This must be awful for you."

Con looked at me, his face composed, as always, his eyes completely devoid of emotion. "You're perfect," he said. "Stupid to the end. You haven't figured it out, have you? There's no Spiro. Spiro is dead. He died in the fire. There was nothing left of him but ashes and his school ring."

"I thought he was never found. There was never a service."

"He wasn't found. There wasn't anything left of him. Just the ring. I stumbled across it and never said anything. I didn't want a service. I wanted to move on, to rebuild my business. If he'd lived he would have ruined me, anyway. He was a moron."

This was the first I'd ever heard Con speak badly of the

dead. And it was of his son. I didn't know what to say. It was true. Spiro was a moron, but it was chilling to hear it from Con. And if Spiro was dead then who was tormenting me? Who blew up Mama Macaroni? I suspected the answer was standing two feet away, but I couldn't put it together. I couldn't imagine solicitous Constantine Stiva, Mr. No Personality, offing Mama Mac.

"So it wasn't Spiro who was leaving me notes and blowing up cars?"

"No."

"It was you."

"Hard to believe, isn't it?"

"Why? Why were you stalking me?"

"Why doesn't matter," Con said. "Let's just say you're serving a purpose. I guess it's just as well that you're here. I don't have to hunt you down."

I put my hand to the gun at my hip, but it was an unfamiliar act, and I was slow. Con was much faster with his weapon. He lunged forward, and I saw the glint of metal in his hand, and I barely registered *stun gun* before I went out.

I WAS IN absolute blackness when I came around. My mind was working, but my body was slow to respond, and I couldn't see. I was cuffed and shackled, and I was blindfolded. No, I thought. Back up. I wasn't blindfolded. I could open and close my eyes. It was just very, very dark. And silent. And stuffy. I was disoriented in the dark, and I was having a hard time focusing. I rocked side to side. Not much room. I tried to sit but couldn't raise my head more than a couple inches. The space around me was minimal. The realization of confinement sent a shock of panic into my chest and burned in my throat. I was in a silk-lined container. God help me. Constantine Stiva had put me in one of his caskets. My heart was pounding and my mind was in free fall. This couldn't be real. Con was the heart and soul of the Burg. No one would ever suspect Con of bad things.

My hands ached from the cuffs, and I couldn't breathe. I was suffocating. I was buried alive. Hysteria came in waves and receded. Tears slid down my cheeks and soaked into the satin lining. I had no idea of time, but I didn't think much time had passed. Maybe a half hour. An hour at most. I had a moment of calm and realized I was breathing easier. Maybe I wasn't suffocating. Maybe I was just suffering a panic attack. I didn't smell dirt. I wasn't cold. Maybe I wasn't buried. Okay, hold that thought. Did I hear a siren far off in the distance? A dog barking?

My confinement stretched on with nothing to break the monotony. My muscles were cramping and my hands were numb. I no longer knew if it was day or night. What I knew with certainty was that Ranger would be looking for me. He'd return from Florida, and he'd do what he does best . . . he'd go into tracking mode. Ranger would find me. I just hoped he'd get to me in time.

I heard a door slam and an engine catch. The casket shifted. I was pretty sure I was being driven somewhere. I hoped it wasn't the cemetery. I strained to hear voices. If I heard voices I'd make noise. I seemed to have air, but I didn't want to chance depleting the oxygen if I didn't hear voices. We were stopping and starting and turning corners.

We stopped, and a door opened and slammed shut, and then I was sliding and bumping along. I'd been to a lot of funerals with Grandma Mazur. I knew what this was. I was moving on the casket gurney. I was out of the hearse or the truck or whatever, and I was being taken somewhere. I was wheeled around corners, and then the motion stopped. Nothing happened for what seemed like years, and finally the lid was raised, and I blinked up at Con.

"Good," he said, "you're still alive. Didn't die of fright, eh?" He looked in at me. "Undertaker humor."

My first thought was that I wouldn't cry. I'd try to stay smart. I'd keep him talking. I'd look for an opportunity to escape. I'd stall for time. Time was my friend. If I had enough time, Ranger would find me.

"I need to get out of this casket," I said.

"I don't think that's a good idea."

"I need to use the bathroom . . . bad."

Con was fastidious to a fault, and he looked genuinely horrified at the possibility of a woman peeing in one of his silk-lined caskets. He cranked the gurney down to floor level and helped me wriggle myself out of the box.

"This is the way it will work," he said. "I don't want you making a mess all over everything, so I'm going to let you use the bathroom. I'm going to release one cuff, but I'll stun-gun you if you do anything dumb."

It took a moment to get my balance, and then I very carefully shuffled into the bathroom. When I shuffled out I felt a lot better. My hands were no longer numb and the cramps in my legs had subsided. We were in a house that looked like a small '70s ranch. It was sparsely furnished with mix-and-match hand-me-downs. The kitchen linoleum was old and the paint was faded. The counters were red Formica dotted with cigarette burns. The white ceramic sink was rust stained. Some of the over-the-counter kitchen cabinets were open and I could see they were empty. The casket was in the kitchen, and I was guessing it had been wheeled in from an attached garage.

"Is this in retaliation for Spiro's death or the fire in the funeral home?" I asked Con.

"Only tangentially. It's a bonus. Although it's a very nice bonus. There've been a couple nice bonuses to this cha- rade. I got to kill Mama Macaroni. Who wouldn't love to do that? And then I got to bury her! Life doesn't get much better. The Macaronis bought the top-of-the-line slumber bed."

I cut my eyes to *my* slumber bed.

"Sorry," Con said. "Molded plastic. Not one of my better caskets. Lined with acetate. Still, it's good quality for peo- ple who haven't set aside funeral expenses. I'd like to put your grandmother in one of these. Her death should be declared a national holiday. What is this morbid obsession she has with the dead? I have to nail the lid down when there's a closed casket. And she's never happy with the cookies. Always wanting the kind with the icing in the middle. What does she think, cookies grow on trees?" Con smiled. "Maybe I'll nail your lid down just to annoy her. That would be fun."

"So, I guess that means you're not going to bury me alive?"

"No. If I buried you alive I'd have to put you back in the casket. And I have plans for the casket. Mary Aleski is on a table back at the mortuary, and she'll be on view in that casket tomorrow. And besides, do you have any idea how much digging is involved in burying someone in a casket? I have a better plan. I'm going to hack you up and leave you here on the kitchen floor. It's important to my plan that you're found in this house."

"Why?"

"This house belongs to Spiro. It's tied up in probate because he hasn't been pronounced dead. If Spiro killed you it would be in this house, don't you think?"

"You still haven't told me why you want to kill me."

"It's a long story."

"Are we in a rush?"

Con looked at his watch. "No. As a matter of fact, I'm ahead of schedule. I'm coordinating this with the last of the Spiro sightings. Spiro will be seen in his car around midnight, and then I'll come back here and kill you, and Spiro will disappear forever."

"I don't get the Spiro tie-in. I don't get anything."

"This is about a crime that happened a long time ago. Thirty-six years to be exact. I was stationed at Fort Dix, and I masterminded a hijacking. I had four friends who helped me. Michael Barroni, Louis Lazar, Ben Gorman, and Jim Runion."

"The four men who were found shot to death behind the farmer's market."

"Yes. An unfortunate necessity."

"I wouldn't have pegged you for a criminal mastermind."

"I have many unappreciated talents. For instance, I'm quite good as an actor. I play the role of the perfect undertaker each night. And as you know I'm a genius with makeup. All I needed was a hat and a jacket, some colored contacts and handmade scars, and I was able to fool you and that pizza delivery boy."

"You always seemed like you enjoyed being a funeral director."

"It has its moments. And I hold a certain prominence in the community. I like that."

Constantine Stiva has an ego, go figure. "So you masterminded a hijacking."

"I saw the trucks come through once a week, and I knew how easy it would be to take one of them down on that isolated back station. Lazar was a munitions expert. I learned everything I know about bombs from Lazar. Gorman had been stealing cars since he was nine. Gorman stole the tow truck we used to drag the armored truck away. Barroni had all kinds of connections to launder the money. Runion was the dumb muscle.

"Do you want to know how we did it? It was so simple. I was on guard duty with two other men. The armored truck pulled up. Runion and Lazar were directly behind it in a car. Lazar had already planted the bomb when the truck stopped for lunch. *Kaboom,* the bomb went off and disabled the truck. Runion killed the other two guards on duty and shot me in the leg. Then Gorman hooked the truck up to the tow truck and hauled it off about a quarter mile down the road into an abandoned barn. I wasn't there, of course, but they told me Lazar set a charge that opened the truck like he'd used a can opener. They killed the truck guards and in a matter of minutes were miles away and seven million dollars richer."

"And no one ever solved the crime."

"No. The army expended so much energy hushing it all up that there wasn't a lot of energy left to investigate. They didn't want anyone to know the extent of the loss. That was very big money back then."

"What happened to the money?"

"There were five of us. We each took two hundred thousand as seed money for start-up businesses when we got out. And we agreed that every ten years we'd take another two hundred thousand apiece until we hit the forty-year mark and then we'd divide up what was left."

"So?"

"We had a vault in the mortuary basement. We had a system that each of us had a number, and it took all of us to open the vault. No one knew, but over the years I'd figured out the numbers. So I borrowed from the vault from time to time. Then you and your grandmother burned my business down. The vault survived, but I didn't. I was underinsured. So I took what was left in the vault and used it to rebuild. Two months ago, Barroni found out he had colon cancer and asked for his share of the money. He wanted to make sure it went to his family. We set the meeting up in the field behind the farmer's market so we could take a vote. I knew they were going to give Barroni the money. And they were going to want their share early, too. We were all at that age. Colon cancer. Heart disease. Irritable bowel. Everyone wants to take a cruise. Live the good life. Buy a new car. They were going to go down to my basement, open the vault, find out I'd stolen the money, and then they would have killed me."

"So you killed them."

"Yes. Death isn't such a big deal when it's happening to someone else."

"How do I fit in?"

"You're my insurance policy.

"Just in case one of my comrades shared the secret with a wife and she came looking for me, maybe with the police, I would confess to telling Spiro about the crime. Of course, it would be my version of the crime and I'd be non-culpable. Easy to believe Spiro would return to extort money and then resort to mass murder. And easy to believe Spiro would be a little goofy and take to stalking you. And I'd be the poor grieving father of the little bastard."

"That's the dumbest thing I ever heard."

"*You* fell for it," Con said. "Actually my original plan was just to leave you a few notes. Then I realized you'd made so many enemies you might not consider Spiro as the stalker, so I had to get more elaborate. Probably I could have stopped after you identified me at Cluck-in-a-Bucket, but by that time I was addicted to the rush of the game. It's too bad I have to kill you. It would have been fun to blow up more cars. I really like blowing up cars. And it turns out I'm good at it."

He was crazy. He'd inhaled too much embalming fluid. "You won't get away with it," I told him.

"I think I will. Everyone loves me. Look at me. I'm above suspicion. I'm the social director of the Burg."

"You're insane. You blew up Mama Macaroni."

"I couldn't resist. Did you like my present to you? The mole? I thought that was a good touch."

"What about Joe? Why did you run him over?"

"It was an accident. I was trying to get home, and I

couldn't get rid of you and your idiot grandmother. I hit the curb and lost control of the car. Too bad I didn't kill him. That was a slow week."

Shades were drawn in the house. I looked around for a clock.

"It's almost ten," Con said. "I need to have Spiro seen one last time, driving the car that will be found in this garage. Sadly, it will be my final Spiro performance. And your body will be found in the kitchen. Horribly mutilated, of course. It seems like Spiro's style. He had a flare for the dramatic. I suppose in some ways the apple didn't fall far from the tree." He held the stun gun up for me to see. "Do you want me to stun you before I put you away or will you cooperate?"

"What do you mean, put me away?"

"I want you to be freshly killed after Spiro is seen driving the car. So I'm going to have to put you on ice for a couple hours."

I cut my eyes to the casket. I really didn't want to go back in the casket.

"No," Con said. "Not the casket. I need to get that back to the mortuary. It was just an easy way to transport you." He was looking around. "I need to find something that will keep you out of sight. Something I can lock."

"Ranger will find me," I told him.

"Is that the Rambo bounty hunter? Not a chance. No one's going to find you until I point him in the right direction."

He turned and looked at me with his pale, pale eyes, I saw his hand move, I heard something sizzle in my head, and everything was black.

————

MY MOUTH WAS dry and my fingertips were tingling. The jerk had zapped me again and stuffed me into something. I was on my back, and I was curled up fetus style. No light. No room to stretch my legs. My arms were pinned under me and the cuffs were cutting into my wrists. No satin lining this time. I was pretty sure I was crammed into some sort of wooden box. I tried rocking side to side. No room to get any momentum and nothing gave. This wasn't as terrifying as being locked in the casket, but it was much more uncomfortable. I was taking shallow breaths against the pain in my back and arms, playing games to occupy my mind, imagining that I was a bird and could fly, that I was a fire-breathing dragon, that I could play the cello in spite of the fact that I wasn't sure what a cello sounded like.

And suddenly there was a very slim, faint sliver of light in my box. I went still and listened with every molecule in my body. Someone had turned a light on. Or maybe it was daylight. Or maybe I was going to heaven. There were muffled sounds and men's voices, and there was a lot of door banging. I opened my mouth to yell for help, but the box opened before I had the chance. I tumbled out, and fell into Ranger's arms.

He was as stunned as I was. He had a vise-like grip on my arms, holding me up. His eyes were dilated black, and the line of his mouth was tight. "I saw you folded up in there, and I thought you were dead," he said.

"I'm okay. Just cramped."

I'd been stuffed into one of the empty over-the-counter

cabinets. How Con had gotten me up there was a mystery. I guess when you're motivated you find strength.

Ranger had come in with Tank and Hal. Tank was at my back with a handcuff key, and Hal was working on the shackles.

"It's not Spiro," I said. "It's Con, and he's coming back to kill me. If we hang around we can catch him."

Ranger raised my bruised and bloody wrist to his mouth and kissed it. "I'm sorry to have to do this to you, but there's no *we*. I've just had six really bad hours looking for you. I need to know you're safe. Sitting in this house waiting for a homicidal undertaker doesn't feel safe." And he clamped the handcuff back on my wrist. "You've had enough fun for one day," he said. And the other bracelet went on Tank's wrist.

"What the . . ." Tank said, caught by surprise.

"Take her back to the office and have Ella tend to her wrists and then take her to Morelli," Ranger told Tank.

I dug my heels in. "No way!"

Ranger looked at Tank. "I don't care how you do it. Pick her up. Drag her. Whatever. Just get her out of here and keep her safe. And I don't want those bracelets to come off either of you until you hand her over to Morelli."

I glared at Tank. "I'm staying."

Tank looked back at Ranger. Obviously trying to decide which of us was more to be feared.

Ranger locked eyes with me. "Please," he said.

Tank and Hal were goggle-eyed. They weren't used to "please." I wasn't used to it either. But I liked it.

"Okay," I said. "Be careful. He's insane."

———

HAL DROVE, AND Tank and I sat in back in the Explorer. Tank was looking uncomfortable with me as an attachment, looking like he was searching for something to say but couldn't for the life of him come up with anything. I finally decided to come to his rescue.

"How did you find me?" I asked him.

"It was Ranger."

That was it. Three words. I knew he could talk. I saw him talking to Ranger all the time.

Hal jumped in from the front seat. "It was great. Ranger dragged some old lady out of bed to open the records office and hunt down real estate. He brought her in at gunpoint."

"Omigod."

"Boy, he was intense," Hal said. "He had every Rangeman employee and twenty contract workers out looking for you. We knew you disappeared at Stiva's because I was monitoring your bike. Tank and me started looking for you before Ranger even landed. You told me you were coming back and I got worried."

"You were worried about me?"

"No," Hal said. "I was worried Ranger would kill me if I lost you." He shot me a look in the rearview mirror. "Well yeah. Maybe I was a little worried about you, too."

"I was worried," Tank said. "I like you."

Hot damn! I leaned into him and smiled, and he smiled back at me.

"We went through the funeral home, and we went

through the undertaker's home," Hal said. "And then Ranger figured they might own property someplace else, so he got the old lady in the tax records to open the office. She found that little ranch house under Spiro's name. It was all tied up because Spiro was never declared dead."

FORTY MINUTES LATER, I got dropped off at Morelli's. I had my wrists bandaged, and I had some powdered-sugar siftings on my black T-shirt. Tank walked me to the door and unlocked the cuffs while Morelli waited, a crutch under one arm, his other hand hooked into Bob's collar.

"She's in your care," Tank said to Morelli. "If Ranger asks, you can tell him I unlocked the cuffs in front of you."

"Do you want me to sign for her?" Morelli asked, on a smile.

"Not necessary," Tank said. "But I'm holding you responsible."

I ruffled Bob's head and slipped past Morelli. He shut the door and looked at my T-shirt.

"Powdered sugar?" he asked.

"I *needed* a doughnut. I had Hal stop at Dunkin' Donuts on the way across town."

"Ranger called and told me you were safe and on your way here, but he wouldn't tell me anything else."

Ranger was going to take Stiva down, and he didn't want anything going wrong. He didn't want to lose Stiva. He wanted to do the takedown himself, without a lot of police muddying the water.

"I accidentally got lost trying to find the memorial ser-

vice and happened to stumble into Con's personal workroom. I tripped an alarm and Con found me snooping."

"I'm guessing he wasn't happy about you snooping?"

"It turns out Spiro is dead. Con said he found Spiro's ring
in the fire debris. Con needed a scapegoat and decided
Spiro was the ghost for the job. So Con's been going around
in mortician's makeup, looking like a scarred Spiro."

"Why did Con need a scapegoat?"

I told Morelli about the hijacking and the money missing from the vault, and I told him about the mass murder.

Morelli was grinning. "Let me get this straight," he said.
"In the beginning, you basically made all the wrong
assumptions about Anthony's involvement and Spiro's
identity. And yet, at the end, you solved the crime."

"Yeah."

"Fucking amazing."

"Anyway, Stiva locked me up in a casket and took me
somewhere to kill me. He left so he could do one last Spiro
impersonation, and while he was gone Ranger found me."

"And Ranger's waiting for him to return?"

"Yep."

"He should have told me," Morelli said.

"Probably didn't want the police involved. Ranger likes
to keep things simple."

"Ranger's a little psycho."

"Marches to his own drummer," I said.

"His drummers are all psycho, too."

I looked at Bob. "Has he been out?"

"Only in the yard."

"I'll take him for a short walk."

I went to the kitchen and got Bob's leash. And while I

was at it I pocketed the keys to the Buick. I was feeling left out. And I was feeling pissed off. I wanted to be part of the takedown. And I wanted to release some anger on Stiva. I'd quit my job in an effort to normalize my life, and he'd sabotaged my plan. Of course, he'd done some good things, too, like blowing up Mama Macaroni and sending my cello to cello heaven. Still, it was small compensation for mowing Joe down and stuffing me into a casket. Maybe I should be feeling charitable because it appeared he was insane, but I just didn't feel charitable. I felt angry.

I snapped the leash on Bob, took him out the front door, and loaded him into the Buick. There was a slight chance we'd both be blown to smithereens, but I didn't think so. Blowing me up wasn't in Stiva's plan. I shoved the key in the ignition and listened to the Buick suck gas. Music to my ears. Morelli wouldn't be happy when he heard the Buick drive off, but I couldn't risk telling him I was going back to help Ranger. Morelli would never let me go.

I'd paid attention when we left the little ranch house where I'd been held captive, and in fifteen minutes I was back in the neighborhood. I cruised by the house. It was dark. Half a block away I spotted the Explorer. Hal and Tank were in the house with Ranger. I backed the Buick into a dark driveway directly across from the little ranch. I sat with the motor running and my lights off. Bob was panting in the backseat, snuffling his nose against the window. Bob liked being part of an adventure.

After ten minutes, a green sedan came down the street. The car passed under a streetlight, and I could see Stiva behind the wheel. He was wearing the hat, and a splash of light illuminated his fake scars. He turned into the ranch house driveway and stopped. The garage door started to slide up. This was my moment. I stomped my foot down on the gas and roared across the street, slamming into the back of the green sedan. I caught it square, sending it crashing through the bottom half of the garage door, pushing it into the back of the garage.

Bob was barking and jumping around in the backseat. Bob probably drove NASCAR in another life. Or maybe demolition derby. Bob loved destruction.

"So what do you think?" I asked Bob. "Should we hit him again?"

"Rolf, rolf, rolf!"

I backed up and rammed the green sedan a second time.

Ranger and Tank ran out of the house, guns drawn. Hal came five steps behind them. I backed up about ten feet and got out. I inspected the Buick. Hard to get a good look in the dark, but I couldn't see any damage by the light of the moon.

Tank played a beam of light from his Mag across the green sedan. The hood was completely smashed, the roof had been partially peeled away by the garage door, and the trunk was crumple city. Steam hissed from the radiator and liquid was pooling dark and slick under the car. Stiva was fighting the airbag.

I took Bob out of the backseat and walked him around on Spiro's front lawn so he could tinkle. I was thinking I'd move back into my apartment tomorrow. And maybe I'd get a cello. Not that I needed it. I was pretty darned interesting without it. Still, a cello might be fun.

Ranger was standing, hands on hips, watching me.

"I feel better now," I said to Ranger.

"Babe."

LETHAL LEGACY

ALSO BY LINDA FAIRSTEIN

Available from Random House Large Print

Killer Heat

LETHAL LEGACY

LINDA FAIRSTEIN

A NOVEL

RANDOM HOUSE
LARGE PRINT

Copyright © 2008 by Fairstein Enterprises, LLC.

Published in the United States of America
by Random House Large Print in association with
The Doubleday Publishing Group, New York.
Distributed by Random House, Inc., New York.

Cover Design by Michael J. Windsor
Cover photographs: sky © charles briscoe-knight/
getty images; new york public library ©
angus oborn/getty images;

The Library of Congress has established a
Cataloging-in-Publication record for this title.

ISBN: 978-0-7393-2770-8

www.randomhouse.com/largeprint

FIRST LARGE PRINT EDITION

10 9 8 7 6 5 4 3 2 1

This Large Print edition published in accord with the
standards of the N.A.V.H.

For librarians—
Guardian angels of the mind and the soul

And for my favorite librarian, David Ferriero
Andrew W. Mellon Director of the New York
    Public Libraries

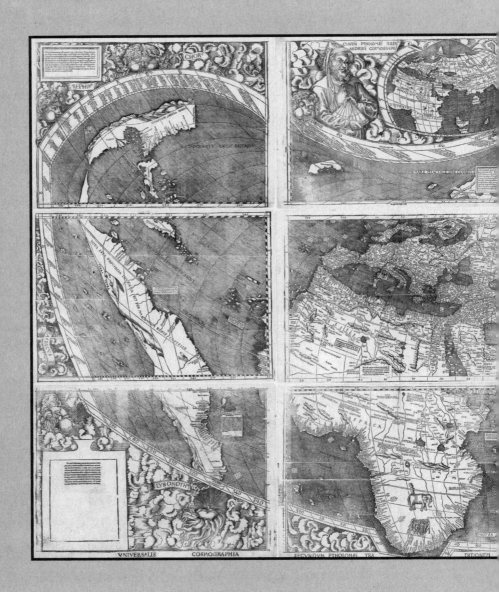

**Geography and Map Division,
Library of Congress**

LETHAL LEGACY

"I want you to open the door for me."

Only silence.

"Look through the peephole," I said. "I'm not a cop. I'm an assistant district attorney."

I stepped back and squared off so the woman inside the basement apartment could check me out. The hallway and staircase had been cleared of men in uniform, including the detail from Emergency Services poised to knock down her door with a battering ram, which was there when I arrived at the scene a short while ago at one o'clock in the morning.

I didn't hear any sound from within. No sense of her movement.

"My name is Alexandra Cooper. You're Tina, aren't you? Tina Barr." I didn't say what my specialty was, that I was in charge of the DA's Office Sex Crimes Prosecution Unit. The police weren't certain she had been assaulted by the man who had earlier invaded her home, but several of them thought she might reveal those details to me if I could gain her confidence.

I moved in against the metal-clad door and pressed my ear to it, but heard nothing.

"Don't lose your touch now, Coop." Mike Chapman walked down the steps and handed a lightbulb to the rookie who was holding a flashlight over my shoulder. "The money on the street's against you, but I'm counting on your golden tongue to talk the lady out so those guys can go home and catch some sleep."

The young cop passed the bulb to Mercer Wallace, the six-foot-six-inch-tall detective from the Special Victims Unit who had called me to the brownstone on the quiet block between Lexington and Third avenues in the East Nineties.

Mercer reached overhead and screwed it in, illuminating the drab, cracked paint on the ceiling and walls of the hallway. "Somebody— most likely the perp—shattered the other one. There are slivers of glass everywhere."

"Thanks, kid," Mike said, dismissing the rookie. "No progress here, Detective Wallace?"

"We haven't got a homicide," I whispered to Mercer. "And they sell lightbulbs at the bodega on Lex. I don't know why you think we needed Mike, but please get him off my back."

"Damn, I've listened to Blondie charm full-on perverts into boarding the bus for a twenty-five-to-life time-share at Sing Sing. I've seen her coax confessions from the lying lips of the deranged and demented. I've watched as weak-willed men—"

Mercer put his finger to his lips and pointed at the staircase.

"Tina, these two detectives are my friends. I've worked with them for more than ten years." I paused to cough and clear my throat. There was still a bit of smoke wafting through the hallway. "Can you tell me why you don't want to open up? Why it is you won't trust us? We're worried about your safety, Tina. About your physical condition."

Mercer pulled at my elbow. "Let's go up for a break. Get some fresh air."

I stayed at the door for another few minutes and then followed Mike and Mercer to the small vestibule of the building and out onto the stoop. It was a mild October night, and neighbors returning to their homes, walking dogs, or hanging around the 'hood were checking on the police activity and trying to figure out what was wrong.

The uniformed sergeant from the Twenty-third Precinct, whose team had been the first responders, was on the sidewalk in front of the building, talking to Billy Schultz, the man who had called 911 an hour earlier.

"What's the situation behind the house?"

Mike asked Mercer as I caught up with them on their way down the front steps.

"Two cops stationed there. Small common garden for the tenants. Back doors from both the first floor and Barr's basement apartment, but no one has moved since they've been on-site."

"What do you know about the girl?"

"Not much. Nobody seems to," Mercer said. He turned to the man standing with the sergeant, whom I guessed to be about forty, several years older than Mike and I. "This is Mike Chapman, Billy. He's assigned to Night Watch."

Mike worked in Manhattan North Homicide, which helped staff the Night Watch unit, an elite squad of detectives on call between midnight and eight a.m., when precinct squads were most understaffed, to respond all over Manhattan to murders and situations, like this one, that the department referred to—with gross understatement—as "unusuals."

"Billy lives on the first floor," Mercer said. "He's the guy who called 911."

"Good to meet you," Mike said. He turned to me. "What's her name?"

"Tina Barr."

"She your friend?" he said to Billy.

"We chat at the mailboxes occasionally. She's a quiet girl. Keeps to herself. Spent a lot of time gardening on weekends in the summer, so I ran into her out back every now and then, but I haven't seen her much since."

"Lived here long?"

"Me? Eighteen years?"

"Her."

"Tina sublets. A year, maybe more."

Mike ran his fingers through his thick black hair, looking from Billy to me. "You sure she's in there?"

"I could hear a woman crying when I first got here," I said. **Whimpering** was a more accurate word.

"Tina was sobbing when I knocked on her door," Billy said.

"But she wouldn't open up for you?"

Billy Schultz adjusted his glasses on the bridge of his nose while Mike scrutinized him. "No, sir."

"Why were you knocking? What made you call 911?"

"Mercer gave us all this, Mike. Let me get back inside."

He held his arm out at me, palm perpendicular like a stop sign. "Don't you want the chronology from the horse's mouth? Primary source. Catch me up, Billy."

I had one hand on the wrought-iron railing but stopped to listen.

"I'm a graphic designer, Detective. Worked late, stopped off for a burger and a couple of beers on my way home," Billy said. He was dressed in jeans and a sweatshirt. There were smudges of ink or paint on his jeans, too dark in color to be blood, I thought. "It was about twelve-thirty when I got near the building. That's when I saw this guy come tearing out the front door, down the steps."

"What guy? Someone you know?"

Billy Schultz shook his head. "Nope. The fireman."

Mike looked to Mercer. "Nobody told me about that. The fire department got here first?"

"Not for real," Mercer said.

"I mean, I assumed he was a fireman. He was dressed in all the gear—coat, boots, hat, even had a protective mask of some kind on. That's why I couldn't see his face."

"Did you stop him? Did he talk to you?"

"He flew by me, like there was a forest fire on Lexington Avenue he had to get to. Almost took me out. Even that didn't seem odd until I looked up the street for his truck but there wasn't one around. Just weird."

"What did you do then?"

"I unlocked the door to the vestibule, and as soon as I got inside, I could smell smoke. I could see little waves of it sort of spiraling upward from the basement," Billy said. "We don't have a super who lives in the building, so there was no one for me to call. I figured whatever happened had been resolved. By the guy I thought was a fireman. But I wanted to check it out, make sure there was nothing still burning."

"Sarge, you want to get me that mask?" Mercer said.

The older man walked to the nearest squad car and reached in for a paper bag while Billy Schultz talked.

"I went downstairs first. It was pretty dark, but I could make out a small pile of rubble in the corner of the hallway, a couple of feet from Tina's door. Nothing was burning—no flames—but it was still smoldering. Kicking off a lot of smoke. That's when I knocked on her door."

"Did she answer?" Mike asked.

"No. Not then. I didn't hear anything. I figured maybe she wasn't home. I ran up to my apartment, filled a pitcher with water, and came back down to douse whatever was still smoking. Figured the other firemen must have gone off to a bigger job and that the last one—the guy who almost plowed me down—was trying to catch up with them."

The sergeant passed the bag to Mercer, who

put on a pair of latex gloves from his pocket before opening it.

"It's when I went downstairs the second time that I heard Tina."

"What did you hear, exactly?" I asked.

Billy cocked his head and answered. "I knocked again, just because I was worried that the firemen might have left her there even though there was still something smoldering in the hallway. She was weeping loudly, then pausing, like to inhale."

"Words," Mike said. "Did she speak any words?"

"No, but I did. I told Tina it was me, asked her if she was all right. I was coughing myself from the smoke. I told her she could come up to my apartment."

"Did she answer you?"

"No. She just cried."

"How do you know it's Tina Barr you were talking to?" Mike asked.

Billy hesitated. "Well, at that point—I, uh—I just assumed it, Detective. She lives there alone."

"What next?"

"I went home to get a bucket and broom. Swept some of the trash into the bucket to throw out on the street—"

Mike glanced at the sergeant. "Yeah, we got

it, Chapman. Looks like amateur smoke bombs."

"The sobbing was so bad by then, I called 911, from my cell. Maybe she was sick, overcome by the smoke. I waited out here on the stoop till the officers came. Three minutes. Not much longer. That's when Tina went berserk. That's when I knew it was her, for sure. I recognized her voice, when she was yelling at the cops."

Mercer removed a large black object from the bag and dangled it in front of us.

"Yeah," Billy said. "That's what the fireman had on his face."

"Found it halfway up the block," the sergeant said. "Right in the perp's flight path."

"That's not department gear," Mike said. "It's a gas mask. Military style."

It was a black rubber helmet, with two holes for the eyes, and a broad snoutlike respirator that would fit over the mouth, with a long hose attached.

"Couldn't see a damn thing," Billy said. "It covered his entire face."

"What did the cops do?" Mike asked.

"I led them down to the basement. They knocked on Tina's door and one of them identified himself, said they were police. That's when she started yelling at them to leave her alone. I mean screaming at them. Freaked out. Sounded like she collapsed—maybe fell onto the floor—crying the whole time."

"What makes you think she's alone in there?"

"We're guessing," Mercer said. "She's the only one to make a sound—no scuffling, no struggling, no other voices. But that's another reason ESU won't leave."

Mike prodded my side with his fingers as we started up the front steps. I went back in the vestibule toward the basement staircase.

"One of the cops told Tina he just wanted to make sure that the fire hadn't affected her," Billy said, drawing a handkerchief from his pocket to wipe his smoke-fogged glasses. "Asked her if she could stand up and look through the peephole at his badge, for identification. She went wild."

"What do you mean?" Mike asked.

"Tina screamed at the cop. Told him that's how the guy got in. The fireman. That he showed her his badge and she opened the door."

"It was the fireman who was inside her apartment? You knew, Coop?"

"That's why Mercer called me. We don't know who the man was, why he was using such an elaborate disguise, why he went inside, and what he did to this woman. Okay? Don't come any closer, Mike. Let me talk to her."

I walked the short corridor to the rear of the hallway, glass crunching under the soles of my shoes.

"Tina? It's Alex Cooper. We're all still here. The police officers won't leave until I convince them that you're unharmed. I'll keep them outside the building if you'll let me in for just a few minutes."

"I'd rank that a toss-up," Mike said. "Ten minutes with you or the quick punch of a battering ram? Tough call."

"You think this helps? You think she can't hear you?" I threw up my arms in frustration as I turned to Mike. "Mercer, please take him upstairs."

The men marched back to the first floor as I made another attempt to persuade Tina Barr to let me in.

"I'm the only one in the basement now, Tina. The men are all outside. I don't want them to break down your door any more than you do. But they're worried that you've been injured. There was a lot of smoke down here. Can you just tell me if you're hurt?"

There was no answer for more than a

minute. Then a soft voice spoke a word or two, which sounded as though the woman was still sitting or lying on the floor inside. I couldn't understand her, so I crouched beside the door and put my ear against it.

"Sorry. What did you say?"

"Not hurt. I'll be okay."

She spoke haltingly, her words caught in her throat.

"Tina, are you having trouble breathing?"

No answer.

"We can give you oxygen, Tina. Is it the smoke? Is there still smoke in your apartment?"

"No."

"The man who was dressed like a fireman, did you let him come into your apartment?"

She was crying again as she tried to speak. "No, no, I didn't let him in."

"But you told the police officer that—"

"I only opened the door because he showed me a gold badge and told me there was a fire. I could smell the smoke and then saw it. I believed him." Tina Barr's words came out phrase by phrase, embedded in sobs. "He forced his way inside. I didn't **let** him in."

"You can trust us, Tina. Now you know that man wasn't actually a fireman. His badge wasn't real." Mercer had already checked that with the department and had been telling that to Barr before I got there. "The cops think the man started the fire himself in order to break in to your apartment."

She was taking deep breaths on the other side of the door.

I took one, too, and tried to get at what had so far been unspoken. "I work with victims of sex crimes, Tina. That's all I do. It's why the police thought I might be able to help. I deal with the most sensitive cases you can imagine," I said, closing my eyes, which burned from the lingering smoke. "Did this man assault you tonight?"

She coughed again.

I didn't know how long he'd been within the apartment before Billy Schultz saw him running from the building at twelve-thirty in the morning.

"Did he awaken you when he knocked, Tina?"

"No."

"Do you know what time it was when you first went to the door?"

"Five," she said.

"Five o'clock in the afternoon?" She must have been confused. "Look, I'm going to have to let the police work on your door, or the back window in your kitchen, Tina. You may be a little woozy. He couldn't have been inside there that long."

There was a noise before Tina Barr spoke next, as though she shifted her position. She had gotten to her feet, perhaps angered by my comment. I stood up, too, as she pounded on the door. "I know exactly what time it was when the man knocked, do you understand? It wasn't the middle of the night, Ms. Cooper. It was five o'clock."

All the cops and I had assumed the events had occurred within minutes of Schultz's arrival home. Fast, like most break-ins, and while the smoke bombs were steaming. We were wrong.

"I apologize, Tina. That's even more reason for me to know what he did to you." I didn't want to suggest the word **rape** to her. I needed **her** to reveal to me what had occurred.

"I don't want to talk to any cops, Ms. Cooper. I'll tell you what happened if that will make them go away."

"I'm alone down here now. The men won't come in." I paused before I spoke again. "I give you my word."

Tina Barr sniffled, then was quiet. I heard the dead bolt turn.

The door opened a few inches and I could see the young woman peering out from behind it, clutching the lapels of her white chenille robe with one hand. Her dark brown hair was disheveled, her eyes reddened from at least an hour of crying, and what looked to be remains of adhesive tape forming a rectangle on the skin around her mouth, where she had probably been gagged.

I reached out a hand to her, hoping to comfort her with a touch, but she recoiled at the movement in her direction.

"You're mistaken if you think this was about a sex crime, Ms. Cooper. He wanted to kill me," Tina Barr said. "That man left me for dead."

TWO

←—————————————————————————

"I don't want to press charges."

Tina Barr was seated in an armchair in the cramped living room of her apartment, and I was opposite her on a small loveseat that was sorely in need of reupholstering.

"That's not even an issue right now, Tina. I'd like to know what happened to you. We don't have a suspect, so there's no one to prosecute."

"You told me you wanted to make sure I was all right. You see I'm not hurt, so now you can leave."

She was unnaturally pale and rested her forehead in her hand, as though she needed that support to keep it upright.

"A couple of minutes ago you told me a man tried to kill you. You told me he was with you in here for more than six hours. How can I walk away from this? You don't look well, Tina. You must be terribly frightened."

"I'm nauseous. I just want to lie down."

I tried to make eye contact with her, but she was staring at the floor.

"Who did this to you, Tina? Do you know that?"

Her entire body trembled. "No idea. There was some horrible black mask covering his face."

I didn't want to press her, to cross-examine her, but it seemed unlikely that her attacker had had the mask on for so many hours. "The whole time he was here? Didn't he ever take it off?"

"I don't know what he did. I don't remember."

I expected her to be a difficult interview after the experience the cops had when they got to the building. But I hadn't thought she would stonewall me once she opened the door.

"You don't remember?"

"I was unconscious the entire time that man was here, Ms. Cooper." Tina lifted her head and looked at me. "He pushed his way in and threw me down. He put a cloth over my mouth and I couldn't breathe any longer. I just felt dizzy and watched the room turn upside down. I thought I was going to die. I don't have any idea what he did after that."

Now I had even more reason to be concerned, and greater need not to express it.

"How are you feeling?"

"I've told you already. I'd like to go to sleep."

"Do you know what he drugged you with?"

Tina rested her head on the back of the chair and snapped at me. "Now how could I possibly tell you that?"

"I didn't think you'd be able to. That's my point. All the more reason to let the doctors examine you, have them test your blood. You've undoubtedly still got something in your system."

"I don't want anyone else coming in here—can you understand that?"

"I'd like to take you to the emergency room. There's an excellent hospital less than ten blocks away."

Tina Barr started to cry again. There was a box of tissues on a desk behind her chair. I crossed the room to get a handful of them, glancing around for any obvious signs of a disturbance. Bookcases lined the walls. End tables, like the desk, were cluttered with a messy array of papers and journals.

"Why don't you take a minute to compose yourself?"

I handed her the tissues and reached out to stand the wastebasket upright. There was a large rag in it, and as I leaned over, it smelled sickeningly sweet. I used a tissue to remove the cloth from the basket and put it in the pocket of my jeans.

"Would you like some water, Tina?"

"I'm too nauseous to drink. I'm very thirsty, but I doubt I can hold anything down."

I retraced my steps to the loveseat. I could get more facts later. I wanted to talk to her about medical treatment. "I just have a couple more questions, okay? When you regained consciousness, were you still here, on the floor?"

She searched out another spot in the dark pattern of the cheap Oriental rug and stared at it. "I was on my bed, Ms. Cooper. I was naked. Completely naked. There was some kind of tape over my mouth, and my hands were tied to the headboard with a pair of my stockings. Loose knots, they were. I was able to work them off easily."

"While the man was still here?"

"No," she said, breathing deeply. "I came around just a few minutes before he left. I could hear him in this room, so I just played dead and didn't move till the door shut."

"Tina, you've got to see a doctor." I was on the edge of the seat cushion, pleading with her to let me take her to Mount Sinai Hospital. "They've got a wonderful advocacy program for victims of violence. I just have to call ahead and someone knowledgeable about the process will be with you through the entire exam."

"I told you before I wasn't raped." Tina got

to her feet and steadied herself before she started walking toward the back of the apartment. "I'm going to be sick."

I stood up to follow her. "Let me—"

"Please don't come inside. I'd like some privacy."

A door slammed and I couldn't hear anything until the toilet flushed and water ran in the sink. The dozens of questions I had would be answered, I knew, when she was made comfortable and felt safe. I needed to get her to the ER as fast as possible. Once crime scene investigators had access to her bedroom, the trace evidence on the linens and clothing might tell us more about what occurred than Tina Barr could.

About ten minutes later, Tina emerged from what must have been her bedroom and bath area. She was dressed in khaki slacks and a cable-knit sweater.

"If I go with you to the hospital, does it mean I'm pressing charges?"

"Not at all. You have weeks to make that decision, if we catch the guy. This is all about your health, about trying to figure out what he did to you. If you aren't examined now, the tests will never yield the same results in two or three days, when you might have second thoughts about all this." I knew that if she had been penetrated by her assailant, the natural forces of gravity would eliminate any fluids that could be tested for DNA. Whatever she had been drugged with would be gone from her bloodstream, too. "It's your own best protection."

"I'd prefer to take a cab, Ms. Cooper. I can do this myself."

"There's an ambulance waiting near the building. We were all so worried about you. I can cut through a lot of administrative red tape if I'm along."

She hesitated again, then went back inside and returned with a small tote. "I'll go with you. Just don't ask me any more questions, okay?"

"Let me call the detectives, so the ambulance is right in front." I pressed Mercer's speed dial on my cell.

"You need me?"

"Ms. Barr and I are coming out. I'm going to ride to Sinai with her in the bus. Maybe you can meet us at the ER. And get rid of the guys with the heavy equipment."

"Done, Alex. Will she let crime scene in to process the apartment?"

I turned to ask her. I wanted the bed linens and bathrobe, the tape and the pantyhose, as soon as possible. I wanted to know if there were any more rags inside, whether he had applied the substance to her face more than once. "Tina, would you mind if the detectives got to work on looking for evidence in your bedroom? Fingerprints, possible DNA sources—"

"Nobody comes in here while I'm gone," she said. "I don't want any other strangers inside my home tonight. Do you understand?"

"Of course I do." I knew Mercer had heard it, too. I shut off the phone.

Tina walked behind me on the staircase, bracing her hands against the wall. When we reached the stoop, I was relieved to see the police cars and trucks were all gone, and that two EMTs were standing at the rear door of the ambulance, with the gurney between them.

I offered her my arm and she accepted it for the short walk. I introduced us to the EMTs, and they asked Tina to sit down so they could lift her inside after I climbed up and wedged myself into a jump seat.

"How you doin'?" the medic asked Tina as his partner got into the driver's seat. "You okay?"

"I'm sick to my stomach, actually."

"Take it slow, Howie. Don't bounce in any potholes," he called out to the driver. "My name is Jorge Vasquez. I'm just gonna get your vitals, miss. Gotta do that."

Tina reclined on the gurney and pushed up her sleeve for the blood pressure cuff.

"How old are you, Ms. Barr?"

"Thirty-three."

"Date of birth?"

She gave the year first, then told him March 14.

"Your height and weight?"

"Five-four." She was six inches shorter than I, and weighed almost the same. "One thirty-five."

"What kind of insurance you got?"

Tina covered her mouth with her hand, as though she was going to be sick again.

"You got insurance?"

"No."

The EMT looked over her head at me and I nodded. The hospital would get its money from the crime victims compensation board if Barr didn't pay. This wasn't the time or place to dicker about who'd foot the bill for the expensive sexual assault examination.

"How about your occupation?"

"I'm—uh—I'm a librarian."

"Nice. You like books. Me, I don't have time to read." Vasquez was filling in the blank spaces on his form. "Who's your employer? Would that be the city?"

"I'm not working at the moment. I quit my last job just a week ago."

"City's got good benefits. You should think about it. Which branch, Ms. Barr? It's regulations. I gotta put something in this box."

"No, it wasn't the city. It was private. It's over."

The driver made the turn onto Madison Avenue and we headed north. Vasquez put his clipboard on his lap, took Tina's pressure, and recorded the numbers.

"You mind if I check your eyes?"

The young woman shook her head from side to side and Vasquez leaned in, studying her pupils and making a note, I guessed, about how dilated they were.

"You want to start with what happened to you, miss?"

"I'm not really sure. I know I was drugged, but that's all I can tell you," Tina said. "And I've got a terrible headache now."

"Any idea what kind of drug?"

"Like I told Ms. Cooper, I don't know. But I'm really thirsty," she said, licking her lips.

"Sorry. You're dehydrated, but the triage nurse will see you in a few minutes. No point giving you anything before that. She may want to start an IV."

We were at the hospital in less than five minutes. It was background information about Tina Barr that I wanted—something to lead me to why she was victimized this way—but Jorge Vasquez had as much pedigree as he needed.

When he opened the rear doors of the ambulance at the hospital receiving bay, Mercer was waiting for me. I stepped around the gurney and jumped down, holding on to his hand.

"I think we're better off keeping Ms. Barr right here till she's called in for triage. It's kind of zooey in there," Mercer said.

"We can hold," Vasquez said. "I could use the break."

"They got a gunshot wound in the chest. Fifteen-year-old kid caught in the crossfire of two dealers. A bad car crash on the FDR Drive—three passengers with head trauma—and the typical assortment of fractures and bellyaches. You know a possible rape won't be seen till daybreak unless you can pull some strings, Alexandra."

Most victims of sexual assault presented to treating physicians without any external physical injury. To an emergency specialist, the trauma had occurred when the crime was committed. The survivor who presented at the hospital was not in need of life-saving treatment like the other medical patients, but rather was there for evidence collection and psychological counseling. Without advocates or forensic examiners on call, these women were often the most neglected emergency room visitors, waiting hours to be evaluated.

"We'll try to get you in as quickly as we can," I said to Tina, leaving her in the care of Vasquez and his partner as I turned to follow Mercer into the ER.

The security guard stood back as Mercer flashed his gold shield and the automatic double doors swung open to admit us. A dozen curtained cubicles—all seemingly occupied—formed a semicircle around the nurses' station, where Mike had settled in with his feet on the counter, eating chocolates from a box on the desk.

"Have you spoken to the head nurse?"

"Yeah, we're somewhere between the heart attack in that corner and the domestic dispute racheted up till the missus settled it by hurling a meat cleaver at the bum's neck," Mike said.

One of the nurses emerged from behind the thin curtains of the first treatment area, and Mike waved him over. "This is Ms. Cooper, Joe. You any good at splinter removal? She's had a stick up her ass for the last couple of months, and I was hoping—"

"We're waiting for one of the SAVI volunteers, Ms. Cooper," Joe said, stripping his bloodied gloves off and dropping them in the hazardous-waste bin along with the syringe in his hand. He was the size of a fullback, a black man with skin as dark as Mercer's, and not in the mood for Mike's humor. "Get you in here as soon as we can. I've got one going up to X-ray and another for admission, just waiting on a room."

"This may not have seemed urgent when the detectives first called," I said, knowing that it might take half an hour for a sexual assault violence intervention program advocate to reach the ER, "but Tina's in worse shape than we thought."

I pulled the rag from my pocket, pinching it on a corner to hold it up. "The perp soaked this in something and knocked her out by putting it over her nose and mouth."

"Nice save, Coop." Mike stood and bent over the counter, sniffing at the rag. "What's your guess, Joe? Ether of some kind? Not so noxious as that. Maybe chloroform?"

Joe didn't want to come closer. "If that's what it was, it's enough to cause a fatal cardiac arrhythmia."

"That baby's going straight to the lab, Coop."

"Tell the EMTs to bring her right in," Joe said. "Let's get your girl worked up."

The three of us headed for the exit, past the waiting area filled with anxious family members and friends, down the driveway and onto the street. The driver had backed out of the bay to leave room for the next arrival and double-parked on Madison Avenue.

Jorge Vasquez was leaning against the side of the red-and-white ambulance. Mercer waved at him as we approached, telling him to move it in and unload the patient.

Vasquez shrugged his shoulders.

"Don't give me that 'not my job' crap," Mike said. "Roll it."

"I'm empty, man," Vasquez said, brushing his hands against each other like he was dusting off crumbs. "The broad took off."

"Took off where?" I asked.

"RMA, Ms. Cooper. I can't be holding no-body against her will."

Tina Barr had refused medical attention, despite the ordeal she'd survived.

"Which way'd she go?"

"No sé," Vasquez said. "She told me she never wanted the cops called in the first place. Jumped out the bus and said to tell you to leave her alone."

THREE

⟶

"I still think we could have beat Tina to her apartment," Mike said, several hours later, as he sat across the desk from me.

"To what end? For some reason, she never wanted any of us involved in the first place. It was the neighbor—not Tina—who called 911."

"I don't know. Should have scooped her up and made her a material witness till we figured out what happened."

"No such thing as getting a material witness order unless there's a pending prosecution," I said, continuing to make notes on a legal pad, charting the chronology of a murder investigation we'd been working on for several months. "You know that."

"Are you going to follow up with her now?"

"I'm giving Tina a day to settle down. By then she'll realize the flashbacks and night sweats won't go away by themselves. She might even welcome the chance to talk about it."

We were in my office in the Sex Crimes Prosecution Unit on the eighth floor of Manhattan's Criminal Courthouse at nine-thirty on

Wednesday morning. Mike had brought me a third cup of coffee and took the lid off after he set out his bagel on top of a file cabinet, using a manila folder as a place mat.

"How come Judge Moffett scheduled a hearing on the Griggs case? You don't even have an arrest yet."

We had been working on the rape-homicide of a nineteen-year-old-girl named Kayesha Avon that had taken place almost eight years earlier. The case had gone cold long ago, but the recent submission to the databank of the DNA profile of a man named Jamal Griggs and the near match that resulted had given Mike a reason to revive the investigation.

"Jamal Griggs doesn't like the idea that we're so interested in his family tree," I said.

Jamal and his brother Wesley, known to us as the Weasel, had floated in and out of the criminal justice system for most of their adult lives. Despite Jamal's homicide conviction as a teenager—or maybe because of it—he and Wesley had become part of the entourage that surrounded and sold drugs to the crews of late thug rappers such as Biggie Smalls and Tupac Shakur.

"I applied for a search warrant to get into the California database to see what it tells us about Wesley's DNA, and must have struck a nerve.

Jamal's new counsel requested a chance to oppose my motion. I need you and Mattie Prinzer," I said, referring to the forensic biologist who headed the lab at OCME, the Office of the Chief Medical Examiner, "to make my case."

"Jamal get himself a new suit? Last I knew he was a poster boy for the Legal Aid Society. How's he paying for a lawyer?"

"I have the feeling we're going to meet the new suit in the courtroom. He's been dispatched from the City of Angels by the Weasel."

"Amazing that Wesley made it out the 'hood," Mike said. The thirty-two-year-old wannabe gangsta had moved from pushing crack cocaine on East Harlem street corners to producing records in Hollywood, while his baby brother was behind bars again for an armed robbery of a gas station in Queens. "I think a proper homecoming would be a sweet thing, Coop."

"I'm a long way from blowing up balloons and mailing out save-the-date cards for the Weasel's return to New York," I said. "Would you give these lab reports to Laura, please, and ask her to make copies? I'll have to turn them over to defense counsel if Moffett makes you two testify."

Mike walked to the door and handed the case file to my secretary. He was wearing his trademark navy blazer with a pale blue button-down shirt and crisply pressed khakis. His dark good looks and irrepressible grin were an appealing combination, and his intelligence and experience made him a trusted partner—like Mercer—in the most difficult cases we'd handled together.

"You think maybe she knew him?"

"Did Kayesha Avon know Wesley Griggs?" I asked.

"No, no, no. I'm thinking about Tina Barr. Maybe she didn't want to cooperate with us because she made the man beneath the mask. Or he actually took it off once he got inside the apartment. If she recognized the guy, could be she knows how dangerous it is for her and that's why she fled the scene."

I was studying Jamal Griggs's pre-sentence report, trying to get a sense of whether he had a favorite modus operandi. "Could be."

"Don't you think that puts her at greater risk now? Don't you need to do something to safe-guard her?"

"And what would that be, since she's expressed herself so clearly? I can't take her hostage if she's so dead set against reporting this."

"Did you ask for a detail to sit in front of Tina's house?"

"The CO turned me down flat."

"Use your juice, Coop. There's a couple of dudes at headquarters who think you walk on bottled water. Call in a chit."

"Yeah, and maybe you can forward my nomination to the Supreme Court in case there's a vacancy. That would be an easier task than getting Commissioner Scully to sign off on a spare RMP for a victim who tied up enormous resources in the middle of the night and then took a hike with no explanation at all."

There was a shortage of both manpower and radio motor patrol cars because of the spike in violent crimes charted since the summer.

"I didn't know you could qualify for the Supremes if you were living in France. There must be some kind of jurisdictional requirement."

I looked up from my notes and bit on the tip of my fountain pen, but I was unable to suppress a smile. "Michael Patrick Chapman. Is that what's bugging you? Have you been working overtime on my love life? All you had to do was ask."

One of the city's most experienced homicide detectives turned scarlet from his brow to the point where his neck disappeared into his shirt collar.

"No need to pry into that, blondie. You're wearing it all over your puss. Be a shame to waste the latest Parisian fashions under long black judicial robes, if you ask me," Mike said. "And that skirt you're wearing is way too short for Judge Moffett. His defibrillator might zap into overtime."

I looked down at the navy blue suit I'd bought on the Avenue Montaigne when I had last visited Luc Rouget, the Frenchman I'd been dating since early summer. Anything not to make eye contact with Mike.

"Make you a deal," I said. "Let's get through this Griggs motion today and we can catch up over dinner. I never meant to hold back anything from you or Mercer. Luc turned up in the middle of a killing spree and my personal life deservedly took a back seat."

"You don't owe me any explanation," he said, shifting away from me. "Skip the talk tonight and just feed me, Coop. But you'll have to take yourself out of that chic getup before cocktails. Too rich for my blood."

"I'll call Mercer. The three of us haven't been out in more than a month. I'm buying."

"What if it's about kinky sex?" Mike asked,

balling up his napkin and tossing it over my head into the garbage.

My turn to blush. "Kinky what?"

"Not you and the French guy, kid. Tina Barr. Maybe she was tied up 'cause she wanted to be. Could explain why she wouldn't talk."

We had seen it all, working sex crimes and homicide. Just when one of us thought there was nothing left to shock, along came a new way for two people to amuse themselves in the privacy of their homes.

"A long shot," I said. "But always a possibility."

"Think about it. Broad's tied up and gagged—there's evidence to support that—but tells you she wasn't raped. Wouldn't be anything to call the cops about if she consented."

I slipped my heels off under the desk before Mike could comment on their style, and replaced them with a sturdier work shoe for our court appearance. "Maybe."

"What do you know about chloroform?" Mike asked. "Pick up anything medically useful from your old man while you were growing up?"

"Wasn't it the first anesthetic used for women in childbirth in the nineteenth century? Till the docs found out it was too toxic."

"Well, it's still around, and it caused three deaths, just in the north, in the last eighteen months," Mike said.

New York County—the island of Manhattan—was split in half by the NYPD for the management of unnatural-death investigations. Mike's office, the Manhattan North Homicide Squad, responded to everything from Fifty-ninth Street to the tip of Spuyten Duyvil, while its southern counterpart took the territory from midtown down to the Battery.

"You're not talking serial killer again?"

"Nope," Mike said, topping off his bagel with a handful of red licorice sticks. "It's a phenomenon called SSD. Sudden sniffers' death. Lieutenant Peterson's been all over these cases lately, he told me yesterday. Easy to buy the ingredients on the Web. Chloroform's a central nervous system depressant. If it doesn't kill you, inhaling it for the high will at least leave you dizzy and tired, with a crushing headache."

"So you think Tina OD'd accidentally, trying to get tuned up for some kind of sexual encounter?" I asked. "I don't know, Mike. She claimed the guy tried to kill her."

"So maybe he did, if you can believe her at this point."

"It's the 'tried to' that stops me short. He was

in there for hours. He certainly had the opportunity."

"She said she played dead, Coop. If her
breathing was shallow enough, maybe the perp
thought he **had** killed her. Could be why he ran
out of the place the way he did."

"It still doesn't explain his disguise," I said.

"I'm just saying you should call her. You're
the hand holder. You're the one who's supposed
to be so good at bonding with your victims."

Mercer and I liked working with survivors of
sexual assault, helping them recover from the
trauma they had experienced, in addition to
bringing the criminal to justice. Mike was used
to the cold finality of death investigations. No
victims with ambivalence about their attackers,
no quirky personalities to soothe and stroke.
Dead bodies and crime scenes might hold puzzles for pathologists and detectives, but unlike
their living counterparts, they never lied.

Laura stood in the doorway with the documents. "Mattie just called. She's going to jump
in a cab as soon as possible. Shall I tell her to go
right to the courtroom?"

"Good idea, Laura. Thanks."

The buzzer on my telephone console rang as
its red light flashed insistently. Paul Battaglia,
the district attorney of New York County for

more than twenty years, had a hotline to each
of his bureau chiefs. He didn't like to wait for
answers to questions handed him by reporters,
politicians, rivals, and concerned citizens.

"Yes, Paul?"

"I need ten minutes of your time," Battaglia
said. "The mayor's looking for where I stand on
that legislative proposal we discussed."

"I'll be over as soon as I finish an argument
I've got in front of Judge Moffett."

"I need you right now, Alexandra. I'm already late for City Hall. I don't expect you to
keep the mayor waiting."

FOUR

Rose Malone, Battaglia's executive assistant and my trusted friend, waved me into his suite without buzzing the intercom. Her lack of a cheerful greeting let me know that the district attorney hadn't started the day in a good mood.

"Do I have a position on this Halloween business, Alexandra?" Battaglia had called me in to discuss a legislative proposal about sex offenders that had become a controversial piece of the city council's agenda. He started walking from his desk to the large conference table at the rear end of his office as soon as he saw me cross the threshold. "Did I make up my mind about what we're going to say?"

"Not as of the last time we discussed it."

"Sit down," he said, his teeth gripping the long unlit cigar in the middle of his mouth. "What is it, just a few weeks until Halloween?"

"Yes."

"I guess the mayor is trying to grandstand here. Show that his balls are bigger than mine. What's he up to?"

"I read the proposal. Half a dozen states and

a lot of local authorities have been trying to place restrictions on registered sex offenders for just that one night a year," I said. "Some communities are requiring them to attend four- or five-hour educational programs on Halloween. In Virginia, they've all got to report to their parole officers between four and eight p.m., so they're not at home to answer the door when kids come trick-or-treating. That's the model the mayor wants to adopt in the city."

"What do I think of it?" Battaglia asked. He was the consummate politician and had enough confidence in his senior staff to let us participate in important decisions, even though he had a long memory for mistakes.

"Pretty useless."

He lifted his glasses off his nose and rested them on top of his forehead. "Sexual predators are one of the major concerns in law enforcement. You've got a holiday here that offers a tantalizing chance for these perverts to have unsupervised contact with kids. The youngsters knock on the door, ask for some candy, and God knows what can happen to them."

"It's one night a year, boss. If the legislature puts some teeth in the laws we've already got, then maybe the police could actually monitor the offenders they're supposed to be tracking."

Battaglia rarely removed the cigar when he

spoke, just stretching the corners of his mouth around it without slurring any of his words. "And the advocate groups? Where do they come down on this?"

"Not impressed. Most children are victimized by people they know and trust, not by strangers. This draft doesn't even distinguish between pedophiles and perps who committed crimes against adults. You won't get any heat from victims' groups if you don't support the proposal. Press for enough money to track the registered offenders 24/7. That's where the real problem is."

Battaglia got up and removed his suit jacket from the back of the chair. That would serve as a dismissal. I stood up to leave the room.

"How about the flip side?" he asked.

"What would that be?"

"Well, that Halloween presents another danger for kids. Offenders could be dressed in costumes, too. Abducting teens or children from the street, or knocking on doors in some kind of disguise."

"I'll tell you, Paul, we haven't seen any problems on Halloween over the years. Late October hasn't been high season for sex crimes."

"You're not hanging me out to dry in front of the press, Alex, are you?"

I assumed Battaglia was joking, and I

laughed as I started for the door. "I wouldn't think of doing that until my pension vests, Paul."

"I'm not kidding. I smell a setup over at City Hall."

I turned to face him, and he removed the cigar from his mouth. "This brouhaha last night, Alex. Some guy broke into a girl's apartment dressed up like a fireman, right?" he said. "How come you didn't call me about it?"

"Well, there isn't actually a case, Paul," I said. His displeasure was visible in his scowl. I had irked him by neglecting to inform him about a matter that I'd miscalculated in importance, but which must have a link to a player in his political world.

"Somebody at City Hall seems to think otherwise. It's all to do with disguises and assaults, isn't it?"

"I wish I could tell you what happened, but the victim hasn't been cooperative with us."

"Get on it, Alex. Bring her in. Find out what this is about."

It hadn't occurred to me while I pleaded with her in the drab hallway outside her basement sublet the night before that Tina Barr had any high-powered clout. I wanted to know who had gotten to Battaglia on her behalf—or on the part of her mysterious assailant, which worried me more.

"You know something about Ms. Barr that I should be aware of?" I asked.

He put his glasses back on and started to read a memo that was on the table. It was an easy way to ignore my question. Either Battaglia had been leaked a tidbit and was looking for me to give him more information, or something so sensitive was involved that he wasn't willing to disclose it.

I tried again. "Is it the victim you're interested in, Paul, or is it the perp?"

"As long as I'm the district attorney, Alexandra, I'll ask the questions," Battaglia said. "You get me the girl."

FIVE

Mike and I zigzagged our way through the hapless gaggle of criminals—some arguing with their public defenders, others waiting with family members or friends—who filled the fifteenth-floor corridor of the criminal courthouse.

"Somebody's got Battaglia wound up about Barr, or knows something about her attacker," I said.

"So when we finish here, I'll drive you to her apartment."

"I just called Mercer. He'll meet us there, too."

He pulled on the large brass handle of the door in the middle of the hallway, holding it back so that we both could enter Part 53 of the Supreme Court of New York County, Criminal Term.

Harlan Moffett was on the bench, his back to the courtroom, seemingly engrossed in the **New York Law Journal**. Mattie Prinzer, the first woman to head the OCME crime lab, was seated alone in the front row. Only the staff was present—no spectators—and a well-dressed man who appeared to be younger than I, sitting at the defense table, the one farther from the empty jury box.

The court clerk saw us enter and signaled to the reporter, then got the judge's attention. "We have the prosecutor, Your Honor. Shall we bring the prisoner in?"

Moffett spun in his chair and folded the newspaper. "Good to see you, Ms. Cooper. Detective, thanks for making yourself available on such short notice. Say hello to your adversary, here. What's your name again, son?"

"Eli Fine." He got to his feet and extended his hand to shake mine after I entered the well and dropped my files on the table.

"You have a chance to meet your client yet?" Moffett was in his seventies, close to mandatory retirement. His once-thick white hair had thinned and faded to a dull gray, but the garnet pinky ring he sported still sparkled as he twisted it while he talked.

"I spent a couple of hours with him at Rikers yesterday, after I flew in."

"Let's have Jamal Griggs," the judge said, motioning to the court officer in charge. "How long you been out of school, Eli?"

"Six years, sir."

"I've been a judge for more than thirty." Moffett had been around long enough to know most of the New York bar that practiced in this forum. The courthouse regulars were used to his schmoozing and put up with his clumsy attempts at humor in hopes he would rule in their favor. The judge didn't bother to clean up his act for strangers.

Fine was biting his lip. "Judge, would you mind if we—?"

The court reporter had worked with Moffett often enough to know to keep her fingers away from the keyboard until the judge signaled that he wanted to go on the record.

"Take off your sunglasses, Mr. Fine. That's what I mind. We're not in Malibu. You admitted in New York?"

"Yes, sir. I graduated from New York Law School. Took the bar both here and California."

"Long as we're legal, son."

The door to the holding pen opened and an officer led Jamal Griggs into the room. He smiled when he saw his lawyer, and waited for his hands to be uncuffed before taking the seat beside him.

Fine was whispering something to Griggs when Moffett interrupted him. "What brings you to town today?"

"Ms. Cooper and her team have been conducting an investigation, and—"

"We've got a habit here, son. We stand up

when we address the court," Moffett said, turning the motion papers over to read the name of Fine's law firm. "Stein, Schlurman, and Fine. Ever try a murder case, son?"

Eli Fine slowly rose to his feet. "Entertainment law, sir. It's our specialty."

"Entertainment lawyers? That's an oxymoron," Moffett said, resting his elbows on the bench and tapping his fingertips together. "Ms. Cooper's had—what is it, dear? Six, seven trials to verdict in front of me. You're not careful, she could take you to the cleaners. What's your motion?"

The young lawyer looked at the reporter. "Are we on the record?"

Moffett rapped the gavel to regain Fine's attention. "When **I** tell you we are. Give me a sense of what you want."

"As you know, Judge, my client is incarcerated for an armed robbery. Despite Ms. Cooper's best efforts to connect Jamal to the unsolved homicide of Kayesha Avon, his genetic profile did **not** match the evidence in the case," Fine said, reading from notes that I expected had been prepared for him by a defense attorney familiar with the language of a criminal law practitioner. "Now she's come before this court on an absurd fishing expedition, having applied for an out-of-state search warrant to get into the California database. I'm here to oppose that application."

"Come all this way to try to stop Ms. Cooper? I'm impressed, son." Moffett rubbed the hem of his sleeve over the garnet stone in his ring, admiring the polishing job when he finished. "Now, what's in that databank that's so damn important to the People of the State of New York?"

"Nothing worth invading the privacy of any citizens of California, sir. The attorney general has taken a strict position on protecting the integrity of the state's database."

"What are you after, Alexandra?"

I was on my feet, ready with my arguments. "We'd like to do a familial search, Your Honor."

Moffett cupped his hand to his ear. "A what?"

"A familial search, Judge. It's a new forensic technique, and we'd like to use it in this matter. The warrant requests the DNA profile of Jamal's brother, Wesley Griggs, which we believe is in the crime scene evidence database of California."

"Wesley's a convicted felon out there?"

"No," I said. That would make our task simpler. His profile would probably be in the FBI's CODIS files if that were the case. "We understand he was present at a drug-related shooting, and that genetic material of his was recovered and processed. He's not in the convicted offender files, but we have reason to believe he's in the evidence databank."

"Why go through all this red tape?" Moffett said. "You asked the AG nicely for it?"

"Yes, Your Honor. But Mr. Fine is right. California is among the toughest jurisdictions on kinship searches. They simply don't allow them at this point, although there is precedent in several other states. There haven't been many cases on point. I've submitted documents to you and have a copy for counsel," I said, passing a memo and stack of scientific treatises to the court officer to give to Eli Fine.

"So you want to make some law here, hon, is that it?" Moffett said, shuffling papers around on his blotter. "Eli, did you brief this for me?"

"No, sir. I figured you'd take oral argument."

"From the land of the hip-shooters, young man," Moffett said, swiveling in his chair and pointing to the elaborate portrait of Lady Justice, standing beneath the flag, with the words **E Pluribus Unum** at her feet. "You know how that translates, Mr. Griggs?"

Jamal leaned forward and squinted at the Latin inscription, then shook his head.

Harlan Moffett stood and adjusted the belt

on his trousers before wagging a finger at the defendant. "**E Pluribus Unum.** Always hire local counsel, Mr. Griggs."

"Judge, I really object to that kind of comment in front of my client," Fine said.

"Move for a change of venue if it suits you. You got some nice racetracks in California. I'd like to hold these proceedings somewhere near Santa Anita myself," Moffett said, taking his seat. He liked the ponies more than he enjoyed writing decisions, since he had an unusually high percentage of reversals by the Court of Appeals. "Maybe I'd better take some testimony."

He pointed at the reporter and made a few comments about the nature of the hearing, then asked me to call my witness. I signaled for Mattie to go out to the witness room to wait for her turn to testify, and I called Mike's name into the record.

Mike Chapman walked to the stand and placed his hand on the Bible that the court officer held out to him. I walked him through his education at Fordham College, where he majored in military history, through his years on the job and early successes that vaulted him to the prestigious homicide squad, and brought him to the current re-investigation of Kayesha Avon's death.

"Did you respond to the scene of the crime, Detective?"

"Yes, ma'am, I did."

"At what location?"

Mike stated the address. "On the rooftop of her apartment building, in the projects at Taft Houses in East Harlem."

I let him describe the heartbreaking sight of the college student's body, after she was abducted from the elevator in her own building on her way home from class.

"Were you present the following day, eight years ago, at Ms. Avon's autopsy?"

"Yes, I was."

"What findings were made by the pathologist?"

"There were six stab wounds in Kayesha's neck and chest, one of which pierced her heart."

"Was there any blood evidence found at the scene?"

"No. No, there was not."

"Any fingerprints?"

"None."

"Any seminal fluid?" I continued.

"Yes. There was semen in her vaginal vault, and also on her right thigh. She appeared to have been sexually assaulted before she was killed."

"Was a genetic profile developed by a forensic biologist at the Office of the Chief Medical Examiner?"

"Yes, ma'am."

"Can you tell us what efforts were made at that time to find a match to that DNA sample?"

"As Your Honor knows," Mike said, "back then, we were in the infancy of databanking. We ran the crime scene samples against the entries—many thousand fewer than there are today—and had the lab make comparisons to specific suspects we developed through the tip hotline."

"Was a match ever declared?" I asked.

"Nope. Not even close."

"What else did you do?"

"Every six months, I asked Dr. Prinzer at OCME to run the evidence against the convicted offender databank, which has been growing steadily, Judge. Kept going back, hoping to get lucky."

Mike had been haunted by the brutality of Kayesha Avon's death. He had refused to give up the investigation to the more recently formed cold-case squad, determined to find the young girl's killer himself, with the help of this revolutionary scientific technique.

"Was Jamal Griggs's DNA profile among the

samples submitted during the last seven and a half years, Detective?" I asked.

"No, ma'am."

"Is it correct that Jamal Griggs had a homicide conviction?"

"Yes, he did. But because he had been a juvenile offender at the time of the murder, his DNA was not included in the databank."

"Do you know the facts of that case?"

"Yeah. I do." Mike paused and stared directly at Griggs. "Jamal was fourteen years old. He had dropped out of school to sell drugs with his big brother, Wesley."

Eli Fine pushed his chair back but seemed uncertain about whether he should be objecting to this line of questioning.

"The girl he killed was sixteen," Mike went on. "Jamal stabbed her in the back when she made the mistake of accidentally busting up a drug sale by knocking on the wrong door."

"Did there come a time when you asked Dr. Prinzer for a comparison to be made to Mr. Griggs's DNA?"

Mike shifted in his seat and ran his fingers through his hair. "Yeah, about three months ago, just after his robbery conviction."

"Would you tell the court what result you were given?"

"Objection, Your Honor."

"On your feet, Mr. Fine," Moffett said. "That's the only way I can overrule you. What grounds?"

"Hearsay."

"You're not offering this for the truth of it, are you, Alex? Dr. Prinzer's going to testify, too, isn't she?" Moffett asked, without waiting for my answers. "Overruled. It's just a hearing, young man. You got no jury. Save your energy for cross-examination."

Fine sat down and scribbled furiously on his legal pad while Mike answered the question. "There was no hit, Ms. Cooper, but Dr. Prinzer told me she had a partial match."

I finished questioning Mike, establishing that every other means of identifying the perpetrator in Kayesha's homicide had been unsuccessful. Moffett needed to understand that a kinship search was our only alternative. Fine went nowhere with his brief cross-examination, and Mike stepped down from the stand.

"The People call Dr. Mathilde Prinzer," I said. She would take the scientific piece of the testimony forward.

It took more than fifteen minutes to list her credentials and establish her unique expertise in this still-evolving field of forensic science. If this case of first impression was to stand up to appellate scrutiny, I wanted the full effect of this brilliant scientist's body of work.

In addition to her daily routine with the five city prosecutors' offices and the NYPD, Mattie had been among the OCME heroes of 9/11, working doggedly with her colleagues to identify victims from thousands of tiny fragments of human tissue.

I ran her through a primer of DNA testing, more familiar to Moffett than to Fine, who had a puzzled look on his face throughout the entire direct.

"When you compare a suspect's DNA profile to a crime scene evidence sample, Doctor, what are the possible outcomes?"

"Traditionally, Ms. Cooper, we have had three results. A match can be declared if you have thirteen loci in common—that is, thirteen places on the chromosome at which the gene for a particular trait resides," Prinzer said, speaking slowly and looking at Fine as she spoke. "A suspect can also definitively be excluded if genetic differences are observed. The third option has been a finding of 'inconclusive' if we don't have enough information to make a positive determination."

"Has the scientific community recently accepted a fourth category?"

"Yes. We have begun to develop indirect genetic kinship analyses, using the DNA of biological relatives, in humanitarian mass disasters and for missing person identifications, situations in which we have only small samples of genetic material. We try to compare those to DNA from surviving relatives. In those instances, we're usually working with partial matches."

"Can you explain to the court the meaning of the term 'partial match'?"

Moffett moved his chair closer to Prinzer.

"Certainly. When we look at the thirteen loci needed to declare a match, there are two physical traits charted at every one of them. You see them as peaks on the Avon case lab report Ms. Cooper provided to you," she said, as Moffett and Fine tried to find the corresponding page. "These peaks—or alleles, as we call them—come in pairs, one from the mother and one from the father."

Moffett nodded as he listened.

"In a partial match, at each of the thirteen critical loci, the profiles being compared have at least one allele in common."

"You could see that on this paper?" the judge asked, bending over the bench and holding out his report to Mattie.

"Oh, yes, Your Honor." She held the report

and pointed to a pair of peaks. "Look right there. In our business, those graphics really stand out."

"And what do they tell you?" I asked.

"In the case of Kayesha Avon, we've got high-stringency matches to Jamal Griggs at eleven of the thirteen loci on his sample. So I know I'm **not** looking at the DNA of the person who contributed the crime scene sample, but in all likelihood I'm staring at the genetic profile of someone closely related to him. Probably Jamal's full sibling."

Probably Wesley the Weasel.

"Has the partial-match technique been used to solve any crimes, to your knowledge?"

"Familial searches have been used with great success in the United Kingdom and Wales," Prinzer said, citing the cases of child predator Jeffrey Gafoor, serial murderer Joseph Kappen, and James Lloyd, the notorious shoe fetish rapist of Rotherham. "In this country, in 2005, the process exonerated a North Carolina man who'd been incarcerated for eighteen years and identified the killer who'd left his DNA on cigarette butts at the crime scene."

"Does the FBI provide information on partial matches, Dr. Prinzer?"

"Not as of this time, Ms. Cooper. My colleagues and I are required to submit a request

for the release of the information sought, along
with the statistical analysis used to conclude
that there may be a potential familial relationship between the suspected perpetrator and the
offender."

"Have you prepared the statistical analysis in
the matter of Kayesha Avon?"

"Yes, I have. To begin with, Justice Department figures confirm that fifty-one percent of
prison inmates in this country have at least one
close relative who has also been incarcerated,"
she said. "And in this case, the donor of the
crime scene semen shares twenty of the twenty-
six alleles with Jamal Griggs."

"Can you tell us what that means, Dr.
Prinzer, with a reasonable degree of scientific
certainty?"

"Yes, I can. It means that we're looking for
Jamal's biological brother. For his full sibling—
same mother, same father. I believe that's whose
semen was in Kayesha Avon's vaginal vault."

I concluded my questioning and watched as
Eli Fine wrangled with Mattie Prinzer. Prosecutors and members of the criminal defense bar
took courses in DNA advances every six
months to keep current with the technology.
The Weasel must have thought his high-priced
mouthpiece could bluff his way through op-

posing the search warrant application, but Fine was in over his head.

Moffett watched Fine struggle for half an hour. Finally the judge stood up and twisted his ring as he began to talk. "Let me help you out here, son."

"Judge, I'm perfectly capable of—"

"Sit down, Mr. Fine. I've got some questions of my own."

Moffett waited until the young man took his seat next to Griggs. "So, Doc, the FBI releases only perfect matches, am I right?"

"Yes, you are."

"But in New York—you're satisfied these partial matches are useful?"

"We're one of the few states that generates them, along with Virginia and Florida. Many more allow law enforcement agencies from other jurisdictions to go into their databases if probable cause is established. We believe kinship searches have an enormous potential to solve crimes, to increase database hits by more than twenty percent all over the country."

"Let me ask you this, Doctor. You know how many brothers Jamal Griggs has?"

I tried to keep a poker face. Moffett was a sleeper, sometimes coming alive mid-trial to hit on the one question that either the assistant DA or defense counsel had overlooked. He'd just handed Fine a gift.

Mattie Prinzer turned her head to the judge. "I have absolutely no idea."

"Step down, Doctor. You know the answer to that, Alexandra?"

"No, sir."

"This Wesley character, is he the only one?"

"I don't believe so, Your Honor."

Moffett snapped his fingers at the court officer nearest the side door of the courtroom. "Get me Chapman."

In less than a minute, Mike walked back into the room.

"You're still under oath, Detective. Have you ever met Mama and Papa Griggs, Chapman?"

"Mrs. Griggs is dead, Your Honor. I have spent some time with Jamal's father, Tyrone."

"And how many little Griggses did they produce?"

"Six children, sir. They have six grown sons."

Eli Fine had one of the biggest shit-eating grins I had ever seen spread across his face.

"Where are they, Chapman, the other four?" Moffett was waving his arm in large circles, swinging the sleeve of his robe as he did.

"Tyrone Junior lives right here in Manhattan. The other three don't check in at home very often."

"How many of the Griggses' sons have rap sheets?"

"Two that I know of, sir," Mike said. "Just Jamal, and then Wesley took a few misdemeanor collars for drugs, before he moved his operation to the coast. None of those were designated for databank entry."

"Let me make it clear, Your Honor," I said. "We'd be more than pleased to take a swab from each one of Jamal's brothers. We happen to know where Wesley is, and we know he has a history of criminal behavior."

Harlan Moffett snapped his fingers again and pointed at the court reporter. "Take a break, Shirley."

The portly middle-aged woman clasped her hands over her stomach.

"You believe in this stuff, Chapman?" Moffett asked. "These familial searches?"

Mike smiled at the judge. "I do."

"You understand what she's talking about, with these peaks and alleles and locusts?" Moffett said, aiming his pinky ring at Mattie Prinzer.

"**Loci,** Your Honor. Soft **c.** Couldn't be easier," Mike said, grinning at Jamal Griggs. "It all comes down to a simple rule of law: Don't do the crime if your brother's doing time."

"Hear that, Jamal?" the judge asked before

turning to Eli Fine. "And your objection to Ms. Cooper's request?"

"Ms. Cooper's plan is a violation of the Fourth Amendment rights of every single citizen whose DNA is in the California database. It's an impermissible invasion of privacy, an unreasonable search and seizure."

Someone in Fine's office had prepped him to regurgitate the key legal buzzwords for his argument.

"Convicted felons give up lots of rights. Who's your client, here? Jamal Griggs or Wesley?"

"Ms. Cooper's made her application in the matter of Kayesha Avon. I'm opposing it on behalf of Jamal Griggs, who has been exonerated in this investigation. People who just happen to be related to criminals haven't given up their own privacy rights. It's genetic surveillance, Your Honor. It violates the Constitution."

"So you're protecting all the nuts and fruits in California, are you? And you, Alexandra?"

"Suppose Detective Chapman and I were working on a vehicular homicide case, a hit-and-run accident with an eyewitness who saw the whole thing. She tells us the make and model of the car and remembers the first three numbers of a six-digit tag. She gives us a partial plate."

"Yeah?"

"Would you expect Chapman to just shrug his shoulders and back off from the investigation, or would you expect him to go to the DMV and search it for all the plates—every single one in existence—that include the numbers he was given?"

"We're not talking about license plates, Your Honor," Fine said. "We're talking about human DNA. African Americans and Latinos make up a disproportionate amount of the database entries in every state, because of their representation in the criminal justice system. This—this wild-goose chase targets minorities and indigents."

"You're not disputing that the science works, then, are you?"

"I'm not conceding a thing. It's an outrage that Ms. Cooper thinks she can go through every name in the database."

"There are no names in there, Judge," I said. "The forensic biologists can't see any individual's name in a database—every entry has a numerical designation. If there is in fact a match between the samples, then the techs have to call the state's CODIS administrator to get the person's name. The identity protections are all in place."

Harlan Moffett stroked his chin again. "You

got any plans to invite Wesley home for Thanksgiving, Jamal? Make it easy for me?"

Jamal Griggs stared Moffett down.

"Tell you what, Mr. Fine. I'll take the matter under consideration. I'll have a decision on this by early next week."

"I assumed you'd rule on this from the bench, Your Honor. I've got to go back to California in the morning."

"The State's waited eight years to figure this out. So they'll wait a few more days. You will, too. Tell Wesley to behave himself this weekend."

Jamal Griggs cocked his head at his lawyer and slammed his open hand on the table.

"I told you, Mr. Griggs, **E Pluribus Unum.** Mr. Fine can't be here, I'll appoint one of the Baxter Street boys to represent you," Moffett said, referring to the court-appointed lawyers who hung out in street-front offices across from the Tombs. "Suit yourself, Mr. Fine. It's in your client's best interest—well, it might be—if you show up for him."

The Weasel was paying good money to keep our noses out of the California database, and Jamal was clearly not interested in disappointing him.

SIX

I left the courtroom with my two witnesses and went back to the office to drop off my papers, eat the sandwich that Laura had ordered in, and explain to her that Mike and I were going to pay a visit to Tina Barr.

There was no traffic on the northbound FDR Drive, so Mike had us on the Upper East Side in twenty minutes, shortly before two o'clock in the afternoon.

Mercer was waiting in an unmarked car almost directly across the street from Barr's brownstone, and Mike continued on until he found a place to park closer to the corner of Lexington Avenue.

"How long have you been here?" I asked when Mercer came up to talk.

"A little over an hour. Have you tried calling her today?"

"Couldn't get a number. She hasn't got a phone—listed or unlisted—and it's a sublet, so if there's a hard line in there, we need to know who the landlord is to get it."

"Reverse directory?"

"Nothing." More and more young people were using their cell phones and BlackBerrys in place of a traditional phone.

"Knock on the door, Coop," Mike said. "It worked for you last night."

Mercer walked me down the block to Barr's building. The vestibule door was locked, so I rang the buzzer next to her name several times, getting no response. Then I started pressing other doorbells until the man in 4E responded on the intercom by asking who was there.

"Police," Mercer said. "I'm trying to get in to speak with Tina Barr."

"Who?"

"The woman who lives in the basement."

The man didn't seem to care much about our visit. He buzzed us in and I followed Mercer down to the basement. I knocked but heard nothing from within.

"Ms. Barr? It's Alexandra Cooper. If you're there, I'd like to talk to you."

We waited a couple of minutes and then I asked Mercer for a scrap of paper from his memo pad. I wrote a note on it, with my cell phone number, and slipped it under the apartment door.

"Let's get comfortable, Alex. We have some time to kill."

The three of us went up to the corner together to buy coffee. "I'll sit at this end of the street," Mike said. "Better chance she'd be coming from Lex than Third, either by bus or subway. You and Mercer should be right in front of the building, so you can run interference before she gets inside."

It was a beautiful fall afternoon, crisp and clear, and we leaned against the hood of Mercer's car, talking about the events of the last month, catching up on Vickee and their young son, Logan.

"Now you see why stakeouts are so tedious," Mercer said, stretching his arms and straightening his back. "Give it another hour and then go on home. I'll call you when we see Tina."

"I can't take the chance she'll batten down the hatches again. Battaglia's ripped."

We took turns walking up and down the street just to stay alert. I checked with Laura for my messages and made calls on several of my cases. The air chilled a bit as the sun slipped behind the tall apartments that lined Central Park West, and I bought another round of coffee before settling in to the front seat of Mercer's car.

"What have you got?" Mercer said, flipping open his cell phone. He listened and then answered. "I see him coming."

It was after six o'clock when Tina Barr's neighbor, Billy Schultz, approached the building from Lexington Avenue. He jogged up the front steps, unlocked the door, and went in. Within the hour, an older couple got out of a taxicab and made their way inside, too. A minute later, a light went on in the third-floor window facing the street.

I heard the sirens before I saw the flashing strobes of the patrol cars that raced into the narrow one-way block from each direction, coming to a stop nose to nose with each other in front of Barr's building.

The passenger in each RMP dashed out of his car and bolted up the steps. Someone—it looked like Schultz's head framed in the narrow space—opened the door, and they disappeared inside.

Mercer was running across the street as I opened my car door, shouting at me. "Stay put!"

Mike raced downhill from the corner, then took the steps two at a time and pushed through the door that had been propped open by one of the cops. I could see the glimmer of the gold detective shield he had palmed.

A crowd began to collect around the front of the building—people on their way home, going out for dinner, heading for a run in the park, or walking dogs.

I tried to get past the driver of the patrol car who had stationed himself at the building's entrance, but he didn't know me and refused to let me in. I showed him my ID, but he wasn't interested in admitting me without orders from a higher-ranking officer.

"You trolling for bodies, Alex?" I turned at the sound of Ray Peterson's voice.

The lieutenant in charge of the homicide squad had pulled in behind one of the RMPs. He had been at too many crime scenes in his career to feel the need to rush, taking his time for a last drag on his cigarette before nodding at the uniformed cop.

"What do you know, Loo?" I was already feeling guilty about not having pushed Tina to talk to me, and now I was panicked at the thought that her attacker had returned. "Is it Tina Barr?"

"That your vic from last night?" Peterson said, patting my back. "We got a corpse, but she doesn't fit that 'scrip. Mike's in there now."

"Yes, we were waiting together for Barr to get home."

"What's he doing leaving you outside with the riffraff? C'mon in. I'm sure you've seen worse."

The officer stepped aside as Peterson guided me up the steps. The commotion was downstairs, and the door to Barr's apartment was open. Peterson led me in, through the little room where I had talked with the distraught woman. Tables and bookcases were overturned, as though the apartment had been ransacked.

Peterson continued down the narrow hallway. I glanced into the bedroom as we passed it, noting the disarray, including empty dresser drawers dumped on the floor.

"Chapman?" Peterson called out as he approached the kitchen.

"Come ahead. I'm out back, in the garden," Mike said. He must have seen me when he looked up to answer the lieutenant. "For Chrissakes, Loo, what'd you bring Coop in for? It looks like a slaughterhouse."

Mercer tried to intercept us before I saw the body, but he was too late. The dead woman was lying facedown, spread-eagled on the wide wooden planks of the kitchen floor, her head split open like a ripe melon. Blood spatter streaked the refrigerator and dotted the ceiling, and what hadn't spurted upward was pooled around her head.

I closed my eyes as Mercer pressed me against his chest. "The lady's too tall to be Barr."

"Who is she?" I asked.

"Don't know yet. Mike's talking to Billy Schultz."

No matter how many crime scenes, autopsies, or morgue visits came up in the course of my work, the individual horror of each circumstance never lost its impact. Peterson liked to tell his men it was time to hang up the job the moment that happened.

I looked again, taking deep breaths to calm myself. There would be a wait for the medical examiner on call, and for CSU to process the apartment and photograph the body. All necessary, but it seemed so cruel to leave her in that position, as a deadly exhibit for the trail of investigators who would be summoned to ferret out clues.

"When do you figure she died, Mercer?"

"It's not what you're thinking, Alex. It didn't happen on your watch. There's rigor, and she's been cooling down. Maybe late morning."

It didn't help to know the body had been there while we had been sitting outside, across the street, for close to five hours.

"Do you remember seeing anyone leave the building?"

"Not a soul," Mercer said. "You okay, Alex? Let's go. C'mon, now—you can't help the lady."

I wondered who the woman was and what connected her to Tina Barr. She looked seven or eight years older than I—in her midforties, perhaps—and almost as tall as my five foot ten. She was dressed in a well-tailored black wool suit, an expensive one, if I was not mistaken.

While one shoe was still in place, the other appeared to have come off as the blow to the back of the head knocked her to the floor.

"I'm coming," I said softly, putting my hands in my pants pocket so that Mike and Mercer, always trying to protect me from the atrocities of our chosen jobs, couldn't see them shaking.

Mike and the lieutenant were huddled in the small backyard behind Barr's apartment, talking with Billy Schultz. He was explaining to Peterson what he must have told Mike minutes ago.

"No, it's not usual for me, if that's where you're going. I'm not a peeper," Schultz said, sort of bobbing in place while he responded to questions. "I poured myself a drink when I got home, came to sit here for a while—won't be many more nights so mild I can do that."

There was a wooden staircase leading down from his first-floor apartment, and two folding beach chairs with a table between them. There was an empty tumbler and an iPod resting beside it.

"Ms. Barr's rear door was open?" Peterson asked.

"Not wide open. It was ajar, which was strange, considering there were no lights on in the kitchen. After what happened here the other night, I didn't want to take any chances."

I was standing behind Mike as he asked the questions. "Tell the lieutenant exactly what you did."

Schultz took a handkerchief out and blew his nose. "Sorry. I've never seen anything like this before. I—uh—I called out Tina's name. Two, maybe three times. When she didn't answer, I pushed the door in a bit more and said her name again. There was no answer, so I turned on the light—and, well, that's when I saw the body."

"Then?"

"I took a few steps in. I was—um—you guys do this every day, but I was pretty overwhelmed."

"Is that blood on your pant leg?" Peterson asked.

"I guess it is. I kneeled down. I wanted to be sure there was nothing I could do for her before I got on the phone."

I had seen that expression on the lieutenant's face before. **Like what the hell did you think you could do for the broad?** is what he wanted to say. But I understood how Schultz felt. I had wanted to touch her, too. I had wanted to cradle her broken head and body and get her off the kitchen floor to a more dignified resting place.

"Did you touch her?"

"Yeah. I tried to find a pulse."

"Make sure you swab him, Mike," Peterson said. "Get his clothes, too."

Schultz's eyes opened wide.

"It's routine, Billy," Mike said. "We need your DNA for elimination purposes. You put yourself in the crime scene. It was the right thing to do, but we just got to account for it, in case you left any trace of yourself there."

"Do you know who she is, Mike?" I asked.

"If you don't mind, try being the silent partner tonight, Coop. You're here by the grace of God and your good friend Mercer Wallace." He was probably rolling his eyes, too. "How long were you in the kitchen, Billy?"

"Less than three minutes," he said, taking his razor-thin cell phone out of his pocket. "I couldn't stay in there. I came back out and called 911. I mean right away."

Peterson lit another cigarette and inhaled, pocketing his lighter, then bent down to examine a large garden ornament that had toppled over on its side, resting next to Barr's back door. Light from within the kitchen reflected on the decorative brass object and its thick wrought-iron base.

That must have been the murder weapon. There was a dark stain covering a dented portion of the brass design, clumped with hair and probably brain tissue, too.

"But you knew who she was," Mike said.

"Minerva Hunt."

"You've met her before?"

"I've seen her in the building occasionally. She's Tina's landlady, if I'm not mistaken. Her name was on the buzzer before Tina moved in. I mean, I've never been introduced to her."

"Did you touch the handbag, Billy?"

"No way."

"How about the tote?"

Schultz hesitated a second too long before answering. "Maybe."

"Whaddaya mean, 'maybe'?" Peterson asked.

"Well, I saw the initials on it. M.H. I just turned it around—it was upside down—to make sure I was reading them right."

"You tell the 911 operator—?"

"That I thought it was Minerva Hunt? Yes, I did."

I took a few steps backward to the door and glanced toward the body. The shoulder strap of the python-skin bag still hung on the woman's shoulder, but the contents had been strewn on the floor. Next to her was a large vinyl tote, the maker's logo—now drenched in blood—gar-

ishly stamped all over it. The gold monogrammed initials of its owner—M.H.—were
hard to miss.

"Just a minute, Billy," Mike said, brushing
past me to walk into the kitchen. His cell
phone was ringing, and he answered it out of
the presence of his witness. "Hello?"

The caller spoke to him and he held up a finger to me. "DCPI."

The deputy commissioner of public information had gotten word of a murder on Manhattan's Upper East Side. Mike would have to
keep that office up to speed on every development, no matter how minor, because news-
hounds would be on the scene in minutes.

"Only a tentative so far. We haven't even
started to look for next of kin," Mike said. "No
driver's license. Nothing confirmed. Peterson's
got a couple of guys back at the office trying to
run it down."

I heard the front door of the apartment slam
shut and footsteps—it sounded like a woman
in spike heels—coming down the hallway. I was
hoping to see Tina Barr, thinking she might
shed some light on this.

"Give me a break, Guido, we just got here.
We're waiting for the ME now," Mike said.
"The broad was DOA, yeah. Don't go with it

yet, but it could be Hunt. Minerva Hunt, okay?"

The Chandleresque brunette—tall, lean, and tough looking—struck a pose in the doorway of the kitchen, dressed also in a well-tailored and probably expensive black suit. She looked through me as though I were invisible, tossed back her hair, and smiled at Mike.

"Now what kind of detective work is that?" she asked him. "Do I look dead to you?"

SEVEN

←————————————————————————————

Minerva Hunt was perched on the corner of
Mike Chapman's desk in the offices of the
Manhattan North Homicide Squad.

Mike seemed to be as interested in her affect
as he was in her appearance. I watched him
look her over again as she glanced around the
room. She was casually coiffed and carefully
made up to accent her dark eyes and full lips.

"Doesn't exactly have the makings of a physical plant for a think tank, does it?" Hunt said,
scanning the room.

The desks that were positioned back to back
with each other had been cheap when they were
purchased twenty years earlier. Computer equipment was usually outdated by the time it was installed. The drunken arrestee groaning on the
bench in the holding pen behind us, who had
beaten his mother-in-law to death just hours ago,
was a harsh reminder of the business at hand.

"Most of the time we get it done," Mike
said. "You feeling better?"

Two hours earlier, when Minerva Hunt first
saw the corpse on the kitchen floor, she had lost

her composure. But the emotional outburst was short-lived, and a frosty veneer had settled over her like a thin sheet of ice.

"Karla Vastasi?" Mike asked, making notes on the steno pad he carried in his jacket pocket.

"Karla with a **K**, Detective. Could I trouble you to ask the lieutenant for one of his cigarettes, Mr. Wallace? And don't tell me about the no smoking rules. I really need it."

"There's a chair for you here, Ms. Hunt," Mike said.

"I'm perfectly comfortable," she said, recrossing her shapely legs, which had caught the attention of the two older detectives working on the far side of the room.

"How long ago did you hire her?"

"She came to me during the winter. I'd say it's been eight or nine months."

"What did she do for you, exactly?"

"I told you, Mr. Chapman. Karla was my housekeeper. That's what we call them now, isn't it? I mean we don't say things like 'maid.' "

"Did she live with you?"

"No. She slept at my apartment occasionally when I traveled. Took care of the dog if I was called away."

"And where is your home?"

"Thanks, Detective," Hunt said to Mercer. She stood up and let him light her cigarette for her, holding her perfectly manicured hands around his. "I've got a town house on Seventy-fifth Street. Between Madison and Park."

"Where did Karla live?"

"Queens. Somewhere in Queens," Hunt said, sticking the edge of a brightly painted red fingernail between her two front teeth while she thought. "The agency will have an exact address for her. Matter of fact, I probably have some receipts from the car service I use. Sometimes I sent her home that way if it was late or she wasn't feeling well."

"Family? Do you know anything about Karla's relatives?"

"There's a sister here in the States. Connecticut, I think. The rest are back home."

"Where's home?" Mike asked.

"Which is the country where the women all have such perfect skin? You know . . . they all come here to be facialists?" Minerva asked, looking at me. "Romania, isn't it? Yes, she's Romanian. The employment agency has all that information."

"How old was she, do you know?"

"She told me she was forty-five."

I guessed Hunt to be a few years older than that.

"Did she have a husband, a boyfriend, a social life?"

"The ex is back in the old country. And no, no social life on my time."

"She's a good-looking woman," Mike said. "Never a guy hanging around?"

Hunt inhaled and flicked her ashes on the floor. "She asked to sleep at the house once or twice because the man she was dating got a bit too possessive, maybe a little rough. But I never went into that with her, and I think they broke up during the summer."

"Let me ask you, Ms. Hunt, did anyone ever get the two of you confused?"

She looked at Mike as though he had just punched her in the face. "Confused? The girl could barely form a proper sentence in English. She cleans house, makes the beds, washes the dishes."

"Physically, Ms. Hunt. Karla was about your height, had a nice figure, hair about the color of yours—"

"And she was the help, detective. I'm not sure who would have had trouble getting that clear. My friends? The dry cleaner? The butcher? I don't know if you meant that as a compliment to her or an insult to me."

"We've got to figure out if whoever killed Ms. Vastasi was looking for her," Mercer said, "or consider the possibility that she was mistaken for you. You own that apartment, don't you?"

"Yes, but I didn't spend any time there."

"You went tonight."

"Obviously. I think that's the second or third time I've set foot in it. And I sent Karla there this morning."

"Why?" Mercer asked.

The detectives were playing Hunt off against each other, Mercer distracting her from Mike's comment that she found so offensive.

"Because I got word that the tenant had moved out. It was rather abrupt, and I wanted to know what shape the apartment was in. I wanted it cleaned out."

Mike flashed me his best I-told-you-so look, then shook his head. Tina Barr was gone. I'd been puzzled by her connection to this tragic event from the moment I saw Karla's body, and now the urgency of Battaglia's directive to find Tina made sense.

"You lived there at one time, didn't you?" Mercer asked. Billy Schultz had told us Hunt's name used to be on the buzzer.

"Never."

"Someone using your name, before Tina Barr moved in?"

"Ridiculous. What reason would anyone have to do that?"

No point pushing her on that tonight. There would be neighbors and witnesses to confirm or deny what Schultz said.

"Ms. Hunt, Karla seemed a bit overdressed to be cleaning an apartment," I said.

She gave me a glance. "Remind me, young lady. Who are you?"

"Alex Cooper. From the district attorney's office."

"Well, then, you're working overtime. I'm so glad I voted for Paul Battaglia, darling. Four times already, or has it been five? 'Don't play politics with people's lives'—that's a good mantra for a prosecutor."

I was tempted to ask her whether she had spoken to Battaglia early this morning, but I knew better than to give her that advantage. I would call him as soon as we took a break.

"The clothes Karla was wearing—"

"They're mine, Ms. Cooper. Old clothes, of course. It's either the staff or the thrift shop. I hate to say I wouldn't have been caught—well, dead—in that outfit again this fall."

From Park to Fifth avenues, it was often hard to tell the matrons from the nannies, au pairs, and housekeepers strolling the sidewalks. The latter often sported last year's fashions, handed down at the end of the season. They carried home leftover food and goody-bag giveaways in the instantly recognizable shopping bags tossed out by their employers: the robin's-egg blue of Tiffany, the bright orange of Hermès, the pale lavender of Bergdorf Goodman, and the shiny black and white of Chanel.

"The tote with your initials on it?"

Hunt stood and crushed the cigarette with the ball of her black patent pump.

"I hate those logo bags, Ms. Cooper. One sees oneself coming and going. It was a gift, and I passed it on to Karla."

"It's a bit odd that she went to clean an apartment without taking some work clothes to change into," I said.

"How do you know she didn't?" Hunt snapped at me. "Maybe she put them down on her way in, somewhere else in the apartment. Maybe the thief took them."

"The police didn't find any clothes."

"We'll give the pad another look," Mike said. He wanted to be the good cop again. He would like the challenge that this arrogant woman presented, perhaps as much as he liked her looks. "The ME was wrapping up when we left to come back here. Taking Karla's body to the morgue. We'll go over the place more carefully in the morning."

"Listen, Detective Chapman," Hunt said, softening as she talked. "I'll try to get a number for her sister. If there's any issue about funeral expenses, I'll take the bill."

"Thanks for that. We'll be doing a lot of

work with you on this investigation, so you might as well get to know us. First thing is, call me Mike."

"Okay, Mike. You do the same."

"Fair enough. Just tell me what you like. Min? Minnie?"

"Minnie's a mouse, Detective. I'm Minerva."

"Minerva, the warrior goddess."

"Now that, Mike, is only a myth." Hunt crossed her arms, and one side of her mouth lifted into a smile. She was practically nose to nose with him. "Just a myth."

There was nothing about military history—from Roman mythology to real-life conflict—that Chapman didn't know.

"The warrior part?" he asked, and Hunt laughed.

"We've got to talk about getting you some coverage," Mercer said. "The lieutenant has someone standing by to take you home. And if you don't mind, we'd like to give you a guard for tomorrow."

The commissioner wouldn't allow the same mistake the department had made, refusing my request to provide protection for Tina Barr.

"I've got my own security. Thanks for the offer, but I don't need yours."

"Security?" Mike asked.

"The gentleman who dropped me off at the

apartment tonight and followed us here. Didn't you make the tail, Detective? You've surprised me again."

Mike chewed on the inside of his cheek.

"What's that about?" Mercer asked. "Why have you got protection?"

"I'm a Hunt. And if you were thinking tomato sauce and ketchup, you'd be wrong."

"I was thinking oil, actually," Mike said. "Something thicker than tomato sauce."

"Even better than that, Detective. Real estate. New York city real estate. My great-grandfather was a partner of John Jacob Astor's. Jasper Hunt was his name. We still own more of Manhattan than it's polite to talk about. Be careful where you walk, Detective. I wouldn't want you stepping on me."

"Well, what makes you Hunts so unpopular you need security 24/7?"

She looked at her watch as she answered. "We're not unpopular in most circles, Mike. But my father made a point of teaching me early on to protect my assets. All of them."

Mercer shook his head at me. He didn't like the direction Mike was going any more than I did.

Minerva Hunt's name was familiar to me from society columns and media coverage of philanthropic events. It made no sense that she, an heiress to a great family fortune, was micromanaging a basement apartment in Carnegie Hill.

"Going back a bit, Ms. Hunt. Perhaps I didn't understand what you meant, but you own the apartment in which Tina Barr was living?" I asked.

"Not that dank little apartment," she said, tsk-tsking at me without missing a beat. "We own the building, Ms. Cooper. The whole row of brownstones on that street."

Then why didn't Billy Schultz recognize her name when he saw it on the buzzer, as he claimed he had before Tina Barr moved in?

"And the tenants pay rent to——?" I asked.

"Not to me, Ms. Cooper. I don't go around collecting with a tin cup on the first of the month. There's a management company, of course."

"Of course," Mike said, taking Minerva's part, as though the questions I was asking made no sense. "What's that called?"

"Mad Hatter Realty."

"Alice in Wonderland?" Mike asked, laughing.

"Don't laugh. My grandfather, Jasper the Second, was mad. Eccentric is what the rich like to call it, but mad is what he was. My father named one of the companies for him."

"So you did have a special relationship with Tina Barr, then?" I asked. "It's not just a coincidence that she lived in your apartment."

"Tina worked for my father for a period of time."

"Doing what?"

"He's a collector, Ms. Cooper. Rare books. It's an inherited trait in the male line of Hunts," Minerva said, talking directly to me for the first time. I thought she was finally giving up her flippant attitude. But she went on. "For generations they've all seemed to love the same things—rare books, expensive wine, and cheap women."

"And Barr?"

"She was cataloging the collection. My father's an old man, Mike. He's close to ninety, and quite incapacitated now. Changed his will more often than I change my shoes. I just made sure she had a place to live while she was working for him."

"Did he fire her?"

"He's not in a condition to fire anyone. Tina quit—that's what Papa's secretary told me."

Minerva Hunt removed her BlackBerry from her pocketbook and dialed a number, pressing the digits with her long nails. Someone picked up on the first ring. "Carmine? Are you in front of the police station? I'll be down in a minute."

"Where did Barr go?"

"Why don't you check with our management office? Perhaps she left forwarding information."

Hunt was pulling on her short leather gloves—a fashion statement or a sign that she was through with us for the night, not protection against the mild weather.

"You have all my numbers," she said. "I expect we'll talk tomorrow."

"Were you looking for anything in particular in that basement apartment?" Mercer asked as she readied herself to leave. "Anything you sent Karla Vastasi to retrieve?"

Minerva Hunt backed up a step or two. "I thought I told you why she was there."

"Just cleaning up, I think you said. Nothing of value you might be interested in?" Mercer said, talking as he walked into Peterson's office, mimicking Hunt's motion with a pair of latex gloves that he put on as she talked.

"I assume Ms. Barr took whatever belonged to her. The apartment was sublet to her furnished. We keep a few of our properties available for help who need temporary lodging. I wanted to make certain that none of the belongings was disturbed. You'll allow me to do that later in the week, I'm sure."

Mercer emerged with an object in the palm of his large hand. It was a small book that appeared to be covered with precious jewels.

Minerva Hunt's eyes widened. Her calfskin-covered fingers reached out toward it.

"You know what this is?" he asked.

"It once belonged to my family," she said, glaring at him while she kept her arm outstretched, in expectation that he'd turn it over. "Where did you get it?"

"The ME found it after you and Alex left the kitchen. It was on the floor, under Karla's body, tucked inside the jacket of her suit."

I could see dark stains on the surface of the gems that must have been Karla Vastasi's blood.

"I want the book, Detective. Do you know how much it's worth?" There was nothing playful about Minerva Hunt's attitude.

"Your hand's going to atrophy hanging out there like that," Mercer said. "Right now, it's evidence in a murder case."

"What is it?" Mike asked.

"The Bay Psalm Book," Hunt said, looking at all of us with disdain for our obvious ignorance. "This was the first book printed in North America, in 1640. Open it carefully, Detective. It will have my grandfather's name inside. 'Ex Libris, Jasper Hunt Jr.' "

Mercer didn't move.

"There weren't a dozen copies that have survived over the centuries, gentlemen. Jasper's wife had one bound this way when their first son was born. My grandfather treasured it," she said. "Kept it by his bedside every night until shortly before he died. It's part of the Hunt Collection at the New York Public Library now."

Mike crossed his arms and whistled. "Guess I ought to renew my library card. Never saw anything close in my bookmobile."

"It hasn't been out of that building in almost forty years. Look at it, will you?"

Mercer placed his pinky on the lower corner of the book and gently lifted the cover.

Minerva Hunt stared at the bookplate and sneered.

EX LIBRIS TALBOT HUNT was written on the cream-colored label, decorated with a heraldic coat-of-arms poised above a globe.

"From the library of Talbot Hunt, my ass," Minerva said, shaking a finger at Mercer.

"Is Talbot related to you?"

"He's my brother, Mike. He's the kind of man who would kill for a book like this."

EIGHT

←

"You believe Carmine Rizzali's got a gig like that?" Mike asked. "His own PI firm, doing security details for the rich and famous. Driving Miss Minerva, maybe even stopping in for dessert. Twenty years on the job, the guy couldn't find a Jamaican on Jamaica Boulevard."

Mike, Mercer, and I had walked Minerva Hunt out of the squad building and turned her over to the ex-cop who guarded her. We drove down Second Avenue for a midnight supper at Primola, one of our favorite restaurants in the East Sixties, not far from my home.

Giuliano, the owner of the upscale eatery, bought us a round of drinks as we waited for Adolfo, the maître d', to take our order before the kitchen closed.

"Carmine looks like he's enjoying the ride as much as Ms. Hunt," Mercer said. "What did you get out of Battaglia, Alex?"

"Don't you remember, Mercer? I give, Battaglia gets. I called to tell him what happened, so he wants me in his office first thing in the morning."

"Was he surprised?"

"Seemed to be when I told him about the murder. Asked for all the details."

"Did he react when he heard Minerva Hunt's name?"

"Didn't skip a beat." I swirled the ice cubes around in the golden brown scotch before taking a long sip.

"Signorina," Adolfo said, "the chef will do anything you'd like."

"Just some soup."

Murder had never been known to have an impact on Mike Chapman's appetite. "Let me start with pasta. Rigatoni—then throw whatever's left in the kitchen on top of it. Chicken parmigiana after that. And back up my vodka before Fenton falls asleep," Mike said, pointing at the bartender. "Mercer?"

"Soup and a salad. That's it for me." He tasted his favorite red wine. "You think it's a coincidence that Karla Vastasi was dressed just like her boss?"

"It's possible," Mike said, gnawing on a breadstick.

"Minerva Hunt sucked you in completely," I said. "The way you were playing with her, I felt like a third wheel."

"Sometimes you are, Coop. I was just trying to keep her loose till we sort out the facts."

"Any looser and she'd have been on your lap. I'm with you, Mercer. The bit with the clothes is too much of a fluke to be unplanned."

"Karla was dressed for success," Mike said. "Just happened to be Minerva's hand-me-downs."

"The same exact shoes—flat grosgrain bow and brass hardware on the front. It's a classic style, and the ones Karla was wearing weren't even scuffed," I said. "That black suit isn't the least bit outdated. I'll bet it's exactly the same one that Minerva had on."

"So we need to find out whether she bought that monogrammed tote herself," Mercer said. "If it wasn't a gift like she claimed, I'm thinking Karla was the canary in the coal mine, sent there to see if it was safe before Minvera went in herself."

Mercer and I were on the same page. Maybe Hunt was supposed to meet someone in Tina Barr's apartment earlier in the day. Maybe there was a dangerous purpose to the rendezvous, and she had sent her unwitting servant inside to keep the appointment.

"Very hot plate, Alessandra," Adolfo said, setting the soup bowl in front of me.

"I suppose we'll find out if that little bejeweled book is very hot, too," Mike said. "Maybe it's stolen and someone was trying to scam

Minerva, tempt her to buy it back. I think I see a date with a librarian in my future."

"Battaglia will be our matchmaker for that," I said. There would be no overture to a major New York institution before he greased the wheels at the very highest levels. No point any of us going in through the back door when he could command the attention of the top dogs.

"Well, whoever committed the murder didn't exactly come to the scene armed. Someone can make a good case that it wasn't premeditated," Mike said. "Never seen a garden ornament as a murder weapon before."

"An armillary sphere."

"It wasn't a spear, Coop. Didn't you see it? Her head was cratered by that big brass-and-iron thing, weighs a ton."

"Sphere. I didn't say **spear.** Probably a Hunt antique," I said. "They were used centuries ago by astronomers, before telescopes."

Mike's cell phone vibrated on the table. He looked at the caller ID on the display and answered with a mouthful of pasta. "Excuse me, Mom. We're just having our supper. No, no, no. I can't talk about it now, 'cause I don't want you to have any bad dreams. I'll call you tomorrow. Yeah, I'll say hello for you. Just tell me the question, okay?"

His widowed mother lived in a small condo

in Bay Ridge, next door to one of his three sisters. Mike's father, Brian, had been a legend in the NYPD—honored for his bravery on countless occasions, and enormously proud that his only son had shown such academic promise. He retired from the department while Mike was at Fordham, but died of a massive coronary two days after handing in his gun and shield. No one who knew Brian and how much his son admired him was surprised when Mike enrolled in the academy the day he got his college diploma.

" 'Night, Ma. Talk to you tomorrow," Mike said, putting down the phone. "The Final Jeopardy category is 'Steel Wheels,' got it?"

"Now, when did you have time to set this up?" Mercer said, laughing.

"I called her when we were in front of Barr's house. I figured we might be outside there for hours. Didn't want to miss my chance to make a score off Blondie. Pony up the money."

Mike's fondness for trivia was the other habit that rarely took a back seat to homicide. He liked to bet on the last **Jeopardy!** question of the night and found a way to be in front of the television whether in the squad room, the morgue, or a neighborhood pub.

"I'm glad you showed a little respect for

Karla Vastasi tonight," I said, smiling at him. "I was touched by your restraint when we were in the kitchen, even though it was showtime."

"I like it when I please you, kid, but in all honesty, I didn't see a TV there, did you?"

"Twenty bucks for the winning question," Mercer said.

"I'm in," I said.

"Double or nothing."

"Well, damn, man. Seems to me you've heard the answer. And your enthusiasm suggests you've already got a good guess tucked away. So I'm holding at twenty," Mercer said.

"Picture your boyfriend Trebek reading the answer, Coop. 'Steel Wheels' it is. Fastest speed at which New York City subway trains are designed to run."

I held up my empty glass to signal to Fenton that I wanted a refill while I stalled. "What is . . . ?"

"It helps if you ride underground every now and then, even though you act like you're allergic to public transportation." Mike hummed the **Jeopardy!** music to time me out. "Hurry it up."

"What is forty-five miles an hour?" Mercer asked.

"Not a bad guess, Mr. Wallace, but not the

right one. Don't be thinking of that City Hall station, Coop. You got big curves like that and grade, the steel wheels go much slower."

"Thanks for the reminder. An afternoon with you two on that platform was enough to keep me in taxis for a lifetime. I'm going with thirty-five."

"And once again, you would be wrong, ma'am. What is fifty-five miles per hour, folks? I'll trust you to pay up after we eat. It's a speed rarely reached because it requires long, uninterrupted acceleration, but that's what they're made to do. My pop used to ride me up front on the trains when I was a kid. Loved all that stuff. No subways in the suburbs, kid. That's one of your problems."

My privileged upbringing in Westchester County, along with my education at Wellesley College and the University of Virginia School of Law, had been made possible by the loving encouragement of my mother and father, Maude and Benjamin Cooper. In addition to her long legs and green eyes, I'd inherited a fraction of the extraordinary compassion Maude exhibited as a nurse. My father and his partner's great contribution to cardiac surgery—a small plastic invention called the Cooper-Hoffman valve—had endowed me with more tangible assets. Despite the enormous differences in our backgrounds, I had never made better friends than Mike Chapman and Mercer Wallace.

"Fortunately," I said, "it's way too late tonight to ask what you think my other problems are."

I pushed the soup bowl away and concentrated on my scotch. The image of Karla Vastasi's crushed head would be with me all through the night.

"There'll be no more picking on you for now," Mercer said. "Soon as Mike finishes his dinner, I'll drop you at home."

My feelings about Mike had grown more complicated over time. His teasing and humor got me through the worst situations imaginable—some devastatingly traumatic to witness, like the one this evening, and others actually life-threatening moments in which he and I had faced off against deranged killers. Occasionally I questioned whether my concern for maintaining our productive professional relationship stopped me from exploring the attraction I felt for him.

"I've got the autopsy in the morning," Mike said. It was part of his duties to attend the medical examiner's procedure. "You'll call me when you finish up with Battaglia?"

"Will do," I said, getting up from the table.

"I hope they've got good insurance at the morgue," Mike said, taking a last slug of his drink. "Between that murder weapon and the little psalm book, there's enough burglary bait there to tempt the dead."

NINE

I was surprised to hear voices when I approached the door to Battaglia's suite. I had assumed that I would beat him to his office, even though he told me to be there at eight a.m. Rose Malone wasn't at her desk yet, so I turned the corner to present myself.

The district attorney stopped midsentence, a cigar gripped between the knuckles of two fingers. "C'mon in, Alexandra. Figure out how to get that damn coffeepot working and then we'll get started. Jill, I'd like you to meet Alex Cooper."

"Hello, Alex. I'm Jill Gibson."

I walked behind the conference table at which the pair were seated, measured the coffee, and started the machine, reminded of how much Rose had spoiled Battaglia.

"Good to meet you," Jill said.

The tabloids were spread out in front of Battaglia. I had picked up copies on my way downtown and seen that the item about Karla Vastasi's murder was buried in a single paragraph near the end of the news section. The difference in status between the housekeeper and the heiress had put this story on the back burner and given us breathing room to work on the case without a media frenzy.

"Jill's an old friend, Alex. Came here two years ago from Yale, where she ran the Beinecke Rare Books Library," he said. "She's the deputy chief executive at our NYPL now—the number three job—and the first woman in that position."

"That's impressive."

There was a quiet elegance about Jill Gibson. She was probably in her mid-fifties, with frosted hair and an easy smile.

"I want you to describe what happened last night," Battaglia said, planting the unlit cigar in his mouth. "It's okay, Alex. I've already told Jill the little I know."

The DA had caught my momentary hesitation. It was unlike him to debrief me about a pending case in the presence of an outsider. It was clear that Jill Gibson had his confidence and might even be the person who alerted him to the situation earlier in the week about Tina Barr.

I described the events from the time Mercer, Mike, and I had arrived uptown to wait for Barr to get home. Battaglia double-tasked, making notes in the margin of a wiretap application that one of my colleagues from the Frauds Bureau had submitted for his signature. He didn't look up until I mentioned Minerva Hunt's name.

Then he asked Jill, "Do you know Minerva?"

"No, I don't. I've seen her around from time to time, but we've never been introduced."

"She's not involved with the library?"

"Not in any major way. Her father's still on the board, and she's called in occasionally on matters that concern him. He was chair at one time, as you probably know. Jasper Hunt the Third. A hugely powerful force there for quite a while, in the 1980s and '90s. And Tally, her brother, is also on the board. From what I understand, Minerva has other interests."

The super rich have plenty of avenues for charitable giving, whether for causes about which they are passionate or for structuring the tax benefits of their estates. Art, ancient or avant-garde; dance, classical or modern; museums, paintings or extinct animals, cultures or ethnic heritage; and poverty, local or global, are among the competing enterprises that attract major donors.

"I think she's disease," Battaglia said, pointing at the coffeepot. "Used to be ballet, but I'm pretty sure Minerva Hunt is running the capital campaign for one of the hospitals."

Naming opportunities at medical centers for pavilions and wings and research facilities were fast becoming ways for baby boomers to insure a jump to the head of the line when a family member needed a heart transplant or an experimental drug for an aggressive illness.

"Ms. Hunt told me her father was very ill," I said. "Do you know what's wrong?"

"He's a recluse," Gibson said. "Old and frail. That's what I've been told."

"I haven't seen Jasper Hunt out and about for the better part of two years now," Battaglia said, putting down the sheaf of papers. "Go back to the murder scene. Tell me exactly what went on. How did Minerva react when she arrived?"

I took Battaglia through the details of the entire evening, including the way Karla Vastasi and Minerva Hunt were dressed. I described the conversation at the squad with Mike and Mercer as I got up to pour coffee for the three of us.

There was only one thing I left out of the conversation. I didn't mention the Bay Psalm Book. I didn't know Jill Gibson or the reason the district attorney trusted her enough to include her in this meeting. The little jeweled treasure was a crucial piece of evidence, and I needed to figure out its connection to the institution where Gibson worked before I leaked its existence.

"Does Chapman have a hunch?" Mike had made arrests in some of the most high-profile murder cases in Manhattan, and Battaglia respected his unerring street sense.

"Nothing he was ready to let me in on, Paul. There was some discussion with Minerva about things that might have been in the apartment. I know Mike vouchered some property to be analyzed at the lab. At least one book, I'm pretty sure."

Jill Gibson seemed more interested in that fact than did Battaglia.

"But no sign of the young woman who lived there?" he asked.

"Nothing. She's a librarian, Jill. Her name is Tina Barr. I thought perhaps you might know her," I said.

"No, I'm afraid I don't," she said, seemingly uninterested in the missing girl. "What kind of books did the detectives find?"

This was a no-win situation for me. If I withheld information that Battaglia wanted Jill Gibson to know, he would be furious with me. But if I disclosed something that was not going to be made public at this point in time, who knew what Gibson would do with the information?

"Is there an actual Hunt collection at the library?" I asked. "I heard Mike say it had something to do with that."

Jill Gibson pulled her chair up to the table. "Their family helped establish the library, Alex, more than a century ago. The collection they've amassed is enormously valuable. We make it a practice not to do anything to disturb the Hunts," she said, making her point to Battaglia.

"Well, I'm certainly going to have to meet with each of them," I said.

"We'll talk about that after Jill leaves, Alex. She and I have had a couple of meetings in the last two weeks about some problems they've been experiencing at the library. It may be that this case isn't an isolated event."

Now Battaglia had my complete attention. "What kind of problems?"

"Do you know the library?" Jill asked.

"I think it's the most magnificent building in New York City," I said, refilling our mugs. The Carrère and Hastings Beaux Art masterpiece, with its massive triple-arched portico, dominated Fifth Avenue at the corner of Forty-second Street.

"You've spent time there?"

"I majored in English literature when I was at college. I was fortunate enough to be admitted for a month between semesters to do research for my senior thesis."

"You might want to know why the Hunts are so important to us, Alex. Why we try to tiptoe around them, keep them out of the headlines," Jill Gibson said. "I'd also be happy to give you private access to their collection. It's got some extraordinary pieces."

"I'd appreciate that."

"New York City came late to the idea of establishing a great library," Jill said. "The French had the Bibliothèque nationale and in London the fabulous domed Reading Room was built at the British Museum.

"These institutions were symbols of civilized societies and cultures, founded in ancient seats of national government, with documents and books descended from kings and noblemen over the centuries. Americans, on the other hand, were struggling to emerge from the shadows of colonialism, with no comparable government funding for these purposes. By the 1890s, our domestic rivals for intellectual prestige—Boston and Chicago—had already built central libraries, and in Washington, the Library of Congress moved out of its home in the Capitol to the first of its own buildings."

"We had no libraries here before that time?" Battaglia asked.

"There are two very different kinds of facilities, Paul. One is what's called a circulating system."

"Elevate the masses by giving the people books," I said, recalling my nineteenth-century history. "Advancement through self-improvement. Weren't they usually the work of well-to-do ladies in their communities, making sure that poor little girls had wholesome stories to read?"

"Exactly. They're what led to the branch libraries, here and all over the country. The other type is the well-endowed reference library. That's how the NYPL developed—as a research facility, in which the books are never allowed to leave the building. We were a gift to the city from some of the richest men in America."

"Who founded it?" I asked.

"It began with private collections. The largest was put together by the first American millionaire, John Jacob Astor," Jill said.

"Jasper Hunt's business partner."

"In some ventures, Alex, that's correct. Astor loved literature and had many literary friends. In fact, Washington Irving was the first president of the Astor Library. By the 1890s, the collection John Jacob had bequeathed to his younger son, William Blackhouse Astor, had more than a quarter of a million books."

"Where could they possibly have been housed?" Battaglia asked.

"Lafayette Street, Paul. That wonderful red-brick brownstone where the Public Theater is today. That was the Astor Library," Jill said. "And the city's other devoted bibliophile was James Lenox, who was also a real estate mogul and a merchant. He built himself a palatial marble library on the Upper East Side—today it's the Frick. From Lenox we got the first Gutenberg Bible brought to America, the original autographed manuscript of George Washington's Farewell Address, and the most complete first editions of Bunyan and Milton."

Jill Gibson was animated now, her eyes sparkling as she expressed her obvious joy for these treasures.

"What brought the Astors and Lenoxes together?" I asked.

"Samuel Tilden, actually, at the end of his life. A bachelor with an immense fortune that he wanted to leave for the public good."

"Nothing like a politician," Battaglia said. "Tilden lost the presidential election to Rutherford Hayes, but he was one of the finest governors of this state."

"Tilden was also a leader of the civic movement bemoaning New York's lack of a great free public library and reading room. He formed a trust to establish one as his legacy to the city, consolidating the unique private collections already in existence and infusing them with fresh funding. The Tilden Trust and Astor and Lenox libraries joined in 1895 to form this new cultural entity—the New York Public Library."

"Public?" Battaglia asked.

Jill Gibson smiled. "Open to the public, but a private, nonprofit corporation governed by a self-perpetuating board of trustees."

"Tight-lipped and tough-minded, that group is."

"Exactly, Paul. The power rests entirely in that board, to this day."

"And the building itself?" I asked.

"The board asked the city to supply a site and maintain the building and grounds—the beginning of this public-private partnership. The city chose Reservoir Square—the huge, gloomy, and obsolete home of the Croton Reservoir, a central crossroads of Manhattan at the time, between Fifth Avenue and Bryant Park."

"Of course. The reservoir was demolished in order to create the library," I said, remembering the process that led to the construction of the vast underground system of tunnels to bring water to the city so long ago.

"You can still see the foundation of the reservoir in our basement," Gibson said. "Sixteen years after the trust was set up—in 1911—at the cost of nine million dollars, close to two hundred million in today's terms, the building was hailed as the greatest modern temple of education."

"What about the Hunts?" I asked. "Was their collection part of the original gift?"

"Jasper Hunt the Second wasn't so quick to get on board. He was skeptical about relinquishing his father's precious books—and those he'd continued to acquire. That reluctance kept the original trustees from inviting him to join the board."

"Who were they?" Battaglia asked.

"Best described, Paul, as twenty-one rich white men past their prime. Social status, gender, and economic standing were intentionally homogeneous, to encourage a harmony of action and purpose," Gibson said. "Schuylers and Cadwaladers, Bigelows and Butlers. Jasper Hunt had the money, but not the class."

"Was it his eccentricity?" I asked.

Jill Gibson laughed. "The library papers suggest that eccentricity was part of his charm. To this group of trustees the Hunts were practically outlaws."

"Even with the Astor business connection?"

"Jasper Hunt the First started life shoeing horses for John Jacob Astor. You know the Astor quote about real estate?"

"No, I don't."

" 'If I could live all over again, I would buy every square inch of Manhattan,' " Jill said. "And Astor came pretty close to doing just that. He took a liking to young Hunt. Brought him into the real estate company before Hunt was twenty years old, funded his first acquisitions, and introduced him to extravagances like the rare books that gave Astor such pleasure. Hunt was smart enough to follow in his master's footsteps."

"Sounds brilliant for a kid who started by shoeing horses," I said.

"Then Astor withdrew from the fur trade and most of his other ventures to concentrate on purchasing land in Manhattan, investing all the proceeds in pushing north of the city limits. His genius was in never selling anything he bought, insisting that others could pay rent to use the properties. Jasper Hunt went along with him, but the younger man's greed tempted him to go a bit too far."

"In what way?" Battaglia asked.

Gibson sat back in her chair. "John Jacob Astor's fur business took him all over the Pacific Northwest, and then to China, where he and his partners traded skins, as well as teas and exotic woods. Then he began to purchase tons of Turkish opium, shipping the contraband to China to smuggle into this country."

"I didn't know Astor dealt in opium," I said.

"Wisely, on his part, he didn't do it for very long. But there was such a fortune to be made that Jasper Hunt couldn't bring himself to cut those ties, as Astor had. Even Junior kept his hand in smuggling for a time."

"And the book collection?" I asked.

"The New York Public Library was a stunning success from the moment its doors opened. People like the Hunts who'd been uncertain about participating began to change their minds."

"Want to top off my coffee, Alex? It's cold," Battaglia said.

I got up and waved a hand at Gibson, who'd raised her eyebrows at the command. "It's not personal. He'd make any of the guys on the legal staff do the same thing."

"You're good at this, Jill," Battaglia said. "You probably know the first book a reader asked for opening day."

"A young émigré came in to request a

Russian-language study of Tolstoy. Not what anyone expected, but a sign of the changing culture of the community. This library is really the soul of the city," Gibson said. "I just love it there."

"I take it that Jasper Hunt Jr. rose to the occasion," I said.

"Two things happened. Within a decade, the library had risen to the front ranks of research institutions, here and abroad. The collections grew in size to more than a million volumes.

"Then, in 1917, the steel magnate Andrew Carnegie retired to embark on a massive philanthropic distribution—his 'gospel of wealth.' He wanted to give his money away in his lifetime, saw libraries as the best gift to any community, and in 1917 promised to build sixty-five branch libraries in New York, provided that the city would maintain them. Can you imagine?" Gibson asked. "Carnegie's plan established more than twenty-five hundred libraries in the English-speaking world."

"So then Junior kicked in," Battaglia said.

"Yes, he did. With his father's rare book collection as well as his own, which he continued to add to for the rest of his life. They've got good genes for longevity, those Hunts," Jill said. "Junior died in 1958, well into his eighties. He hoped that his possessions would buy him a place on the board along the way. But that never happened."

"Jasper the Third finally made it," Battaglia said. "The old boy is still kicking around."

"The family had divested themselves of the smuggling operation, contributed a few million dollars to the library, and become model citizens by the 1920s," Jill said.

"And Tally?" Battaglia asked. "Do he and his father get along?"

"In the boardroom," Jill said, "everyone's on his best behavior. The real intrigue doesn't happen inside the library walls."

I couldn't take my eyes off the small color photograph on a document to the right of Battaglia's hand as I refilled his mug. It was a copy of an employee identification tag from the New York Public Library, dated earlier in the year. The woman who'd posed for the camera to get her security clearance was the elusive Tina Barr.

TEN

"I'm going to step out and let you finish your business with Jill," I said. "Why don't you call me when she's gone, Paul?"

I was reeling from seeing Barr's face on a library document just moments after Gibson told me she didn't know the girl.

"What's the matter? You see a ghost?" Battaglia asked.

"Yes, I did. The one I've been trying to channel since you told me to find her."

I was angry about being a pawn in the middle of their deal. Jill Gibson had lied to me, and the district attorney let her do it.

Jill leaned over and tapped her finger on the table. "You've tipped your hand, Paul. It's the photograph."

Battaglia wasn't rattled. He had a reason for playing this the way he had chosen, and irking me was of no consequence to him.

"Sit down, Alexandra. Pouting doesn't become you." He waved at me with the lighter that he held to the tip of the cigar. "Jill's in the middle of some professional difficulties and I'd just agreed to open an investigation when the Barr girl got herself tied up the other night."

"Got herself what? Not exactly the way I'd describe that attack, Paul. What do you know that I don't? I understand how sensitive the issues are at an institution like the library."

"We've spent so many decades dealing with the renovation and modernization of the building itself, Alex, that we've dropped the ball on most of the other problems," Jill said. "They've festered and grown."

"Tell her why you were brought in," Battaglia said, puffing on the cigar that was plugged into the middle of his mouth.

"I spent the first twenty years of my career at the NYPL, so I know the collections—and the characters—quite well. In the century since we opened, there was never any relationship between the research library—this central building—and the branches. I'm heading the long-overdue consolidation of the two divisions. There are now ninety-three branches, so that's a big enough undertaking of its own. But at the same time I've walked into a firestorm."

"Why?" I took my seat across from Jill Gibson.

"There are personal issues involving some of our trustees that have spilled into the boardroom. Battles over family fortunes have us in and out of court. A century ago, Samuel Tilden's nieces and nephews fought tooth and nail to break his testamentary trust so that the library would never be created, from the first day of probate. Brooke Astor's estate wasn't the first to be dragged through a court of law—by her own son, no less—and it won't be the last."

"That can't be unusual for museums or any other institutional beneficiaries, can it?"

"Certainly not. But we aren't a museum, Alex. That's one of the things that makes our situation unique."

"What do you mean?"

"Very often, when trustees or benefactors of the library die, we inherit not only their manuscripts and books. We get other works of art, too. But we're a library and a research institute. We can't care for great art, nor can we curate it. Most of the time, we can't even hang it on our walls. And yet, if we violate the wishes of the dearly departed, we're likely to lose everything else bequeathed to us."

"So there's been trouble in-house because you've been selling art that the library owns?"

Jill looked to Battaglia before she answered.

"That's part of it. I think it's what Paul refers to as our lack of transparency. One of the committees made the decision to deaccession a major painting a few years ago that had been left to us by one of our most famous donors, and after the full board learned about the transaction, some of the trustees really thought it was grounds for murder."

"Tell me more about it."

"Forget it, Alex," Battaglia said, drawing back his lips around the cigar. "I've got someone on that."

"From the U.S. Attorney's Office?" I asked. The feds had jurisdiction over matters involving culturally significant works of art, but it was unusual for Battaglia to want to share a major investigation with them.

"Nobody mentioned the feds, did they?"

"Who did you assign to it, Paul? I'll work with him," I said. "We'll make it a joint investigation. Whatever has been going on might have something to do with Barr's assault, or the murder of Karla Vastasi."

"Someone's been stealing from the library, Alex," Jill said. "That's the reason I called Paul for help. Whoever it is—or they are—has got to be stopped. We've got treasures under our roof worth millions of dollars, some of them not even cataloged, and we're starting to bleed from the losses."

Now I felt guilty for holding back the information about the jeweled book that had been found under Vastasi's body.

"What do you know about the Bay Psalm Book?" I asked.

Battaglia's eyes narrowed as he listened to Jill's answer. "It's a very rare piece of Americana. Interestingly enough, the Puritans considered Hebrew to be the 'mother' of spiritual languages and used it in many of their services. The book is a makeshift translation of David's Psalms from the original Hebrew into English, printed in Massachusetts when the first presses were set up. It's one of the most important items that came to the library with the Lenox collection."

Now Battaglia shifted his gaze to me. "I guess your memory's improving, Alex. Is that the book the cops found last night?"

"Can't be the same. The one they vouchered came from the Hunt collection, not from Lenox. Minerva was quite emphatic about its history."

Jill Gibson's elbows were on the table and she rested her head in her hands. "The police have it? Is it covered with precious stones?" she asked without looking up.

"Yes."

"That will be another blow to Leland Porter," Jill said, referring to the library's president. "I don't think anyone's aware that the Hunt piece had gone missing."

"Stolen or deaccessioned?" Battaglia asked. "We've got to know that before we go looking for bad guys. You'll check on that, Jill. Does it literally have jewels on the binding?"

"Yes, it does. Jasper Hunt took a perfectly interesting piece of history—not important literature—and turned it into a garish little objet d'art, a personal vanity. It's been locked away in a library vault for as long as I can remember," Jill said. "The only one we display—the one that scholars work with—is the Lenox version of the Bay Psalm Book. Thank you, Alex, for letting me know about this."

I couldn't tell whether my revelation would come back to bite me or not.

"Do you know where Tina Barr is?" I asked Gibson.

"No, I don't."

"But you know her, don't you?"

Jill grimaced as she looked to Battaglia again. "I'm sorry I lied to you before. I, uh—I wasn't sure Paul wanted me to tell you the story. Yes, she used to work in our library. She trained there as a conservator."

"What exactly do conservators do?" I asked.

"It's a field that requires great skill. They're responsible for the preservation of all our rare documents and books. They've got to be knowledgeable about the history of the materials, and have enough scientific education to understand the structural stability and characteristics of whatever they're working on. Tina's young, but she's one of the best."

"When did she stop working at the library?"

"She was full-time with us until a year ago. Then she started working with Jasper Hunt," Jill said. "But that isn't unusual. All the private collections of that quality have conservators, and because we have our own lab, many of them—like Tina—do their work right in our facility."

"So it wasn't a problem that she went to work for Hunt?"

"Of course not. We viewed it as an advantage for Tina to catalog everything in his home. We expect to get the rest of his collection some day. It's been promised to us."

"Unless one of his children convinces him to change his will," Battaglia said.

"But Tina's no longer working for Mr. Hunt," I said. "That's what Minerva told us."

"I didn't know anything about her current situation," Jill said. I thought her voice was beginning to tremble. "I had no reason to, until she called me this week."

"When did she call?" I asked, looking at Battaglia out of the corner of my eye.

"It was very early yesterday morning, the day

after she was attacked. She awakened me, in fact, on Wednesday."

No wonder Battaglia had known about Barr's assault when he called me into his office a couple of hours later.

"What did she say? What did she tell you?"

"That she was terrified," Jill said. "She told me she was going to take some time off, leave the city for a while. I guess Tina thought of me as an ally, from the old days when she was first hired at the library. She wanted to know if I would help her get her job back when she returned."

"Did you agree?"

"Certainly. I told her to come in to see me that very day. I wanted to make sure she was all right. I even mentioned that I knew the district attorney and perhaps he could help with her case. I had no idea that you had been called out on the matter during the night."

"And did she come in?"

"Tina said she'd be there yesterday," Jill said, lowering her voice, "but she never showed up. Then Paul called me late last night to tell me about the woman who was murdered in Tina's apartment. To ask if I knew her."

"Did you?"

"No, no, no. Absolutely not."

"I'm going to ask you again," I said, trying

to make eye contact. "Do you know where Tina is now?"

Jill pursed her lips and shook her head.

"Do you know whether she had taken another job? Was she working for someone else?"

This time Jill nodded, just as someone knocked on the door.

"Come in," Battaglia said.

I turned my head to see Patrick McKinney, the head of the trial division, striding toward the table. He was senior to me, and although I reported directly to Battaglia on sex crimes, McKinney had oversight for all homicides and other felonies. The district attorney respected his investigative abilities, but McKinney was rigid, humorless, and small-minded, and made it his regular business to stab me in the back whenever an opportunity presented itself.

"Morning, boss. Sorry I'm late. Good morning, Jill," McKinney said, shaking hands with her. Battaglia must have put him in charge of the library issues that Jill had brought to him. "Alex, I wish you had called me last night. I just spent fifteen minutes getting up to speed with the chief of d's. He had to fill me in on the Vastasi murder himself. You talking about Tina Barr?"

"I was just explaining to Alex that she had

recently left Jasper Hunt to start working for another one of our patrons," Jill said.

"Who is he?" I asked.

"His name is Alger Herrick. She was quite happy," Jill said. "It was actually a much better fit for her than Jasper Hunt."

"Why is that?"

"Herrick is also a collector, with a special interest in cartography."

Battaglia's lips drew back again. "Maps."

"Most conservators have a specialty, Alex. The work has increasingly become so technical that they usually develop an expertise in one area. For Tina, it's been rare maps," Jill said. "And Alger is much younger than Jasper Hunt. He's in his mid-fifties—a very vibrant personality."

"You've talked to him about Tina?" I asked, glancing from Jill Gibson to Pat McKinney.

"He's as puzzled by her disappearance as the rest of us," Jill said.

McKinney seated himself next to Battaglia. "I'm on it, Alex."

"Did Tina tell you why she was terrified?" I asked.

"Well, given what had happened to her the night before, there wasn't much reason to ask," Jill said. "The attack made her even more anxious to get out of the apartment, too. Minerva Hunt was furious with her."

"Did she tell you why?"

"Minerva hates Alger Herrick. They've crossed swords in some business deals, is all I know," Jill said. "Tina couldn't move out fast enough once Minerva knew she was working with Alger."

"It's crazy to double-team this, boss," McKinney said to Battaglia. "Karla Vastasi's death wasn't a sex crime. Alex and I can sort this all out ourselves."

I could almost feel the point of his elbow digging into my side from across the wide oak table. "I'd like to find Tina Barr before anyone causes her more distress, Pat. The woman is still my victim."

"Tina Barr isn't anyone's victim, Alex. She's a thief," Pat McKinney said. "Don't wrap your bleeding heart around her. She's a forger—and a common thief."

ELEVEN

"I disagree with Battaglia," Mike said.

It was two-thirty on Thursday afternoon, and he was eating his second hot dog, leaning against the blue brick wall of the building that housed the morgue on First Avenue at Thirtieth Street.

"I was hoping you would."

"Not about taking you off the murder case. About how you look when you pout."

"Maybe you'll ask the lieutenant to go to bat for me. Keep me on the team."

"You should get your feelings hurt more often, Coop. Kind of cute. You look almost vulnerable."

"All these years together and I thought you liked edgy and cool. You want to see vulnerable, watch McKinney try to undermine me."

"Nah, that's when you go all pit bull on me. Did Battaglia set ground rules?"

"For the time being, I can work with you and Mercer on Tina Barr. I guess setting up this interview with Alger Herrick, the man she's been working for lately, is my consolation prize.

Pat's sitting on the larger matter of the library, and the DA may force him to let me in on it."

"What's McKinney's reason for bumping you off Vastasi's murder?"

"I may be needed as a witness if there's an arrest and trial, so I can't be the prosecutor. What did we see during the surveillance? Did I touch the body or the evidence? What did Billy Schultz and Minerva Hunt say to me? That's why I thought we could get back to work on Barr. The two crimes can't be unrelated."

"Why did McKinney call Tina Barr a thief?" Mike asked.

"He interviewed Jill Gibson last week, before any of this happened. She was talking about some of the things that have disappeared from the library in the last couple of years. In order to get your hands on the most valuable items you'd really need to have special access to the best collections. That's why the executives think most of the thefts had involved insiders."

"This Gibson woman fingered Tina Barr?"

"No, she actually likes Barr. But it's clear that the conservators work on materials from different parts of the library. Her name was one of the common denominators that kept coming up as the individual curators were interviewed. It's McKinney who's drawn a bead on her."

"Stealing these priceless objects for herself,"

Mike said, "and the best she could do was live in a basement in one of the Hunts' buildings?"

"Thefts to order, Mike. That's apparently the big scam. Rich collectors are all scrambling for the same limited goods. They know that thousands of these artifacts are shelved in stacks that nobody ever sees, or warehoused for decades, like the little book Karla Vastasi hid inside her jacket. And Barr was courted by many of these collectors because she's so extraordinarily talented and had such unique access inside the building."

"You have time to Google this Alger Herrick after Battaglia booted you from the inner sanctum?"

"Yes," I said. "McKinney only interviewed him by phone, last week when Herrick was still in England. That was about the problems at the library, so Barr's name came up in the conversation, but I thought we should go deeper."

"He was here in New York when Barr was attacked?"

"Yes, and for Vastasi's murder, too," I said. "He arrived last weekend."

"You want a bite?" Mike asked, holding his hot dog out to me.

"Thanks, I had lunch at my desk." I took a napkin from his hand and wiped the mustard from the corner of his mouth.

Mike grinned at me. "The guy must be a real gent if you're cleaning me up for him."

"Very upper-crust, this Mr. Herrick. He's English, he's rich, and he's very proper. I thought it would be refreshing for him to meet you."

"Four fifty-five Central Park West. If he's so rich, how come he's living in the DMZ?" The area that bordered the park on the Upper West Side, north of Ninety-sixth Street, has seen more than its share of violent crime.

"According to the search I did today, when that landmark building was renovated and apartments went on the market three years ago," I said, "Alger Herrick paid eight million dollars for the most coveted space in the joint."

"And just seven years ago," Mike said, shaking his head, "it was like a big old haunted house. The deadbeat hotel next door was a crack den and it was worth your life to walk down the block without being robbed by junkies or hit up by prostitutes."

"So you know the building?"

"Had a nightmare of a case in four fifty-five back then. Three teenage boys from the 'hood killed up on the third floor, execution style, 'cause they were playing in there and witnessed a buy. The place had such a spooky history, most of the neighbors would cross the street rather than pass by too close to it. Only things inside were stray cats, dead pigeons, and half-dead crackheads."

"I'd never heard of it until I just read the story about Herrick."

"It was the New York Cancer Hospital in the 1880s," Mike said. "The first one of its kind in the country to devote itself to the care of cancer patients."

"The photo of it online looks more like a French château. The article said it was built with money from the Astor family. I guess they really did round up a load of real estate."

"Wait till you see it. It's got turrets on each side, round towers like in a castle," Mike said. "The architect actually designed them on the theory that germs and dirt wouldn't collect in corners. I can't exactly say we had a guided tour, but Peterson and I got to know every nook and cranny in the place. It was the predecessor to today's Memorial Hospital on the East Side."

Mike's late fiancée, Valerie Jacobsen, had been treated at Memorial a couple of years before—successfully—for breast cancer, only to be killed in a skiing accident. During those months, he had applied himself to learning as much about the disease as he knew about military history.

"And now it's been transformed into elegant

co-op apartments," I said. "Maybe it'll bring the rest of the neighborhood along with it."

"Everything in New York used to be something else," Mike said, tossing his trash into a pail on the corner as we waited for the light to change. "These old buildings have stories, Coop. They're here to tell us who we were, who we used to be."

"Herrick's home seems to have mostly sad stories."

"The mother of one of the boys who was killed there became a one-woman campaign to clean it up. Learned everything there was to know about its history. She told me she used to sit in the same desolate room where her kid was offed, just staring out at the park, thinking about how many people had come to the end of their lives in that forsaken place."

"Back when it was built," I said, "cancer was incurable. Treatment was just palliative."

"Patients went to that hospital to die, eased by morphine and champagne, Sunday carriage rides in the park," Mike said. "Story was that the hospital whiskey bill was higher than the one for medical supplies. Even Marie Curie came to visit."

"She did?" I asked as we crossed the broad street, dodging taxis and buses, to get to Mike's car.

"The Curies discovered radium in 1898, and doctors here pioneered the first techniques to burn cancers away with it. The largest repository of radium in the country was kept in a steel vault right in that building."

"I don't know that I could live in a place like that," I said. "Too many ghosts."

"Life goes on," Mike said. "The Octagon— the old lunatic asylum on Roosevelt Island— has been turned into a housing development, and the building where more than a hundred people died in the Triangle Waist Company fire in 1911 is a biology lab at NYU now. Like a phoenix from the ashes."

I had just cleared the passenger seat of half a dozen empty soda cans, a tie, a book on the Crimean War, and a gross of Tic-Tac boxes when I heard Mike's beeper go off.

He looked at the display and slammed the car door. "It's Peterson."

My cell was in my hand. I speed-dialed Mike's boss and handed him the phone.

"Hey, Loo, what's up?" Mike listened to the answer. "Got it. Yeah, she just bought me lunch at the medical examiner's outdoor café. We're on it."

"Detour?" I asked.

"Quick stop on Ninety-third Street," Mike said.

"Tina's apartment? Why?"

"Because Billy Schultz played hookey from his office today. He's working from home."

"So?"

Mike was driving up First Avenue, weaving between cars to catch the lights while he talked. "Precinct guys spent the morning canvassing the buildings that face the garden behind the apartment. Got a rear-window thing going on. Remember Billy told us he hadn't seen much of Tina since the summer? Well, the little old lady who takes the fresh air on her fire escape saw Billy out back with Tina over the weekend. Saturday, right around dusk."

"Doing what?"

"Digging."

"You mean gardening?"

"I would have said it if that's what I meant. She says digging. With a great big shovel and mounds of dirt. No pansies, no tulips, no vegetables."

"Why didn't he tell us?" We were cruising past the United Nations, and Mike put on his whelper to cut a course through the slow-moving traffic. "Did you see any disturbance in the garden?"

"Actually, Coop, I was distracted by the broad on the floor with the bad headache. I thought there was a messy patch in the yard, and I just figured it was where the perp pulled the armillary out of the ground to whack her. Anyway, Crime Scene will have photos," Mike said. "Peterson's got a uniform outside his apartment, rope-a-doping him into answering questions about all the other tenants till we get there. And I buried the lead."

"What's that?" I held the dashboard as Mike slammed on the brakes to avoid an Asian deliveryman, then accelerated again.

"That gas mask the cops picked up a few doors away from the building the night Barr was attacked?" Mike asked.

"Don't look at me. Look at the road," I said. "What about it?"

"Preliminary on the DNA inside the mask. There's a mixture, of course," Mike said. "I'd expect that with something like a mask—especially if it isn't brand new. And one of the profiles matches Billy Schultz."

"Are you serious? I never thought of him that way for a minute. He was wearing the damn thing?"

"Skin cells, sweat. I don't know what else they got."

Once we passed the turn-off for the Fifty-ninth Street Bridge, we made the left onto Ninety-third Street in less than three minutes.

I could see an officer talking to Schultz on

the sidewalk as we pulled up in front of the building. He looked over when he heard the car door shut and started up the steps as Mike approached.

"Yo, Billy," Mike said. "I need a couple of minutes of your time."

Schultz was wearing a plaid flannel shirt, sleeves rolled up, and he frowned as he checked his watch before telling Mike that he had to get back upstairs for a conference call. "I can't talk to you now."

"A guy could get a complex. Only person who's ever happy to see me is my mother," Mike said. "It's just a little thing."

"Really, I've got to make a call."

"This Minerva Hunt thing's got me puzzled." Mike was doing his best Columbo imitation, a look of complete befuddlement on his face. He seemed too dense to be able to figure out much of anything. "When you phoned 911, you told the operator you thought the dead woman was Minerva Hunt, right?"

Schultz looked annoyed. "That's what I said."

"That you'd seen her in the building on other occasions."

"Exactly."

"You were standing with me when the

real Minerva Hunt walked into the kitchen, weren't you?"

"In the garden, yes."

"Did you see her?"

"I did."

"I'm just trying to get straight which of the two women you'd seen around the building before that night. That's all I want to know."

"The way you came speeding up the street, I thought it was something more urgent," Schultz said, seemingly relieved that was the reason for our visit. "I—uh—I was mistaken when I called for help. The outfit, the general physique, the bag with her initials. I couldn't really see her face—it was such a mess—I just jumped to that conclusion. As soon as I saw that other woman talking to you, I knew I'd been wrong."

"Very helpful, Billy. I didn't mean to hold you up," Mike said with a wave of his hand. "What are you growing this time of year? Pumpkins?"

"Excuse me?"

"In your garden. My lieutenant asked me to find out what's in bloom."

"It's all put to bed, Detective. Come back next spring and see what we've got," Schultz said, heading up the stairs.

"The big dig, Billy. Last Saturday. What was that about?"

Schultz continued on his way.

"People saw you with Tina out in the yard. You want to tell me what you were doing together?"

Schultz stopped but didn't answer.

"Don't be going back out there for a while, Billy. Cops are on their way to seal it up now, till we have a chance to check it out. It's off-limits."

The man turned to look at us, clearly displeased. "Tina asked to borrow my shovel, okay? I didn't ask her why. I didn't need to know. I took it down to her and talked for a minute or so. That's her little plot. I don't care what she does with it."

"But you told us you hadn't talked to her—" I said.

"Maybe I just forgot. It was such an insignificant exchange, I simply forgot."

Mike took a step closer and put his hand on the railing of the staircase. "Easy to understand, Billy. A lot easier to understand than the fact that you left your droppings in that freaking mask you ran around in the other night."

"What are you talking about? That's not my mask," Schultz said, angered. He raised his voice and his face flushed.

"The lab got your DNA sample last night, and they say it looks pretty good that you were the guy who had his mug in that contraption. You forget to tell us that, too? Why don't we take this conversation inside, Billy. Your place or mine?"

"Don't come any closer, Detective. Yeah, did I see the fireman—the guy who ran out of here—throw something on the ground? Sure I did. It was only two, three car lengths up the street. Yeah, I picked it up and looked at it— and maybe I did just hold it up over my face. I couldn't figure how he could see out of it. Then I just dropped it back down. Figured your buddies would pick it up."

"I think you'd be doing yourself a favor if you came up to the squad and sat down to go over all this a little more carefully, you know?"

"I'll do you a bigger favor," Schultz said, opening the vestibule door and shouting before he disappeared inside. "I'll have my lawyer call you."

TWELVE

A doorman admitted us at the entrance of the elegantly restored Gothic building on Central Park West and directed us to the concierge.

"We're here to see Alger Herrick," I said, taking in the opulence of the décor in the lobby. The architectural detail of the last century had been carefully preserved, but there were discreet signs pointing to an indoor lap pool and the spa.

"He's expecting you?"

"Yes. I'm Alexandra Cooper."

The concierge rang the apartment, and when someone answered, he announced me. "Take that elevator to your left."

"And what floor do I press?"

"The lift only goes to Mr. Herrick's home."

I followed Mike into the small elevator and pressed the button that said Up. Seconds later, it came to a stop and the door opened.

"Good afternoon, Ms. Cooper. I'm Alger Herrick," he said, extending his right hand to help me step off. His left hand was tucked into the pocket of a charcoal gray cashmere sweater, set off against a yellow ascot that framed his long, narrow face.

Mike introduced himself as I moved onto a small balcony that hung above the main room of the apartment. It took my eyes a minute to adjust to the dim light, and then I looked around at the vaulted ceiling and the large stained-glass windows that ringed the cavernous space of the perfectly appointed room.

"I was in here years ago, but I'd never recognize the place," Mike said, whistling softly as he moved in behind me. "This used to be the hospital's chapel, wasn't it?"

"Precisely, Detective. Did you know it in the old days—after the hospital closed—when these glorious rooms were filled with decay?" Alger Herrick asked. "This was indeed the chapel of St. Elizabeth of Hungary. Patron saint of the suffering."

I felt a chill run down my spine.

"I had a rather long conversation with your colleague, Mr. McKinney, from my home in London late last week," Herrick said. "Thursday evening, I believe."

He led us down the winding staircase of the duplex and seated us in the living room, waiting for the butler to return with our ice water and his tea.

"Things have happened since then," Mike

said. "A woman's been killed in the apartment Tina Barr was living in, and Barr herself has disappeared."

"Yes, I got back to town on Sunday. Jill Gibson called yesterday, asking about Tina. Apparently she seemed to have left without a trace."

"Were you surprised?"

"I was, Mr. Chapman. She's been working with me for several weeks," Herrick said, "and I thought we were getting on very well. I owe her quite a large amount of money, so I assume she'll be in touch with me about that."

"Do you know anything about her family, her next of kin?" I asked. "Any idea where she might have gone?"

"Her father died when she was very young. I know that. Tina spoke of her mother. I understand she lives in one of those artists' colonies on the west coast of Mexico."

"Would you have the mother's name, or an address for her?"

"I'm afraid not. No reason for me to have it."

Herrick was standing a few yards away from me, but I could barely see his face because of the lack of light in the room.

"You mind turning up the wattage?" Mike asked, also frustrated by not being able to gauge the expressions on Herrick's face.

Herrick walked to a panel near the staircase

and pushed the dimmer. The mountings on the wall, all in gilded frames, were maps—oceans and continents, familiar territories and foreign names.

"Sorry, Mr. Chapman. I'm so used to living at lamp level—that's what we call it when you work with ancient documents—that I forget others aren't accustomed to it. The objects in my collection, whether on parchment or vellum or paper, are better protected by low lighting. That's why it's so dark in here," Herrick said. The dimness added to the solemnity of the room. "I'd only got to know Tina a little better about a month ago. We hadn't worked out the details for her fees yet."

"Hope you figure it out before next April," Mike said. "She'll have taxes to pay."

"Frankly, Detective, Tina wanted to be paid off the books. Cash. I was quite uncomfortable with that. I gave her some money up-front, to get her going, but I hadn't formalized our arrangement."

The butler returned with our drinks and handed me water in a heavy crystal double-highball glass. While Mike questioned Herrick, I checked out the sumptuous fittings of the old chapel and admired the brilliant colors of the antique hand-drawn maps and charts.

"Where did you meet Tina?" Mike asked.

"At the New York Public Library. I'd seen her there over the years, exchanged pleasantries and such, and I was aware that she'd built up a good reputation for herself," Herrick said, resting his teacup on the mantel above the fireplace. "It seemed the perfect opportunity for both of us, with my collection and her skill."

"Wasn't she already working for someone else?"

"Jasper Hunt. She'd been hired by someone to do some projects for the old man himself."

"Not hired by him?"

"Jasper? Entirely gaga at this point, Detective. At least, that's what I heard. It was probably one of his children, trying to get their greedy hands on his treasures," Herrick said, taking a sip of his tea. "You've met them, have you?"

"Tell me what you know," Mike said.

"Talbot's a bookman. That's how collectors are known. The father always favored him because Tally's got the same nose for books as Jasper, the same appreciation—had it since he was a child. He's probably close to fifty now, a bit younger than me. Been very involved in running the family property empire, expanding it to pass on to his children."

"So they get on, father and son?"

Alger Herrick ran his finger along the edge

of the mantel. "There are others closer to Jasper who could tell you more than I."

"But you've heard rumblings. You must have had something in mind when you hired Tina Barr away."

"Idle gossip around the library," Herrick said. "Tally's getting impatient, hoping to keep some of his father's fortune in the family. Make sure it isn't all given away. That sort of thing."

"Even to the library?" Mike asked. "Even though he's on the board?"

"I have the impression that Tally would like to have control of something substantial at this point in his life. Something of his very own. There's a certain feeling of entitlement that comes over a man like that by the time he's reached middle age. His grandfather was such an eccentric that no one's quite sure how much of the fortune is still intact. A lot of the Hunt money has already been given away, and Jasper himself kept threatening to change the provisions of his will. Mind you, that's just the talk."

"And Minerva?"

Alger Herrick raised his teacup. "I'll have to switch to something stronger than this, Detective, if we're to talk about that viper. I have a bad taste in my mouth at just the mention of her name."

"Why so?"

"You seem intrigued by that one, Ms. Cooper," Herrick said. He caught me staring at a beautifully drawn map of the European coastline, the compass roses highlighted in gold paint. "By all means have a closer look."

"Minerva Hunt," Mike said, drawing Herrick back to the conversation. "Why do you dislike her?"

"She's a lightweight, Mr. Chapman. A complete cipher. Minerva's a girl who was handed every advantage in life on a silver plate, and she still hasn't worked out what to do with it all. Other than the income she derived from it, the family business never interested her. Books were Tally's thing, so that put her off becoming a bibliophile. But even on a personal level, I know she's been a great disappointment to Jasper," Herrick said. "He confided that to me years ago."

"How long have you known Jasper Hunt?"

"My goodness. Half my life, I suppose. It's a small world we collectors live in. Very few of us with the means to indulge ourselves in this market. Jasper used to keep a flat in London, where I have a house. He was always there for the big sales and auctions. I learned a lot from him, from the time when I was just an eager young man. Jasper Hunt had a brilliant eye."

"When did you first meet Tally and Minerva?" Mike asked.

"I think they were both still at university. Tally at Oxford, where his father had done a year as well. The old man had his eye on me for Minerva," Herrick said, shaking his head at the thought. "He introduced me to her one weekend. She was in her first year at Bryn Mawr then."

"So you dated?" Mike asked.

"Heavens, no. I was already engaged at the time. You've met her, haven't you?"

"Yes, briefly."

"Tough as nails, is that what you Americans say? I don't know about you, Detective," Herrick said, smiling at Mike, "but I like my women a bit softer."

"I'll drink to that," Mike said, winking at me. "Fragile. Almost vulnerable."

"Indeed."

"Did you see Tina this week, after your return?"

"She was here on Monday," Herrick said. "She was working upstairs in my study."

"On what?" Mike asked.

"She finished her first big project for me—I let her audition on a piece of moderate value. And then she's been sorting through some of

my recent acquisitions, trying to help me determine which items are candidates for restoration."

"When did you talk with her next?"

Herrick put his right hand in the deep
pocket of his sweater, lowered his head, and
started to pace around the perimeter of the
room.

"Not again," he said. "I haven't spoken to
her since."

"Were you concerned when she didn't show
up yesterday?" Mike asked.

"Not at all. No. She wasn't supposed to
come in. She was planning to spend the day at
the library. Tina was only working for me part-
time. Due back today, actually."

Herrick paused in front of one of the
chapel's stained-glass windows. The tapered
conical ceiling rose almost thirty feet over his
head, and although he was a tall man, he
seemed almost overwhelmed by the space of the
once-hallowed room.

"Have you done anything to try to find her?"

"I should think, Mr. Chapman, that responsibility falls on you. I barely know the woman,
and if she chooses to take a holiday as a result
of the break-in that Jill Gibson described to me,
there'll be plenty of work for her when she returns."

"Mr. Herrick," I said, standing to approach him, "what does Tina Barr have to do with Minerva Hunt?"

"I haven't any idea, to be honest with you. Tina told me she'd met Minerva at Jasper's home. The woman frightened her, quite frankly. I told Tina that she frightens lots of people."

"You've done business with Minerva?"

"I'd hardly describe it as business. Every now and then she goes after something I'm keen on. She's got in my way from time to time. Nothing serious, mind you."

"But I thought you said she doesn't collect?" I said.

"Not books, Ms. Cooper," Herrick said, doubling back to the fireplace, crossing in front of it, pausing beside an enormous wooden stand, almost as tall as he, in which an antique globe was mounted. "Maps. Minerva Hunt likes to dabble in rare maps."

"Like you."

"I'm not a dabbler, Detective. With me, it's a passion," Herrick said. "I'm trying too hard to point out the differences between us, that's true. There's nothing scholarly about my interests. They're purely visual. Very different from book collecting, I can assure you. I just go after the best-looking things."

His self-deprecating comment was meant to belittle Minerva Hunt.

"You've got hundreds of books here, too," Mike said, pointing up to the balcony from which we'd descended on our way in.

"Atlases mostly," Herrick said. "You can circumnavigate the globe with those books, Mr. Chapman."

"Did Jill Gibson tell you about the murder in Tina's apartment last night?" I asked.

"She did. She called me a little while ago. Minerva's maid, was it? Carrying one of Tally's books. Something like that. I'm just glad Tina wasn't at home when the bastard got there. Looking for something valuable, no doubt. How did the woman die?"

"Fractured skull, Mr. Herrick," Mike said. "Split her head in half and crushed her brain. No use for the patron saint of the suffering, 'cause she didn't suffer very long."

Herrick didn't react. "You think the killer knows Tina Barr?"

"I don't know anything about him at this point, who he knew or what he wanted. Only that he was at least your height, 'cause the woman was tall, and the blow that took her down struck the crown of her head."

"Heavens, Detective. The world is full of

people as tall as I am. Even Minerva Hunt fits the bill."

"I'd say you'd need a pair of strong arms to heave that thing," Mike said. "I think Minerva would be afraid she'd ruin her manicure."

Mike was baiting his subject, trying to get a rise out of him.

Alger Herrick took his hands out of his sweater pockets. There was a glint of metal against the dark wooden globe as he reached to spin it. The oceans and continents began to whirl around on the solid wooden stand, and I could see that where his left hand should have been there was only a single hook.

THIRTEEN

"Did I startle you, Mr. Chapman?" Herrick asked. "I don't want you putting me at the scene of the crime without getting to know me a little better."

"You called me on that one, sir. I'm sorry if I was rude."

"Just obvious, Detective. I was born without a hand—a defect the doctors assume was caused by the medication my mother was taking during pregnancy. I'm used to people's stares and gasps. I've got a modern prosthesis I wear when I'm out, in case you're wondering. But this is what I had when I was growing up, and it suits me fine. Now what were we discussing?"

"Mike and I are trying to get to know the world that Tina Barr moved in," I said. "It's hard to imagine that books and maps, and the quiet reading rooms of the public library, would expose her to danger, but the two attacks this week took place in her apartment. Perhaps you could tell us about some of the people she worked with. You, Mr. Herrick, tell us about yourself."

Herrick crossed the center of the long room and seated himself at a desk near my chair. I wanted to understand Tina Barr, and if my appeal to his vanity guided me to learn about things in which she had immersed herself, it would be time well spent.

"I don't like talking about myself, Ms. Cooper, but I can tell you all you want to know about these beautiful things," he said, sweeping his good arm around in a circle.

"When did you start collecting?"

"My life has been a matter of great good luck, after a very bumpy start," Herrick said. "I was deposited on the steps of an orphanage in Oxfordshire, or so I'm told, by a single mother—a teenager herself—who must have been overwhelmed at the prospect of taking care of a child as handicapped as she thought I would be. I don't remember anything about that part of my life, so you needn't imagine all sorts of stories about eating gruel and being forced to pick pockets as a child. Shortly before my fourth birthday, I was adopted by the Herricks, a local family who had lost their only son to polio about five years earlier.

"My adoptive father, Charles, was a wonder-

fully kind man, a barrister who made a respectable living. They gave me a loving home,
and an introduction to material comforts."

"I wouldn't think many barristers could af-
ford these digs," Mike said.

"About the time I was a teenager, my father
came into a large inheritance, Mr. Chapman.
You know about primogeniture, of course. He
was the third son of a third son and so on. But
when his uncle died without any heirs—his uncle Algernon, in fact, for whom I was named
when they adopted me—the old fellow left
most of his estate, including his home and his
library, to my father. Hence to me."

"I like stories with happy endings."

"So do I, Detective, so do I. And yes, I've
tried to make a contribution of my own. If Jill
hasn't told you, I've been a member of the
Council of the Stock Exchange. Investments
and such. Very lucky indeed," Herrick said.
"Have either of you ever heard of Lord Wardington?"

"No, no, I haven't," I said.

"He was a mentor of my father's, known to
everyone as Bic. His family had built a spectacular library over several centuries, and he himself amassed the greatest collection of atlases in
England. I used to spend hours at Wardington
Manor as a child. I was painfully shy—because

of this," Herrick said, examining his hook as he spoke. "So I was more than happy to spend my time in the silence of the great reading room there."

"That's easy to understand."

"Bic was incredibly generous to me. He saw that I loved old books—I loved smelling them and touching the rich Moroccan leather. There were early English Bibles and Shakespeare Folios, incredibly fine incunabula—"

"What's that?" Mike asked.

"Books from the infancy of printing, Detective. From before 1500. The books were my friends—my only friends, in fact, for a long time—but it was maps that fascinated me the most. My father had a pair of globes. Not as fine as this one, but they were brightly colored and they towered above me, and I never tired of making them spin.

"And it was at Wardington Manor that I discovered atlases," he went on. "Bic continued the tradition of acquiring books for the family library, but he became obsessed, much as I have, with maps."

"Why is that?" I asked. "They're quite beautiful, but what makes them so special to collectors?"

Herrick opened the oversize leather-bound book in front of him and turned to look at the pages he had selected. "Think of how the ancients must have imagined the world, Ms. Cooper, long before most of them were ever able to travel it, to take measure of it in their journeys. There have been maps as long as there have been walls or vellum on which to write and draw. Who was the first man to give us a mathematical picture of the universe? Do you know?"

Both Mike and I shook our heads.

"Ptolemy, of course, in his **Cosmographia,** which was based on voyages and itineraries of early travelers, and on their fantasies as well. About AD 150. His was the first account to locate places in terms of longitude and latitude. For hundreds of years afterward, monks and madmen all over Europe were able to draw maps of what they believed to be the world."

"Where's Mercer when we need him?" Mike said.

"Excuse me?"

"We've got a friend named Mercer Wallace whose father was a mechanic at LaGuardia Airport," Mike said. "Has a thing for maps, too, only not rare ones. His dad used to hang all the airline routes on the walls in Mercer's room when he was a kid, teaching him about faraway places. So he also grew up on maps. Bet he'd love to hear this."

"Then you must bring him with you next time," Herrick said, smoothing the page and running his forefinger over the outline of the northern coast of Africa. "Everything changed with the invention of the printing press, of course. Imagine the amazement of people seeing printed maps for the first time."

Herrick prodded the book with his hook to swivel it around, allowing us to see the two-page illustration, colored in red and green inks, the seas a pale blue, with odd-looking creatures lurking on the corners.

"This is Ptolemy's Atlas. The very first one ever printed, Ms. Cooper. Presented in Bologna in 1477."

The images were breathtaking in their complexity and surprising in their accuracy depicting the landmasses bordering the Mediterranean.

"Twenty-six maps in the volume, done with double-page copperplate engravings, and then hand-colored. Taddeo Crivelli's work—he was a genius. There are only thirty-one copies of this atlas in the world, and only two in private hands. Go ahead, touch it. I promise it won't bite."

Mike reached over me to feel the paper. He lifted the page and studied the image on the underside before sitting back.

"Did that say anything to you, Mr. Chapman?"

"Like what?"

"Like whether what I'm telling you is true? I'm teasing you, Detective, but Tina Barr is skilled enough to call my bluff on that. The real Bologna Ptolemy that I own is in England under lock and key. That one's worth more than a million pounds. I bought it at Sotheby's, when Lord Wardington sold most of his collection a few years ago. This is a much later edition—you'll even find America in here—and it's damaged by those small wormholes and some tears in its margin. Hasn't nearly a fraction of the value of the Bologna printings. The green coloring has seeped through the paper, as sixteenth-century green often does."

"I'll give you a hundred bucks for it," Mike said, smiling.

"I'm afraid you'd be fifty thousand pounds short." Herrick smiled. "You must understand that with the Age of Discovery, Detective, came an explosion of new information. Sea monsters disappeared from the edges of the ocean and distant places began to take on more precise shapes. California is discovered, as you see in these subsequent volumes. For two hundred years—to the European mind—it was drawn as an island. Brilliant to watch the history of the world unfold through these documents. There was a military purpose to them, too."

"That must have been critical," Mike said.

"Usually a hanging offense for a merchant or soldier to share a country's maps with a foreign power. That handsome example on the wall that you were admiring earlier," Herrick said to me, "is the **Neptune François,** a collection of sea atlases commissioned by Louis XIV to give the French navy an important advantage over the British. Meticulous engravings they were— all about navigation—so soundings and rhumb lines and the markings for every little coastal port were of major importance."

"Did it help the French in battle?"

"Well, it would have, Mr. Chapman, if the charts hadn't been copied quite so quickly by the Dutch and distributed abroad. With the advent of printing, scholars of every nation were able to compare and revise, leading to a considerable advance in geographical knowledge."

"Help me understand," I asked. "What's more valuable? The individual maps, like those hung on the walls here, or the bound atlases?"

"Ah, now you've hit on a point of contention. Scratch the surface of this and you'll find real scoundrels, Ms. Cooper."

I was looking for a stronger word to describe our perp, but I'd settle for some direction instead.

"Unlike rare books," Herrick said, "maps were not greatly prized by collectors until thirty or forty years ago. Lord Wardington's a perfect example. The family amassed books for generations, going back over four hundred years. He focused his attention on maps and created what was indisputably the world's best private collection in the last four decades."

"Why the disparity?"

Herrick pursed his lips and frowned. "Individual maps—the kind that sailors and traders and explorers used every day—were just utilitarian pieces of paper. Not many were considered works of art, with elaborate decorations and fine calligraphy—the kind that wind up bound in atlases. They were essentially untethered documents to be used in their own time— not carefully maintained, without any record of their provenance—just meant to get the traveler or the sailor from one place to another.

"The better maps wound up in books— printed, then hand-colored, and bound in all of the wonderful ways you see in collections. They were only sold separately when the books were damaged. You want to point a finger at the enemy?" he said, chuckling softly. "It's the modern dealers."

"Dealers?" I asked.

"They're the atlas-breakers. They're the ones who manipulate the market, trying to keep up with old-fashioned supply and demand."

"What's an atlas-breaker?"

"Remember I told you that this was a purely visual passion, not a scholarly one?" Herrick said. "The desirability of old maps—out of books and on the walls—was strictly a result of the fact that fashionable interior designers discovered how attractive they are, back in the 1970s and '80s. English country style, if you will. The maps became more highly sought after than the books that held them, so dealers started hoarding the atlases and dismembering them. Taking the maps out and selling them separately was far more profitable than finding one buyer for the whole book."

"Are there many of these dealers around New York?" Mike asked.

"You're both too young to have known Book Row," Herrick said. "Fourth Avenue, between Union Square and Astor Place, was a bibliophile's paradise for almost a hundred years. All that's left of it these days is the Strand. So, in fact, there are only a handful of serious dealers at this point, working in the price range we're talking about. I can tell you exactly who they are, if that's what you need."

"I think what we need is to figure out where Tina Barr fits in this picture," I said. "What kind of person is she?"

"I can't help you there. I only know her professionally. She's incredibly well trained and has a great eye for detail. That's one she finished for me just last week."

I walked to the wall between two tall windows and studied the minuscule calligraphy on another exquisitely rendered old map.

"Saxton's cartographic survey of England and Wales," Herrick said, "commissioned by Elizabeth the First."

"Is Tina capable of reproducing something as beautiful as this?"

"These days, Ms. Cooper, digital processing would make it possible for almost anyone to reproduce documents such as that one."

"I mean, a copy good enough to fool—well, to fool a dealer or a collector."

"Are you talking about a forgery? Heavens, no, Ms. Cooper. To begin with, one would have to have the proper vellum, which would be pretty difficult to come by these days. The best quality vellum was made from the skins of unborn animals. In England, you know, we still print our Acts of Parliament on it, but you'll never find something that could be dated and matched to the original. On top of that, she'd have to be a first-rate artist, not just a meticulous restorer. Then I'd say we'd need to give her three or four years to work on it."

"What is it that Tina did on the map you started her with?"

"Minor repairs, mostly. Decades ago, when maps were mounted for display—like this one was, in Hampton Court—they were first backed with muslin. The glue that held it in place was very destructive. So Tina removed the backing, cleaned up the tears and discoloration, and deacidified it."

"Where did she do the work?"

"There's a state-of-the-art facility in the public library—the Goldsmith Conservation Laboratory. She did it there."

"Are you on the board of the library?" Mike asked.

"No, Mr. Chapman, but I make handsome contributions. You'll find I'm quite welcome there."

"You must have a system for doing background checks on your employees," I said. "I assume you don't just meet a conservator and invite him in with free access to possessions as valuable as yours."

Herrick stood up and leaned against the desk. "There's a very serious vetting process, and Tina passed with flying colors. I never considered her a security risk."

"There are people at the library who think she—"

"People at the library should take their heads out of their books and stop pointing fingers at the worker bees. Every time there's been a major problem, it's a trustee or a donor who was responsible."

"What do you mean?" I asked.

"All the new money on the board—hedge fund managers and the like who think that if they splash enough cash around they can buy themselves some instant class—it's created considerable tension at the library. There's a man called Jonah Krauss waiting like a vulture for that last great dame to die— the one before Brooke Astor—so he can sell some of her collection."

Mike was making notes of the names.

"And I can't think why they'd go after Tina Barr when the real map thief was paroled just a few months ago."

"The **real** map thief?" I asked.

"Eddy Forbes, Ms. Cooper. The chap Minerva Hunt was in bed with," Herrick said. "I don't mean that literally, but I don't doubt for a minute that she subsidized his travels."

"What travels?"

"Eddy Forbes flooded the market with stolen goods, Detective. Some of the finest maps the world has ever seen, stolen right from under the noses of all the brass at the public library, on Jill Gibson's watch at the Beinecke, from the Boston Library, the British Reading Room, The Hague—shall I go on or do you get my point?"

"How did Forbes get access to all those collections?"

"He was a dealer, of course. A dealer, a scholar—so he liked to think—and a complete fraud. It's always the inner circle, Ms. Cooper. That's where you've got to look, not at the earnest young worker bees."

"I don't understand," Mike said, reaching out to touch the four folio-size volumes stacked on Herrick's desk. "How does the librarian, or the security guard, let you get out the door? You walk out of a library and nobody notices you're carrying these great big books in their fancy leather jackets with shiny gold lettering? Maybe once you could fit one in a shopping bag, but most of these are even too large for that."

Herrick opened the desk drawer again and removed a small object with his right hand. He rested it on the blotter and closed the finely

tooled cover of his sixteenth-century copy of
Cosmographia. Then he reached for an even
larger black leather-bound book with gold lettering on its spine.

"No need to wince, Ms. Cooper," Herrick
said, holding up an X-Acto knife—a short,
sharp blade mounted on a metal body the size
of a pen. "I'm not going to cut anyone's throat."

With a single swipe, he ran the blade down
the length of the page, separating it from the
binding of the book. He rolled it up and
slipped it through the cuff of his sweater.

"Don't fret, either. This book was already
disemboweled by one of the thieves before I bid
on it. Here's the rub, Detective. Steal a single
page from a first folio of Shakespeare and you
walk away with nothing of value. An interesting
sheet of paper, perhaps, but of no value in the
marketplace without the entire folio."

Herrick held up his arms, as if in triumph
for making the page disappear. "But slip just
one sheet like this up your sleeve—a single
map, say, from John Smith's great atlas of Colonial America—and you walk out of the library
with a ready-to-sell, largely untraceable treasure
worth hundreds of thousands of dollars."

FOURTEEN

"Much less punishing than my last encounter with the police," Alger Herrick said as he led us up the staircase to the elevator.

I turned my head to look at Mike. "And what was that?"

"I was on my way to the country from London a few years ago, after a spectacular score I made at auction. Mercator's atlas—1595. The first book in the history of the world to be called an atlas, in fact," Herrick said. "My wife took me out to dinner to celebrate, and I'm afraid I should have known better than to drive."

"Wind up in the hoosegow?" Mike asked. He dismissed my concern with a smirk.

"No incarceration, Detective. Had my license taken away for a few months, plus a hefty fine, but not as hefty as the purchase I'd just made," Herrick said, opening the door to the elevator. "If I can be of help with any introductions, I'd be happy to do that. I'm hoping Tina will calm down and come back to work before too long."

"We'd like very much to find her," I said. "Thanks for your time."

"Pleasure."

Mike made small talk on the way down in the elevator, waiting to get away from the building's workers before he asked me about Herrick. "I don't know about you, but I'd still bet there's enough grit in that guy's upper crust that he could swing our murder weapon or just about anything else."

"You just don't like him because he doesn't share your affection for Minerva."

"We've got to get back on her dance card, don't you think? Fill in some blanks."

"Tomorrow morning when I get to the office, I'll sit down with McKinney and stroke him. You've got to talk to all the Hunts—Minerva, Tally, Jasper. As long as I make Pat feel like he's in charge, I'm sure he'll let me go along with you. See what you can schedule."

"Did you open a grand jury investigation on Barr today?"

"Yes," I said. "Right before lunch. Laura's typed up subpoenas for her cell phone records, credit card—anything to tell us if Tina's on the move. It's sad that she doesn't really have a network of any kind."

"All that freelance work—some of it in the library and a lot of it at either Jasper Hunt's home or Herrick's—so it wasn't like she was in a setting where somebody would be concerned during the first day or two if she didn't show up."

"You think there's any point in talking to the guys at Missing Persons again? Don't you think it would help to get her photo out on the news?"

"Catch-22. Tina Barr's an adult, for one thing. With no signs of foul play after she walked away from the ambulance, you got the forty-eight-hour rule," Mike said. "Nobody's complained that she's missing, Coop."

It was well known in law enforcement that the overwhelming number of adults who vanish without any indication of criminal activity do so voluntarily.

"We're just going on forty-eight hours now. Maybe I can push Battaglia to leak her disappearance to the press. Think that's the way to go?"

"Start making your lists of things to do, kid. We'll find her," Mike said, unlocking the car. "I'll drop you off at your place."

"You don't have an extra ticket for tonight? Can't sneak me in?"

He started the ignition and grinned at me. "Who squealed?"

"Vickee called. Told me Mercer snagged four seats right behind third base." The Yankees had won two out of three games in the division playoff series and were back at the stadium tonight, looking to clinch. "I'm insanely jealous."

"He's invited Ned and Al," Mike said, referring to two of my favorite detectives from the Special Victims Unit. "And I'm his date. Sorry to disappoint you."

"Then you might as well scoot me home," I said. "It's after four-thirty."

"I'm psyched. Haven't been to a game since July. We make it to the pennant, your pal Joan is going to collect on my promise. Told her last year I'd take her."

My best girlfriends—in the office and apart from it—all adored Mike and had gotten to know him well over the years. They liked his intelligence and his humor, too, but mostly appreciated the way he covered my back in every conceivable circumstance.

Nina Baum and Joan Stafford were my two closest confidantes, lifelong buddies with whom I'd been through every triumph and tragedy. Nina, my college roommate, lived on the West Coast with her husband and son, while Joan and her husband split their time between New York and Washington, D.C.

"Joanie's in town. I'll be watching at her place tonight," I said as we went through the underpass in Central Park. "She'll never let you

welsh on that one, so you'd best get on that advance ticket line at the crack of dawn. And
count me in on that round."

"Deal."

By the time we made a rough plan about
our approach to the witnesses we needed to interview, we were less than a block from my
apartment.

"I'll jump out here, Mike. I need to stop at
the cash machine and pick up some groceries."

"Call you in the morning," he said, pulling
over to the curb.

"Only if we win. If you don't pull the Yankees through tonight, I may hand you back
over to McKinney."

He whelped at me once as he drove away,
and the coven of little old ladies on the corner
of the street turned to stare.

I did some errands and walked another block
to my apartment, enjoying the opportunity to
be at home much earlier than was usual. Neither of the doormen stepped out to greet me as
I approached, but one of the porters came running from the mail room when he heard my
footsteps. "Sorry, Ms. Cooper. Need a hand?"

"I'm fine, thanks. Where's Vinny?" I said,
walking to the elevator.

"He's on meal and Oscar went home sick.
I'm trying to cover, but it's been crazy busy."

When the elevator reached the lobby, I pressed twenty and rummaged through my tote for my keychain, replaying the information that had unfolded throughout the day.

If Billy Schultz was telling the truth about recognizing Minerva Hunt, why had she been to Tina Barr's apartment on other occasions? Was it weird, or was it just natural curiosity that led him to pick up the mask that the perpetrator had worn—if he had not in fact been the masked intruder?

I turned the key in the lock and went inside, flipping on the foyer light. I left the bag with the orange juice and English muffins next to the credenza and started down the hallway toward the linen closet with the cosmetics I'd bought at the drugstore.

The bedroom door ahead of me was closed. In a split second I reminded myself that it was Thursday and that my housekeeper had not been in today. I was sure I had left the door open, as always, and I slowed my pace.

I heard noise from within—a sound like the closing of a dresser drawer. I began to back up, wondering for how long the building's entrance had been unsecured this afternoon, and whether someone who didn't belong here had gotten inside. My thoughts flashed to members of the Latin Princes gang, whose leader I had successfully prosecuted, and who had stalked me relentlessly during the summer.

I scrambled to retrace my steps to the front door, and as I turned, the long strap of my tote caught on the door handle of the guest bedroom. The contents dumped out as I bent to unhook it, and the drugstore purchases scattered onto the floor.

I let go of everything and dashed to the foyer. I could hear the bedroom door opening and my adrenaline kicked in as I ran faster. In that short sprint, I was breathing as rapidly as if I'd completed a 5K race. I pulled on the doorknob just as I heard the man's voice.

"Alexandra? **C'est toi?**"

I exhaled and steadied myself against the door, throwing my head back, thinking how unnerved I'd been by the thought of an intruder.

"Have I upset you, **mon ange?** This was meant to be such a great surprise," Luc Rouget said as he stepped over the packages to make his way toward me, wearing only the towel that was draped around his waist. "Are you all right, Alex?"

I nodded and smiled. He wrapped me in an embrace and I held on to him with all my strength.

FIFTEEN

We were still in bed together nearly an hour later, Luc cradling me in his long, slender arms, laughing about the fact that Joan Stafford's wonderful plan to help him surprise me had almost backfired.

"I'm telling you, we both thought it was foolproof," Luc said. "I had to be in Washington last night to meet with some investors, so we took the shuttle up together today and had lunch around the corner at Swifty's. So perfectly American, that place. Then Joan brought me up here to settle me in. **Faites comme chez vous,** she told me, and so I did."

Joan and I had always had keys to each other's apartments, and the doormen knew her as well as they knew my parents and brothers.

"I'm delighted you made yourself at home," I said, kissing the tip of his nose.

"We did all the shopping at Grace's Marketplace so that I could fix you a delicious dinner by the time you got here from the office. But Joanie said you never, never get out before seven, eight o'clock. **Jamais, jamais.**"

"I rarely do. But we were working on an investigation uptown, not far from here. I've had a few late nights this week, so it was a treat to be early. I don't know why I was so jumpy."

Luc brushed back the curls from around my forehead and kissed me on the mouth, long and tenderly. "Are you feeling better now?"

"Like a different person."

"I don't want you to be someone else, Alexandra. I made love to you, not to any other woman."

"I'm not the least bit confused about that," I said, rolling onto my side to sit up.

"Because if you are, then I'm happy to try to remind you." Luc reached up and playfully pulled me down beside him. He ran his finger slowly down my spine, then along the back of my leg, kissing the crook of my knee. "Looks exactly like you, feels exactly like you, and tastes deliciously the same as you did last time."

"I might taste even better after I clean up."

"Take one of your luxurious bubble baths, darling. I'm going to start preparing dinner."

"Will I be the guinea pig for any new tastings?"

Luc's father, Andre Rouget, was a great French restaurateur who'd changed the culinary scene in New York City when he founded Lutèce in a townhouse on the East Side. Luc had followed in his father's footsteps in a French village called Mougins, where his elegant four-star restaurant was a destination for locals and travelers in the south of France. He'd been courted by several backers to reopen Lutèce and restore the reputation of the famous eatery, and was making frequent trips to America to move the plan forward.

"No, no. I've had my nose in so many French menus these last few weeks that I decided to cook Italian tonight. **Ça va?**"

"**Ça va bien.** Anything I can do to help?"

"In the kitchen?" Luc asked. "Then I would really be concerned I was with an imposter. You just relax, Alexandra. I don't need a sous-chef; I need a hungry woman."

I went into the bathroom and ran the hot water, sprinkling in bath salts that I'd brought back from Paris.

The relationship with Luc had no emotional complications. He was mature at forty-eight and quite direct. Divorced after fifteen years of marriage to an unfaithful woman, Luc was devoted to the two children whose custody he shared with his ex. I liked that about him, and looked forward to meeting the boys he so adored.

The only issue that nagged at me as I found myself falling in love was what Nina teasingly

referred to as his "GU"—the geographic unde-
sirability of his faraway home. Luc's spending
so much time in the States as he explored his
new business venture made it easy for me to
stay focused between his visits, but the reality
was that most of the time we were separated by
an ocean and the craggy foothills of the Mar-
itime Alps.

When I finished bathing, I pulled on a pair
of leggings and a five-year-old navy blue sweatshirt with Jeter's name and number 2 on the
back. If I couldn't be at the Yankee game, at
least I could carry the colors. I swept my hair
into a ponytail and dabbed Luc's favorite perfume behind my ears and on my throat.

The telephone rang as I was about to leave
my bedroom. Luc came toward me from the
kitchen. "You want me to answer?"

"I'm just screening," I said. "I'm hoping it's
not business."

It took most of the guys I dated a while to
understand that whenever senior prosecutors
were working investigations, phones and beep-
ers went beyond the boundaries of eight-hour
workdays.

"I'm at the stadium, Coop." Mike's voice
talking to my answering machine jolted me as
though he had just stepped into the bedroom
between Luc and me. "Can't find a frigging

television anywhere. If you haven't left for Joan's yet, be sure you catch **Jeopardy!** for us. I'll speak to you tomorrow."

I took Luc's glasses off the bridge of his nose and kissed his forehead.

"Ah, that's one of your detective friends, **non?** You and Joan have talked about him. He calls about this trivia game, too?"

I continued down the hallway toward the kitchen, changing the subject. "The sauce smells fabulous. What is it?"

"He's the one Joanie told me—how do you say?—has a crush on you."

"We've been friends since my rookie year in the office. I think he'd laugh out loud at that suggestion."

"I'd like to meet these guys who get to spend so much time with you," Luc said, reaching around me, as he kissed the nape of my neck, to put out the wineglasses.

"Next time you're here we can do that," I said, dreading the thought of my favorite alpha-dog detective going head-to-head with my very confident French lover. "That way maybe I can get an actual arrival date from you."

Luc turned me around and pulled me in, kissing me again and again. "So much for my surprise."

I wrapped my arms around his slim shoulders and kissed him back. "I love your surprise. I'm very happy tonight."

"Then I'll let you in on my schedule. On Saturday I fly to San Francisco. I've got meetings in Napa and Sonoma, with vintners. Then to Los Angeles, Houston, Atlanta—"

"Food tastings everywhere?"

"Poor me, right? And then I'm back here in about ten days. You think you can get away for a weekend on Martha's Vineyard? You tend to the fireplace and I'll keep you well fed."

Luc didn't want to hear that my answer depended on the progress of the investigation.

"That gives me something to dream about."

He took me by the hand and led me back to the kitchen. "I know this isn't your forte, but I'm going to give you this wooden spoon and have you stir for me while I check on the chicken."

"I didn't think you trusted me enough to let me near one of your creations."

"I've got a lot riding on this dish, Alexandra. You know puttanesca sauce?" Luc asked. "Named for the Neapolitan ladies of the night. Legend has it that when these women brought home sailors to entertain, this recipe was used as an aphrodisiac."

"Then I'll stir more vigorously," I said.

Over dinner, I told Luc some of the details

of the case. He had used his warmth and charm, ever since we met months earlier, to get me to open myself to him.

"You're not drinking," he said. "Won't you have some wine?"

"I'm so tired after this crazy week we've had. Just these few sips are enough."

"How's my sauce working?"

I rubbed my stomach and nodded. "Those girls in Naples knew exactly what they were doing."

Luc stood up and blew out the candles. "I think I know what I'd like for dessert."

I led the way back to the bedroom and we undressed as though we'd been apart for weeks, making love again before falling asleep in each other's arms.

When the telephone rang, I could see the time on the clock radio next to my bed. It was after one in the morning and I grabbed the receiver before the second ring.

"Sorry to wake you, Coop."

"That's all right. I fell asleep early."

"Before we gave up the grand slam in the top of the eighth, I hope."

"Yeah," I said, sitting up to get my bearings, knowing that Mike wouldn't be calling at this hour unless there was a break of some kind in the case. "I was exhausted."

"I got worse news than the loss, kid," Mike said. "Tina Barr is dead."

Luc grabbed my hand and squeezed it when he heard me groan.

"They found her body wrapped up in a tarp, just off Sixth Avenue, inside Bryant Park." That was less than a city block away from the rear door of the New York Public Library. "She's been dead for at least twenty-four hours, Coop. Looks like a dump job."

SIXTEEN

Crowds lined the sidewalk at the intersection of Sixth Avenue and Forty-second Street, even though it was two o'clock in the morning. The uniformed cops who had picked me up at my apartment muscled through the onlookers and lifted the yellow police tape that kept them out of the park so we could duck under it.

Huge bright floodlights were mounted on a metal catwalk that framed an enormous JumboTron screen. Below the massive structure, dozens of NYPD men and women were still scrambling to secure the perimeter of the crime scene and push back the cameramen who were trying to climb the low wall to photograph the activity.

"Over here, Alex," Mercer called out. "Watch your step."

The old cobblestone-and-gravel path was littered with debris, and on both sides of it there were tall stacks of folding chairs and wheeled pallets loaded with objects covered with canvas and strapped in place. Fall plantings had been trampled and expensive landscaping would have to be restored.

"Tina?"

"Body's there," Mercer said, pointing to the far side of the plaza beyond the metal super-structure that framed the screen. "The ME got here fifteen minutes ago. She'll finish up soon."

"What's all this?" I asked, looking around at the equipment that cluttered the twin prome-nades of the beautifully landscaped park that ran the length of a football field.

"There was an event here last evening. One of the mayor's goodwill gestures," Mercer said. "Had the JumboTron put up yesterday, and bused in Scout troops—a few thousand kids— from all over the city to see the game. Free. Everybody was pretty orderly when it broke up at the end, and then the workmen started to take the place apart."

I followed him to the edge of the walkway, staring off at the group of cops who were stand-ing shoulder to shoulder, holding up sheets around what was obviously the body of Tina Barr.

"That's when someone found her?"

"Yeah. Her body was wrapped in one of these tarps, just like all the other gear they were about to load up and move out of here."

"Do you think she was—?"

"Fully clothed. Doesn't look like a sexual assault, Alex."

I could see the medical examiner, a short, plump woman with dark skin, emerge from behind the sheeting that had given her some privacy to examine the body. Mercer led me in her direction.

"Detective Wallace, Ms. Cooper," the doctor greeted us as she pulled off her gloves and handed them to her assistant. "Not exactly the best conditions for what I've had to do, but if you'd like to step into my temporary office, you can see what the young lady looks like for yourselves."

Mike was kneeling beside the body of Tina Barr, studying her face. He didn't move when Mercer and I came inside the makeshift morgue.

"As you can see, Ms. Cooper, the killer slit her throat."

Dr. Assif delivered her preliminary clinical findings in a flat monotone. The detective standing behind Tina's head shone his flashlight on the corpse as she spoke.

"Butchered her," Mike said, without picking up his head. "Mercer, would you tell Hal Sherman I want some more photos?"

It was almost impossible to recognize the

face of the woman I had talked with after the attack in her home a few nights ago. There was a long incision across her neck, and a deep wound that exposed layers of muscle beneath the skin. Her vacant eyes were open toward the night sky, and her mouth was agape.

"He's working on the tarp now. Crime Scene's trying to figure a way to move it downtown without losing anything," Mercer said. "He'll be right back."

Barr's body was resting on a clean sheet that the ME's crew had brought with them. The tarp in which she'd been wrapped would be processed for clues.

"She must have bled buckets," I said. There were dark stains all over the front of her short-sleeved V-neck sweater.

"Clothes are a mess," Mike said. "But there's nothing on the tarp."

"Probably because she was killed a day or so before she was placed inside it," Dr. Assif offered.

"Any other signs of a struggle?" I asked.

"I'll know more, of course, when we get her clothes off," the doctor said. "But it doesn't appear to be the case now. No other bruising on her arms or chest. No defensive injuries. I want you guys to bag her hands before she's moved, but I don't see any broken fingernails either."

"How is that possible?"

"Let me examine the wound margins and pattern on the neck, Ms. Cooper. I'll have a better sense of whether I think she was attacked from behind, and what kind of weapon you're looking for."

"Let me know if it's a small sharp blade, like an X-Acto knife," Mike said.

I thought of Alger Herrick as he slit through the long page of the old book.

"Wouldn't you expect her to have time to fight her attacker, or at least to scream?" I couldn't think of a place in Manhattan so remote that no one would hear such a commotion.

"You're thinking of exsanguination," Assif said. "You're assuming that your victim bled to death—slowly. But a postmortem X-ray will tell me if the injury caused a fatal air embolism."

Mike stood up. "That would figure, Doc."

"When one of the larger neck veins is penetrated," the pathologist explained to me, "air is sucked into the vessels because of the negative pressure in the veins. That air mixes with blood and instantly forms a foam, causing a valve lock in the ventricular chamber of the heart."

"Then Tina may have gotten off a gasp or

two, but the embolism brings on an extremely rapid collapse," Mike said.

I listened to them talk about the sudden death that might have resulted from this slice across the victim's neck, but I couldn't take my eyes off the gruesome sight of her discolored, distorted face.

"The body's very well preserved," Assif said. "She must have been in a cool place, not exposed to the elements. No small animals or even insects."

Hal Sherman, a longtime crime scene investigator, pulled back one of the sheets and stuck his head in. "I thought I gave you everything you need, Chapman. Hey, Alex—that's a pretty mean cut, isn't it?"

"Take a few straight over her head, will you?" Mike asked. "I want to check her pockets, so stand by."

Hal was ready with his camera and flash. He moved in over Tina Barr's body and focused his lens on her face and neck while Dr. Assif backed out of the way.

"Did the guys in the office check the weather service for you, Mercer?" Mike asked. "What time is sunrise?"

"Six-thirteen."

"Then tell the lieutenant we need sixty,

maybe eighty uniformed guys here at six-eleven this morning to walk a grid," Mike said. "I don't care where the commissioner pulls them from. They're going to have to eyeball every piece of equipment that moves out of here, talk to every single stagehand who set up this gig. Maybe looking in the grass for a knife or blade—anything sharp that could have done the job. Probably a complete waste of time, but it's got to be done."

"You think Tina was dumped here before the game?" I asked.

"Hard to know. The outside of the tarp was a mess. Footprints all over it. Could have been dumped here—wheeled over on one of these dollies—while the crew was busy unloading everything. The park must have looked like an anthill on fire, getting stuff in place for the game."

Mike lifted the edge of Tina Barr's sweater and reached into her right pants pocket. There was nothing in his gloved hand when he removed it.

I kneeled down beside him.

"Jeez, Coop. What the hell did you do? Put a clove of garlic in your Chanel bottle?"

I covered my mouth with my hand. "Sorry."

"Something I don't know? You're being stalked by a vampire? At least you and Joanie had time for a good dinner," Mike said, reaching across Tina's body into her other pocket. "Here's something."

He sat back on his heels and held up a small laminated tag on a long chain. "It's her library ID—the original one," Mike said. "She must have been dying to get back in there to get a book."

I stood up and turned away from the body. There was no point in trying to change Mike's ways, to discourage the black humor that got him through the relentlessly dark territory of his work.

"Maybe she was dying to get out," I said.

He turned to look at me for the first time since I had arrived at the scene. "Not a bad thought. Wouldn't have been a long haul to get her here, but where the hell could she have been inside that place that was so isolated? It's for scholars and students, for Chrissakes. Me, I think there's just some kind of symbolism in this. Somebody making a statement by dumping her right at the back door of the library."

Hal snapped close-ups of the tag, front and back, and Mike placed it in a paper bag to send to the lab. He went back into the woman's pocket, withdrew a folded slip of paper, and opened it to read.

"Hey, Coop. Isn't this a call slip?"

He lifted the small rectangular piece so that I could see it. "Yes," I said. "It's got Tina's name on it and Tuesday's date."

Mike lifted the corner and below it was a pink slip, then a yellow one, both attached at the end to the top paper. "It's still in triplicate. Looks like she didn't submit it."

"What book was she asking for?"

"**Alice's Adventures in Wonderland,** an 1866 edition. Mercer, you got a bag for this?" Mike asked. "Maybe she realized her landlady, Minerva Hunt, really is a Mad Hatter."

"Just a minute, Mike," Hal Sherman said. "There's some writing on the back."

He took a photograph of the front of the slip, then Mike turned it over.

"What does it say?" I asked.

Hal bent over and started to read. " 'The evil that men do . . .' "

"That's all?" Mike said.

"Why? There should be more?"

" 'The evil that men do lives after them,' " Mike said, picking up the paper after Hal took a picture of it, and getting to his feet. "Finish it off, Coop."

" 'The good are oft interred with their bones.' "

Mike winked at Hal. "**Julius Caesar,** Detective Sherman."

"Quite the poet, Mikey," Hal said, backing away from Tina Barr. "I'm impressed."

"Coop knows her Shakespeare. I know my Roman generals."

One of the cops holding up the sheets lowered a corner to tell Mike that the men were ready to put Tina Barr in a body bag and get her into the ambulance.

We all stood still, silent for a moment, saying our own goodbyes to the slain woman. Then Mike nodded at one of the officers, signaling for the morgue attendants to take her away.

As I moved to make room for the men, the quiet within our space was broken by the shrill ring of a cell phone. A second ring, and I realized the sound was coming from somewhere on Tina's body.

Mike kneeled again and slid his hand beneath her, pulling something from her rear pants pocket. "You answer it, Coop. It's a woman they're expecting to hear," he said, passing me the razor-thin phone eerily buzzing for its dead owner.

I flipped it open and muffled my voice with my hand, saying, "Hello."

The caller waited a few seconds, then disconnected. I could have sworn I heard him laugh before he did.

SEVENTEEN

I was waiting in the lobby of my building when Mike and Mercer pulled in the driveway just after seven a.m. that morning.

"Did you two get any sleep?" I asked, climbing into the back seat.

"Catnap on cots up at the squad," Mercer said. "How about you?"

"I rested." No matter how many murder victims I had seen, it never got easier to find a peaceful zone that wasn't already inhabited by killers and cops.

"No whining, then, Coop," Mike said. "We got a long day ahead of us."

"You never heard that girl whine, Mr. Chapman. Mind your mouth."

I had been comforted to have Luc beside me when I got home several hours ago, holding me and not asking any questions once I told him the bare outline of what had happened. At six, I had gotten out of bed again to call Battaglia with the news, knowing that he would prefer to be awakened with information from me rather than learning it from a newspaper headline on his doorstep.

"What's first?" I asked.

"How about the New York Pubic Library?" Mike said. "Thanks for giving me Jill Gibson's number. I phoned her after you left, to tell her about Tina. She agreed to be here early to have security let us in. Said we'd meet her at seven-thirty."

Mercer opened the lid on a cardboard cup of black coffee and passed it to me as Mike pulled out of the driveway.

"Still no contact for Tina's mother?"

"The lieutenant is sending someone to the Mexican consulate first thing. See if they can smoke her out that way."

"My paper hasn't been delivered yet. Is there a story?"

Mercer held up the **Times** and tabloids. "Lucky for us, the body was found too late for the morning news. May give us a few hours' jump on talking to people."

"I've got to get through to legal at the phone company. Let them know that subpoena I sent out covers the call that came in this morning," I said. Tina Barr was dead, but her cell phone account was still live.

"Freaked me out when that sucker started to ring," Mike said.

Mike got onto the drive in Central Park, looping around to the West Side and exiting on Central Park South. He cruised down Seventh Avenue, turning east onto Forty-second Street— the Deuce, in police parlance—and parked beside the corner entrance to Bryant Park.

The mild weather was a break for the cops. Plainclothes detectives were lined up along the balustrade on the western border of the park, doing one-on-one interviews with men who appeared to be from the JumboTron construction crew. Huge trucks bordered the avenue, waiting to be loaded with equipment that should have been taken off-site in the early hours of the morning, before Tina Barr's body was found.

We walked over and Mike listened in on ten minutes of an interview. "This'll take all day. They're checking each guy's ID so they can run record checks. Getting them to re-create every minute of the setup and breakdown, whether there were any strangers lurking around," he said, shaking his head. "And the bus lanes will be tied up till midnight with these trucks stuck on the street."

Commuters emerged from the corner subway station, confused to find the cheerful breakfast and sandwich kiosks within the park still shuttered and closed, cordoned off by police tape.

We started down the path toward the library building. The phalanx of uniformed cops that Mike had demanded were already in place, clustered in groups to search for anything that might provide a clue.

"Look at all the litter," I said. Ice-cream wrappers and soda cans had been discarded by kids who had watched the ball game. "I can't imagine any items of evidentiary value would survive the presence of the Scout troops."

"Yeah, I wouldn't get my hopes up, Coop. Hair bags and hotheads," Mike said. "Looks like all the commish came up with on short notice to do the search are old-timers who never made it out of uniform and kids fresh from the academy. Cross your fingers."

"They've found needles in bigger haystacks," Mercer said.

"It's kind of ironic that whoever killed Barr left her here," Mike said, stopping to stomp his foot on the ground. "You know what's underneath this park?"

"No," I said.

"Dead people. Nothing but dead people."

"What do you mean?"

Bryant Park was a green oasis in the middle

of one of the city's busiest commercial districts. Thousands of office workers in nearby skyscrapers escaped their buildings every day—until the middle of winter, when it was turned into a skating rink—to eat lunch, read books, meet friends, enjoy the carrousel, and relax in the atmosphere of a French formal garden.

Mike turned and walked backward, sweeping his hand around the park. "During the Revolutionary War, this site was a killing field for Washington's troops when they fled the British after the Battle of Long Island."

"Well, they're surely not below the park now," I said.

"Listen to me, Coop. The whole feng shui of this place is death. After the war, the city made this ground a potter's field. Final resting place for the indigent and unbefriended. Dead folk down there, one on top of the other, I'm telling you."

"I thought this place used to be the site of the reservoir," Mercer said.

"No, no, no. The reservoir was right over where the library stands," Mike said, pointing at the back of the elegant structure. "This spot was the burial ground. I know there's dead people under here, Coop. It's a fact. The city decommissioned the potter's field in the 1850s to build a crystal palace for the first World's Fair.

When that burnt down, they turned it into
a park.

"When my old man came on the job—the
1970s—Bryant Park was one of the most
treacherous places in Manhattan. Dope dealers
ran the place, he used to tell me. All crime all
the time."

"Over here, Sarge," a voice called out, and a
hand went up in the air. The three of us
stopped in our tracks.

"Whaddaya got?"

The young cop was wading through a bed of
pachysandra. "Used condoms. Do I pick 'em up?"

The sergeant's answer was drowned out by
three other officers yelling that they had also
found condoms. "Everything goes to the lab."

Mike continued walking east. "Be prepared.
Isn't that the Scouts' motto? Glad they came to
the game with condoms. Maybe they were
cross-pollinating with the Brownies while the
Yankee bullpen was falling apart. Those techs
are going to have their hands full, testing all the
crap that turns up."

At the end of the pathway, we found an exit
onto Forty-second Street and left the park to elbow our way to the front of the library, which
stretched down two long blocks. The midtown
crossroads at the corner of Fifth Avenue was a
hub of pedestrian and vehicular traffic.

"Is that Gibson?" Mike said.

I looked ahead and could see Jill, talking on her cell, as she paced below the statue of one of the two spectacular marble lions—iconic New York City landmarks—that stood on guard at the foot of the terraced steps of the great building.

I introduced her to Mike and Mercer, reminding her that Mike was the detective who had called her early that morning.

"I'm heartbroken about this, Alex. It's just unthinkable that someone could have done this to Tina. We were all so willing to help her, but I couldn't get her to come in," Jill said, turning to lead us up the first tier of steps. "I've called security. They're sending someone to the front door to open up."

"You ought to put some mourning ribbons around the lions' necks," Mike said, patting the large paw of the one to his right as he passed by it.

"You know their names, Mike?" Jill asked.

"I didn't know they had names."

"During the Great Depression, Mayor La-Guardia called them Patience and Fortitude. He felt those were the qualities New Yorkers needed to endure the hardships of the times."

"The same traits will serve us well this week," Mercer said.

Mercer was as quiet and steady as ever, knowing that we were moving deeper into a tangled thicket of characters and motives, that we had a series of crimes that would not be solved as quickly as Mike might like. Mike, on the other hand, was long on fortitude and short, as always, on patience.

We continued our climb, and I admired the stunning array of sculptures and reliefs—sphinxes, winged horses, allegorical figures, and literary inscriptions—that decorated the massive portico of the library. At the very top, we passed under one of the arches and waited at the front door for a worker to admit us.

Mike reached into his jacket pocket and removed some folded papers. "This is a Xerox of the call slip that Tina had in her pocket when she was killed," Mike said. "The one I mentioned to you on the phone."

Jill Gibson read the notations on the first piece of paper—Tina's name, the date, and the book she must have been about to request. On the second page was the partial quote that had been scrawled on the back of that slip.

Jill looked at them both again, just as the man inside opened the series of locks and pulled back the huge wood-and-glass door.

"Tina didn't write this," Jill said. "Someone made this call slip out in her name."

"You mean one of the librarians?"

"Well, you saw the original, Mike. Was it made out in pencil or in ink?"

"The front side, with her name and the book title, was done in ink. The notation on the back—see how faint it is here on the copy? That was written in pencil."

"The librarians in the reading room don't allow ink in there. Most research libraries are like that. You can only use pencil," Jill said. Her hand was trembling as she folded the slip in half. "I know Tina's handwriting well, Detective. It's quite distinctive, whether in print or script. She didn't write that information on the call slip. And it's unlikely any of the librarians did, either. Certainly not in ink."

Mike took the papers back and compared the two writing styles. I knew what he was thinking. We'd have to bring in another expert—someone familiar with the very unscientific field of handwriting analysis. One clue that seemed promising at two o'clock in the morning now created a new level of obfuscation.

"The second page—that quote on the back of the slip—that's Tina's writing," Jill said. "But she didn't fill out this form. We have several early editions of the Lewis Carroll work, all of them quite rare. Maybe another person asked her to make the request to see one of these books."

Maybe someone who didn't want to be associated with the request filled out the call slip, counting on the fact that he—or she—could persuade Tina to deliver it and retrieve the book. Maybe it was the person who killed her.

EIGHTEEN

"Where are the books?" Mike asked. "I don't see a frigging book in here."

Mike, Mercer, and I were standing in the middle of Astor Hall, one of the most magnificent interior spaces in New York. Jill had gone off to find the chief security officer to ask him to guide us through the enormous building.

"It's not a lending library, Mike. It's a home for scholars to use, for research," I said. "Books have to be accessed through a formal system. They're not out on open shelves, and they never leave."

"Unless they're stolen. So where the hell are they?"

"Upstairs, in carefully maintained private collections," I said. "And under your feet, in the stacks. You'll see."

Mercer was walking around the great vaulted space. "Looks like we've time-traveled back to inside a medieval castle."

The great hall, dressed entirely in white marble, had a self-supporting vaulted ceiling that covered the space between the two broad staircases leading up to the second floor. Four giant torchères—also marble—stood sentry around the large, empty room.

"Did you see her hand shake?" I said, whispering so that my voice didn't echo throughout the hall.

"Jill's?" Mercer asked. "I missed that."

"When Battaglia and I were talking to her yesterday and McKinney jumped in, he referred to Tina Barr as a thief and a forger."

"And you said Jill didn't seem to buy in to that."

"Yes. But someone working in here must think so."

"What's your point?" Mike asked, standing under one of the arches across the room.

I walked toward him so that I didn't have to shout. "How can Jill say for sure that the writing on the call slip wasn't done by Tina?"

"You mean, if Tina was capable of forgery, maybe she intentionally wanted it to look like someone else wrote it out?"

"That's possible. Once she turned in the original slip, it would become the permanent record that the library would have for the request. That's who they'd look to if the book went missing."

Mercer came up behind me. "It's also possible Jill got the shakes 'cause she recognized the penmanship on the slip, Alex. Maybe it's given her an idea about who wrote it but she chose not to tell you just yet."

We heard her approach on the marble staircase and stopped talking.

"Why don't you come this way?" Jill said, pausing halfway down.

We crossed the room, our footsteps echoing throughout the hall, and followed Jill as she turned and walked up to the second floor. At the top, a man about my height with a thick build was standing cross-armed, dressed in a drab green uniform.

"This is Yuri," Jill said, introducing him to each of us. "None of the security supervisors is here yet. He's one of our engineers, so just tell us what you'd like to see and we can get started."

"Top to bottom," Mike said. "Entrances, exits, any way in or out of this place."

"Obviously," Jill said, "we've just come in the front door."

"Is that how the public enters?"

"Most of the time, Detective. There's also a smaller entrance on the Forty-second Street side. Yuri," she said, "why don't we start upstairs and work our way down?"

"What's your security like?"

"Since September 11 it's been a lot tighter.

Our doors open at ten most weekdays. Guards check bags on the way in and on the way out."

"I saw two metal detectors at the door," Mike said. "They good enough to catch a thief with a razor blade or knife coming through?"

"So you know how the bad guys used to cut out the desirable pages?" Jill was a few steps ahead of us, with Yuri. "A thing of the past, Mike. Between metal detectors and the arrest of a few major map thieves, those particular tools have become obsolete."

Yuri was leading us up another flight of stairs.

"You mean people don't steal old prints or maps out of books anymore?"

"Sadly, the thefts go on. It's just that the methods change. The bad guys have moved on to dental floss."

"Floss?"

"Try it, Detective. Wet some floss. Soak it for a while to stiffen it up. Keep it moist by balling it up inside your cheek when you get to the library. The thieves have found it just as effective for ripping out pages with exactly the same result. Takes about ten minutes to soften up the old paper by applying the floss to it, so it's a bit more nerve-racking than the old-fashioned technique. But it works just fine."

"Not even against the penal law. Armed with

a dangerous instrument—wet dental floss," Mike said, trying to catch up with Jill. "You sure got a lot of steps."

"All part of the master plan. The first floor has that grand open space, and a periodical room that the public was allowed to use from our earliest days. Then up to the second floor—you'll see our offices later—where the private collections are housed, and then up to the third level, to the great reading room. The nineteenth-century design idea was to lift the scholars away from the noise and pollution of the street so they could get their work done in the lightest, airiest part of the library. Still a good idea. Is this where you did your college research, Alex?"

"The reading room? Yes, it is."

"It's been completely restored to its original condition. You'll hardly recognize it," Jill said, pausing at the top of the steps.

Yuri took a key from among the many on the ring that dangled from his belt. While he unlocked the massive wooden doors, I looked up to the barrel vault on the ceiling, at the brilliant painting of Prometheus bringing the gift of fire to man, which soared in the rotunda overhead.

He stood back to let us into the room. Mike and Mercer entered before me, and both seemed stunned by the beauty—and size—of the Rose Reading Room.

"Go ahead," Jill said. "There's a quarter of an acre of space in here, meant to accommodate seven hundred scholars. It's one of the largest uninterrupted rooms in the city—almost the full length of two blocks. For me, it's the heart of the place."

Library table after library table with aisles on either side lined up in rows from end to end. Atop each were lamps and ports to service laptops at each station.

"It practically glows in here now," I said.

The large multipaned windows that flanked the room flooded it with morning light. "Can you imagine?" Jill asked. "That glass was all painted black during World War Two, and stayed dark until only a few years ago, with this recent renovation."

I walked along the parquet floors in search of the table at which I'd situated myself day after day to work on my senior thesis more than fifteen years ago. I looked up at the ceiling—perhaps the most beautiful in the city—for a marker among the hanging chandeliers, a gilded cherub whose once-tarnished wings now gleamed again. She was still surrounded, as I remembered her, by coffers ornamented with angels and satyrs, and luminous paintings of blue skies and puffy white clouds in the style of the old masters.

I sat in one of the chairs and leaned back to take in the murals and all the detail that seemed to have been refurbished to its original brilliance.

"Don't get too comfortable, Coop," Mike said. "What's the process, Jill? Say Tina wanted to get this book, this particular edition of **Alice in Wonderland.** What would she have had to do?"

Jill walked to the center of the long room, which was divided by the catalog area.

"She would have come here, as she'd done many times before," Jill said, placing her hand on the top of the counter. "Tina—or any researcher—hands in the call slip to the clerk and is given a delivery number. The clerk figures out where the book is, whether in a collection upstairs or below us in the stacks, and sends for it using a pneumatic tube system."

"Pneumatic tubes?" Mike asked. "I thought they went out with covered wagons."

"Old systems die hard in the library business. We're trying to convert to something a little more current—electronic—but that will still take years to effect."

"Did she need a letter of introduction?"

"Tina's credentials are well established here,

Detective. As newcomers, each of you would have to start out with references, but not someone with whom we're familiar. The letters in support of her application would still be on file."

"Makes an inside job even easier to pull off," Mike said. "Your staff develops a comfort level with the researcher when they see her here regularly."

"Quite true."

Mike took the papers out of his pocket again and smoothed them on the countertop.

"So how does the clerk know which copy of **Alice in Wonderland** to fetch?"

Jill had her back against the wooden partition and was talking to all of us. "She would have asked Tina to specify that. They'd have looked in the card catalog to see where the different volumes are."

"Let's do that," Mike said. "Where's the catalog?"

"Not in little wooden boxes anymore, Detective, if that's what you're thinking. Those books against the wall—eight hundred of them— reproduce the original catalogs. Everything else is online now. It's a program called CATNYP— Catalog of the New York Public Library. One can access it here, of course, but also from anywhere in the world."

"So Tina, or anyone she was working with for that matter, might have looked for the existence of a book from a computer in her own apartment?"

"Quite easily."

"Why don't you show us how?" Mike said.

Jill didn't seem eager to comply. She looked at her watch, but it was still too early to be expecting anyone on staff to appear.

"C'mon. I'd like to see the way it works."

Jill walked behind the counter and logged on to one of the computers. We watched as she typed in the request. Mike stepped in to look over her shoulder.

"We've got several early copies in the Central Children's Room, but that collection isn't housed in this building anymore. Tina knew that, so she wouldn't have been looking for any of those by putting a slip in here," Jill said, moving her finger down the screen. "Okay, in the Special Collections section, we have one in Arents. An 1866 edition."

"What's Arents?"

"George Arents was an executive at P. Lorillard in the early part of the last century. You know, one of the big tobacco companies. He bequeathed us his library in 1944—it's called the Tobacco Collection, because every book and artifact in it is related to that subject."

"So why would **Alice in Wonderland** be shelved there?" Mike asked.

"The caterpillar with the hookah," I said. "Smoking opium on his mushroom."

"Exactly. Then I see another 1866 edition in the Berg Collection," Jill said. "Quite the rare piece. Very valuable. It's the author's presentation copy to Alice Liddell, inscribed by Carroll to her. The first approved edition, bound in blue morocco. You can certainly have a look at that one."

"Alice Liddell's father was the dean of Christ Church in Oxford," I explained to Mike and Mercer. "Charles Dodgson—he used the pen name Lewis Carroll—was a math tutor at the college, and friendly with the Liddells. He first told his stories of a girl's adventures after falling in a rabbit hole to Alice, who was believed to be his inspiration for them, and later published the book."

Jill Gibson was scanning the catalog. "That's all I find for 1866."

"How about in the Hunt Collection?" Mercer asked, leaning his elbows on the counter.

"Let me see," she said, scrolling down to that field. "There's an 1865 edition, but that one was never approved. The author and illustrator didn't like the quality of the drawings. And there are letters of Carroll's, some of his correspondence. There are also originals of some of the pictures he took of Alice. You may not know, but Carroll's hobby was photography."

"I've seen some of the images—ten-year-old Alice posed half naked," I said. "Guess that's what started the speculation that Lewis Carroll was a pedophile."

"We'll never know, will we?" Jill said.

"Coop would have gotten to the bottom of it. Load the old boy's hookah with something to suppress the urge and pack him off to prison," Mike said, pushing the copy of the call slip in front of the keyboard. "You know, Jill, I kind of got the feeling you've seen this handwriting before."

She kept her eyes on the screen in front of her. "I never said that. Maybe I spoke too quickly. It's quite possible Tina printed the words herself. I shouldn't have jumped to another conclusion. Here's the original of Lewis Carroll's diary covering the period he wrote the book. That's in the Hunt Collection."

"Pat McKinney thinks Tina was a forger, Jill. Do you?"

"She was an artist, Detective. Very skilled at her work."

"I'd like you to look at this slip of paper again, Jill. Why won't you do that?"

She clasped her hands and rested them on the countertop, looking down at the copy.

"You were so emphatic a short time ago that the words on here weren't written by Tina Barr. Isn't that because you recognized the penmanship as someone else's?" Mike asked. He was standing so close to her that he seemed to have her pinned in place, pressuring her to answer. "You shook like a leaf when I handed you this paper outside the library. Why, Jill?"

She pushed Mike's arm away from her and turned to face him. "There are people in the library—employees as well as board members—who didn't trust Tina. Alex knows that. Mr. McKinney was talking to many of them for his investigation, and all the while I've been defending the girl. Then you show me this," Jill said, picking up the paper from the countertop. "I'd hoped never to see this writing in one of my libraries again."

"Who do you think it is?"

"A man named Eddy Forbes. I don't suppose you know about him."

"A map thief," Mike said. Alger Herrick had talked about Forbes yesterday. Herrick said he'd been released from jail and was involved in some kind of deal with Minerva Hunt.

"The most prolific map thief we've ever

come up against. And a lot of what he stole was from the Beinecke Library in New Haven, during my tenure there," Jill said, bowing her head.

"You were blamed for the lax security?" Mercer asked.

"By some. There were others who thought worse."

"That you partnered with him on proceeds of what he stole from your library?"

"Yes, Alex. I fought that battle once and won. I was lucky I had friends among the trustees here who believed in me. They let me come back to work. That won't be the case a second time, if it turns out Eddy Forbes had a plan to use Tina—and perhaps someone else on the inside."

"I thought his specialty was maps," I said. "That doesn't seem at all connected to Alice and her adventures underground."

"If Forbes is involved, count on the fact that there's a map in the mix."

"Was Tina capable of imitating someone's signature?"

"Probably so. In this digital age, the ability to copy or even to forge has been made so much easier by all the technology available. Almost anyone could do it, let alone someone as artistically gifted as Tina."

"Why did Pat McKinney tell me—tell the

district attorney—that Tina Barr was a forger and a thief?" I asked.

"I haven't known Minerva Hunt and her brother, Talbot, to be aligned on very many issues for as long as I've been around. But both of them have accused her, to the president, of stealing from the family collection in the past few months." Jill Gibson started to lead us out of the catalog area, back to the hallway. "Quite frankly, until I looked at this call slip and made the link between Tina and Eddy Forbes, I didn't believe it for a minute."

Mercer was walking the length of the room, bending down to check beneath the desktops, examining the volumes along the wall.

Yuri followed behind him like a shorter, stubby shadow, protecting his turf.

At the far corner of the room there was a narrow opening.

"Where does that lead to?" Mercer asked.

"Goes nowhere. Is attic. Is only air handlers for the building," Yuri said.

"Is there an exit up there?"

"Is nothing, I told you."

Jill Gibson waved them off. "Nothing there. No one except engineering's allowed in the attic. The public doesn't have access."

"But is there an exit from the library?" Mercer asked.

Yuri was beginning to stutter. He had a burly build, and he lurched forward, swinging his thick arms as he walked. "You—you want see? Is just roof."

Mercer stepped aside as Yuri turned the corner, and the three of us followed. A small caged elevator was the only thing in the small dark space behind the reading room.

We all fit in it, tightly crunched together.

It was a quick ride—maybe fifteen seconds—up to the attic, literally, to the rafters below the library roof.

"Careful, miss," Yuri said, pointing to the catwalk. "No slip."

The space was remarkably clean and open, with giant metal pipes that circulated fresh air throughout the building.

I held on to the wooden railing as Yuri led us along the open walkway to a narrow ladder, and above it, a small hatch. Mercer climbed up behind him and stepped outside for a few seconds before rejoining us.

"Where does it go?" Mike asked.

"No egress to the street. Kind of a dead end," Jill said. "It's an interior courtyard, and it's covered."

"What if the guy was a jumper?"

"I'm afraid he'd go right through the glass roof directly below. You didn't want to take my word for it, but that hatch is above the Bartos Forum. That's the part of the library covered entirely in glass, to replicate the old Crystal Palace. Have you had enough, gentlemen?"

Jill seemed anxious to move us out of this space. She started along the catwalk, leading us back to the elevator.

"What are those things?" Mike asked, pointing at two huge cylindrical tanks.

I knew he was as surprised as I that the attic was so exposed, not likely to have been used to conceal a body.

"Water tanks, Mike. More than a century old. Cork-insulated barrels that sit right on top of the world's largest plaster ceiling, with the library's entire water supply running through them," Jill said, pausing to look over at the giant casks. "Fire and water, Detective, are the two things a librarian has most to fear."

Mike steadied himself on the beam and crouched down, looking under the barrels to make certain nothing was behind them.

"Hold on, folks," he said, shimmying himself forward till his head and shoulders disappeared beneath one of the water tanks. "You more afraid of fire and water than dead bodies in your belfry?"

We all stopped in a line behind Jill Gibson. "What?" she asked in a shrill voice.

"You're moving too fast for me, lady," Mike said. "I just wanted to get your attention. There's no body in here, but it looks like a nice pile of overdue library books. Might get yourself a healthy fine paid, if you come across the thief."

Mike worked himself back out from underneath the tank, and Yuri scrambled to help him up on his feet.

"Ms. Gibson, I swear," Yuri said. "Was here yesterday, eleven o'clock in the morning. Once every twenty-four hours, check under tank for leaks. No leaks. Was nothing there. Myself did it. Myself."

"We'll discuss that later, Yuri. Be still." Jill wasn't interested in his protestations. She stepped off the catwalk and I followed her over to where Mike had moved the small pile of books. "May I have them, please?"

"I think they're ours for the time being," Mike said, removing gloves from his pants pocket before he lifted the cover of the first slim volume. **"Tamerlane,** 1827. Edgar Allan Poe."

"One of thirteen existing copies in the world, Detective. Fifty printed—his first published poem. A treasure, to say the least."

"From . . . ?"

"It was kept in a vault in the Berg Collection. That's on the second floor, Mike. I'll show you where."

"Walt Whitman's **Leaves of Grass,** 1860," Mike said. "You caught a break here. It's only a third edition."

"That particular copy has actually got greater value than the firsts," Jill said, nervously poised over Mike's shoulder. "It's called the Blue Book. Whitman kept it at his desk while he worked as a clerk at the Department of the Interior, constantly making edits in it. The secretary found it and thought it so obscene that Whitman was fired on the spot."

The four books beneath that were larger. Three were brilliantly colored illuminated manuscripts of Petrarch's poems, Horace's works, and Aesop's fables, all with spectacular calligraphy done on ancient vellum. Mike read the titles aloud to us, including the fourth one, which was an archive of the paintings of Asher Durand.

Jill Gibson exhaled. "That will raise some board eyebrows."

"Why's that?" Mercer asked.

"Durand was a nineteenth-century artist," she said. "His work helped define the Hudson River School. And it's his great painting— **Kindred Spirits**—which was bequeathed to us and which we sold for a fortune in 2005."

"Over the heated objection of many of your trustees," I said.

"That's putting it mildly."

"Can you give us a breakdown later of who was for and against it?" Mercer said.

"Certainly."

Mike lifted the oversize folio that had been at the bottom of the pile. "John James Audubon, **Birds of America,** volume one."

"Heads will roll," Jill said. "That's from the Hunt Collection—one of its jewels—and worth a king's ransom today. If Jasper gets word that we haven't had the ability to protect the best things he's given us, we stand to lose all the rest."

Mike gently lifted the cover. "Talk about the emperor's new clothes. These birds either flew the coop, Coop, or somebody beat us to them."

He held the book up for us to see inside, and it was clear that pages had been sliced out of it. Only blank parchment was left between the ends of the fine leather bindings.

As Mike stood up with the heavy tome in his arms, he flipped through the few remaining sheets in it. He turned the last page, and a two-foot-long fragment of a larger antique map—not bound into the old book—slipped out and fluttered to the floor.

Jill reached down for it as Mike yelled out, "Don't touch it."

I kneeled beside her and looked at the detailed engraving: a piece of the Asian continent, and the figure of a man standing beside a map of the world. The cartouche over his head proclaimed him to be Amerigo Vespucci.

"What's he got to do with birds?" Mike asked.

"Nothing at all," Jill said, steadying herself with one hand on the floor, the other clasped to her chest. "What you may be looking at is a piece of the most valuable map ever made, in a little village in France, in 1507."

"How valuable is it? Worth enough to kill for?" he said, trying to make out the detail in the woodcut engraving.

"If all twelve sections of this puzzle actually do exist, there's only one other map like it in the world. The price tag on it would be close to twenty million dollars."

"That's a staggering number," I said. "Maybe enough to turn Tina Barr into a thief."

"I don't know why she wouldn't have been tempted by it," Jill Gibson said. "Half the members of my board would sell their souls to own this map."

NINETEEN

←—————————————————————————————→

"If you're looking for the Holy Grail of rare maps," the petite librarian said to us, grinning as she gazed at the woodcut that Mike had placed on the table in front of her, "this is as good as it gets."

Bea Dutton was in charge of the map division of the library, home to more than half a million of them and more than twenty thousand atlases and books about cartography. Jill had called her to come in to the office early, moments after Mike made his find, and she appeared within the hour.

"Did you know this map was missing?" Mike asked.

"What do you mean?" Bea said. Her white cotton gloves—a tool of her trade—looked more civilized than Mike's plastic ones. She was short and slight, and leaned her elbows on the long trestle table to get a good look at her subject.

"I'm sure you must know exactly when something as precious as this disappeared from your collection."

"You've made a bad assumption, Detective. We've never had a map like this under our roof. I can't even imagine what this portion of it was doing here. I've been waiting a professional life-time to see if another one of these treasures came to market. The only known original in the world is in the Library of Congress. Didn't Jill tell you?"

"This is your bailiwick, Bea," Jill said. "I've seen it on your wish list but really didn't know whether or not we owned any of the individual panels."

"Let me explain what you've found here," Bea said, inviting Mercer, Mike, and me to sit around the table. We were on the first floor of the library, in an elegant room with dark wood paneling, three long tables, and copies of anti-quarian maps of all varieties mounted in gilded frames along its walls. Only the coat of arms of the City of New York on each pedestal of the tables betrayed that we weren't being enter-tained in a fancy British manor home. "That is, if I can take my eyes off it. You're looking at one of the pieces of what many people call Amer-ica's birth certificate."

Mercer looked closely at the ancient draw-ing. "How so?"

"This panel is part of a map that was the very first document in the world on which the word 'America' appears as the name for a body of land in the Western Hemisphere."

Mike bent forward to look for the notation.

"Not on this particular fragment, Mike. Remember, there are twelve pieces of this beauty, each the same size as this. Once joined together, the map is four feet tall by eight feet wide. It's quite an unusual masterpiece."

"Who created it?" I asked. "What made it so special?"

"The primary author was Martin Waldseemüller, a German cleric and cartographer who spent his life in Saint-Dié, France, part of a small intellectual circle there. Until this was published in 1507, the European body of knowledge about the world's geography was entirely based on the second-century work of Ptolemy. This map," Bea said, tapping her gloved finger on the table, "radically changed the worldview."

"In what way?" Mike asked.

"Think of it, Detective. The Spanish and Portuguese kept returning to Europe at the end of the fifteenth century with dramatic news of explorations down the African coast and across the Atlantic, where no Europeans had ever been before. To us, this map looks incredibly accurate, but to his contemporaries, Martin's map

ignited a great deal of debate. It presented a revolutionary vision of the world."

"Why?"

"This was the first document ever created
that depicted a Western Hemisphere, standing
alone between two oceans, the first to represent
the Pacific as a separate body of water, and the
first to give the new world its own name:
'America.' In those times, they were completely
radical ideas."

Mercer's huge frame was bent over the table
as he examined the fine print in the woodcut.
"Used to be, according to Ptolemy, the Atlantic
stretched from Europe and Asia right over to
Japan, Cathay, and India, with a little bit of
terra incognita along the way."

"Exactly," Bea said.

"What about Columbus?" Mike asked. "He
was over here before Vespucci. How come he
didn't get the whole caboodle named for Christo-
foro instead of Amerigo?"

"Well, that's another reason this map was so
controversial. Both men made several voyages
across the Atlantic. Vespucci enjoyed more
popularity throughout Europe because he
wrote many publications that were read widely
by intellectuals and explorers—he was a best
seller in his day—and he actually went farther

down the coastline of South America, convinced there was another ocean, entirely separate, on the western side of that landmass," Bea said. "Columbus, on the other hand, died in disgrace. Do you remember your history?"

"Yeah, I guess he did the first Terra Nova perp walk, didn't he?" Mike said. "He was the governor of Hispaniola, and the king had him arrested for mismanagement."

"Right. He also maintained, till his dying day, that he had reached Asia on one of his voyages. It was Vespucci who realized that both he and Columbus had come upon another continent—not Asia, not the Indies—that most Europeans didn't know existed. So he got the credit," Bea said. "It's kind of remarkable when you think that this single obscure mapmaker—as great as he was—chose the name for the entire Western Hemisphere."

"And that he named it for a man who was still alive at the time, Amerigo Vespucci. No waiting for the verdict of history or going the traditional route of naming it for a mythological figure," Mercer said, straightening up.

"Then he feminized it," Bea said. "Don't forget that, Alex. Asia and Europa got their names from mythical women—so that tradition of the feminine ending of a continent remained intact."

"But it's this little group of clerics and geographers who were so taken by Vespucci's writings that they placed his name on this map?" I asked.

"No longer Terra Incognita or Terra Nova, as the new world was called by the ancients. Martin and his team just went ahead and christened these lands America—their very own idea," Bea said, "and as soon as this work was published, cartographers everywhere adopted that name for the Western Hemisphere."

"How many of these maps were printed at the time?" Mercer asked.

"A very sizable run for those days, actually. One thousand copies."

"What became of them all, do you think?"

Bea smoothed her curly red hair with the back of her glove. "Like many objects of intellectual interest in the sixteenth century, part of the plan was to distribute them as widely as possible across Europe, to spread the new knowledge that the explorers were acquiring with each trip they made. That broad dissemination accounts for the loss of many things, and makes the ones that made it through time, warfare, pillaging, and the usual historical turmoil so very rare."

"And its size?" I asked.

"Another problem indeed. The larger an old

map, the rarer it has usually become. The huge size and very inconvenience of form of this one certainly quickened its destruction. It was so much greater than many of the charts of the day, folded once—never bound—inside an elephant folio. So the mere difficulty of keeping twelve large panels like this one in pristine condition, and not allowing the dozen sections of it to be separated, was an enormous obstacle to its survival."

"What's an elephant folio?" Mike asked.

"It's the term for a very large book, Detective. Usually greater than two feet tall. That Audubon in which you found the map is actually a double elephant folio—easy to conceal your map in because it's so large. Let me show you something."

Bea got up from the table and disappeared behind the reference desk, returning minutes later with a volume of elephant-folio size.

"This one is a book of reproductions of famous maps," she said, placing it beside the piece that Mike found inside the Audubon. "It will give you an idea of how startling the real thing is when you see all the panels joined together, as originally planned."

She unfolded the enormous pages and spread them before us. The dozen individual engravings came together as a gigantic rectangular map of the world, separated by the seams of the individual pieces. The portion that Mike had discovered in the library's attic, stashed under a water tank, was one from the top panel, in the third of four columns.

"It's not only beautifully drawn," I said, scanning the continents and islands, oceans and seas, and their relationships to one another. "But you're right. It's incredibly accurate for its time."

"Men who'd never left their villages in Europe combined their own dreams of the greater world with this outpouring of information from the explorers," Bea said. "Today, there is no more terra incognita. From your handheld GPS you can pull up a satellite image of your own backyard, or an atoll in the Pacific. These early maps charted the unknown, and they're remarkably exciting for that reason."

"You say there's a complete original of this one at the Library of Congress?" Mike asked. "When was that found?"

"Don't get too excited, Detective. More than a century ago. This sheet you stumbled over this morning is the first fresh sighting in a hundred years."

"Tell us about the last one."

Bea Dutton was as enthusiastic as she was knowledgeable about her cartographic history.

"Have you ever heard of a German Jesuit priest named Josef Fischer?"

None of us had.

"A brilliant scholar and perhaps a bit of a rogue. There's a very rare piece at Yale called the Vinland Map, purchased for the library there by the great philanthropist Paul Mellon. Had it been proved to be authentic, it would have shown that the Vikings predated Columbus's voyages to this continent by fifty years."

"Sounds like you don't think it's real," Mike said.

"Carbon-fourteen analysis dates the parchment to the 1430s, Mike, but a chemical study of the ink puts us in the 1920s. It's on old paper—the kind you can slice right out of an ancient book, sad to say—but the ink gave it away."

"So Father Fischer's a fraud?"

"Well, most of us in the field think the only person he was trying to defraud—and embarrass—with his doctored map was the führer."

"Then I'm all for the old boy already," Mike said. "How's that?"

"Hitler was using Norse history as Nazi propaganda. He likened the Norse to Aryans by claiming that their territorial ambitions were similar to his own empire-lust," Bea said.

"So Fischer put the Roman Catholic Church in the mix," Mike said. "Didn't want the Nazis to get away with their propaganda without a little bit of religion thrown in."

"There's a lot of Catholic imagery in the Vinland Map," Bea said, pointing out notations with her white glove in the same book of reproductions. "Father Fischer was so outraged by the Nazi persecution of the Jesuits that he just teased Hitler by creating this fake document. If the führer wanted to believe the Vikings led the way to the new world, Fischer wouldn't let him have that victory unless he accepted that the Catholic Church was also along for the ride."

"So what did Father Fischer have to do with finding my map?" Mike asked.

"See, you've got the fever already," Bea said. "**Your** map, is it?"

Mike smiled at her. "I've got a lot of empty wall space in my crib. You tell me what I'm looking for and let's go for the whole dozen panels. I'll let you come visit any time you'd like."

"That's a deal, Mike," Bea said, continuing her story. "Fischer was doing research in 1901, in a private library in a German castle. As happens with so many important discoveries in history, Fischer simply lucked upon something he'd never set out to find—in this case, a dusty portfolio in an obscure corner of a nobleman's home. Cartographers had been searching for remnants of this particular lost map for so long that they had begun to believe the great Vespuccian model never really existed as such."

"A complete accident, then?"

"Exactly. Prince Waldburg's ancestors had collected maps for generations. While Fischer was studying papers of the early Norsemen in Greenland—his own personal area of interest—he came across a large manuscript that had been in the family for generations. It was a prize collection of the famous sixteenth-century globe maker named Johannes Schöner that had been acquired centuries earlier. Schöner, we figure, had purchased the Waldseemüller map of 1507 in order to incorporate its new worldview in his work so that he could use it to make his own globes more up-to-date."

"What a find," Mercer said.

"And especially because the twelve panels had never been assembled. Each one was carefully concealed inside the pages of this enormous folio, untouched for four centuries," Bea said, shifting her attention back to the segment that Mike had found just a couple of hours earlier. "I'd say this looks just about faultless, too."

"What became of the one that Father Fischer found?" Mike asked.

"It stayed in private hands—at the castle—for another hundred years. In 2003, one century and ten million dollars later, this map became the crown jewel of the Library of Congress. The **universalis cosmographia.**"

"What?" I asked.

"The world map of 1507 is how we know it as librarians. **Universalis cosmographia secundum Ptholomaei traditionem et Americi Vespucii aliorumque lustrationes.** That's its formal name."

"A map of the world according to the tradition of Ptolemy and the voyages of Amerigo Vespucci," Mike said, smiling at Bea, who looked surprised by his translation ability. "You don't think those nuns at parochial school liked me for my good behavior, do you? My Latin wasn't half bad."

She flipped back to the copy in her book of reproductions and again unfolded it before us.

"What are the chances that Mike's find is a forgery?" Mercer asked.

Bea Dutton frowned. "Because of what I told you about Father Fischer?"

More likely Mercer had asked that question because of rumors about Tina Barr.

"Yeah."

"The Vinland Map presented an entirely different issue. The Vikings were the greatest explorers of the Middle Ages—nobody disputes that. They just never made maps. Not a single one," Bea said. "They didn't have a concept of the world that encouraged any of them to draw diagrams, so lots of scholars were skeptical about its authenticity from the get-go. Then there's the ink. You know how ink is made?"

I'd never given it a thought. "Actually, I have no idea."

"It's the reaction between iron in ferrous sulfate and tannin from oak trees. Together they oxidize on a page and literally burn the letters or drawings into the paper. Over centuries, the blackened mark starts to turn brown."

"And the Vinland Map ink?" Mercer asked.

"Document examiners subjected it to microprobe spectroscopy, which yielded a synthetic substance—something called anatase—that was in the ink. And that wasn't manufactured until World War One. Heave-ho to the Vikings."

"And this?"

"Look closely at it, Mercer." Bea pushed the tip of the antique panel closer to us and started to explain it to us. "This is exquisitely elaborate, do you see?"

There was a masterfully drawn portrait of Vespucci, holding his navigational instruments, at the top of the large panel. Below him was the upper portion of the map, representing an area that was bordered by the Arctic Ocean, and below it a landmass with tiny writing that described interior regions and portrayed the topography of the area. Behind Vespucci was a chubby-cheeked figure—the northeast wind—blowing across the frigid waters.

"The detail is astonishing," I said.

"See the inset?" Bea asked. On the upper-left quadrant of the panel was a small world map. "It's actually different than the larger image, if you were to see them all assembled. As Vespucci completed more voyages, the latest descriptions were added to these smaller insets."

"Too detailed to forge?" I asked.

"Not only that, Alex. The Vinland Map is just ink on parchment. This one is a woodcut. It's truly a work of art, and I'd say impossible to re-create today. After all, we do have one original in Washington against which any discoveries like the one you made this morning can be compared."

Mike was poring over the reproduction that Bea had unfolded. "Every section of this map tells its own story, doesn't it?"

"That's one of the things that's so magical about it," she said.

The margins of the twelve panels were festooned with figures of the wind and sea, and cartouches that chronicled the most important features of these newly charted territories.

"Could be the reason that this piece of the map was stored in that particular book might point us to whatever Tina Barr—or her killer— was looking for," Mike said, nodding to Mercer. "Maybe something in one of these images, or a link to the part of the world that's portrayed in the fragment we found, you know?"

"The section of the map featuring Amerigo himself is stuck inside a book about American birds. Not a bad idea," Mercer said. "Bea, is there any way to get a copy of the full map that's reproduced here in your book?"

"You want the four-by-eight-foot version, I guess."

Mike was right. If the stack of books deposited under the water tanks in the last twenty-four hours was connected to Tina Barr's death, then this high-priced piece of a jigsaw puzzle might prove to be a clue.

"We've got a photocopy machine behind the reference desk that duplicates folio-size pages," Bea said. "Just give me a minute and you'll each have one to go."

She disappeared around the corner just as there was a loud banging on the door.

"Ignore it," Jill said. "We don't open to the public until ten."

"There'll be no public today," Mike said, checking his watch. "Crime scene techs will be swarming all over the library within the hour. Nobody's getting in till the whole place is worked over."

The banging didn't stop. "May I check?" Jill asked.

Mike stood up as she walked to the door.

"Goddammit!" a voice thundered at her. "Get your foot out of the way and let me in."

"I've got some police officers with me," I heard her whisper to the man in the hallway. "Why don't you wait in my office and I'll meet you there shortly."

"The hell with the police," he said, pushing open the door so that Jill tripped over herself getting out of his way. "I'm here to get what belongs to me."

There was no mistaking Talbot Hunt. The physical resemblance to his sister, Minerva, was striking, and the air of Hunt arrogance as he approached Mike Chapman was equally identifiable. He was tall and whippet thin, with straight dark hair and dark eyes.

"Talbot, I'd like you to meet Detectives Chapman and Wallace," Jill said, trying to catch up with Hunt. "And Assistant District Attorney Alexandra Cooper."

"I've already wasted two hours of my time yesterday with your colleagues," Hunt said. "That business about my sister's housekeeper—"

" 'Business'? Oh, you mean the fact that she was murdered in an apartment your sister owns, dressed exactly like her," Mike said. "And the idea that she might have been killed because she was carrying a book that belongs to you, or that **you** say belongs to you."

"Who says differently? Is it Minerva?" Hunt asked, talking to Mike but repeatedly glancing over at the map on the table.

"I don't remember anyone inviting you here this morning," Mike said.

"Some members of Ms. Gibson's staff seem to place more value than she does on the library's relationship with my family. Now I'd like to see the Audubon volume that you found," Hunt said. "And my map."

"**Your** book of psalms, **your** birds, **your** map," Mike said, shaking his head. "I just can't imagine the commissioner is looking to turn these things back over to you until he's damn sure nothing that has gone on involves **your** indictment, Mr. Hunt."

Hunt took a few steps toward the trestle table and Mercer stood to block his approach.

Bea came back into the room with her arms full of copies of the map, and stopped short when she saw Talbot Hunt.

"It's a panel from the world map, isn't it?" Hunt asked. "Am I right, Ms. Dutton?"

"You are, Mr. Hunt."

"That is mine, Detective," he said, each word separated by a dramatic pause, as though a nail had been driven between them as he spoke. "My father's lawyers will want to speak to you as soon as I reach them."

"You're telling me you knew about the existence of this particular map?" Mike asked. "That you knew it was here, at the library?"

Hunt didn't seem to want to answer that question.

"Bea, I thought you said you've never seen one of these panels," Mike said. "That the library never owned one."

"That's true," the petite woman said, holding her ground. "I haven't, and we don't."

"The world map of 1507," Hunt said. "Martin Waldseemüller. The only known original is in the Library of Congress."

"Tell me something I don't already know, Mr. Hunt." Mike peeled back the wrapper on a pack of Life Savers and popped one into his mouth.

"I can do that, Detective. I can tell you something almost nobody in the world knows," Hunt said. "There's another original of that 1507 map that survived. My grandfather bought it from the Grimaldis—the royal family of Monaco— more than a century ago."

Bea Dutton's head practically snapped as she turned it to look at Talbot Hunt. "You have the other pieces to complete this map?"

"We can race against each other to find the missing panels, Mr. Chapman, if you won't agree to return this one to me," Hunt said, choosing to ignore the earnest librarian. "I can leave you to your own devices."

"That's how come they gave me a gold shield," Mike said, crunching the mint between his teeth.

"I can assure you that if you fail, someone else is bound to die."

TWENTY

Talbot Hunt was seated at the head of the table, one leg crossed over the other and his hands touching at the fingertips. "For the moment, Detective, wouldn't you say that I'm in the driver's seat?"

Mike was pacing, his back to Hunt as he walked away from us. "Coop?"

"I'm not bargaining with possessions—no matter how valuable—in exchange for information connected to two murders, Mr. Hunt. Either you talk to us, or you tell it to the grand jury," I said. "The decision about who owns these things will be made in a courtroom, not because you're here to bully us. I assume the library can establish what belongs in this building and what doesn't. Things that have been donated to the Hunt Collection—"

"And all those other things they are desperately hoping will be left to them," he said, glaring at Jill Gibson. "Fortunately, while my father is still breathing, everyone here is likely to be on his best behavior. It takes so little time to change a codicil these days."

"How did your grandfather get the map?" Mike asked. "And how come nobody knows he had it?"

"There are a few people aware of the fact—some more dangerous, more desperate to find it than others."

"Your sister, Minerva? Is she one of them?"

"Did you ever see a pig looking for truffles, Detective? My sister would have her carefully sculpted snout deep in the dirt if it would help her find the rest of the panels."

"Why would any of this cause someone to be desperate?" Mercer asked.

"Because the more time that passes before the pieces of the map are reunited, the greater the likelihood they will never be found," Hunt said.

"And there's much less value to the individual pieces than to the work as a whole," Mike said. "But if your grandfather bought it intact, how did it get broken up?"

"Because Jasper Hunt Jr. was mad."

"Your sister mentioned that."

"First honest thing I've heard out of her mouth in ages," Hunt said. "We hardly knew him—he died when we were very young—but the stories about him are legion. He was all about games and pranks and tricks, Mr. Chapman. The older he got, the more difficult. Like many rich men, he wanted to take it all with him. Very torn about whether he should create a legacy that would outlive him or go out like a pharaoh, with all his worldly goods surrounding him for the long ride."

"How did he come to buy the map?" I asked.

"According to my father, Grandpapa was thirty years old when the discovery of this map was made by Josef Fischer. The news spread worldwide, of course, and even though Jasper's interest was primarily in books, like most collectors he was fascinated with the idea that one could still uncover such treasures, untouched over time, in a personal library. And so he made a plan."

"And what was that?" Mike asked.

"Jasper asked his curator to study the small royal families of Europe, like the Waldburgs of Wolfegg Castle, where the map was found. Kingdoms, principalities, and duchies that had libraries in 1507, when the great map was printed, and had perhaps managed to hang on to those residences throughout the four intervening centuries. It was well known that royals were among the first to buy these documents at the time they were printed."

"Sounds reasonable," Mercer said.

"By the time they finished a careful survey of

European history three years later, Jasper was surprised to see how few of the existing properties had not been pillaged or changed hands numerous times. So he and his curator—and his personal banker—decided to embark on a grand tour of the continent."

"Just to search for that map?" I asked.

"The ostensible purpose was that the great American book collector Jasper Hunt Jr. was making a pilgrimage to Europe's oldest royal libraries in order to add to his own. But Grandpapa was also counting on the fact that while many of these princes had retained their titles, they had lost most of their riches and their long-gone feudal lifestyles. Some of them might be ready to offer to sell him valuable works—maybe even the great world map."

"But wouldn't there already have been a feeding frenzy, after the announcement of the discovery of the one map?"

"Actually not, Mr. Wallace," Hunt said. "You see, Prince Waldburg had no intention of selling his. The great excitement at the time was that it existed at all, and in such perfect condition. Cartographers everywhere wanted to see and study it, but the prince made it clear that there was never to be a price tag placed on the map, so it was never assigned a commercial value in the marketplace. A century later—just a few years ago—we all learned that the Library of Congress had made known its interest in acquiring the map."

"So your grandfather never knew that it was worth millions of dollars?" I asked.

"Grandpapa had a great eye for the rare and beautiful, but not even he could have guessed the price this would have ultimately been worth. No one could have."

"How did he find it?"

"In 1905, they were traveling through Belgium and the Netherlands, actually making some magnificent purchases of incunabula and very old illustrated manuscripts, when Jasper was summoned by Prince Albert of Monaco—Albert the First," Hunt said. "The two had known each other for quite some time because Albert had married a rich American girl from New Orleans whose family was well acquainted with the Hunts. It seems that Albert got word of Jasper's search, and from Jasper's perspective, the Grimaldi family was high on his list of prospects. They had ruled Monaco since the thirteenth century, and being in such an important strategic position on the Mediterranean seaport, would likely have been interested in a map of the New World at the time it first appeared."

"Yeah, but the Grimaldis had been chased

out of town at least once," Mike said. "They didn't retain possession of their palace for that whole passage of time."

Talbot Hunt's furrowed brow suggested his puzzlement at Mike's display of knowledge, which was doubtless some factoid of military history. "You're right, Detective. That, too, was part of Prince Albert's story.

"Don't forget that Monaco is built on top of a rock, Detective—literally, a fortress atop a great cliff above a strategic harbor, with ramparts constructed all around to reinforce it. Before the Grimaldis fled the palace during the French Revolution, they were able to stash many of their treasures—crown jewels, the art collection amassed by Prince Honoré, and a good portion of the royal library—inside a series of catacombs built into the rock in medieval times. Everything still high and dry when the next generation was restored to the palace thirty years later."

"Why did Albert contact your grandfather?"

"Word had spread throughout these European principalities about the questions Jasper was asking during his travels. And Albert was an unusual prince for his time, far more interested in intellectual pursuits than most others. In fact, he is best remembered as an explorer—

a very serious oceanographer—which explains his attachment to maps."

"There's a great oceanographic museum in Monaco, isn't there?" I asked.

"Indeed. And it was founded by Albert—in 1906."

"One year after your grandfather met with him."

"And thanks to Grandpapa's largesse," Talbot Hunt said. "You see, Princess Alice—the rich American wife—left Albert a few years earlier, after he slapped her in the face during an evening at the opera, when he learned she was having an affair with a famous composer."

"Like you say, Coop"—Mike pointed at me—"nothing new about domestic violence."

"And when Alice walked out, she took her sizable dowry with her. By selling the 1507 world map to my grandfather, Prince Albert pocketed a small fortune for himself and was able to establish the oceanographic museum and library, which is still thriving today."

"Nobody in the principality complained that he was deaccessioning such a rare document?"

"Ms. Cooper, I daresay not many people knew of its existence. My father claims that Albert told Grandpapa that the panels of the great map had been protected because they were inside a series of books—books that had intrigued Albert from the time he was a young child."

"Do you know which books?" I asked.

"Certainly. Some time after the Grimaldis returned to power in 1814, the royal library acquired the entire collection of the **Description de l'Égypte.** All twenty-four volumes. Where the pieces of the map had been stored for safekeeping during the revolution, I don't suppose we'll ever know. But whoever found them thereafter decided that the double elephant folios of the Napoleonic expedition would be just the right size to protect the panels."

"What are they?" Mike asked.

"The Description of Egypt was the largest publication in the world at that time—in its physical size, not in the number of copies—and a very prized possession, too," Jill Gibson explained. "Napoleon led a failed invasion of Egypt in 1798."

"I know that. The British defeated him in the Mediterranean and his troops were cut off from France," Mike said. "He abandoned his army and went home."

"But a horde of civilians accompanied the military, and stayed on in Egypt to create an exhaustive and meticulously drawn catalog of everything from the obelisks and large statues along the Nile, to the great tombs, to the flora and fauna," Jill said.

"And the very last volume of the first edition of the Description of Egypt is an atlas—the book that captured the imagination of the young Prince Albert, and the one in which he found the even older map," Talbot Hunt said. "The map he sold to Jasper."

"Do you know where your grandfather kept his panels?"

"I wouldn't be searching for them today if I knew where they were." Hunt stood up and frowned at Mike.

"I mean, did he display them, or did he hide them inside other volumes?"

"He was a bookman, Mr. Chapman. Ten, twenty, thirty years after he bought the world map, there had never been another peep about the original one. Nothing about its existence or its value since the first news accounts of its discovery. My father told me that Grandpapa lost interest in it, just like everyone else."

"So Jasper Hunt bought this map a hundred years ago," Mike asked, "let me guess—for sport?"

"Why do very rich men collect rare objects, Mr. Chapman? Paintings, coins, motor yachts, Arabian stallions, Ming vases?"

"Got me on that one. I gave up on collecting when my mother threw out nine shoe boxes full of my baseball cards after I moved out of the house."

"So other very rich men can't claim the ultimate prize," Hunt said. "If there were two of these maps in the world, and a reclusive prince owned one of them, then Jasper Hunt Jr. wanted the other. It sat in his library, in a specially made leather box, for thirty years after the idea of owning it had captured his fancy, and by then no one in the world seemed to give a damn about it. He was long onto other, more talked-about treasures. He didn't live long enough to see the revived interest in his forgotten map."

"Does anyone—perhaps your father—understand why the twelve panels of your grandfather's map became separated?" I asked.

Talbot Hunt cleared his throat. "You can't make sense of an eccentric. If my father knows why, he's never told me."

Either that was true or Hunt wasn't letting go of any other family secrets in front of Bea Dutton and Jill Gibson.

"Did your grandfather own a first edition set of this Napoleonic expedition?"

"Yes, he did, Mr. Chapman," Hunt said. "But my father gave that to the library—oh, I'd

say twenty years ago or more. Our curator—
and the accountants—will have a record of that
gift."

"Bea," Mike said, standing up and rapping
on the trestle table with his fisted hand. "So
where's the atlas? Let's have a look."

"We can locate it for you, certainly. And pull
it," Jill said. "Why do you ask?"

"That's the volume in which Prince Albert
found his copy of the map. Maybe Jasper was
playing on that fact, if he was such a prankster.
This panel we just found," Mike said, sweeping
his arm over the trestle table, "was nested inside
the Audubon folio, which used to belong to
Grandpa Hunt. Maybe the killer was looking
for places the map might have been concealed
by the old man as one of his tricks, in another
one of his books. Was that his brand of eccentricity?"

Talbot Hunt nodded. "Grandpapa wanted
to keep my father on a leash, never assuming
he would inherit everything without working
at it."

"Wouldn't an atlas be part of the collection
in this very room?" Mike asked.

"You want to know how things disappear,
Mr. Chapman?" Hunt said, almost bellowing.
"Certainly there are maps and atlases in here.
But there are more maps in the general stacks,

and yet again others in the various rare-book rooms. We've got one collection in the building—the Spencer—that's just about rare bindings. The curator there doesn't give a damn if he's got roadways or rodents between the covers—it's all about the leather and decoration on the outside of the books. If there's even a drawing of a tobacco leaf—say, in a depiction of the Virginia colony—in one of the cartouches, then that map might be housed in the Arents Collection. The maps are spread out everywhere throughout the library."

"Why isn't the Hunt Collection all in one room, like most of the others?" I asked.

"Because the library didn't have enough space to maintain it that way by the time his gift was made," Hunt went on. "The Audubons, for example, and the Egyptian expedition volumes—well, he agreed to the library's plan to let them reside where its curators deemed they were most appropriate."

"So where are these particular books?" Mike asked.

Jill Gibson spoke more calmly. "At the time of Napoleon's travels, Egypt was considered part of the Orient. So they're in our Orientalia section—Asian and Middle Eastern."

"You see what I mean, Chapman? They run these great libraries like a shell game," Hunt said, walking to the far side of the room. "I can't tell you how many millions we've given to these people over the years. I've got every damn right to pull the plug and demand an accounting immediately."

"Surely the card catalogs have—" I started to say.

"They tell us nothing, Ms. Cooper," Hunt said. "Maps are rarely mentioned in library catalogs, and those within the atlases aren't ever individually described. Take a razor to a page and it's hard to prove what was ever there. They're unmoored, maps. Unmoored and generally ignored. Not like books at all."

Jill looked at her watch. "Perhaps some of the curators have arrived. I can call and have someone bring us the Egyptian atlas."

"I don't think you understand the plan," Mike said. "There are cops at every door of this place by now. No one is touching any of these books unless we're along for the ride. And no one's entering the building until the crime scene detectives have been over every inch of this place."

"That could take days. You can't close the public library."

"Faster than you can say Dewey decimal system, lady," Mike said, tapping me on the shoulder. "Coop, call Battaglia. Tell him to get on the horn with the commissioner. The pair of them can shut this mother down in a minute."

"I'll wait in Jill's office, then," Talbot Hunt said.

"Mercer, why don't you escort Mr. Hunt to the nearest exit?"

"These are **my** books, Chapman."

"That's not so," Jill said. "You've got no personal claim to any of the things your grandfather gave to us."

"Don't embarrass yourself, Mr. Hunt," Mike said, pointing at the neatly embroidered letters—TH—on Hunt's shirt, just visible below the sleeve of his jacket. "I don't have monogrammed handcuffs. You wouldn't want to be photographed when I eject you wearing metal bracelets."

"I'll hold you personally responsible, Detective," Hunt said, turning his back to us.

"For what?"

Hunt's freshly polished loafers snapped like gunshots on the bare floor as he stomped toward the exit of the map room. He was furious, but couldn't express a reason that made any sense. "For the loss of . . . of . . . of any valuable property that should have been rightfully restored to me."

"Shoulda, woulda, coulda. You didn't even know the frigging map existed for most of your life," Mike said as Mercer followed after Hunt. "Tell me the real story about it, why don't you? Or sue me. Maybe you actually need all the savings I got in my piggy bank."

"Would you mind telling us where you spent the evening last night?" I asked as Hunt pulled open the door.

"I wasn't in Bryant Park, Ms. Cooper. I'm not a baseball aficionado."

"Strikes me as a much more sporting type, Blondie, doesn't he?" Mike said, sneering at Hunt. "Cold-blooded and calculating. Fox hunting, deer shooting, and all those genteel upper-class pastimes where you kill things for the fun of it."

"Tina Barr isn't worth anything to me dead, Mr. Chapman," Talbot Hunt said, glancing back over his shoulder. "You ought to talk to my sister, Minerva. There's a girl who knows how to hold a grudge."

TWENTY-ONE

Bea Dutton and Jill Gibson sat together at the farthest table from the reference desk, staring off in different directions, like two schoolkids in detention. I had used the landline to call Paul Battaglia, to tell him the latest developments and get his help with Commissioner Scully.

Mercer returned within minutes. "You're growing quite a crowd outside, Mike."

"Front steps?"

"The employees come in through the service entrance on Fortieth Street. Seems like most of them hadn't heard any news reports about the body in the park."

"Is the detail in place?"

"Yeah. Chief of d's has everything covered. A fresh Crime Scene crew is unloading now. They should be in the lobby in five."

Mike walked to where Bea and Jill were sitting. "Bea, I'm going to have a uniformed cop sitting here with you for the day. Just to make sure no one gets past the door and tries to come in."

She smiled at him wanly. "You mean just so I don't start doing my own treasure hunt, don't you?"

"A little of both."

"I've got an appointment—some engineers from the city due at eleven."

"Why?"

"There's a problem under the old Penn Station railroad tunnels. They need a footprint—a vertical search—before there's any structural damage. It sounds pretty urgent."

"What can you do for them?"

Bea Dutton explained. "I can search the particular property or plot of land back before the time of the Civil War, when maps of the city were created for insurance companies. You can see exactly what structures existed at any location over time, and what the topographical conditions are. There was flooding in the sub-basement of the Empire State Building last spring—"

"Flooding from what?" Mike asked.

"There's a stream that cuts through the southwest quadrant of the building, way underground. It shows on the old maps, before midtown was built up. Because of all the snow last winter, the stream swelled with the spring melt and dumped six inches of water into that sub-basement. The engineers need to get into the train tunnels before the snowstorms start, to make sure they can prevent any potential for collapse."

"And you can help them with that, Bea?"

"Like I said, the old maps give you a historical footprint of every inch of the city."

"They'll have to wait another day," Mike said, rolling his eyes at her request as he walked back to the desk. "Give the guy a call and cancel your date. We may need you as we go along."

"What did the DA say?" Mercer asked.

"Expect this place to be swarming with cops within the hour," I said. "Between Scully and the mayor, we'll have everything we need."

"Let's get moving," Mike said to me. "Mercer, you mind going back out to get one of the rookies to babysit Bea?"

"Done."

"Keep yourself busy, Bea, baby. Do me a historical footprint of Bryant Park. Where the murder was," Mike said, trying to make her smile again, while he summoned Jill to the desk. "So where exactly was Tina Barr working when she was here?"

"Well, most recently she spent time upstairs in the reading room. And of course she had access to some of the special collections."

"We've been upstairs, Jill. Which collections?" Mike was tapping his fingers on the countertop.

"I can't be certain. We'll have to talk with the curators."

"How about the conservation laboratory?" I asked.

"Well, yes. Tina used to have access there, when she worked here."

"Do all your employees?"

"Oh, no. It's kept quite secure. Very few people have clearance to get in there."

"Why?" Mike asked, heading for the door and waving at Jill and me to follow.

"It's where the most fragile items in the library are taken for repair. They're often left out on worktables overnight, with strict environmental controls. We've got only four conservators working in there, and a lot of expensive equipment."

"Take us in," Mike said, holding open the door.

"I—I can't. If none of the conservators is inside, I'd have to have the code in my library identification tag to be swiped at the entrance. I've no reason to have one."

"I've got Tina's." Mike reached into his jacket pocket and removed Barr's ID—the one he had found with her body the night before. "Just lead the way."

"That won't work," Jill said, clutching at her own plastic card dangling from the chain around her neck. "She was supposed to have surrendered it when she quit. It should have been deactivated."

"Let's give it a try." Mike took out his cell and called Mercer. "We're going down to the conservation lab. Before you come back in, check at the employees' entrance, where all the staff is waiting. See if you can scoop up a conservator to give us a guided tour."

Jill moved into the dark hallway and started a reluctant march to the far end of the building. Uniformed cops had taken up positions inside the front door and at the bottom of each of the grand staircases. We continued to the end of the corridor, and through an exit that led to steep steps down to the basement.

As we descended, I could see where the white marble and granite of the library foundation rested upon the actual rough red brick of the old reservoir walls, built almost two centuries ago.

If there were lights in the corridor, Jill didn't know where the controls were, so we made our way slowly through this windowless subterranean maze. Metal trolleys and dollies were everywhere, parked on angles against the wall like dozens of abandoned cars. They were obviously used to transport books of every size, and could easily accommodate something larger.

Jill stopped in front of the double doors marked with the conservation lab sign. Mike raised Tina's pass to the small electronic pad below the bell. As he moved it back and forth, the buzzer sounded, and Mike turned the knob to open the door.

Jill hesitated before stepping over the threshold and flipping on the light switch.

I followed her in and looked around. The grace and elegance of the library rooms above bore no resemblance to this workhorse in the underbelly of the building. Large tables, most covered with tools of all shapes and sizes, filled the center, and along the sides were smaller cubicles that appeared to be stations for the staff.

"Why does it smell so bad?"

"Chemicals, Mike. There are a lot of toxic materials used in this work. Solvents of all kinds, ammonium hydroxide—things that draw acids out of old paper. The students actually have to study organic chemistry before they're accepted into a conservators' program."

Mike was snooping around all the machinery in the room.

"This was the library's original bindery," Jill said, pointing to an enormous wooden table straight ahead of us, "so when they have to repair the spine of an eighteenth-century rare book, they've still got to dissolve a block of animal glue. Hot animal glue, layers of it, from cattle, rabbits, tigers—more than a century's worth—adds to the foul odor in here."

The doorbell rang and Mike turned back to admit Mercer, who was accompanied by a young woman. She was slightly built, with auburn hair, and a long fringed scarf doubled around her neck.

"Good morning, Lucy," Jill said. "You've met Mr. Wallace. This is Alex Cooper, from the DA's Office, and Mike Chapman, another detective."

"It's true about Tina?"

"I'm afraid so," she said, completing our introductions to Lucy Tannis.

"Why did you want to see me?"

"The detectives need to understand what goes on down here, and whatever you know about what Tina was working on."

"Or who she was working with," Mike said.

"I don't know very much. It's not like she confided in any of us."

"Had you known her very long?"

Lucy shrugged. "A few years. There aren't many of us trained in this field, Detective. The four of us who work here full-time, we're a pretty tight-knit group. Spend most of our days together in this little hole below ground, which seems odd to most outsiders. But we get to touch some of the most exquisite works on paper ever created."

"And Tina?" Mike asked.

"She just didn't fit. Good at what she did, no question about that. But she was cold as ice and never really seemed to enjoy her work the way the rest of us do. At least not lately."

"Did you see her this week?"

Lucy thought for a moment and then nodded. "Twice. Tina was here twice. She was in for a little while on Monday morning. I remember that because I was sort of surprised to see her. She was working for some rich guy— from England, I think—and she needed to pick up some supplies."

That would have been a day before she was attacked in her apartment.

"And Wednesday. I'm sure it was Wednesday. She got here right as I was cleaning up to leave. But you'd know that, Jill?"

"Sorry? Why would I know?" Jill said, looking surprised.

"Tina told me she was here to see you that evening. That you had asked her to come in for a meeting. She seemed pretty nervous about it."

"I told you, Alex. I—I wanted her to come in, but she never showed up," Jill said, turning to me to protest Lucy's suggestion that she had actually seen Tina on Wednesday. "But that was to make sure she was okay after—well, after Tuesday's break-in."

"Well, she was still here when the three of us left, shortly after five," Lucy said.

I couldn't get a fix on Jill Gibson. I wanted to trust her, but as fragments of information developed, I wasn't sure that I could.

"Can you give me a sense of what you've been working on recently?" Mike asked Lucy, trying to make her more comfortable before he went back to the details of her last encounter with Tina.

Lucy waited for Jill to nod at her and started to explain. "Sure. You can see on this table over here, I've been doing some restoration on a copy of the Declaration of Independence."

Mike was on top of it in a second, leaning over to study the document. "In Jefferson's hand?"

"Yes, one of two that survived. And repairing a tear in the last letter that Keats wrote to Fanny Brawne."

I tried to make out words in the script that the dying poet had penned to the lover he left behind in London when he ran off to Rome.

"Most of the time we're working on a dozen

things at once. There are tidemarks on this manuscript of **Native Son** that I've got to get started on today."

"Tidemarks?" I asked.

"Water stains. I've got to try to remove them. And foxing is the probably the most common thing we see. That's mildew to you. It occurs when ferrous oxide—F Ox in chemistry—is attracted to the paper and activated by humidity."

"I can see why you love this," I said. "I realize it's very hard work, but I envy the opportunity you have to enjoy these riches every day. And the other conservators?"

"One is rehousing some sixteenth-century prints on the far side of the room, and another is working on new bindings for books in which the bindings have failed. See this?" Lucy asked. "Post-it notes are the bane of my existence."

"How so? I couldn't live without them," I said. "I wouldn't remember half the things I have to do."

"What holds them in place are little globules of adhesive that explode when you stick them to a page. The adhesive is stronger than the paper, so it eats away and makes the paper translucent if left there too long. That's a constant problem for us. We go from the excitement of saving documents of great historical importance to the tedium of repairing everyday damage caused by a reader's carelessness."

"What was Tina doing?" Mike asked.

"Same stuff as us, when she worked for the library," Lucy said. "Right now, I'm not sure. She was given permission to use the lab—as long as someone else from staff was in here—'cause she was doing private consulting with some of the big donors."

"Did you see her with any maps? Atlases?"

"From time to time, Detective. She liked working on maps. She had a great talent for that."

"And recently? In the last few weeks?"

"No. I'm sure of that."

"Why?"

" 'Cause I would have noticed. Old maps are so beautiful, so visual—none of us would have missed seeing them in these close quarters."

"Where did she work?"

"Whatever table was free. Sort of depended on what she was handling."

Mercer was more interested in the tools that were mounted on the walls and grouped in coffee mugs on shelves above each cubicle. "Tell us about these."

Lucy loosened her scarf and unbuttoned the

top button of her blouse. I looked at the clear skin on her neck and flashed back to the sight of the deep wounds that brought Tina Barr's life to an end. No wonder Mercer was examining the array of knives displayed above the workstations.

"About what? My tools?"

"Yeah."

"Each of us has a set, Mr. Wallace," Lucy said, walking to her desk in the next alcove. "Part of the conservation process is that we each create our own tools, to fit our styles, the size of our hands, the kind of work we do. Mine are over here."

She picked up an ivory-colored piece about the size of a ruler with a sharp, pointed end. "This is a bone folder. It's made from the bones of a cow's leg."

So much for the refined life of a library conservator—animal glue and spare body parts.

"I bought it at an art supply store, then ground and burned it until it fit exactly the shape I like to work with."

"What do you use it for?" I asked.

"It's got thousands of functions here. Leather bruises very easily when it's wet, so if I'm working on an old binding, I'll smooth it carefully with this. Or turn damp pages of a book that's got water damage." Lucy began to point out her equipment with the tapered end of the bone folder.

Above her head were mason jars and coffee mugs filled with a mix of household objects and art tools. Pens, pencils, and brushes were clustered in some, while others held tweezers and an assortment of dental picks.

Then there were knives, several dozen of them in all sizes in a large plastic tub on her shelf. "Why so many knives?" I asked.

"They look like weapons, not tools," Mike said. "Sharp?"

"Razor sharp," Lucy said, reaching for one to hand to Mike. "We have to keep them that way. We're cutting all the time—from fine paper to edging the leather on bindings."

"Mercer, check those shapes," Mike said.

Lucy described their importance. "These are lifting knives, and these are scalpels I use to carve fine lines. These are skifes, and the blades that go with them."

"Skifes?"

Lucy slowed down and smiled at me. "Taxidermists' tools. They're used to skin dead animals. Gets the top layer off without puncturing the flesh. Serves the same purpose on book bindings. And these are paring knives."

"May I see one?" Mike asked.

"Sure," Lucy said, standing on tiptoe to remove one from the mug in which it was standing.

The knife was about seven inches long, with an angled steel blade and wooden handle. Mike held it in his left hand and with his right thumb tested the cutting edge. "Wicked."

He passed it to Mercer, who studied the beveled edge. "We ought to take a few of these to the morgue. They'd make a pretty distinctive cut."

"Was Tina . . . ?" Lucy couldn't finish the sentence.

"We're not sure what happened to her yet," Mike said. "We're just trying to help the medical examiner out. Did Tina keep her tools here?"

"Some of them," Lucy said. "They're in this next cubicle."

The three of us followed her to the desktop at which Tina had been working. Her station had been left in perfect order. It was a smaller space than Lucy's, and there were fewer tools displayed, but Tina had been spending only part of her time at the library.

"Would you know if any of her knives or scalpels was missing?" Mike asked.

"I haven't any idea. These things are our security blankets. I can look at my shelves in the morning and be able to tell you exactly where everything is. But that's unique to each conservator, and we never touch each other's tools."

"Visitors," Mercer said. "Did anyone visit Tina while she was here?"

Lucy thought for a few seconds. "When she was on staff, of course people from other departments dropped in to talk about their needs, or just take a break. Lately? The usual people coming by to queue up their projects, beg us to jump the line. Some of them know Tina, so they chatted."

"Any outsiders?"

"Just one that I can think of, several weeks ago."

"Do you know who he was?" Mike asked.

"She, actually. It was a woman. And I didn't know her."

"Can you describe her?"

Lucy closed her eyes and pulled up an image. "An attractive woman, about fifty years old. Tall and really thin, a little overdressed and jeweled for eleven in the morning."

A good shot Tina's visitor was Minerva Hunt. "Did they arrive together?"

"No. She rang the bell and one of my colleagues let her in. She asked to see Tina, so I assumed it was someone she was working with."

"Do you know any of the Hunts?" Mike asked.

Lucy looked over her shoulder to see whether Jill was in earshot, and when it seemed she was far enough away, Lucy leaned back against one of the worktables.

"Not personally," she said. "Sometimes we joke about the collectors. We know some of their books so well, we feel like we've lived with them. In my imagination, I've been talking to Jasper Hunt the Third for years, even though we've never been introduced. His father had exquisite taste, that's for sure."

"Have you met either of his children?" Mike asked. "Talbot or Minerva?"

"Just his leather-bound babies, Detective."

"The woman who came to see Tina," I said. "Do you remember how long she stayed?"

"I don't think she was there more than ten or fifteen minutes."

"What did she want?"

Lucy looked away from me. "None of my business. I don't know."

"But your desks are so close to each other. They're back to back."

"They argued, okay? That's all I know. The woman seemed to have a bad temper. I didn't hear words, but she was displeased about something Tina had done. She sort of chewed Tina out, and then she left."

"Did Tina talk about it at all?"

"Not to me. Not to any of us, I'd guess," Lucy said. "But as soon as the woman left, Tina broke down and started crying. I asked if she was okay, and she said she was just upset and needed to go outside for some fresh air. That's all I know."

"What day was that?" Mercer asked.

Lucy was beginning to understand there was some importance to what she had observed. I wondered if that would jog her memory.

"Two, maybe three weeks ago. You can ask my colleagues if they can place it. The only other person who engaged Tina in any kind of—well, **personal** conversation was Mr. Krauss. But he actually came to see me. Sort of surprised him that she was here, and I guess he asked her what she was doing."

"Krauss?" Mike asked, looking at me for help in placing the name.

"Would that be Jonah Krauss?" I asked Lucy. I remembered that Alger Herrick had mentioned his name to us.

"Exactly. He's on our board. Drops in every now and then—a lot of the trustees do—to see what we're working on and what we might need."

"Did Krauss know Tina?"

Lucy pushed a lock of hair behind her ear. "He certainly seemed to. I can't imagine he has a clue who I am, but once he caught sight of her, he made a beeline right for her and called her by name."

"Did you——?"

"I didn't hear a word, Detective, and it all seemed very cordial. I just thought it was strange that they knew each other."

There was an index card tacked to the wall on the side of Tina's desk. "What's that?" I asked.

"Might be the list of things she had in the works. I track mine on my laptop, but everyone does it differently."

I pulled the thumbtack and the card came off with it.

"Is this Tina's handwriting?" I asked.

Lucy glanced at the card. "Yes. She always printed."

I thought of the call slip that had been in Tina's pocket. This was not written in the same style. I read the list to Mike as Mercer walked off, making his way around the far end of the large room.

" 'The Nijinksy Diaries—Performing Arts Collection. The Grunwald Correspondence— Rare Books. The Whistler Sketches— drypoint—Art and Architecture.' "

Lucy Tannis interrupted me. "That can't be current, Ms. Cooper. Those are all items from collections in this library. Tina had finished those projects. I saw the papers down here when they were assigned to her. She's only doing private work now."

I skipped to the bottom of the list. "What does this mean, Lucy? 'The Hunt Legacy.' What's that?"

She squinted to look at the words, then shook her head. "I'm pretty familiar with the Hunt Collection. I've never seen that expression before."

I passed the card to Mike, who pocketed it as Mercer called his name.

"Wassup?"

"In here, in the back room. You and Alex come quick. Leave the girl."

Mercer's voice had an urgency to it that I rarely heard. I broke into a trot and made my way around the old wooden tables that filled the room.

There was an archway into the adjacent space, a darkened work area that had large mechanical equipment—paper cutters and a standing book press—and along one side of the room, where Mercer was waiting, three huge stainless steel chests were lined up end to end.

"These are freezers," he said, lifting the lid

of the first one to show us the books—four
of them—inside. "Remember how cool Tina's
body was?"

"Yes, but this doesn't look like it's been disturbed at all," I said.

Mercer lifted the closure of the second one
and revealed a single volume, folio size, resting
in its icy storage container.

When he shifted to the third freezer and
hoisted its heavy lid, I gasped. The book inside
was small and slim, its gold calf binding elabo-
rately decorated with gilt designs and lettering:
The Poems of Elizabeth Barrett Browning.

The cold blast of air from within the chest
couldn't hide the dark red stain, most likely
blood, that had seeped into the pale calfskin—
and three strands of brown hair that had frozen
onto the cover of the old book.

TWENTY-TWO

"What's with the freezers?" Mike asked Lucy.

"Why? Do you think . . . ?"

Jill had gone over to Lucy when she heard us run to the back. She was standing with her arm around the girl, who seemed to be trying to absorb the fact that Tina's body may have been concealed right under her nose.

"How often do you open them?"

"Not—not often. Not for months at a time," Lucy said.

"What are they for?"

"Disaster recovery. Freezing the books stops mold from doing more destruction. It kills insects that have infested them. You want to do some damage control to a hurt volume, you put it in the freezer, record that in the log in the back room, and nobody opens it again for six months."

"And everybody working down here knows that?" Mike asked.

"Yes. But not just us. All the curators upstairs know it, too. So do most of the collectors we deal with," Lucy said, wide-eyed with concern, as though Mike were accusing her of Tina's murder.

"Frozen coffins," Mike said to none of us in particular. He was trying to get a signal on his phone. "How frigging convenient. Plenty of room for a short broad. Odor proof—and it already stinks in here. An unwelcoming basement room with no windows for anyone to peek inside. Whoever killed her could have kept her on ice for weeks, if the mayor hadn't made the evening so convenient for a nearby disposal."

"The thermostat's right on top," Mercer said. "I imagine he turned up the temperature till he took the body out."

"Same effect. Cool but not so stiff he couldn't move her after the rigor passed," Mike said. "By the time somebody discovered a body, there'd be so much contamination in this room that no forensics would be of any value."

"Cell phones don't work down here," Lucy Tannis said. "You can use the landline near the door."

"Why don't you wait here with Lucy while I grab the Crime Scene crew?" Mike said to Mercer. His impatience was palpable. "She can explain this place to the guys. You show them what you found. I'll take Coop and Jill with me. We'll make that map room the command post."

Mike took the stairs three at a time, yelling back at us to wait for him in Bea Dutton's office.

There was no reason for me to separate Jill and Bea at this point. I walked to a corner of the room, away from them, to call Pat McKinney and give him an update. I was unlikely to get any goodwill out of letting him be the one to tell Battaglia about the developments, but it was worth a try.

By the time I finished answering McKinney's questions, Mike had returned.

"Did you catch up with the guys?"

"Yeah," he said. "They're going to process the conservation lab first. You going downtown to your office?"

"That makes the most sense. If you need a warrant drafted or any subpoenas, I'll be at my desk."

"Excuse me, Mike," Bea said as she approached us. "Are you going to keep me locked up all day? I don't want to be a nuisance, but if your plan is just to make me sit here, I'll go stir-crazy."

I could tell that he liked her manner—feisty and direct.

"Now how about that assignment I gave you? That should keep you busy."

She laughed at him. "A historical footprint of Bryant Park? Who do you think prepared the one that was actually used when the place was restored twenty years ago?"

Mike walked me to the door, and I turned to thank Jill for her cooperation.

"Dead bodies, right? Like I told Alex, nothing but dead bodies down there."

"Dead wrong, Detective," Bea said, wagging a finger at him.

"What do you mean?"

"Books. Eighty-eight miles of books."

"What happened to the bodies?" Mike asked.

I stopped in the doorway, thinking about the spot near Sixth Avenue where Tina Barr's body was found. It was a long city block away from the conservation lab just below us on the Fifth Avenue side of the library. "What do you mean, there are books under the park?"

"The entire piece of land below Bryant Park was turned into an underground extension of the library a while back."

I let go of the door and it closed behind me. Mike rubbed his hands together and then scratched his head. "Connected to this building?"

"By a one-hundred-and-twenty-foot-long tunnel," Bea said, coming alive again as she explained the setup to us. "They couldn't build an extension that would change the appearance of the main library, because that's landmarked. So when the park was closed for restoration, the old Revolutionary War battleground and the potter's field were dug up. Originally, the stacks were right beneath us in this section, but we outgrew that space ages ago. The Bryant Park extension has greater capacity than this entire library."

"How do we get there?" he asked, ready to dash off to the nearest stairwell.

It had never occurred to any of us when Barr's body was found the night before that below the park was a cavernous structure that coupled with this one.

"May I show them, Jill?" Bea turned to ask.

"Yes, of course. Whatever they need."

"Does anyone work in there?"

"There are two levels underground. That's where the conveyor system that takes books up to the call desk winds up, so there are always a few staffers on the first floor throughout the day to pull the requested volumes and ship them back upstairs. The lower floor is usually deserted."

"And books?"

"Just a few million of them," Bea said as I held open the door.

"Valuable ones?"

"Everything here is valuable to somebody."

Her short legs couldn't move fast enough for Mike. This time, she led us down the other direction of the long corridor to a service elevator, trying to keep up with Mike's pace. She had to catch her breath as we waited for the doors to open, and then waited again for the old lift as it creaked and groaned to deliver us down to the north end of the basement.

When we got out, she told Mike that the entrance to the stacks was only accessible from the stairwell straight ahead. This time, he started off and I ran with him, leaving a slightly bewildered Bea Dutton alone in the quiet hallway, with an order for her to ask one of the cops in the main lobby to send some men to help us.

The two of us pounding down the steps made as much noise as a small herd of ponies, the sound reverberating through the great empty space. The granite and marble so prominent throughout the rest of the library building ended abruptly at this point. There was a long, sloping steel ramp that started at the bottom tread, and I grabbed on to the red metal handrail along the wall to keep my balance as we rounded corners, racing farther below ground.

The path flattened and the narrow entryway

opened onto a cluttered workspace that looked like a scene from a Victorian novel—industrial, impersonal, damp, and cold.

Mike stopped to scope the area—a handful of unoccupied desks, piles of books ready to be restacked and shelved, and ahead of us and on the floor below, several acres of volumes, row after row of shelves, that formed this enormous hidden book vault beneath the formal gardens of Bryant Park.

"It's like a catacomb of forgotten books," Mike said, his hands on his waist.

I ventured past the desks to the beginning of the tightly packed shelves that stretched out in the distance farther than either of us could see. The space was musty and airless. It was impossible to think that anyone really knew what was among the pages relegated to this dank reserve.

"What are we looking for exactly?" I asked.

"A way out."

"We just got here. Bea said it's the only entrance."

"What she said is that it's the only entrance from within the library. I'll never look at the park the same way again," Mike said. "I want to see if there's an exit near the Sixth Avenue side."

"Why don't we wait for someone to guide us through it?" I asked.

"You and your damn claustrophobia again. Let's go over it fast, kid, before we've got the whole department tied up here," Mike said, brushing past me. "You're looking for blood, a weapon, clothing. Any sign this was part of the killer's escape route. And another staircase."

Mike headed off down the first row to our right. I watched him as he loped along, ignoring the books shelved from floor to ceiling on both sides of him, looking instead at the floor, pausing to pick up a scrap of paper, which he eyeballed and then slipped into his pocket.

I took the left half, setting off on a slow jog to look for anything out of place. By the time I reached the end of the third row, I was coughing so badly from the dust that I had to stop and clear my throat.

"You okay?" Mike shouted.

"I'll be fine. Why do you sound so far away?"

"I got smart, Coop. I'm going down to the other end, closer to Sixth Avenue. I'll work my way back from there. Meet you in the middle. You just keep going."

Every now and then I bent over to pick up a blank call slip that had fallen out of book, but none had any writing on it.

I trolled through the Slavic and Baltic sections and was in the middle of an archive of Islamic manuscripts from the Asian and Middle Eastern collection when I saw something shiny on the floor, between two of the tall racks of books. From a distance, it appeared to be shaped like one of the scalpels I had seen at Lucy Tannis's desk.

I stepped out of the aisle between the already overcrowded mechanically operated shelves to get closer to the object so that I could better tell if it was something for the Crime Scene cops to pick up. But as I knelt down, I could see that it was a silver-colored ballpoint pen, its body matted with enough dust for me to know that it had been on the floor there for some time.

Another two rows farther on and something else caught my eye. Also metallic, but this was shorter in length and much flatter than the pen.

It was a few yards in from the long aisle, and I got right on top of it, kneeling again to inspect it. It was a small key, and it wasn't covered with dust. I had no idea if it had any significance to our search.

I held on to the edge of a divider to steady myself, making a mental note of what row I was in—between large folios of the designs for the Royal Pavilion at Brighton and watercolor plates illustrating dress during America's colonial period—when the entire bookshelf behind me began to move, quickly and quietly, pinning me against the one that I had grasped.

Someone was trying to crush me between the heavy compact movable shelves, and I screamed for Mike as my wrist twisted and I fell onto my side.

TWENTY-THREE

Yuri—the engineer who had taken us up to the attic this morning—was the first person to reach me. "Was accident, miss. Was my accident."

"What are you doing down here, Yuri?" Mike asked. "What hurts, Coop?"

I was sitting up, massaging the fingers of my left hand. "My tailbone, my wrist, and mostly my pride. You think everybody on Forty-second Street heard me scream?"

"Miss Jill send me. Miss Jill make me come."

"You moved the shelves? Why'd you do that?" Mike shouted at Yuri.

The man was flustered and struggling to express himself. "I don't see nobody in aisle. Shelves not on line."

"On line?"

Jill Gibson walked up behind Mike in the company of two uniformed cops. "He means aligned. I'm sure he means aligned."

"Let him tell me what he means," Mike said. "Why'd you touch the controls?"

"Is my job, Mr. Mike. In morning, I check things and make even again."

At the end of each long row was a round handle, like the steering wheel of a car. I had passed scores of them in the last few minutes, and knew when cranked they compacted the shelves to allow more inventory. But I never gave a thought to anyone's activating them while one of us was between the densely packed bookcases.

"Alex couldn't have gotten trapped in there," Jill said. "I'm sure the movement just frightened her. There are motion sensors that won't let the shelves close completely if something—someone—is in between them."

"Is there a way to override that?" Mike asked.

"Well, I guess any system can be meddled with," Jill said. "There's probably an override. Yuri, you didn't happen to do anything—?"

"Everybody's got a dose of Columbo in him," Mike said. "Just jump in with your questions, Jill. Then you can lift the fingerprints and pick up the evidence and find the little double helixes. You've seen it all on television and it looks so easy, doesn't it? Well, you know what? My buddies in blue here will take Yuri upstairs and he'll have a chance to explain exactly what happened. How's that for law and order?"

Mike stooped beside me and lifted my chin to look me in the eye. "You ready to dance yet, kid?" he said. Then he reached out to take my right hand to pull me up.

"Just about. I need your handkerchief for a minute."

I didn't want Jill or Yuri to see the key I had stopped to pick up, but I didn't want to touch it either. I dabbed at my nose and then reached under my calf to adjust my shoe, palming the key inside the white cotton square Mike had given me.

"Alley-oop, Blondie."

I stood up and brushed myself off.

"I came down here because I thought I could save you some trouble," Jill said. "I didn't know quite what you were looking for, but I can certainly tell you about the emergency exit."

"Maybe Bea should have thought of that," Mike said, annoyed with Jill Gibson.

"She doesn't know about it. Most people who work here have no reason to know. The space was designed and built with a single entrance—the way you came in—to better protect the books against both theft and the elements," Jill said. "But we failed all the fire department codes on the first inspection."

"So what did you do?"

"Yuri can show you, if you'll allow him. Down at the far end—"

"Near Sixth Avenue?" Mike asked.

"Yes. There are two emergency hatches, small steel plates, just about two foot square, that were dug into the ceiling."

"Are they kept locked?"

"Just latched on the inside. That's the whole point. No one can get them open from above, but theoretically, whoever was down here could be evacuated. If someone was working and, say, a fire broke out—worst-case scenario—he'd have to be able to push the hatch up. There's a short folding ladder that drops down."

"And bingo—you're in Bryant Park. Watching the Yankees give up a five-run lead," Mike said. "And from up top?"

"The plates are camouflaged with dirt and shrubbery this time of year. No one can get close enough to walk on them because of the little railing around the plants, and yet the bushes are light enough to let you lift the lid beneath them."

I remembered arriving at the park last night and noting the disarray of the greenery in the area where all the heavy equipment was standing.

Mike took me aside while he talked to the two young officers who were waiting for an assignment. "We're killing the Crime Scene Unit with this case. They're working another part of the library now, so one of you needs to stay put till they arrive. Keep this guy Yuri with you. Let him show you these hatches Ms. Gibson is talking about, so they can check them over, inside and out, okay?"

They both nodded.

Mike handed one of them a card with his phone number on it and told them to call with any questions or developments.

Jill asked me what we wanted her to do.

"Let's go up to your office," I said. "I'd like to get a list of your trustees—names and addresses."

"The president of the library and the board chair are in China, on a major acquisition trip," she said, looking glum. "I'm hesitant to do anything involving our trustees until I can reach them."

"Look, Jill, these are names I can get off your website or in your annual report. We need to talk with some of these people today. Now. Before facts and misinformation start to appear in the news. All I'm asking for is to speed this up by giving us a way to get to the folks we need. We'll get it done with or without you."

She pursed her lips. "Which ones do you want?"

"I'm not playing that game, Jill. We want them all."

She started walking briskly up the long ramp

that led to the elevator. Mike and I were several paces behind her.

"Stay on her ass, Coop. I'll be back to get you. Let me slip outside and see if I can spot the hatch while the crime scene's still taped off. See if it was disturbed recently."

Mike separated from us in the lobby of the building, and Jill and I continued on to her office, past another uniformed cop who'd been posted at the door. She encouraged me to take a seat in the anteroom, but I insisted on following her to her desk.

Reluctantly, she opened a file drawer and removed a list of the current board members and handed it to me.

I scanned it and could see that the addresses of the names that interested me most—Jasper Hunt and Jonah Krauss—were nearby, on the East Side of Manhattan.

I asked Jill about other members whose names had not come up so far in the case, in part to educate myself and in part to let her think we'd be moving too fast, with too many trustees, for her to try to run interference.

When we finished talking, I used her phone to call Laura and let her know I'd been sidetracked by the discovery of Barr's body.

"Don't worry about it. It's Friday and very quiet down here."

"Any calls?"

"McKinney's secretary. Says he wants you to check in with him by the hour if you're not coming in today. Battaglia's orders. I'm only the messenger."

"Not to worry. I'm behaving like Pat's new best friend."

"And Moffett's law secretary called about that familial search issue in the Griggs case," Laura said. "Is Mr. Fine the defendant's lawyer?"

"Yes."

"Moffett let him go back to California 'cause he hadn't finished writing his decision, so he won't announce it until Wednesday, when Fine can be back in town. I've got you calendared to be up in court at ten a.m."

"Thanks, Laura. We've waited eight years for a good lead in Kayesha's case. One more week won't be a deal breaker."

"I'll call you if anything else comes up. Tell Mike not to work you too hard."

Ten minutes later, Mike came through the door of Jill's office. He had been running, I guessed, from the way he was panting.

"You mind stepping out, Jill? I need a minute with Alex."

She was almost bristling now, put out in

every way possible and cut off from her staff. She left the room without answering.

"First of all, it's like a mob scene on the street. We'll have to try to duck out with some cover on the Fortieth Street side, unless you want your puss all over the news. The staff comes and goes by the old carriage entrance— shipping and receiving now—so maybe an RMP can pull in and take us to my car."

"Employees?"

"Nah. Lieutenant Peterson's playing hardball out there. He's let a few of the curators in, in case CSU needs them as they work their way around. Everybody else has been told to take the day off and come back on Monday."

"What then?"

"I haven't seen so many guys in uniform since the Paddy's Day parade. Only this time they're sober," Mike said. "And if you think that good-looking army of cops—and the shitload of yellow tape that's wrapped around the entire circumference of Bryant Park—hasn't attracted every crime reporter in town, you'd be mistaken."

"And the hatch?"

"Couldn't have made it easier unless somebody shot the body out of a rocket launcher."

"How?"

"Look, Coop. Yesterday afternoon, that end of the park was teeming with workmen. Say our boy was anywhere in the 'hood and saw the staging area setting up for the ball game. Here's his golden opportunity."

"Well, you're assuming he's familiar with the library."

"Damn right I am. This scheme wasn't launched by some junkie looking to get high. Five o'clock last night, the whole place goes dark. Everybody scatters for home."

"Tina's dead?"

"Killed in the lab. What did Dr. Assif say? Maybe the evening before. No struggle. She knew the guy, I'm thinking. Trusted him. Maybe they were hanging out together for a reason. Hoist on her own petard."

"What?"

"The weapon. I'll bet the weapon came right off the top of her desk," Mike said. "Now back to last night."

"Yeah, but if the killer doesn't work in the lab, how did he get back in to get her body?"

"He had her ID tag. Swiped it and came back. Covered her little body with a tarp, took it out of the freezer, and dollied it down the hall, down the ramp, down to the stacks."

"It must be so sinister there at night."

"Nobody around to get in his way. Push up

the hatch and roll one more tarp among all the others," Mike said. "Count on the fact that he's a Red Sox fan to even think of screwing up a Yankee game like that."

"It's incredibly risky," I said. "Smarter just to leave the body in the freezer. Who knows when it would have been found?"

"You're not thinking, Blondie. My guy didn't go there for the body. That was just pure carpe diem. Carpe corpse. My killer went back for the books."

"What books?" I asked.

"The ones I found under the water tank. The one that had the map inside," Mike said, doodling on a paper on Jill's blotter. "I'm figuring he might have had them stashed in the freezer with Barr's body, then moved them upstairs last night after he disposed of her."

"So when did he leave the library?"

"Who says he left?"

"That's a chilling thought."

"You know how enormous this place is—above and below ground? That's why nobody's getting in until it's swept by Scully's finest."

"What if he just walked **out** the door this morning?"

"Who?"

"Your killer. I mean, security wasn't letting people in, but nobody said anything about let-

ting anyone out. Especially with all the commotion outside, and the staff gathering at the
entrance. What if he passed for a detective and
just walked into the crowd?"

Mike's eyebrows raised. "You think too
much. That's one of your problems."

"So why am I wasting time with this list of
trustees, Mike? Your scenario doesn't quite fit
what I'd assume would be the modus operandi
of all the deep-pocketed Seconds and Thirds,
the Juniors and Seniors who sit on this board.
Or Minerva Hunt."

"Partners in crime. Some grunt getting paid
to do the dirty work. What did Jill Gibson tell
you the other day? That map thieves steal to order. We ought to talk to that master thief, Eddy
Forbes. See if his parole officer can lean on him
to squeal. If he's got anything to give, maybe
you can cut him a deal. Forbes can't be the only
library rat ever running around loose in the
stacks. He might know some of the other
players."

"I'm yours for the day," I said.

"Start making your wish list. Your afternoon
itinerary," Mike said, opening Jill's office door.
"I just need to call the morgue and see when
they're going to autopsy Barr, grab Mercer, and
then we're off."

Jill was sitting in the alcove of the executive

suite. She stood up as we came toward her, and Mike asked if he could use the phone on the desk.

I was staring at a portrait that hung on the end wall of the narrow room as Mike dialed.

"Jasper Hunt," Jill said to me. "The First. Done by the great Thomas Eakins, while he was teaching in New York at the Art Students League in the 1880s."

It wasn't the striking figure of Hunt that had caught my attention.

"Look at that, Mike," I said. "Look at his hand."

"I'll be damned. It's Hunt and his armadillo."

"Armillary, not armadillo," Jill said, in a humorless effort to correct Mike. "The brass rings represent the principal circles of the heavens."

I walked closer to look at the detail. Jasper Hunt's hand was resting on the brass skeleton of the sphere.

"It's the one." There was no question from the markings and detail portrayed that it was the weapon that had killed Karla Vastasi.

"You know the painting?" Jill asked. "We're so fortunate that Mr. Hunt gave this to us. You don't see many Eakinses outside of Philadelphia."

I couldn't think of anything else except con-

necting the lethal antique to Jasper Hunt himself. But Jill continued explaining the significance of the art to us.

"Important men often had their portraits
done with their armillaries. It was such a complex device that it was used to represent the
height of wisdom."

"Sit tight for a few hours, Jill. We'll call you
later." Mike hung up the phone. "Saddle up,
Coop."

He broke into a run and I trailed behind
him, out of the executive suite, down the great
staircase to the lobby. "I'm all turned around,"
he said. "Which way is the map division?"

I pointed to the north end of the hall and
tried to stay with him as he picked up speed.
He threw open the door and startled Bea, who
was sitting at her computer.

"How long will it take you to work up a historical footprint?"

"Depends on the location. You picked a
good day, Detective," she said, winking at him.
"I seem to have some time on my hands.
What's the address?"

Mike gave her the number of the brown-
stone on East Ninety-third Street in which Tina
Barr had last lived, the building in which Karla
Vastasi had been murdered.

"There's a whole row of houses there that have been in the Hunt family for more than a hundred years. Tell me anything about those properties you can learn from your maps, Bea. Dig me up some footprints as fast as you can."

TWENTY-FOUR

It was only eleven-thirty in the morning, but I felt as though a week had passed since Mike called me about Tina Barr's body.

A patrol car had backed in to the receiving bay of the library and the three of us were able to get through, without incident, the crowd of photographers, reporters, and local ghouls feasting on rumors of the dead girl in the park.

Mike examined the key wrapped in his handkerchief. It was old-fashioned—a long, cylindrical shaft with a notched tip, and an ornate bow to grasp and turn.

"You got an evidence bag?" he asked the driver of the patrol car.

"Yeah."

Mike dropped the key in the manila envelope and made a note of the cop's name and shield number. "Get this down to the lab right now and voucher it. Ask for Ralph Salvietti. He's been assigned to the case. Tell him Chapman needs this yesterday, okay?"

It was a short drive up Park past the corner

of Fifty-ninth Street, where a new luxury tower had opened a couple of years ago amid the stately old buildings that lined the avenue for the next thirty-five blocks.

We were throwing out ideas as we walked to the building, adding to the ever-growing list of chores.

"Who's going to check with the shipping companies and post office to see whether Tina mailed some of her belongings off, like to her mother?" I asked. "She must have done something with her possessions when she cleaned out of the apartment."

"I got Al Vandomir doing postal, UPS, FedEx, and all the storage locations near the apartment and the library," Mercer said.

Every item one of us thought to add to the list led to three or four more. The squad working on each murder—Karla Vastasi and now Tina Barr—would be expanded to a task force and the media would pump up the fear factor across the city. Any witnesses we couldn't reach today would be on notice of the scope of the investigation by the time the morning news dropped on their doorsteps.

I asked the concierge for Jonah Krauss's office, and we were directed to the forty-third floor. The elevator interior was sleek and high-tech, with two small-screen televisions—one that ran the local all-news station and the other, a stock ticker.

When we got off, an attractive young receptionist greeted us with a polished plastic smile. "How may I help you?"

Over her head was a sign with the company name and logo: MONTAUK WHELK MANAGEMENT.

"We're here to see Mr. Krauss."

She looked at a schedule on her desk and frowned. "Is he expecting you?"

"It's a condolence call," Mike said. "One of those sudden-death things."

"Oh, my," she said, startled by the news. "Jonah is in the gym. He should be finished there in a few minutes. Is it somebody close to him? May I tell him about it?"

"Thanks, but we've got to do it ourselves," Mike said. "What block is the gym on? We can pick him up."

She pointed at a frosted-glass door twenty feet away. "It's right there. But he's wheels-up from the Thirty-fourth Street heliport in an hour and I've got to get him there. Are you guys the police or something?"

"Something. And I'm wheels-up from the morgue at four o'clock, so we should be fine."

The girl swallowed hard and told us to take a seat.

"What's a hedge fund, anyway?" Mike asked me.

I sunk into a leather sofa and took my lip gloss out of my pocket. "They're private investment funds, usually only open to a limited range of investors. Hedge funds are exempt from direct regulation by the SEC, the way brokerage firms or mutual funds are managed. So they're considered riskier than a lot of traditional investments."

"Riskier how?"

"They often invest in distressed securities—like companies going into bankruptcy. Many of them aren't very transparent, since they don't have to disclose their activities to regulators. Sort of secretive."

"Like you, Coop," Mike said. "Krauss runs one?"

"The thumbnail sketch on the library contact sheet said Krauss manages hedge funds. Forty-six years old, graduate of Dartmouth, with homes in Manhattan, Montauk, and Lyford Cay. Still on his first wife—Anita."

"That's refreshing," Mercer said.

"And still wanting to use his new money to elbow out the good ole boys on the board to be the chair, according to Alger Herrick."

"Don't you think it's supposed to be **wealth** management?" Mike asked me, looking at the firm's name on the wall sign.

"I get that all the time," the girl said, looking up at Mike. I hadn't realized she could hear us talking. "Don't you know what a channeled whelk is?"

Mike reached for one of the candies in a silver bowl on her desk. "I'm drawing a blank."

"They're these clams that are in the ocean all over the eastern tip of Long Island, and the white part of the whelk is the most valuable. That's what wampum comes from—you know, Native American money. And Jonah is from Montauk, so it's his play on words."

"Must have a great sense of humor, your boss."

"Excuse me. Jonah, these guys—and her," she said, waving in my direction. "They're here to see you."

Teeth whiteners must have come with the firm's annual bonus. Jonah Krauss picked up his head and flashed a broad smile at us as he crossed between the reception desk and our seating area. "Whatever you're selling, come back next week," he said. "I told you time was tight today, Britney. I'm out of here."

The girl couldn't have been anything but a Britney.

"They're cops, Jonah," she said, standing up to grab his arm before he disappeared between the sliding glass doors that opened automatically as he neared them.

Krauss turned to look at the three of us. Still smiling—more cheesily than did most people on whom we dropped in—he introduced himself and offered a handshake to each of us. His curly brown hair was still wet from the shower I assumed he had taken after his workout. He was dressed in a warm-up suit and sneakers, ready for his weekend getaway.

"What's this about, folks?"

"A homicide investigation," Mercer said.

"Really? Murder?" Krauss said, some of the sparkle gone. "Who died?"

"Tina Barr."

"Tina? From the library? She does conservation work. Let's take this inside my office, shall we? Brit—hold all my calls and tell the pilots to expect a delay."

The doors parted again and we followed Krauss a few steps to another set of doors that slid apart on our approach.

I stood at the threshold, surprised by the sight. Most corporate executives who pay forty-third-floor midtown rents want forty-third-floor Manhattan views, river to river.

Instead, Krauss had created a thoroughly

modern, high-tech, translucent glass-and-steel library—carefully lighted and hermetically sealed—within the core of this new business tower. The only clue that we were anywhere near a corporate office was the four television screens—one in a bookcase on each wall, so that they could be viewed from every angle in the room—on which the Bloomberg channels ran continuously.

"No windows?" Mike asked as Jonah glanced at the numbers as they glided by.

"Can't do. The books have to be protected from the sun, from any dampness or dust that seeps in," Krauss said. "But it suits me fine. I'd rather be surrounded by them all day than staring out at the city. The kids who work for me have their offices on the perimeter. Big views, so they can dream bigger. Keeps them hungry. Want to tell me about Tina?"

"Somebody killed her," Mike said.

"How did it happen? Why?"

In the fifteen-second intervals when Krauss wasn't distracted by the ticker, he seemed genuinely surprised by the news.

"We're still trying to figure that out. Nobody from the library called you?"

"What does her murder have to do with the library?"

"Everything, apparently. How well did you know Tina Barr?"

"Not much better than I know you, Detective. I met her when she worked at the library. I guess you got to me because I'm on the board. She was handling some important restoration projects, the kind of thing it interests me to learn about. I looked over her shoulder a few times, but that's as close as it got."

Mercer was making his way around the room, tilting his head to study the titles of the books. "Did she do any work for you directly?"

"No. No, she didn't. I have someone in England who handles all my books. I just hadn't any need for Tina's services, although I admired her talent. Look, guys, what happened to her?"

"Somebody killed her," Mike said.

"Where? I wasn't sure Tina was still in town."

"I expect it happened in the basement of the public library."

"**What?**" Krauss seemed truly shocked. He sat at his desk, gesturing to us to take seats as well, giving Mike his complete attention. "That's impossible. Right under our roof? That's got to be the safest place in town."

"Once upon a time, maybe."

"And who do you think is responsible? A

workman? A trespasser? I know our security isn't foolproof, Detectives, but the idea of a murder inside the building is preposterous."

"More likely it's going to be someone who knew Tina," Mercer said. He was standing behind me, his large body framed by shelves of books with gilt and silver-tooled decorations and lettering on their spines.

"Such a quiet girl. I can't imagine she made many enemies. How can I help?"

"When's the last time you spoke with her?" Mercer asked.

"A month ago, maybe two. I hosted a cocktail party for the opening of our Dickens exhibit. We've got an extensive collection that hadn't been seen all together in a dog's age. I know Tina was there. Everyone in the conservation lab had done some work on that over the last couple of years, and I thanked her for that. I don't think—wait a minute," Krauss said. "I did see her again."

"When?" Mike asked.

"Within the last couple of weeks. I had stopped in at the lab because one of the girls had been working on an illuminated manuscript of Petrarch's poems. Stunning little book—brilliant pigments and elaborate detail. I was surprised to see Tina there. I didn't think she worked at the library any longer."

"And so you went over to talk to her?" Mike said.

"Actually, no. She said hello to me, and then—then she asked me a question, something to do with an investment idea I'd had earlier. Something I'd abandoned a while back. She was at her desk, and I guess we chatted for three or four minutes."

"Had Tina ever talked with you about investments?" I asked.

His expression suggested my question was ridiculous. "Never."

"Then why?"

Krauss put his hands in the pockets of his warm-up jacket and swiveled his chair back and forth. "I had a crazy idea a few years ago. Tried to put together a consortium of investors to acquire something for the library. Some bull—excuse me, Ms. Cooper—some cockamamie plan that started with board gossip. I was surprised Tina even knew anything about it."

"But she did," Mike said.

"Well, Detective, she wanted to." Krauss took his left hand out of his pocket and looked at his watch. "I had nothing to tell her."

"What was your plan?"

"I was approached by a guy who goosed me to do a joint venture. Wanted me to put up most of the money to try to buy a valuable property that would fetch a fortune, if the damn thing even existed. I figured I could find some buddies in the business to ride it with me, but the whole thing turned out to be a hoax."

"Who told you about it?" Mike asked.

Krauss threw back his head. "You don't want to know."

"Try me."

"His name's Eddy Forbes."

"The map thief?"

Krauss gave Mike a thumbs-up. "What's this? Know your library felons? At the time Forbes sniffed me out, he was a scholar and a private dealer, helping some of my fellow trustees elevate their tastes and shape their collections. He fooled a lot of people in the library world."

"What is it that Forbes wanted you to buy?"

"An old map, Mr. Chapman."

It was the answer I expected from the lead-in Krauss gave us. What he didn't expect was Mike's comeback.

"The 1507 Waldseemüller world map?"

Krauss turned on the dental brights again. "Anytime you get tired of working for the department, I might have a job for you, Detective. Now, how'd you know about that?"

"Some guys are good at missing persons. I got a sixth sense about missing things," Mike said. "Seems like everybody on your board wants a piece of it."

"Yeah, but they're just spinning their wheels. 'Cause if Eddy Forbes couldn't find it or steal it, then that map is just one more piece of the legend of Jasper Hunt Jr., made up to get the rest of the rich boys buzzing."

"You gave up on the project?" Mike asked.

"I shouldn't have gotten involved in the first place. I'm not into maps," Krauss said. "There was a well-known bibliophile named Holbrook Jackson, famous for saying, 'Your library is your portrait.' Look around this room. There's not a single map on display."

"So why did you entertain Forbes's folly to begin with?"

"The deal, Detective. The deal always grabs me. Could have been searching for a rare map or Captain Kidd's sunken treasure or King Solomon's mines. It would have been spectacular if the damn thing even existed," Krauss said, picking up a model helicopter from his desk and twirling the rotors as he talked. "People would have been throwing money at me left and right if I'd come up a winner. Instead I got hosed. Probably all went to Forbes's defense attorney anyway."

"And you haven't heard from Forbes since?"

"That's one of the conditions of his probation," Krauss said. "He can't be anywhere near a library and he can't communicate with any staff or trustees."

"Why'd he pick you in the first place if he knew you didn't care about maps?" I asked.

"Money."

"Everybody on your board has money."

"Hard to get those tough old guys to part with their dough. Most of their money is older than they are." Krauss smiled again. "I figure there's always more to be made where the last pot of gold came from."

I was certain that Alger Herrick had told us that Minerva Hunt was involved in a deal with Eddy Forbes.

"Didn't you try to discuss this consortium idea with Jasper Hunt the Third? Doesn't he still sit on the board with you?" I asked.

"What was that saying about Boston Brahmins? The Lowells talk only to Cabots, and the Cabots talk only to God?" Krauss asked of no one in particular, reciting the singsong doggerel. "The Hunts talk only to Astors . . . and maybe to God, as long as he isn't a Jew or a black man. Or even worse, a woman. Jasper hasn't been on the scene much the last four or five years. And he's not exactly a fan of mine."

"Why's that?"

Krauss wound the screw on the side of the

helicopter and launched it, watching it crash to the carpet beside him. "I guess he doesn't like my style."

"How about Talbot Hunt?" I asked. "How well do you know him?"

"Only in the boardroom."

"Get along?"

"I wouldn't turn my back on Tally for very long," Krauss said. "We have different ideas about the direction the library should be going. Nothing deadly, I wouldn't think."

"Didn't he have any interest in Forbes's idea? After all, the map was supposed to have been his grandfather's purchase."

"I don't think Eddy Forbes and Talbot Hunt are on the same page either. Would have surprised me if they were even before all of Forbes's legal troubles. Besides, Talbot's sister, Minerva, wanted a piece of the action. I'm sure once she was in, her brother wouldn't have been a likely partner. There's bad blood between those two."

"But you know Minerva?"

"We've met a handful of times. Eddy introduced us. She was willing to put up some of the seed money. She'd done that for Forbes before. I guess she was the one who told him the story of the missing map. He had access to most of the inner circle then. Minerva got all psyched up when the Library of Congress bought the only original that was thought to exist, be-cause she remembered hearing stories about the second one—her grandfather's—when she was a kid."

"So what was in this for you?" Mike asked.

Krauss leaned over and picked up his little toy. "Like I said. I put up a couple of million dollars. A few partners kicked in. We find this sucker? Forbes told me it would sell for maybe twenty million today."

"Sell . . . to the library, you mean?" I asked.

"Not likely. We'd get a much bigger bang from a private collector. That's what Eddy Forbes did. He helped these map nuts build their collections. The whole time, he was prob-ably stealing from one of them to feed the others."

"Maybe it's naïve of me," I said, "but I just assumed that as a member of the board, your loyalty would be to the library."

Krauss launched the whirlybird again and this time it circled his desk and came to a gen-tle landing on the table beside me. "You know why I get in trouble at the library? 'Cause I happen to think the place should be all about books. Screw the maps, screw the art. That's why so many of those guys have no use for me."

"But the maps—" I started to say, thinking

of Alger Herrick's description of their beauty and importance.

"So your cousin Sally marries a dentist from St. Louis and moves out there, Ms. Cooper. You stroll up Madison Avenue to some over-priced gallery looking for a wedding present and you buy a map of the city as it looked in 1898, framed and all. Three hundred bucks. Probably sliced out of an atlas in a library—maybe even by the master thief himself, Mr. Forbes," Krauss said, standing up and walking to a bookshelf behind his desk. "Or your buddy builds himself a ranch in Montana—Jewish investment banker cowboys—we're resettling Montana and Wyoming like they were the promised land. Some shyster will sell you a hand-colored print of whatever prairie town you want, at whatever your price point. It's not great art, it's not even a book you can hold and read and reread. What's the point?"

"Did you inherit your collection?" Mercer asked.

"I didn't inherit squat, Detective. My father sold used cars in Merrick, Long Island."

"How did you get into this . . . this . . ."

"Addiction. That's what it is. The first time I ever bought a book—I mean an old book, something I didn't have to read for school or to get me through a long plane ride—I was in Paris, walking around those little shops on the Left Bank after dinner one night. It was my first time there, I was flush with my first Wall Street bonus and some serious Bordeaux, and I stopped to look at the titles. I needed something for the flight home. I saw **Gatsby** and picked it up. I'd always loved the story when I was in college, figuring out how I could get me a piece of the American dream. You should have heard the proprietor scream when I pulled that copy off the shelf."

"Why?" Mike asked.

"F. Scott Fitzgerald. **The Great Gatsby.** I'm not talking about the paperback you read in high school," Krauss said, moving his hand along the bookshelf and lifting out a small volume, running his hand lovingly over the dust jacket, protected in its mylar sleeve. "This is the first edition. Modern firsts, that's how I started. Have you ever seen a more perfect image? It's totally iconic."

Jonah Krauss handed me the book. The jacket was cobalt blue, and the features of a woman's face looked down on an amusement park version of New York City at night.

I turned it over and noted the faint spots on the rear cover and the slightly faded lettering on the spine.

"Open it."

"That's okay?"

"Open it," he said again.

I lifted the cover and read. **Ernest—I think this book is about the best American novel ever written. Scott Fitz. 1925.**

"See what I mean?" Krauss took the book back and turned the pages. "Fitzgerald handled this himself. You touch these things, you imagine who held them before you did, you smell them and breathe in the print, the history, the romance. Guess what I paid?"

I had a few modern firsts, but nothing like this. "I can't."

"Fifteen years ago, thirty-five thousand bucks. My entire bonus and then some, gone in a flash," Krauss said, snapping his fingers.

"I'll be lucky if my pension's that good," Mike said under his breath.

"Stopped the Frenchman in his tracks when I told him to wrap it up for me. At auction today, it would draw double. After that I had to have everything Fitzgerald I could find. Hemingway next. Dos Passos. Wolfe. It's totally addictive."

"You obviously moved on to older collectibles, too," I said, scoping the room.

"I had to teach myself about them. See, the great private libraries have been amassing rare books for centuries." Krauss crossed the room, pausing in front of the Bloomberg, then continued on to shelves stocked with leather-bound books of all sizes. "I didn't know Keats from Yeats, Samuel Johnson from Samuel Pepys. But I'm a quick study."

He stopped in front of a shelf on which an open book rested in a cradle, two matching volumes standing beside it. He picked them up and offered them to Mike and me to admire. Each was bound in black leather, inlaid with mother-of-pearl. "Beautiful, huh?"

The silver writing, embellished with an intricate floral design, announced that we were looking at Charlotte Brontë's **Jane Eyre.** "Three volumes, 1847. The library has a set of its own, without the inlay. It's even got the writing desk Brontë used when she traveled."

His excitement seemed quite genuine, and he clearly wanted us to appreciate the collection.

"Do you have any atlases?" Mike asked. I figured he was testing Krauss about his interest in maps.

"Not my thing," Jonah Krauss said, as he saw Mercer reach for a book that was displayed on a shelf at the far end of the room. "Whoa, you don't want to pick that one up, Detective. Some of the pages are loose."

"Sorry," Mercer said, replacing the large book on its stand and repeating the title on the spine. "It looks like the court record of an old English trial. The 1828 proceedings against the murderer Aaron Keyes."

Krauss looked nervous. He stepped in front of Mercer and rested his fingers on the open page. "It's, uh . . . different."

"Different how?" Mercer asked.

"It's . . . it's an anthropodermic binding, Mr. Wallace. Extremely rare. Most unusual to find."

"Anthropodermic?" Mike asked. "Help me out, Coop. Means what?"

"Don't know."

"The binding is made from human skin," Jonah Krauss said, folding his arms and speaking quietly. "That inquest record is bound in the skin of the murderer, Detective."

Mike lowered his head. "It doesn't get much creepier than that."

"Aaron Keyes raped and killed a young girl in the English countryside. He was sentenced to be hung, and after that his skin was tanned and used to make this binding."

"Human skin?" Mike asked. "You're not joking?"

"Not at all, Detective. Most libraries don't want books like these, of course—although Harvard has a few—but many private collectors do. It's a very specialized market, human skin. Not for everyone's taste."

Krauss turned away from the book and went back to his desk. His lips parted and the whitener on his teeth reappeared. "Lighten up, guys. It's from the murderer, not the dead girl."

Mike Chapman wasn't amused. "Like you said, Mr. Krauss. Your library is your portrait."

TWENTY-FIVE

"That's frigging sick," Mike said, when Krauss stepped out of the room to give Britney a new ETA for his pilots.

"Doesn't make him a killer," Mercer said.

"Sorry," Krauss said when he returned. "What else can I do to be useful?"

"Let's go back to your last conversation with Tina Barr, when she asked you about the consortium looking for the map," Mike said.

"I didn't have anything more to say," Krauss said, packing some folders into a soft leather briefcase. "I told her it was a bust, okay? I thought maybe she was getting mixed up with the wrong people. I cautioned her to be careful."

"Careful of the wrong people? Alger Herrick? Minerva Hunt, or her father? That's who Tina was working for most recently."

"When she asked me the question, I was actually worried that Eddy Forbes had gotten to her. He's a very seductive guy."

"You think he went after Tina as a romantic interest?" I asked.

Jonah dismissed me with the back of his hand. "Not that kind of seductive. He was a genius at scamming the best collectors. Had his own gallery and a handful of rich clients who trusted his judgment implicitly. Forbes had the cunning to steer some of these serious collectors to donate important works to the library, and once the transaction was complete, he stole from those very treasures."

"Don't people bother to ask what the source of a rare sixteenth-century map is when they go to buy it?"

"A guy like me might **hondel** a bit, Ms. Cooper. Bargain hard, ask questions, get tough in a negotiation. That's my nature. Eddy just has to whisper in the ears of those old buzzards that some fourth-generation blowhard had gone through the family fortune and had to break up the jewels. All hush-hush, 'cause every one of these dynasties has had deadbeat offspring who might come to the same end. Circle the wagons. Building, inheriting, and disposing of these library pieces has a tremendous element of secrecy involved."

"Secrecy?" I asked.

"In the antiquarian business, knowing where the books are—the atlases, the maps—whose hands they're in, that knowledge is power. It's money. And a great many of these things that have been in families for generations aren't even insured. They couldn't possibly be, at today's prices. There are things inventoried in the great private collections of the world that haven't been seen for decades, so it's impossible to know what's become of them," Krauss said, holding his forefinger to his lips. "That's why I told Tina Barr to be careful."

I didn't like Jonah Krauss, and he could smell that.

"You want to tell us about yesterday afternoon? About where you were last night?" Mike asked.

"You guys are serious, right? I don't believe this. I ran a meeting in our conference room till six-thirty. Britney can give you the names of all the attendees. Then my driver picked me up and took me to the Bronx. Is that a crime?" Krauss reached into his warm-up jacket and pulled out the thinnest phone I'd ever seen. He pressed an icon and then hit zoom. "Have a look, Detective. Yankee Stadium with my boys. Right up until the bitter end."

"Great seats," Mike said, passing me the phone. Krauss had taken snapshots of his two young sons from his box, right over the dugout.

I handed him back the phone and he put

both hands up in the air. "Who sent you here, really? Some of those trustees just hate my guts, don't they? Try to mix me up in a murder case."

"Who hates you?" Mercer asked. "And why?"

"Now, that's something I really don't have time to answer today."

"Put your bag down, Jonah, and take a seat," Mike said. "Give it a try."

"If you had any idea of the turmoil inside the public library—inside most libraries— you'd be able to understand the depth of the animosity, Detective. It all looks so scholarly and benign from the outside, but there are real battles being fought," Krauss said, refusing to sit.

"Over what?"

"Start with the future of the library. What do you think the biggest problem is?"

"Funding," I guessed. "Money to keep a facility like this—"

"We're pouring money into it, Ms. Cooper. The problem is that ten years from now, who's going to need a library?" Krauss was snarling at me. "Our attendance has been plunging for years, not just in New York but all over the world. Research libraries like ours in particular. The computer and the Internet are killing us, making us obsolete. We've been given a conservative estimate that at least ninety-five percent of all scholarly inquiries begin on Google."

"But these rare books in research libraries are so unique," I said.

"And sooner or later, every one of these beauties will be digitized. We've got fifty-three million items in this library, and already, the images from hundreds of thousands of them are available on the Web. How do we stay relevant? What if we just become a damned book museum? Those are some of the things we fight about."

"Where are you in these battles?"

"I'm trying to move the dinosaurs forward. That's part of their animosity. Within the next decade, Google will have digitized fifteen million of our works. I'm all for scanning the great libraries of the world. Sit at home in Dubuque with your laptop and look at everything we've got. Why not?"

"Because there's something so different to holding the physical book," I said, remembering my own research in the great reading room. "Coleridge and Keats—each of them annotated the margins of their books with their thoughts, their ideas. You can see what mattered to them when you read their own work, and how that affected their creative process."

"Paper disintegrates, Ms. Cooper. Books crumble, unless you can provide the environment in which to protect them, as I can."

"There are things a computer will never be able to tell us. I remember doing my thesis research at my regular seat in the reading room, next to the same quiet guy every day. He was a medical historian, trying to track down the history of disease outbreaks in eighteenth-century England," I said, talking more to Mercer and Mike than to Jonah Krauss, who finished packing up his briefcase. "I couldn't understand why he kept sniffing the papers he was studying. It seemed so odd."

"You cross-examine him?" Mike asked.

"Gently. He told me he was reading letters from an archive that came from the Cotswolds. At the time, people took to sprinkling vinegar on the correspondence, in hopes that it would disinfect them and stop the spread of cholera. He could still trace the scent on some of the old paper."

"A very romantic notion, Ms. Cooper, but it's not the future. Any chance I can be released for the weekend?"

"What's the source of your disagreements with the Hunts?" Mercer asked.

"Look, Detective, we've buried the sword. It's been almost five years. I assume Jasper's gotten over it. You might want to keep an eye on Tally. I think he'd pull out the rug from everything to get his father's bequests."

I thought of the bejeweled book that had been found with Karla Vastasi's body. Minerva Hunt said it had been given to the library years earlier, when her grandfather died, but the "Ex Libris" plate bore Talbot Hunt's name.

"Why do you say that?"

"Five years ago, Ms. Cooper, when I led the charge to deaccession an Asher Durand painting, Jasper Hunt literally threatened my life," Jonah Krauss said, spreading his palms as he leaned on the desk. "Check with your commissioner. I had police protection 24/7."

"All because of a painting?" Mike asked. "This library's got more action than any crack den in Bed Stuy."

"A very famous work of art, detective. **Kindred Spirits,** it's called."

"What's so deadly about that?"

"It was one of the library's sacred cows, Mr. Chapman. My committee made a decision to sell it, and quite frankly I thought the board would just rubber-stamp us. Turned out I was wrong."

"What's the story?"

"Durand is one of the best-known artists of the Hudson River School founded by Thomas Cole.

Landscape paintings. Cole's best friend was the poet William Cullen Bryant," Krauss said.

"Bryant Park?" Mike asked.

"Exactly. Together, Cole and Bryant became leaders of New York City's civic and cultural life."

"Why was the painting in the library in the first place, and not an art museum?" I asked.

"You're catching on, Ms. Cooper. Bryant's daughter gave the painting to the Lenox Library in 1904. So when this building opened, and the park was created in her father's name, it seemed like a fitting home. But it just moved around from one end of a dark hallway to another. In my view, it didn't belong here at all."

"So your committee decided to sell it. Was there an auction?"

"That was another one of my problems," Krauss said. "We didn't hold a public auction. You know that like most other major cultural institutions, our endowment dropped precipitously after September eleventh. We figured a healthy sale of a few pieces of our art would rally some investment income to buy important books that we wanted. We are, after all, a library."

"So there was a silent auction instead?"

"Yes. Sotheby's acted as our agent, and interested parties were invited to submit sealed bids."

"How much did it bring?" Mike asked.

"Thirty-five million dollars. Highest price ever paid for an American painting," Krauss said, the side of his mouth pulling up, as though he couldn't suppress a smile. "Me, I'm not the sentimental type. I thought it was a great deal."

Mike whistled. "What museum had that kind of money?"

"The Met was outbid, Detective. The Wal-Mart heiress Alice Walton bought the Durand for a small museum her family plans to open soon in Arkansas."

"Attention all Wal-Mart shoppers! At that price, it went to a discount store? What were you smoking, Jonah?"

"The art critics wanted to stone me, the **Times** said the sale was the crime of the century—that **Kindred Spirits** is a national treasure that belongs in New York—and the rest of the board caved in to the public outcry."

"What spooked Jasper Hunt to go after you personally?" Mike asked.

"He said that we'd never be able to attract future donors. They'd be put off by the fact that their own bequests might eventually be disposed of in some secret way. But I think it was all about Hunt himself."

"What do you mean?" I asked.

"When my committee was figuring out what to deaccession, we stumbled on a few things that had come in to the library through Jasper the Second—Hunt's father," Krauss said. "Things the library doesn't really need. We've had a Gutenberg Bible from the time this library was built, right? Printed in 1455—a simply amazing accomplishment, for the man to invent a movable press that re-created the finest Gothic scripts of his age. Maybe one hundred and eighty of them printed, and close to fifty survive. Ours is usually on display on the third floor. James Lenox donated it when the library was built—the first Gutenberg that was ever brought to America. You've seen it, haven't you?"

"Yes." It was one of the centerpieces of the library's collection.

"Well, Jasper Hunt gave us another one, not in such good shape as the Lenox gift. Questionable provenance. Why do we need it locked up in a vault somewhere underground when we could sell it for a healthy price?"

"Still sounds like it would be a pretty desirable thing to have, from a curator's standpoint," I said.

"J. P. Morgan set the standard for Jasper Hunt, and that's not a compliment. Neither one was a very picky shopper. They both bought up English and European estates by the boatload. Morgan's library has three Gutenbergs. I say one is enough. His advisors had the good sense to make him get rid of the objects that didn't enhance his collection—medieval tapestries, Egyptian sculpture, second-class art. We could sell the excess and get things our curators really want and need."

"Was that what you wanted to deaccession?" Mike asked. "His Gutenberg Bible?"

"It wasn't at the top of my list, but it was there. I would have preferred to start with a gaudy little prayer book that came from his father's collection. Extremely rare volume when Jasper Hunt the First bought it, but then he had it covered in jewels—to commemorate his son's birth."

Mike cocked his head. He was obviously thinking of the object that had been found with Karla Vastasi's body.

"Rumor has it that the president of Cartier offered the Hunts a king's ransom to buy it. Seems the jewels were chosen and set by Louis Cartier himself, and the current managers of the business are peeved that it's collecting dust in storage."

It appeared that everyone had lost the significance of the prayer book's original purpose.

"What became of Jasper's death threat?" I asked.

"Sort of withered and lost its energy, just like he did," Jonah Krauss said, snapping the lock on his case. "Three or four months of aggravation, then he was on to his next enemy. Now, I'd like to get a start on my weekend, Ms. Cooper. Any objections?"

Krauss had the briefcase in his right hand, and with his left he reached down to pick up a gym bag.

"That looks like it weighs a ton," Mike said. "Let me help you out with it."

"Part of the reason I lift weights, Detective. I've got twenty-five pounds of catalogs for the winter auctions, in addition to my own paperwork."

"One last thing, Mr. Krauss. You got any idea where Jasper Hunt's little jeweled book is now? I mean, like where in the library is it, if I wanted to see it today?"

Krauss held open the door for us, then stopped and turned to answer Mike. "I haven't a clue. Last I heard, Tally was taking lessons from the ne'er-do-well son of Brooke Astor. I made such noise about selling off the things that didn't belong in our collection that he

started to try all kinds of tricks to break his father's will, transfer some of the bequests made
to the library ages ago out from under our
roof."

"But how could he do that?" Mike asked.

Krauss pressed a button at the side of the
glass door and it seemed to zap every system in
his room, dimming lights, turning off electron-
ics, and sealing the exit.

"I assume his lawyer explained the legal lia-
bility to him, Mr. Chapman. I guess that's why
he probably resorted to theft."

TWENTY-SIX

"You see his pecs?" Mike asked Mercer as he held open the car door and ushered me into the back seat. "Bet Krauss could lift that armillary sphere with two fingers. Smash the daylights out of Karla Vastasi. Good we got there in time so nobody skinned her to decorate his library."

"There's no middle ground with you," I said. "It's easy to dislike the guy, but what's a motive for him to be snooping around Tina's apartment? Killing Vastasi?"

"They're all so greedy, Coop. The Hunts spend generations coveting and buying and preserving all these things, and this clown's ready to discard them all."

"Krauss is new to the ˙˙'hood, but he has surely learned fast," Mercer said. "Those Hunts, though, I think it's in their genes. I can't figure how Tina Barr got caught up in this."

"It wouldn't be the first time I got fooled by someone who wasn't what she appeared to be," I said.

"Did you hear back from Minerva Hunt?" Mike asked.

I checked my cell for messages. "Nothing new."

"You called her?"

"Twice since you told me to this morning. Why don't you try your magic? She seemed to like you."

Mike didn't answer.

"I get it," I said, ruffling the hair at the nape of his neck. "She hasn't returned your calls either. That's why you're hounding me."

He flipped open his cell and dialed information. "Yeah, operator. In Manhattan, Rizzali Investigations. Connect me."

Someone answered the phone.

"Mike Chapman here. Homicide. Looking for my buddy Carmine. You got his cell for me?"

Apparently, whoever was in charge didn't want to give that out.

"Okay, patch me through," Mike said, waiting for the receptionist to make the connection. "Yo, Carmine. How's things? Someday I'm going to have my own secretary, too. You're living the good life, man. You working with Ms. Hunt today?"

I could hear the gruff voice barking back at Mike.

"Where at? No, no. I don't want to see **her**. I want to make you a hero, Carmine. Ms. Hunt dropped an earring in the office the other night. I'll hand it off to you, you give it back to her," Mike said. "Why would I kid you? One high-maintenance broad on my hands is enough. Where are you? Yeah, right now."

Mike gassed the car and we were off.

"Where to?" I asked.

"He's parked at the corner of Fifth Avenue and Eighty-third Street. I tell you, Minerva may pay him a lot more than the City of New York did, but Carmine is still one dumb schmuck. Take off one of your earrings, kid."

I instinctively clasped my hands to my ears and covered the small gold hoops. "I like this pair. Way too simple for Minerva Hunt. Can't have it."

"Once she tells him he's crazy, Carmine'll give it back to me. I'm just trying to get to the broad."

I unhooked one earring and passed it to Mike.

"What did you find out about that tote that Karla Vastasi was carrying?" he asked.

"Oops, I dropped the ball on that. Didn't think it would be important until we saw her again."

"You're about to get your wish, if I know Carmine."

I dug my cell out of my handbag and it was

my turn to call information. "Bergdorf Good-man," I said, and accepted the operator's request to dial the number of the department store that carried the distinctive bag.

"I'm wondering if you can help me," I told the saleswoman when the switchboard connected me. "I was with a friend of mine last week. She had one of those open totes with the geometrical pattern—that French line that you've carried for the last couple of years."

She mentioned the designer's name, reminded me that Bergdorf's had the exclusive, told me the exorbitant price, and asked if I wanted to purchase one.

"Yes, but before I make the trip over, I want to be sure I can get exactly the same color, same monogram style. I'm not sure if she got if from you, or while she was traveling."

The woman groaned at my insistence. "Who's your friend?"

"Minerva Hunt."

"Ms. Hunt?" I could envision the saleswoman standing at attention at the sound of the name. "Yes, of course. She has that bag in three colors. Would you like the black or the navy? We can stamp the monogram on overnight. I don't think we have the burgundy in stock."

"Too bad. That's the one I wanted."

"Would you like me to special-order it for you?"

I had already disconnected the phone as I announced to the guys, "Minvera lied. Remember when she said that tote was a gift to her and that she didn't like it? Well, she bought three of them herself."

"You think people go to their doctor and say they've got a bellyache when their ears hurt? Or a sore throat when its hemorrhoids?" Mike asked. "But they've got no problem lying to the prosecutor. See how smart she is and whether she can figure out the truth."

Mike squared the block in front of the Metropolitan Museum of Art and pulled in on Fifth Avenue, behind Carmine's Mercedes S500. I looked through the list of library trustees and found Jasper Hunt III. "I think Minerva may have dropped in on her father. He lives on this block."

"Twofers, kid. May be our first break."

Carmine was wiping the side of the car with a chamois until he looked up and saw Mike. He dropped the polishing cloth on the hood and headed toward us.

"Coming at my bait," Mike said, "faster and dumber than a guppy swimming up for food. Maybe he thinks Minerva'll give him a reward."

"Carmine's looking pretty buff himself,"

Mercer said. "He could hoist a garden ornament over my head, don't you think?"

"No question about it."

"Got the earring, Chapman?" Carmine said, his thick hand gripping Mike's door.

"In my pocket. Let me get out," Mike said, stepping onto the sidewalk as he fumbled with his jacket. "You waiting to get in to see the Monets?"

"Nah, she stops by to check on her father every couple of days," Carmine said, pointing his thumb over his shoulder. "Lemme see."

"Minerva have you working last night? We could have taken you to the Yankees game with us, isn't that right, Mercer?" Mike was checking Carmine's whereabouts—maybe Minerva Hunt's, too. "Here it is."

"Had a breather last night. She didn't want no company, and me and my goomada had a quiet night at home. No charity balls, no Thursday-night shopping spree. Like doing a day tour, back when I was in your shoes."

Mercer got out of the car and opened my door.

"Whoa. You told me you weren't looking for Minerva. Where you all going?" Carmine asked. "Hey, these ain't hers. She don't have anything without sparkles. Someone else dropped this. Check the projects, you jerk."

"Could have fooled me," Mike said. "I was sure it was Minerva's. What number, Coop?"

"Right here—the one with the green awning."

Mike straightened his blazer and adjusted his tie as he approached the doorman.

"Jasper Hunt," Mike said, displaying his gold shield. "And no, he isn't expecting us, but his daughter will be by the time her hired goon gets off the phone."

Carmine's face was red and his eyes bulging as he stood on the sidewalk with his phone in hand.

The doorman spoke to someone on the intercom and gestured to the elevator. "You want the penthouse."

The three of us got in, and Mercer pressed the button while Mike sat on the red velvet bench behind. The mahogany paneling and brass trim were complemented by the small oil painting over Mike's head. "This is decorated nicer than my apartment," he said. "And I think it's bigger."

"You've refused all my offers to help you put your place together," I said.

"I didn't say I wanted it to look like a brothel, with all your fancy tassels and pillows and stuff."

I remembered how his fiancée, Val, had

transformed the small space of the dark walk-up he referred to as "the coffin," and I bit my tongue rather than remind him of her.

There was only one apartment on the floor, and as the elevator door opened, we were greeted by a woman in a white uniform. Before she could say a word, Minerva Hunt stepped in front of her.

"Why don't you go out for a walk, Martha. Father won't need you while I'm here."

"Yes, mum. I'll just be getting my jacket."

"So, Detective, Carmine tells me you're a bit desperate to see me."

"Actually, I stumbled into him while we were on our way to meet your father."

"Oh, he can't be talking to you, sir," the woman, whom I assumed to be a nurse, said to Mike as she reached for a jacket in the hall closet.

"I'm dealing with this, Martha," Minerva said, her long arm stretched across the door frame. "We've just finished lunch and he's rest-ing, Mr. Chapman."

"I'm famished. Must be some leftovers. What do you feel like, Mercer?"

Minerva let down her arm so that the nurse could exit, and Mike stepped into the foyer of the apartment. "Cook has plenty of roast beef left, Miss Minerva."

"So you're in, Detective," Minerva said, turning her back to us and following Mike into the living room. "Exactly what is it you want?"

Mike had crossed through to the living room, an enormous space flooded with early-afternoon light from the tall windows that provided a view over the top of the museum and the fall foliage of Central Park. The antique furniture and old masters paintings were extraordinary.

"I'm about to leave," Minerva said, looking over her shoulder at Mercer and me. "You've got no business being here. If your issues are with me and about my housekeeper, then let's go somewhere to talk."

"We need to speak to your father. This is bigger than Karla Vastasi. It's about the library now," I said. She didn't give any hint that she knew about the murder of Tina Barr. "I'd like you to stay until we've finished with him."

Her navy turtleneck sweater and pencil skirt showed Minerva Hunt's slim frame to advantage. She tugged at her collar and pulled it up against her chin. "He's too weak to do this so unexpectedly. I'll get you the number for his lawyer—Justin Feldman. Let him set the appointment for you."

I smiled at Minerva. "I've got Mr. Feldman's number on my phone," I said. "He's a great litigator and a powerful adversary, Ms. Hunt. I've worked with him often. I didn't realize he did estate work, too."

She practically slapped the phone out of my hand. "No, that's right. He's not—um—not handling those matters. You tell me right now what anything has to do with my father's estate. The man isn't dead yet."

"Temper, temper, Minerva," Mike said. "We'll explain that to him ourselves."

Sliding pocket doors opened and a butler appeared, summoning Ms. Hunt. "I'll be right in. Why don't you show my friends out?"

"We'll take a couple of roast beefs on rye before we go, and I'll stay with Minerva, if you don't mind."

The butler looked more perplexed than the nurse had been. Minerva pushed the doors wider apart and led us down a hallway, past the grand dining room and a parlor to a cheerful sunroom that caught the southern exposure.

Seated in a leather armchair was an elderly man dressed in a black jacquard smoking jacket, and perfectly groomed. A large yellow cat sat on his lap, stroked by the man's trembling, liver-spotted hand. A second one, identical in color, was curled against his slipper.

"This is my father, Jasper Hunt. Father, these gentlemen are from the police department. Ms.

Cropper—is that your name, dear?—works for Paul Battaglia. You remember Paul, don't you?"

Jasper Hunt lifted his head and met us with a vacant stare.

"We're having a family chat," Minerva said. "I know you've met my brother, Tally. Perhaps you'd like to meet father's favorite children."

"Siblings?" Mike asked.

"Of course. They're in the will—doesn't that make it so?" she said, approaching her father. "That's Patience, on his lap, and Fortitude, on the floor. Golden Maine coons. Longhairs. Have I got them right, Papa?"

The old man smiled and kept stroking.

"Little library lions, Detective. When Leona Helmsley kicked the bucket a few years ago," Minerva said, referring to the hotel magnate known as the Queen of Mean, "she left twelve million dollars to her dog. Gave Father all kinds of bad ideas. I've done everything reasonable to change his mind, but for now I'm sweet as I can be to those pussies. I may have to adopt them one day."

"Good afternoon, Mr. Hunt," Mike said, getting on one knee to try to make eye contact with the patriarch of this unusual family. "Pleased to meet you."

Hunt's eyes followed the sound of Mike's voice, but he made no response.

I turned at the sound of footsteps behind me as Talbot Hunt came into the room.

"I forgot to tell you we've got visitors, Tally," Minerva said as her brother stopped in his tracks. "I think you've met them before."

"And I forgot to tell you when I arrived that Tina Barr is dead," Talbot Hunt said. "Murdered, of all things. In the library."

TWENTY-SEVEN

It was obvious that Talbot Hunt had come to his father's home after leaving us at the library this morning. I wondered whether it was a coincidence that he and Minerva met here.

"I thought maybe you were organizing a memorial service for Tina," Mike said. "Seems like she had something to do with all of you."

"Why don't we move into the office?" Talbot said.

"Because my first order of business is to talk with your father."

"I think you're smart enough to see he's not having a good day," Minerva said.

Mike stood up, took her arm, and walked with her to the door of the room, out of Jasper Hunt's earshot. "What's his condition?"

"He's old, Mr. Chapman. In case you hadn't noticed. He's infirm."

"Any dementia?"

Minerva looked at her brother, and neither answered quickly. "He's clear most of the time," Tally said.

"I guess he has to be if you're trying to

change the will. Isn't that so?" Mike asked. "We got a little bit of Brooke Astor going on here?"

The great Mrs. Astor, who spent half a century distributing her husband's fortune—more than one hundred million dollars—wound up with her estate in the middle of an ugly battle. The will she had signed years earlier—leaving much of the Astor trust to New York institutions she loved, such as the library—had a subsequent codicil bequeathing most of those same assets to her only son.

"I don't get it, Detective," Tally said.

"The issue was Mrs. Astor's competence— her mental competence—at the time the codicil was signed," I said.

"Mrs. Astor was a dear friend of my father's," Minerva said. "I'm familiar with the case. I just don't see what it has to do with us."

"Hello, Minerva." I heard a weak voice from across the room. "Who's here with you?"

"Your turn, Coop. You're good with the old guys."

"Father, I think it's time for you to take a nap."

I started toward Jasper Hunt and kneeled beside Fortitude, who raised up and started to rub herself against my leg, her bushy tail tickling my face and her big tufted feet padding the carpet like a miniature lion's.

"Don't marginalize me, Minerva. Who's this nice young lady here? Have we met?"

He reached out to touch my cheek and I held my hand over his. "I'm Alexandra Cooper, Mr. Hunt. I'm a lawyer. A prosecutor, actually."

"Bully, Ms. Cooper. Doing justice, are you?"

"We're trying, Mr. Hunt."

Mercer was attempting to steer Tally out of the room, but he stood firm.

"Have you met my babies?"

"Patience and Fortitude," I said. "They're beautiful."

"They're smart, young lady. Better than beautiful. Never caused me a moment's trouble. The only price for their loyalty is a small bit of food."

"Are you too tired to talk to me for a few minutes, Mr. Hunt?"

He was staring at Patience, and I turned to look at the foursome behind me. Minerva and her brother seemed frozen, fearful that Jasper would betray whatever secrets this dysfunctional family held close.

"I'm always tired. But I like to talk to young girls."

"We've just come from the public library. We know how generous you've been to them over the years."

"I used to have a wonderful library of my own.

Right here. It's all gone, plundered by thieves."
Hunt lifted his bent forefinger in the air.

"That's not true, Father. I'll be happy to
show Ms. Cooper your library," Tally said. "It's
an extraordinary collection, as you might
imagine."

Hunt grasped at my hand. "Yesterday I took
a long walk in the park—Central Park. Do you
know it? I couldn't find my way home. It was
frightening, actually. I walked for miles and
miles and still couldn't get out of the park."

"Don't get agitated, Father," Minerva said,
coming up beside up. "That was just a dream
you had. You haven't walked in the park for
years."

"Did you say your name was Alice?"

"Almost, sir. It's Alex. Alexandra."

"Did you ever meet Alice?"

"Sorry?" I looked to Minerva for help.

"Alice Liddell. The girl for whom **Alice in
Wonderland** was written. My grandfather had
an obsession with that child—or maybe with
the book. I think this is Papa's long-term memory at work."

"Would you like me to come back with **Alice**?" I asked the old man. "With that book?
Perhaps read to you?"

Why did that children's story play such a recurring role in these events?

Jasper Hunt looked up at me and smiled. "Of course I'd like that."

"Do you remember a young woman named Tina? Tina Barr?"

His eyes closed and he repeated the name several times, as though trying to locate it in a crumbling memory bank.

"Do we know her, Minerva?" he asked.

"Yes, Father. That nice girl who was helping you with your books. Cataloging the collection, restoring some of your Melvilles."

"Then I know her, if my daughter says I do. Was that your question?" He looked at me again.

"Do you remember talking with her?"

He closed his eyes and shook his head from side to side two or three times.

"Did you know that she left you to go to work for Alger Herrick?"

"Herrick? There's a lucky man," Hunt said. "I once thought he'd be a fine match for my Minerva. She didn't agree—did you, dear?"

Minerva Hunt cackled like a witch. "I'm glad you remembered that."

"What became of Alger? Have I seen him about?"

"He's got a wonderful apartment here in New York, Mr. Hunt," I said. "Full of the most magnificent maps."

"You can't read maps, young lady," he said, almost scolding me. "You can't hold them, fondle the smooth bindings, finger the parchment and vellum, and caress them, as you can books. I don't care for maps. Herrick's folly, not mine."

"Tally told me that your father had a map," I said, checking with Talbot Hunt as I tried to get to the subject. The son looked grim, avoiding my eyes. "One of the rarest in the world. It had a dozen separate pieces, twelve panels."

"Did you know my father was mad, young lady? Absolutely mad."

"She wants to know about the Waldseemüller map, Father," Tally said, his arms folded and his words sharp.

"They all want the map, boy. I wouldn't have any visitors if it weren't for that damn map, you know. How long has it been since you've been by to see me?"

"Don't take it personally, Father. Tally's afraid he might run into me if he came to call," Minerva said, smoothing the front of her skirt. "Two hours together and it already seems like a month."

The old man mumbled something under his breath. I thought I heard him say, "Even the Jew."

I leaned closer to him. Had Jonah Krauss been to see him, too?

Minerva queried him. "Even a few what, Papa?"

Jasper Hunt's chin rested on his chest and his eyes closed again. His short defense of book-men—his ancestors and himself—and the troublesome questioning about the map had seemed to devour all his energy.

"My father's a doctor, Mr. Hunt. He's a brilliant man, and an especially kind one, too."

Hunt's glassy eyes fixed on me while I talked.

"It's a remarkable legacy he's set in place," I said, looking back at Minerva and Tally to see if either of them reacted to the sound of that word. "Your father, sir—and your grandfather—their philanthropic giving has been a stunning gift to so many great institutions. What do you think the Hunt legacy is?"

"Still searching for that, are you? My father would find it amusing, I'm sure. Tried to take it all with him, in case there was no one left to care. He'd be so pleased that we're sitting here today, trying to figure what he was all about, talking about him. That keeps him alive in a strange way, doesn't it?"

"Searching for what, exactly?" I wanted to go back to that.

" 'The evil that men do lives after them,' " Jasper Hunt said. "That's usually the case, isn't it?"

I froze at the sound of the Shakespearean

words that had been scrawled on the paper found with Tina Barr's corpse.

"But what evil?" I asked. "Your father was good and generous to so many people."

"He quoted that phrase all the time. Probably figured no one would long remember his good deeds. Just his madness," Hunt said, his eyelids fluttering closed. "Is it time for a cocktail, Tally?"

Minerva answered. "Not yet, Father. You need your medications."

I could see that the conversation was a strain, and I stood up, patting the hand that held the golden cat.

Minerva picked up a small silver bell and rang it until the butler appeared in the doorway. "Will you help me settle Father inside?"

"Certainly, madam."

"Mind if we ask you a few more questions?" Mike said to Tally Hunt as he led us toward the living room.

"I should think you'd have your fill of answers by now."

Mike showed that he wasn't leaving by settling in to the deep pillows of a sofa covered in a silk damask print with birds and butterflies. "So, it looks like you shot up here for a surprise visit as soon as you saw the panel of the map that we found this morning."

"Hardly seems to be illegal, Detective."

"Who tipped you off to it?"

"It wasn't Jill, if that's where you're going. The library is a closed world, a tight one. Word travels fast."

"Your father's trust and estate lawyer?" Mike asked. "Your sister doesn't seem to know."

Talbot stood by one of the windows that overlooked the museum. "It was that fellow Garrison. Francis X. Garrison."

"The lawyer Brooke Astor's son used to try to defraud his mother," I said. "Battaglia indicted him."

"I've been interviewing for a new lawyer, actually. Haven't hired one yet. I've been my father's business advisor for years. I've taken good care of his affairs."

"I'd think you'd have a hard time convincing a surrogate's court judge about any changes to the will that have been made in your favor lately, considering the condition of his health," Mercer said.

"My father is not the least bit delusional, Mr. Wallace. He has occasional problems with his short-term memory, but he's quite sound. He's demonstrates solid comprehension of things he needs to know—just dangle a dollar sign in front of him. Mrs. Astor lived to be one hundred and five, you will recall, and made frequent amendments to her will in the last five years of her life."

"That's what tied her estate up in court for so long, isn't it?" I asked. "Deciding whether her son had taken advantage of her deterioration to divert millions of dollars intended for the New York Public Library to his own pockets."

"Despite her fortune, Ms. Cooper, she was living in squalor. Her apartment was looted and most of her servants were let go," Talbot Hunt said. "Don't lecture me about my father's condition. There are enough millions to go around. Even for the damn cats."

"Tell us about the Bay Psalm Book," Mercer said, moving closer to Talbot Hunt. "We know its significance to your great-grandfather. But how did it come to be in your possession?"

He didn't like answering our questions, but it was clear that he wanted to stake his claim to the valuable little book.

"Understand, Detective, that the moment my sister comes into the room, this conversation will cease," Hunt said, fuming as he glanced at the hallway. "This is between my father and myself. It has nothing to do with Minerva."

"All right."

Talbot Hunt talked to Mercer. "My father's instincts were good enough, just several years ago, for him to see the writing on the wall. Our fellow trustees had the gall to start deaccessioning several important objects—paintings, manuscripts, archives of writers who had fallen into obscurity—that kind of thing."

"The **Kindred Spirits** sale."

"Exactly." Once again, Hunt raised his eyebrows, seemingly surprised that the NYPD was up to speed on art and literature.

"My grandfather kept that prayer book, which celebrated his birth, next to his bed—at home or abroad—for all of his life. He wanted the library to have it, to treasure it as he had. He never expected it would be warehoused or he wouldn't have willed it to them. When Jonah and his allies wanted to put the book up for sale, my father wouldn't stand for it."

"Was that the person your father was referring to?" I asked. "Does he call Jonah 'the Jew'?"

Talbot Hunt studied me as if to divine my genetic fingerprint.

"Yes, I'm Jewish. I can deal with it, Mr. Hunt. Jonah Krauss came here to discuss the lost map with your father?"

"Apparently so, Ms. Cooper. I wasn't aware of that. I know he despised Jonah from the time he set foot in the boardroom. No class, new money—that sort of thing. You know what I mean."

Jewish. That was mostly what Talbot Hunt meant. "So your father made a deal?"

"Yes."

"With whom?"

"Leland Porter, the president of the library."

"How convenient that Porter is somewhere in Outer Mongolia this weekend," Mike said.

"Well, I assume that's the way Father got the psalm book back. Leland is the only person in a position to negotiate something at that level."

"Are you telling me you don't **know**?"

"The key word is supposed to be 'transparency,' Mr. Chapman. But behind the scenes, where many of these transactions occur, it's thick as mud."

"Thick as thieves, we say in my business."

"My father wanted me to have the Bay Psalm Book. In exchange, he told me he was giving the library something they wanted even more."

"What's that?" Mike asked, looking to me to vet the credibility of Talbot Hunt's answer.

"A book of illustrations—twenty rather macabre watercolors—that were done by William Blake in 1805. **Designs for Blair's Grave,** it's called. The poet kept a set of the paintings for himself. Had them bound into book form. Simple, but quite striking—a meditation on mortality and redemption."

"That must be the only complete set," I said. There had been a major controversy just a few years earlier, when Sotheby's had broken up a recently discovered group of nineteen plates from the same work—unbound—for sale at auction.

"That's correct, Ms. Cooper. If you know that, then you're aware that it's worth many more millions than our prayer book."

"And the library owns that volume of watercolors now?"

"The library's Berg Collection is strong on Blake. They've coveted this for a very long time. Pleaded with my father to pass it on to them. The book is in their hands, not to be displayed until after Father's death—at his own direction—to avoid controversy about the transaction."

Footsteps in the hallway announced Minerva's return.

Her gait was firm and fast. She walked past me and directly to her brother, stopping only to slap him across the face before she turned away.

"If you paid any attention to your father you'd know there was an intercom in every room, so the nurses can hear him if he calls for anything," she said. "What else have you swindled me out of, you selfish bastard? What else, besides that precious little book?"

TWENTY-EIGHT

Mike stood up and stepped between the spoiled siblings.

"No secrets anymore, Mr. Hunt. Looks like your sister trumped you on this one. When did the psalm book disappear from your home?"

"Check with his wife, Detective. She probably took it to the consignment shop for resale, along with those dreadful things she calls clothes. She'd have dug those jewels out with her teeth, were it possible."

"About three weeks ago, Mr. Chapman," Talbot Hunt said. "And leave Josie out of it, Minerva."

"She is out of it, Tally. Always has been. Father despises her. Imagine, Detective, leaving her church-mouse-of-a-husband minister for Talbot Hunt. True love, I'm sure."

"Why didn't you report the theft to the police?"

"Not very complicated, is it? I knew it had to be an inside job—someone who understood the personal value of its worth to me. Nothing else was disturbed in the entire apartment. I figured it was about blackmail, and that at the right moment, I'd be contacted. One can't very well call the police about a theft of an object for which one doesn't even have proper title. The Bay Psalm Book still belongs to the New York Public Library, in theory."

"Where were you when the theft occurred?" Mercer asked.

"I was—I mean, we were," Talbot said, correcting himself immediately to protect his wife from Minerva's sharp tongue, "we were in Millbrook."

"The family estate, Mr. Wallace. My great-grandfather bought land in Dutchess County before he died. My grandfather loved it there, too. A big horse farm," Minerva said. "Just not big enough for all of us at any one time."

"Who else besides you and your wife lives in the apartment?"

"The children are away at college. It's just the two of us. And a housekeeper, but she traveled with us to the country."

"Do you mind if we get some guys in to go over the place with you?"

Talbot Hunt **pfumphed** for a few seconds. "I told you, it's been weeks. There's no harm in it, certainly, but what do you expect to find?"

"You never know. We might catch a break," Mike said. "Where exactly did you keep the psalm book?"

Hunt stared at his sister but didn't speak.

"Do you have a library in your home?"

"Yes. Yes, I do. But that isn't where I had it."

"Like I give a damn, Tally. Tell the man, will you? I'm not after your books."

"Then how come your maid was clutching it when she died?" he shouted at her. "Who were you expecting to meet there? Your low-life buddy Eddy Forbes?"

"Imagine one family with this much dirty laundry, Mr. Chapman. It's lifesaving that my brother married a washerwoman," Minerva said. "You see, Tally couldn't keep the book in his safe—the one in the bedroom closet—because that's where the cow keeps her jewelry. Don't be shocked, Ms. Cooper. Father always called Josie the cow. Suits her dead on."

"How do you know about the safe in your brother's bedroom closet?" Mike asked.

"Because Tally's first wife—his **late** first wife—was a very dear friend of mine. I went there often when she was alive to borrow some of the pieces my mother had left to her. And yes, she died of natural causes—don't think I wasn't on his case about that."

"There's a bureau in my dressing room, Detective. I kept the book in a false drawer. Actually locked in that drawer, at the base of the bureau."

"Locked . . . with a key?"

"Yes."

"Do you still have the key?" I asked, thinking of the one I found on the floor in the stacks.

"I do. It's at home. You can have it if you like."

"Was the lock broken?"

"Not at all. Picked, I'd say."

"Who knew about the drawer?"

"Well, obviously, my wife."

Minerva crossed her arms and let out a long, low "moo."

"I'm not sure anyone else would know."

"The housekeeper?"

"Certainly, she cleans in there, but I can't imagine she'd be involved. She's been with me for twenty years, Mr. Chapman."

"Anyone else?" Mike asked. "Workmen, guys doing construction or repairs, people in the building?"

"It's a Park Avenue building. Quite secure. And no one was doing any work for us inside the apartment."

"Who was helping you in the library?" Minerva asked, rearranging the French tulips in a vase near the sofa. "You've always had someone to watch out for the books. Who now, Tally?"

"The same curator I've had for years. He'll be happy to talk with you. He's only there one day a week."

Minerva Hunt snapped the stem off one of the flowers and focused her attention on her brother. "That's not what I mean, Tally. Who's your book doctor these days, hmmm? Who's been doing your preservation assessments? Mending your tears? Checking your clamshell boxes?"

Talbot Hunt was trying to ignore Minerva, but she was like a steam engine picking up speed.

"Now I see it," she said. "Tell the nice detectives what they ought to know."

"It has nothing to do with this."

"Tina Barr was working for my father, Mr. Chapman. She was treated well here, as you might guess. Then all of a sudden she quit. Quite abruptly."

"And started working for Alger Herrick," Talbot said.

"Only part-time," I said. That's what Herrick had told us.

"You hired her away from Father, didn't you? You knew Tina had all the information about his collection that you weren't able to get from him yourself. How far in did you let her, Tally?"

His face was red and he looked like he was ready to spit at his sister.

"She wanted the extra work. She didn't enjoy it here. This is more like a mausoleum than a library. I was doing her a favor, Minerva. Can you understand that?"

"How far did you go, Tally? That's all I asked."

"It's not what you think," he said, gritting his teeth.

"You were sleeping with her, weren't you?"

"Stop it!" he shouted at Minerva. "Don't be such a fool."

"A fool to figure it out, or to say it in front of the detectives?"

I'd only seen Tina Barr in the immediate aftermath of her first victimization. It was hard to think of the distraught young woman as anyone's paramour.

Talbot Hunt started toward the foyer.

"Didn't figure she was your type, Mr. Hunt," Mike said, following him. "So what kind of favor did you do for her? How long did your affair go on?"

Hunt stopped long enough to say, "Hardly an affair, Detective. Tina came on to me, that's all it was. She was lonely—and, well . . . things happened."

"I get lonely myself, Mr. Hunt. Doesn't mean I crawl into bed with the first weasel that comes along," Mike said. "What kind of things? Did you and she have a sexual relationship?"

He looked past Mike at Minerva, his teeth clenched.

"I won't tell Josie," Minerva said. "You must understand, Mr. Chapman, he's terrified of his wife. He's already given her far too much stake in Hunt properties, and she dangles that over his head like a sword."

"Did you sleep with Tina Barr in the bedroom of your apartment?" Mercer asked. "Where you kept the book?"

Hunt took too long to think. The answer must have been yes.

"But where was your wife?" Mike asked.

"One of the cats must have his tongue, Detective. Josie spends most of her weekends in Millbrook. Tally's to the manor born, of course. And she's to the barn born—but to the manor well-adjusted. Loves living the grand country life there."

Mercer stepped closer to Talbot Hunt, pressing Mike's arm to encourage him to move away. "We need to have this information, sir. Did Tina Barr know about the psalm book?"

"Of course she did. She's a—she was a very

accomplished conservator. It interested her as much as anyone else in our world."

"Were you intimate with her?"

They were face-to-face, ten steps away from Minerva and me, in the darkened foyer.

"Yes, Mr. Wallace, I was."

"We're going to need to know when that relationship started and when it ended."

"I told you that it wasn't a relationship. I'll try to give you any specifics I remember."

"Did she spend time in the bedroom of your apartment?"

"Yes, Mr. Wallace. Are you through humiliating me? Yes, she did."

"Did she have a key to your apartment?"

"Of course. She was doing work there for me. I trusted her with my entire collection. Why wouldn't I give her a key?"

Mercer's voice seemed to get lower with every question he asked. "Did she know where the drawer was, the one in which you locked the book when you left town?"

Talbot Hunt paused for several seconds. "I—I guess she might have. It's possible she saw me fetch it from the bureau after a weekend away."

Minerva turned away, reached for a small silver bell on one of the tables, and rang it. "I think I need a drink."

"My sister, the virgin queen. Hard to take criticism on this subject from you."

Mercer tried to keep Talbot focused on Tina Barr. "After you realized the book was missing, did you talk about it with Tina?"

No wonder he hadn't called the police. He'd first have to explain the probable suspect to his wife.

"I'm really not sure. I must have mentioned it to her."

Minerva was more incredulous than I was. She didn't let the appearance of the butler interfere with her response. He stood silently and waited for her order. "How could you not have known, Tally? I don't even spend time at the library, but I know that she'd lost their trust, too."

At my first meeting in Battaglia's office with Jill Gibson, Pat McKinney had called Tina Barr a forger—and a thief.

"A vodka gimlet," Minerva said.

"Now, madam? At this hour?"

"Now, Bailey. Right now," Minerva said. "If you didn't know it, Tally, then you're the last one in town. The girl shared a bed with the master thief, too, before he got caught. Tina Barr used to run with Eddy Forbes."

TWENTY-NINE

"If you don't feed me," Mike said, "I'm going to put some mustard on my shoe and eat it. Then I might start on your toes."

It was midafternoon, and the list of things we had to do and people we had to find and interview continued to grow.

"That's about as dysfunctional a family unit as I can imagine," Mercer said, shaking his head. "All the money in the world and the two cats are probably the only living things Hunt can trust."

"Coop's starving me. I can't even think, man."

"Let's not waste time on a meal. Pull up in front of P. J. Bernstein's," I said, referring to my favorite Upper East Side deli. "I'll hop out and get sandwiches while you call the feds and get an address on Eddy Forbes."

"Make it two turkey clubs for me, a bag of chips, a cream soda, and you got a deal. Mercer?"

"Ham and provolone on rye toast."

We were less than five minutes away from the Third Avenue classic deli. Mike double-parked while I ran in and placed my order with the counterman.

"What do you know?" I asked as I climbed into the back seat.

"The lieutenant just called. They had to let Billy Schultz go. His alibi for last night held up just fine. Three other guys working late with him. That's the bad news."

"What's the good?"

"His office is less than ten blocks away from the library. Think they need to work those alibi witnesses a little harder."

"I still don't like his DNA in the mask from the first break-in at Barr's apartment," I said. "His explanation strikes me as weird."

"I told you the lab said it's a mixture, Coop. Enough saliva there to get another profile—it just doesn't match anyone in the databank." Mike had spread a napkin across his lap, holding half a sandwich in his right hand as he navigated uptown again with his left.

"Tell her what Peterson said about the phone call," Mercer said.

"Traces back to a booth on the corner of Sixth Avenue and the Deuce."

"So this creep lurked around the library and watched until Tina's body was found— and about to be bagged—and then dialed up her cell?"

"We're dealing with a freaky-deaky guy, in case you hadn't figured that," Mike said, looking at me in the rearview mirror. "C'mon, girl, you still gotta eat."

"The whole damn crew is freaky," Mercer said. "You got a sister-brother act that's as ugly as anything in Greek mythology, a too-nosy neighbor whose DNA winds up in an important piece of crime scene evidence, a one-armed guy who lives in the chapel of an old cancer hospital, a library executive who lied to Alex the first time they met, the most successful map thief in recent times now on parole, and a young turk with books bound in human skin who was so anxious to be wheels-up that—"

"I'll be wheels-up his ass if he neglected to tell us about his visit to Jasper Hunt," Mike said. "And this dead girl—may she rest in peace—gets more complicated by the hour. What was she doing in bed with Talbot Hunt? And Eddy Forbes?"

"What did you learn about Forbes?"

"Sentenced to only three years, over the objection of just about every library director in the galaxy. Got out seven months ago, with some time off for good behavior. Reports to his parole officer in Maine every week."

"Didn't he ever live in the city?"

"Yeah, in Chelsea, but he lost his lease when

he went to jail. The feds seized all his books, maps, papers. They're still in the process of trying to match up the stolen things with libraries that haven't even missed them yet."

"Any family here?" I asked.

"A younger brother on the West Side. Chow down and I'll have you there in no time."

I nibbled at the corner of my sandwich. "Who's his brother?"

"Name is Travis Forbes. That's all I know at the moment. Don't get pushy."

"Well, where?"

"First floor in a brownstone on West One Hundred and Fourth Street, off the park."

We had visited Alger Herrick in his opulent apartment only one block away. "That's close to where Herrick lives."

"A universe apart, actually. This area's still a run-down bunch of tenements." Mike had devoured the first sandwich before we entered the transverse drive. He washed it down with a swig of soda and a handful of chips before starting on the second one.

When we reached 104th Street, Mike turned in to the block. School had let out for the day, and kids, most of them black and Hispanic, had clustered on the sidewalk. The department Crown Vic—an obvious intrusion in the 'hood—caught the attention of most of them, who watched with interest as we got out of the unmarked car.

I climbed the steps and opened the vestibule door. The name T. Forbes was next to a buzzer, and I pressed it. Several seconds later, I heard a voice through the intercom.

Mike nudged me out of the way. "Travis Forbes?"

A man answered. "Yes."

"Mike Chapman. NYPD. I'd like to talk with you."

There was no response.

"You there, Forbes?"

A dark-skinned kid who appeared to be about twelve years old had followed Mercer up the steps.

"He don't let nobody in, dude. He real shy or something."

"You know him?" Mercer asked.

"I seed him around. Yo, you know his brother real famous. Got locked up. Got took away in handcuffs. His picture was in the paper and they even looks alike," the kid said, totally animated. "You the man?"

Mike pressed the intercom again. "I am. But I guess Mr. Forbes doesn't think so."

"You give me ten dollars if I get you inside?"

"Not by breaking in," Mercer said. "You live here?"

"Down the street." The kid smiled and tsked at the suggestion he might do something illegal. "Naw. Hit four-C. Ms. Jenkins."

I pressed the buzzer.

It must have taken almost a minute for her to get to the intercom. "Hello?"

"Give me the ten," the kid said to Mercer, who took a bill out of his pocket.

"Yo, Ms. Jenkins? It's Shalik. You need anything from the store?"

"Milk. I need milk and a loaf of bread, dear."

"Let me in so's I can get the money."

The buzzer sounded and Shalik opened the door for us. He pointed to a door behind the stairwell. "That his," he said, starting the climb to the fourth floor.

Mike went ahead of me and pounded on Travis Forbes's door. The three of us waited in the hallway, and Shalik stopped in place.

"Police," Mike said, banging again.

"Do you have a warrant?" the voice inside responded.

"You watch too much television, Travis. Open up. I just need some information about Eddy."

"He's not here."

"That's a good start. Now open the door."

"You can't come in. I've just got a robe on. I'm dressing to go out."

"As long as you're not gonna expose yourself to me, crack the door."

I heard the lock disengage and the door opened several inches, coming to a sharp stop as it strained against the small chain that secured it. I could see a shock of brown hair, but the man's face was shadowed.

"We want to talk to you, and I'm not gonna do it in the hallway," Mike said.

"How many of you are there?"

"Three of us."

Travis Forbes paused. "There isn't room for you. It's a very small apartment."

"I'll send in my thinnest partner. She'd fit in a closet," Mike said. "Put some clothes on. I'm not moving till you do."

"Give me a few minutes then," Forbes said. He closed the door and walked away from it.

Mercer backed up and turned around. "Let me check out the building. Wouldn't want to spook him out the window. There a fire escape?" he asked Shalik.

"Yeah. Go through the back alley. You could climb up it, see all the crazy shit he got piled in there."

Mercer left as the kid came down the steps and approached Forbes's door, squeezing his wiry frame between Mike and me.

"Whoa, Shalik. Where're you going?" Mike asked.

The kid turned the knob and gently pushed on the door till it caught against the chain. He slipped his skinny arm through the space—just several inches wide—twisting his body as he slid the metal catch out of place.

"Future perps of America," Mike said. "You can't do that, Shalik."

"I be done," he said, standing back from the door, which swung open. "You look, Mr. Detective."

From the floor to the ceiling of the entryway, with only enough room for a single individual to pass through, were stacks upon stacks of books, magazines, and yellowed newspapers, piled on top of one another and towering over my head. They were so densely packed together that although they gave the illusion of being about to tumble over, there wasn't anywhere for them to fall.

"Get on your way, Shalik. Scram," Mike said. He had one foot in the hallway and one over the threshold. "You call the lieutenant, Coop. Tell him to stand by. Tell him we've got a Collyer situation."

THIRTY

I knew Mike well enough to do as he directed before I asked why. He was on his cell to Mercer, asking if he'd seen any sign of Travis Forbes from the alley behind the building.

"Well, he hasn't come back out yet. Call if you spot him."

"What's a Collyer?" I asked as we waited in the quiet hallway, the door still ajar.

"Cops, firemen—all 911 responders—that's the designated expression for a house so full of junk it's treacherous to get inside, or back out," Mike said, reaching up to pull newspapers off the top of the nearest pile. "Look at this. Dated three years ago. You never heard of the Collyer brothers?"

"No."

"Two very rich guys who lived in Harlem in the 1930s. Well educated, from a prominent family, but really eccentric. They saved every piece of junk they could find on the street. Hoarders, they were. Hermit hoarders," he said, reaching up to the second pile. "Here you go, catalogs from rare book auctions in London."

Still no sign of Travis. Mike handed two of the catalogs to me. "2002," I said. "A little late to put a bid in."

"Homer Collyer, the older brother, went blind. So the younger one began to save newspapers," Mike said, sweeping his arm across the piles of Forbes's out-of-date dailies.

"Why?"

"In case Homer ever regained his sight, Coop. Then he'd have all the news that he'd missed to read. They even booby-trapped the whole place against thieves. So the younger one got stuck in one of his own traps and buried in the rubble, while Homer starved to death. Rats took care of the rest of him."

"I get the point."

"You get a call to a Collyer, you don't know what to expect to find under the debris. Junk? Stolen books? Maybe a body or two?"

Mike's phone rang. He listened and then repeated to me what Mercer told him. "Travis just peeped out the back. Made eye contact with Mercer. Maybe now he'll move our way."

"Hey!" Forbes called out from the far end of the hallway. "You can't come in here. You can't just break the lock."

"I swear I didn't," Mike said. "I guess it

just—just fell. What have you got here, Travis? You know how dangerous it is to keep paper jammed in here like this? A regular fire hazard."

Travis Forbes was either embarrassed by Mike's discovery or simply didn't like to make eye contact. I guessed him to be in his late twenties, about my height, with a sad expression lingering within the intense gaze of his dark, bespectacled eyes.

"I understand," he said.

"What's with yesterday's news?" Mike asked.

"I started saving things for Eddy. Things I didn't think he could get in prison. It's—it's just a habit."

"Somewhere along the way, I guess Eddy told you the federal can is like summer camp, no? The **Times**, the **Journal**—that's all those swindlers and crooks read."

"I told you, it's a habit. It's what I do."

"You into rare books, too?" Mike asked, taking the catalog from my hand.

"No. No, I'm not. I—I was keeping that for Eddy."

"This auction took place years before your brother's arrest, years before he went to prison," I said.

"Then he must have given it to me to hold for him," Travis said, shrugging. "I've got lots of Eddy's stuff."

"The feds ever been here?" Mike asked.

"These things were released to me after Eddy got in trouble. He had to give up his apartment and had nowhere to store them. The FBI went through everything he owns. They know all about it."

It was as obvious to Travis Forbes as it was to me that Mike wanted to get inside and ferret through every piece of paper, looking for stolen books and maps, or anything else of value. It was also obvious he didn't have a leg to stand on, other than the one that was planted inside the door.

"Who lives here with you?" Mike asked.

There was a wooden board on a slice of the wall beside the door, with several jackets hanging on pegs.

"Nobody."

"You collect clothes, too?" There were windbreakers in different colors and weights on top of one another, and a workman's denim jacket with the label of a Maine utility company on the sleeve, covering the upper part of a white lab coat.

Forbes didn't answer.

"When was the last time Eddy was in town?"

"He hasn't been here since before he was sent away. I haven't seen him."

"Pets. You got pets?"

"Tropical fish. I have an aquarium."

I imagined Forbes sitting alone in his fortress of useless papers and old books, staring at brightly colored fish in a tank. He seemed far too aloof and cold to be a companion to any warm-blooded animal.

"What do you do, Travis?"

"I wait tables."

"Where?"

"Near the Columbia campus, on Broadway. Place called the Lion's Pub."

"How long have you been doing that?" I asked.

"Since I ran out of money to finish graduate school, a year and a half ago. I'm a neurobiologist. At least, I will be when I complete the program."

"What are your hours there?"

"Eight p.m. till we close. Four in the morning."

"And last night?" I asked.

"Same," Travis said, while I tried to penetrate his blank stare. "What does this have to do with my brother?"

My exhaustion had me seeing suspects at every turn. If Travis Forbes had the same access to the library that his brother once enjoyed, he could have found his way to Tina on Wednesday evening, in the conservators' office, and back again to move the body last night. But if his alibi held tight, he wouldn't have been standing on a nearby street corner—with us in his sights—at the time the body was found and the ghoulish, laughing caller rang on Tina's cell.

"Do you know a girl named Tina Barr?" Mike asked, refocusing the conversation.

"Who?"

"A friend of your brother's."

"Eddy's a lot older than I am. We never really socialized together."

"This is someone he worked with," Mike said. "A conservator. Restores rare books and old maps."

"I know what a conservator does, Detective," Travis said, growing more churlish by the question. "Ask Eddy. You must have his number."

"Why don't you give it to me, just in case?" The ex-con was likely to have two phones—one that his probation officer used and one for his friends and family.

"I'll have to ask him if he wants me to do that."

"I'll wait."

"Not in here, you won't," Travis said, taking his hands out of his pockets to try to close his front door, dislodging Mike's foot.

Mike tried to keep his balance by grabbing at the jamb with his left hand while his right one settled on Travis Forbes's wrist. "Sorry. I get it. We're out."

Travis shook loose of Mike's accidental grasp. At the same moment, we both saw the cuts on the back of Travis Forbes's left hand. Long narrow strips of red-lined flesh protruded from both ends of a bandage strip.

"What's with the scratches, pal?" Mike asked. "Your fish got fangs?"

The soft-spoken young man covered his bad hand with the good one. "Leave me alone."

"You ought to have that looked at," Mike said. "Could get yourself a nasty infection. I got a doc who'll check it out for you."

Mike wanted to see the injury, just as I did. He wanted to compare the size and shape of the wound to the marks on Tina Barr's neck. Maybe she had tried to defend herself with one of the sharp tools from her own desk.

"I've already been treated," he said, putting both hands back in his pants pocket.

"By whom?"

Footsteps charging down the staircase over-head signaled the reappearance of Shalik, on his way from Ms. Jenkins's apartment to run her errands.

"How'd you get those cuts?" Mike asked. "You drop a steak knife on the job? I'm trying to help you out here."

Now only Mike's fingers on the door jamb prevented it from closing. "Who cut you?"

Shalik stopped to listen to the conversation, squatting on one of the steps, his nose between railings of the banister. But Travis Forbes didn't speak.

Shalik let out a low hissing sound, and Forbes's head snapped up to look at him.

"Quiet, kid," Mike said. "I'm asking you once more, Travis, before I tell Ms. Cooper here to get me a subpoena to photograph your hand. Who cut you?"

"Hisself."

Shalik repeated the word he had said the first time, when I had misheard him.

"Look in his pocket, man. He do it at night sometimes in the summer, sitting on the stoop. He crazy, Detective."

"A subpoena for what?" Travis Forbes said, withdrawing his right hand from his pocket again. He spread it open and in it was a razor blade. "Talk to my shrink. I didn't think my problem was illegal."

Travis Forbes unbuttoned the cuff of his shirt and started to roll up his sleeve. Scars lined his inner arm, and marks that looked like they'd been left by lighted cigarette butts dotted the skin on the outer side.

Mike's hand dropped to his side.

"Take care of yourself, Travis," he said, backing away. "Here's my card if I can do anything to help."

THIRTY-ONE

"I gotta tell you, Mercer, I took one look at the guy's messed-up paw and I was ready to throw the cuffs on and collar him," Mike said, turning off Central Park West for the ride through the park to my apartment. "We gotta slow this down before I make a mistake."

"I never saw Mike turn on a dime so fast," I said from the back seat, patting him on the shoulder. "He went from executioner to social worker in a heartbeat."

"Yeah, well, what makes you such an expert on self-mutilation, kid? I don't think I've ever had one of these."

"Alex and I have seen more than our share of it because the highest incidence is among teenage girls."

"Does it mean that Travis Forbes is suicidal?" Mike asked.

"Not necessarily," Mercer said. "It's a form of intentional self-harm without actually having the wish to die."

"So why do they do it? I mean, not the psychobabble, but what do you know about it?"

"The docs tell me that self-mutilation is some sort of outlet for strong negative emotions," I said. "Usually anger or shame. Anger at someone else that's then directed against the self."

"So maybe he's embarrassed about Eddy," Mike said. "Mad at him for ruining the family name, being such a jerk to get caught. Is it always done by cutting?"

"Knives and razors," Mercer said. "They're the most popular. Biting or bruising yourself, pulling out hair, putting out cigarettes on your skin."

"That fourteen-year-old we had last year," I said to Mercer. "Remember? The one whose mother blamed her when the baby brother died?"

"Yeah. The shrink said she was dissociating. That her mind just split off that memory, which was too painful to keep in her conscious awareness. Whenever she hurt herself, she felt alive again."

"Well, I should have given Shalik a bigger reward. He saved me from making a fool of myself with Forbes."

"And it doesn't seem that Travis has his brother's book interests. I mean, you wouldn't keep rare books in a junk heap like that," Mercer said.

"We've still got to get to Eddy. His name just comes up in this too many times to ignore," Mike said. "I'm dropping you at home, Coop?"

"Please."

"I'll hang with you for the autopsy," Mercer said to Mike.

It was almost four when I got out of the car and walked into my lobby. I stopped for the mail and went upstairs, as anxious to know whether Luc was waiting for me there as I was to step into the shower and clear my head of the day's confusion.

I unlocked the door and went inside. "Luc?"

He didn't answer, and I was almost relieved to have a brief respite to myself.

There was a bouquet of white lilies on the table in the foyer, and a piece of notepaper next to the vase.

Darling—Must be you had a very busy day. I missed hearing your voice, even to tell me you had no time to talk. Joan reserved for the four of us at 7:30 at Patroon. Très Americain, **which suits me fine. Dreaming of a great steak, a serious Burgundy, and a night with you. Am off to some appointments and will see you there.** À toute a l'heure, ma princesse.

I didn't want to leave the comfortable cocoon of my home. I wanted to give Luc all my attention before he left for the West Coast in the morning.

His professional world—completely luxe and extravagant—was so diametrically opposed to the trauma that surrounded my colleagues and me that sometimes it was hard for me to imagine how we communicated at times like this. An overdone salmon, not enough mustard in the vinaigrette, or a table that couldn't turn over on time seemed to me, an outsider, to be the kind of urgencies restaurateurs confronted. I knew there was more to Luc's business than that, but on days like this one, it all seemed so frivolous.

I went into the bedroom and stripped off my clothes. I tried to sneak into the bathroom to turn on the water for a steaming hot shower without glancing at myself in the mirror, but there was no escaping how tired I looked, and how overwrought I felt.

I dried off and wrapped the towel around me as I slipped under the comforter to take a short nap, setting the alarm to make sure I didn't oversleep.

At six-thirty, I awakened and put myself together for the evening. My wardrobe palette was heavy on pale blues and greens, even for fall and winter, but I didn't feel like color tonight. I dressed in black—a clingy sweater and a short pleated skirt.

The makeup helped, and a crystal barrette to hold back my hair added some sparkle around my face.

I was ready to go downstairs to find a taxi when my phone rang. Caller ID displayed the telephone exchange of the morgue.

"Hey, Coop. Just thought you'd like a heads-up, give Battaglia a shout about the autopsy results," Mike said. "Dr. Assif called it. Fatal incised wound associated with an air embolism in the jugular vein. The cut is longer than it is deep. Killer just hit the right place. Tina would have collapsed immediately. No struggle. No defensive wounds."

"And the weapon?"

"It's not any of the ones we submitted for comparison, but Assif likes the angles on those conservators' paring knives. She'll be testing a slew of them."

"So sad," I said. "And still no news of Tina's mother?"

"Commissioner Scully has the State Department on it now. I'll let you know what we hear," Mike said. He hesitated before speaking again, and for some reason I couldn't explain, I stayed on the line. "Coop? Everything okay?"

"Just thinking about the week, the two women. Tina Barr and Karla Vastasi."

"You sound down."

"I just took a nap. I'll shake it off."

"Want company? Me and Mercer—"

"No—"

"Sorry. Forgot I was dealing with the grammar police. Mercer and I can come over for a while."

"Thanks, Mike. You need to chill as much as I do."

"Call you tomorrow, then. Double or nothing on **Jeopardy!**"

I left a message on Battaglia's home machine. In another effort to put the day behind me, I dabbed perfume behind my ears and down the length of my throat.

I wrapped a long cashmere stole around my shoulders, applied a new layer of lipstick, and headed for the lobby.

Oscar held the door open for me and I waved good-bye, grateful for the crisp autumn weather.

I walked to the end of the driveway on Seventy-first Street, knowing the odds were better that I'd find a yellow cab from there. The Marymount College auditorium was just down the block, and weekend nights there was a steady flow of drop-offs for theatrical events at the school.

I stepped off the sidewalk and raised my arm in the air. Three or four cabs were lined up on the far side of the one-way street, queuing to discharge their fares. Another that was already empty flashed his headlights and lurched in my direction.

When I got into the cab, I leaned toward the opening in the Plexiglas partition and spoke to the driver. "Good evening. I'd like to go to Forty-sixth Street, between Lex and Third."

"You got it." He started the meter running and I sat back, my head against the window.

After the second light, he made the turn onto Lexington Avenue on our way downtown. The reggae music coming from the speaker behind my head was too loud, but there was no point getting into a squabble during the short ride.

"You got a team, miss?"

"Excuse me?"

"I aksed you if you got a team. Baseball."

The driver was looking at me in the mirror. I could see only the outlines of his black face highlighted by white teeth.

I returned the smile. "Yankees. I'm a Yankee fan."

"Dodgers. I like the Dodgers."

"You're lucky—you got Joe Torre."

"That's not why they my team. It's Los Angeles. I got family in Los Angeles."

"Nice," I said, looking at the designer windows at Bloomingdale's as we drove by.

"You got family, miss?"

There was no winning. Tell the guy I wasn't interested in his chatter and I'd be lucky if all he did was call me rude.

"You hear me?"

"I do."

"Where? Where they be?"

I smiled wanly this time. "All spread out."

"Sisters and brothers?"

"Two brothers."

"Here in New York?"

"No."

We were speeding past the nondescript buildings on Lexington till we were stopped by a red light at the rear entrance to the Waldorf, mercifully close to my stop.

"I aksed you where they be?"

His voice had an edge to it now. I put my hand on the door handle, grabbing a ten-dollar bill from my purse. Then I did what I told every nervous tourist to do in a yellow cab, and looked below the partition for the driver's permit and photo. The plastic sleeve that was supposed to hold his identification was empty.

"Texas," I lied. "Texas and Minnesota. You want to release the lock, please?" I was pulling at it, but the driver clearly had the controls.

The light changed and he floored the gas pedal, throwing me back against the seat.

"Good to know, miss. Case I want to do my own family search," he said, laughing at my growing panic. "And you ought to leave Wesley right where he's at in Los Angeles. Be real good for your health to do that."

How many days and nights had this cabbie been waiting for me to come out of my building alone?

"It's Griggs, Miss Prosecutor. Anton Griggs."

"Open the door," I screamed at him, trying to grab my phone.

He braked to a halt on the corner of Forty-seventh Street and I heard the click of the lock. I practically fell onto the pavement as I pushed at the door and jumped out of the cab, scraping my arm against the rough edge of the door. The shawl caught on the exposed metal as I slammed it shut.

"You let Wesley be, girl," he called out to me. " 'Cause I got more brothers than you got brains."

My chest was heaving as Anton Griggs sped away, the cashmere stole hanging from the side of the cab like a limp body being dragged through the city streets.

THIRTY-TWO

"You sound like you can't breathe," Mercer said. "Slow down, Alex."

I had practically run the block and a half to the restaurant before calling Mercer.

"I'll be all right. Are you with Mike?"

"He's on the phone in Dr. Assif's office. Why?"

"I want you to know what happened," I said, describing the nightmare cab ride and how I had played right into the patient hands of Anton Griggs. "Obviously, you have to tell the lieutenant, and I'll call Battaglia, but hold off on Mike for tonight. He's likely to go ballistic and head off after Anton and Tyrone Griggs. We don't need any more trouble."

"And the judge?"

"I'll tell him in chambers on Monday. It's smarter to have one of the guys from the DA's squad handle this. I need Mike as a witness in the underlying murder case."

"I'll run Anton Griggs. You get a plate number?"

"Not even a partial. I wasn't thinking. I just wanted out."

"Understood. You want me to stay at your place tonight?"

"No, thanks. I've got—well, um, Luc is in town. We're having dinner with Joan and Jim. I'll be fine."

"Sounds like Anton had his moment if he was going to do anything more than scare the pants off you."

"A total success at that."

"You're on the street? I heard a car honking."

"Just going into the restaurant, I promise."

"I'll check in with you in the morning. You got your Saturday ballet class?"

"I've just done my best leap. I'll play hooky tomorrow."

"You know Battaglia will put someone on you the minute you call him," Mercer said. "I'd just as soon have it be me."

"So would I. But I want to wait till Luc goes to the airport in the morning. I'd like a semblance of a normal social life for the evening."

"You're entitled to that. We'll talk."

Ken Aretsky welcomed me to Patroon with his usual warmth and charm. We embraced and exchanged kisses. "Good to see you, Alex. I hope you're not coming down with something."

"No, Ken. Why?"

"Well, you're all flushed and perspiring a bit."

That was a polite way of telling me I was sweating and shaking. "The traffic was wild. I had to sprint the last couple of blocks."

"Better for me. That's bound to make you even hungrier," he said, leading me into the dining room, where New York's power brokers gathered to make deals over the superb food for which Aretsky was known. "Joan's at the table. Jim took Luc upstairs to show him the private dining rooms and the rooftop bar. Happy to know I'm getting you into my business."

"That's entirely Luc's doing, I'm afraid."

Ken led me to the banquette in the front corner of the room and left me to bask in Joan Stafford's effusive greeting.

I slipped onto the seat beside Joan, and after we hugged she asked to be brought up to the minute on everything I'd been doing.

"Sweetheart, did you even have time to see the news tonight? Your case is all over it. What did that poor girl do to deserve to die like that?"

"Isn't it tragic?"

"I know you can't tell me anything, but it's so dreadful. We like to think of libraries as up-lifting sanctuaries, but there have been murders and thefts associated with the best of them.

Someone walked out of Cambridge University with a million dollars' worth of rare books a couple of years ago when my play was in rehearsal in London."

"I didn't know about that one. It's mind-boggling, isn't it?"

"Mark Antony plundered the entire library of Pergamon so he could give it to Cleopatra as a wedding present. Nothing new under the sun."

A novelist and playwright, Joan knew more about literature than anyone I had ever encountered. Brilliant, funny, and incredibly chic, she was happily married to an expert in foreign affairs who wrote a nationally syndicated column. Joan and my college roommate, Nina Baum, were the most loyal of friends, and I leaned on their shoulders during my more serious investigations.

"So I'm learning. And the characters who people this world—"

"Tell me about it. I go to those library benefits, and let me remind you that it isn't all classy trustees like Louise Grunwald and Gordon Davis. The NBC reporter said the Hunts might be involved in this brouhaha," Joan said as Stefan, the maître d', came over to fill my flute with champagne. "You don't want to find

yourself between Minerva Hunt and a rat-
tlesnake. She'll take your eyes out in a flash."

"How about Jonah Krauss?" I asked. Joan
had one of the grandest homes in East Hampton, where she'd been summering all of her life.
There were few people of substance there that
she didn't know.

"You're talking very north of the highway
now, Alex," she said, referring to the less fancy
neighborhoods on the far side of Route 25,
which split the Hamptons in half, where many
of the newly rich had built their McMansions.

"We met with him this afternoon. He's actually got a book bound in human skin."

"Check his wife's plastic surgeon. She's had
so much work done, they probably had enough
left over to bind an encyclopedia," Joan said,
clinking her glass against mine. "Listen, sweetheart, when the reporters come after you on
this one, promise me you'll trowel on some
foundation. You came in here all flushed and
now you're so white, you look as though you've
seen a ghost."

"I thought I had, Joanie."

"You must just be exhausted. Let's give you
some delicious comfort food and send you
home to bed. Here come the guys," she said,
pointing at Jim and Luc, who had stopped in

the bar to talk with Ken. "Things going okay with Luc?"

"He's wonderful to me and it's been very exciting. There can't be a worse week for him to be here, though. I've been so unavailable on every level—physically and emotionally."

"If I see your head fall into the bisque during dinner, I'll kick you under the table," she said, reaching out and squeezing my hand.

"I'll stay awake," I said, as Joan's usual good humor restored my calm.

"Not to worry."

Luc came directly to my side, bending over to kiss me on each cheek before he and Jim took seats opposite us. "I was so worried that Mr. Battaglia wouldn't give you the night off, darling. How do you feel?"

"Better, for the three of you."

Luc lifted his glass for a toast to Joan and Jim, then turned his attention back to me.

"I'm going to miss you terribly, Alexandra. You look stunning tonight."

"Please don't—"

"She's right to stop you, Monsieur Rouget. Or I'll never believe anything you tell me," Joan said, wagging a finger at Luc. "She looks drawn and tired and thin. Awful is how she looks. Stunned, not stunning."

"My English doesn't need correction, **chère**

madame. After all, Alex was called out by the police in the middle of the night. She's had absolutely no rest, and she's got me to deal with, too."

"You were there?" Joan said, turning to me. "You had to go out to the scene? You didn't tell me that."

"Let's talk about somebody else's week, okay?"

"I just sit in a room and make up stories all day. This was one of the mornings the muse decided not to visit. Can't I ever come out to a crime scene with you?" Joan asked. "Mike would let me, wouldn't he?"

"He adores you. Of course he would," I said. "Did you accomplish anything today, Luc?"

"For me, it was very exciting. I was just telling Ken that I think I've found a property, a townhouse very much like the original Lutèce, also on the East Side, in the Fifties. As soon as I talk with my advisors, I'm going to make a bid on the building."

"You must be so happy," I said, pleased to disengage from my own worries and participate in Luc's enthusiasm.

"How divine," Joan said, lifting her glass again. "I'll give the opening party."

"**Pas si vite,** Joan. It won't happen that fast," Luc said, talking to Joan but looking at me. We both knew she enjoyed the role of matchmaker and was trying to push us together at a speed greater than we could deal with.

Jim's diplomatic skills saved the moment, and he arranged for Stefan to take our order. He had just interviewed the British prime minister earlier in the day and had marvelous insights into the economic conference about to start at the United Nations.

By the time Joan and I shared a profiterole that made up for all the calories I had missed during the week, I was ready to fold. Jim's car was parked in front of the restaurant, and they offered to drop us off on the way home.

I took Luc's arm for the short walk to the car, searching the dark street to make sure Anton Griggs hadn't circled back to wait for me again.

"So who's the killer?" Joan asked as she buckled her seat belt.

"You're worse than Battaglia. Give me a week or so, will you?" I said, as Luc gently hugged me closer.

"How's your Flaubert?" Joan asked.

"**Madame Bovary.** That's it."

"Luc," she said, completely focused on the homicide case again. "You know **Bibliomanie?**"

"**Bien sûr.**"

"It was the first story Flaubert published, Alex. And it was based on an historical event, wasn't it, Luc?"

"Oui. C'est vrai," he said. "Fra Vincente was a monk in Barcelona in the Middle Ages. A bibliomaniac."

"He became so obsessed with owning a particular rare book about the mystery of St. Michael that he killed to get his hands on it. A monk, Alex. Just think what some of your characters might do. I'll get you a copy so you can read it."

"That's the last thing I want to do, Joanie."

"You see? I've got all this useless information," she said, throwing her arms up in false despair. "If only I could try a case. Where did I go wrong?"

Jim stopped in front of the door and Luc helped me out of the car.

The champagne had relaxed me, and I let Luc take me by the hand and lead me into the bedroom. I was relieved that no light was flashing on my answering machine, and ready to shut down the professional part of my life that so often intruded on my spirit.

We made love—Luc's tenderness and sincerity piercing the steel-like armor that I subconsciously developed to protect myself against the world in which I worked. I slept soundly until early morning, when he awakened me by making love to me again.

It was so pleasantly normal to lounge in my robe with my lover on a Saturday morning, to do the **Times** crossword puzzle, sip coffee, enjoy the omelet Luc whipped up with French cheeses he'd stocked in my refrigerator.

When eleven o'clock came and the doorman called to tell us that Luc's car service was waiting for him, he pulled me onto his lap and held me tight.

"It's only going to be a week or so, darling. I'll be back very soon," he said.

I walked him to the door and said a cheerful good-bye, then closed it behind me, taking the paper into the bedroom so I could curl up and finish the puzzle.

He'd barely had time to get into the car when my phone rang. The caller ID showed it was Mercer.

"Good morning," I said. "I really admire your timing."

"I have more respect than you think for the good things in life, Alex."

"Where are you?"

"Closer than you'd like me to be."

"I promise I'll call Battaglia and tell him about Anton Griggs. I'm not going anywhere."

"I'm in the lobby. The doorman just pointed

out your friend to me. Thought the least I could do was give you the morning."

"I'm okay, Mercer. Really."

"It's not about you, Alex. Sergeant Pridgen's the squad commander in the sixth precinct now. Called me about a victim of his who's hospitalized in St. Vinny's. I'm going down to talk to her, and I'm sure you'll want to come along."

"What's it about?" I asked, throwing the paper to the side.

"Her apartment was broken into a few nights back. The guy knocked her out with chloroform, just like Tina Barr."

THIRTY-THREE

Pridgen was waiting for us outside the patient's room on the fourth floor of St. Vincent's Hospital, pacing the quiet hallway. We had worked with him in the SVU when we'd had our first cold hit, just after Mercer was shot by a desperate killer.

"Good to see you both," he said. "Wish I could sit down, but the chief of d's ripped me a new one at yesterday's COMPSTAT."

"Been there," Mercer said.

The brilliant Computerized Statistics program originated with the NYPD in 1994 as an aggressive approach to crime reduction and resource management. Weekly meetings of the department's seventy-six precinct commanders, on Friday mornings at headquarters' most high-tech facility, were designed to improve the flow of information between supervisors.

"The captain made me go yesterday 'cause he thought my case was so unique," Pridgen said. "I stood at the podium, laid out the facts, and that crew leaped on me like I was a rookie just out of the academy. 'Why didn't you do this? Why didn't you think of that? Why didn't you call Special Victims?' How was I supposed to know about your case? It wasn't in the papers or anything. And mine wasn't a sex assault."

"But one of the execs figured they might be related?" I asked. "Is that why they made you hook up with Mercer?"

"I got a push-in with a bastard who chloroforms the vic. Those guys think I didn't question her as good as you would have about a sex crime. They think I might have missed something. Said you had a similar case a few days earlier."

"Let's hear what you've got," Mercer said.

Pridgen's plaid polyester jacket was so worn, it almost shined. His cheap tie wasn't knotted, just crossed—detective style—below the open collar of his shirt.

"Jane Eliot—one tough broad," he said. "Eighty-one years old."

"Your witness?" Mercer asked.

"Yeah. I mean, I know we've had sex crimes with women older than that, but my guys asked her about it. She passed out and all, but her clothes were never disturbed. All we got is a push-in with a guy who ransacked the apartment."

"Take anything?"

"Don't look like she had much of any value.

Not even electronic stuff. She hasn't been back there to tell us whether anything's missing."

"Can we talk to her?" I asked.

"Yeah. She doesn't see too good. Has real thick cataracts."

Pridgen opened the door to the room and announced himself as we went in. "Hey, Miss Eliot, how's it going? Pridgen here."

"I'm doing well. Though the social worker says they won't release me until Monday," she said. "Observation and all that."

The handsome woman, perfectly erect in a vinyl hospital chair with her feet on the ottoman, was dressed in a housecoat, listening to the opera on a small portable radio.

"I brought you those friends I told you about. This here is Ms. Cooper, and the big guy is Detective Wallace."

"How do you do?" she asked, shifting her head as though trying to make us out. "I'm Jane Eliot."

"I'm Alex and he's Mercer. I guess you know who we are."

"I do. And I know you're not here for my blood or my temperature, so that's just fine," she said, smiling at us. "Pridgen, would you bring in a few chairs?"

I explained our purpose to Jane Eliot, without mentioning Tina Barr, and told her we needed to do another interview, to probe even more thoroughly.

"It's rather odd for me, Alex. I've lived such an ordinary life for so very long that I can't understand all this interest."

"Why don't we work backward, then?" I said, sitting on one of the chairs that the sergeant had brought into the room. "Get the worst over with first. When did this happen?"

I wanted the facts, and I also wanted to know how clear she was.

"Wednesday. It was shortly before noon," Jane Eliot answered without any hesitation. "I've got my favorite shows to listen to, so I know exactly what day and time it was."

"Where do you live?"

"Greenwich Village," she said. "On Bedford, between Morton and Commerce streets."

"How lovely. Such a pretty area." The historic district of tree-lined streets and small townhouses was one of the safest parts of the city. "That's the block where Edna St. Vincent Millay's house is, if I'm not mistaken."

"Precisely, young lady. The narrowest house in the Village—nine and a half feet wide. Are you a poet as well as a lawyer?" Eliot asked, leaning over to pat me on the knee.

No question she was as sharp as a tack. I laughed. "No, ma'am. All lawyer."

"I've been there for many, many years—on the first floor, thank goodness. I don't think I could climb those steps very well anymore."

"Do you live alone, Miss Eliot?"

"Yes, dear. Always have."

"How large is your apartment?"

"Just a small parlor, my bedroom, the kitchen, and a little den."

"Why don't you tell us exactly what you remember about Tuesday?"

"Certainly. I was waiting to get my local news and weather, enjoy the chatter on one of those midday shows. There was a knock on my door, which surprised me, because the buzzer hadn't rung."

"There's an outer entrance that's kept locked?"

"Always."

"What did you do?"

"I was in the den, turning on the television, so I walked through the apartment to the living room. The knocking came again, and I asked who was there."

"Did someone respond?"

"Oh, yes. The young man spoke to me. Told me he had a package."

"For you?"

"That's what has me feeling foolish. I don't

get many packages, other than an occasional fruitcake from my niece and nephews around the holidays. Can't give them away fast enough." She was spunky and quick to smile. " 'Not for me, you don't.' That's what I told him."

"What did he say?"

"That it was a delivery for my neighbor. He even had the name and apartment right. Miss Ziegler in two-C. Then he told me to look through the peephole so I could see his uniform."

While Jane Eliot was talking, I heard Mercer ask the sergeant whether there was a list of names in the building's vestibule. He nodded and mouthed the word "yes."

"My vision isn't too good these days," she said, "but I can make out shapes and colors. I can see, Mercer, that you've got a very large frame, that you're a tall man, black skinned. And you're quite tall yourself, Alex, with lovely golden hair."

"Thank you."

"Mine was red," Jane Eliot said. "Fiery red. Well, there he was in one of those brown jackets. You know that delivery service that's all done up in brown?"

Tina Barr's assailant had dressed in a fireman's uniform but lost his mask at the crime scene. Was he enough of a chameleon to change his disguise less than twenty-four hours later?

"Tell me about Miss Zeigler," I said. "Have you ever taken packages for her before?"

"Heavens, yes. It's hard for someone like me, without a computer, to understand how she does it, but the girl buys everything online— her books, her clothes, and sometimes even her food. She works for a travel magazine so she's on the road often, and I'm used to accepting deliveries for her."

"Had she asked you to take anything in this week?"

Jane Eliot bit her lip. "It's not that I like to look foolish, Alex. But she doesn't always re-member to ask me."

"There's nothing wrong with what you did, Miss Eliot. What happened isn't your fault. I don't blame you for opening the door," I said. "Would you tell us what happened when you did?"

She inhaled deeply and continued speaking. "The fellow pushed his way in, and that's when I lost my balance. I didn't fall, thank the Lord, but I grabbed for the bench behind me and sat down on it. That's when he dropped the parcel—a small box—and I thought maybe he had stumbled on something.

"Then he bent over, not to get the box, but

to get me," she said, becoming a bit emotional. "He covered my mouth with a cloth, with some kind of fabric that he'd soaked in something dreadful. I thought I was going to die, young lady. I—I couldn't breathe. I got so dizzy. I remember the room spinning, and that's all."

"A few more things, if you don't mind," I said, letting her recover from reliving those frightening moments. "Can you tell us anything about the man who did this?"

"Nothing that Sergeant Pridgen found very helpful."

"Now, Miss Eliot," Pridgen said. "You've been terrific."

"You called him a young man, Miss Eliot. And I understand you have cataracts, but do you have any idea how old he was?"

"Look at me, Alex. I call everyone young."

My turn to bite my lip.

"He was white, I know that for sure. He was an adult, not a teenager. But I couldn't see his features, if that's what you're asking."

"No marks on his face, when he got up close to you?"

"Clean shaven is all I can say. Usually I can make out facial hair if a man's got it. Didn't see any of that."

"Did his uniform have any markings on it? Could you see?"

"You mean like the name of the company? I'm sorry. I just couldn't tell you that."

"We've checked those services, Alex. These days, they've got their scanners current to the second. They can account for all their drivers in the area," Pridgen said. "He wasn't legit."

"Was the box still there when you came to?" Mercer asked.

"I never saw it again."

"What's the next thing you remember?" I asked.

"My goodness, it was hours later. Almost five o'clock. There I was, right on the very same bench. Like I was Sleeping Beauty, gone for a long nap and never been missed."

"Were you injured?"

"I—I didn't know. There's no cushion on that old bench, so I was stiff as a board. And awfully dizzy still, with a terrible headache. Must have been that stuff he had on the cloth. The doctors think it was chloroform."

"But nothing broken?"

"How many times have they had me to X-ray, Mr. Pridgen? MRIs and all these other fancy tests."

"I'm going to ask you something very personal, Miss Eliot. Sergeant Pridgen has explained what my job is, why Mercer and I work together," I said. "We need to know whether this man touched any part of your body before you lost consciousness."

Jane Eliot sat up straighter and talked more seriously. "Now, why would anybody want to do **that**?" she asked. "I'm an old, old lady. Of course he didn't touch me."

It was the specifics I had to establish, whether she wanted to hear them or not.

"What had you been wearing, Miss Eliot? Can you tell us that?"

"Pridgen knows. A housecoat, like this one, but light green. They button up the front so it's easier for my arthritic shoulders than lifting over my head."

"And was your clothing disturbed?"

"Hard to disturb a wrinkled housecoat, isn't it?"

"Do you have any sense that this man might have touched your breasts?"

She put one arm to her chest and chuckled. "They were right where I left them, Alex. He didn't have anything to do with them."

"And your undergarments? Did you have any type of underwear on?"

"These young men probably don't remember the word 'girdle.' I wear a firm girdle, and support hose for the circulation in my legs. Might take a construction crew to get through all of that."

"I'm glad to know that you weren't molested," I said, "and that nothing was broken. Do you have any idea why someone would want to break in to your home?"

"I've been sitting here going on four days. Plenty of time to think about it," Jane Eliot said. "He was either just a fool, or he broke in to the wrong apartment."

"Do you have any valuables there?" I asked. "Has anyone had a chance to see what was missing?"

"I taught elementary school till they put me out to pasture at sixty-five. Fourth grade mathematics. Multiplication tables and time tests—everything that became obsolete with the new math. I'm at an age at which I give my possessions away, Alex. Never had the money for fine things, and don't like the clutter. Had a sweet set of porcelain dolls people brought me from all over the world, but I gave them to my niece years ago."

"No cash that you kept in the house? No jewelry?"

"I was wearing the only piece of gold I own. Couldn't have missed it if he was looking for something pricey to steal. It's bright and shiny, and practically the size of an alarm clock," Jane Eliot said. "Show her, Pridgen."

He walked to the bedside table and picked up the watch, noting its heft before passing it to me. "I'll tell you what, Miss Eliot. If you had cracked the bum over the head with this, he'd have been a goner."

"Wish I'd thought of it then," she said. "It's a man's watch, Alex. It was given to my father after fifty years at his job. The big size—and the large numbers—suit me well. I've worn it ever since he's been gone."

"Fifty years," Pridgen said to Mercer. "Today most guys would be lucky to get a bologna sandwich and a pat on the back after working someplace half a century."

I examined the striking face of the old timepiece. The famous French maker's name written on the dial added value to the watch, which appeared to be made of solid gold.

"He obviously missed the opportunity to take this—it's such a beautiful keepsake. I'm sure that would have been a terrible loss to you. Were there any other things like this that you had hidden away? Any reason for him to ransack your rooms?"

"Not a blessed thing for him to find, I promise you."

I turned the watch over in my hand and read the inscription on the back of it. **To Joseph Pe-**

ter Eliot with gratitude for fifty years of devoted service. September 1, 1958. Trustees of the New York Public Library.

I had begun to think the connection to Tina Barr was a coincidence. But now my adrenaline surged.

"Miss Eliot," I said, "your father worked for the library?"

"Started there right out of high school, Alex, as assistant to the chief engineer."

"And you, did you have any direct association with the place yourself?"

"My dear, I was born in the New York Public Library during a snowstorm in 1928."

"Not literally?"

"Yes, quite literally, young lady. There was an entire apartment within the library where the chief engineer and his family lived, till they threw us out. Needed the room after the Second World War. Until I went off to college, Alex, the public library was my home."

THIRTY-FOUR

"Have I tired you, Miss Eliot?" I asked. "I think you've triggered some information that can help us figure out why you were attacked."

"I'm just getting warmed up for you. Do go on. I'd like to be helpful."

"A girl was murdered this week. A conservator who used to work at the library but was involved with private collectors most recently."

"I heard something about it on the radio this morning. Terribly sad."

"Mercer and I have been all through the library. No one said anything about an actual apartment within it. Is that what you mean?"

"In 1908, even before the library opened, a man named John Fedeler was named chief engineer. There was a seven-room apartment built for him to live in with his family, and when it came time for him to retire eighteen years later, that's when my father got the job and we moved in."

"What was it like then?" I asked.

"Quite a spectacular space, really, especially coming from a tenement in Hell's Kitchen, where my parents had lived. It was an enormous duplex, with an entrance on the mezzanine floor, facing the central courtyard of the building. All paneled in the finest walnut. Big fireplaces and leather armchairs that my mother used to sit in at night, reading to us."

Jane Eliot seemed to delight in her reminiscences. "It's where I was raised, Alex. We were the envy of all the children at school."

"What's become of that apartment, do you know?" I asked, as Mercer drew his chair in as close to her as mine.

"I get invited back every few years, a bit like a dog and pony show, to some of those luncheons. The president occasionally puts me on display as the only baby ever born inside the place," Eliot said. "But the whole apartment is broken up now."

"What's it used for?"

"The top floor, where we children lived, that's all become administrative offices. There was a wonderful spiral staircase, so we could go up and down without entering the library hallway. I suppose that's still in place. Our kitchen is the reproduction center—Xeroxing and that kind of thing. And the family living chambers are where some of the special collections are sorted out."

"You're saying the apartment was self-contained, is that right?" Mercer asked. "But were you allowed into the library itself?"

"That was the great fun of it, of course. I mean, we always had to wait until all the offices were closed for the evening, but gradually, as time went by, Father let us have the run of the place. After dark, mostly, when it was quite spooky, full of great shadows that came from the streetlights outside, and an eerie quiet that settled over the enormous hallways."

"The books, Miss Eliot," I asked. "Did you have access to the books?"

"Mercy, yes. We thought the whole place was just a playground for the three of us. Roller-skating down those hallways in the evening, playing hide-and-seek in that great reading room.

"Christmas Day, once, George and our cousins decided to play stickball in the corridor on the third floor," she went on, rubbing her hands together as she pulled up images from her youth. "He just went into one of the collections—things weren't all locked up back then—and grabbed the biggest books he could find to be the bases. Turned out they were all important double folios. Rare volumes of prints and such, worth a fortune. George got the whipping of a lifetime for that."

"George?" Mercer said, trying to keep up with her.

"My older brother was George Eliot," she said. "Mind you, my mother didn't even have a high school education. When my father got the job there, she decided to name all her children after writers. She didn't know George Eliot was a woman until she began to educate herself with all the wonderful treasures under our roof."

"For whom were you named?" I asked.

"Jane Austen. I'm Jane Austen Eliot. I had a big sister, too. Edith Wharton Eliot. Both my siblings are gone now, but my niece and nephews are very good to me."

"I can appreciate that—mine are, too," I said. "Tell us more about the books, if you don't mind."

"I've always loved books, of course, and that may be because I grew up surrounded by them. They were the center of the universe in our family."

"Did you have books of your own?"

"Our father made it very clear to us that everything in the library was very special, that none of it belonged to us. But for every holiday the trustees would present us with books. I remember our birthdays in particular. After we returned from school, if it was a birthday, we'd get called to the president's office, all dressed up in our best, and one of the board members would give us a gift, explaining the importance of the particular book and its author."

"Sounds like a fine little ceremony."

"Oh, it really was. I got my first **Pride and Prejudice** that way. They were always heavy on Austen for me, of course. I've had a lifetime of pleasure because of those gifts, Alex. It made the loss of my vision even more painful."

"The books that were presented to you, Miss Eliot, were they ordinary things you could buy in a store?"

"There's no such thing as an ordinary book, is there? But these were always particularly un-usual. Beautifully bound in Moroccan leather, or fixed up in those—what do you call them?—clamshell boxes, I think. I can still remember how it felt to hold and smell them for the first time."

"Did you know the trustees?"

"Most of them knew my father well, of course. He was responsible for making sure that their treasures were safe and protected, at least according to the methods available back then. He made sure their great institution ran like a smoothly sailing ship. And my mother catered some of their smaller meetings—everything homemade, right in our kitchen. She was really a saint."

"These gifts you received," Mercer asked, "were they new books?"

"Some were, some weren't, as I recall it." Jane Eliot put her elbow on the arm of the chair and closed her eyes to think. "Later, as I learned more about these things, I'd have to assume that we got some of the castoffs, either second or third editions of books that were of no value to the great collectors, or copies that had been damaged by tears or discolorations. Still, Alex, they opened the world to me. All the classics, all the great literature you could imagine. The three of us were grateful to have them."

I could hardly contain my excitement. The perp must have staged this burglary to get at something Jane Eliot owned, something she didn't even realize was of value.

"The books that you were presented with, Miss Eliot, are they still in your apartment?"

She stretched her right leg and groaned, bending to tug at her hose. "I gave them away ten years ago, maybe more. What's the use, I thought? I'd read and reread them, when I had my sight. Time to let the next generation enjoy."

"But you know where they are?" Mercer asked.

"Gone to my great-nieces and -nephews."

"How lucky they are to have them," I said. "Is your family here, in the city?"

"Gosh, no. Some of them are upstate in Buffalo, and others are out in Santa Fe. Must be several hundred books, all split up between the relatives."

I sat back in my chair, as deflated as the burglar must have been to come up empty after ransacking Eliot's apartment.

"Not a single one that you kept for yourself?" Mercer asked.

"Help me up, Pridgen, will you?" Jane Eliot said. "My joints get all locked tight if I sit too long."

The sergeant helped her get to her feet.

"Walk with me, please," she said, linking arms with Mercer and with me as we stood up. She moved toward the door of the room. "There was only one that I kept. Had to keep, actually. Edith's daughter would have nothing to do with it."

"Why is that?" I asked.

She winced as she put her weight on her left leg. "My sister, Edith, had a very special book presented to her on her twelfth birthday. I remember so well because I was terribly envious when she brought it back to the apartment."

"What was it?"

"You may be able to make more sense of what happened than I ever did," Eliot said. "Because of your job, I mean. Nobody talked about things like that back then. It was a copy of **Alice in Wonderland**. Quite a dazzling one."

Mercer and I exchanged glances over Jane Eliot's head.

"Dazzling?" he asked. "How so? Was it old?"

"Indeed it was—old and wonderfully illustrated with those drawings by John Tenniel that became so famous. The date in it was 1866."

I thought of the call slip that had been found in Tina Barr's clothing.

"Did it ever belong to the library?" I asked.

"Not this one, I don't believe. Most of our gifts were donations from one trustee or another. From time to time, books were quietly deaccessioned from the collections of course, especially if some more desirable copy came along. But we could tell if that were the case. There were markings inside the jackets with the name of the library branch, and those were crossed through to show that the book had been discarded, so we knew we wouldn't get in any trouble."

"Edith's gift sounds very special."

"Oh, yes. That was obvious. It was bound in the most glorious red leather, with gold lettering on the spine and gilt designs all over the cover. And then there was its size—we'd never had books of our own quite that big."

Jane Eliot let go of my arm and drew an outline in the air. "You know, sort of double folio, if you're familiar with that."

"I've seen other copies of the early editions, though, and I never knew any to be oversize," I said.

"Well, you're right. The manuscript was of average size, for an illustrated work of that period, I'm sure. But this particular edition had been mounted on larger parchment pages and bound into this folio because it also included a rare set of prints of the photographs that Charles Dodgson—Lewis Carroll, you know—took of young Alice."

"The photographs were inside the book?" I asked.

"There was a pocket sewn into the back of the book. That's where the photos were. We could take them out and look at them, spread them out on the living room floor," she said. "In fact, that's what got Edith in trouble with Mother."

Jane Eliot shuffled down the hallway of the hospital, continuing to talk to us.

"Why?" I asked.

"The book wasn't a problem. We'd all read the story dozens of times. But those photographs? My goodness. Must have been weeks after Edith's birthday, Mother happened upon the picture of that child dressed as a beggar maid, with her bare shoulders—you know the one I mean?"

"Yes, Miss Eliot. It's a very famous image."

"Well, it convinced my mother that Dodgson was a pedophile. She wouldn't have us looking at a little girl displaying herself that way."

"Alex was just telling me that story about him," Mercer said. "I'd never heard it before."

"What did your mother do?" I asked.

"That was the last we saw of the book, until she lay on her deathbed. She forbade Edith to have it, which created its own stir at the time. Then Mother asked one of the curators in the children's collection to do some research about Dodgson. What she learned was that Alice Liddell's mother had a big falling out with him. Tore up all the correspondence that he'd had with Alice. That inflamed my mother even more."

Mercer tried to frame a question. "Because she thought he'd been . . . ?"

"Inappropriate, sir. That's as explicit as we

got in those days," Eliot said. "It seems Mrs. Liddell found every letter the man sent to her daughter—mind you, she was only eleven or twelve at the time, and he was a grown man—and she ripped them to shreds. That's a fact. And then, when Dodgson died, he left thirteen volumes of diaries. A record of his entire life. But someone in his family was worried enough about the contents to destroy the four years—every page of them—that detailed his friendship with Alice."

"So your mother confiscated the book," I said.

"First thing she did. Poor Edith—the girl had a tantrum over that. I can still hear her screams. The next thing was, my mother had it in her head to go after the trustee who'd given my sister the book. She found some letters he'd written to Edith after the day he met her, telling her how proud he was of her school grades."

"How did he know about them?" Mercer asked.

"Some of the trustees—the nice ones—used to ask us questions like that when they came to see Father, or on the holidays. Harmless enough. What books did we like? What subjects were we studying? We were the library's little family, you see. But Edith kept the notes this man had sent her, offering to take her out in his automobile—nobody had cars in those days—show her parts of the city she hadn't seen. He didn't have a daughter, he said. Just a boy. Said he wanted to be her friend."

"I can understand why that upset your mother," I said. "Edith was only twelve at the time, right?"

"Yes, ma'am. Just like Alice Liddell. So Mother went on a rampage. I was there the afternoon she came home and told Edith that she had walked all the way up Fifth Avenue to his mansion, the day after a terrible snowstorm. Knocked on the door and demanded to see the man. She wanted to give him back his book. Can you imagine her taking on such a rich and powerful person as a trustee of the New York Public Library?" Eliot asked, proud of her mother's spirit. "She came back and told Edith there'd be no more presents from him, and no more visits."

"Miss Eliot," I said, trying not to get ahead of myself. "Do you know the man's name? The trustee who gave Edith the book?"

Her slippers scuffed along the linoleum floor.

"Of course I do," she said. "It was Jasper Hunt. Jasper Hunt. Edith said he called himself the Mad Hatter. Oh, she was very peeved at Mother for ruining her fun."

Jasper Hunt Jr., the eccentric owner of the rarest map in the world.

"Did Edith ever tell you what she meant by her 'fun'?" I asked.

"Not what you're thinking, Alex. No, no. Mr. Hunt never did anything improper, Edith assured me of that. But Mother's concern was with his intentions. And for Edith, it seemed like she'd been deprived of a great adventure, a chance to be treated like a grown-up. In hindsight, I'd say Mother nipped something in the bud."

"And the book—how did you come to have the book?"

"Mr. Hunt was very patient with my mother. He brought her inside, had her served tea and pastries, and removed the photographs that had offended her. He told her that she must keep the book. That one day it would be worth a lot of money and she couldn't deprive Edith of that."

"So your mother returned home with the book?" Mercer asked.

"Yes, but she had made such a fuss about the whole thing that she never admitted it to us. Not till just before she died. She'd kept it on a shelf in her linen closet all those years. Finally told Edith to take it and have it appraised."

"But you said Edith didn't want it."

"She was stubborn, my sister," Jane Eliot said. "She felt it had spoiled her birthday. Didn't want anything to do with it. The whole episode had embarrassed her with the staff and all that. You know how girls that age are."

"I sure do," I said. "Did you ever show the book to a dealer?"

"A couple of years ago, after Edith passed on, I called someone at the library. I wouldn't know how to find a reputable dealer. The president's assistant gave me the name of a man who worked closely with them, she said. I've forgotten it at this point. Anyway," Jane Eliot said, "by the time I got around to contacting him, my letter was answered by the FBI. They told me the fellow was in jail. Now, that was quite a shock, since it was the library folks who had recommended him to me."

"It must have been Eddy Forbes," I said.

"Forbes. That could have been the name."

"Did you describe the book to him in your letter?"

"Yes. That was the point of speaking with him, wasn't it? I had left several phone messages, too. After that," Jane Eliot said, "it just didn't seem worth bothering, if even the dealers

turned out to be thieves. I really wasn't interested in its dollar value. I don't want for anything, and my relatives have plenty of other rare
books. It wasn't mine, after all."

"So you have it still?"

"I did, until just a few months ago," Jane
Eliot said, stopping in her tracks. "I gave it
back."

"Back?" I asked. "To the library?"

"No, no. I did my genealogy, dear. Easy to
do with folks as well known as the Hunts. It
turns out that old Mr. Hunt had one son, just
as he had told my mother. Jasper Hunt the
Third, who's even older than I am. I wasn't
about to give anything to him."

She squeezed my hand and smiled again.

"But I learned there's also a granddaughter.
A woman named Minerva. So I wrote her a
note. I told her about the book, about our family's connection to the library," the old woman
said, pointing toward the door of her room and
directing us toward it. "I left out my mother's
suspicions about Minerva's grandfather, of
course."

"Did she return your correspondence?"

"She didn't seem the least bit interested at
first. I didn't get a reply for several weeks. Then
I wrote again. My writing isn't too neat, because
of my vision. Of course, I can't see the detail on

the pages of that old book very well anymore, but I tried to describe how beautiful it was. I told her about the map that the Mad Hatter had tucked in that pocket in the back, with the photographs."

Mercer jumped in before I could open my mouth. "There was a **map**?"

"When my mother was dying and she told Edith and me about the book, she said that Mr. Hunt had insisted she keep the map. The very first day we had opened the book, we saw the map, of course. George spread it out on the floor at once, but it wasn't nearly so interesting to us as the photographs."

"But why was there a map?" he asked.

"Do you remember that Alice—the one in Wonderland—went to a tea party?"

"Sure, the Mad Hatter and the March Hare were there," I said. "But what did the map have to do with the tea party?"

Jane Eliot slowly started to move again. "Let me think what Mother said. It was a big old map, folded up several times, as I recall. It was a picture of the island of Ceylon. Mr. Hunt said that's where the tea came from. The tea for the party."

Jasper Hunt certainly lived up to his reputation for eccentricity.

"He told Mother to leave the map right

where it was. That it would increase the value of the book, in the end. He said he wanted to make up for alarming her, to do right by Edith," Jane Eliot said. "So Mother saw no harm in keeping it. Like Jasper told her, he loved the library, too, and knew that we did. She had her piece of the Hunt legacy."

THIRTY-FIVE

"Is that how your mother referred to Jasper Hunt's gift?" I asked.

"At the end of her life, when she talked about him."

"Were those her words, or his?"

"I don't have any idea," Jane Eliot said.

"Did you finally get Minerva Hunt's attention?" Mercer asked, helping to lower the woman into her chair.

"She couldn't have been more gracious. Came all the way downtown to visit me. She really seemed so pleased that I had thought of her. Brought me a beautiful plant."

"And left with the book?" Mercer asked.

As Mike liked to say, that's why the rich were rich. Minerva Hunt exchanged a potted plant for a rare book and a piece of one of the most valuable puzzles in the world.

"Oh, yes. Such a sentimental lady. She seemed almost in tears about it. Turned the pages of the book, kept stroking the map, too, though she never took it out to open it up."

"What did Minerva talk to you about, Miss

Eliot?" I asked. "Did she speak about her grandfather?"

"I talked mostly. About the library and such. She asked some questions."

"Like what?"

"She was very curious about the other books we'd gotten as kids. Were any of them quite as big as this one? But they weren't," Eliot said, scratching her head as she recalled the conversation. "She wanted to know if I'd told anyone else about Edith's gift. That's what she was most interested in."

"And have you?" Mercer asked.

"Certainly, but years ago. No one's listened to me in ages. There was a time, after Jasper Hunt was gone, and my mother, too, that I made a few speeches at the library, to the trustees. They always seemed to enjoy stories of what we did there as kids. It kind of brought the great institution to life."

"Did you mention the map?" he said.

"No. It never really made an impression on me as a child, Mercer. I saw it so briefly, and now I can't really see at all. At those meetings, I described how we lived, the significance of the books that were given to us, particular books— like **Alice in Wonderland**—that sort of thing."

"Did that satisfy Minerva?" I asked.

"A touch of sibling rivalry, I guess," Jane

Eliot said with a chuckle. "She was more concerned about whether her brother knew about the map. I can't pull up his name at the moment, but she wanted to be very sure I hadn't sent a letter to him before she'd responded to me."

"You hadn't?"

"No, no. Young people would call it sexist, but I thought that lovely book should go to a girl. I was hoping maybe Minerva had children, but she told me she doesn't."

"In your correspondence with Eddy Forbes, Miss Eliot," Mercer said, "did you mention the map that was inside your copy of **Alice in Wonderland**?"

"I certainly did. I remembered what Jasper Hunt had told Mother about its value."

"And you've never heard from Forbes himself?"

"Thank goodness, no. And the FBI wasn't interested at all. They only wanted to know if I'd done any other business with Forbes. They didn't even come to see me."

There was no reason for the feds, at that time, to have thought there was any significance to Jane Eliot's attempt to reach Eddy Forbes.

"Was there anything else Minerva mentioned?"

"No, Alex. Not that I can think of. She hugged me quite warmly before she left. I figured I'd made a new friend. She seemed so concerned about my health, too. Just lovely."

"But you haven't heard from her since?"

"Actually, I haven't. It sounds as though you think my old copy of **Alice** had something to do with this attack on me. Am I right?"

"We'll let you know as soon as we figure it out, Miss Eliot. I promise you that," I said. "Can we do anything to make you more comfortable here before we leave?"

"Take me with you," she said, chuckling again.

"You'll go home in grand style when you're released. The sergeant will get you there in a blue and white chariot. We'll have your place all straightened up."

I knew she'd be shocked to see her home turned upside down, and to know there was fingerprint powder on most of her furniture. Someone from Witness Aid would be on top of helping with her homecoming.

Pridgen walked us to the elevator as Mercer speed-dialed Lieutenant Peterson. "Loo? Don't worry—I've got Alex covered for the day. She's going to be with me. This Jane Eliot push-in is definitely a piece of our case—Tina Barr and Karla Vastasi. You need a uniformed cop posted at her hospital door, 24/7, in case this creep decides to come back at her."

Mercer listened to Peterson's reply and gave me a thumbs-up.

"And I'm about to call Chapman. Seems his heartthrob, Minerva Hunt, has been keeping secrets from him. Looks like she's lied to us from the start. I think it's time to round her up and hold her fancy pedicured toes to the fire."

THIRTY-SIX

"So everybody's keeping secrets from me, huh?" Mike said, combing his fingers through his hair. "First Minerva Hunt and then you. All of a sudden I find out you're so worried about my temper, you won't even call me when one of the Griggs takes you for a ride. Do you honestly think I'd do something stupid to compromise Kayesha Avon's case after eight long years?"

The three of us were standing in front of Tina Barr's building. Mike had been on his way to the apartment when Mercer reached him as we left the hospital room.

"I apologize," I said. "It just seemed smarter at the time to let someone else in the squad handle last night's episode."

"It would have seemed smarter to me at the time not to get in the frigging cab with Anton Griggs. He's got a rap sheet longer than the Holland Tunnel."

"You didn't mention that when you testified at the hearing."

"Don't give me attitude, Coop. Anton

doesn't bother with his birth name too often. He's got a different alias for just about every arrest. Most of the collars are in Jersey, so I missed it first time around, okay?"

"What's the plan, Mike?" Mercer asked, ever the peacemaker. "I told Alex not to call you. Let her be."

"Falling on your sword for her again, huh? Do it too often and there'll be permanent puncture wounds in your heart," Mike said, tapping his fingers on his chest. "Don't say anything, Blondie. It's only a joke."

I felt a pang of guilt and looked away.

"Bea Dutton is on the subway, on her way to meet me here. She wants to show me the historical footprint of these buildings."

While we waited, Mercer told Mike the details of our interview with Jane Eliot.

He had barely finished the story when Mike pulled out his cell phone.

"Slow it down," Mercer said. "Who are you calling?"

"Carmine Rizzali. If I find that useless thug who she pays to protect her, we'll know where Minerva Hunt is."

I could see Bea walking from Lexington Avenue, waving as she saw us standing on the steps of the brownstone.

Mike slapped the phone shut. "Doesn't even

go to voice mail. Guess he's catching on," he said. "Yo, Bea. What have you got for me?"

"Can we go inside, so I can spread out my maps?"

"Sure," Mike said, leading us down to the basement apartment—the scene of Tina's assault and Karla's murder. Crime scene tape was still draped across the doorway, but Mike had brought a key with him.

When we reached the kitchen table, Bea unzipped her bag. "What do you know about these buildings?" she asked.

"Only that there's lousy karma in this basement lately."

"It didn't start out that way," she said. "You know something about the Hunts, I take it?"

"Nothing good," Mike said. "Educate me."

"Jasper Hunt and John Jacob Astor became partners in the real estate business. What Manhattan properties Astor didn't buy, Hunt did."

Bea Dutton spread out one of her maps on the table.

"Here's where we're standing," she said, pointing at East Ninety-third Street on a copy of a fairly primitive map of the city. "This row of brownstones was built in 1885. Pretty swell digs at the time."

Mike squinted and looked at the writing. "Now, how can you tell when it was built?"

"I did the vertical search for you," Bea said, knowing she had captured Mike's interest. "The 1884 maps don't show any of the structures. The next year, here they are."

"Why were these maps created annually?"

"Did you ever hear of the Great Fire of 1835?"

Mercer and I were shaking our heads, but Mike answered, "Yes. It destroyed hundreds of buildings in lower Manhattan."

"That's right," Bea said. "Everything that was in today's Wall Street area. These are called Sanborn maps, made by a company right after that fire. They were done for insurance purposes, for claims. Sanborn had the idea for these very detailed maps, showing every structure on the island. Can you see?"

Her finger pointed from building to building as she talked. "The brick buildings, like these, were colored in pink. Things built for industrial use were green. And down the block a bit, you see the yellow ones? Those represent wood frame houses—more likely to burn, less likely to get a good insurance rate."

"Why is this one both pink and yellow?" Mike asked.

"A brownstone, but with a wooden porch in the backyard. I want you to hold that thought, because it's going to come in handy a few maps down the road," Bea said. "In the meantime, I can also tell you **why** these homes were built."

"We're all ears."

"Jasper Hunt—the great-grandfather of Tally and Minerva—wanted a residence for his mistress. Close to Fifth Avenue, but not so close his wife would be able to smell her perfume," Bea said.

"Now, how do you know that?" Mike asked, patting her on the back.

"I've got a library card, Mr. Chapman. It serves me well. There were tabloids even back in those days. Five buildings in this row. The one we're in was completed first, and then the one next door was built for the mother of his mistress—a deal the young lady was smart enough to insist upon. The other three weren't quite as grand, but Mr. Hunt built them for servants and staff."

"And Minerva was still using the basement for the hired help," Mercer said, referring to Tina Barr.

"The next structural change to note is in 1912," Bea said, layering her maps on top of each other. "Something very interesting has been added to the rear of this building."

"What's that?" Mike asked. "Can we see it?"

"Look closely. Attached to one side of the pink drawing that represents the house, there's a small black rectangle."

"Got it," Mike said. "But what does it mean?"

"It's an indication that some kind of chamber was added out in the yard—something that would be impervious to fire and water. That's what the black color code tells us. It's not as deep as the basement we're in, which was really helpful for me to know."

"Why?" I asked.

"Remember yesterday, when Mike made me cancel my meeting with the Department of Transportation about the flooding in the Empire State Building? The men were coming to study the Viele map, so that gave me the idea to search out this site on that."

"I know you're the map maven," Mike said. "But I'm trying my best to follow this."

"Let me make it easy for you," she said. From her briefcase she removed another thick paper, which she unfolded, revealing a vividly colored reproduction of a topographical map of Manhattan. "See there? Egbert Viele, 1865."

This one had a street grid superimposed on the island, but no structures or buildings. Instead, it showed a city full of ponds, natural springs, and streams, from its southern to northern tips, before it was paved over and populated.

"This is Greenwich Village," Bea said. "You can see Minetta Stream coursing below Washington Square. And there's a creek, just underneath Broadway in the Twenties. This blue line, up in Harlem, right around One Hundred and Fortieth Street? That's also a stream."

And then her fingertip led our eyes to First Avenue, just east of the Hunt buildings. "And that, my friends, is an underground pond, where water pools and collects—to this very day, no doubt. The stream that leads from it comes right below our feet. You can't possibly trace them today, but every architect in the city still uses this map—like an X-ray of the island—to find out where the leaks are coming from."

"So what's your deduction, Sherlock?" Mike asked the diminutive librarian.

"Elementary," she said. "Who owned the buildings by 1912?"

"You've got better sources on the Jasper Hunts than I do," Mike said.

"Jasper Junior had just come into his own. Don't forget, he did his world tour, visiting all the European principalities, in 1905. By 1912, according to the yellow journalists of the day,

Junior took over where his father left off. He moved his late father's mistress in with her mother, next door, and brought his own to live right here."

How had Minerva first described the predilections of the Hunt men? Rare books, expensive wine, and cheap women. Jasper Hunt Jr. had a wife, a mistress, and, later in life, perhaps an inappropriate interest in young girls like Edith Wharton Eliot.

"So what is this chamber he built in the backyard made of—Kryptonite?" Mike asked.

"Not so deep as this basement, where we're standing," Bea said. "After all, if something was likely to flood in here, it would be ruined. Seems to me, if a man had valuables he wanted to protect—"

"And if Jasper was more than a little bit eccentric, enough so not to entrust things to a bank vault . . ."

"Maybe he built his own vault, right in his babe's backyard?" Bea said. "Maybe that's where she kept her jewels."

Mike straightened up and smiled for the first time that afternoon. "Or maybe that's where he kept the panels of the great map of 1507. High and dry, locked in a waterproof, fireproof chamber where nobody was likely to look. Had to get past his lady love to get to the yard.

Buried his treasure under his father's favorite garden ornament."

"Don't tell me Billy Schultz didn't know what his neighbor was digging for," Mercer said, crossing the kitchen floor in three strides to open the back door.

Mike was on his tail just as quickly. "That's a pretty deadly vertical search that landed Tina Barr so permanently horizontal."

THIRTY-SEVEN

I had gone upstairs to knock on Billy Schultz's door before returning to the backyard, but there was no answer. Both Mike and Mercer were digging with garden spades when I joined them and said he wasn't home. Bea had pulled the collar up on her raincoat and watched them work from a bistro chair set out behind the house.

"You ever get your hands in the dirt up on the Vineyard?" Mike asked. "You have any idea what we've got here?"

I knelt down beside him. "The top couple of inches is mulch. These look like tulip bulbs," I said, lifting out several plantings below the surface. "Some people plant them in the fall."

Mike jabbed his small shovel into the dirt again. "Too bad Tina didn't stick around for the spring bloom."

"She's still the victim," I said. "Is there another shovel?"

"Not until Billy Schultz gets home."

Whoever tended the little garden kept it densely packed with perennials and small shrubs. Mercer was pulling them out to get a better angle as he dug.

Minutes later, I heard the sound of metal clanging against metal. "I'm in," Mercer said.

Bea jumped to her feet and both of us clustered behind him. Mike saw the hole in the ground left by Mercer's uprooting of a dwarf pine and started digging furiously. Seconds later, the tip of his shovel struck against some kind of metal vault.

"Right where it shows on the map," Bea said.

Both men scrambled to excavate the dirt on top of the buried chamber.

Just like on the diagram Bea had shown to us, the exterior of the rectangular chest was almost ten feet long bordering the rear of the house, and only three feet wide.

"It looks like it's split into compartments," Bea said, peering in over Mike's shoulder.

"Can you tell from your map," Mike asked as he continued to throw dirt back onto the flagstone path adjacent to the site, "whether there were peepers way back then in the buildings behind us?"

He raised a valid point. It wouldn't have been a very good hiding place if everyone around could see the dig.

"It appears from the maps I've examined that Hunt enclosed these first two buildings—

the ones for his mistress and her mama—with a common wall," she said, pointing to the brick surround, which was about twenty feet tall. "The family held on to the property behind us until almost 1930, when those apartments that back up on it were constructed."

"See that stump?" Mercer said. "Bet there was a big old shade tree right there that might have given some cover."

"You gentlemen need to understand something about topography," Bea said. "The reason this chamber was displayed on the map is because at some point, the top of it must have been visible, on the surface of the ground. A hundred years later, with shifts in the land, it settled in a little deeper."

"So what are you telling us?" Mike asked.

"That this would have been much more accessible to Jasper Hunt when he wanted to get to it," Bea said. "Probably only covered with a thin layer of sod."

Mike and Mercer were both kneeling at ends of the chest. "Doesn't seem to be any opening on my end," Mike said. "Totally airtight. How about you?"

"Same."

Bea looked pensive as she walked back to the house. "Could be another way at it, don't you think?"

I followed her into the kitchen, where she turned to study the cabinet doors high above the sink, out of reach to both of us. "You've got me on height, Alex."

I dragged one of the chairs over and stepped on the seat of it to climb to the lip of the old sink. I pulled at the latch, too useless a location to have ever been replaced by any of the tenants.

It stuck for my first few attempts, then opened wide as I yanked again, practically dislodging me from my perch. Bea reached out to steady my legs.

The thick layer of dust that coated the interior shelf had recently been disturbed. Streaks across the width of the space suggested someone had reached inside.

"You might be right, Bea," I said.

"Hey, Mike," she called out. "Come help us."

Mercer and Mike were behind me seconds later.

"Make yourself useful, Bea," Mike said. "I'll hold her legs."

He put his hands around my calves, squeezing them to reassure me that all was okay between us.

I reached back and ruffled his thick black hair.

Mercer opened several closet doors until he found a stepladder. He helped me down and, with his great height added to the three steps, was halfway inside the cabinet when he called out, "There's a false front here."

He leaned to the side, pulling out the piece of wood that formed the crossbar for the single shelf.

In the space behind the center cabinet—a good four feet wide—was the side of the metal chamber we had seen from above.

Directly in front of Mercer, in the seam of the concealed door, was a keyhole—an old-fashioned design, which looked like it would accommodate a notched tip turned with an ornate bow.

"Call the lab, Mike," I said. "Get someone up here with the key that I found in the library stacks."

THIRTY-EIGHT

"It's a fake," Bea Dutton said, her gloved hands spreading the parchment that appeared to be a panel of the 1507 world map across one end of my dining room table, after we'd made the short drive from East Ninety-third Street.

We had waited forty minutes in the basement apartment until one of the forensic biology lab techs appeared with the key that I had found along the path the killer probably took to dispose of the body of Tina Barr.

Mercer had opened the locked chamber to reveal a watertight series of metal chests within chests—like a small version of the caskets in Napoleon's tomb—and removed them from the hidden compartment.

The smallest one was fitted with a velvet lining large enough to hold double-folio-size prints. Only one thing—a piece of the map—rested within the case. Mercer removed it and Mike called the lieutenant to tell him we were on our way to my apartment to determine what it was.

"How can you tell it's a fake?" I asked.

"Remember what I said yesterday about forgeries of something as detailed as this piece? The fact that it's a made from a woodcut, not just a drawing?" Bea asked. "It would be next to impossible to pull off."

Bea put on her reading glasses and began to examine the paper more closely.

Mike was looking over her shoulder. "Which of the twelve parts is it?"

"**Winturn Eurus.** The easterly skies. That's the coast of India, with Tibet above it, and the island of Java off to the side. It's one of the easier panels to try to copy because so much of it is just water rather than the finely documented landmasses, which require minuscule writing and exquisite particularity."

Bea rubbed the edge of the parchment between her fingers. "The texture is the first giveaway," she said, starting to explain the flaws. "Most experts could tell right off the bat."

"Someone like me, Bea, who doesn't know rare maps," I said. "Would it fool me?"

"Stevie Wonder could tell this one's a forgery, Coop. Get with the program." Mike pulled at a strand of hair that had fallen between my eyes. "Make yourself comfortable, Bea. Want a soda?"

He walked into the kitchen and helped himself to a soft drink.

"Nothing, thanks. Do you have that photocopy of the entire map I made for you at the library?"

"I got it," Mercer said. He had brought a stack of work up from the car and sorted it out from the pile he had dropped on the credenza on his way inside.

"Let's lay it out on the table. Do you mind if I move your flowers, Alex?" Bea asked.

Mike lifted the vase of white lilies. "More where those came from, Bea. Guess this guy didn't get so lucky. The place usually looks like a funeral home when she's put out her best stuff."

Bea ignored him. "Grab me some tape and a few pads."

Mike knew his way around my place. He left the room, then returned from my office with what Bea requested.

"You guys keep going on your end. Let me play with the map a bit," she said.

Mercer, Mike, and I set ourselves up around the coffee table in the living room. It was late in the afternoon, and the three of us were trying to use a quiet Saturday to regain the territory and figure out what we had to work with so far in the murders of Tina Barr and Karla Vastasi.

"You liked what the old broad had?" Mike asked.

"Jane Eliot?" I said. "Absolutely."

"But the guy who broke in to her place didn't bother with a mask. So why would he bother with the fireman outfit the first time he hit Tina Barr's place?"

I leaned back and put my feet up on the sofa. "Maybe he thought she'd make him, recognize him."

Mercer nodded. "Possible. Didn't mean to kill her if he could find what he was looking for in the apartment."

"Jane Eliot can't see well enough to describe her assailant," I said. "If he knew her vision was impaired and was confident she had no reason to identify him from any previous encounter, he didn't have to go to the trouble of hiding his face. Besides that, he'd lost the gas mask."

"Alex has a point," Mercer said. "The delivery uniform he wore to break in to Eliot's was a disguise of sorts."

Mike had found a deck of cards in the drawer of the coffee table and was playing solitaire while we talked.

"Did you ever follow up with the lab on that DNA profile in the mask?" I asked Mike.

"I'm on it. Partial match to Billy Schultz, but it's a combo, so they can compare it to other samples we submit."

"So how you doing on profiles?" Mercer asked. "Whose DNA have we got?"

"Schultz's, obviously. But his alibi works for Tina's murder," Mike said. "And I gave the lab the Hunts."

"Which Hunts?" I asked.

"Let's see," he said, folding his losing hand and shuffling again. "Minerva's first."

"I know they're only amendments," I said, too tired to go at Mike full force. "But they are still part of the Constitution. Hope the seizures were lawful, but then if they were, I probably would have known about them."

"That cigarette butt she crushed to death in the squad room the other night? Abandoned property," Mike said.

"I'll give you that," I said with a smile. "Nice work."

"Think of it, a woman inside a fireman's uniform and mask. Who'd guess that? You automatically assume it's a guy."

Bea Dutton looked over at us every now and then as we tried to put the clues together.

"You're right, Mike. It would never occur to me, hearing that description, to think of a Minerva Hunt—or a Jill Gibson."

"What are you saying about Jill?" Mike asked.

"Forget I mentioned it. It's just a personal thing."

"I'm gonna talk to you about that, Bea," Mike said. "You can't hold back if you think there's something that might be useful to us."

"Sorry. I just think she plays both sides of the street. She means well, but she's in a difficult position, as an administrator, between sucking up to the board and keeping her staff squared away."

I made a note on the top of my pad to get back to Bea Dutton.

"So what did you get from Talbot Hunt?" I asked.

"Swiped a cocktail napkin that the butler missed in the living room yesterday. Figured the one with lipstick was Minerva's and the one without was her brother's."

"Swiped doesn't work for me."

"Don't get in a swivet about it, Coop. I didn't take it from **his** house. He doesn't have any standing at Papa's pad. Give me any illegal search bullshit and I'll have a seizure."

"I'll remember to argue that when I'm taking heat in the hearing."

"Who else should we look at for DNA?" Mercer asked. "I'd like to go back into Forbes's apartment. See what he's got going on."

"Ask Shalik to scoop up some Band-Aids for

you while Travis is picking himself clean on the stoop," Mike said. "I want Alger Herrick. The man with the golden arm."

"Because you think he's dirty?" Mercer asked.

" 'Cause he likes maps so much."

"We have Herrick's DNA," I said.

Mike's head snapped in my direction. "Promise me you went back to his house and got your sample the old-fashioned way. None of this swabbing and drooling stuff."

"Not my type, Mikey."

"So what'd I miss?"

"Herrick told us he'd been stopped for drunk driving back in England," I said.

"And the Brits do DNA on every infraction, no matter how minor," Mike said. "So Scotland Yard has Herrick's DNA profile in the hopper."

"Frankly, I don't see him playing dress-up," I said. "And he certainly didn't do Jane Eliot. She described a young man."

Mercer stood by the window and dialed his phone. "Hey, Loo. Get on the horn with that deputy inspector in London who owes you. Alger Herrick—he's got a genetic fingerprint on file there. Ask them to transmit it to the lab, stat, will you?"

Peterson must have assured him he would before Mercer thanked him and hung up.

"Jonah Krauss is another story," Mike said. "Walked out of his office gym all pumped and ready to fly out of town. No question he's strong enough to heave that garden ornament."

"Kinky enough for the first night attack on Tina?" Mercer asked.

"Hey, his favorite display item is a book made out of human skin," Mike said. "Plus he has access to all those subterranean spaces in the library."

"Don't forget his connection to Minerva Hunt," I said.

"That's a pretty slimy trio—Krauss, Minerva, and Forbes the map thief, all trying to figure out how to find the panels of the great treasure."

Bea Dutton had been assembling the pieces of the photocopied map. It covered almost the entire top of the dining table. "Want to see what I've been up to?"

"Sure," Mike said, throwing down the cards and walking toward her.

I stood and stretched, and we all took up positions on one side of the table, our backs to the window with the high, sweeping view over the city.

Bea stood in the center, flattening the enormous map with her small hands. "Okay. So we've talked about the twelve panels, right?"

She reached to a chair beside her and raised the image we had found earlier in the day. "You asked if this fake could fool anyone, Alex, and I'd have to say the answer is not anyone knowledgeable, and not for very long. The paper isn't a fit, it's probably been stained by tea—yes, just an ordinary tea bag—to discolor it a bit, age it some. The drawing itself is rather crude."

Bea juxtaposed the parchment next to its copy on the map. It formed part of the border on the right, in the midsection.

Mike looked at the pieces side by side. "I kept thinking of Karla Vastasi when we found this thing in the apartment today," he said, referring to Minerva Hunt's housekeeper.

"Why Karla?" I asked.

" 'Cause she was set up, Coop. No doubt in my mind that Minerva sent her in, dressed in the madam's clothes, to meet someone who wouldn't have a clue if she was Minerva Hunt or not."

"Rules out Alger Herrick," Mercer said. "And Jonah Krauss."

"But rules in the possibility that she had brought that tote bag to carry something out—something just about the size of one of these panels," Mike said, pointing to the map. "And she wouldn't be expected to know if it was genuine or not."

"She had the psalm book, too," I said.

"Maybe she—or the killer—found it there. If Tina Barr is the one who stole it from Talbot Hunt's apartment, she might have been hiding it on her own."

"Waiting for the best offer," Mercer said.

"I smell a cross," Mike said. "Somebody double-teaming someone else. Mild-mannered Tina Barr, the pawn in a treacherous double cross, with stakes so high she couldn't even imagine what a dangerous position she put herself in working with any of these greedy bastards."

"So this document is a fake," Mercer said, turning his attention back to Bea. "Let's start with that. What else can you tell us?"

"Let's take this puzzle piece by piece. There's got to be a logic to the way Jasper Hunt broke it up and concealed the panels."

"Like his son said, Bea, you can't assume that with a complete eccentric."

"Nonsense, Mike. Maybe what Hunt did won't seem logical, but there had to be some kind of method to his madness, especially if he ever hoped to see these pieces reunited."

And especially if Jasper Hunt ever hoped to leave this map as part of his legacy.

"What makes you think so?" I asked.

"So far, the two panels found weren't hidden

randomly," she said. "What's the most important feature of the piece you found yesterday
morning in the library?"

Mike was quick to answer. "The inset about
the New World as a separate continent, with
the portrait of Amerigo Vespucci. Mr. America,
himself."

"And where did you find it, Mike?" Mercer
said, following Bea's lead. "Tucked inside a rare
volume of Audubon's **Birds of America.** Not
all that crazy, is it?"

I thought of Jane Eliot's story and looked at
the photocopy of the large map, placing my finger on the lower right section that featured
Ceylon and Madagascar. "Jasper put this one in
the back of his very unique edition of **Alice in
Wonderland** because it made him—the Mad
Hatter of the family—think of Ceylonese tea."

"Ten to go," Mike said. "All we need is a list
of the double-folio-size books that Jasper Hunt
bequeathed to the library. Feeling lucky, Bea?"

"You get the commissioner to open the
doors for us tonight, give me a handful of curators," Bea said, "and maybe I'll give you the
world. Jasper Hunt's world."

THIRTY-NINE

The combined forces of Commissioner Keith Scully and District Attorney Paul Battaglia were enough to open the great doors of the New York Public Library on Saturday evening at seven p.m.

Jill Gibson, obviously not pleased to be in the dark about what had prompted the gathering of her senior curators and her own police escort, stepped out of a patrol car as we approached the side door.

Uniformed cops had been stationed at all the entrances for almost forty-eight hours now, as investigators continued to work on processing the vast spaces within the sub-basements of the library.

"Excuse me, Alex?" Jill called out. "May I talk with you a minute?"

"Whatcha got, Jill?" Mike said, stepping between us.

"I'd like to ask Alex a few questions."

Mike tapped my shoulder to keep me moving. "She's fresh out of answers, but we're looking, Jill. We're holding court in the map division."

The sergeant in charge moved us through the doors of the old carriage entrance and down the twisting corridors until we could see our way to Bea's department at the farthest end of the main floor.

Curators from the various private collections were seated at the trestle tables. Arents, Berg, Pforzheimer, and the rare books division were represented. A dozen young cops, at Mike's request, stood around the room, ready to help.

Mike sat on the edge of one of the tables and started to explain what he wanted the librarians to do.

"How fast can you get together a list of the volumes donated to this institution by Jasper Hunt the Second?" Mike asked.

Jill Gibson didn't wait to be acknowledged. "If you'll allow me to go to my office, I can print that out for you immediately."

Mike looked toward one of the rookie cops at the door and told him to take her there. Jill seemed shocked to be under guard in her professional home.

One of the men spoke up before she left. "It's not that simple, Detective. Many of the Hunt gifts have been in and out of the library over time. I think each of us, in our own collections, could be more helpful than any master list."

Jill's lips clamped together.

"What do you mean?" Mike asked.

"Take World War Two, for example. You know the windows in the reading room were entirely blacked out," the man said. "There were legitimate fears of an air raid, and decisions had to be made about the safety of the most valuable books."

"I get it."

"The Gutenberg Bible, Washington's Farewell Address, the Medici **Aesops,**" he went on. "Things like these were actually carried off-site for protection."

"And some of the books that were taken away were once the property of Jasper Hunt?" Mike asked. "Is there some confusion about where they were housed after they were returned?"

"That, of course, Mr. Chapman. As well as the fact that some of the finest volumes simply never came back to us."

"Because the Hunts kept them?"

The man looked to Jill Gibson before he answered, aware that he was crossing a line. "That's my understanding. Jasper Hunt Jr., as well as several trustees, decided, rather quietly, it might be a good time to reclaim some of the things they'd given away."

"Don't wait around, Jill," Mike said. "Something you already knew, apparently, and didn't feel the need to tell me. Go ahead and get me your list anyway."

Then he turned to Dutton. "You're up, Bea. Tell them what you need."

She addressed her colleagues, apologized for not being able to say exactly what we were after, and asked them to brainstorm for any insights that went beyond card catalogs, computer lists, and digitization.

"Let's talk about the Napoleonic **Description de l'Égypte**," Bea said.

She was starting with the most obvious hiding place—the one in which Prince Albert of Monaco had found the copy that Jasper Hunt Jr. purchased in 1905. It was logical that Hunt might have chosen to mimic the Grimaldis. Talbot had told us the day before that his father—probably unknowingly—had given a set of the twenty-volume classic to the library just two decades ago.

"Orientalia," one of the men said. "I believe we have three sets of the Napoleonic expedition, all in Orientalia."

"You know that's not politically correct," the older woman beside him joked. "It's the Asian and Middle East department now."

"Yeah. Rugs are the only things left you can call Oriental," Mike said. "People—and I guess books—are Asian."

I could tell he liked his new team. They were smart and sincere, and seemed to love the rare objects in their care.

"Any of you seen them, these books?"

A man in a madras plaid shirt, with a crew-neck sweater tied around his shoulders, raised his hand. "I'm Bruce. Bruce Havens. I used to work in that department. The Napoleonic expedition volumes have been completely digitized. You can view the entire thing online, without leaving home. The originals are locked away. Only scholars with a really good reason to see them can get access under a curator's supervision."

"Do you know the three copies, Bruce?"

"Let's say I've seen them, Bea. Is that what you mean?"

"Provenance, Bruce. What's their provenance?"

"Whew. It's a tough issue in that particular collection. Much of what came in was without designation."

Bea turned to us to explain. "Bruce means a lot of the photographs and foreign-language volumes were—what's a polite word?—pilfered by explorers during their travels."

"Sort of like the Elgin Marbles?" Mike asked.

"You got it," Bea said to him. "Bruce, do you know the donors of the three Egyptian sets?"

"The prize of the three was a Lenox endowment. An absolutely pristine set of books, in a contemporary French speckled calf, board edges with gilt roll tool. Exquisite."

"Under lock and key now?"

"Yes, it is. I know you're interested in whether any of them are Hunt acquisitions," Bruce said, "but I simply don't know."

"Any of them submitted to the conservators for repair?" I asked.

"Possibly, but not on my watch. They were actually shelved in the stacks."

Mike heard the word "stacks" and stood up, signaling to one of the cops. "This gentleman's going to take you downstairs to look for something. Stay with him."

"I wouldn't have access, Detective."

"Why not?"

"In each department, there are cages—metal cages," Bruce said. "Sort of wire mesh, where the rare books are locked."

"Who's got the keys?" Mike asked.

Bea answered. "We each have control of our own section. The front office has all the masters."

Mercer walked to the door. "I'll take them to Jill Gibson and make sure she gives up the key. You keep at it with Bea."

"What's next?" Mike asked her.

"The Most Noble and Famous Travels of Marco Polo," Bea said. "How many different versions of that would you think we have?"

"Jill will know," one of the men said.

"Forget Jill." Bea was on a tear.

The older woman spoke. "We've got the Elizabethan translation by John Frampton in the Berg Collection. It was an Astor gift," she said. "Not the Hunts'."

"I know," Bea said. "I've got a version with large folding maps, but it came to us recently out of Lord Wardington's collection."

I recognized Wardington's name. He had been a mentor to Alger Herrick.

"There must be half a dozen of those spread around," another man said.

"You." Mike pointed at him as he spoke. "Take two cops and scout them out. Any copies you find come right back to this room before anyone cracks the cover, okay?"

Bea was calling on the remaining curators. "Think Hunt, ladies and gents. And then give me regions of the world. Japan, China, Africa, America—North and South."

"I've got a huge box that Jasper Hunt donated," a young woman said. "Erotic color prints of the Ming period. Sort of Chinese sex life from Han to Ch'ing."

"We'll take it," Bea said.

"You got pornography here?" Mike asked.

"Art, Mr. Chapman," Bea answered with a laugh. "Only the French library system has the backbone to exhibit the stuff, if that isn't true to type. The rest of us just keep it hidden. Handwritten manuscripts by the Marquis de Sade, English 'flagellation novels,' Parisian police reports about nineteenth-century brothels, and shelves full of Japanese prints and Chinese illustrations. Some of them courtesy of Jasper Hunt."

"Sounds like the Jasper Hunt who collected photographs of Alice Liddell," I said.

"The Slavic and Baltic Collection has an elephant-folio chromolithographed account of the coronation ceremonies of Alexander the Second, the Tsar Liberator," another voice chimed in, catching Bea Dutton's enthusiasm for her task.

Mike paired the young man with a cop, and they were off to search.

"We've got several editions of the Edward Curtis American Indian photographs that are in folio form in our rare-books division," a man said, standing and ready to move.

"You want Americana, Detective, we should give those a shot."

"Tell me more."

"Curtis took more than two thousand photographs of native Americans between 1907 and 1930 in an effort to document their lives. Tried to sell five hundred sets but went bankrupt before he could."

"Are they Hunt connected?"

"The set I know was donated by J. P. Morgan. That usually made Hunt try to find something as good, or more elegantly bound. I'd like to look."

"Go for it."

Mike, Bea, and I were now alone in the room with a few of the officers still waiting to be assigned to a task. I imagined the library coming alive at night, just like in Jane Eliot's stories, with curators and cops unlocking the cages and exploring the deep recesses of storage areas and stacks.

"I want you to see my thinking," Bea said, unfolding and respreading the copy of the 1507 map on one of the trestle tables. "Track these books and drawings as they report back to us.

"It's going to be a long night, guys, but maybe we can match some of these panels to the parts of the world they represent." She cleaned the lenses of her glasses on the hem of her sweater, then took a red marker from her pocket and numbered each of the map sections from one to twelve, starting in the top left corner. "Keep an eye on me, Mike. I've got some atlases to search, too."

"I'd trust you with my firstborn, Bea. Need any help?"

"Come into my cage, if you don't mind."

We walked through the room and behind the reference desk, past Bea's personal work area. She removed a key chain from her pants pocket and shuffled through the assortment until she found the one that opened the gate to a space that reminded me of safe-deposit vaults.

"These are where the oldest maps are stored," she said, weaving between chest-high rows of long metal filing cabinets with large horizontal drawers. "The loose ones, of course."

Farther back, out of sight from the front desk, was shelf after shelf of old books, all over-sized and many of them splendidly decorated.

"All the great cartographers are represented here," she said. "Mercator, Ortelius, Blaeu, Seller."

"Are you looking for something in particular?" Mike asked.

"One of my favorite map-meisters, Detective. Claudius Ptolemaeus."

"I know. I know all about Ptolemy," Mike said, looking at the shelves above Bea's head. "First guy to give us a mathematical picture of the universe. AD 150, right?"

He was quoting the information he had learned from Alger Herrick.

"You're a quick study, Mike."

His head was moving from side to side as he scanned the shelves. "The guy is everywhere. What do you want?"

"Once the printing press was invented, illustrated books of every kind became available. Ptolemy's work was translated from the Greek text into all the European languages. The Romans tried to outdo the Florentines, Strassburg's scholars thought they could color the maps more beautifully than in Ulm. Vicenza, Basel, Venice, Amsterdam—all over the continent printers were racing to get these maps in the hands of the rich and the royal. First, second, third editions. It may seem like a lot of them to you, but each volume in its own way is quite rare."

"Any of these come from Jasper Hunt's collection?" I asked.

"Sore point, Alexandra," Bea said.

"Why?"

"There it is, Mike. You mind lifting it down?" Bea had spotted the volume she wanted. "It's a Strassburg Ptolemy. 1513."

He handed her the large book, and she caressed it as she carried it to her desktop. "Contemporary Nuremberg binding of blind-stamped calf over wooden boards."

The front cover was decorated in an elaborate fleur-de-lis pattern with a leafy border, gilt flowers, and gryphons adding to its striking appearance.

"Only thirty-three copies of this work survived," Bea said. "And before the Second World War, this library owned a pair."

"The gift of Jasper Hunt?" I asked.

"At the time, yes, it was. He decided to take one of these atlases back. Long before my time, mind you, but no one here ever saw it again, though I'll bet Jill will still include it on the list of our acquistions she gives you tonight."

"Sure, rather than agitate—or challenge—any of the Hunt heirs," Mike said. "Why are you looking for this version?"

"Because it might have been exactly the kind of idea that would have amused our eccentric friend Jasper Hunt Jr.," Bea said. "Remember—no use of the word 'America' appeared in any cartography until the 1507 map. It certainly never entered into anything Ptolemaic. But with the development of the press and the incorporation of all the new explorations of the period, the Strassburg Ptolemy of 1513 was the first book to print a solo map of America. Only America. The first map devoted uniquely to this continent."

Bea was turning pages in the great volume with painstaking care as she talked.

"A fitting place for Jasper to hide the panel from our map that depicts America," Mike said.

"Yes, but I think I'm striking out," she said, separating and flattening the pages as she went.

"There is a second copy of this book though," I said. "It never surfaced again?"

"Only in rumors," Bea said. "And then from the mouth of Eddy Forbes."

"How reliable was he at gossip?"

"Almost as good as he was at stealing," she said. "In the 1940s, the deals between collectors were a lot different than they are today. With the Internet, we can all keep track of books and maps—who's got something to sell and who's in line to buy. Back then, there was much more discretion, many more one-on-one interactions, and lots of secrecy."

"What did Eddy tell you?" Mike asked.

"His story was that after the war, Jasper Hunt sold the second Strassburg atlas to Lord Wardington. He was always unhappy when the library didn't treat his bequests like they were their most important gifts of the year. He represented to the buyer, of course, that he had the title free and clear." Bea pushed the glasses to the top of her head. "It didn't take long for Wardington, who was a real gent, to learn the truth. He returned the map to Hunt at once to let him make amends with the library."

"But Hunt never did that," Mike said.

"Much to my regret," Bea said. "Now, I had this conversation well before Eddy got in trouble."

"You mean before he got caught for all the trouble he'd been causing."

"Right again, Mike." Bea closed the large book and rested her hand on its lid. "Eddy told me that when Lord Wardington returned the book to Jasper Hunt, the old boy kept it for a while—he had no intention of ever letting it collect dust in our stacks again. Eventually, he gave the book to his granddaughter, Minerva."

"What?" Mike seemed stunned.

"I'm only the messenger, Detective. That's what Eddy said, and he knew Minerva Hunt— they'd had some dealings with each other. Why wouldn't I believe him? None of this had any significance until you found that panel under the water tank yesterday. Till you told me this map—which I wasn't even certain existed— might be connected to the murder of Tina Barr."

Mike was circling the table now, punching his right fist into the palm of his left hand.

"We've got to get to Eddy Forbes, Coop. You talk to the feds on Monday," Mike said. "What else did he tell you, Bea?"

"Of course, my angle was selfish, too. I asked

about the map because I wanted to get it back from the family. Have it here, where it belonged," the librarian said. "Eddy told me that for most of her life, Minerva had kept the atlas in her father's library. She had no use for it, and no real idea of its value. Then, shortly before his arrest, Eddy Forbes reintroduced her to Alger Herrick, who offered to pay her dearly for the atlas, not withstanding its clouded provenance."

"For a reason?"

"Herrick's collection is heavy on Ptolemy," Bea said. "He's got the most important library of maps in private hands, now that Lord Wardington is gone."

"Yes, he told us about his Bologna Ptolemy," I said. "But Herrick also said Minerva dabbled in maps. Why wouldn't she have wanted to hold on to it?"

"If you ask me, you're making too much of the fact that Alger Herrick was after that book. It's much more like the rivalry between the Red Sox and the Yankees," Bea said. "Herrick's a Ptolemy guy. He's been trying to corner the market on all the great editions of that work."

"And Minerva?" I asked.

"Strictly Mercator," Bea said, handing the book back to Mike to reshelve.

"Sorry? I don't get what you mean."

"Mercator was one of the greatest sixteenth-century geographers, Alex. Mercator maps? Every schoolkid knows them."

"Sure," I said, recalling the famous images of the cylindrical projection maps, with parallels and meridians and perpendicular chartings all neatly aligned.

"Gerardus Mercator. His maps were designed for marine navigation, so that sailors could use a straight line to determine their position at sea, even without instruments."

"What's it called when sailors do that?" I asked.

Mike brushed back his hair and answered. "Dead reckoning."

Bea Dutton wagged her finger at Mike. "That's just what Eddy Forbes said about that girl. Back then, I thought he was joking. He said she was total Mercator all the way."

"What did he mean?" I asked.

"If Minerva Hunt is doing the reckoning," he used to say, "anyone who gets in the way of the straight line between her and whatever she's after, the odds are they'll be dead. That's what he meant by dead reckoning."

FORTY

By nine o'clock, curators and cops had been returning to the map division room in rolling waves, like eager kids gathering clues on a scavenger hunt.

Bea was in charge of examining each volume they found in hopes of coming across a panel of the missing map, but none of the rare books and atlases yielded any treasure. Jill Gibson sat glumly in a corner of the room, checking her master list against the items that had been retrieved, noting those that were reported to be missing from their proper places.

"I'm so hungry, I'm losing it," Mike said.

"There are some places in the neighborhood," Bea said. "We could take a walk."

"No time for that. Coop, you got enough cash for about eight pizzas to feed these guys?"

I dug into my pants pocket and handed him my money.

"We can't eat in here, Mike," Bea said. "You can lock me up before I let you get food into this room."

"Deal." He signaled to one of the rookies. "Send your partner for as many pies as this will buy. Anything but anchovies. Get me some tarps from the Crime Scene wagon. Set them up on the ground at the receiving dock."

Mike turned to Bea. "A little brisk for an al fresco picnic, but that's what I'm offering."

"Accepted."

While we waited for the takeout order, Bea continued to study the books, most of them from the Hunt Collection. I caught glimpses of the Asian sex lithographs, the Curtis photos, and several versions of Marco Polo's journals. The erotic drawings were as visually stunning as the sepia prints of Native Americans and the brilliant notations made by the great Italian traveler, but nothing she searched turned up any unexpected bonus.

Twenty-five minutes later, when our dinner arrived, Mike and I—joined again by Mercer—led our bleary-eyed soldiers out to the freight entrance and tried to get our minds off work while we ate.

"I bet you're real good at trivia," Mike said to Bea. He was sitting cross-legged on a tarp while she parked herself on one of the steps a few feet away.

"Not many topics. Why?"

"Mercer, the Coopster, and I bet on the **Final Jeopardy!** question most nights. I'm asking you to be my teammate, okay?"

"I won't be much help."

Mike was on his second slice of pepperoni and sausage. "You were taking your crazy cab ride last night, kid, so I know you didn't see the show. And Mercer was with me. Lucky that I've got TiVo and no life. Twenty bucks, everybody. Coop, I'm taking it out of your change."

"Help yourself. It would have been the first time you ever gave me change."

"The category is **Animals. Animals,** ladies and gents."

"No fair, Chapman. You know the Q and A," Mercer said.

"Double or nothing. I'll keep my mouth shut, and if Bea gets it, I'm buying dessert."

"So what's the answer?" Mercer asked.

Mike did his best Alex Trebek imitation. "The answer is . . . Oldest living animal on the planet. Oldest living animal on the planet."

"Wait a minute, Bea," I said. "I've got another idea, another possible literary hiding place for Jasper Hunt."

"Hold that thought, Coop," Mike said. "I'm looking to score."

"I give up. This is more important. Whales, elephants, rhinoceri."

"Bad sport, Blondie. Don't spoil it for the others."

Bea was wiping the crumbs from her veggie pizza off her sweater. "Tell me, Alex. What are you thinking?"

"Aw, Bea. Give me an old animal," Mike said. "In the form of a question."

"What's a snail?"

"Bad answer, Bea. You're letting me down. Mercer?"

"What's a . . . ?"

"I'll give you a hint. Coop's favorite restaurant in the world. Martha's Vineyard. The Bite."

The Quinn sisters' tiny shack by the side of the road in Chilmark served the very best chowder and fried clams I'd ever tasted. But Mike revealed the question before I could shift my train of thought from rare books to shellfish.

"What's an ocean quahaug?" Mike said. "Trebek said some researchers dredged up a four-hundred-year-old clam near Iceland this year. It's got growth rings, just like trees, so you can tell its age. Check your chowder next time. Those old quahaugs could get chewy."

He was eating his third piece of pizza, with no sign of slowing down.

I went back to the thought I had while Mike

was quizzing us. "Bea, I'm sure the library must have a good sampling of Shakespearean originals."

"Absolutely. I'm not familiar with them, but I know we have several copies of the four folios. Someone in this group will be able to tell us," she said. "And we'll find out if any have to do with Jasper Hunt. What's his connection to the Bard?"

Mike wiped his mouth. "Slip of paper on the corpse. 'The evil that men do lives after them. The good is oft interred with their bones.' "

Bea bent down to help me stack the empty boxes and collect the trash. "So why are you looking for the books?"

"Because Hunt was into pranks and tricks," I said. "Seems like it would have appealed to that eccentric part of him to hide pieces of the map in a Shakespearean folio, if that was his favorite passage. Make it hard for his greedy heirs to put them back together."

"Maybe that was the evil part of him," Bea said, straightening up. "Maybe the good—the rest of the panels to complete the map—maybe they're interred with his bones."

Mike Chapman was on his feet faster than a bolt of lightning could strike a tree.

"You're my girl, Bea. Didn't Talbot tell us

that his grandfather wanted to go out like a pharaoh, surrounded by all his worldly goods? Let's find out where Jasper Hunt was laid to rest. Let's see what's buried with his bones."

FORTY-ONE

I rang Jasper Hunt the Third's apartment, and the butler answered.

"He's asleep, madam. Do you know the hour?"

"I apologize for calling so late. I'm trying to find out where his father is buried. Would you happen to know?"

"Certainly, madam. In Millbrook, on the family estate. We shall all be in Millbrook one day, God willing."

I thanked him and hung up.

We were back in Bea's office. The helpful curators were still searching for books, with a new emphasis on volumes related to Shakespeare.

Mike was on Bea's computer. He had Googled Jasper Hunt's obituary and was reading aloud to us. "Yeah, looks like Junior and his father were laid to rest beside their wives—no mention of mistresses—and their beloved pets. The reinterment took place in the 1980s, when Jasper Three created a plot for them on the back forty of the horse farm—immediate family, servants, and still plenty of room for Patience and Fortitude. Looks like the Dutchess County society event of the season."

"Does it say why there was a reinterment?" I asked.

"Guess they had a layover someplace else, Coop. I see a road trip up the Hudson in your future," Mike said. "No mention of books, Bea."

"Bibliomaniacs have done it forever," she said. "Put their favorite books in their burial chambers with them. You're the military buff. You know the name Rush Hawkins?"

"Civil War general. Led a volunteer cavalry troop called Hawkins's Zouaves."

"Well, he built himself a mausoleum in Providence so he could be surrounded by all his books after he shuffled off his mortal coil," Bea said. "Elizabeth Rossetti, too."

"The writer's wife?" I asked.

"Yup. Dante Gabriel Rossetti placed his unpublished poems in his young bride's grave at Highgate Cemetery, along with a Bible. The poet had a change of heart a year later and reclaimed his work for publication—somewhat dampened by exposure. The vellum pages are at Harvard now. It's been done forever."

"Worth considering," I said.

"You're good at exhumations, Coop."

My only other experience like that had been the sad task of reexamining the body of a teenage girl whose original autopsy had missed the telling signs that motivated her killer.

"How long do you want to keep the staff going at this tonight?" Bea asked.

"I think most of them are about to hit a wall," I said. "Maybe we should knock off and start them fresh in the morning."

My cell phone vibrated and I reached for it to see whether it was a call I wanted to take.

"We can secure everything right here," Mike said. "We'll have a detail at this very door around the clock."

Bea grimaced. It was obvious she didn't like the idea of entrusting all these treasures to outsiders who didn't respect the integrity of each book, atlas, map, and document the way these curators did.

"I promise you, they'll be fine," I said, pressing the talk button as I recognized the number of Howard Browner, one of the senior forensic biologists at the DNA lab. "Howard? It's Alex."

"Am I catching you at a bad time?"

"Still working, Howard. You, too?"

"Yeah."

Browner—whom Mike called the Brainiac— was brilliant and dedicated to his work, one of the first experts in DNA technology who had trained many of us in this evolving science since its introduction in the criminal justice system.

Mike spun his finger in a circle, telling me to hurry the call so we could help Bea close up. I rolled my eyes at him.

"You have something for me?" I asked.

"I've been in the lab all day. Got handed this assignment late afternoon. It's kind of interesting, along the lines of what Mattie's been working on with you for the Griggs case."

"Wrap it up, Coop," Mike said.

"Thanks for thinking of me, Howard. I'm sort of tied up with Mike right now." Interesting was not what I needed at the moment. "Can it wait till Monday?"

"Sure, Alex. It's just a bench hunch."

Browner wasn't calling about a match in the databank but something his gut instinct was feeding him as he looked at profiles at his bench, as the lab workspaces were called.

"You mean a familial search?" I asked. "Is it Wesley Griggs?"

Despite Mike's prodding, I was anxious for a development that might impact Judge Moffett's decision.

"No. Nothing new on that front."

"I'll call you first thing when I get to the office, Howard. Okay? You know how Mike is. We're trying to shut down for the night."

"Understood. Just make a note to tell me if the father of one of your witnesses is still around. I'd like to get a swab from him."

"A witness in which murder case?" I asked. "Are you talking Griggs?"

Mike stood still and put his hands on his waist, staring at me as I listened to Browner.

"No, no, Alex. They've added me to the team on the Barr-Vastasi homicides. I'm working on a cigarette butt Chapman submitted."

"That's got to be the one he picked up from the floor of the squad. The smoker is a woman named Minerva Hunt," I said. "What's so interesting about it?"

"I had it right on my bench when the fax came through from London a few hours ago. I'm looking through all the profiles, and I see that the smoker and this guy, the drunk driver from England—well, they've got an allele in common at each one of thirteen loci we've tested. They match perfectly," Browner said, his normally flat delivery lifted a decibel with excitement. "I know how you like this forensic stuff, Alex."

My mind was racing to make the connection between the players. "Tell me what it means, Howard."

"I can't be certain till I get a paternal swab, but if I enjoyed betting as much as Mike does, I'd have to say I'm looking at a half brother and sister here. Same father, different mothers. Isn't that wild?"

Alger Herrick—the infant who'd been abandoned by his teenage mother on the steps of an orphanage in England—was in all likelihood the illegitimate child of Jasper Hunt III, the blood brother of Talbot and Minerva Hunt.

FORTY-TWO

"You think old Jasper ever figured that out?" Mike asked.

We had secured the map room, arranged for rides home for Bea and her colleagues, and were walking from the side door of the library to Mike's car, shortly after midnight.

"Not back in Minerva's college days, when he tried to fix her up with Herrick," I said, recalling his story. "And I've got no sense that any of them realize it now."

"This might be the most unwelcome familial search since Dick Cheney found out he's related to Barack Obama."

"The only resemblance I see is greed," Mercer said.

"The genetic Hunt predisposition you mentioned yesterday," Mike said. "Meanwhile, they're ready to rip each other's throats out over old books and maps. I say Coop charms some drool out of Jasper, we firm this up, and sit them all down for a reality check."

"Chapman!" a woman's voice called from half a block away.

We all stopped and turned, and saw Teresa Retlin, a detective from the burglary squad, jogging after us.

"Don't you answer your phone? Your voice mail box is full," she said. "I'm too old to be chasing you down in the middle of the night."

"Didn't stop you ten years ago, Terry. I think the phone's out of juice," Mike said. "And so am I. What's up?"

He pivoted and moved forward while Retlin tried to keep pace.

"Got a baby snitch for you."

"For me? What's he snitching about?"

"Name is Shalik Samson. Says you want what he's got."

The three of us stopped short to listen to Terry Retlin.

"That twelve-year-old?"

"Fourteen," she said. "Just small for his age. Neighbor saw him breaking in to the back window of an apartment an hour ago and called 911. The kid starting throwing your name around before I could cuff him."

"Where is he now?" Mike asked.

"In my care, Chapman. I have to take him to a juvenile facility till Monday morning," she said, handing Mike a business card. "Says he found this in the garbage. That you gave your

card to a guy named Travis Forbes—the vic in
my burglary—and Forbes threw it out."

Mike laughed and shook his head from side
to side. "Piece of work. Where's your car?"

"My partner's over there," she said pointing
across Fortieth Street.

Mercer and I followed Mike to the parked
RMP. "Shalik, my man," Mike said, bracing
himself against the roof of the car and leaning
down to talk to the boy. "What brings you to
the library tonight?"

"I got locked up for helping you, Detective.
You give me twenty bucks and I'll tell you."

"You got that wrong, Shalik. I don't pay guys
to break the law."

"I got you into that building, didn't I? You
paid me yesterday."

"Tell it to the judge, Shalik. We're outta
here," Mike said, tapping the car. "Take him
away, Terry."

"No! Mr. Mike!" Shalik shouted.

"What's on your mind? It's getting too late
for nonsense."

"I was going in there tonight for you, Mr.
Mike. Tell you what he up to," Shalik said.
"Find out why he all dressed up like a cop."

"What? Let him out of the car, Terry," Mike
said, as Mercer stepped up to open the door

and stand beside the skinny kid to make sure he didn't try to run. "Tell me about that, Shalik."

The boy knew he had the attention of all the grown-ups. His jeans drooped so low, they barely covered his rear end; the pant legs crumpled on top of his sneakers. He pushed them even lower when he shoved his hands in his pockets as he considered what to say to us.

"You talk to the judge for me? It's my third time."

"I'll sing to the judge, Shalik. You tell me about Travis."

"I seen him before in all these different clothes," he said. "Dressin' stupid and stuff sometimes when he go out. But he always go out alone. And I never seen him in no police officer's uniform. He ain't no cop."

I thought of Tina Barr's attacker and the fireman's gear. I remembered the man in a brown uniform who had broken in to Jane Eliot's apartment.

"Travis Forbes's coatrack, Mike," I said. "All those jackets that were hanging in the hallway, remember? I'll get a warrant to see what kind of stuff he's got there."

"You know real cops, Shalik," Mercer said. "Did his uniform look real?"

"It do. It really do. Had a hat, too, and a shiny silver badge."

"Did he see you?" Mike asked. "Or did he just keep on walking down the street?"

Shalik's chest puffed up. "He didn't walk nowhere."

"What did he do?"

"He had a chauffeur, Mr. Mike. Big fat guy gets out of a limousine and opens the door for him. Travis, he like got in the back with his date."

"His date?" Mike said. "You're doing real good for me, Shalik. Tell me, did you see the woman?"

"Dark-haired lady. Skinny. Skinnier than her," he said, tipping his elbow toward me. "Older than her, too. Long red fingernails. Smoking a cigarette."

Travis Forbes dressed himself like an NYPD cop for a night on the town with Minerva Hunt. Now all we had to do was figure out where Carmine Rizzali had driven them.

FORTY-THREE

Mercer had his arm around Shalik's shoulder, trying to cut him a deal.

"We're taking him from here, Terry," Mike said.

"I could lose my shield for this, anything happens to the kid. Rules are different for juvies."

"I'll stay with him," I said. "I'll go to the judge myself."

She walked back to her car, got inside, and slammed the door, while Mike and I followed Mercer and Shalik down the dark side street until we hit Fifth Avenue and went around the block.

"How are we going to raise the fat bastard?" Mike asked. "Yesterday he wouldn't even take my call."

"Let Alex do the talking. He won't blow her off so fast," Mercer said.

"You'd better script it for me."

"Tell him you've got something urgent to discuss with Minerva," Mike said. "He must have driven her to Jane Eliot's apartment. Let him know the old lady's talking about what she gave to Minerva. He'll want to collect on that tidbit. Makes him look useful. Eliot's safe, isn't she, Mercer?"

"Cops are with her in the hospital room. Not a problem."

"If TARU can find his cell phone pings, we're in business," Mike said, as he and I got into the front seat of the car. The Technical Assistance Response Unit had the latest gadgetry and technology to solve almost every communication and surveillance problem investigators needed.

"Who's this? Hey, Sonny—Mike Chapman here. I got two known numbers; one's going to place a call to the other. The caller's in the car with me, midtown. If I give you both, can you pinpoint the other guy's location for me?"

The answer was short and obviously positive.

"Ready for me? First one is Assistant District Attorney Alexandra Cooper," Mike said, dictating my number. "The receiver is Carmine Rizzali. Yeah, used to be on the job. I need to find him pronto. The nearest cell phone tower would be great. Coop'll dial him to see if he picks up. I'll stay on with you."

I punched Carmine's number into my key pad. My caller ID would be blocked, so he'd have to answer in order to know who was calling at this late hour.

One ring and Carmine spoke into the phone. "Hullo?"

"Carmine? It's Alex Cooper. I met you with Mike—"

"Is this more of his bullshit?"

"No, no. This is something urgent that I'm trying to speak to Ms. Hunt about, just between the two of us. I think Mike's on his way to her home now—"

"What is he, nuts? It's the middle of a Saturday night. She ain't even there."

"Look, there's a woman who lives in the Village, on Bedford Street. She's made a complaint that Minerva Hunt stole something from her. I . . . uh . . . I—" I held my hand out, palm upward, trying to figure a direction to go.

Mike just nodded at me and mouthed the words **You're doing fine.**

"She didn't steal nothing. I drove her there myself. The lady had a present for her. All very civilized."

"I think Mike's blowing this totally out of proportion," I said. "I disagree with him completely. I thought you might want to give her a heads-up, and maybe I can set up a meeting with her tomorrow."

He wasn't ready to trust me.

"Is Minerva with you now?"

"Cute, Ms. Cooper. Real cute. Then you tell

the homicide dick whatever I tell you, so I'm just the schmuck who's out of a job."

He disconnected me the second he finished the sentence.

"Sonny? You got a location for me?" Mike asked. "Thanks, buddy. I owe you big-time."

He dropped the phone on the seat and started the engine, making the turn from Forty-second Street onto Fifth Avenue.

"You did good, Blondie. It seems that Carmine took the odd couple downtown—Second Avenue, between Second and Third streets. Nearest cell tower is in front of Provenzano's, a funeral home."

"A little late for a condolence call, isn't it?" Mercer said.

Traffic moved well on the straight run south to the point at which Broadway intersected Fifth Avenue, then Mike wound his way farther east.

As we crossed Third Street, I could see the limousine parked on the west side of Second Avenue.

Mike pulled over to the curb, several cars behind Carmine, and turned off the engine and headlights. "What do you think, Mercer? Him sitting in the limo all these hours, don't you think all that weight would have flattened one of his tires by now?"

"I could do that," our young charge said.

"You stay with me, Shalik."

"C'mon, Coop," Mike said. "Let's all have a look around."

As we got out, Mike walked ahead and peered into the window of Carmine's car. Then he kneeled down. I tried to keep Shalik occupied while Mike scored one of the tires with his Swiss Army knife.

"I don't think he should eat such heavy meals at night," Mike said, coming back to get us. "He's sleeping like a baby. Least they can't make such a quick getaway if Minerva and Travis aren't happy to see us."

Mercer was on the sidewalk, checking out the block on either side of the avenue. "There's a pizza joint, a Thai restaurant, and a neighborhood pub. We can look in each of those."

He kept one arm on Shalik's shoulder, and I walked on the other side of the kid, closer to the buildings. We watched as Mike tried the front door of the funeral home, but it was locked and all the lights were out.

We passed an alleyway fronted by a wrought-iron gate, and kept going. The night was clear and getting cooler. Mike went into each of the open restaurants and bars on both sides of the street but didn't spot Hunt or Forbes in any of them.

"Go another block north," Mercer said. Mike did, while I tried to find out from Shalik whether he had gotten inside Travis Forbes's apartment before getting caught.

By the time Mike doubled back, the kid had described how the cops had arrived and nabbed him just after he'd jimmied the back door and wriggled in.

"No trace of them," Mike said. "Time to interrupt Carmine's dream cycle and have a chat. Worst he can do is call and alert them that we're here to break up the party."

We turned around and started walking back toward the limousine.

The light from the street lamp bounced off the gold paint on the narrow archway above the wrought-iron fence that closed off the alley to my left.

I read the words on the large sign, first to myself and then aloud: NEW YORK MARBLE CEMETERY. INCORPORATED IN 1831.

Below them was a smaller tablet, also engraved. I held on to one of the bars of the fence as I read again: A PLACE OF INTERMENT FOR GENTLEMEN.

"Gents like Jasper Hunt Jr. and his cronies," Mike said. "Get the kid in the car, Coop. I'm going in."

FORTY-FOUR

→

"Stay here, Alex," Mercer said. "I don't know how Mike thinks he's going to get past this gate."

Shalik Samson grabbed two of the vertical iron bars with his hands and tried to shake them. "You put me on your shoulders," he said to Mercer, "I could be over that easy."

"Getting you out might be the problem. Let go of those."

Traffic was light on this part of the avenue, and there were no pedestrians to bother us.

"You think somebody inside?" Shalik asked, craning his neck to look up at Mercer. "It look like a little park in there."

Mike was studying the lock, which was a single keyhole. There was no sophisticated equipment in place to protect the entrance, which seemed well groomed and tended.

"Pretty clever. If you're going to break in to someplace right on the street," he said, "dress Travis Forbes up like a cop to give you cover."

Shalik was back against the bars, standing on

the sharply pointed pieces that jutted up from the base of the heavy gate.

"Cut it out, Shalik. You'll hurt yourself," Mike said. "Coop, I told you to put him in the car."

"Yo, look! It ain't even locked no more."

The teenager had reached his slim arm between the bars and retrieved a metal rod that must have temporarily held the bars in place. Someone had indeed broken in to the old cemetery, and in all likelihood was still somewhere inside.

Shalik pushed on the right side of the gate, and it creaked open against his weight. Before I could stop him, he ran ahead down the alleyway, which was bordered on both sides by brick walls.

Mercer gave chase and overtook him twenty feet away, where the passage opened onto a large grassy area, almost the length of a football field but half as wide. He put his hand up to his lips and told the boy to be quiet.

I closed the gate behind me and caught up with Mike, who had stopped to read a plaque on the wall.

"What does it say?" I asked as he turned away and headed toward Mercer.

"The oldest nonsectarian cemetery in the city. A hundred and fifty solid marble vaults," he said, breaking into a trot. "All of them were built underground as a health precaution against nineteenth-century contagious disease."

We were suddenly in a gardened oasis in the middle of the East Village that I had never known existed.

The tall walls around the open green space seemed to be made completely of stone, many parts obscured by the bushes and trees that had grown up around the borders.

Mercer was deputizing Shalik, trying to extract a promise from him to stay close and obey directions.

Mike jogged along the perimeter of the north wall, stopping at smooth marble tablets to note names of the occupants of the subterranean vaults. I was just a few steps behind him.

"Charles Van Zandt. Uriah Scribner. James Tallmadge," Mike said, stopping to run his hand over the names, one above the other, as he read them from the engravings.

Ten feet farther along, another tablet, with numbers I assumed corresponded to the graves below. Some listed three or four vaults, though only one or two individuals' names had been added to the list of the dead.

There were Auchinclosses and Randolphs, Phelpses and Quackenbushes, grand names that together created a history of New York City. I paused at the marker for the infant son of Frederick Law Olmsted, the man who had landscaped Central Park.

Mike crossed to the south wall and continued his search. Before he had moved very far along, he signaled me to join him.

"Here they are, kid. Jasper Hunt. Jasper Hunt Jr.," he said, showing me the names of father and son, and their wives, the first dates for the family patriarch etched in the wall more than a century ago. "Four Hunts, six burial vaults."

Beneath the neatly carved names and dates were the numbers: 61, 62, 63, 64, 65, 66.

"They were obviously buried here originally, before the reinterment," I said.

"And Minerva must know what's in Millbrook—and what isn't. She'd certainly have access to the family digs up on the property."

"So maybe when they moved the bodies, nobody gave any thought to whether there was anything in these other two vaults they owned—whether any books were interred with the Hunt bones. There was certainly no record of other descendants on this plaque."

"Wait here with Mercer," Mike said.

"What are you going to do?"

"There's got to be a way to get below to the vaults."

"Mike, let's get help."

"And if something bad's going on right now? You going to live with yourself if somebody's down there, left for dead?"

Mercer was motioning to Mike. "Check out that corner."

The dim light filtering in from the street and wind blowing the bushes played tricks with my vision. It looked like Mercer was right—that there was a hatch open in the southwest end of the enclosed area, a wooden door of some sort, against the far wall of the garden.

Mike sprinted forward and I followed, practically slamming into him when he stopped short just ten feet from the spot.

He was fixed on something on the ground.

I knelt beside him and saw the body of a man—short, overweight, middle-aged—slumped beneath a small evergreen bush, his feet protruding into the pathway from beneath the branches.

FORTY-FIVE

"He's alive," Mike said.

I looked up to see Mercer and Shalik standing over us. Mike was already dialing 911 to ask for an ambulance and backup.

"Move the kid, Mercer. Get him out of here."

There was something white on the ground, next to the man's head. It was a handkerchief, and when I picked it up—ignoring all crime scene protocol—it reeked of sickly sweet chloroform.

I told Mike and stuffed the cloth in my pants pocket, then reached for the card in the man's outstretched hand. It identified him as a caretaker of the New York Marble Cemetery.

"Figures," Mike said. "They'd need a guide to find the old Hunt property. Also useful for Travis Forbes, the chloroform kid, to be in a cop's uniform to get close enough to knock the guy out, probably before Minerva stepped out of the car."

Mercer was on the ground, trying to do CPR on the fallen man before the medics arrived. He took a pen-size LCD flashlight from his pocket and passed it to Mike, who was on his way toward the opening. I hurried after him.

"You're not gonna like this, Coop. I'll go alone."

We had been in claustrophobic situations often enough for Mike and Mercer to know they were a problem for me. But I couldn't imagine letting Mike, who had covered my back more times than I could count, go down without a partner.

He took his blazer off and threw it on the ground, unholstering his gun as he put his hand on the top of the hatch.

Mike started down into the entrance shaft of the burial space and cleared the short staircase. I listened for voices, but heard none.

I put my foot on the top step and, afraid to lose the light that Mike was leading with, hurried down ten more until I touched the earthen floor.

I stood up straight and looked around the grim necropolis. On either side of me were narrow passageways that led between enormous stone vaults. Long slate shelves supported some of the coffins, mostly made of stone, which were stacked on top of one another.

I stayed as close to Mike as I could get while he moved the light over the dirt, then up and down among the coffins, looking for names of the dead and numbers of their vaults.

We had passed the forties, seen the markers

for Deys and Cruikshanks, Wetmores and Wheelocks—adults and far too many infants, typical of the mortality rates of that century.

As we came to the intersection that marked the divide between the vaults numbered in the fifties from those in the sixties, Mike's flashlight framed a woman's face.

Minerva Hunt was seated on the ground, her hands tied behind her with a length of rope. A silk scarf—probably her own—served as a gag between her teeth, wrapped around the back of her head.

Next to her, Travis Forbes was holding a taxidermist's skife—the sharp tool designed to skin dead animals.

"Forget it, Forbes," Mike said.

"No, you forget it." He pressed the edge of the blade to Minerva's slender neck and the first drops of blood spurted out. "I can end it for her much faster than you can shoot."

"I have no doubt you can. I've seen your work."

I could picture the deep, gaping wound in Tina Barr's neck.

Minerva Hunt's eyes were opened wide with fear, flitting between Travis Forbes's hand and something behind me.

I turned to look but saw only the massive outlines of stone caskets and slate shelves.

Travis pulled at Minerva's arm to get her to her feet. "Give me the gun, Detective, or I'll cut her throat."

"Did you get what you wanted?" Mike asked. "Can't kill her before she lays the golden egg, can you?"

Again Minerva Hunt's eyes darted from Forbes to the staircase through which we had entered. I glanced back, hoping to see Mercer and the cops he had summoned, but no one was there.

"Make yourselves comfortable, Mr. Chapman," Forbes said, positioning the terrified woman between himself and Mike. If Mike had considered firing his gun at Forbes, he had missed his brief opportunity.

"Ms. Hunt and I have to go," Forbes said, pushing Minerva to take baby steps forward. "We haven't finished our conversation. Pick yourself out a slab and get some rest while we find a less crowded place to talk."

Minerva looked to the staircase again, then jerked back her head, just as I heard the hatch crash to a close.

This time, Mike flashed his light in that direction. Against the blackness of the wall, it caught Alger Herrick's shiny chrome hook.

FORTY-SIX

"There's a shaft at the other end, Forbes," Alger Herrick said, coming down the steps. "You've got to take her that way. There's another detective outside here."

Forbes was focused on Mike's gun. He tried to move Minerva around and drag her away from where we stood. Strapped to him was a backpack, open at the top, which appeared to have a large book—the size of a double folio—sticking out of it.

"Hurry, Forbes."

"I want his gun."

"We can do better than that," Herrick said, coming up directly behind me. "We'll take his girl."

Mike pointed his pistol at Herrick, but it was too late. The man was upon me, the cold steel of his prosthesis gripping my forearm.

"Let go of me. I'll walk," I said, trying to shake myself loose.

He held me tight, angling so that I was always between him and Mike, and led me around the central burial chambers to an earthen path parallel to the one on which Mike stood, inches away from Minerva Hunt and Travis Forbes.

"Shoot, Mike!" I yelled. "Shoot Forbes."

The stark confines of this dungeonlike underground chamber smelled of death.

Forbes responded with a laugh, a loud, guttural laugh. What was Mercer doing up above that he couldn't hear us? Probably helping to load the injured man into an ambulance.

Hunt tried to speak—or maybe she was crying. All that emerged from behind the gag was a muffled noise.

Herrick turned the corner, and for the first time I could see that the fieldstone cap had been removed from vault 65, marked with the name Jasper Hunt II. Books were strewn about, no doubt the result of this unusual break-in undertaken by Herrick and Forbes. The old eccentric had in fact gone to his grave—the first time—with some of his beloved treasures.

Minerva Hunt had played right into their hands, trusting Travis Forbes to help her search for the missing panels of the great map. She'd fallen prey to the same double cross that had proven lethal to Tina Barr.

"In fact, Detective, why don't you come over here?" Herrick said, pushing me faster, understanding the urgency with which he had to escape before more police arrived. "There's a vacancy. Several of them, to be honest."

Mike wasn't giving up his gun, and Herrick seemed confident he wouldn't find a way to use it, with both Minerva and me serving as human shields.

"Drag her, if you can't pick her up," Herrick shouted to Forbes. "If he kills her, just run. Let's get out of here with what we have."

Herrick was ready to sacrifice Minerva Hunt, confident perhaps that she had nothing more of value to give to him.

"Minerva is your **sister**," I screamed as loud as I could. "Let her be, dammit. She's your blood sister."

Alger Herrick froze at my words, reflexively tightening his grip on my arm. I winced at the pain, but knew I had shocked him.

"**Her** father is **your** father," I said, listening as he took deep breaths, startled by the information. His chest heaved against my back. "You're a Hunt, too. We've got the DNA to prove it."

Mike steadied his gun with both hands, aiming at the spot where Forbes was moving with Minerva. "You're entitled to the damn map. You didn't have to kill to get it."

This was no time to correct Mike on the fine points of the law. I didn't think Alger Herrick would expect to go to court now to collect on the Hunt fortune.

"I never murdered anyone, you fool," Herrick said. "**He** did. He's your killer."

Herrick pulled at me again, moving me farther into the darkness, farther away from Mike.

Now I could hear pounding from the direction of the entrance shaft. Mercer and the backup team must be trying to get to us, but Herrick had found a way to secure the hatch from within.

"I'll give you three seconds to let Minerva go," Mike said, moving in toward Travis Forbes and his hostage. "Kill her, and you die, too."

Alger Herrick heard the commotion. "Drop her, Forbes. Run as fast as you can go to the other end. There's a staircase just like the one we came in. Beat them out of here with the book—they'll think you're an officer, too. You'll walk right through them."

Forbes's fake—or stolen—uniform might serve him well in the confusing mix of cops responding to a call for help. I didn't care if it did. I didn't care about the missing panels of the rare map and whether they were lost forever. I wanted to get out of this hellhole, with Mike, alive.

Travis Forbes was beginning to fidget like a caged animal. Herrick would give him up as

Tina and Karla's killer, claiming not to have known his young accomplice was going to use violence. It would make no difference to a jury, but Herrick must have thought it would save his neck.

Mike was gaining on him. "You wanna cut somebody? Cut yourself, Forbes. Slice your own throat."

Over my shoulder, I thought I saw a sliver of light in the farthest remove of the room. I looked again down the dirt corridor of death, but all was darkness.

Had there been movement, or was my mind frozen with fright? It was getting harder to breathe in the dank, airless space. I knew there was a chance that none of us would make it out alive.

Suddenly, I heard a loud grunt from Travis Forbes. He lifted Minerva Hunt off the ground and threw her at Mike. She couldn't even brace herself for the fall, her hands still bound behind her.

It looked like Mike's gun—the glint of silver flashing against the black backdrop—fell to the ground as he tried unsuccessfully to catch Minerva. He was knocked backward by the impact of her body against his own.

Forbes was running in the direction Herrick had sent him, unburdened by his captive. And

Alger Herrick was moving faster, too, pulling me with him, while Mike tried to extricate himself from beneath Minerva Hunt.

I was coughing now as dust particles from the ground scuffed up by the skirmish seemed to choke my airway. My own sense of panic made it harder for me to regain control.

"Forbes," Herrick yelled out. "Are you there?"

I could still hear his footsteps running away from us. I reached in my pocket for a handkerchief to cover my mouth.

The first thing I touched was the heavy piece of cotton cloth, the one that had been doused with chloroform to knock out the cemetery guide.

"Stop!" I said, pleading with Alger Herrick. "I can't breathe."

His good hand, the right one, smacked the side of my head so hard that I saw stars. "I need you with me. Just keep moving."

"I'll be back for you. You'll do fine," I heard Mike say to Minerva.

He must have gotten to his feet and retrieved his gun. He'd be coming after us.

Just then I heard a thud from the direction in which Travis Forbes had run.

"Forbes?" Herrick shouted again. "Have you found the steps, man?"

There was no answer.

Herrick seemed distracted by the silence. I thought—and maybe he did, too—that Forbes had reached the exit and dropped the lid on us after he escaped.

I pulled my arm from Herrick's viselike grip, but he yanked me back, face-to-face. I swung my free hand up from my side, covering his nose with the chloroform-soaked cloth, using my height to my advantage.

The silver hook released its hold as Herrick tried to swat me away. I pressed the rag to him again, not knowing whether there was enough of the gas on it to overwhelm him.

He swiped at my neck with the hook, and I stepped back. He must have scored a cut. I felt a trickle of blood seeping behind my ear.

"Get down, Coop," Mike said, rushing out of the dark.

Before Mike could reach me, Alger Herrick fell to his knees.

I didn't know if chloroform had done its job, or if he was brought down by Shalik Samson, who cracked him on the back of his legs with a baseball bat.

FORTY-SEVEN

→

The night watchman at the Provenzano funeral home had opened it up for the chief of detectives while he was waiting for us to be led out of the cavernous burial ground.

Mercer brought me inside the large parlor, decorated for old-fashioned comfort—sofas and armchairs of burgundy silk, with antimacassars—meant to soothe grieving relatives. It wasn't where I wanted to be right now, but I had no choice in the matter.

Detectives and uniformed cops, huddling in small groups to gossip about the case now that the emergency had passed, moved out of the way as I walked through the room.

I lowered myself onto one of the sofas and rested my head against the pillow.

The watchman was telling some of the officers about the old cemetery. "I bet you didn't even know it was here, did you? We get asked about it all the time," he said. "It was because of the terrible contagion in Manhattan back then—yellow fever, tuberculosis, scarlet fever. The city banned aboveground graves, so these

rich guys decided to excavate this block and
build marble vaults ten feet under. Regular
plague pits, they must have been."

I shivered, wrapping a blanket around myself as I waited for Lieutenant Peterson to clear
the room.

I saw a couple of the guys who were leaving
make way for Shalik Samson. Mercer brought
him over to me to say good night.

"You saved us, you know," I said to him,
mustering a smile.

"You gonna say that to the judge?"

"Of course I will, if you tell me how you
did it."

"Mercer was helping that sick man, you
know? He made me go wake up the chauffeur
'cause the amb'lance took so long. Carmine—
that guy? He had a baseball bat in the car.
Guess he thought I was gonna rob him. Mercer
was like gonna shoot him if he didn't drop the
damn thing."

"How'd you get down into the burial vault?"

"That way you went in got locked, you
know," Shalik said. It happened when Alger
Herrick dropped the lid. "Me and Mercer, we
just went around the whole garden, all along
that crumbly stone wall, looking for another
entrance. Had to be, he kept telling me.

Couldn't have just one way in or out for all those bodies."

"And you found it," I said.

"Back behind a tree. Mercer didn't fit, but I did."

I hadn't been wrong. That sliver of light I thought I saw had been Shalik opening the lid of the second hatch.

"So you tripped the guy with the backpack?"

"Dude didn't even see me. That dungeon's as black as I am."

"What do you think, Mercer? Gold shield?" I asked.

"First, we're taking him home. I'm not ready to give Shalik any commendations yet, but we'll get those charges thrown out."

The kid high-fived me, and Mercer handed him off to the cops who were going to drive him home.

Mike came into the room a minute later. He had cleaned himself up, and brought some hydrogen peroxide and a bandage to cover the cut on my neck.

"You know the river Styx, Loo? Greek mythology?" Mike asked as he leaned over me, dabbing the small wound before he dressed it. "The river of hate, it was called. An old guy named Charon ferries the dead across the river to the underworld. I swear, Coop and me—we were on that ferry tonight."

"I don't care if the whole magilla is made of marble or papier-mâché," Peterson said. "Couldn't get me down in there for all the money in the world. Are you telling me, Alex, that Alger Herrick is the half brother of Minerva and Talbot Hunt?"

"The lab is hot on this new familial search technology. Howard Browner says he can prove it with a sample from the father."

"Think of it, Loo," Mike said. "Jasper the Third spent a lot of time in England, liked the ladies—young ones—as much as he liked his books. Herrick's mother was a single girl who deposited him in an orphanage. Alex thinks Hunt's father might even have paid to steer the infant to a good home. Placed him so well, they wound up with the same friends."

Mercer sat down beside me and held my hand. "You want us to put this together for you?" he asked the lieutenant.

"It's all about the map, isn't it? The rarest map in the world?"

"Seems to be."

The backpack that Travis Forbes had been wearing when Shalik brought him down with the first blow of the bat was on a table next to me.

While Mercer talked, Mike removed the large folio from the bag. It was a volume of the Napoleonic expedition to Egypt—the atlas of the world—the same book in which the Grimaldis had concealed the panels for centuries.

All conversation ceased as Mike lifted the cover. There were four folded sheets of paper, which he slowly and carefully opened before us.

"The four corners of the earth," he said. "Magnificent, Coop. Aren't they?"

We all leaned in to look. The three of us had seen a fake earlier in the day, and a real one in the library, under Bea's tutelage. Experts would confirm it for us, but everything about these papers looked authentic.

The first one, the top left section of the entire map, represented the North American continent, with exquisite drawings of Zephir and Chor—the wind and the sea—surrounding the land.

The second piece, from the top right position, was Cathay and Japan, mapped with more detail than the previous segment, since they had actually been described as a result of Marco Polo's thirteenth-century journeys.

Mike opened the third of the large pages that would form the bottom right corner. Below the Spice Islands of Indonesia was the legend written by the mapmaker, attributing the name of America to Vespucci.

The bottom panel, to the west, documented the extension of the new land—the South American continent—that Vespucci had explored as far down as the River Plata. The word **America** showed up for the first time, south of what is now Brazil.

"You're looking at history, Loo. Not many people beside the Hunts even knew this baby existed, and as time went by, scholars began to think it was a myth."

"How'd the Barr girl get mixed up in all this?" Peterson said, an unlit cigarette dangling from his mouth.

"Eddy Forbes, the map thief, he seems to have been the driving force keeping the legend of this treasure alive. First he tried to get Minerva to back him in finding the panels. You'll have to ask her, but I don't think she believed him until Jane Eliot called her a few months back to give her a gift—a book she didn't want, which happened to have a piece of the map inside," I said. "I'd guess it was Eddy Forbes who educated Minerva about the Strassburg Ptolemy, and the panel inside it. That's the book that Grandpa Hunt reclaimed from the library during the war."

"Eddy had a romance with Tina Barr at one time," Mike said. "Once you interrogate him, check their phone records. I bet you'll find they were still in touch. He may be a convicted felon, but he's still a scholar. I'm sure he did all his research on the Hunts. He probably set Tina up with Minerva, suggested that she move into the apartment. That would have enabled him to steal the panel right out from underneath her nose."

"Using Tina," Peterson said, "like Eddy Forbes seems to have used everyone else over the years—librarians, curators, trustees. So why the gas mask? Do you think that Billy Schultz had anything to do with all this?"

"Nothing at all. I'd bet it's just what he claimed," Mercer said. "The guy did the right thing and called the police after Tina was attacked. He probably was just stupid enough to pick up the gas mask and try it on."

"Will you have someone call the lab in the morning?" I asked, rubbing my forehead to ease the tension headache that was building up. "Run that mixed sample against Travis Forbes."

Peterson stood up and rested his elbow on the mantel over the fireplace with the faux logs. "Why'd Travis go in with a mask? Did Tina know him?"

"He told us she didn't," I said. "But Travis apparently looks so much like his brother, Eddy, he was afraid she'd make him."

"Why was he there?" the lieutenant asked again.

The three of us—Mike, Mercer, and I—had lots of time to work through these answers. Now we were only making educated guesses.

"Because the double cross was already under way," I said. "Tina had quit her job with the Hunts and was working for Alger Herrick. Is he talking?"

"Not yet," Peterson said. "Your boss has Pat McKinney at the station house doing the questioning."

I closed my eyes and groaned.

"Get her some pain relievers and a scotch," Mike said.

"I hope that jackass remembers to separate Herrick and Forbes." I was joking with Mike, trying to regain my sea legs, but it would be like McKinney to screw up the most basic rules in his rush to get back in the case.

"Don't be such a control freak," Mike said to me, walking over to a uniformed cop and handing him some bills. "There's a pub on the corner of Third Street. Fill a plastic cup with Dewar's and don't spill any of it running back. Coop's indicted guys for less than that."

"This was the once-in-a-lifetime score, Loo," Mercer said. "Herrick wanted to put this map together to cap his collection, no matter what it cost him."

"And Forbes?" Peterson asked.

"For him, it was his last great scam. Lead these greedy fools like the pied piper, and his endgame, with his brother's help, was to wind up with this masterpiece for himself," Mike said. "Sell it to the highest bidder—twenty, maybe thirty million."

"For this, Tina Barr had to die?" the lieutenant said.

"She must have panicked when Travis showed up in the library, just a night after she'd been attacked," Mike said.

"Tina walked away from the emergency room because she knew this was all tied into the stolen books and maps," I said. "She wasn't giving up a thing that would lead us in that direction, even if she didn't know exactly who Travis was the first time she encountered him."

"But she probably recognized him when he came into the conservation lab in the library," Mike said. "And in her own devious little mind, began to put the pieces together. Realized she was in way over her head, playing with the bad guys."

"Too late to help herself," I added, thinking

of what Jill Gibson had first told Battaglia. "That's why some of the people in the library thought she was a thief. She really had been in bed with Eddy Forbes."

"That's why Travis killed Tina with one of her own tools," Mercer said. "He didn't go to the library meaning to do it. He was probably looking for the key that opened the compartment in the basement. Maybe Eddy sent him to get the job done right the second time. The key might have dropped out of her clothing when he was carrying her through the stacks, after she was dead, without his knowing it. I doubt the murder was premeditated—just a flare-up about the missing goods that ended with him slitting her throat."

"That's what Travis Forbes does," Mercer said. "He cuts. He mutilates. She couldn't have known that."

"Then he dumped Barr's body the next night. Probably called Herrick when he took off for his night job at the pub," Mike said. "Must have been Herrick who watched us bag the body. He's the one who called Tina's cell phone—and laughed."

That would chill the jurors as much as it had sickened me.

"It's the housekeeper who gets lost in all this," I said. "Karla Vastasi."

"That has to be Minerva's doing," Mike said. "She in the hospital, Loo?"

"Yeah."

"Let me at her when she's ready to squeal. Minerva had Karla dressed up as her double, carrying a forged copy of one of the panels in her tote. Travis had never met Minerva—wouldn't know her if he fell over her," Mike said.

"My money's on Eddy Forbes," I said.

"I read you. You think Eddy was waiting in Barr's apartment with Travis that afternoon. **He** knew the lady in black wasn't Minerva and realized the panel she was carrying was a fake. Queered the whole deal."

"Karla saw that Tina had left behind another treasure when she moved out—the jewel-encrusted psalm book," I said. "The one Tina stole from Talbot's bedroom. So Karla tried to take it to her mistress, clutched on to it with what turned out to be her life. One of the Forbes boys caught her and went ballistic. Whacked her over the head with the garden ornament."

The pieces were coming together as nicely as the panels of the great world map of 1507.

"You better get some sleep, Alex," the lieutenant said. "Battaglia wants all of us in his office at ten o'clock."

"Don't stretch out here," Mike said, sweeping his arm along the back of the old sofa. "You stay still for very long, they'll find a box that fits."

"Make me a better offer," I said as Mercer helped me to my feet.

"That cemetery had me craving some fresh air. Feel like walking up the avenue to the pub? I could use a drink out of a real glass."

I thanked the rookie who'd returned with the plastic cup of scotch. "Give that one to the lieutenant. I've got a date."

Out on the sidewalk in front of Provenzano's funeral home, I looped arms with Mike and Mercer. I took several deep breaths of the cool October air, steadied myself between my friends—fortitude and patience—and headed off into the night for a bracing bit of cheer as our manhunt ended.

FORTY-EIGHT

"That's no way to spend a Saturday night," Luc said exactly a week later, when he returned from his trip. "I can't let you sit in front of a television set eating popcorn with this great wine."

"It's a whole lot better than the way I spent the last one. Besides, if you tell me you don't want to watch my Yankees play a World Series game, we've got a real deal breaker here."

We had flown up to the Vineyard that morning, after all the drama of the past week had played out in court.

Travis Forbes had been charged with the murders of Tina Barr and Karla Vastasi. His brother, Eddy, was indicted, too, for acting in concert with Travis on the Vastasi killing—proved by cell phone records and credit card receipts for gas and food.

Travis had rolled over on Alger Herrick and implicated him in the deadly plot to find the twelve panels of the priceless map, though Battaglia hadn't needed to promise any leniency. The detectives had continued to build a rock-solid case against the Englishman, who was indeed the illegitimate son of Jasper Hunt III.

Luc and I had walked down the path from my Chilmark home to watch the sun set, sipping a glass of chilled Corton-Charlemagne that he had brought with him. We had made love in the afternoon, slowly and without any distractions this time, and I was dressed in one of his shirts as I lay back in the sand, wiggling my toes in the cool water of Menemsha Pond.

Luc had driven to the store while I napped fitfully, still not able to get images of this case out of my head.

"Everything at Larsen's Fish Market looked **merveilleuse,** darling. I decided on those sweet little bay scallops," he said.

"I adore them."

"Lemon, garlic, fettucine."

I looked at him and cocked an eye. "How do you eat food like that at a ball game?"

I heard Mike's voice in the back of my head ordering a hot dog and a cold beer.

"Trust me. It will be better than anything you get at the stadium."

"For starters?"

Luc stood up and dug his toes into the sand as the gentle waves receded. "Clams. Fresh ones."

"Let me help."

I sat up and we scratched below the surface until we filled a towel with a dozen quahaugs.

"That lady at the library, the one you really liked," Luc said, sitting beside me as a bright red ball of sunlight started to slip down behind the hills of Aquinnah.

"Bea?"

"So she was right about the places that the eccentric Mr. Hunt hid the panels of the map."

"She was dead on," I said.

"You think they will ever find the entire thing?" Luc asked.

"So far we're more than halfway there. Four that Hunt tried to take to the great hereafter with him, the one that Jane Eliot gave to Minerva, the other that Minerva had all along—in the Strassburg Ptolemy—and the one that Mike found inside the library, under the water tank."

"You said Bea found others?"

"Yes, during the week, when the search continued, two of the curators discovered pieces tucked inside books from the Hunt Collection, just as Bea had predicted," I said. "And Talbot Hunt is cooperating now."

The Friday morning we first met Talbot at the library, he had hinted at the fact that he was in the race to find the entire map. He had un-

earthed one not long ago in an atlas he inherited from his grandfather, which he'd ignored
until Tina Barr began to work with him.

"So that accounts for ten of the twelve," Luc
said. "What will become of the map, if it is ever
put together?"

I sipped at the wine, then stretched out
again in the sand, watching the crown of the
sun disappear.

"The Hunts have finally agreed on something, after a lifetime of acrimony and unpleas-
antness. A substantial piece of damage control,"
I said. "They've made a gift of the map to the
New York Public Library, along with a sizable
contribution for the restoration of the Hunt
Collection. The money will also help the library try to find the last two pieces."

"Are you getting cold, darling?"

"No, I'm fine. I don't want to go in yet."

The involuntary chill that swept over me
had nothing to do with the weather. There
would be hearings and trials to follow, a system
trying to make sense of the senseless deaths of
two young women.

"You can get this off your mind now, can't
you?"

Judge Moffett had approved my application
for the familial DNA search of Wesley the
Weasel Griggs. A homicide case that had lan-

guished for eight years might now be solved by science, and I would have a new challenge to fill the fall days.

"Tonight, yes," I said, as Luc swept back my hair and put his lips against my forehead.

"And tomorrow?"

"Yes." I laughed as he moved his lips to the tip of my nose.

Months earlier, after Joan and Jim's wedding, Luc had embraced me for the first time in this secluded cove. All the best memories of my life were connected to this peaceful, glorious island.

"And Monday, after I've flown home to France?"

"Hard to predict," I said. **"Au revoir, mon amour."**

"Tuesday?" he asked, entwining his legs with mine in the shallow water that lapped at our feet.

"Maybe."

"Only maybe? I've got some serious work to do before I leave," Luc said.

I put my arms around his neck and we kissed each other, over and over again. Then I pulled him to his feet and led him up the hill to the outdoor shower. I wanted to wash off the sand from the beach—and some of the grit I carried with me, always, from my job.

"C'mon, Luc," I said. "Time to play ball."

ACKNOWLEDGMENTS

My earliest childhood memories of books are of those from which my mother read to me every night before I went to sleep. I still have the frayed volumes of poems by Robert Louis Stevenson and A. A. Milne, and the stories of Beatrix Potter and E. B. White. I remember the first time she took me to the public library in our small city, and with what delight I left that day carrying the three books the librarian entrusted to me. Our favorite weekly excursion—an hour of pure happiness with my mother—was the trip downtown to return the small stack I had selected and replace it with another.

Most bibliophiles love reading **about** books, too, and for me, the opportunity to do some of my research with literary treasures was a thrilling experience. One foundation for my exploration was a 1923 tome I picked up at an antiquarian book fair—Harry Miller Lydenberg's **History of the New York Public Library**. I studied Phyllis Dain's **A Universe of Knowledge**, Nicholas Basbanes's **A Gentle Madness**, Ingrid Steffensen's **The New York**

Public Library: A Beaux Arts Landmark, and a slim little book published by Educare Press, **The Waldseemüller World Map** (1507).

One of the most riveting articles I relied on for an understanding of the world of rare map collectors appeared in **The New Yorker**'s Annals of Crime, called "A Theft in the Library" by William Finnegan. As always, my research notebooks were teeming with clippings from the **New York Times**, whether about the structural bones of Manhattan buildings or transparency in the boardroom's of libraries and museums, or even the obituaries of long-forgotten individuals.

Perhaps the most extensive private collection devoted to cartography was in the unique library of England's Christopher Henry Beaumont Pease, the second Baron Wardington. The essay written by Lord Wardington for Sotheby's 2006 sale of Important Atlases from his library captured the passion these treasures inspired, and the elegant descriptions in that catalog helped me design the volumes that line the bookshelves of my fictional characters.

My dear friends Cynthia and Dan Lufkin invited me to their spectacular apartment when they moved to a landmarked building on Central Park West several years ago. It's still a mystery to me how elements of their stunning home took such a sinister turn in my imagination, but I am grateful for that introduction to the chapel over cocktails.

Dr. Cecilia Crouse, chief of the Palm Beach Sheriff's Office forensic science laboratory, is a woman I admire enormously. She solves crimes, saves lives, does justice every day, and trains scores of young scientists to do the same. Cece is a great force for good against evil in this world, and she remains my DNA guru.

Paul LeClerc, President of the New York Public Library, has the most splendid professional home in America. He has called libraries "the memory of humankind, irreplacable repositories of documents of human thought and action," and I agree with him that the NYPL is such an institution, par excellence.

David Ferriero, Andrew W. Mellon Director of the New York Public Libraries, was my brilliant personal guide through all the amazing wonders of the great library. The NYPL was founded in 1895, he said, with the mission of making the accumulated knowledge of the world freely accessible to all, without distinction as to income, religion, nationality, or other human condition. David knew that I was likely to invent murder and mayhem within the historic walls of the central library as a result of the time he spent with me, but still he led me from the rooftop to the basement stacks and through every secret passageway in between, and put me in the hands of each scholarly curator and conservator along the way.

My lifelong love affair with librarians reached a fever pitch while working on this book. David's enthusiasm for the world he inhabits is impressive and infectious. He and Zelman Kisilyuk led me from the rooftop through the treacherous stacks with great care. Isaac Gewirtz educated me about the Berg Collection; John Lundquist let me explore the Asian and Middle Eastern works; Shelly Smith and her colleagues in the Barbara Goldsmith Preservation Division helped me understand the critical nature of their work—and the incomparable gift bestowed on the NYPL by Barbara; and Alice Hudson, and her assistant chief Matthew Knutzen, thrilled me with their displays of the breathtaking and vulnerable riches of the Lionel Pincus and Princess Firyal Map Division. I borrowed a bit of Alice's wisdom and spirit to enliven the plot.

Everyone should have a friend like Louise Grunwald. She's smart, beautiful, funny, wise, and fiercely loyal to her many, many friends. Her quiet generosity never ceases to amaze me, and she exercised it this time to open the massive doors of the NYPL and place me into the hands of David Ferriero.

My team at Doubleday—led by Steve Rubin and Phyllis Grann—is the class of the field in the publishing world and includes Alison Rich, John Pitts, John Fontana, and Jackie Montalvo. To Esther Newberg and everyone at ICM—especially Kari Stuart—goes my gratitude for helping make my dream of a writer's life come true.

Wherever you are, use your libraries and support them. And when you are in New York City, come visit the great New York Public Library and behold its treasures.

My mother was the kindest person I have ever known, with the most enormous heart and a dazzling smile that invited all comers to share in her happiness. Among the very best things she ever did for me—and there are many—was to nurture my love of books and reading. She is forever, as I said in the dedication of my second novel, simply the best. Dearest Bobbie, rest in peace.

And like all the books before it, this one is for Justin, always—my first reader, my great warrior.

LINDA FAIRSTEIN, one of America's foremost legal experts on crimes of sexual assault and domestic violence, ran the Sex Crimes Unit of the District Attorney's Office in Manhattan for more than two decades. Her first novel, *Final Jeopardy*, which introduced the character Alexandra Cooper, was published in 1996 to critical and commercial acclaim. Her nonfiction book, *Sexual Violence*, was a *New York Times* Notable Book in 1994. She lives with her husband in New York and on Martha's Vineyard.

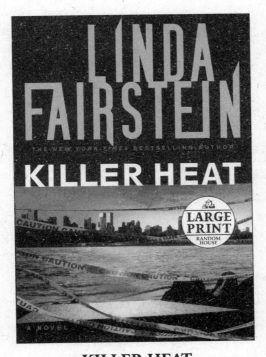